D0336120

Compton Mackenzie

The Adventures of Sylvia Scarlett

JOHN MURRAY

The Early Life and Adventures of Sylvia Scarlett first published in
Great Britain in 1918
Sylvia and Michael first published in Great Britain in 1919
Complete edition first published in Great Britain in 1950

This paperback edition first published in 2012 by John Murray (Publishers)
An Hachette UK Company

1

© The Society of Authors 1918, 1919

A CIP catalogue record for this title is available from the British Library

ISBN 978-1-84854-768-1
E-book ISBN 978-1-84854-769-8

Typeset in Sabon by Hewer Text UK Ltd

Printed and bound by Clays Ltd, St Ives plc

John Murray policy is to use papers that are natural, renewable
and recyclable products and made from wood grown in sustainable forests.
The logging and manufacturing processes are expected to conform to
the environmental regulations of the country of origin.

John Murray (Publishers)
338 Euston Road
London NW1 3BH

www.johnmurray.co.uk

To Faith

Forword to New Edition

In April 1915 after finishing my novel *Guy and Pauline* I went to Gallipoli. Then in the autumn of that year I went to Athens and later to Syra in the Cyclades where I remained until September 1917. In the small hours of the blazing summer of 1916 I wrote a novel in twelve episodes called *No Papers* which was intended for serialisation in the United States to fulfil a contract entered into shortly before the outbreak of the First World War. The central figure of this story was the girl who appears in *Sylvia Scarlett* as Queenie Walters. When my house was shot to pieces and sacked by Boeotian Reservists brought into Athens by the anti-Venizelists to settle with their opponents, the manuscript of *No Papers* disappeared; it was probably supposed to be a document of value to the Intelligence of the pro-German party. Full compensation was paid by the Greek Government a couple of years later, and some of the incidents were used in *Sylvia Scarlett*. Apart from *No Papers* I wrote nothing from the moment I landed on the Peninsula until I left the Aegean two and a half years later except two or three dispatches from Gallipoli, innumerable Intelligence reports and about six thousand telegrams.

On my arrival back in London the Chief of the Secret Service wanted me to become his Number Two at Headquarters with the idea of succeeding him a year or two after the war. I told him my ambitions did not lie in that direction but that, although I was unwilling to work with him as his heir-presumptive, I would serve him as his vizier. I need not have worried. Twenty-four hours later he sent for me to say that on his announcing to his staff the proposed appointment he had received a round robin signed by all of them to let him know their desire to resign if it was made. Unlike the frogs in Aesop's fable they did not want King Stork. So in the end I went to Capri on indefinite leave and full pay. The full pay of a Captain in the Royal Marines was not enough to maintain a villa in Capri and by now a long period of earning nothing from my own profession had swallowed up all my money. It was therefore imperative to write a novel.

A week after I got back, on November 3rd, 1917, St. Silvia's Day, I sat down to begin *Sylvia Scarlett*.

I was extremely tired after the arduous and exciting time of building up an organization which started in October 1915 with £150 a month to cover all its expenses and which by September 1917 was requiring £12,000 a month and the services of over 40 officers, naval and military. This fatigue made me subject from time to time to the attacks of an acute neuralgia in the sciatic nerve. Looking back to those days, I am rather astonished now that I was able to write all but the last two and a half chapters by the middle of January 1918, when pain asserted itself and I was unable to finish the book until May. However, by January my publisher Martin Secker had decided that the shortage of paper would make it impossible to publish a novel of over 300,000 words and it was decided to publish the first two parts under the title *The Early Life and Adventures of Sylvia Scarlett* in the spring of 1918 and to wait until the following spring to publish the third part under the title *Sylvia and Michael*. So, in March 1918 the first volume duly appeared printed on a foul flaccid greenish paper. As I remember, 12,000 copies, all the available paper ran to, were sold within a week or two, and then the book was out of print for more than a year.

The reception by the critics was mixed. Those who liked the book were more than generous in their praise, but many of the old brigade were shocked by its apparent contempt for all the conventions that even as late as this still exercised their power. Undoubtedly it was a handicap to bring it out incomplete, and when in due course *Sylvia and Michael* was published all except a few critics were completely bewildered. This was the first novel affected by weariness and disgust of the war and most of the critics at that date had been left behind by the march of time; they still thought war should inspire lofty and romantic notions in a novelist's mind. Moreover, they were suspicious of a writer who failed to live up to the label they had affixed to him. The fact that Sylvia Scarlett herself (whose name was suggested by a novel Stevenson never wrote to be called *Sophia Scarlett*) had already appeared in *Sinister Street* added to the puzzle of the changed style.

The explanation was simple enough. I had spent two years squeezing telegram after telegram I wrote into the fewest words possible and by now I was almost unable to use a single adjective or adverb of mere decoration. When every word costs nearly two shillings to send adjectives and adverbs do not stand a chance with the blue pencil. Furthermore I had read Stendhal and been bewitched by his theory of unnecessary decoration, and the demand that his characters should express so much of themselves in direct speech. Finally it was imperative to write *Sylvia Scarlett* as quickly as possible in order to relieve the financial situation for myself. I wrote and revised for twelve hours a day until I cracked after writing about 280,000 words in eighty days; the remaining 20,000 took me a hundred days.

To add to the difficulties I lacked writing paper, and the first part of the book was written on the back of the manuscript of *Guy and Pauline*. The typing was done by my wife, and as a tribute to the ribbons of those days it may be mentioned that the blue part of one ribbon on an old L. C. Smith No. 2 typewriter I had bought very cheaply in New York held out for half the manuscript. Later the red part of the same ribbon served D. H. Lawrence to type out for himself his *Fantasia of the Unconscious*. I can see him now like a caryatid bringing back that grand old typewriter on his head along the cliffs of Capri, a bottle of Benedictine in one hand to be opened in celebration.

I mentioned above the character of Queenie Walters; it will probably be obvious that she is a portrait and that some of the incidents I have used were based on real incidents in her strange life. On the other hand Sylvia Scarlett herself is entirely a creation of my own fancy, although some of her adventures in Russia and Roumania were related to me by a French woman from her own experience. The character of Mrs. Gainsborough was entirely my own invention, but about nine years after she had first appeared in *Sinister Street* I met her in the flesh. Mrs. O— looked like Mrs. Gainsborough, Mrs. O— dressed like Mrs. Gainsborough, and Mrs. O— talked like Mrs. Gainsborough. Nobody could have acquitted me of painting an exact portrait if I had happened to meet her before I wrote *Sylvia Scarlett*. This appearance in real life of an eccentric character evoked earlier from my own imagination has happened to me several times but most uncannily in the case of Mrs. Gainsborough.

D. H. Lawrence read *Sylvia Scarlett* when he was in Capri. 'It's so like life,' he murmured in that high dreamy voice he used for his most benevolent mood. If Lawrence was right the book will still be readable. If he was wrong it will now be unreadable.

COMPTON MACKENZIE

Contents

Prelude

At six o'clock on the morning of Ash Wednesday in the year 1847, the Honourable Charles Cunningham sat sipping his coffee in the restaurant of the Vendanges de Bourgogne. He was somewhat fatigued by the exertions that as *le lion* of the moment he had felt bound to make, exertions that had included a display of English eccentricity and had culminated in a cotillon at a noble house in the Faubourg St. Germain, the daughter of which had been assigned to him by Parisian gossip as his future wife. Marriage, however, did not present itself to his contemplation as an urgent duty; and he sipped his coffee, reassured by the example of his brother Saxby, who with the responsibility of a family succession remained a bachelor. In any case the notion of marrying a French girl was preposterous; he was not to be flattered into an unsuitable alliance by compliments upon his French. Certainly he spoke French uncommonly well, devilishly well for an Englishman, he told himself; and he stroked his whiskers in complacent meditation.

Charles Cunningham had arrived at the Vendanges de Bourgogne to watch that rowdy climax of Carnival, the *descente de la Courtille:* and now through the raw air they were coming down from Belleville, all sorts of revellers in masks and motley and rags. The noise of tin trumpets and toy drums, of catcalls and cocoricots, of laughter and cheers and whistling came nearer. Presently the road outside was thronged for the aristocrats of the Faubourg St. Germain to alight from their carriages and mix with the mob. This was the traditional climax of Carnival for Parisian society: every year they drove here on Ash Wednesday morning to get themselves banged on the head by bladders, to be spirted with cheap scent and pelted with sugar plums, and to retaliate by flinging down hot *louis* for the painful enrichment of the masses. The noise was for a time deafening; but gradually the cold light of morning and the melancholy Lenten bells cast a gloom upon the crowd, which passed on toward the boulevards, diminishing in sound and size at every street-corner.

The tall fair Englishman let himself be carried along by the retreat, thinking idly what excitable folk foreigners were, but conscious, nevertheless, of a warmth of intimacy that was not at all disagreeable, the kind of intimacy that is bestowed on a man by taking a pack of friendly dogs for a country walk. Suddenly he was aware of a small hand upon his sleeve, a small hand that lay there like a white butterfly; and, looking down, he saw a poke-bonnet garlanded with yellow rosebuds. The poke-bonnet was all he could see; for the wearer kept her gaze steadily on the road, while with little feet she mimicked his long strides. The ineffable lightness of the arm laid on his own, the joyous mockery of her footsteps, the sense of an exquisite smile beneath the poke-bonnet, and the airy tremor of invitation that fluttered from the golden shawl of Siamese crêpe about her shoulders tempted him to withdraw from the crowd at the first opportunity. Soon they were in a by-street, whence the clamour of Carnival slowly died away, leaving no sound upon the morning air but their footfalls and the faint whisper of her petticoats where she tripped along beside him.

Presently the poke-bonnet was raised; Charles Cunningham beheld his companion's face, a perfect oval, set with eyes of deepest brown, demurely passionate, eyes that in this empty street were all for him. He had never considered himself a romantic young man; when this encounter had faded to a mere flush upon the dreamy sky of the past, he was always a little scornful of his first remark, and apt to wonder how the deuce he ever came to make it.

'By Jove, *vous savez, vous êtes tout à fait comme un oiseau.*'

'*Eh, alors?*' she murmured in a tone that was neither defiance nor archness nor indifference nor invitation, but something that was compounded of all four and expressed exactly herself. '*Eh, alors?*'

'*Votre nid est loin d'ici?*' he asked.

Nor did he blush for the guise of his speech at the time: afterwards it struck him as most indecorously poetic.

'*Viens donc,*' she whispered.

'*Comment appelez-vous?*'

'*Moi, je suis Adèle.*'

'*Adèle quoi?*' he pressed.

'*Mais Adèle alors, tout simplement ça.*'

'*C'est un peu – vous savez – un peu,*' he made a sweep with his unoccupied arm to indicate the vagueness of it all.

'I love you,' she trilled: deep down in her ivory throat emotion caught the trill and made of it a melody that set his heart beating.

'*Vraiment?*' he asked very solemnly; then laying syllable upon syllable in a kind of amazed deliberation, as a child builds a tower of bricks, he began to talk to her in French.

'*Mais, comme tu parles bien,*' she told him.

'*Tu m'inspires,*' he murmured hoarsely.

Afterwards, when he looked back at the adventure, he awarded this remark the prize for folly.

The adventure did not have a long life; a week later Charles Cunningham was called back to England by the news of his brother's illness. Before Lent was out, he had become the Earl of Saxby, who really had to think seriously of marriage and treat it with more respect than the Parisian gossip over which Charles Cunningham had idly mused at six o'clock of Ash Wednesday morning in the year 1847. As for Adèle, she met in May the owner of a travelling booth, a widower called Bassompierre with a small son, who had enough of the gipsy to attract the irresponsible Adèle and enough of the bourgeois to induce her to marry him for the sake of a secure and solid future. She need not have troubled about her future, the deep-voiced Adèle; for just when November darkens to December she died in giving birth to Juliette. The gipsy in Albert Bassompierre accepted as his own daughter Juliette; the bourgeois in him erected a cross in the cemetery and put a wreath of immortelles in a glass case to lie on Adèle's tomb. Then he locked away the few pieces of jewelry that life had brought her, hung another daguerreotype beside the one of his first wife, and wrapped Juliette in a golden shawl of Siamese crêpe. Lightly the two daguerreotypes swung to and fro; and lightly rocked the cradle where the baby Juliette lay sleeping, while the caravan jolted southward along the straight French roads where the poplars seemed to be commenting to one another in the wind.

For eighteen years the caravan jolted along these roads, until young Edouard Bassompierre was old enough to play leading man throughout the repertory and thereby most abruptly plunge his predecessor into old age. At the same time Juliette was allowed to act the soubrettes; her father was too much afraid of the leading lady to play any tricks of suddenly imposed senility with her. It was on the whole a jolly life, this vagrancy from fair to fair of all the towns of France. It was jolly, when the performance was done, to gather in the tent behind the stage and eat chipped potatoes and drink red wine with all the queer people whose voices were hoarse with crying their wares all the day long.

Then came, one springtime, the fair at Compiègne. Business was splendid, for the Emperor was there to hunt the wild boar in the forest. Never had old Albert Bassompierre beaten his big drum so confidently at the entrance of his booth; never had Edouard captured so many young women's hearts: both of them were too much occupied with their own triumphs to notice the young officer who came every night to the play. The Emperor left Compiègne in April; when he departed, the young officer departed also, accompanied by Juliette.

'*Ah, la vache,*' cried old Bassompierre, 'it's perhaps as well her mother didn't live, for she might have done the same.'

'You should have let her play the lead,' said Edouard.

'She can play lead in real life,' replied old Bassompierre. 'If she can,' he added fiercely.

But when Juliette wrote to him from Paris and told him how happy she was with her lover, the gipsy in Bassompierre drove out the bourgeois, and he sent his daughter her mother's jewelry and the golden shawl; but he kept the daguerreotype, for after all Juliette was not really his daughter and Adèle had really been his wife.

Three years passed; Juliette lived in a little house at Belleville with two baby girls called Elène and Henriette. When in after years she looked back to this time, it seemed to her smothered in roses, the roses of an operatic scene. Everything indeed in retrospect was like that – the arrival of her lover in his gay uniform, the embowered kisses, the lights of Paris far below, the suppers on the verandah, the warm Sunday mornings, the two babies asleep on the lawn and their father watching them, herself before a glass and her lover's face seen over her shoulder, the sudden sharp embrace; all were heavy with the intolerable sense of a curtain that must fall. Then came the war; there was a hurried move down to stuffy apartments in Paris; ready money hastily got together by the young officer, who spoke confidently of the large sum it was, since after all the war would be over in a month and the Prussians have had their lesson; and at last a breathless kiss. The crowds surged cheering through the streets, the two babies screamed disapproval of their new surroundings, and Juliette's lover was killed in the first battle; he had only time to scribble a few trembling lines:

Mon adorée, je t'ai flanqué un mauvais coup. Pardonne-moi. Mes dernières pensées sont pour toi. Adieu. Deux gros bécots aux bébés. J'ai parlé pour toi à mon père. Cherche argent – je t'embrasse follement follem

Yet when she received this letter, some impulse kept her from going to her lover's father. She could not bear the possibility of being made to realise that those debonair years of love were regarded by him as an intrigue to be solved by money. If André's mother had been alive, she might have felt differently; now she would not trouble a stricken family that might regard her tears as false: she would not even try to return to her own father. No doubt he would welcome her; but pride, all the strange and terrible pride that was henceforth to haunt Juliette's soul forbade her.

xvi

It was impossible, however, to remain in Paris; and without any reason for her choice she took her babies to Lyon and settled down in rooms overlooking the Rhône to await the end of the war. When she had paid the cost of the journey and bought herself the necessary mourning, she found she had nearly eleven thousand francs left: with care this could surely be made to last three years at least; in three years much might happen. As a matter of fact much happened almost at once; for the beauty of Juliette, a lustrous and imperial beauty, caught the fancy of Gustave Lataille, who was conductor of the orchestra at one of the smaller theatres in Lyon. To snare his fancy might not have been enough; but when with her dowry she captured also his imagination, he married her. Juliette did not consider it wrong to marry this sombre, withered, and uncommunicative man of forty, for whom she had neither passion nor affection. He struck her as essentially like most of the husbands she had observed hitherto; and she esteemed herself lucky not to have met such an one before she had been granted the boon of love. She must have inherited from that unknown father her domestic qualities; she certainly acquired none from Adèle. From him, too, may have come that pride which, however it may have found its chief expression in ideals of bourgeois respectability, was nevertheless a fine fiery virtue and supported her spirit to the very last.

Juliette and Lataille lived together without anything to colour a drab existence. Notwithstanding his connection with the theatre, Lataille had no Bohemian tastes; once when his wife suggested after a visit from her father that there seemed no reason why she should not apply for an engagement to act, he unhesitatingly refused his permission; when she attempted to argue, he reminded her that he had given his name to Elène and Henriette, and she was silent. Henceforth she devoted herself to sewing, and brought into the world four girls in successive years – Françoise, Marie, Marguerite, and Valentine. The last was born in 1875, soon after the Latailles had moved to Lille, where Gustave had secured the post of conductor at the principal theatre. Juliette welcomed the change, for it gave her the small house of her own that she had long wanted: moreover nobody in Lille knew at first hand of the circumstances in which Gustave had married her, so that Elène and Henriette could go to school without being teased about their mother's early lapse from the standards of conduct that she fervently desired they would adopt.

Unfortunately the conductor had enjoyed his advancement only a year when he was struck down by a paralytic stroke. With six small children and a palsied husband upon her hands Juliette had to find work. Partly from compassion for her ill-fortune, but chiefly because by now she was a most capable seamstress, the management of the theatre engaged her as wardrobe-mistress; and for five years Juliette sustained her husband, her children, and her house. They were years that would have rubbed the bloom from most women; but Juliette's beauty seemed to grow rather than diminish. Her personality became proverbial in the town of Lille; although as wardrobe-mistress she was denied the public triumph of the footlights, she had nevertheless a fame of her own that was considered unique in the history of her profession. Her pride flourished on the deference that was shown her even by the management; between her beauty and her sharp tongue she achieved an authority that reached its height in the way she brought up her children. Their snowy pinafores, their trim stockings, their manners, and their looks were the admiration of the *quartier*; and when in the year 1881 Gustave Lataille died, the neatness of their new black dresses surprised even the most confirmed admirers of Madame Lataille's industry and taste. At no time could Juliette have seemed so beautiful as when after the funeral she raised her widow's veil and showed the attendant sympathizers a countenance unmarked by one tear of respectable emotion. She was far too proud to weep for a husband whom she had never loved, and whose death was a relief; when the neighbours expressed astonishment at the absence of any outward sorrow, she flung out a challenge to fate:

'I have not reached the age of thirty-four, and brought up six children and never once been late with so much as a ribbon, to cry for any man now. He'll be a wonderful man that will ever make me cry. Henriette, don't tug at your garter.'

And as she stood there, with great brown eyes burning beneath a weight of lustrous black hair, she seemed of marble without and within.

Nevertheless, before six months had passed, Madame Lataille fell impetuously in love with a young English clerk of twenty-one called Henry Snow; what is more she married him. Nobody in Lille was able to offer a credible explanation of her behaviour. People were willing to admit that his conduct was comprehensible notwithstanding the fourteen years of her seniority; and it says much for the way Juliette had impressed her personality upon a dull provincial world that Henry Snow's action should have been so immediately understood. Before the problem of her conduct, however, the world remained in perplexity. Financial considerations could not have supplied a motive; from all accounts the Englishman was unlikely to help; indeed, gossip said that even in his obscure position he had already had opportunities of showing that, such as it was, the position was better than he deserved and unlikely to be bettered in the future. Nor could his good looks have attracted her, for he was insignificant; and since Englishmen in the experience of Lille were, whatever their faults, never insignificant, the insignificance of Henry Snow acquired an active quality that contradicted its characterization and made him seem not merely unattractive but positively displeasing. Nor could she have required someone to help in managing her six children; altogether the affair was a mystery, which gathered volume when the world began to grasp the depth of the feeling that Henry Snow had roused in Juliette. All the world loves a lover, but only when it is allowed to obtrude itself upon the love. Juliette, absorbed by her emotion and the eternal jealousy of the woman who marries a man much younger than herself, refused to admit any spectators to marvel at the development of the mystery. She carried on her work as usual; but instead of maintaining her position as a figure she became an object of curiosity, and presently because that curiosity was never gratified an object of suspicion. The lover-loving world began to shake its head and calumny whispered everywhere its commentary: she could never have been a *femme propre*; this marriage must have been forced upon the young Englishman as the price of a five-year-old intrigue. When some defender of Juliette pointed out that the clerk had only been in Lille three years, that his name had never been connected with hers, and that in any case he was only twenty-one now, calumny retorted with a long line of Henry Snows; presently the story of Juliette's life with André Duchesnil was dragged to light, and by an infinite multiplication of whispers her career from earliest youth was established as licentious, mercenary, and cruel.

For a while Juliette was so much wrapped up in her own joy that she did not observe the steady withdrawal of popular esteem. Having made it clear to everybody that she wished to be left alone with her husband, she supposed she had been successful and congratulated herself accordingly, until one day a persistent friend, proof against Juliette's icy discouragement, drove into her that the *quartier* was pitying Henry Snow, that things were being said against her, and that the only way to put a stop to unkind gossip was to move about among the neighbours in a more friendly fashion.

Gradually it dawned upon Juliette that her friend was the emissary of a universally accepted calumny, the voice of the *quartier*, the first to brave her, and only now rash enough to do so because she had public opinion at her back. This did not prevent Juliette from showing her counsellor the door to the street, nor from slamming it so abruptly that a metre of stuff was torn from her skirt; yet when she went back to her room and picked up her needlework, there came upon her with a shock the realisation of what effect all this might have on Henry. If the world was pitying him now, it would presently be laughing; if he were laughed at, he would grow to hate her. Hitherto she had been so happy in her love that she had never stopped to consider anything or anybody. She remembered now Henry's amazement when, in the first tumultuous wave of passion dammed for so many years, she refused to let herself be swept away; she recalled his faint hesitation when first she spoke of marriage and gave him to understand that without marriage she would not be his. Even then he must have foreseen the possibility of ridicule, and he had married her only because she had been able to seem so desirable. And she was still desirable; he was still enthralled; he was still vain of her love; yet how was the flattery of one woman to mitigate for a man the contempt of the crowd? Mercifully he was an Englishman in a French town, and therefore it would take longer for the popular feeling to touch him; but soon or late it would strike home to his vanity. Something must be devised to transfix him with the dignity of marriage: they must have a child; no father could do anything but resent and despise laughter that would be directed against his fatherhood. Juliette's wish was granted very shortly afterwards; and when she told her husband of their expectation she held him close and looked deep into his eyes for the triumph she sought. Perhaps the fire in her own was reflected in his, for she released him from her embrace with a sigh of content.

Through the months of waiting Juliette longed for a boy: it seemed to her somehow essential for the retention of Henry's love that she should give him a boy: she could scarcely bear another girl, she who had brought into the world six girls. Much of Juliette's pride during those months was softened by her longing; she began once more to frequent the company of her neighbours in her zest for the least scrap of information that might help the fulfilment of it. There was no fantastic concoction she would not drink, nor any omen she would not propitiate: half the saints in the calendar were introduced to her by ladies that knew them and vouched for the interest they would take in her pregnancy. Juliette never confided to anybody her reason for wanting a boy; and nobody suspected it, since half a dozen girls were enough to explain any woman's desire for a change. One adviser discovered in a tattered volume of obstetrical theory that when the woman was older than the man the odds were on a male child. Juliette's researches to gather confirmation of this remark led her into discussions about unequal marriages; and as the time of her confinement drew near she became gentler and almost anxious to discuss her love for Henry Snow, so much gentler and less reserved, that those who had formerly whispered loudest and most falsely to one another now whispered sympathetically to her.

On the day before Juliette's confinement her husband came in from work very irritable.

'Here, when's this baby going to be born? I'm getting a bit annoyed. The men at the office are betting on its being a boy. It makes me look a fool, you know, that sort of thing.'

She clutched his arm.

'Which do you want, Henri? Tell me, *mon amour, mon homme.*'

'I don't care which it is, as long as you're quick about it and this betting stops.'

That night she was delivered of a girl, and because it was his she choked down the wild disappointment and loved Sylvia the best of all her seven girls.

THE EARLY LIFE AND
ADVENTURES OF
SYLVIA SCARLETT

BOOK I

Sylvia and Philip

I

The first complete memory of her father that Sylvia possessed was of following her mother out into the street on a clear moonlight night after rain and of seeing him seated in a puddle outside the house, singing an unintelligible song which he conducted with his umbrella. She remembered her mother's calling to him sharply, and how at last after numerous shakings and many reproaches he had walked into the house on all fours, carrying the umbrella in his mouth like a dog. She remembered that the umbrella was somehow wrong at the end, different from any other umbrella she had ever seen, so that when it was put into the hall-stand it looked like a fat old market woman instead of the trim young lady it should have resembled. She remembered how she had called her mother's attention to the loss of its feet and how her mother, having apparently realized for the first time her presence at the scene, had promptly hustled her upstairs to bed with so much roughness that she had cried.

When Sylvia was older and had become in a way her mother's confidante, sitting opposite to her in the window to sew until it was no longer possible to save oil for the lamp, she ventured to recall this scene. Her mother had laughed at the remembrance of it and had begun to hum the song her father had snug:

> La donna è mobile
> La da-di la-di-da.

'Shall I ever forget him?' Madame Snow had cried. 'It was the day your sister Elène was married, and he had been down to the railway-station to see them off to Bruxelles.'

Sylvia had asked what the words of the song meant, and had been told that they meant women were always running about.

'Where?' she had pressed.

'Some of them after men and others running away from them,' her mother had replied.

'Shall I do that when I'm big?' Sylvia had continued. 'Which shall I do?'

3

But it had been time to fetch the lamp, and the question had remained unanswered.

Sylvia was five when her sister Elène was married; soon afterwards, Henriette married too. She remembered that very well, because Marie went to join Françoise in the other bedroom, and with only Marguerite and Valentine left, they no longer slept three in a bed. This association had often been very uncomfortable, because Marguerite would eat biscuits, the crumbs of which used to scratch her legs; and worse than the crumbs was the invariable quarrel between Marguerite and Valentine that always ended in their pinching one another across Sylvia, so that she often got pinched by mistake.

For several years Sylvia suffered from being the youngest of many sisters, and her mother's favourite. When she went to school, she asked other girls if it were not nicer to have brothers, but the stories she heard about the behaviour of boys made her glad there were only girls in her house. She had practical experience of the ways of boys when at the age of eight she first took part in the annual *féerie* at the Lille theatre. On her first appearance she played a monster; though all the masks were very ugly, she, being the smallest performer, always got the ugliest, and with the progress of the season the one that was most knocked about. In after years these performances seemed like a nightmare of hot card-board-scented breath, of being hustled down the stone stairs from the dressing-room, of noisy rough boys shouting and scrambling for the best masks, of her legs being pinched by invisible boys while she was waiting in the wings, and once of somebody's twisting her mask right round as they made the famous entrance of the monsters, so that, being able to see nothing, she fell down and made all the audience laugh. Such were boys!

In contrast with scenes of discomfort and misery like these were the hours when she sat sewing with her mother in the quiet house. There would be long silences broken only by the sound of her mother's hand searching for new thread or needle in the work-basket, of clocks, of kettle on the hob, or of distant street-cries. Then her mother would suddenly laugh to herself and begin a tale so interesting that Sylvia's own needlework would lie idly on her knee, until she was reproved for laziness, and silence again enclosed the room. Sometimes the sunset would glow through the window-panes upon her mother's work, and Sylvia would stare entranced at the great silken roses that slowly opened their petals for those swift fingers. Sometimes it would be a piece of lace that lay on her mother's lap, lace that in the falling dusk became light and mysterious as a cloud. Yet even these tranquil hours had storms, as on the occasion when her mother had been working all day at a lace cap which had been promised without fail to somebody at the theatre who required it that night. At six o'clock she had risen with a sigh and given the cap to Sylvia to hold while she put on her things to take it down to the theatre. Sylvia had stood by the fire, dreaming over the beauty of the lace; and then without any warning the cap had fallen into the fire and in a moment was ashes. Sylvia wished she could have followed the cap when she saw her mother's face of despair on realizing what had happened. It was then that for the first time she learnt how much depended upon her mother's work; for during all that week, whenever she was sent out on an errand, she was told to buy only the half of everything, half the usual butter, half the usual sugar, and what was stranger still to go to shops outside the *quartier*, at which Madame Snow never dealt. When she enquired the reason of this, her mother asked her if she wanted all the *quartier* to know that they were poor and could afford to buy only half the usual amount that week.

Sylvia, when the first shame of her carelessness had died away, rather enjoyed these excursions to streets more remote, where amusing adventures were always possible. One Saturday afternoon in April, she set out with a more than usually keen sense of the discoveries and adventures that might befall her. The first discovery was a boy on a step-ladder, polishing a shop window; the second discovery was that she could stand on the kerb-stone and never once fail to spit home upon the newly polished glass. She did this about a dozen times, watching the saliva dribble down the pane and speculating with herself which driblet would make the longest journey. Regretfully she saw that the boy was preparing to descend and admire his handiwork, because two driblets were still progressing slowly downward, one of which had been her original fancy for the prize of endurance. As she turned to flee, she saw on the pavement at her feet a golden ten-franc piece; she picked it up and grasping it tightly in her hot little hand ran off, not forgetting, even in the excitement of her sudden wealth, to turn round at a safe distance and put out her tongue at the boy to mark her contempt for him, for the rest of his class, and for all their handiwork, especially that newly polished window-pane. Then she examined the gold piece and marvelled at it, thinking how it obliterated the memory of the mother-o'-pearl button that only the other day she had found on the dust-heap and lost a few hours afterwards.

It was a wonderful afternoon, an afternoon of unbridled acquisition, which began with six very rich cakes and ended with a case of needles for her mother that used up her last *sou*. Coming out of the needle shop, her arms full of packages, she met a regiment of soldiers marching and singing. The soldiers expressed her triumphant mood, and Sylvia marched with

5

them, joining in their songs. She had a few cakes left and, being grateful to the soldiers, she handed them round among them, which earned her much applause from passers-by. When the regiment had arrived at the barracks and her particular friends had all kissed her farewell and there were no more bystanders to smile their approbation, Sylvia decided it would be wise to do the shopping for her mother. She had marched farther than she thought with the soldiers; it was nearly dusk when she reached the grocer's where she was to buy the small quantity of sugar that was all that could be afforded this week. She made her purchase, and put her hand into the pocket of her pinafore for the money; the pocket was empty. Everything in the grocer's shop seemed to be tumbling about her in a great and universal catastrophe. She searched feverishly again; there was a small hole; of course, her mother had given her a ten-franc piece, telling her to be very careful indeed of the change, which was wanted badly for the rent. She could not explain to the man what had happened and, leaving the packet on the counter, she rushed from the shop into the cruel twilight, choked by tearless sobs and tremors of apprehension. At first she thought of trying to find the shops where she had made her own purchases that she might recover such of the money as had not been eaten; but her nervous fears refused to let her mind work properly, and everything that had happened on this luckless afternoon seemed to have happened in a dream. It was already dark; all she could do was to run home, clutching the miserable toys to her heart and wondering if the needle-case could possibly allay a little, a very little of her mother's anger.

Madame Snow began as soon as Sylvia entered the house by demanding what she had been doing to be so late in coming home. Sylvia stammered and was silent; stammered again and let fall all her parcels; then she burst into a flood of tears that voiced a despair more profound than she had ever known. When her mother at last extracted from Sylvia what had happened she too wept; and the pair of them sat filling the room with their sobs, until Henry Snow appeared upon the scene and asked if they had both gone mad.

His wife and daughter sobbed a violent negative. Henry stared at the floor littered with Sylvia's numerous purchases, but found there no answer to the riddle. He moved across to Juliette and shook her, urging her not to become hysterical.

'The last bit of money I had, and the rent due on Monday!' she wailed.

'Don't you worry about money,' said Henry importantly. 'I've had a bit of luck at cards,' and he offered his wife a note. Moreover, when he heard the reason for all this commotion of grief, he laughed, said it might have happened to anyone, congratulated Sylvia upon her choice

6

of goods, declared it was time she began to study English seriously and vowed that he was the one to be her teacher, yes, by George, he was, and that to-morrow morning being Sunday they would make a start. Then he began to fondle his wife, which embarrassed Sylvia, but nevertheless because these caresses so plainly delighted her mother, they consoled her for the disaster. So she withdrew to a darker corner of the room and played with the doll she had bought, listening to the conversation between her parents.

'Do you love me, Henri?'

'Of course I love you.'

'You know that I would sacrifice the world for you? I've given you everything. If you love me still, then you must love me for myself – myself alone, *mon homme*.'

'Of course I do.'

'But I'm growing old,' protested Juliette. 'There are others younger than I. *Ah, Henri, amour de ma vie*, I'm jealous even of the girls. I want them all out of the house. I hate them now, except ours – ours, *ma poupée*.'

Sylvia regarding her own doll could not help feeling that this was a most inappropriate name for her father; she wondered why her mother called him that and decided finally that it must be because he was shorter than she was. The evening begun so disastrously ended most cheerfully; when Françoise and Marie arrived back at midnight, they escaped even the mildest rebuke from their mother.

Sylvia's father kept his promise about teaching her English, and she was granted the great pleasure of being admitted to his room every evening when he returned from work. This room until now had always been a Bluebeard's chamber, not merely for Sylvia, but for everyone else in the house. To be sure Sylvia had sometimes, when supper was growing cold, peeped in to warn her father of fleeting time, but it had always been impressed upon her that in no circumstances was she to enter the room; though she had never beheld in those quick glimpses anything more exciting than her father sitting in his shirt-sleeves and reading in a tumble-down arm-chair, there had always been the sense of a secret. Now that she was made free of this apartment she perceived nothing behind the door but a bookcase fairly full of books, nothing indeed anywhere that seemed to merit concealment, unless it were some pictures of undressed ladies looking at themselves in a glass. Once she had an opportunity of opening one of the books and she was astonished, when her father came in and caught her, that he said nothing; she felt sure that her mother would have been very angry if she had seen her reading such a book. She had blushed when her father found her; when he said nothing and even laughed in a queer unpleasant sort of a way, she had blushed still more deeply. Yet whenever she had a chance, she read these books afterwards and henceforth regarded her father with an affectionate contempt that was often expressed too frankly to please her mother, who finally became so much irritated by it that she sent her away to Bruxelles to stay with Elène, her eldest married sister. Sylvia did not enjoy this visit much, because her brother-in-law was always making remarks about her personal appearance, comparing it most unfavourably with his wife's. It seemed that Elène had recently won a prize for beauty at the Exposition, and though Sylvia would have been suitably proud of this family achievement in ordinary circumstances, this continual harping upon it to her own disadvantage made her wish that Elène had been ignobly defeated.

'Strange her face should be so round and yours such a perfect oval,' Elène's husband would say. 'And her lips are so thin and her eyes so much lighter than yours. She's short too for her age. I don't think she'll ever be as tall as you. But of course everyone can't be beautiful.'

'Of course they can't,' Sylvia snapped. 'If they could, Elène might not have won the prize so easily.'

'She's not a great beauty, but she has a tongue. And she's smart,' her brother-in-law concluded.

Sylvia used to wonder why everyone alluded to her tongue. Her mother had told her just before she was sent to Bruxelles that the priest had put too much salt on it when she was christened. She resolved to be silent in future; but this resolve reacted upon her nerves to such an extent that she wrote home to Lille and begged to be allowed to come back. There had been diplomacy in the way she had written to her father in English rather than to her mother in French. Such a step led her mother to suppose that she repented of criticizing her father; it also prevented her sister Elène from understanding the letter and perhaps writing home to suggest keeping her in Bruxelles. Sylvia was overjoyed at receiving an early reply from her mother bidding her come home, and sending stamps for her to buy a picture-postcard album, which would be much cheaper in Belgium; she was enjoined to buy one picture-postcard and put it in the album, so that the customs-officials should not charge duty.

Sylvia had heard a great deal of smuggling and was thrilled by the illegal transaction, which seemed to her the most exciting enterprise of her life. She said good-bye to Bruxelles without regret; clasping her album close, she waited anxiously for the train to start, thinking to herself that Elène only kept on putting her head into the carriage window to make stupid remarks, because the compartment was crowded and she hoped someone would recognize her as the winner of the beauty competition at the Bruxelles Exposition.

At last the train started; and Sylvia settled down to the prospect of crossing the frontier with contraband. She looked at all the people in the carriage, thinking to herself what dangers she would presently encounter. It was almost impossible not to tell them, as they sat there in the stuffy compartment, scattering crumbs everywhere with their lunches. Soon a pleasant woman in black engaged Sylvia in conversation by offering her an orange from a string-bag. It was very difficult to eat the orange and keep a tight hold of the album; in the end it fell on the floor, whereupon a fat old gentleman sitting opposite stooped over and picked it up for her. He had grunted so in making the effort that Sylvia felt she must reward him with more than thanks; she decided to divulge her secret and explain to him and the pleasant woman with the string-bag the history of the album. Sylvia was glad when all her other fellow-travellers paid attention to the tale, and she could point out that an album like this cost two francs fifty centimes in Lille, whereas in Bruxelles she had been able to buy it for two francs. Then, because everybody smiled so encouragingly, she unwrapped the album and showed the single picture-postcard, discoursing upon the ruse. Everybody congratulated her, and everybody told each other anecdotes about smuggling, until finally a tired and anxious-looking woman informed the company that she was at that very moment smuggling lace to the value of more than two thousand francs. Everybody warned her to be very careful, so strict were the customs-officials; but the anxious-looking woman explained that it was wrapped round her and that in any case she must take the risk, so much depended upon her ability to sell this lace at a handsome profit in France.

When the frontier was reached, Sylvia alighted with the rest of the travellers to pass through the customs, and with quickening heart she presented herself at the barrier, her album clutched tightly to her side. No, she had nothing to declare, and with a sigh of relief at escape from danger she watched her little valise safely chalked. When she passed through to take her seat in the train again, she saw a man whom she recognized as a traveller from her own compartment who had told several anecdotes about contraband. He was talking earnestly now to one of the officials at the barrier and pointing out the anxious woman, who was still waiting to pass through.

'I tell you she has two thousand francs' worth of lace wrapped round her. She admitted it in the train.'

Sylvia felt her legs give way beneath her when she heard this piece of treachery. She longed to cry out to the woman with the lace that she had

9

been betrayed, but already she had turned deathly pale at the approach of the officials. They were beckoning her to follow them to a kind of cabin, and she was moving towards it hopelessly. It was dreadful to see a poor woman so treated, and Sylvia looked round to find the man who had been the cause of it, but he had vanished.

Half an hour afterwards, the woman of the lace wearily climbed into the compartment and took her seat with the rest; her eyes were red, and she was still weeping bitterly; the others asked what had happened.

'They found it on me,' she moaned. 'And now what shall I do? It was all we had in the world to pay the mortgage on our house. My poor husband is ill, very ill, and it was the only way to save him. I should have sold that lace for four thousand francs, and now they have confiscated it and we shall be fined a thousand francs. We haven't any money. It was everything – everything. We shall lose our house and our furniture, and my husband will die. Oh, *mon dieu, mon dieu!*'

She rocked backwards and forwards in her grief; nothing that anyone could say comforted her. Sylvia told how she had been betrayed, everybody execrated the spy and said how careful one should be to whom one spoke when travelling; but that did not help the poor woman, who sobbed more and more despairingly.

At last the train came to its first stop in France, and the man that had denounced the poor woman suddenly jumped in, as they were starting again, and took his old seat. The fat gentleman next to Sylvia swelled with indignation; his veins stood out, and he shouted angrily at the man what a rascal he was. Everybody in the carriage joined in abusing him; the poor woman herself wailed out her sad story and reproached him for the ruin he had brought upon her. As for Sylvia, she could not contain herself, but jumped up and with all her might kicked him on the shins, an action that made the fat gentleman shout: '*Bravo! Vas-y! Encore, la gosse! Bravo! Bis! Bis!*'

When the noise had subsided, the man began to speak.

'I regret infinitely, madame, the inconvenience to which I was unfortunately compelled to put you, but the fact is that I myself was carrying diamonds upon me to the value of more than 200,000 francs.'

He suddenly took out a wallet from his pocket and emptied the stones into his hand, where they lay sparkling in the dusty sunshine of the compartment. Everybody was silent with surprise for a moment; when they began to abuse him again, he trickled the diamonds back into the wallet and begged for attention.

'How much have you lost, madame?' he enquired very politely.

The woman of the lace poured forth her woes for the twentieth time.

'Permit me to offer you these notes to the value of six thousand francs,' he said. 'I hope the extra thousand will recompense you for the temporary inconvenience to which I was unfortunately compelled to put you. Pray accept my deepest apologies, but at the same time let me suggest greater discretion in future. Yet we are all human, are we not, monsieur?' he added, turning to the fat gentleman next to Sylvia. 'Will you be very much surprised when I tell you that I have never travelled from Amsterdam but I have found some indiscreet fellow-traveller that has been of permanent service to me at temporary inconvenience to himself? This time I thought I was going to be unlucky, for this was the last compartment left; fortunately that young lady set a bad example.'

He smiled at Sylvia.

This story, when she told it at home, seemed to make a great impression upon her father, who maintained that the stranger was a fool ever to return to the carriage.

'Some people seem to think money's made to throw into the gutter,' he grumbled.

Sylvia was sorry about his point of view, but when she argued with him, he told her to shut up; later on that same evening he had a dispute with his wife about going out.

'I want to win it back,' he protested. 'I've had a run of bad luck lately. I feel to-night it's going to change. Did I tell you I saw the new moon over my right shoulder, as I came in?'

'So did I,' said his wife. 'But I don't rush off and gamble away other people's money for the sake of the moon.'

'You saw it too, did you?' said Henry eagerly. 'Well, there you are!'

The funny thing was that Henry was right; he did have a run of good luck, and the house became more cheerful again. Sylvia went on with her English studies; but nowadays even during lessons her father never stopped playing cards. She asked him once if he were telling his fortune, and he replied that he was trying to make it. 'See if you can pick out the queen,' he would say. And Sylvia never could, which made her father chuckle to himself with pleasure. About this time, too, he developed a habit of playing with a ten-centime piece. Whenever he or anyone else was talking, he used to fidget with this coin; in the middle of something important or interesting it used to jingle down on the floor, and everybody had to go on hands and knees to search for it. This habit became so much the intrinsic Henry Snow that Sylvia could never think of him without that ten-centime piece sliding over his long mobile hands, in and out of his prehensile fingers: and though with the progress of time he ceased to drop the coin very often, the restless motion always irritated her.

When Sylvia was eleven, her uncle Edouard came to Lille with his caravan and brought the news of the death of her grandfather. She was not much impressed by this, but the caravan and the booth delighted her; and when her uncle asked if he might not take her away with him on a long tour through the south of France, she begged to be allowed to go. Her mother had so often held her spellbound by tales of her own wandering life that, when she seemed inclined to withhold her permission, Sylvia blamed her as the real origin of this longing to taste the joys of vagrancy, pleading so earnestly that at last her mother gave way and let her go.

Uncle Edouard and Aunt Elise, who sat in the box outside the booth and took the money, were both very kind to Sylvia, and, since they had no children of their own, she was much spoilt. Indeed there was not a dull moment throughout the tour; for even when she went to bed, which was always delightfully late, bed was really a pleasure in a caravan.

In old Albert Bassompierre's days the players had confined themselves to the legitimate drama; Edouard had found it more profitable to tour a variety show interspersed with one-act farces and melodramas. Sylvia's favourites in the company were Madame Perron, the wife of the *chanteur grivois*, and Blanche, a tall, fair, noisy girl who called herself a *diseuse*, but who usually sang indecent ballads in a powerful contralto. Madame Perron was Sylvia's first attraction, because she had a large collection of dolls with which she really enjoyed playing. She was a *femme très propre*, and never went farther with any of her admirers in the audience than to exact from him the gift of a doll.

'*Voilà ses amours manquées,*' her husband used to say with a laugh.

In the end Sylvia found her rather dull, and preferred to go tearing about the country with Blanche, who, though she had been a scullery maid in a Boulogne hotel only a year ago, had managed during her short career on the stage to collect more lovers than Madame Perron had collected dolls. She had a passion for driving; Sylvia could always be sure that on the morning after their opening performance in any town, a waggonette or dog-cart would be waiting to take them to some neighbouring village, where a jolly party would make a tremendous noise, scandalize the inhabitants and depart, leaving a legacy of unpopularity in the district for whichever of Blanche's lovers had paid for the entertainment with his purse and his reputation. Once they arrived at a village where a charity bazaar was being held under the direction of the *curé*. Blanche was presented to him as a distinguished actress from Paris who was seeking peace and recreation in the depths of the country. The *curé* asked if it would be presuming too far on her good nature to give them a taste of her art in the cause of holy charity, a speech perhaps from Corneille or Racine. Blanche assented immediately and recited a piece stuffed so full of spicy *argot* that the rustic gentility understood very little of it, though enough to make them blush, all except the priest, that is, who was very deaf and asked Blanche when she had finished if it were not a speech from *Phèdre* she had declaimed, thanking her very earnestly for the pleasure she had given his simple parish-folk, a pleasure, alas, which he regretted he had not been able to enjoy as much as he should have enjoyed it before he became deaf.

On another occasion they drove to see the ruins of an ancient castle in Brittany, and afterwards went down into the village to drink wine in the garden of the inn, where an English family was sitting at afternoon tea. Sylvia stared curiously at the two little girls who obeyed their governess so promptly and ate their cakes so mincingly. They were the first English girls she had ever seen, and she would so much have liked to tell them that her father was English, for they seemed to want cheering up, so solemn were their light blue eyes and so high their boots. Sylvia whispered to Blanche that they were English, who replied that so much was very obvious, and urged Sylvia to address them in their native tongue: it would give them much pleasure, she thought. Sylvia, however, was too shy; so Blanche in her loudest voice suddenly shouted:

'Oh, yes! Tank you! I love you! All right! You sleep with me? Goddambleudi!' The English family looked very much shocked, but the governess came to their rescue by asking in a thin throaty voice for the 'attition,' and presently they all walked out of the garden. Blanche judged the English to be a dull race, and mounting on a table began a rowdy dance. It happened that, just when the table cracked, the English governess came back for an umbrella she had left behind and that Blanche, leaping wildly to save herself from falling, leapt on the governess and brought her to the ground in a general ruin of chairs and tables. Blanche picked up the victim and said that it was all very *rigolo*, which left Miss as wise as she was before, her French not extending beyond the tea-table and the chaster portions of a bedroom. Blanche told Sylvia to explain to Miss that she had displayed nothing more in her fall than had given much pleasure to all the world. Sylvia, who really felt the poor governess required such practical consolation, translated accordingly, whereat Miss became very red and, snatching her umbrella, walked away muttering, 'Impertinent little gipsy.' When Blanche was told the substance of her last remark, she exclaimed indignantly:

'*Elles sont des vrais types, vous savez, ces gonzesses. Mince, alors! Pourquoi s'emballer comme ça? Quelle race infecte, ces anglais! Moi, je ne peux pas les souffrir.*'

Sylvia listening to Blanche's tirade wondered if all the English were like that. She thought of her father's books, and decided that life in France must have changed him somehow. Then she called to mind with a shiver the solemn light blue eyes of the little girls: England must be a cold sort of a place, where nobody ever laughed: perhaps that was why her father had come away. Sylvia decided to remain in France, always in a caravan if possible, where no English miss could poke about with bony fingers in one's bread and butter.

Sylvia acquired a good deal of worldly wisdom from being so continuously in the society of Blanche, and for a child of eleven she was growing up somewhat rapidly. Yet it would have been hard to say that the influence of her noisy friend was hurtful, for it never roused in Sylvia a single morbid thought. Life in those days presented itself to her mostly as an amusing game, a game that sometimes caused tears, but tears that were easily dried, because after all it was only a game. Such was the situation created on one occasion by the unexpected arrival of Blanche's *fiancé* from his regiment, the 717th of the line.

The company was playing at St. Nazaire at the time, and Louis Moreau telegraphed from Nantes that he had been granted a *congé* of forty-eight hours.

'*Mince, alors!*' cried Blanche to Sylvia. 'And, you know, I don't want to give him up, because he has 30,000 francs and he loves me *à la folie*. We are only waiting till he has finished his military service to get married. But I don't want him here. First of all, I have a very *chic* lover, who has a *poignon fou* and doesn't care how much he spends, and then the lover of my heart is here.'

Sylvia protested that she had heard the last claim too often.

'No, but this is something much greater than a *béguin*. It is real love. *Il est très trr-ès beau garçon, tu sais*. And, *chose très drôle*, he also is doing his military service here. *Tout ça ne se dessine pas du tout bien, tu sais, mais pas du tout, tu comprends! Moi, je ne suis pas veinarde. Ah, non, alors, c'est le comble!*'

Blanche had been sufficiently agile to extract the usual waggonette and pair of horses from the *chic* lover to whom she had introduced the real lover, a tall cuirassier with fierce moustaches, as her brother; but the imminent arrival of Louis was going to spoil all this, because Louis knew well that she did not possess a relative in the world, in fact, as Blanche emphasized, her solitary position had been one of her charms.

14

'You'll have to get rid of Monsieur Beaujour.' This was the rich lover.
'And lose my horses? *Ah, non, alors!*'

'Well, then you'll have to tell Marcel he mustn't come near you until Louis has gone.'

'And see him go off with that Jeanne at the Clair de la Lune Concert!'

'Couldn't Louis pay for the horses?' suggested Sylvia.

'I'm not going to let him waste his money like that; besides he'll only be here two nights. *C'est assommant, tu sais.*' Blanche sighed.

In the middle of the discussion Louis arrived, a very short little *sous-officier* with kind watery eyes and a moustache that could only be seen properly out of doors. Louis had not had more than five minutes with his *fiancée* before M. Beaujour drove up with the waggonette and pair. He was the son of a rich shipping agent at St. Nazaire, with a stiff manner that he mistook for evidence of aristocratic descent, and bad teeth that prevented him from smiling more than he could help.

'I shall tell him you're my brother,' said Blanche quickly. Louis began to protest.

'*Sans boniment,*' Blanche went on. 'I must be pleasant to strangers in front. Madame Bassompierre insists on that, and you know I've never given you any cause to be really jealous.'

M. Beaujour looked very much surprised when Blanche presented Louis to him as her brother; Sylvia, remembering the tall cuirassier with the fierce moustaches that had also been introduced as Blanche's brother, appreciated his sensations. However, he accepted the relationship and invited Louis to accompany them on the drive, putting him with Sylvia and seating himself next Blanche on the box; Louis, who found Sylvia sympathetic, talked all the time about the wonderful qualities of Blanche, continually turning round to adore her shapely back.

M. Beaujour invited Louis to a supper he was giving that evening in honour of Blanche, and supposed perhaps a little maliciously that Monsieur would be glad to meet his brother again, who was also to be of the party. Louis looked at Blanche in perplexity; she frowned at him and said nothing.

That supper, to which M. and Mme Perron with several other members of the company were invited, was a very restless meal. First, Blanche would go out with the host, while Marcel and Louis glared alternately at each other and the door; then she would withdraw with Louis, while M. Beaujour and Marcel glared and fidgeted; finally she would disappear with Marcel, once for such a long time that Sylvia grew nervous and went outside to find her. Blanche was in tears; Marcel was stalking up and down the passage, twisting his fierce moustaches and muttering his annoyance. Sylvia was involved in a bitter discussion about the various degrees of Blanche's love, and in the end Blanche cried that her whole life had been shattered, and rushed back to the supper-room. Sylvia took this opportunity of representing Blanche's point of view to Marcel, and so successful was she with her tale of the emotional stress caused by the conflict of love with prudence that finally Marcel burst into tears, called down benedictions upon Sylvia's youthful head and rejoined the supper-party, where he drank a great quantity of red wine and squeezed Blanche's hand under the table for the rest of the evening.

Sylvia, having been successful once, now invited Louis to accompany her outside. To him she explained that Marcel loved Blanche madly, that she, the owner, as Louis knew, of a melting heart, had been much upset by her inability to return his love, and that Louis must not be jealous, because Blanche loved only him. Louis' eyes became more watery than ever, and he took his seat at table again, a happy man until he drank too much wine and had to retire permanently from the feast. Finally Sylvia tackled M. Beaujour, and recognizing that he was probably tired of lies told him the truth of the situation, leaving it to him as an *homme supérieur* to realize that he could only be an episode in Blanche's life and begging him not to force his position that night. M. Beaujour could not help being flattered by this child's perception of his superiority and for the rest of the entertainment played the host in a manner that was, as Madame Perron said, *très très-correcte*.

However, amusing evenings like this came to an end for Sylvia, when once more the caravan returned to Lille. Her uncle and aunt had so much enjoyed her company that they proposed to Madame Snow to adopt Sylvia as their own daughter. Sylvia, much as she loved her mother, would have been very glad to leave the house at Lille, for it seemed, when she saw it again, poverty-stricken and pinched. There was only Valentine now left of her sisters, and her mother looked very careworn. Her father, however, declined most positively to listen to the Bassompierres' proposal, and was indeed almost insulting about it. Madame Snow wearily bade Sylvia say no more, and the caravan went on its way again. Sylvia wondered whether life in Lille had always been as dull in reality as this, or if it were dull merely in contrast with the gay life of vagrancy. Everybody in Lille seemed to be quarrelling: her mother was always reproaching Valentine for being late and her father for losing money and herself for idleness in the house. She tried to make friends with her sister, but Valentine was suspicious of her former intimacy with their mother, and repelled her advances. The months dragged on, months of eternal sewing, eternal saving, eternal nagging, eternal sameness. Then one evening, when her mother was standing in the kitchen, giving a last glance at everything before she went down to the theatre, she suddenly threw up her arms, cried in a choking voice, 'Henri!' and collapsed upon the floor. There was nobody in the house except Sylvia, who though she felt very much frightened tried for a long time without success to restore her mother to consciousness. At last her father came in, and bent over his wife.

'Good God, she's dead!' he exclaimed, and Sylvia broke into a sweat of horror to think that she had been alone in the twilight with something dead. Her father struggled to lift the body on the sofa, calling to Sylvia to come and help him. She began to whimper, and he swore at her for cowardice. A clock struck and Sylvia shrieked. Her father began to drag the body toward the sofa; playing cards fell from his sleeves on the dead woman's face.

'Didn't she say anything before she died?' he asked.

Sylvia shook her head.

'She was only forty-six, you know,' he said; in and out of his fingers, round and round his hand, slipped the ten-centime piece.

For some time after his wife's death Henry Snow was inconsolable, and his loudly expressed grief had the effect of making Sylvia seem hard, for she grew impatient with him, especially when every week he used to sell some cherished piece of furniture. She never attempted to explain her sentiments when he accused her of caring more for furniture than for her dead mother: she felt it would be useless to explain them to him, and suffered in silence. What Sylvia found most inexplicable was the way in which her father throve on sorrow, and every day seemed to grow younger. This fact struck her so sharply that one day she penetrated the hostility that had been gathering daily between her and Valentine, and asked her sister if she had observed this queer change. Valentine got very angry; demanded what Sylvia meant; flung out some cruel sneers; and involved her in a scene with her father, who charged her with malice and underhanded behaviour. Sylvia was completely puzzled by the effect of her harmless observation and supposed that Valentine, who had always been jealous of her, had seized the opportunity to make further mischief. She could never understand why Valentine was jealous of her, because Valentine was really beautiful, and very much like her mother, enviable from any point of view, and even now obviously dearer to her stepfather than his own daughter. She would have liked to know where the caravan was now; she was sure that her father would no longer wish to forbid her adoption by Uncle Edouard and Aunt Elise.

The house grew emptier and emptier of furniture; Sylvia found it so hard to obtain any money from her father for current expenses that she was often hungry. She did not like to write to any of her older sisters, because she was afraid that Valentine would make it appear that she was in the wrong and trying to stir up trouble. Summer passed into autumn, and with the lengthening darkness the house became unbearably still; neither her father nor her sister was ever at home; even the clocks had now all disappeared. Sylvia could not bear to remain indoors; for in her nervous hungry state old childish terrors were revived, and the great empty loft at the top of the house was once again inhabited by that one-legged man with whose crutches her mother used to frighten her when naughty long ago. There recurred, too, a story told by her mother on just such a gusty evening as these of how when she first came to Lille she had found an armed burglar under her bed, and of how the man had been caught and imprisoned. Even her mother, who was not a nervous woman, had been frightened by his threats of revenge when he should be free again, and once when she and her mother were sewing together close to the dusky window her mother had fancied she had seen him pass the house, a large pale man in a dark suit. Supposing he should come back now for his revenge? And above all these other terrors was the dread of her mother's ghost.

Sylvia took to going out alone every evening, whether it rained or blew, to seek in the streets relief from the silence of the desolate house. Loneliness came to seem to her the worst suffering imaginable, and the fear of it that was bred during these months haunted her for years to come.

In November about half-past eight of a windy night, Sylvia came back from one of her solitary walks and found her father sitting with a bottle of brandy in the kitchen. His face was haggard; his collar was loose; from time to time he mopped his forehead with a big blue handkerchief and stared at himself in a small cracked shaving-glass that he must have brought down from his bedroom. She asked if he were ill, and he told her not to worry him, but to go out and borrow a railway time-table.

When Sylvia returned she heard Valentine's angry voice in the kitchen, and waited in the passage to know the cause of the dispute.

'No, I won't come with you,' Valentine was saying. 'You must be mad! If you're in danger of going to prison, so much the worse for you. I've got plenty of people who'll look after me.'

'But I'm your stepfather.'

Valentine's laugh made Sylvia turn pale.

'Stepfather! Fine stepfather! Why, I hate you. Do you hear? I hate you! My man is waiting for me now, and he'll laugh when he hears that a convict wants his stepdaughter to go away with him. My mother may have loved you, but I'd like her to see you now. *L'amour de sa vie. Son homme! Sa poupée, sa poupée! Ah, mais non alors! Sa poupée!'*

Sylvia could not bear any longer this mockery of her mother's love, and bursting into the kitchen she began to abuse Valentine with all the vulgar words she had learnt from Blanche.

Valentine caught her sister by the shoulders and shook her violently:

'Tu seras bien avec ton père, sale gosse!'

Then she smacked her cheek several times and left the house.

Sylvia flung her arms round her father.

'Take me with you,' she cried. 'You hate her, don't you? Take me, father.'

Henry rose, and in rising upset the bottle of brandy.

'Thank God,' he said fervently. 'My own daughter still loves me.'

Sylvia perceived nothing ludicrous in the tone of her father's speech, and happy tears rose to her eyes.

'See! here is the time-table. Must we go to-night? Shan't we go to-night?'

She helped her father to pack; at midnight they were in the train going north.

II

The amount of brandy that Henry Snow had drunk to support what he called his misfortune made him loquacious for the first part of the journey; while he and Sylvia waited during the night at a railway-junction, he held forth at length not merely upon the event that was driving him out of France, but generally upon the whole course of his life. Sylvia was glad that her father treated her as if she were grown up, because having conceived for him a kind of maternal solicitude, not so much from pity or affection as from the inspiration to quit Lille for ever which she gratefully owed to his lapse, she had no intention of letting him re-establish any authority over herself: his life's history poured forth while they paced the dark platform or huddled before the stove in the dim waiting-room confirmed her resolve.

'Of course, when I first got that job in Lille it seemed just what I was looking for. I'd had a very scrappy education, because my father who was cashier in a bank died, and my mother who you're a bit like – I used to have a photograph of her but I suppose it's lost like everything else – my mother got run over and killed coming back from the funeral. There's something funny about that, you know. I remember your mother laughed very much when I told her about it once. But I didn't laugh at the time I can tell you, because it meant two aunts playing battledore and shuttlecock – don't interrupt, there's a good girl. It's a sort of game. I can't remember what it is in French. I daresay it doesn't exist in France. You'll have to stick to English now. Good old England, it's not a bad place. Well, these two aunts of mine grudged every penny they spent on me, but one of them got married to a man who knew the firm I worked for in Lille. That's how I came to France. Where are my aunts now? Dead, I hope. Don't you fret, Sylvia, we shan't trouble any of our relations for a long time to come. Then after I'd been in France about four years I married your mother. If you ask me why, I can't tell you. I loved her; but the thing was wrong somehow. It put me in a false position. Well, look at me! I'm only thirty-four now. Who'd think you were my daughter?

'And while we're talking on serious subjects, let me give you a bit of advice. Keep off jealousy. Jealousy is hell; and your mother was jealous well French women are more jealous than English women. You can't get over that fact. The scenes I've had with her. It was no good my pointing out that she was fourteen years older than me. Not a bit of good. It made her worse. That's why I took to reading. I *had* to get away from her sometimes and shut myself up. That's why I took to cards. And that's where your mother was wrong. She'd rather I gambled away her money, because it's no use to pretend that it wasn't her money, than go and sit at a café and perhaps observe – mind you, simply observe another woman. I used to drink a bit too much when we were first married, but it caused such rows that I gave that up. I remember I broke an umbrella once, and you'd really have thought there wasn't another umbrella in the whole world. Why, that little drop of brandy I drank to-night has made me feel quite funny. I'm not used to it. But there was some excuse for drinking to-night. I've had runs of bad luck before, but anything like these last two months I've never had in my life. The consequence was I borrowed some of my salary in advance without consulting anybody. That's where the manager had me this afternoon. He couldn't see that it was merely borrowing. As a matter of fact the sum wasn't worth an argument; but he wasn't content with that, he actually told me he was going to examine – well – you wouldn't understand if I tried to explain to you – it would take a commercial training to understand what I've been doing. Anyway, I made up my mind to make a bolt for it. Now don't run away with the notion that the police will be after me, because I very much hope they won't. In fact I don't think they'll do anything. But the whole affair gave me a shock, and

Valentine's behaviour upset me. You see, when your mother was alive, if I'd had a bad week, she used to help me out; but Valentine actually asked *me* for money. She accused me of all sorts of things, which luckily you're too young to understand; and I really didn't like to refuse her, when I'd got the money.

'Well, it's been a lesson to me, and I tell you I've missed your mother these last months. She was jealous; she was close; she had a tongue; but a finer woman never lived, and I'm proud of her. She used to wish you were a boy. Well, I don't blame her. After all, she'd had six girls; and what use are they to anybody? None at all. They might as well not exist. Women go off and get married and take somebody else's name, and it's finished. There's not one of your sisters that's really stayed in the family. A selfish crowd, and the worst of the lot was Valentine. Yes, you ought to have been a boy. I'll tell you what, it wouldn't be a bad idea if you *were* a boy for a bit. You see in case the French police make enquiries, it would be just as well to throw them off the scent; and, another thing, it would be much easier for me till I find my feet in London. Would you like to be a boy, Sylvia? There's no reason against it that I can see, and plenty of reasons for it. Of course it means cutting off your hair, but they say that's a very good thing for the hair once in a way. You'll be more free too as a boy, and less of a responsibility. There's no doubt a girl would be a big responsibility in London.'

'But could I be a boy?' Sylvia asked. 'I'd like to be a boy if I could. And what should I be called?'

'Of course you could be a boy,' her father affirmed enthusiastically. 'You were always a bit of a *garçon manqué*, as the French say: I'll buy you a Norfolk suit.'

Sylvia was not yet sufficiently unsexed not to want to know more about her proposed costume. Her father pledged his word that it would please her; his description of it recalled the dress that people in Lille put on to go shooting sparrows on Sunday.

'*Un sporting?*' Sylvia queried.

'That's about it,' her father agreed. 'If you had any scissors with you, I'd start right in now and cut your hair.'

Sylvia said she had scissors in her bag; and presently she and her father retired to the outer gloom of the junction, where, undisturbed by a single curious glance, Sylvia's curls were swept away by the wind.

'I've not done it quite so neatly as I might,' said her father, examining the effect under a wavering gas-jet. 'I'll have you properly cropped to-morrow at a hairdresser's.'

Sylvia felt cold and bare round the neck, but she welcomed the sensation as one of freedom. How remote Lille seemed already, utterly, gloriously far away! Now arose the problem of her name.

'The only boy's name I can think of that's anything like Sylvia is Silas, and that's more Si than Sil. Wait a bit. What about Silvius? I've seen that name somewhere. Only we'll call you Sil for short.'

'Why was I ever called Sylvia?' she asked.

'It was a fancy of your mother's. It comes in a song called *Plaisir d'amour*. And your mother liked the English way of saying it. I've got it. Sylvester! Sylvester Snow! What do you want better than that?'

When the train approached Boulogne, Henry Snow gave up talking and began to juggle with the ten-centime piece; while they were walking along to the boat he looked about him furtively. Nobody stopped them, however; and with the kind of relief she had felt when she had brought her album safely over the frontier Sylvia saw the coast of France recede. There were many English people on the boat, and Sylvia watched them with such concentration that several elderly ladies at whom she stared in turn thought she was waiting for them to be sick, and irritably waved her away. The main impression of her fellow-travellers was their resemblance to the blind beggars that one saw sitting outside churches: she was tempted to drop a *sou* in one of the basins, but forbore, not feeling quite sure how such humour would appeal to the English. Presently she managed to engage in conversation an English girl of her own age, but she had not got far with the many questions she wanted to ask, when her companion was whisked away, and she heard a voice reproving her for talking to strange little girls. Sylvia decided that the strangeness of her appearance must be due to her short hair, and she longed for the complete transformation. Soon it began to rain; the shores of that mysterious land to which she actually belonged swam towards her. Her father came up from below, where, as he explained, he had been trying to sleep off the effects of a bad night. Indeed he did not recover his usual jauntiness until they were in the train, travelling through country that seemed to Sylvia not very different from the country of France. Would London after all prove to be very different from Lille? Then slowly the compartment grew dark, and from time to time the train stopped.

'A fog,' said her father, and he explained to her the meaning of a London fog.

It grew darker and darker, with a yellowish-brown darkness that was unlike any obscurity she had ever known.

'Bit of luck,' said her father. 'We shan't be noticed in this. Phew! It is thick. We'd better go to some hotel close by for to-night. No good setting out to look for rooms in this.'

22

In the kitchen at Lille there had been a picture called *The Impenitent Sinner*, in which demons were seen dragging a dead man from his bed into flames and darkness; Sylvia pointed out its likeness to the present scene at Charing Cross. Outside the station it was even worse: there was a thunderous din; horses came suddenly out of the darkness; everybody seemed to be shouting; boys were running along with torches; it was impossible to breathe.

'Why did they build a city here?' she enquired.

At last they came to a house in a quieter street, where they walked up high narrow stairs to their bedrooms.

The next morning her father took Sylvia's measurements and told her not to get up before he came back. When she walked out beside him in a Norfolk suit nobody seemed to stare at her; when her hair had been properly cut by a barber and she could look at herself in a long glass, she plunged her hands into her trouser-pockets and felt securely a boy.

While they were walking to a mysterious place called the Underground, her father asked if she had caught bronchitis, and he would scarcely accept her word that she was trying to practise whistling.

'Well, don't do it when I'm enquiring about rooms, or the people in the house may think it's something infectious,' he advised. 'And don't forget your name's Sylvester. Which reminds me it wouldn't be a bad notion if I was to change my own name. There's no sense in running one's head into a noose, and if enquiries *were* made by the police it would be foolish to ram my name right down their throats. Henry Snow. What about Henry White? Better keep to the same initials. I've got it. Henry Scarlett. You couldn't find anything more opposite to Snow than that.'

Thus Sylvia Snow became Sylvester Scarlett.

After a long search they took rooms with Mrs. Threadgould, a widow who with her two boys, Willie and Ernie, lived at 45 Pomona Terrace, Shepherd's Bush. There were no other lodgers, for the house was small; and Henry Scarlett decided it was just the place in which to stay quietly for a while until the small sum of money he had brought with him from Lille was finished, when it would be necessary to look for work. Meanwhile, he announced that he should study very carefully the advertisements in the daily papers, leaving everybody with the impression that reading advertisements was a most erudite business, a kind of scientific training that when the moment arrived would produce practical results.

Sylvia meanwhile was enjoined to amuse herself in the company of Mrs. Threadgould's two boys, who were about her own age. It happened that at this time Willie Threadgould the elder was obsessed by Secret Societies, to which his brother Ernie and many other boys in the neighbourhood had recently been initiated. Sylvia was regarded with suspicion by Willie, until she was able to thrill him with the story of various criminal associations in France and so become his lieutenant in all enterprises. Most of the Secret Societies that had been rapidly formed by Willie and as rapidly dissolved had possessed a merely academic value; now with Sylvia's advent they were given a practical intention. Secrecy for secrecy's sake went out of fashion: muffling the face in dusters, giving the sign and countersign, lurking at the corner of the road to meet another conspirator were excellent decorations; but Sylvia pointed out that they led nowhere and produced nothing; to illustrate her theory she proposed a Secret Society for ringing other people's bells. She put this forward as a kind of elementary exercise; but she urged that, when the neighbourhood had realized the bell-ringing as something to which they were more continuously exposed than other neighbourhoods, the moment would be ripe to form another Secret Society that should inflict a more serious nuisance. From the Secret Society that existed to be a nuisance would grow another Secret Society that existed to be a threat, and finally there seemed no reason why Willie Threadgould (Sylvia was still feminine enough to let Willie think it was Willie) should not control Shepherd's Bush and emulate the most remarkable brigands of history. In the end Sylvia's imagination banished her from the ultimate power at which she aimed: the Secret Society for Ringing Other People's Bells did its work so well that extra policemen were put on duty to cope with the nuisance, and an inspector made a house-to-house visitation, which gave her father such a shock that he left Pomona Terrace the next day and took a room in Lillie Road, Fulham.

'We have been betrayed,' Sylvia assured Willie. 'Do not forget to avenge my capture.'

Willie vowed he would let nothing interfere with his vengeance, not even if the traitor turned out to be his own brother Ernie.

Sylvia asked if he would kill him, and reminded Willie that it was a serious thing to betray a Secret Society when that Society was doing something more than dress up. Willie doubted if it would be possible to kill the culprit, but swore that he should prefer death to what should happen to him.

Sylvia was so much gratified by Willie's severity that she led him into a corner where, having extracted his silence with the most solemn oaths, she betrayed herself and the secret of her sex: then they embraced. When they parted for ever next day, Sylvia felt that she had left behind her in Willie's heart a romantic memory that would never fade.

Mrs. Meares who kept the house in Lillie Road was an Irishwoman whose husband had grown tired of her gentility and left her. She did not herself sum up her past so tersely as this, but Sylvia was sure that Mr. Meares had left her because he could no longer endure the stories about her royal descent. Perhaps he might have been able to endure his wife's royal descent, because after all he had married into the family and might have extracted some pride out of that fact; but all her friends apparently came from kings and queens too; Ireland, if Mrs. Meares was to be believed, consisted of one large poverty-stricken royal family, which must have cheapened the alliance for Mr. Meares. It was lucky that he was still alive, for otherwise Sylvia was sure that her father would have married their new landlady, such admiration did he always express for the manner in which she struggled against misfortune without losing her dignity. This from what Sylvia could see consisted of wearing silk skirts that trailed in the dust of her ill-kept house and of her fanning herself in an arm-chair, however cold the weather. The only thing that stirred her to action was the necessity of averting an ill-omen. Thus, she would turn back on a flight of stairs rather than pass anybody descending; although ordinarily when she went upstairs she used to sigh and hold her heart at every step. Sylvia remembered her mother's scrupulous care of her house, even in the poorest days; she could not help contrasting her dignity with this Irish dignity that was content to see indefinite fried eggs on her table, cockroaches in the bedroom, and her placket always agape. Mrs. Meares used to say that she would never let any of her rooms to ladies, because ladies always fussed.

'Gentlemen are so much more considerate,' said Mrs. Meares.

Their willingness to be imposed upon made Sylvia contemptuous of the sex she had adopted, and she tried to spur her father to protest when his bed was still unmade at four o'clock in the afternoon.

'Why don't *you* make it?' he suggested. 'I don't like to worry poor Mrs. Meares.'

Sylvia, however contemptuous of manhood, had no intention of relinquishing its privileges; she firmly declined to have anything to do with the making of beds.

The breakfast-room was placed below the level of the street: here in an atmosphere of cat-haunted upholstery and broken springs, of over-cooked vegetables and dingy fires, yet withal of a kind of frowsty comfort, Sylvia sometimes met the other lodgers. One of them was Baron von Statten, a queer German, whom Sylvia could not make out at all, for he spoke English as if he had been taught by the maid-of-all-work with a bad cold, powdered his pink face and wore three rings, yet was so poor that sometimes he stayed in bed for a week at a stretch, pending negotiations with his laundress. The last piece of information Sylvia obtained from Clara the servant, who professed a great contempt for the Baron. Mrs. Meares, on the other hand, derived much pride from his position in her house, which she pointed out was really that of an honoured guest, since he owed now nearly seven weeks' rent; she never failed to refer to him by his title with warm affection. Another lodger was a Welsh pianist called Morgan, who played the piano all day long and billiards for as much of the night as he could. He was a bad-tempered young man with long black hair and a great antipathy to the Baron, whom he was always trying to insult; indeed once at breakfast he actually poured a cup of coffee over him.

'Mr. Morgan!' Mrs. Meares had cried. 'No Irishman would have done that.'

'No Irishman would ever do anything,' the pianist snapped, 'if he could get somebody else to do it for him.'

Sylvia welcomed the assault, because the scalding coffee drove the Baron to unbutton his waistcoat in a frenzy of discomfort, and thereby confirmed Clara's legend about the scarcity of his linen.

The third lodger was Mr. James Monkley, about whom Sylvia was undecided; sometimes she liked him very much, at other times she disliked him equally. He had curly red hair, finely cut red lips, a clear complexion and an authoritative, determined manner, but his eyes instead of being the pleasant blue they ought to have been in such a face were of a shade of muddy green and never changed their expression. Sylvia once mentioned Mr. Monkley's eyes to Clara, who said they were like a fish.

'But Monkley's not like a fish,' Sylvia argued.

'I don't know what he's like, I'm sure,' said Clara. 'All I know is he gives anyone the creeps something shocking whenever he stares, which he's for ever doing. Well, fine feathers don't make a summer and he looks best who looks last, as they say.'

One reason for disliking Mr. Monkley was his intimacy with her father: Sylvia would not have objected to this if it had not meant long confabulations during which she was banished from the room and, what was worse, thrown into the society of Mrs. Meares, who always seemed to catch her when she was trying to make her way downstairs to Clara.

'Come in and talk to me,' Mrs. Meares would say. 'I'm just tidying up my bedroom. Ah, Sil, if God had not willed otherwise I would have had a boy just your age now. Poor little innocent!'

Sylvia knew too well this counterpart of hers and hated him as much in his baby's grave as she might have done were he still her competitor in life.

'Ah, it's a terrible thing to be left as I've been left, to be married and not married, to have been a mother and to have lost my child. And I was never intended for this life. My father kept horses. We had a carriage. But they say, "Trust an Irishwoman to turn her hand to anything." And it's true. There's many people would be wondering how I do it with only one maid. How's your dear father? He seems comfortable. Ah, it's a privilege to look after a gentleman like him. He seems to have led a most adventurous life. Most of his time spent abroad, he tells me. Well, travel gives an air to a man. Ah, now if one of the cats hasn't been naughty just when I'd got my room really tidy! Will you tell Clara, if you are going downstairs, to bring up a dustpan? I don't mind asking you, for at your age I think you would be glad to wait on the ladies like a little gentleman. Sure, as your father said the other day, it's a very good thing you're in a lady's house. That's why the dear Baron's so content; and the poor man has much to try him, for his relations in Berlin have treated him abominably.'

Such speeches inflicted upon her because Monkley wanted to talk secrets with her father made her disapprove of Monkley. Nevertheless, she admired him in a way; he was the only person in the house who was not limp, except Mr. Morgan the pianist, but he used to glare at her, when they occasionally met, and seemed to regard her as an unpleasant result of being late for breakfast, like a spot on the tablecloth made by a predecessor's egg.

Monkley used to ask Sylvia sometimes about what she was going to do. Naturally he treated her future as a boy's future, which took most of the interest out of the conversation; for Sylvia did not suppose that she should be able to remain a boy very much longer. The mortifying fact, too, was that she was not getting anything out of her transformation: for all the fun she was having, she might as well have stayed a girl. There had been a brief vista of liberty at Pomona Terrace; here, beyond going out to buy a paper or tobacco for her father, she spent most of her time in gossiping with Clara, which she could probably have done more profitably in petticoats.

Winter drew out to spring; to the confabulations between Jimmy Monkley and Henry Scarlett were now added absences from the house that lasted for a day or two at a time. These expeditions always began with the friends' dressing up in pearl-buttoned overcoats very much cut in at the waist. Sylvia felt that such careful attention to externals augured the great secrecy and importance of the enterprise; remembering the effect of Willie Threadgould's duster-shrouded countenance upon his fellow-conspirators, she postulated to herself that with the human race, particularly the male portion, dress was always the prelude to action.

One morning after breakfast when Monkley and her father hurried off to catch a train the Baron said in his mincing voice:

'Off ra-cing again! They do enjoy themselves-s-s.'

She asked what racing meant, and the Baron replied:

'Hors-s-se-ra-cing, of cour-se.'

Sylvia, being determined to arrive at the truth of this business, put the Baron through a long interrogation from which she managed to learn that the jockeys wore coloured silk jackets and that in his prosperous days the Baron had found the sport too exciting for his heart. After breakfast Sylvia took the subject with her into the kitchen, and tried to obtain fuller information from Clara, who with the prospect of a long morning's work was disinclined to be communicative.

'What a boy you are for asking questions. Why don't you ask your dad when he comes home, or that Monkley? As if I'd got time to talk about racing. I've got enough racing of my own to think about, but if it goes on much longer, I shall race off out of it one of these days, and that's a fact. You may take a pitcher to the well, but you can't make it drink, as they say.'

Sylvia withdrew for a while, but later in the afternoon she approached Clara again.

'God bless the boy! He's got racing on the brain,' the maid exclaimed. 'I had a young man like that once, but I soon gave him the go-by. He was that stuffed up with halfpenny papers he couldn't cuddle anyone without crackling like an egg-shell. "Don't carry on so, Clara," he said to me, "I had a winner to-day in the three-thirty." "Did you?" I answered very cool. "Well, you've got a loser now," and with that I walked off very dignified and left him. It's the last straw, they say, as gives the camel the hump. And he properly gave me the hump. But I reckon, I do, that it's mugs like him as keeps your dad and that Monkley so smart-looking. I reckon most of the racing they do is racing to see which can get some silly josser to give them his money first.'

Sylvia informed Clara that her father used to play cards for money in France.

'There you are, what did I tell you?' Clara went on. 'Nap, they call it, but I reckon that there Monkley keeps wide enough awake. Oh, he's an artful one, he is. Birds and feathers keep together, they say, and I reckon your dad's cleverer than what he makes out to be.'

Sylvia produced in support of this idea her father's habit of juggling with a penny.

'What did I tell you?' Clara exclaimed triumphantly. 'Take it from me, Sil, the two of them has a rare old time with this racing. I've got a friend

Maudie Tilt who's in service, and her brother started off to be a jockey, only he never got very far because he got kicked on the head by a horse when he was sweeping out the stable, which was very aggravating for his relations, because he had a sister who died in a galloping consumption the same week. I reckon horses was very unlucky for them, I do.'

'My grandmother got run over coming back from my grandfather's funeral,' Sylvia proclaimed.

'By the hearse?' Clara asked, awestruck.

Sylvia felt it would be well to make the most of her story and replied without hesitation in the affirmative.

'Well, they say to meet an empty hearse means a pleasant surprise,' said Clara. 'But I reckon your grandma didn't think so. Here, I'll tell you what, my next afternoon off I'll take you round to see Maudie Tilt. She lives not far from where the Cedars bus stops.'

About a week after this conversation Clara, wearing balloon sleeves of last year's fashion and with her hair banked up to support a monstrous hat, descended into the basement, whence she and Sylvia emerged into a fine April afternoon and hailed an omnibus.

'Mind you don't get blown off the top, miss,' said the conductor with a glance at Clara's sleeves.

'No fear of that. I've grown a bit heavier since I saw your face,' Clara replied, climbing serenely to the top of the omnibus. 'Two, as far as you go,' she said, handing twopence to the conductor when he came up for the fares.

'I could go a long way with you, miss,' he said, punching the tickets with a satisfied twinkle. 'What a lovely hat!'

'Is it? Well, don't start in trying to eat it because you've been used to green food all your life.'

'Your sister answers very sharp, doesn't she, Tommy?' said the conductor to Sylvia.

After this display of raillery Sylvia felt it would be weak merely to point out that Clara was not a sister, so she remained silent.

The top of the omnibus was empty except for Clara and Sylvia; the conductor, whistling a cheerful tune, had descended again.

'Saucy things,' Clara commented. 'But there, you can't blame them. It makes anyone feel cheerful to be out in the open air like this.'

Maudie's house in Castleford Road was soon reached after they left the omnibus; when they rang the area-bell, Maudie herself opened the door.

'Oh, you did give me a turn,' she exclaimed. 'I *thought* it was early for the milkman. You couldn't have come at a better time because they've both gone away. She's been ill, and they'll be away for a month. Cook's gone for a holiday, and I'm all alone.'

Sylvia was presented formally to the hostess; and when at Clara's prompting she had told the story of her grandmother's death, conversation became easy. Maudie Tilt took them all over the house and, though Clara said she should die of nervousness, insisted upon their having tea in the drawing-room.

'Supposing they come back,' Clara whispered. 'Oh, lor! Whatever's that?'

Maudie told her not to be silly, and went on to boast that she did not care if they did come back, because she had made up her mind to give up domestic service and go on the stage.

'Fancy!' said Clara. 'Whoever put that idea into your head?'

'Well, I started learning some of the songs they sing in the halls, and some friends of mine gave a party last January and I made quite a hit. I'll sing you a song now, if you like.'

And Maudie, sitting down at the piano, accompanied herself with much effect in one of Miss Vesta Victoria's songs.

'For goodness' sake keep quiet, Maudie,' Clara begged. 'You'll have the neighbours coming round to see whatever's the matter. You have got a cheek.'

Sylvia thoroughly enjoyed Maudie's performance and thought she would have a great success. She liked Maudie's smallness and neatness and glittering dark eyes. Altogether it was a delightful afternoon, and she was sorry to go away.

'Come again,' cried Maudie, 'before they come back, and we'll have some more.'

'Oh, I did feel frightened,' Clara said, when she and Sylvia were hurrying to catch the omnibus back to Lillie Road. 'I couldn't enjoy it not a bit. I felt as if I was in the bath and the door not bolted, though they do say stolen fruit is the sweetest.'

When she got home, Sylvia found that her father had returned also, and she held forth on the joys of Maudie Tilt's house.

'Wants to go on the stage, does she?' said Monkley who was in the room. 'Well, you'd better introduce us, and we'll see what we can do, eh, Harry?'

Sylvia approved of this suggestion and eagerly vouched for Maudie's willingness.

'We'll have a little supper-party,' said Monkley. 'Sil can go round and tell her we're coming.'

Sylvia blessed the persistency with which she had worried Clara on the subject of racing; otherwise, bisexual and solitary, she might have been moping in Lillie Road. She hoped that Maudie Tilt would not offer any objections to the proposed party, and determined to point out most persuasively the benefit of Monkley's patronage, if she really meant to go on the stage. However, Maudie was not at all difficult to convince and showed herself as eager for the party as Sylvia herself. She was greatly impressed by her visitor's experience of the stage, but reckoned that no boys should have pinched her legs or given her the broken masks.

'You ought to have punched into them,' she said. 'Still I daresay it wasn't so easy for you, not being a girl. Boys are very nasty to one another, when they'd be as nice as anything to a girl.'

Sylvia was conscious of a faint feeling of contempt for Maudie's judgment, and she wondered from what her illusions were derived.

Clara, when she heard of the proposed party, was dubious; she had no confidence in Monkley, and said so frankly.

'No one wants to go chasing after a servant girl for nothing,' she declared. 'Every cloud's got a silver lining.'

'But what could he want to do wrong?' Sylvia asked.

'Ah, now you're asking. But if I was Maudie Tilt I'd keep myself to myself.'

Clara snapped out the last remark and would say nothing more on the subject.

A few days later under Sylvia's guidance James Monkley and Henry Scarlett sought Castleford Road. Maudie had put on a black silk dress, and with her hair done in what she called the French fashion she achieved a kind of Japanese piquancy.

'*N'est-ce pas qu'elle a un chic?*' Sylvia whispered to her father.

They had supper in the dining-room and made a good deal of noise over it, for Monkley had brought two bottles of champagne, and Maudie could not resist producing a bottle of cognac from her master's cellar. When Monkley asked if everything were not kept under lock and key, Maudie told him that if they couldn't trust her they could lump it; she could jolly soon find another place; and anyway she intended to get on the stage somehow. After supper they went upstairs to the drawing-room; and Maudie was going to sit down at the piano, when Monkley told her that he would accompany her, because he wanted to see how she danced. Maudie gave a most spirited performance, kicking up her legs and stamping until the ornaments on the mantelpiece rattled. Then Monkley showed Maudie where she could make improvements in her renderings, which surprised Sylvia very much, because she had never connected Monkley with anything like this.

'Quite an artist is Jimmy,' Henry Scarlett declared. Then he added in an undertone to Sylvia, 'he's a wonderful chap, you know. I've taken a rare fancy to him. Do anything. Sharp as a needle. I may as well say right out that he's made all the difference to my life in London.'

Presently Monkley suggested that Maudie should show them over the house, and they went further upstairs to the principal bedroom, where the two men soused their heads with the various hairwashes left behind by the master of the house. Henry expressed a desire to have a bath and retired with an enormous sponge and a box of bath-salts. Monkley began to flirt with Maudie; Sylvia, feeling that the evening was becoming rather dull, went downstairs again to the drawing-room and tried to pass the time away with a stereoscope.

After that evening Monkley and Scarlett went often to see Maudie, but much to Sylvia's resentment they never took her with them. When she grumbled about this to Clara, Clara told her that she was well out of it.

'Too many cooks spoil the soup, which means you're one too many, my lad, and a rolling stone doesn't let the grass grow under its feet, which means as that Monkley's got some game on.'

Sylvia did not agree with Clara's point of view; she still felt aggrieved at being left out of everything. Luckily when life in Lillie Road was becoming utterly dull again, a baboon escaped from Earl's Court Exhibition, climbed up the drain-pipe outside the house, and walked into Mrs. Meares' bedroom; so that for some time after this she had palpitations whenever a bell rang. Mr. Morgan was very unkind about her adventure, for he declared that the baboon looked so much like an Irishman that she must have thought it was her husband come back; Mr. Morgan had been practising the Waldstein Sonata at the time and had been irritated by the interruption of a wandering ape.

A fortnight after this, there was a scene in the house that touched Sylvia more sharply, for Maudie Tilt arrived one morning and begged to speak with Mr. Monkley, who being in the Scarletts' room at the moment looked suddenly at Sylvia's father with a question in his eyes.

'I told you not to take them all,' Henry said.

'I'll soon calm her down,' Monkley promised. 'If you hadn't insisted on taking those bottles of hairwash she'd never have thought of looking to see if the other things were still there.'

Henry indicated his daughter with a gesture.

'Rot! the kid's got to stand in on this,' Monkley said with a laugh. 'After all it was he who introduced us. I'll bring her up here to talk it out,' he added.

Presently he returned with Maudie, who had very red eyes and a frightened expression.

32

'Oh, Jimmy,' she burst out. 'Whatever did you want to take that jewelry for? I only found out last night and they'll be home to-morrow. Whatever am I going to say?'

'Jewelry?' repeated Monkley in a puzzled voice. 'Harry took some hairwash, if that's what you mean.'

'Jewelry?' Henry murmured, taking the cue from his friend. 'Was there any jewelry?'

'Oh, don't pretend you don't know nothing about it,' Maudie cried, dissolving into tears. 'For the love of God give it to me, so as I can put it back. If you're hard up, Jimmy, you can take what I saved for the stage; but give us back that jewelry.'

'If you act like that, you'll make your fortune as a professional,' Monkley sneered.

Maudie turned to Sylvia in desperation.

'Sil,' she cried, 'make them give it back. It'll be the ruin of me. Why, it's burglary. Oh, whatever shall I do?'

Maudie flung herself down on the bed and wept convulsively. Sylvia felt her heart beating fast, but she strung herself up to the encounter, and faced Monkley.

'What's the good of saying you haven't got the jewelry,' she cried, 'when you know you have? Give it to her, or I'll – I'll go out into the middle of the road and shout at the top of my voice that there's a snake in the house, and people will have to come in and look for it, because when they didn't believe about the baboon in Mrs. Meares' room, the baboon was there all the time.'

She stopped and challenged Monkley with flashing eyes, head thrown back, and agitated breast.

'You oughtn't to talk to a grown-up person like that, you know,' said her father.

Something unspeakably soft in his attitude infuriated Sylvia, and spinning round she flashed out at him.

'If you don't make Monkley give back the things you stole, I'll tell everybody about *you*. I mean it. I'll tell everybody.'

She stamped her feet.

'That's a daughter,' said Henry. 'That's the way they're bringing them up nowadays – to turn round on their fathers.'

'A daughter?' Monkley echoed with an odd look at his friend.

'I mean son,' said Henry weakly. 'Anyway it's all the same.'

Monkley seemed to pay no more attention to the slip, but went over to Maudie and began to coax her.

'Come on, Maudie, don't turn away from a good pal. What if we did

33

take a few things? They shouldn't have left them behind. People deserve to lose things, if they're so careless.'

'That's quite true,' Henry agreed virtuously. 'It'll be a lesson to them.'

'Go back and pack up your things, my dear, and get out of the house. I'll see you through. You shall take another name and go on the stage right away. What's the good of crying over a few rings and bangles?'

But Maudie refused to be comforted.

'Give them back to me. Give them back to me,' she moaned.

'Oh, all right,' Monkley said suddenly. 'But you're no sport, Maudie. You've got the chance of your life and you're turning it down. Well, don't blame me if you find yourself still a slavey five years hence.'

Monkley went downstairs and came back again in a minute or two with a parcel wrapped up in tissue paper.

'You haven't kept anything back?' Maudie asked anxiously.

'My dear girl, you ought to know how many there were. Count them.'

'Would you like me to give you back the hairwash?' Henry asked indignantly.

Maudie rose to go away.

'You're not angry with me, Jim?' she asked pleadingly.

'Oh, get out,' he snapped.

Maudie turned pale, and rushed from the room.

'Silly bitch,' Monkley said. 'Well, it's been a very instructive morning,' he added, fixing Sylvia with his green eyes and making her feel uncomfortable.

'Some people make a fuss about the least little thing,' Henry said. 'There was just the same trouble when I pawned my wife's jewelry. Coming round the corner to have one?' he enquired, looking at Monkley, who said he would join him presently and followed him out of the room.

When she was alone, Sylvia tried without success to put her emotions in order. She had wished for excitement; now that it had arrived, she wished it had kept away from her. She was not so much shocked by the revelation of what her father and Monkley had done (though she resented their cowardly treatment of Maudie) as frightened by what might ultimately happen to her in their company. They might at any moment find themselves in prison, and if she were to be let out before the others, what would she do? She should be utterly alone and should starve: or what seemed more likely, they would be arrested and she should remain in Lillie Road, waiting for news and perhaps compelled to earn her living by working for Mrs. Meares. At all costs she must be kept informed of what was going on. If her father tried to shut her out of his confidence, she would appeal to Monkley. Her meditation was interrupted by Monkley himself.

34

'So you're a little girl,' he said suddenly. 'Fancy that.'

'What if I am?' challenged Sylvia, who saw no hope of successfully denying the accusation.

'Oh, I don't know,' he murmured. 'It's more fun, that's all. But, look here, girl or boy, don't let me ever have any more heroics from you. D'ye hear? Or, by god, I'll—'

Sylvia felt that the only way of dealing with Monkley was to stand up to him from the first.

'Oh, shut up,' she broke in. 'You can't frighten me. Next time, perhaps you'll tell me beforehand what you're going to do, and then I'll see if I'll let you do it.'

He began to laugh.

'You've got some pluck.'

'Why?'

'Why, to cheek me like that.'

'I'm not Maudie, you see,' Sylvia pointed out.

Presently a spasm of self-consciousness made her long to be once more in petticoats, and, grabbing wildly at her flying boyhood, she said how much she wanted to have adventures. Monkley promised she should have as many as she liked, and bade her farewell, saying that he was going to join her father in a saloon-bar round the corner. Sylvia volunteered to accompany him, and after a momentary hesitation he agreed to take her. On the stairs they overtook the Baron very much dressed up, who in answer to an enquiry from Monkley informed them that he was going to lunch with the Emperor of Byzantium.

'Give my love to the Empress,' Monkley laughed.

'It's-s nothing to laugh at,' the Baron said severely. 'He lives in West Kensington.'

'Next door to the Pope, I suppose,' Monkley went on.

'You never will be serious, but I'll take you there one afternoon, if you don't believe me.'

The Baron continued on his way downstairs with a kind of mincing dignity, and Mrs. Meares came out of her bedroom.

'Isn't it nice for the dear Baron?' she purred. 'He's received some of his money from Berlin, and at last he can go and look up his old friends. He's lunching with the Emperor to-day.'

'I hope he won't knock his crown in the soup,' Monkley said.

'Ah, give over laughing, Mr. Monkley, for I like to think of the poor Baron in the society to which he belongs. And he doesn't forget his old friends. But there, after all, why would he, for though I'm living in Lillie Road, I've got the real spirit of the past in my blood, and the idea of meeting the Emperor doesn't elate me at all. It seems somehow as if I were used to meeting Emperors.'

On the way to the public-house Monkley held forth to Sylvia on the prevalence of human folly, and vowed that he would hold the Baron to his promise and visit the Emperor himself.

'And take me with you?' Sylvia asked.

'You seem very keen on the new partnership,' he observed.

'I don't want to be left out of things,' she explained. 'Not out of anything. It makes me look stupid. Father treats me like a little girl; but it's he who's stupid really.'

They had reached the public-house, and Henry was taken aback by Sylvia's arrival. She for her part was rather disappointed in the saloon-bar: the words had conjured something much more sumptuous than this place that reminded her of a chemist's shop.

'I don't want the boy to start learning to drink,' Henry protested.

Monkley told him to give up the fiction of Sylvia's boyhood with him: to which Henry replied that though, as far as he knew, he had only been sitting here ten minutes, Jimmy and Sylvia seemed to have settled the whole world between them in that time.

'What's more, if she's going to remain a boy any longer, she's got to have some new clothes,' Monkley announced.

Sylvia flushed with pleasure, recognizing that co-operative action of which preliminary dressing-up was the pledge.

'You see I've promised to take her round with me to the Emperor of Byzantium.'

'I don't know that pub,' said Henry. 'Is it Walham Green way?'

Monkley told him about meeting the Baron, and put forward his theory that people who were willing to be duped by the Emperor of Byzantium would be equally willing to be duped by other people with much profit to the other people.

'Meaning you and me?' said Henry.

'Well, in this case, I propose to leave you out of the first act,' Monkley said. 'I'm going to have a look at the scene myself. There's no one like you with the cards, Harry, but when it comes to the patter I think you'll give me first.'

Presently, Sylvia was wearing Etons at Monkley's suggestion and waiting in a dream of anticipation; the Baron proclaimed that the Emperor would hold a reception on the first Thursday in June. When Monkley said he wanted young Sylvester to go with them, the Baron looked doubtful; but Monkley remarked that he had seen the Baron coming out of a certain house in Earl's Court Road the other day, which seemed to agitate him and make him anxious for Sylvia to attend the reception.

Outside the very commonplace house in Stanmore Crescent, where the Emperor of Byzantium lived, Monkley told the Baron that he did not wish anything said about Sylvester's father. Did the Baron understand? He wished a certain mystery to surround Sylvester: the Baron after his adventure in Earl's Court Road would appreciate the importance of secrecy.

'You are a regular devil, Monkley,' said von Statten in his most mincing voice. Remembering the saloon-bar, Sylvia had made up her mind not to be disappointed if the Emperor's reception failed to be very exciting; yet on the whole she was impressed. To be sure, the entrance hall of 14 Stanmore Crescent was not very imperial; but a footman took their silk hats, and, though Monkley whispered that he was carrying them like flower-pots and was evidently the jobbing gardener from round the corner, Sylvia was agreeably awed, especially when they were invited to proceed to the antechamber.

'In other words, the dining-room,' said Monkley to the Baron.

'Hush, don't you see the throne-room beyond?' the Baron whispered.

Sure enough, opening out of the antechamber was a smaller room in which was a dais covered with purple cloth. On a high Venetian chair sat the Emperor, a young man with dark bristling hair in evening dress. Sylvia stood on tiptoe to get a better look at him; but there was such a crush in the entrance to the throne-room that she had to be content for the present with staring at the numerous courtiers and listening to Monkley's whispered jokes, which the Baron tried in vain to stop.

'I suppose where the young man with a head like a door-mat and a face like a scraper is sitting is where the Imperial family congregates after dinner. I'd like to see what's under that purple cloth. Packing cases, I'll bet a quid.'

'Hush, hush, not so loud,' the Baron implored. 'Here's Captain Grayrigg, the Emperor's father.'

He pointed to a very small man with pouched eyes and a close-cropped pointed beard.

'Do you mean to tell me the Emperor hasn't made his father a field-marshal? He ought to be ashamed of himself.'

'My dear man, Captain Grayrigg married the late Empress. He is nothing himself.'

'I suppose he has to knock the packing-cases together and pay for the ices.'

But the Baron had pressed forward to meet Captain Grayrigg and did not answer: presently he came back very officiously and beckoned to Monkley, whom he introduced.

'From New York City, Colonel,' said Monkley with a quick glance at the Baron.

Sylvia nearly laughed, because Jimmy was talking through his nose in the most extraordinary way.

'Ah! an American,' said Captain Grayrigg. 'Then I expect this sort of thing strikes you as quite ridiculous.'

'Why, no, Colonel. Between ourselves I may as well tell you I'm over here myself on a job not unconnected with royalty.'

Monkley indicated Sylvia with a significant look.

'This little French boy who is called M. Sylvestre at present may be heard of later.'

Jimmy had accentuated her nationality; Sylvia, quick enough to see what he wanted her to do, replied in French.

A tall young man with an olive complexion and priestly gestures, standing close by, pricked up his ears at Monkley's remark, when Captain Grayrigg had retired, he came forward and introduced himself as the Prince de Condé.

Monkley seemed to be sizing up the Prince; then abruptly with an air of great cordiality he took his arm.

'Say, Prince, let's go and find an ice. I guess you're the man I've been looking for ever since I landed in England.'

They moved off together to find refreshment; Sylvia was left in the antechamber, which was filled with a most extraordinary crowd of people. There were young men with very pink cheeks who all wore white roses or white carnations in their buttonholes: there was a battered-looking woman with a wreath of laurel in her hair who suddenly began to declaim in a wailful voice. Everybody said 'Hush,' and tried to avoid catching his neighbour's eye. At first, Sylvia decided that the lady must be a lunatic whom people had to humour, because her remarks had nothing to do with the reception and were not even intelligible; then she decided that she was a ventriloquist who was imitating a cat. An old gentleman in a kilt was standing near her, and Sylvia remembered that once in France she had seen somebody dressed like that, who had danced in a tent; this lent colour to the theory of their both being entertainers. The old gentleman asked the Baron if he had the Gaelic, and the Baron said he had not; whereupon the old gentleman sniffed very loudly, which made Sylvia feel very uncomfortable, because though she had not eaten garlic she *had* eaten onions for lunch. Presently the old gentleman moved away, and she asked the Baron when he was going to begin his dance; the

Baron told her that he was the Chief of a great Scottish clan and that he always dressed like that. A clergyman with two black and white dogs under his arms was walking about and protesting in a high voice that he couldn't shake hands; and a lady in a Grecian tunic standing near Sylvia tried to explain to her in French that the dogs were descended from King Charles I. Sylvia wanted to tell her she spoke English, because she was sure something had gone wrong with the explanation owing to the lady's French; but she did not like to do so after Jimmy's deliberate insistence upon her nationality.

Presently a very fussy woman with a long stringy neck, bulging eyes, and arched fingers came into the antechamber and wanted to know who had not yet been presented to the Emperor. Sylvia looked round for Jimmy, but he was nowhere to be seen, and being determined not to go away without entering the throne-room she said loudly:

'*Moi, je n'ai pas encore vu l'empereur.*'

'Oh, the little darling,' trilled the fussy woman. '*Venez avec moi, je vous présenterai moi-même.*'

'How beautifully Miss Widgett speaks French,' somebody murmured, when Sylvia was being led into the throne-room. 'It's such a gift.'

Sylvia was very much interested by a large orange flag nailed to the wall above the Emperor's throne.

'*Le drapeau impériale de Byzance,*' Miss Widgett said. '*Voyez-vous l'aigle avec deux têtes? Il était fait pour sa majesté impériale par le Société du roi Charles I de* West London.'

'King Charles again,' Sylvia thought.

'*Il faut baiser la main,*' Miss Widgett prompted. Sylvia followed out the suggestion; and the Emperor, to whom Miss Widgett had whispered a few words, said:

'*Ah, vous êtes Français,*' and to Miss Widgett, 'Who did you say he was?'

'I really don't know. He came with Baron von Statten. *Comment vous appelez-vous?*' Miss Widgett asked, turning to Sylvia.

Sylvia answered that she was called Monsieur Sylvestre, and just then a most unusual squealing was heard in the antechamber.

'*Mon dieu, qu'est-ce que c'est que ça?*' Sylvia cried.

'*C'est le – comment dit-on* bagpipes *en français? C'est le "baagpeep" vous savez,*' which left Sylvia as wise as she was before. However, as there was no general panic, she ceased to be frightened. Soon she saw Jimmy beckoning to her from the antechamber, and shortly afterwards they left the reception, which had interested Sylvia very much, though she regretted that nobody had offered her an ice.

Monkley congratulated Sylvia upon her quickness in grasping that he had wanted her to pretend she was French, and by his praise roused in her the sense of ambition, which, though at present it was nothing more than a desire to please him personally, marked nevertheless a step forward in the development of her character; certainly from this moment the old fear of having no one to look after her began to diminish, and though she still viewed with displeasure the prospect of being alone, she began to have a faint conception of making herself indispensable, perceiving dimly the independence that would naturally follow. Meanwhile, however gratifying Monkley's compliment, it could not compensate her for the ice she had not been given, and Sylvia made this so plain to him that he invited her into a confectioner's shop on the way home and gave her a larger ice than any she had seen at the Emperor's.

Ever since Sylvia had made friends with Jimmy Monkley, her father had adopted the attitude of being left out in the cold, which made him the worst kind of audience for an enthusiastic account of the reception. Mrs Meares, though obviously condescending, was a more satisfactory listener, and she was able to explain to Sylvia some of the things that had puzzled her, amongst others the old gentleman's remark about Gaelic.

'This keeping up of old customs and ceremonies in our degenerate days is most commendable,' said Mrs. Meares. 'I wish I could be doing more in that line here, but Lillie Road does not lend itself to the antique and picturesque; Mr. Morgan too gets so impatient even if Clara only hums at her work that I don't like to ask that Scotchman to come and play his bagpipes here, though I daresay he would be only too glad to do so for a shilling. No, my dear boy, I don't mean the gentleman you met at the Emperor's. There is a poor man who plays in the street round here from time to time and dances a sword dance. But the English have no idea of beauty or freedom. I remember last time I saw him the poor man was being moved on for obstructing the traffic.'

Clara put forward a theory that the reception had been a Church Treat. There had been a similar affair in her own parish once, in which the leading scholars of the Sunday School classes had portrayed the Kings and Queens of England. She herself had been one of the little princes who were smothered in the Tower, and had worn a pair of her mother's stockings. There had been trouble, she remembered, because the other little prince had been laced up so tightly that he was sick over the pillow that was wanted to stuff out the boy who was representing Henry VIII and could not be used at the last moment.

Sylvia assured her that nothing like this had taken place at the Emperor's, but Clara remained unconvinced.

40

A week or two passed: the reception was almost forgotten, when one day Sylvia found the dark-complexioned young man with whom Monkley had made friends talking earnestly to him and her father.

'You understand,' he was saying. 'I wouldn't do this if I didn't require money for my work. You must not look upon me as a pretender. I really am the only surviving descendant in the direct line of the famous Prince de Condé.'

'Of course,' Monkley answered. 'I know you're genuine enough. All you've got to do is to go back – well here he is,' he added, turning round and pointing to Sylvia.

'I don't think Sil looks much like a king,' Henry said pensively. 'Though I'm bound to say the only one I ever saw in real life was Leopold of Belgium.'

Sylvia began to think that Clara had been right after all.

'What about the present King of Spain then?' Monkley asked. 'He isn't much more than nine years old, if he's as much. You don't suppose he looks like a king, do you? On the Spanish stamps he looks more like an advertisement for Mellin's food than anything else.'

'Naturally the *de jure* King of Spain who until the present has been considered to be Don Carlos is also the *de jure* King of France,' said the Prince de Condé.

'Don't you start any of your games with Kings of France,' Henry advised. 'I know the French well, and they won't stand it. What does he want to be king of two places for? I should have thought Spain was enough for anybody.'

'The divine right of monarchs is something greater than mere geography,' the Prince answered scornfully.

'All right. Have it your own way. You're the authority here on kings. But don't overdo it. That's all I advise,' Henry said finally. 'I know everybody thinks I'm wrong nowadays,' he added with a glance at Monkley and Sylvia. 'But what about Condy's fluid?'

'What about it?' Monkley asked. 'What do you want Condy's for?'

'I don't want it,' said Henry. 'I simply passed the remark. Our friend here is the Prince de Condé. Well, I merely remark "What about Condy's fluid?" I don't want to start an argument, because, as I said, I'm always wrong nowadays, but I think if he wanted to be a Prince he ought to have chosen a more recherché title, not gone routing about among patent medicines.'

The Prince de Condé looked enquiringly at Monkley.

'Don't you bother about him, old chap. He's gone off at the deep end.'

41

'I knew it,' Henry said. 'I knew I should be wrong; that's right, laugh away,' he added bitterly to Sylvia.

There followed a long explanation by the Prince of Sylvia's royal descent, which she could not understand at all. Monkley, however, seemed to be understanding it very well, so well that her father gave up being offended and loudly expressed his admiration for Jimmy's grip of the subject.

'Now,' said Monkley, 'the question is, who are we going to touch?'

The Prince asked if he had noticed at the reception a young man, a rather good-looking, fair young man with a white rose in his buttonhole. Monkley said that most of the young men he had seen in Stanmore Crescent would answer to that description, and the Prince gave up trying to describe him except as the only son of a wealthy and distinguished painter – Sir Francis Hurndale. It seemed that young Godfrey Hurndale could always command the paternal purse; and the Prince suggested that a letter should be sent to his father from the secretary of the *de jure* King of Spain and France, offering him the post of Court painter on his accession. Monkley objected that a man who had made money out of painting would not be taken in by so transparent a fraud as that; and the Prince explained that Sir Francis would only be amused, but that he would certainly pass the letter on to his son who was an enthusiastic Legitimist; that the son would consult him, the Prince de Condé; and that afterwards it lay with Monkley to make the most of the situation, bearing in mind that he, the Prince, required a fair share of the profits in order to advance his great propaganda for a universal Platonic system of government.

'At present,' the Prince proclaimed, becoming more and more sacerdotal as he spoke of his scheme. 'At present I am a lay member of the Society of Jesus, which represents the Platonic tendency in modern thought. I am vowed to exterminate republicanism, anarchy, socialism, and to maintain the conservative instincts of humanity against—'

'Well, nobody's going to quarrel with you about spending your own money,' Monkley interrupted.

'He can give it to the Salvation Army if he likes,' Henry agreed.

The discussion of the more practical aspects of the plan went on for several days. Ultimately it was decided to leave Lillie Road as a first step and take a small house in a suburb; to Sylvia's great delight, for she was tired of the mustiness of Lillie Road, they moved to Rosemary Avenue, Streatham. It was a newly built house and it was all their own, with the Common at one end of the road, and better still with a back-garden. Sylvia had never lived where she had been able to walk out of her own door to her own patch of green: moreover, she thoroughly enjoyed the game of being an exiled king that might be kidnapped by his foes at any moment. To be sure, there were disadvantages; for instance she was not allowed to cultivate an acquaintanceship with the two freckled girls next door on their right, nor with the boy who had an air-gun on their left; but generally the game was amusing, especially when her father became the faithful old French servant, who had guarded her all these years, until Mr. James Monkley, the enthusiastic American amateur of genealogy, had discovered the little king hidden away in the old servant's cottage. Henry objected to being ordered about by his own daughter, but his objections were overruled by Jimmy, and Sylvia gave him no rest.

'That damned Condy says he's a lay Jesuit,' Henry grumbled. 'But what am I? A lay figure. I suppose you wouldn't like me to sleep in a kennel in the back-yard?' he asked. 'Another thing I can't understand is why on earth you had to be an American, Jimmy.'

Monkley told Henry of his sudden impulse to be an American at the Emperor's reception.

'Never give way to impulse,' Henry said. 'You're not a bit like an American. You'll get a nasty growth in your nose or strain it or something. Americans may talk through the nose a bit; but you make a noise like a cat that's had its tail shut in a door. It's like living in a Punch and Judy show. It may not damage your nose, but it's very bad for my ears, old man. It's all very fine for me to be a French servant. I can speak French; though I don't look like the servant part of it. But you can't speak American, and if you go on trying much harder, you very soon won't be able to speak any language at all. I noticed to-day when you started talking to the furniture fellow, he looked very uneasy. I think he thought he was sitting on a concertina.'

'Anyway, he cleared off without getting this month's instalment,' Monkley said.

'Oh, it's a very good voice to have when there are duns kicking around,' Henry said. 'Or in a crowded railway carriage. But as a voice to live with, it's rotten. However, don't listen to me. My advice doesn't count nowadays. Only,' and Henry paused impressively, 'when people advise you to try linseed oil for your boots as soon as you start talking to them, then don't say I didn't warn you.'

Notwithstanding Henry's pessimism Monkley continued to practise his American; day by day the task of imposing Sylvia on the world as the King of Spain and France was being carefully prepared, too carefully it seemed to Sylvia, for so much talk beforehand was becoming tiresome. The long delay was chiefly due to Henry's inability to keep in his head the numerous genealogical facts that were crammed down his throat by the Prince de Condé.

'I never was any good at history even when I was a boy,' Henry protested. 'Never. And I was never good at working out cousins and aunts. I know I had two aunts and hated them both.'

At last Henry's facts were considered firmly enough implanted to justify a move; and in September the Prince and Monkley sat down to compose their preliminary letter to Sir Francis Hurndale. Sylvia by now was so much accustomed to the behaviour of her companions that she never thought seriously about the fantastic side of the affair. Her own masquerade as a boy had been passed off so successfully even upon such an acute observer as Jimmy, until her father had let out the secret by a slip of the tongue, that she had no qualms about being accepted as a king. She realised that money was to be made out of it; but the absence of money had already come to seem a temporary discomfort to relieve which people in a position like her own and her father's had no reason to be scrupulous. Not that she really ever bothered her head with the morality of financial ways and means: when she spent the ten-franc piece that she thought she had found, the wrong had lain in unwittingly depriving her mother whom she loved: if she had not loved her mother, she might have still had scruples about stealing from her; but stealing from people who had plenty of money and with whom there was no binding link of affection would have been quite incomprehensible to her. Therefore the sight of Jimmy Monkley and her father and the Prince de Condé sitting round a spindle-legged tea-table in this new house that smelt pleasantly of varnish was merely something in a day's work of the life they were leading, like a game of cards. It was a much jollier life than any she had yet known; her alliance with Jimmy had been a very good move; her father was treated as he ought to be treated by being kept under; she was shortly going to have some more clothes.

Sylvia sat watching the trio, thinking how much more vividly present Jimmy seemed to be than either of the other two – the Prince with his greenish complexion never really well shaved and his turn-down collar that made his black suit more melancholy, or her father with his light plaintive eyes and big ears. She was glad that she was not going to resemble her father except perhaps in being short and in the shape of her wide nose: yet she was not really very short; it was only that her mother had been so tall; perhaps, too, when her hair grew long again, her nose would not seem so wide.

The letter was finished and Jimmy was reading it aloud:

Sir,

I have the honour to ask if, in the probable event of a great dynastic change taking place in one of the chief countries of Europe, you would welcome the post of Court painter, naturally at a suitable remuneration. If you read the daily papers, as no doubt you do, you will certainly have come to the conclusion that neither the present ruling house nor what is known as the Carlist party has any real hold upon the affections of the Spanish People. Verb. sap. Interesting changes may be foreshadowed, of which I am not yet at liberty to write more fully. Should you entertain the proposal I shall be happy to wait upon you with further particulars.

I have the honour to be, Sir,
You obedient servant
Josephe-Erneste,
Prince de Condé

'Do you know what it sounds like?' said Henry. 'Mind I'm not saying this because I didn't write the letter myself. It sounds to me like a cross between a prophecy in Old Moore's Almanack and somebody trying to sell a patent knife-cleaner.'

'There's a good deal in what you say,' Monkley agreed in a dissatisfied tone.

Henry was so much flattered by the reception of his criticism that he became compassionate to the faults of the letter and tried hard to point out some of its merits.

'After all,' said Jimmy. 'The great thing is that the Prince has signed it. If his name doesn't draw Master Godfrey, no letters are going to. We'll send it off as it is.'

So the letter was sent: two days afterward the Prince arrived with the news that Godfrey Hurndale had called upon him, and that he had been inexpressibly happy at the prospect of meeting the *de jure* King of France and Spain.

'Bring him round to-morrow afternoon about tea-time,' said Monkley. 'You haven't forgotten the family history, Henry?'

Henry said that he had not forgotten a single relation, and that he damned them severally each morning in all their titles while he was dressing.

The next afternoon Sylvia sat in an arm-chair in the presence-room, which Henry supposed was so called because none of the furniture had been paid for, and waited for Godfrey Hurndale's coming. Her father put on the rusty black evening-dress of the family retainer, and Jimmy wore a most conspicuous check suit and talked so loudly and nasally that Henry was driven to a final protest:

'Look here, Jimmy, I've dressed up to help this show in a suit that's as old as one of those infernal ancestors of Sil's, but if you don't get less American, it'll fall to pieces. Every time you guess, I can hear a seam give.'

'Remember to talk nothing but French,' Monkley warned Sylvia when the bell rang. 'Go on, Harry, you've got to open the door. And don't forget that *you* can only speak French.'

Monkley followed him out of the room, and his voice could be heard clanking about the hall as he invited young Hurndale into the dining-room first. Henry came back and took up his position behind Sylvia's chair: she felt very solemn and excited, and asked her father rather irritably why he was muttering. The reason, however, remained a mystery, for the dining-room door opened again; and heralded by Monkley's twanging invitation Mr. Hurndale stood shyly in the entrance to the presence-room.

'Go right in, Mr. Hurndale,' Monkley said. 'I guess His Majesty's just about ready to meet you.'

Sylvia, when she saw the young man bowing before her, really felt a kind of royal exaltation and held out her hand to be kissed.

Hurndale reverently bent over it and touched it with his lips; so did the Prince, an action for which Sylvia was unprepared and which she rather resented, thinking to herself that he really did not shave and that it had not only been his grubby appearance. Then Hurndale offered her a large bunch of white carnations, and she became kingly again.

'*François*,' she commanded her father. '*Mets ces œillets dans ma chambre.*'

And when her father passed out with a bow Sylvia was indeed a king. The audience did not last long: there were practical matters to discuss, for which His Majesty was begged to excuse their withdrawal. Sylvia would have liked a longer ceremony. When the visitor had gone, they all sat down to a big tea in the presence-room, and she was told that the young man had been so completely conquered by her gracious reception of him that he had promised to raise five hundred pounds for her cause: his reward in addition to royal favours was to be a high class of the Order of Isabella the Catholic. Everybody, even Henry, was in high good humour. The Prince did not come to Streatham again; but a week later Monkley got a letter from him with the Paris postmark.

Dear Mr. Monkley,

Our young friend handed me a cheque for £200 the day before yesterday. As he seemed uncertain about the remainder of the sum promised I took the liberty of drawing my share at once. My great work requires immediate assistance, and I am now busily occupied in Paris. My next address will be a castle in Spain, where perhaps we shall meet when you are looking for your next site.

Most truly yours,
Josephe-Erneste,
Prince de Condé.

Jimmy and Henry stared at one another.

'I knew it,' said Henry. 'I'm always wrong; but I knew it. Still, if I could catch him, it would take more than Condy's Fluid to disinfect that pea-green welsher after I'd done with him.'

Monkley sat biting his lips in silence; and Sylvia recognizing the expression in his eyes that she dreaded formerly, notwithstanding that he was now her best friend, felt sharply her old repugnance for him. Henry was still abusing the defaulter when Monkley cut him short.

'Shut up, I rather admire him.'

'Admire him?' Henry gasped. 'I suppose you'd admire the hangman, and shake hands with him on the scaffold. It's all very fine for you. You didn't have to learn how Ferdinand the Fifty-Eighth married Isabella the Innocent, daughter of Alphonso the Eighth, commonly called Alphonso the Anxious. Condy's Fluid! I swallowed enough of it, I can tell you.'

Monkley told him gruffly to keep quiet; then he sat down and began to write, still with that expression in his eyes: presently he tore up the letter and paced the room.

'Damn that swine,' he suddenly shouted, kicking the spindle-legged table into the fireplace. 'We wanted the money, you know. We wanted the money badly.'

Shortly before dawn the three of them abandoned the new house in Streatham, and occupied rooms in Kennington Park Road: Monkley and Sylvia's father resumed the racing that had temporarily been interrupted by ambition: Sylvia wandered about the streets in a suit of Etons that was rapidly showing signs of wear.

One day early in the new year, Sylvia was leaning over the parapet of Waterloo Bridge and munching hot chestnuts. The warmth of them in her pockets was grateful: her pastime of dropping the shells into the river did not lack interest: she was vaguely conscious in the frosty sunshine of life's bounty, and she offered to the future a welcome from the depths of her being: meanwhile there still remained forty chestnuts to be eaten.

Her meditation was interrupted by a voice from a passer-by who had detached himself from the stream of traffic that she had been disregarding in her pensive greed; she looked up and met the glance of a pleasant middle-aged gentleman in a dark grey coat with collar and cuffs of chinchilla, who was evidently anxious to begin a conversation.

'You're out of school early,' he observed.

Sylvia replied that she did not go to school.

'Private tutor?' he asked; and partly to save further questions about her education, partly because she was not quite sure what a private tutor was, she answered in the affirmative.

The stranger looked along the parapet inquisitively.

'I'm out alone this afternoon,' Sylvia said quickly.

The stranger asked her what amused her most, museums or theatres or listening to bands; and whether she preferred games or country walks. Sylvia would have liked to tell him that she preferred eating chestnuts to doing anything else on earth at that moment; but, being unwilling to create an impression of trying to snub such a benevolent person, she replied vaguely that she did not know what she liked best: then because such an answer seemed to imply a lack of intelligence that she did not wish to impute to herself, she informed him that she liked looking at people, which was strictly true, for if she had not been eating chestnuts she would certainly have still been contemplating the traffic across the bridge.

'I'll show you some interesting people, if you care to come with me,' the stranger proposed. 'Have you anything to do this afternoon?'

Sylvia admitted that her time was unoccupied.

'Come along, then,' said the middle-aged gentleman, a little fussily, she thought; and forthwith he hailed a passing hansom. Sylvia had for a long time been ambitious to travel in a hansom; she had already eaten thirty-five chestnuts, only seven of which had been bad: she decided to accept the stranger's invitation. He asked her where she lived and promised to send her home by cab when the entertainment was over.

Sylvia asked if it was a reception to which he was taking her. The middle-aged gentleman laughed, squeezed her hand and said it might be called a reception, adding with a chuckle, 'a very warm reception in fact.' Sylvia did not understand the joke, but laughed out of politeness.

There followed an exchange of names, and Sylvia learnt that her new acquaintance was called Corydon.

'You'll excuse me from offering you one of my cards,' he said, 'I haven't one with me this afternoon.'

They drove along for some time during which the conversation of Mr. Corydon always pursued the subject of her likes and dislikes. They drew clear of the press of traffic and bowled westward toward Sloane

48

Street; Sylvia, recognizing one of the blue West Kensington omnibuses, began to wonder if the cab would take her past Lillie Road, where Jimmy had specially forbidden her to go, because he and her father owed several weeks' rent to Mrs. Meares and he did not want to remind her of their existence. When they drew nearer and nearer to Sylvia's former lodging, she began to feel rather uneasy and wish that the cab would turn down a side-street. The landmarks were becoming more and more familiar, and Sylvia was asking herself if Mrs. Meares had employed the stranger to kidnap her as a hostage for the unpaid rent, when the cab turned off into Redcliffe Gardens and soon afterwards pulled up at a house.

'Here we are,' said Mr. Corydon. 'You'll enjoy yourself most tremendously, Sylvester.'

The door was opened by a servant who was apparently dressed as a brigand, which puzzled Sylvia so much that she asked the reason in a whisper. Mr. Corydon laughed.

'He's a Venetian. That's the costume of a gondolier, my dear boy. My friend who is giving the reception dresses all his servants like gondoliers. So much more picturesque than a horrible housemaid.'

Sylvia regarded this exotic Clara with considerable interest; the only other Venetian product of which she had hitherto been aware was blinds.

The house, which smelt strongly of incense and watered flowers, awed Sylvia with its luxury; and she began to regret having put foot in a place where it was so difficult to know on what she was intended to tread. However, since Mr. Corydon seemed to walk everywhere without regard for the softness of the carpets, Sylvia made up her mind to brave the silent criticism of the gondolier and follow upstairs in his footsteps. Mr. Corydon took her arm and introduced her to a large room where a fume of cigarette-smoke and incense blurred the outlines of the numerous guests that sat about in listening groups, while someone played the grand piano. There were many low divans round the room, to one of which Mr. Corydon guided Sylvia, and while the music continued she had an opportunity of studying her fellow-guests. They were mostly young men of about eighteen rather like the young men at the Emperor's reception; but there were also several middle-aged men of the same type as Mr. Corydon, one of whom came across and shook hands with them both when the music stopped.

'So glad you've come to see me,' he said in a voice that sounded as if each word were being delicately fried upon his tongue. 'Aren't you going to smoke a cigarette? These are Russian. Aren't they beautiful to look at?'

He proffered a green cigarette case; Sylvia who felt that she must take advantage of this opportunity to learn something about a sphere of life which was new to her, asked him what it was made of.

'Jade, my dear. I brought such heaps of beautiful jade back with me from China. I've even got a jade toilet-set. My dear, it was dreadfully expensive.'

He giggled; Sylvia, blowing clouds of smoke from her cigarette, thought dreamily what funny things her father would have said about him.

'Raymond's going to dance for us,' he said turning to Corydon. 'Isn't it too sweet of him?'

At that moment somebody leapt into the middle of the room with a wild scream and began to throw himself into all sorts of extraordinary attitudes.

'Oh, Raymond, you're too wonderful,' the host ejaculated. 'You make me feel quite Bacchic.'

Sylvia was not surprised that anybody should feel 'back-ache' (she had thus understood her host) in the presence of such contortions. The screaming Raymond was followed into the arena by another lightly clad and equally shrill youth called Sydney; and both of them flung themselves into a choric frenzy, chasing each other round and round, sawing the air with their legs, and tearing roses from their hair to fling at the guests, who flung them back at the dancers. Suddenly Raymond collapsed upon the carpet and began to moan.

'What's the matter, my dear?' cried the host, rushing forward and kneeling to support the apparently agonized youth in his arms.

'Oh, my foot,' Raymond wailed. 'I've trodden on something.'

'He's trodden on a thorn. He's trodden on a thorn,' everybody said at once.

Raymond was borne tenderly to a divan, and was so much petted that Sydney became jealous and began to dance again, this time on the top of the piano. Presently everybody else began to dance, and Mr. Corydon would have liked to dance with Sylvia; but she declined. Gondoliers entered with trays of liqueurs, and Sylvia, tasting *crème de menthe* for the first time found it so good that she drank four glasses, which made her feel rather drowsy. New guests were continually arriving, to whom she did not pay much attention until suddenly she recognized the Baron with Godfrey Hurndale, who at the same moment recognized her. The Baron rushed forward and seized Sylvia's arm: she thought he was going to drag her back by force to Mrs. Meares to answer for the missing rent, but he began to arch his unoccupied arm like an excited swan, and called out in his high mincing voice:

'Blackmailers-s-s! blackmailers-s-s!'

'They blackmailed me out of four hundred pounds,' said Hurndale.

'Who brought him here?' the Baron cried. 'It's-s-s true. Godfrey has been persecuted by these horrid people. Blackmailers-s-s!'

All the other guests gathered round Sylvia and behaved like angry women trying to mount an omnibus. Mr. Corydon had turned very pale, and was counting his visiting cards. Sylvia could not understand the reason for all this noise; but vaguely through a green mist of *crème de menthe* she understood that she was being attacked on all sides and began to get annoyed. Somebody pinched her arm, and without waiting to see who it was she hit the nearest person within reach, who happened to be Mr. Corydon: his visiting cards fell on the floor, and he grovelled on the carpet trying to sweep them together. Sylvia followed her attack on Mr. Corydon by treading hard on Sydney's bare toes, who thereupon slapped her face; presently everybody was pushing her and pinching her and hustling her, until she got in such a rage and kicked so furiously that her enemies retired.

'Who brought him here?' Godfrey Hurndale was demanding. 'I tell you he belongs to a gang of blackmailers.'

'Most dreadful people,' the Baron echoed.

'Antonio! Domenico!' the host cried.

Two gondoliers entered the room, and at a word from their master they seized Sylvia and pushed her out into the street, flinging her coat and cap after her. By this time she was in a blind fury, and, snatching the bag of chestnuts from her pocket, she flung it with all her force at the nearest window, and knew the divine relief of starring the pane.

An old lady that was passing stopped and held up her hands.

'You wicked young rascal, I shall tell the policeman of you,' she gasped, and began to belabour Sylvia with her umbrella. Such unwarrantable interference was not to be tolerated; Sylvia pushed the old lady so hard that she sat down heavily in the gutter: nobody else was in sight, and she ran as fast as she could until she found an omnibus, in which she travelled to Waterloo Bridge: there she bought fifty more chestnuts and walked slowly back to Kennington Park Road, vainly trying to find an explanation of the afternoon's adventure.

Her father and Monkley were not back when Sylvia reached home; she sat by the fire in the twilight, munching her chestnuts and pondering the whole extraordinary business. When the others came in she told her story, and Jimmy looked meaningly at her father.

'Shows how careful you ought to be,' he said. Then turning to Sylvia he asked her what on earth she thought she was doing when she broke the window.

'Suppose you'd been collared by the police, you little fool. We should have got into a nice mess thanks to you. Look here, in future you're not to speak to people in the street, do you hear?'

Sylvia had no chestnuts to throw at Jimmy, so in her rage she took an ornament from the mantelpiece and smashed it on the fender.

'You've got the breaking mania,' said Henry. 'You'd better spend the next money you get on coconuts instead of chestnuts.'

'*Oh, ta gueule!* I'm not going to be a boy any longer.'

III

While her hair was growing long again, Sylvia developed a taste for reading: she had nothing else to do, for it was not to be supposed that with her hair cropped close she could show herself to the world in petticoats. Her refusal any longer to wear male attire gave Monkley and her father an excuse to make one of their hurried moves from Kennington Park Road, where by this time they owed enough money to justify the trouble of evading payment. Henry had for some time expressed a desire to be more central; and a partly furnished top floor was found in Fitzroy Street – or, as the landlord preferred to call it, a self-contained and well-appointed flat. The top floor had certainly been separated from the rest of the house by a wooden partition and a door of its own, which possibly justified the first half of the description, but the good appointments were limited to a bath that looked like an old palette, and a geyser that was not always safe according to Mrs. Bullwinkle, a decrepit charwoman, left behind by the last tenants together with some underlinen and two jars containing a morbid growth that might formerly have been pickles.

'How d'ye mean, not safe?' Henry asked. 'Is it liable to blow up?'

'It went off with a big bang last April and hasn't been lit since,' the charwoman said. 'But perhaps it'll be all right now. The worst of it is I can never remember which tap you put the match to.'

'You leave it alone, old lady,' Henry advised. 'Nobody's likely to do much bathing in here; from what I can see of it that bath gives more than it gets. What did the last people use it for – growing watercress or keeping chickens?'

'It was a very nice bath once,' the charwoman said.

'Do you mean to say you've ever tried it? Go on! You're mixing it up with the font in which you were baptized. There's never been any water in this bath since the flood.'

Nevertheless, however inadequately appointed, the new abode had one great advantage over any other they had known, which was a large raftered garret with windows at either end that ran the whole depth of the house. The windows at the back opened on a limitless expanse of roofs and chimneys: those in front looked across to a dancing academy on the top floor but one of the house opposite, a view that gave perpetual pleasure to Sylvia during the long period of her seclusion.

Now that Sylvia had become herself again, her father and Monkley insisted upon her doing the housework, which, as Henry reminded her, she was perfectly able to do on account of the excellent training she had received in that respect from her mother. Sylvia perceived the logic of this and made no attempt to contest it; though she stipulated that Mrs. Bullwinkle should not be considered as helping her.

'We don't want her,' Henry protested indignantly.

'Well, tell her not to come any more,' Sylvia said.

'I've shoo'd her away once or twice,' said Henry. 'But I expect the people here before us used to give her a saucer of milk sometimes. The best way would be to go out one afternoon and tell her to light the geyser. Then perhaps when we came back she'd be gone for good.'

Nevertheless Mrs. Bullwinkle was of some service to Sylvia, for one day, when she was sadly washing down the main staircase of the house, she looked up from her handiwork and asked Sylvia, who was passing at the moment, if she would like some books to read, inviting her downstairs to take her choice.

'Mr. Bullwinkle used to be a big reader,' the charwoman said. 'A very big reader. A very big reader indeed he used to be, did Mr. Bullwinkle. In those days he was caretaker at a Congregational chapel in Gospel Oak, and he used to say that reading took his mind off of religion a bit. Otherwise he'd have gone mad before he did, which was shortly after he left the chapel through an argument he had with Pastor Phillips, who wrote his name in the dust on the reading-desk, and which upset my old man, because he thought it wasn't at all a straightforward way of telling him that his services wasn't considered satisfactory. Yes,' said Mrs. Bullwinkle with a stertorous sniff, 'he died in Bedlam, did my old man. He had a very queer mania: he thought he was inside out, and it preyed on his mind. He wouldn't never have been shut up at all, if he hadn't of always been undressing himself in the street and putting on his trousers inside out to suit his complaint. They had to feed him with a chube at the last, because he would have it his mouth couldn't be got at through him being inside out. Queer fancies some people has, don't they? Oh, well, if we was all the same, it would be a dull world I suppose.'

Sylvia sat up in the big garret and read through one after another of the late Mr. Bullwinkle's tattered and heterogeneous collection. She did not understand all she read; but there were few books that did not give her on one page a vivid impression, which she used to elaborate with her imagination into something that was really a more substantial experience than the book itself. The days grew longer and more sunny, and Sylvia dreamed them away, reading and thinking and watching from her window the little girls pirouette in the shadowy room opposite: her hair was quite long now, a warm brown with many glinting strands.

In the summer Jimmy and Henry made a good deal of money by selling a number of tickets for a non-existent stand in one of the best positions on the route of the Diamond Jubilee procession; indeed they felt prosperous enough to buy for themselves and Sylvia seats in a genuine stand. Sylvia enjoyed the pageant, which seemed more like something out of a book than anything in real life. She took advantage of the temporary prosperity to ask for money to buy herself new clothes.

'Can't you see other people dressed up without wanting to go and do the same yourself?' Henry asked. 'What's the matter with the frock you've got on?'

However, she talked to Monkley about it and had her own way. When she had new clothes, she used to walk about the streets again, but though she was often accosted, she would never talk to anybody. It was a dull life really, and once she brought up the subject of getting work.

'Work!' her father exclaimed in horror. 'Good heavens, what will you think of next? First it's clothes. Now it's work. Ah, my dear girl, you ought to have had to slave for your living as I had, you wouldn't talk about work.'

'Well, can I have a piano and learn to play?' Sylvia asked.

'Perhaps you'd like the band of the Grenadier Guards to come and serenade you in your bedroom while you're dressing?' Henry suggested.

'Why shouldn't she have a piano?' Monkley interposed. 'I'll teach her to play. Besides, I'd like a piano myself.'

So the piano was obtained: Sylvia learned to play, and even to sing a little with her deep voice; and another regular caller for money was added to the already long list.

In the autumn Sylvia's father fell in love, and brought a woman to live in what was henceforth always called the flat, even by Henry, who had hitherto generally referred to it as the Hammam.

In Sylvia's opinion the advent of Mabel Bannerman had a most vitiating effect upon the life in Fitzroy Street. Her father began to deteriorate immediately. His return to England and the unsurveyed life he had been leading for nearly two years had produced an expansion of his personality in every direction. He had lost the shiftless insignificance that had been his chief characteristic in France, and though he was still weak and lacking in any kind of initiative, he had acquired a quaintness of outlook and faculty for expressing it which disguised his radical futility under a veil of humour. He was always dominated by Monkley in practical matters where subordination was reasonable and beneficial, but he had been allowed to preserve his own point of view which with the progress of time had even come to be regarded as important. When Sylvia was much younger she had always criticized her father's behaviour; but like everybody else she had accepted her mother's leadership of the house and family as natural and inevitable, and had regarded her father as a kind of spoilt elder brother whose character was fundamentally worthless and whose relation to her mother was the only one imaginable. Now that Sylvia was older, she did not merely despise her father's weakness; she resented the shameful position that he occupied in relation to this intruder. Mabel Bannerman belonged to that full-blown, intensely feminine type that by sheer excess of femininity imposes itself upon a weak man, smothering him, as it were, with her emotions and her lace, and destroying by sensuality every trait of manhood that does not directly contribute to the justification of herself. Within a week or two Henry stood for no more in the Fitzroy Street house than a dog that is alternately patted and scolded, that licks the hand of its mistress more abjectly for each new brutality and that asks as its supreme reward permission to fawn upon her lap. Sylvia hated Mabel Bannerman: she hated her peroxide hair: she hated her full moist lips: she hated her rounded back and her shining finger-nails spotted with white: she hated with a hatred so deep as to be for ever incommunicable each blowsy charm that went to make up what was called 'a fine woman.' She hated her inability ever to speak the truth: she hated the way she looked at Monkley, who should have been nothing to her: she hated the sight of her drinking tea in the morning: she hated the smell of her wardrobe, and the pink ribbons which she tied to every projection in her bedroom: she hated her affectation of babyishness: she hated the way she would make Henry give money to beggars for the gratification of an impulsive and merely sensual generosity of her own: she hated her imbedded garters and smooth legs.

'Oh, God,' Sylvia cried aloud to herself once, when she was leaning out of the window and looking down into Fitzroy Street. 'Oh, God, if I could only throw her into the street and see her eaten by dogs.'

Monkley hated her too: that was some consolation. Now often, when he was ready for an expedition, Henry would be unable to accompany him, because Mabel was rather seedy that morning; or because Mabel wanted him to go out with her; or because Mabel complained of being left alone so much. Monkley used to look at him with a savage contempt; and Sylvia used to pray sometimes that he would get angry enough to rush into Mabel's room and pound her, where she lay so softly in her soft bed.

Mabel used to bring her friends to the flat to cheer her up, as she used to say, and when she had filled the room she had chosen for her sitting-room (the garret was not cosy enough for Mabel) with a scented mob of chattering women, she would fix upon one of them as the object of her jealousy, accusing Henry of having looked at her all the evening. There would sometimes be a scene at the moment, when half the mob would cluster round Mabel to console her outraged feelings and the rest of it would hover about her rival to assure her she was guiltless: Sylvia, standing sullenly apart, would ponder the result of throwing a lighted lamp into the middle of the sickly sobbing pandemonium. The quarrel was not so bad as the inevitable reconciliation afterwards, with its profuse kissing and interminable explanations that seemed like an orchestra from which Mabel emerged with a plaintive solo that was the signal for the whole scene to be lived over again in the maddeningly reiterated accounts from all the women talking at once. Worse even than such evenings were those when Mabel restrained, or rather luxuriously hoarded up her jealousy until the last visitor had departed; for then through half the night Sylvia must listen to her pouring over Henry a stream of reproaches, which he would weakly try to divert by argument or more weakly try to dam with caresses. Such methods of treatment usually ended in Mabel's dressing herself and rushing from the bedroom to leave the flat for ever; unfortunately she never carried out her threat.

'Why don't you go?' Sylvia once asked, when Mabel was standing by the door fully dressed with heaving breast, making no effort to turn the handle.

'These shoes hurt me,' said Mabel. 'He knows I can't go out in these shoes. The heartless brute!'

'If you knew those shoes hurt, why did you put them on?' Sylvia asked scornfully.

'I was much too upset by Harry's treatment of me. Oh, whatever shall I do? I'm so miserable.'

Whereupon Mabel collapsed upon the mat and wept black tears, until Henry came and tried to lift her up, begging her not to stay where she might catch cold.

'You know when a jelly won't set?' Sylvia said, when she was recounting the scene to Monkley afterwards. 'Well, she was just like a jelly, and father simply couldn't make her stand up on the plate.'

Jimmy laughed sardonically.

These continued altercations between Mabel and Henry led to altercations with their neighbours underneath, who complained of being kept awake at night. The landlord, a fiery little Jew, told them that what between the arrears of rent and the nuisance they were causing to his other tenants he should have to give them notice. Sylvia could never get any money for the purposes of housekeeping except from Jimmy, and when she wanted clothes it was always Jimmy whom she must ask.

'Let's go away,' she said to him one day. 'Let's leave them here together.'

Monkley looked at her in surprise.

'Do you mean that?'

'Of course I mean it.'

'But if we left Harry with her, he'd starve and she'd leave him in a week.'

'Let him starve,' Sylvia cried. 'He deserves to starve.'

'You hard-hearted little devil,' Monkley said. 'After all, he is your father.'

'That's what makes me hate him,' Sylvia declared. 'He's no right to be my father. He's no right to make me think like that of him. He must be wrong to make me feel as I do about him.'

Monkley came close and took her hand.

'Do you mean what you said about leaving them and going away with me?'

Sylvia looked at him; and, meeting his eyes, she shook her head.

'No, of course I don't really mean it, but why can't you think of some way to stop all this? Why should we put up with it any longer? Make him turn her out into the street.'

Monkley laughed.

'You *are* very young, aren't you? Though I've thought once or twice lately that you seemed to be growing up.'

Again Sylvia caught his eyes and felt a little afraid, not really afraid she said to herself, but uneasy as if somebody she could not see had suddenly opened a door behind her.

'Don't let's talk about me, anyway,' she said. 'Think of something to change things here.'

'I'd thought of a concert party this summer. Pierrots, you know. How d'ye think your father would do as a Pierrot? He might be very funny, if she'd let him be funny.'

Sylvia clapped her hands.

'Oh, Jimmy, it would be such fun.'

'You wouldn't mind if she came too?'

'I'd rather she didn't,' Sylvia said. 'But it would be different somehow. We shouldn't be shut up with her as we are here, I'll be able to sing, won't I?'

'That was my idea.'

Before Henry met Mabel he would have had a great deal to say about this concert party; now he accepted Monkley's announcement with a dull equanimity that nettled Sylvia. He received the news that he would become a Pierrot just as he had received the news that, his nightshirt not having been sent back that week by the laundress, he would have to continue with the one he was wearing.

Early summer passed away quickly enough in constant rehearsals; Sylvia was pleased to find that she had been right in supposing that the state of domestic affairs would be improved by Jimmy's plan. Mabel turned out to be a good singer for the kind of performance they were going to give, and the amount of emotion she put into her songs left her with less to work off on Henry, who recovered some of his old self and was often really funny, especially in his duologues with Monkley. Sylvia picked out for herself and learnt a few songs, most of which were condemned as unsuitable by Jimmy: the one that she liked best and in her own opinion sang best was the *Raggle Taggle Gipsies*, though the others all prophesied for it certain failure. Monkley himself played all the accompaniments and by his personality kept the whole show together; he also sang a few songs which, although he had practically no voice, were given with such point that Sylvia felt convinced that his share in the performance would be the most popular of the lot. Shortly before they were to start on tour, which was fixed for the beginning of July, Monkley decided that they wanted another man who could really sing, and a young tenor known as Claude Raglan was invited to join the party. He was a good-looking youth, much in earnest, and with a tendency toward consumption, of which he was proud.

'Though what there is to be proud of in losing one of your lungs I don't know. I might as well be proud because I lost a glove the other day.'

Henry was severe upon Claude Raglan from the beginning: perhaps he suspected him of admiring Mabel. There was often much tension at rehearsals on account of Henry's attitude; once, for instance, when Claude Raglan had sung *Little Dolly Daydream* with his usual romantic fervour, Henry took a new song from his pocket and having planted it down with a defiant snap on the music-stand, proceeded to sing:

58

> *'I'll give him Dolly Daydreams*
> *Down where the poppies grow;*
> *I'll give him Dolly Daydreams*
> *The pride of Idaho.*
> *And if I catch him kissing her,*
> *There's sure to be some strife,*
> *Because if he's got anything he wants to give away,*
> *Let him come and give it to his wife.'*

The tenor declared that Henry's song, which was in the nature of a derisive comment upon his own, could only have the effect of spoiling the more serious contribution.

'What of it?' Henry asked truculently.

'It seems to me perfectly obvious,' Claude said with an effort to restrain his annoyance.

'I consider that it won't hurt your song at all,' Henry declared. 'In fact I think it will improve it. In my opinion it will have a much greater success than yours. In fact I may as well say straight out that if it weren't for my song I don't believe the audience would let you sing yours more than once. "Cos no one's gwine ter kiss dat gal but me!" ' he went on, mimicking the indignant Claude. 'No wonder you've got consumption coming on! And the audience will notice there's something wrong with you, and start clearing out to avoid infection. That's where my song will come in. My song will be a tonic. Now don't start breathing at me, or you'll puncture the other lung. Let's try that last verse over again, Jimmy.'

In the end after a long discussion, during which Mabel introduced the most irrelevant arguments, Monkley decided that both songs should be sung, but with a long enough interval between them to secure Claude against the least impression that he was being laughed at.

At last the company, which called itself The Pink Pierrots, was ready to start for the South Coast. It took Monkley all his ingenuity to get out of London without paying for the dresses or the properties, but it was managed somehow; and at the beginning of July they pitched a small tent on the beach at Hastings. There were many rival companies, some of which possessed the most elaborate equipment, almost a small theatre with railed-off seats and a large piano; but Sylvia envied none of these its grandeur. She thought that none was so tastefully dressed as themselves; that there was no leader so sure of keeping the attention of an audience as Jimmy was; that no tenor could bring tears to the eyes of the young women on the Marina as Claude could; that no voice could be heard farther off than Mabel's; and that no comedian could so quickly gain the sympathy of that large but unprofitable portion of an audience – the small boys – as her father could.

Sylvia enjoyed every moment of the day from the time they left their lodgings, pushing before them the portable piano in the morning sunshine, to the journey home after the last performance, which was given in a circle of rosy lantern light within sound of the sea. They worked so hard that there was no time for quarrelling except with competitors upon whose preserves they had trespassed: Mabel was so bent upon fascinating the various patrons, and Henry was so obviously a success with the unsentimental small boys that she never once accused him of making eyes even at a nursemaid. Sylvia was given a duet with Claude Raglan, and, whether it was that she was conscious of being envied by many of the girls in the audience or whether the sentimental tune influenced her imagination, she was certainly aware of a faint thrill of pleasure – a hardly perceptible quickening of the heart – every time that Claude took her in his arms to sing the last verse. After they had sung together for a week, Jimmy said the number was a failure and abolished it, which Sylvia thought very unfair, because it had always been well applauded.

She grumbled to Claude about their deprivation, while they were toiling home to dinner (they were at Bournemouth now, and the weather was extremely hot), and he declared in a tragical voice that people were always jealous of him.

'It's the curse of being an artist,' he announced. 'Everywhere I go I meet with nothing but jealousy. I can't help having a good voice. I'm not conceited about it. I can't help the girls sending me chocolates and asking me to sign the postcards of me which they buy. I'm not conceited about that either. There's something about my personality that appeals to women. Perhaps it's my delicate look. I don't suppose I shall live very long, and I think that makes women sorry for me. They're quicker to see these things than men. I know Harry thinks I'm as healthy as a beef-steak. I'm positive I coughed up some blood this morning, and when I told Harry he asked me with a sneer if I'd cleaned my teeth. You're not a bit like your dad, Sylvia. There's something awfully sympathetic about you, little girl. I'm sorry Jimmy's cut out our number. He's a jolly good manager and all that, but he does not like anybody else to make a hit. Have you noticed that lately he's taken to gagging during my songs? Luckily I'm not at all easy to dry up.'

Sylvia wondered why anybody like Jimmy should bother to be jealous of Claude. He was pleasant enough, of course, and he had a pretty girlish mouth and looked very slim and attractive in his Pierrot's dress; but nobody could take him seriously except the stupid girls who bought his photograph and sighed over it when they brushed their hair in the morning.

The weather grew hotter, and the hard work made them all irritable; when they got home for dinner at midday it was impossible to eat, and they used to loll about in the stuffy sitting-room, which the five of them shared in common, while the flies buzzed everywhere. It was never worth while to remove the make-up; so all their faces used to get mottled with pale streaks of perspiration, the rouge on their lips would cake, and their ruffles hung limp and wet, stained round the neck with dirty carmine. Sylvia lost all enjoyment in the tour, and used to lie on the horse-hair sofa that pricked her cheeks, watching distastefully the cold mutton, the dull knives and the spotted cloth, and the stewed fruit over which lay a faint silvery film of staleness: round the room her fellow-mountebanks were still seated on the chairs into which they had first collapsed when they reached the lodgings, motionless like great painted dolls.

The weather grew hotter: the men, particularly Henry, took to drinking brandy at every opportunity; toward the end of their stay in Bournemouth the quarrels between him and Mabel broke out again, but with a difference, because now it was Henry who was the aggressor. He had never objected to Mabel's admirers hitherto, had indeed been rather proud of their existence in a fatuous way and derived from their number the satisfaction of a showman. When it was her turn to take the hat, he used to smirk over the quantity of postcards she sold of herself and call everybody's attention to her capricious autography that was so successful with the callow following. Then suddenly one day he made an angry protest against the admiration which an older man began to accord her, a pretentious sort of man with a diamond ring and yellow cummerbund, who used to stand with his straw hat a-tilt and wink at Mabel, tugging at his big drooping moustache and jingling the money in his pockets.

Everybody told Henry not to be foolish; he only sulked and began to drink more brandy than ever. The day after Henry's outbreak, the Pink Pierrots moved to Swanage, where their only rivals were a troupe of niggers, upon whom Henry was able to loose some of his spleen in a dispute that took place over the newcomers' right to plant their pink tent where they did.

'This isn't Africa, you know,' Henry said. 'This is Swanage. It's no good your waving your banjo at me. I know it's a banjo all right, though I may forget, next time I hear you play it.'

'We've been here every year for the last ten years,' the chief nigger shouted.

'I thought so by your songs,' Henry retorted. 'If you told me you got wrecked here with Christopher Columbus I shouldn't have contradicted you.'

'This part of the beach belongs to us,' the niggers proclaimed.

'I suppose you bought it off Noah, didn't you, when he let you out of the ark?' said Henry.

In the end, however, the two companies adjusted their differences, and removed themselves out of each other's hearing: Mabel's voice defeated even the tambourines and bones of the niggers. Swanage seemed likely to be an improvement upon Bournemouth, until one day Mabel's prosperous admirer appeared on the promenade and Henry's jealousy rose to fury.

'Don't you tell me you didn't tell him to follow you here,' he said, 'because I don't believe you. I saw you smile at him.'

Monkley remonstrated with Mabel, when Henry had gone off in a fever of rage to his room, but she seemed to be getting a certain amount of pleasure from the situation.

'You must cut it out,' Monkley said. 'I don't want the party broken up on account of you and Henry. I tell you he really is upset. What the deuce do you want to drag in all this confounded love business now for? Leave that to Claude. It'll burst up the show, and it's making Harry drink, which his head can't stand.'

Mabel looked at herself in the glass over the fireplace and patted her hair complacently.

'I'm rather glad to see Harry can get jealous. After all, it's always a pleasure to think someone's really fond of you.'

Sylvia watched Mabel very carefully and perceived that she actually was carrying on a flirtation with the man who had followed her from Bournemouth: she hoped that it would continue and that her father would get angry enough with Mabel to get rid of her, when the tour came to an end.

One Saturday afternoon, when Mabel was collecting, Sylvia distinctly saw her admirer drop a note into the hat, which she took with her into the tent to read and tore up: during her next song Sylvia noticed that the man with the yellow cummerbund was watching her with raised eyebrows and that, when Mabel smiled and nodded, he gently clapped his hands and went away.

Sylvia debated with herself the advisability of telling her father at once what she had seen, thus bringing things to an immediate climax and getting rid of Mabel for ever, even if by doing so the show were spoilt. But when she saw his glazed eyes and realized how drunk he was, she thought she would wait. The next afternoon, when Henry was taking his Sunday rest, Mabel dressed herself and went out. Sylvia followed her and, after ascertaining that she had taken the path towards the cliffs to the east of the town, came back to the lodgings and again debated with herself a course of action. She decided in the end to wait a little longer before she denounced Mabel; later on, when her father had woken up and was demanding Mabel's company for a stroll in the moonlight, a letter was brought to the lodgings by a railway porter from Mabel herself to say that she had left the company and had gone away with her new friend by train. Sylvia thought how near she had been to spoiling the elopement and hugged herself with pleasure; but she could not resist telling her father now that she had seen the intrigue in progress and of her following Mabel that afternoon and seeing her take the path towards the cliffs. Henry seemed quite shattered by his loss, and could do nothing but drink brandy, while Monkley swore at Mabel for wrecking a good show and wondered where he was going to find another girl, even going so far as to suggest telegraphing on the off-chance to Maudie Tilt.

It was very hot on Monday, and after the morning performance Henry announced that he did not intend to walk all the way back to the lodgings for dinner. He should go to the hotel and have a snack. What did it matter about his being in his Pierrot's rig? Swanage was a small place, and if the people were not used to his costume by now, they never would be. It was no good anyone's arguing; he intended to stay behind this morning. The others left him talking in his usual style of melancholy humour to the small boy, who for the sum of twopence kept an eye on the portable piano and the book of songs during the hot midday hours. When they looked round, he was juggling with one of the pennies to the admiration of the owner. They never saw him alive again; he was brought back dead that evening on a stretcher, his pink costume splashed with blood. The odd thing was that the hotel carving knife was in his pocket, though it was proved conclusively at the inquest that death was due to falling over the cliffs on the east side of the town.

Sylvia wondered if she ought to blame herself for her father's death, and she confided in Jimmy what she had told him about Mabel's behaviour. Jimmy asked her why she could not have let things alone and made her very miserable by his strictures upon her youthful tactlessness, so miserable indeed that he was fain to console her and assure her that it had all been an accident due to Henry's fondness for brandy – that and the sun must have turned his head.

'You don't think he took the knife to kill himself?' she asked.

'More likely he took it with some idea of killing them and being drunk fell over the cliff. Poor old Harry! I shall miss him, and now you're all alone in the world.'

That was true, and the sudden realization of this fact drove out of Sylvia's mind the remorse for her father's death by confronting her with the instancy of the great problem that had for so long haunted her mind. She turned to Jimmy almost fearfully.

'I shall have you to look after me?'

Jimmy took her hand and gazed into her eyes.

'You want to stay with me then?' he asked earnestly.

'Of course I do. Who else could I stay with?'

'You wouldn't prefer to be with Claude for example?' he went on.

'Claude?' she repeated in a puzzled voice. And then she grasped in all its force the great new truth that for the rest of her life the choice of her companions lay with herself alone. She had become at this moment grown up and was free like Mabel to choose even a man with a yellow cummerbund.

IV

Sylvia begged Monkley not to go back and live in Fitzroy Street; she felt the flat would be haunted by memories of her father and Mabel. It was as well that she did not want to return there, for Jimmy assured her that nothing would induce him to go near Fitzroy Street: a great deal of money was owing, and he wished the landlord luck in his dispute with the furnishing people, when he tried to seize the furniture for arrears of rent. It would be necessary to choose for their next abode a quarter of London to which he was a stranger, because he disliked having to make detours to avoid streets where he owed money. Finsbury Park was melancholy: Highgate was inaccessible: Hampstead was expensive and almost equally inaccessible; but they must go somewhere in the North of London, for there did not remain a suburb in the West or South, the tradesmen and house-owners of which he had not swindled at one time or another. On second thoughts, there was a part of Hampstead that was neither so expensive nor so inaccessible, which was reached from Haverstock Hill: they would look for rooms there. They settled down finally in one of a row of old houses facing the southerly extremity of the Heath, the rural aspect of which was heightened by long gardens in front that now in late summer were filled with sunflowers and hollyhocks. The old-fashioned house, which resembled a large cottage both without and within, belonged to a decayed florist and nursery gardener called Samuel Gustard, whose trade was now confined to the sale of penny packets of seeds, though a weather-beaten signboard facing the road maintained a legend of greater glories. Mr. Gustard himself made no effort to live up to his signboard; indeed he would not even stir himself to produce a packet of seeds, for if his wife were about, he would indicate to her with the stem of his pipe which packet was wanted, and if she were not about, he would tell the customer that the variety was no longer in stock. A greenhouse kept from collapse by the sturdy vine it was supposed to protect ran along the fence on one side of the garden: the rest was a jungle of coarse herbaceous flowers, presumably the survivors of Mr. Gustard's last horticultural effort about ten years ago.

The money made by the tour of the Pink Pierrots did not last very long, and Jimmy was soon forced back to industry. Sylvia nowadays heard more about his successes and failures than when her father was alive, and she begged very hard to be allowed to help on some of his expeditions.

'You're no good to me yet,' Monkley told her. 'You're too old to be really innocent and not old enough to pretend to be. Besides people don't take schoolgirls to race meetings. Later on, when you've learnt a bit more about life, we'll start a gambling club in the West End and work on a swell scale what I do now in a small way in railway-carriages.'

This scheme of Jimmy's became a favourite topic; and Sylvia began to regard a flash gambling hell as the crown of human ambition. Jimmy's imagination used to run riot amid the splendour of it all, as he discoursed of the footmen with plush breeches; of the shaded lamps; of the sideboard loaded with hams and jellies and fruit at which the guests would always be able to refresh themselves, for it would never do to let them go away because they were hungry, and people were always hungry at three in the morning; of the smart page-boy in the entrance of the flats who would know how to reckon up a visitor and give the tip upstairs by ringing a bell; and of the rigid exclusion of all women except Sylvia herself.

'I can see it all before me,' Jimmy used to sigh. 'I can smell the cigars and whisky. I'm flinging back the curtains when everyone has gone and feeling the morning air. And here we are stuck in this old cucumber-frame at Hampstead! But we'll get it, we'll get it. I shall have a scoop one of these days and be able to start saving, and when I've saved a couple of hundred, I'll bluff the rest.'

In October Jimmy came home from Newmarket and told Sylvia he had run against an old friend, who had proposed a money-making scheme which would take him away from London for a couple of months. He could not explain the details to Sylvia, but he might say that it was a confidence trick on the grand scale and that it meant his residing in a Northern city. He had told his friend he would give him an answer to-morrow, and wanted to know what Sylvia thought about it.

She was surprised by Jimmy's consulting her in this way: she had always taken it for granted that from time to time she should be left alone. Jimmy's action made her realize more clearly than ever that to a great extent she already possessed that liberty of choice, the prospect of which had dawned upon her at Swanage.

She assured Jimmy of her readiness to be left alone in Hampstead; when he expatiated on his consideration for her welfare she was bored and longed for him to be gone; his solicitude gave her a feeling of restraint; she became impatient of his continually wanting to know if she should miss him, and of his commendation of her to the care of Mr. and Mrs. Gustard, from whom she desired no interference, being quite content with the prospect of sitting in her window with a book and a green view.

The next morning Monkley left Hampstead; and Sylvia inhaled freedom with the autumn air. She had been given what seemed a very large sum of money to sustain herself until Jimmy's return: she had bought a new hat: a black kitten had adopted her: it was pearly October weather. Sylvia surveyed life with a sense of pleasure that was nevertheless most unreasonably marred by a faint breath of restlessness, an almost imperceptible discontent. Life had always offered itself to her contemplation whether of the past or of the future as a set of vivid impressions that formed a crudely coloured panorama of action without any emotional light and shade, the intervals between which like the intervals of a theatrical performance were only tolerable with plenty of chocolates to eat. At the present moment she had plenty of chocolates to eat, more in fact than she had ever had before, but the interval was seeming most exasperatingly long.

'You ought to take a walk on the Heath,' Mr. Gustard advised. 'It isn't good to sit about all day, doing nothing.'

'You don't take walks,' Sylvia pointed out. 'And you sit about all day, doing nothing. I do read a book, anyway.'

'I'm different,' Mr. Gustard pronounced very solemnly. 'I've lived my life. If I was to take a walk round Hampstead, I couldn't hardly peep into a garden without seeing a tree as I'd planted myself. And when I'm gone, the trees will still be there. That's something to *think* about that is. There was a clergyman came nosing round here the other day to ask me why

I didn't go to church. I told him I'd done without church as a lad, and I couldn't see why I shouldn't do without it now. "But you're growing old, Mr. Gustard," he says to me. "That's just it," I says to him. "I'm getting very near the time when if all they say is true I shall be in the heavenly choir for ever and ever amen, and the less singing I hear for the rest of my time on earth the better." "That's a very blasphemous remark," he says to me. "Is it?" says I to him. "Well, here's another. Perhaps all this talk by parsons," I says, "about this life on earth being just a choir practice for heaven won't bear looking into. Perhaps we shall all die and go to sleep and never wake up and never dream and never do nothing at all never. And if that's true," I says, "I reckon I shall bust my coffin with laughing when I think of my trees growing and growing and growing and you preaching to a lot of old women and children about something you don't know nothing about and they don't know nothing about and nobody don't know nothing about." With that I offered him a pear, but he walked off very offended with his head in the air. You get out and about, my dear. Bustle around and enjoy yourself. That's my motto for the young.'

Sylvia felt that there was much to be said for Mr. Gustard's attitude, and she took his advice so far as to go for a long walk on the Heath that very afternoon. Yet there was something lacking; when she got home again, she found that the book of adventure which she had been reading was no longer capable of keeping her thoughts fixed. The stupid part of it was that her thoughts wandered nowhere in particular and without attaching themselves to a definite object. She would try to concentrate them upon Jimmy and speculate what he was doing, but Jimmy would turn into Claude Raglan; and when she began to speculate what Claude was doing, Claude would turn back again into Jimmy. Her own inner restlessness made her so fidgety that she went to the window and stared at the road along the dusky Heath. The garden-gate of next door swung to with a click, and Sylvia saw a young man coming toward the house. She was usually without the least interest in young men, but on this after-noon of indefinable and errant thought she welcomed the least excuse for bringing herself back to a material object; and this young man, though it was twilight and his face was not clearly visible, managed to interest her somehow, so that at tea she found herself asking Mr. Gustard who he might be and most unaccountably blushing at the question.

'That'ud be young Artie, wouldn't it?' he suggested to his wife. She nodded over the squat teapot that she so much resembled:

'That must be him come back from his uncle's. Mrs. Madden was only saying to me this morning, when we was waiting for the grocer's man, that she was expecting him this evening. She spoils him something shocking. If you please, his highness has been down into Hampshire to see if he would like to be a gentleman-farmer. Whatever next, I should like to know? Why, he can't be long turned seventeen. It's a pity his father isn't alive to keep him from idling his time away.'

'There's no harm in giving a bit of liberty to the young,' Mr. Gustard answered, preparing to be as eloquent as the large piece of bread and butter in his mouth would let him. 'I'm not in favour of pushing a young man too far.'

'No, you was never in favour of pushing anything, neither yourself nor your business,' said Mrs. Gustard sharply. 'But I think it's a sin to let a boy like that moon away all his time with a book. Books were only intended for the gentry and people as have grown too old for anything else, and even then they're bad for their eyes.'

Sylvia wondered whether Mrs. Gustard intended to criticize unfavourably her own manner of life, but she left the defence of books to Mr. Gustard, who was so impatient to begin that he nearly choked:

'Because I don't read,' he said, 'that's no reason for me to try and stop others from reading. What I say is "liberty for all." If young Artie Madden wants to read, let him read. If Sylvia here wants to read, let her read. Books give employment to a lot of people: binders, printers, papermakers, booksellers. It's a regular trade. If people didn't like to smell flowers and sit about under trees, there wouldn't be no gardeners, would there? Very well then: and if there wasn't people who wanted to read, there wouldn't be no printers.'

'What about the people who write all the rubbish?' Mrs. Gustard demanded fiercely. 'Nice idle lot of good for nothings they are, I'm sure.'

'That's because the only writing fellow we ever knew got that servant girl of ours into trouble.'

'Samuel,' Mrs. Gustard interrupted. 'That'll do!'

'I don't suppose every writing fellow's like him,' Mr. Gustard went on. 'And anyway the girl was a saucy hussy.'

'Samuel! That will do, I said.'

'Well, so she was,' Mr. Gustard continued defiantly. 'Didn't she used to powder her face with your Borwick's?'

'I'll trouble you not to spit crumbs all over my clean cloth,' said Mrs. Gustard. 'Making the whole place look like a birdcage!'

Mr. Gustard winked at Sylvia, and was silent. She for her part had already begun to weave round Arthur Madden a veil of romance, when the practical side of her suddenly roused itself to a sense of what was going on and admonished her to leave off dreaming and attend to her cat.

Upstairs in her bedroom she opened her window and looked out at the faint drizzle of rain, which was just enough to mellow the leafy autumnal scents and diffuse the golden beams of the lamps along the Heath. There was the sound of another window's being opened on a line with hers; presently a head and shoulders scarcely definable in the darkness leant out, whistling an old French air that was familiar to her from earliest childhood, the words of which had long ago been forgotten. She could not help whistling the air in unison; and after a moment's silence a voice from the head and shoulders asked who it was.

'A girl,' Sylvia said.

'Anybody could tell that,' the voice commented a little scornfully. 'Because the noise is all woolly.'

'It's not,' Sylvia contradicted indignantly. 'Perhaps you'll say I'm out of tune? I know quite well who you are. You're Arthur Madden, the boy next door.'

'But who are you?'

'I'm Sylvia Scarlett.'

'Are you a niece of Mrs. Gustard?' the voice enquired.

'Of course not,' Sylvia scoffed. 'I'm just staying here.'

'Who with?'

'By myself.'

'By yourself?' the voice echoed incredulously.

'Why not? I'm nearly sixteen.'

This was too much for Arthur Madden, who struck a match to illuminate the features of the strange unknown. Although he did not succeed in discerning Sylvia, he lit up his own face, which she liked well enough to suggest they should go for a walk, making the proposal a kind of test for herself of Arthur Madden's character and deciding that if he showed the least hesitation in accepting she would never speak to him again. The boy, however, was immediately willing; the two pairs of shoulders vanished; Sylvia put on her coat and went downstairs.

'Going out for a blow?' Mr. Gustard asked.

Sylvia nodded.

'With the boy next door,' she answered.

'You haven't been long,' said Mr. Gustard approvingly. 'That's the way I like to see it. When I courted Mrs. Gustard, which was forty years ago come next November, it was in the time of toolip planting, and I hove a toolip bulb at her and caught her in the chignon. "Whatever are you doing of?" she says to me. "It's a proposal of marriage," I says, and when she started giggling I was that pleased I planted half the toolips upside down. But that's forty years ago, that is; Mrs. Gustard's grown more

69

particular since, and so *as* she's washing up the tea-things in the scullery, I should just slip out, and I'll tell her you've gone out to get a paper to see if it's true what somebody said about Buckingham Palace being burnt up to a cinder.'

Sylvia was not at all sure that she ought to recognize Mrs. Gustard's opinion even so far as by slipping out, and thereby giving her an idea that she did not possess perfect liberty of action. However, she decided that the point was too trifling to worry about and, with a wave of her hand, she left her landlord to tell what story he chose to his wife.

Arthur Madden was waiting for her by his gate, when she reached the end of the garden; while they wandered along by the Heath, indifferent to the drizzle, Sylvia felt an extraordinary release from the faint discontent of these past days, an extraordinary delight in finding herself with a companion who was young like herself and who like herself seemed full of speculation upon the world which he was setting out to explore, regarding it as an adventure and ready to exchange hopes and fears and fancies with her in a way that no one had ever done hitherto; moreover, he was ready to be most flatteringly impressed by her experiences, even if he still maintained she could not whistle properly. The friendship between Sylvia and Arthur begun upon that night grew daily closer. Mrs. Gustard used to say that they wasted each other's time, but she was in the minority: she used to say also that Arthur was being more spoilt than ever by his mother; but it was this very capacity for being spoilt that endeared him to Sylvia, who had spent a completely free existence for so long now, that unless Arthur had been allowed his freedom she would soon have tired of the friendship. She liked Mrs. Madden, a beautiful and unpractical woman, who unceasingly played long sonatas on a cracked piano; at least she would have played them unceasingly, had she not continually been jumping up to wait on Arthur, hovering about him like a dark and iridescent butterfly.

In the course of many talks together Arthur told Sylvia the family history. It seemed that his mother had been the daughter of a gentleman, not an ordinary kind of top-hatted gentleman, but a squire with horses and hounds and a park; his father had been a groom and she had eloped with him, but Sylvia was not to suppose that his father had been an ordinary kind of groom; he too came from good stock, though he had been rather wild. His father's father had been a farmer in Sussex, and he had just come back from staying at the farm where his uncle had offered to give him a start in life, but he had found he did not care much for farmwork. His mother's family would have nothing to do with her beyond allowing her enough to live upon without disturbing them.

'What are you going to do?' Sylvia asked.

Arthur replied that he did not know, but that he had thoughts of being a soldier.

'A soldier?' said Sylvia doubtfully. Her experience of soldiers was confined to Blanche's lovers, and the universal connotation in France of soldiery with a vile servitude that could hardly be justified.

'But of course the worst of it is,' Arthur explained, 'there aren't any wars nowadays.'

They were walking over the Heath on a fine November day about Martinmas; presently, when they sat down under some pines and looked at London spread beneath them in a sparkling haze, Arthur took Sylvia's hand and told her that he loved her.

She nearly snatched her hand away and would have told him not to be silly, but suddenly the beauty of the tranquil city below and the wind through the pines conquered her spirit: she sat closer to him, letting her head droop upon his shoulder; when his clasp tightened round her unresisting hand, she burst into tears, unable to tell him that her sorrow was nothing but joy, that he had nothing to do with it nor with her, and yet that he had everything to do with it, because with no one else could she have borne this incommunicable display of life: then she dried her tears and told Arthur she thought he had better become a highwayman.

'Highwaymen don't exist any longer,' Arthur objected. 'All the jolly things have disappeared from the world – war and highwaymen and pirates and troubadours and crusaders and maypoles and the Inquisition. Everything.'

Gradually Sylvia learnt from Arthur how much of what she had been reading was mere invention, and in the first bitterness of disillusionment she wished to renounce books for ever; but Arthur dissuaded her from doing that, and they used to read simultaneously the same books so as to be able to discuss them during their long walks. They became two romantics born out of due season, two romantics that should have lived a century ago and that now bewailed the inability of the modern world to supply what their adventurous souls demanded.

Arthur was inclined to think that Sylvia had much less cause to repine than he; the more tales she told him of her life, the more tributes of envy he paid to her good fortune. He pointed out that Monkley scarcely differed from the highwayman of romance; nor did he doubt but that if all his enterprises could be known he would rival Dick Turpin himself. Sylvia agreed with what he said, but she urged the inequality of her own share in the achievement. What she wanted was something more than to sit at home and enjoy fruits in the stealing of which she had played no part. She wanted none of Arthur's love unless he were prepared to face the problem of living life at its fullest in company with her. She would let him kiss her sometimes, because unhappily it seemed that even very young men were infected with this malady and that if deprived of this odious habit they were liable to lose determination and sink into incomprehensible despondency. At the same time Sylvia made Arthur clearly understand that she was yielding to his weakness, not to her own, and that, if he wished to retain her compassion, he must prove that the devotion of which he boasted was vital to his being.

'You mustn't just kiss me,' Sylvia warned him, 'because it's easy. It's very difficult really, because it's very difficult for me to let you do it. I have to wind myself up beforehand just as if I were going to pull out a loose tooth.'

Arthur gazed at her with wide-open liquid eyes; his mouth trembled.

'You say such cruel things,' he murmured.

Sylvia punched him as hard as she could:

'I won't be stared at like that. You look like a cow, when you stare at me like that. Buck up, and think what we're going to do.'

'I'm ready to do anything,' Arthur declared, 'as long as you're decent to me. But you're such an extraordinary girl. One moment you burst into tears and put your head on my shoulder, and the next moment you're punching me.'

'And I shall punch you again,' Sylvia said fiercely, 'if you dare to remind me that I ever cried in front of you. You weren't there, when I cried.'

'But I was,' he protested.

'No, you weren't. You were only there like a tree or a cloud.'

'Or a cow,' said Arthur gloomily.

'I think that if we did go away together,' Sylvia said meditatively, 'I should leave you almost at once, because you will keep returning to things I said. My father used to be like that.'

'But if we go away,' Arthur asked, 'how are we going to live? I shouldn't be any use on race-courses. I'm the sort of person that always gets taken in by the three-card trick.'

'You make me so angry when you talk like that,' Sylvia said. 'Of course, if you think you'll always be a fool, you always will be a fool. Being in love with me must make you think that you're not a fool. Perhaps we never shall go away together; but if we do, you'll have to begin by stealing bicycles. Jimmy Monkley and my father did that for a time. You hire a bicycle and sell it or pawn it a long way off from the shop it came from. It's quite easy. Only of course, it's best to disguise yourself. Father

72

used to paint out his teeth, wear blue glasses, and powder his moustache grey. But once he made himself so old in a place called Lewisham that the man in the bicycle shop thought he was too old to ride and wouldn't let him have a machine.'

Sylvia was strengthened in her resolve to launch Arthur upon the stormy seas of an independent existence by the placid harbour in which his mother loved to see him safely at anchor. Sylvia could not understand how a woman like Mrs. Madden, who had once been willing to elope with a groom, could bear to let her son spend his time so ineffectively. Not that she wished Mrs. Madden to exert her authority by driving him into a clerkship, or indeed into any profession for which he had no inclination; but she deplored the soft slavery which a fond woman can impose, the slavery of being waited upon that is more deadening than the slavery of waiting upon other people. She used to make a point of impressing upon Mrs. Madden the extent to which she and Arthur went shares in everything, lest she might suppose that Sylvia imitated her complaisance, and when Mrs. Madden used to smile in her tired way and make some remark about boy and girl lovers, Sylvia used to get angry and try to demonstrate the unimportance of that side of life.

'You funny child,' Mrs. Madden said. 'When you're older, how you'll laugh at what you think now. Of course, you don't know anything about love yet, mercifully for you. I wish I were richer; I should so like to adopt you.'

'Oh, but I wouldn't be adopted,' Sylvia quickly interposed. 'I can't tell you how glad I am that I belong to nobody. And please don't think I'm so innocent, because I'm not. I've seen a great deal of love, you must remember, and I've thought a lot about it, and made up my mind that I'll never be a slave to that sort of thing. Arthur may be stupidly in love with me, but I'm very strict with him and it doesn't do him any harm.'

'Come and sing your favourite song,' Mrs. Madden laughed. 'I'll play your accompaniment.'

All the discussions between them ended in music; Sylvia would sing that she was off with the raggle-taggle gipsies, stamping with her foot upon the floor of the old house until it shook and crossing her arms with such resolution that Arthur's eyes would grow larger than ever, as if he half expected to see her act upon the words and fling herself out into the December night, regardless of all but a mad demonstration of liberty.

Sylvia would sometimes sing about the gipsies to herself while she was undressing, which generally called forth a protest from Mrs. Gustard, who likened the effect to that of a young volcano let loose.

Another person that was pained by Sylvia's exuberance was Maria, her black cat, so called on account of his colour before he was definitely established as a gentleman. He had no ear for music and he disapproved of dancing; nor did he have the least sympathy with the aspirations of the lawless song she sang. Mrs. Gustard considered that he was more artful than what anyone would think, but she repudiated as 'heathenish' Sylvia's contention that she outwardly resembled Maria.

'Still I do think I'm like a cat,' Sylvia argued. 'Perhaps not very like a black cat, more like a tabby. One day you'll come up to my room and find me purring on the bed.'

Mrs. Gustard exclaimed against such an unnatural event.

Sylvia received one or two letters from Jimmy Monkley during the winter, in which he wrote with considerable optimism of the success of his venture and thought he might be back in Hampstead by February. He came back unexpectedly, however, in the middle of January; and Sylvia was only rather glad to see him: she had grown fond of her life alone and dreaded Jimmy's habit of arranging matters over her head. He was not so amiable as formerly, because the scheme had only been partially successful and he had failed to make enough money to bring the flash gambling hell perceptibly nearer. Sylvia had almost forgotten that project; it seemed to her now a dull project, neither worthy of herself nor of him. She did not attempt on Jimmy's return to change her own way of spending the time, and she persisted in taking the long walks with Arthur as usual.

'What the devil you see to admire in that long-legged, saucer-eyed, curly-headed mother's pet, I don't know,' Jimmy grumbled.

'I don't admire him,' Sylvia contradicted. 'I don't admire anybody except Joan of Arc. But I like him.'

Jimmy scowled. Later on that day, Mr. Gustard warned Sylvia that her uncle (as such was Jimmy known in the lodgings) had carried on alarmingly about her friendship with young Artie.

'It's nothing to do with him,' Sylvia affirmed with out-thrust chin.

'Nothing whatever,' Mr. Gustard agreed. 'But if I was you I wouldn't throw young Artie in his face. I've never had a niece myself, but from what I can make out an uncle feels something like a father; and a father gets very worried about his rights.'

'But you've never had any children, and so you can't know any more about the feelings of a father,' Sylvia objected.

'Ah, but I've got my own father to look back upon,' Mr. Gustard said. 'He mostly took a spade to me, I remember, though he wasn't against jabbing me in the ribs with a trowel, if there wasn't a spade handy. I reckon it was him as first put the notion of liberty for all into my head. I never set much store by uncles though. The only uncle I ever had died of croup when he was two years old.'

'My father didn't like his aunts,' Sylvia added to the condemnation. 'He was brought up by two aunts.'

'Aunts in general is sour bodies, specially when they're in charge and get all the fuss of having children with none of the fun.'

'Mr. Monkley isn't really my uncle,' Sylvia abruptly proclaimed.

'Go on, you don't mean it?' said Mr. Gustard. 'I suppose he's your guardian?'

'He's nothing at all,' Sylvia answered.

'He must be something.'

'He's absolutely nothing,' she insisted. 'He used to live with my father, and when my father died, he just went on living with me. If I don't want to live with him, I needn't.'

'But you must live with somebody,' said Mr. Gustard. 'There's a law about having visible means of support. You couldn't have a lot of kids living on their own.'

'Why not?' Sylvia asked in contemptuous amazement.

'Why not?' Mr. Gustard repeated. 'Why, because everyone would get pestered to death. It's the same with stray dogs. Stray dogs have got to have a home. If they haven't a home of their own, they're taken to the Dogs' Home at Battersea and cremated, which is a painless and mercenary death.'

'I don't call that much of a home,' Sylvia scoffed. 'A place where you're killed.'

'That's because we're speaking of dogs. Of course, if the police started in cremating children, there'd be a regular outcry. So the law insists on children having homes.'

Sylvia tried hard to convince Mr. Gustard that she was different from other children, and in any case no longer a child; but though the discussion lasted a long time he would not admit the logic of Sylvia's arguments; in the end she decided he did not know what he was talking about.

Monkley so much disliked Sylvia's intimacy with Arthur that he began to talk of moving from Hampstead, whereupon she warned him that if he tried to go away without paying the rent, she would make a point of letting Mr. Gustard know where they had gone.

'It strikes me,' Monkley said, and when he spoke, Sylvia was reminded of the tone he had used when she had protested against his treatment of Maudie Tilt: 'It strikes me that since I've been away you've taken things a bit too much into your own hands. That's a trick you'd better drop with me, or we shall quarrel.'

Sylvia braced herself to withstand him as she had withstood him before; but she could not help feeling a little apprehensive, so cold were his green eyes, so thin his mouth.

'I don't care if we quarrel or not,' she declared. 'Because if we quarrelled, it would mean that I couldn't bear you near me any longer, and that I was glad to quarrel. If you make me hate you, Jimmy, you may be sorry, but I shall never be sorry. If you make me hate you, Jimmy, you can't think how dreadfully much I shall hate you.'

'Don't try to come the little actress over me,' Monkley said. 'I've known too many women in my life to be bounced by a kid like you. But that's enough. I can't think why I pay so much attention to you.'

'No,' Sylvia said. 'All the women you've known don't seem to have been able to teach you how to manage a little girl like me. What a pity!'

She laughed and left him alone.

There was a halcyon week that February, and Sylvia spent every day and all day on the Heath with Arthur. People used to turn and stare after them, as they walked arm-in-arm over the vivid green grass.

'I think it's you they stare at,' Sylvia said. 'You look interesting with your high colour and dark curly hair. You look rather foreign. Perhaps people think you're a poet. I read the other day about a poet called Keats who lived in Hampstead and loved a girl called Fanny Brawne. I wish I knew what she looked like. It's not a very pretty name. Now I've got rather a pretty name, I think; though I'm not pretty myself.'

'You're not exactly pretty,' Arthur agreed. 'But I think if I saw you I should turn round to look at you. You're like a person in a picture. You seem to stand out and to be the most important figure. In paintings that's because the chief figure is usually so much larger than the others. Well, that's the impression you give me.'

Speculation upon Sylvia's personality ceased when they got home; Monkley threatened Arthur in a very abusive way, even going as far as to pick up a stone and fling it through one of the few panes of glass left in the tumbledown greenhouse in order to illustrate the violent methods he proposed to adopt.

The next day, when Sylvia went to fetch Arthur for their usual walk, he made some excuse and was obviously frightened to accompany her.

'What can he do to you?' Sylvia demanded in scornful displeasure. 'The worst he can do is to kill you, and then you'd have died because you wouldn't surrender. Haven't you read about martyrs?'

'Of course I've read about martyrs,' said Arthur rather querulously. 'But reading about martyrs is very different from being a martyr yourself.

76

You seem to think everybody can be anything you happen to read about. You wouldn't care to be a martyr, Sylvia.'

'That's just where you're wrong,' she loftily declared. 'I'd much sooner be a martyr than a coward.'

Arthur winced at her plain speaking.

'You don't care what you say,' was his reproach.

'No, and I don't care what I do,' Sylvia agreed. 'Are you coming out with me? Because if you're not, you shall never be my friend again.'

Arthur pulled himself together, and braved Monkley's threats: on a quiet green summit he demanded her impatient kisses for a recompense; she, conscious of his weakness and against her will made fonder of him by this very weakness, kissed him less impatiently than was her wont, so that Arthur under the inspiration of that rare caress vowed he cared for nobody and for nothing, if she would but always treat him thus kindly.

Sylvia, who was determined to make Jimmy pay for his bad behaviour, invited herself to tea with Mrs. Madden; afterwards, though it was cloudy and ominous, Arthur and she walked out on the Heath once more, until it rained so hard that they were driven home. It was about seven o'clock when Sylvia reached her room, her hair still tangled with moisture, her eyes and cheeks on fire with the exhilaration of that scurry through the rain. She had not stood a moment to regard herself in the glass, when Monkley following close upon her heels shut the door behind him and turned the key in the lock. Sylvia looked round in astonishment; by a trick of candlelight his eyes gleamed for an instant, so that she felt a tremor of fear.

'You've come back at last, have you?' he began in a slow voice, so deliberate and gentle in its utterance that Sylvia might not have grasped the extent of his agitation, had not one of his legs affected by a nervous twitch drummed upon the floor a sinister accompaniment. 'You shameless little bitch. I thought I forbade you to go out with him again. You've been careering over the Heath. You've been encouraging him to make love to you. Look at your hair – it's in a regular tangle, and your cheeks – they're like fire. Well, if you can let that nancified milksop mess you about, you can put up with me. I've wanted to long enough, God knows: and this is the reward I get for leaving you alone. You give yourself to the first bloody boy that comes along.'

Before Sylvia had time to reply, Monkley had leapt across the room and crushed her to him.

'Kiss me, damn you, kiss me. Put your arms round me.'

Sylvia would not scream, because she could not have endured that anybody should behold her in such an ignominious plight. Therefore she

77

only kicked and fought, and whispered all the while with savage intensity, 'You frog! you frog! You look like a frog! Leave me alone!'

Monkley held her more closely and forced her mouth against his own, but Sylvia bit through his underlip till her teeth met. The pain caused him to start back and tread on Maria who, searching in a panic for better cover than the bed afforded, had run between his legs. The cat, uttering one of those unimaginable wails with which only cats have power so horribly to surprise, retired to a corner where he hissed and growled: in another corner Sylvia spat forth the unclean blood and wiped from her lips the soilure of the kisses.

Monkley had had enough for the present: the pain and sudden noise had shaken his nerves; when the blood ran down his chin bedabbling his tie, he unlocked the door and retired, crying out almost in a whimper for something to stop a bad razor cut. Mrs. Gustard went to the wood-shed for cobwebs; but Monkley soon shouted down that he had found some cotton-wool, and Sylvia heard a cork being drawn. She made up her mind to kill him that night, but she was perplexed by the absence of a suitable weapon, and gradually it was borne in upon her mind that if she killed Monkley she should have to pay the penalty, which did not seem to her a satisfactory kind of revenge: she gave up the notion of killing him and decided to run away with Arthur instead.

For a long time Sylvia sat in her bedroom, thinking over her plan: then she went next door and asked Arthur to come out and talk to her about something important. They stood whispering in the wet garden, while she bewitched him into offering to share her future: he was dazed by the rapidity with which she disposed of every objection he brought forward. She knew how to get enough money for them to start with: she knew how to escape from the house, and because the creeper beneath Arthur's window was not strong enough to bear his weight, he must tie his sheets together: he must not bring much luggage: she would only bring a small valise, and Maria could travel in her work-basket.

'Maria?' echoed Arthur in dismay.

'Of course. It was Maria who saved me,' said Sylvia. 'I shall wait until Monkley is asleep: I expect he'll be asleep early, because he's drinking brandy hard now; then I shall whistle the last line of the raggle-taggle gipsies and slither down from my window by the ivy.'

She stuffed Arthur's reeling brain with further details and, catching him to her heart, she kissed him with as much enthusiasm as might have been mistaken for passion. In the end between coaxing and frightening him, threatening and inspiring him, Sylvia made Arthur agree to every-thing and danced back indoors.

'Anybody would think you were glad because your guardian angel's gone and sliced a rasher off of his mouth,' Mr. Gustard observed.

By ten o'clock all was quiet in the house: Sylvia chose with the greatest care her equipment for the adventure: she had recently bought a tartan frock which not having yet been worn she felt would excellently become the occasion; this she put on, and plaited her tangled hair in a long pigtail: the result was unsatisfactory, for it made her look too prim for a heroine; she therefore undid the pigtail and tied her hair loosely back with a nut-brown bow. It was still impossibly early for an escape, so Sylvia sat down on the edge of her bed and composed herself to read the escape of Fabrizio from the Sforza tower in Parma. The book in which she read this was not one that she had been able to read through without a great deal of skipping; but this escape which she had only come across a day or two before seemed a divine omen to approve her decision. Sylvia regretted the absence of the armed men at the foot of the tower, but said to herself that after all she was escaping with her lover, whereas Fabrizio had been compelled to leave Clelia Conti behind. The night wore away; at half-past eleven Sylvia dropped her valise from the window and whistled that she was off with the raggletaggle gipsies – oh. Then she waited until a ghostly snake was uncoiled from Arthur's window.

'My dearest boy, you're an angel,' she trilled in an ecstasy when she saw him slide safely down into the garden. 'Catch Maria,' she whispered. 'I'm coming myself in a moment.' Arthur caught her work-basket, and a faint protesting mew floated away on the darkness. Sylvia wrapped herself up, and then very cautiously, candle in hand, walked across to the door of Monkley's room and listened. He was snoring loudly. She pushed open the door, and beheld him fast asleep, a red and white beard of cotton-wool upon his chin: then risking all in an impulse to be quick, though she was almost stifled by fear, she hurried across the room to his trunk. He kept all his money in a tin box: how she hoped there was enough to make him rue her flight. Monkley never stirred: the box was safe in her muff: she stole back to her room, blew out the candle, flung the muff down to Arthur, held her breath when the coins rattled, put one leg over the sill, and scrambled down by the ivy.

'I wish it had been higher,' she whispered, when Arthur clasped her with affectionate solicitude where she stood in the sodden vegetation.

'I'm jolly glad it wasn't,' he said. 'Now what are we going to do?'

'Why, find a bus, of course,' Sylvia said. 'And get as far from Hampstead as possible.'

'But it's after twelve o'clock,' Arthur objected. 'There won't be any buses now. I don't know what we're going to do. We can't look for rooms at this time of night.'

'We must just walk as far as we can away from Hampstead,' said Sylvia cheerfully.

'And carry our luggage? Supposing a policeman asks us where we're going?'

'Oh, bother policemen. Come along, you don't seem to be enjoying yourself nearly as much as I am. I care for nobody. I'm off with the raggle-taggle gipsies – oh,' she lightly sang.

Maria mewed at the sound of his mistress's voice.

'You're as bad as Maria,' she went on reproachfully. 'Look how nice the lamp-posts look. One, two, three, four, five, six, seven, I can see. Let's bet how many lamp-posts we pass before we're safe in our own house.'

They set out for London by the road along the Heath. At first trees overhung the path, and they passed pool after pool of chequered lamp-light that quivered in the wet road: followed a space of open country where they heard the last whispers of a slight and desultory wind: soon they were enclosed by mute and unilluminated houses on either side, until they found themselves on the top of Haverstock Hill faced by the tawny glow of the London sky, and stretching before them a double row of lamp-posts innumerable and pale that converged to a dim point in the heart of the city below.

'I think I'm rather frightened,' Sylvia said. 'Or perhaps I'm a little tired.'

'Shall we go back?' Arthur suggested.

'No, no, we'll just rest a moment or two, and I'll be all right.' They sat down on their bags, and she stroked Maria pensively.

Sylvia was relieved when the silence was interrupted by a policeman: she felt the need of opposition to drive away the doubts that took advantage of that first fatigue to shake her purpose.

'Now then, what are you doing?' he demanded gruffly.

'We're sitting down,' Sylvia informed him.

'Loitering isn't allowed here,' the policeman said.

'Where is it allowed, please?' she asked sweetly.

'Loitering isn't allowed nowhere,' the policeman declared.

'Well, why did you say it wasn't allowed here?' she continued. 'I thought you were going to tell us of a place where it was allowed.'

Arthur jogged Sylvia's elbow and whispered to her not to annoy the policeman.

'Come along now, move on,' the policeman commanded; in order to emphasize his authority he flashed his bull's-eye in Sylvia's face. 'Where do you live?' he asked after the scrutiny.

'Lillie Road, Fulham. We missed the last train from Hampstead, and we're walking home. I never heard of any rule against sitting on one's own luggage in the middle of the night. I think you'd better take us to the police-station. We must rest somewhere.'

The policeman looked puzzled.

'What did you want to miss your train for?' he asked.

'We didn't want to miss it,' Sylvia gently explained. 'We were very angry when we missed it. Come on, Arthur, I don't feel tired any longer.'

She got up and started off down Haverstock Hill, followed by Arthur.

'I'm sorry you can't recommend any proper loitering-places on the road,' said Sylvia turning round, 'because we shall probably have to loiter about thirty-six times before we get to Lillie Road. Good night. If we meet any burglars, we'll give them your love and say there's a nice policeman living on Haverstock Hill who'd like a chat.'

'Suppose he had run us in?' Arthur said, when they had left the policeman behind them.

'I wanted him to at first,' Sylvia replied. 'But afterwards I thought it might be awkward on account of Monkley's cash-box. I wish we could open it now and see how much there is inside, but perhaps it would look funny at this time of night.'

They had nearly reached the bottom of Haverstock Hill and there were signs of life in the squalid streets they were approaching.

'I don't think we ought to hang about here,' Arthur said. 'These are slums. We ought to be careful; I think we ought to have waited till the morning.'

'You wouldn't have come, if we'd waited,' Sylvia maintained. 'You'd have been too worried about leaving your mother.'

'I'm still worried about that,' said Arthur gloomily.

'Why? You can send a postcard to say that you're all right. Knowing where you are won't make up for your being away; in any case you'd have had to go away soon. You couldn't have spent your whole life in that house at Hampstead.'

'Well, I think this running away will bring us bad luck.'

Sylvia made a dramatic pause and dropped her valise on the pavement.

'Go home then. Go home and leave me alone. If you can't enjoy yourself, I'd rather you went home. I can't bear to be with somebody who is not enjoying himself as much as I am.'

'You can't be enjoying this walking about all night with two bags and a cat,' Arthur insisted. 'But I'm not going home without you. If you want to go on, I shall go on too. I'm feeling rather tired. I expect I shall enjoy myself more to-morrow.'

Sylvia picked up her valise again.

'I hope you will, I'm sure,' she said. 'You're spoiling the fun by grumbling all the time like this. What is there to grumble at? Just a small bag which makes your arm ache. You ought to be glad you haven't got mine to carry as well as your own.'

After another quarter of an hour among the ill-favoured streets, Sylvia called a rest; this time they withdrew from the pavement into the area of an unoccupied house, where they leaned against the damp brick wall quite exhausted, and heard without interest the footsteps of the people who went past above. Maria began to mew, and Sylvia let him out of the basket: a lean and amorous tom-cat in pursuit of love considered that Maria had prejudiced his chance of success, and their recriminations ended in a noisy scuffle, during which the lid of a dustbin in the next area was upset with a loud clatter; somebody, throwing open a window, emptied a utensil, partly over Arthur.

'Don't make such a noise. It was only a jug,' Sylvia whispered. 'You'll wake up all the houses.'

'It's your damned cat making the noise,' Arthur said. 'Come here, you brute.'

Maria was at last secured and replaced in his basket; and Arthur asked Sylvia if she was sure it was only a jug.

'It's simply beastly in this area,' he added. 'Anything's better than sitting here.'

After making sure that nobody was in sight, they went on their way, though by now their legs were so weary that from time to time the bags scraped along the pavement.

'The worst of it is,' Sylvia sighed, 'we've come so far now that it would be just as tiring to go back to Hampstead as to go on.'

'Oh, *you're* thinking now of going back?' Arthur jeered. 'It's a pity you didn't think of that when we were on Haverstock Hill.'

'I'm not thinking at all of going back,' Sylvia snapped. 'I'm not tired.'

'Oh, no,' said Arthur sarcastically. 'And I'm not at all wet really.'

They got more and more irritable with one another. The bow in Sylvia's hair dropped off, and with all the fretful obstinacy of fatigue she would go wandering back on their tracks to see if she could find it: but the bow was lost. At last they saw a hansom coming towards them at a walking pace, and Sylvia announced that they would ride.

'But where shall we drive to?' Arthur asked. 'We can't just get in and drive anywhere.'

'We'll tell him to go to Waterloo,' said Sylvia. 'Stations are always open; we can wait in there till the morning and then look for a house.'

She hailed the cab; with sighs of relief they sank back upon the seat exhausted. Presently an odd noise like a fishmonger's smacking a cod could be heard beside the cab, and leaning out over the apron to see what was the cause of it, Arthur was spattered with mud by a piece of the tyre, which was flogging the road with each revolution of the wheel. The driver pulled up and descended from the box to restrain it.

'I've been tying it up all day, but it will do it,' he complained. 'There's nothing to worry over, but it fidgets anyone, don't it, flapping like that? I've tied it up with string and I've tied it up with wire, and last time I used my handkerchief. Now I suppose it's got to be my bootlace. Well, here goes,' he said, and with many grunts he stooped over to undo his lace.

Neither Sylvia nor Arthur could ever say what occurred to irritate a horse that with equanimity had tolerated the nuisance all day; but suddenly it leapt forward at a canter, while the loose piece of tyre slapped the road with increasingly rapidity and noise. The reins slipped down; but Sylvia, who had often been allowed to drive with Blanche, managed to gather them up and keep the horse more or less in the middle of the road. After the cab had travelled about a mile, the tyre that all day had been seeking freedom achieved its purpose, and lancing itself before the vehicle in a swift parabola, looped itself round an ancient ragman who was shuffling along the gutter in pursuit of wealth. The horse chose that moment to stop abruptly, and an unpleasant encounter with the ragman seemed inevitable; already he was approaching the cab, waving in angry fashion his spiked stick and swearing in a bronchial voice; he stopped his abuse, however, on perceiving the absence of the driver, and muttered to himself:

'A lucky night, so help me! A lovely long strip of indiarubber! Cor! what a find!'

Then he turned round and walked away as fast as he could, stuffing the tyre into his basket as he went.

'I wonder whether I could drive the cab properly if I climbed up on the box,' said Sylvia thoughtfully.

'Oh no, for goodness' sake, don't do anything of the kind,' Arthur begged. 'Let's get down while the beast is quiet. Come along, we shall never be able to explain why we're in this cab. It's like a dream.'

Sylvia gave way so far as not to mount the box, but she declined to alight and insisted they ought to stay where they were and rest as long as they could: there were still a number of dark hours before them.

'But, my dear girl, this beast of a horse may start off again,' Arthur protested.

'Well, what if it does?' Sylvia said. 'We can't be any more lost than we are now. I don't know in the least what part of London we've got to.'

'I'm sure there's something the matter with this cab,' Arthur woefully exclaimed.

'There is,' she agreed. 'You've just set fire to it with that match.'

'I'm so nervous,' said Arthur. 'I don't know what I'm doing. Phew! what a stink of burnt hair. Do let's get out.'

He stamped on the smouldering mat.

'Shut up,' Sylvia commanded. 'I'm going to try and have a sleep. Wake me up if the horse tries to walk into a shop or anything.'

But this was more than Arthur could stand, and he shook her in desperation.

'You shan't go to sleep. You don't seem to mind what happens to us.'

'Not a bit,' Sylvia agreed. Then suddenly she sang at the top of her voice, 'for I'm off with the raggle-taggle gipsies – oh!'

The horse at once trotted forward, and Arthur was in despair.

'Oh, damn,' he moaned. 'Now you've started that horrible brute off again. Whatever made me come away with you?'

'You can go home whenever you like,' said Sylvia coldly.

'What's the good of telling me that when we're tearing along in a cab without a driver?' Arthur bewailed.

'We're not tearing along,' Sylvia contradicted. 'And I'm driving. I expect the horse will go back to his stable if we don't interfere with him too much.'

'Who wants to interfere with the brute? Oh, listen to that wheel. I'm sure it's coming off.'

'Here's a cab shelter,' Sylvia announced encouragingly. 'I'm going to try and pull up.'

Luckily the horse was ready enough to stop, and both of them got out. Sylvia walked without hesitation into the shelter; followed by Arthur with the bags. There were three or four cabmen inside, eating voluptuously in an atmosphere of tobacco-smoke, steam, and burnt grease. She explained to them about the cab's running away, was much gratified by the attention her story secured, and learnt that it was three o'clock and that she was in Somers Town.

'Where are you going, Missie?' one of the cabmen asked.

'We were going to Waterloo, but we don't mind staying here,' Sylvia said. 'My brother is rather tired and my cat would like some milk.'

'What did the driver look like, Missie?' one of the men asked.

Sylvia described him vaguely as rather fat, a description which would have equally suited any of the present company, with the exception of the attendant tout, who was exceptionally lean.

'I wonder if it 'ud be Bill?' said one of the cabmen.

'I wouldn't say it wasn't.'

'Wasn't Bill grumbling about his tyre this morning?'

'I don't know if it was his tyre: he was grumbling about something.'

'I reckon it's Bill. Did you notice if the gentleman as drove you had a swelling behind his ear?' asked the man who had first propounded the theory of the missing driver's being Bill.

'I didn't notice,' said Sylvia.

'About the size of a largish potato?' the theorist pressed encouragingly.

'I'm afraid I didn't notice,' said Sylvia.

'It must be Bill,' the theorist decided. 'Anyone wouldn't notice that swelling in the dark, specially if Bill had his collar turned up.'

'He did have his collar turned up,' Arthur put in.

'There you are,' said the theorist. 'What did I tell you? Of course it's Bill. No one wouldn't see his swelling with his coat turned up. Poor old Bill, he won't half swear when he has to walk home to-night. Here, Joe,' he went on, addressing the attendant tout. 'Take Bill's horse a bit of a feed.'

Sylvia and Arthur were given large slices of bread and butter and large cups of coffee: Maria had a saucer of milk: life was looking much more cheerful. Presently a burly cabman appeared in the entrance of the shelter and was greeted with shouts of merriment.

'What ho, Bill, old cock! Lost your ruddy cab, old sporty? Lor! we haven't half laughed to think of you having to use your bacon and eggs to get here. I reckon you didn't half swear.'

'Who are you getting at, you blinking set of mugs? Who's lost his ruddy cab?' demanded Bill.

'That's not the driver,' Sylvia said.

'I thought it couldn't be Bill,' said the theorist quickly. 'As soon as I heard she never noticed that lump behind his ear, I thought it wasn't Bill.'

'Here, less of it, you and your lumps behind the ear,' said Bill aggressively. 'You'll have a blurry lump behind your own blurry ear, Fred Organ, before you knows where you are.'

Sylvia could not refrain from observing the famous lump with a good deal of curiosity, and she wondered how anybody could ever have supposed it might not be noticed, for she should have described it as more like a beetroot than a potato.

A long discussion about the future of the driverless cab ensued; and finally it was decided that Joe the tout should lead it to the police station if it were not claimed by daylight, after which the company turned to the discussion of the future of the abandoned fares. Sylvia had by this time evolved an elaborate tale of running away from a stepfather whose conduct to Arthur, herself and Maria had been extremely brutal.

'Knocked the cat about, did he?' exclaimed the theorist, whose name was Fred Organ. 'I never could abide people as ill-treated dumb animals.'

Sylvia went on to explain that they had intended to throw themselves on the mercy of an aunt who lived at Dover and with that intention had been bound for Waterloo, when they lost their driver. On being told that they were going to the wrong station for Dover, she began to express fears of the reception her aunt might accord them. Did anyone present know where they could find lodgings, for which of course they would pay, because their mother had provided them with the necessary money?

'That's a mother all over,' said Fred Organ with enthusiastic sentiment. 'Ain't it, boys? Ah, I wish I hadn't lost my poor old mother.'

Various suggestions about rooms were made, but finally Fred Organ was so much moved by the emotional details with which Sylvia continually supplemented her tale that he offered to give them lodgings in his own house near Finsbury Park. Sylvia would have preferred a suburb that was barred to Monkley, but she accepted the offer, because with Arthur turning out so inept at adventure it seemed foolish to take any more risks that night.

Fred Organ had succeeded to the paternal house and hansom about two years before. He was now twenty-six, but his corpulence made him appear older; for the chubby smoothness of youth had vanished with continual exposure to the weather, leaving behind many folds and furrows in his large face. Mr. Organ senior had bought Number Fifty-three Colonial Terrace by instalments, the punctual payment of which had worried him so much as probably to shorten his life, the last one having been paid just before his death. He had only a week or two for the enjoyment of possession, which was as well; for the house that had cost its owner so much effort to obtain was nearly as ripe for dissolution as himself, and the maintenance of it in repair seemed likely to cause Fred Organ as much financial stress in the future as the original purchase had caused his father in the past.

So much of his history did Fred Organ give them while he was stabling his horse, before he could introduce them to his inheritance. It was five o'clock of a chill February morning, and the relief of finding herself safely under a roof after such a tiring and insecure night compensated Sylvia for the impression of unutterable dreariness that Colonial Terrace first made upon her mind, a dreariness quite out of accord with the romantic beginning to the life of independence of which she had dreamed. They could not go to bed when they reached the house, because Fred Organ, master though he was, doubted if it would be wise to wake up his sister to accommodate the guests.

'Not that she'd have any call to make a fuss,' he observed. 'Because if I says a thing in Number Fifty-three, no one hasn't got the right to object. Still I'd rather you got a nice first impression of my sister Edith. Well, make yourselves at home. I'll rout round and get the kitchen fire going.'

Fred routed round with such effect that he woke his sister, who began to scream from the landing above:

'Hube! get up, you great coward! There's somebody breaking in at the back. Get up, Hube, and fetch a policeman before we're both murdered.'

'It's only me, Ede,' Fred called out. 'Keep your hair on.'

When Sylvia saw Edith Organ's curl-papers, she thought the last injunction was rather funny. Explanations were soon given and Edith was so happy to find her alarm unnecessary that she was as pleasant as possible and even invited Sylvia to come and share her bed and sleep late into the morning; whereupon Fred Organ invited Arthur to share his bed, which Arthur firmly declined to do notwithstanding Sylvia's frown.

'Well, you can't go to bed with the girls,' said Fred.

'Oh, Fred, you are a . . . oh, he is a . . . oh, isn't he? Oh, I never. Fancy! what a thing to say. There! Well! Who ever did? I'm sure. What a remark to pass,' Edith exclaimed quite incoherent from embarrassment, pleasure, and sleep.

'Where's Hube?' Fred asked.

'Oh, Hube!' snapped Edith. 'He's well underneath the bedclothes. Trust Hube for that. Nothing'd get him out of bed except an earthquake.'

'Wouldn't it then?' said a sleek voice, and Hube himself, an extremely fat young man in a trailing nightgown, appeared in the doorway.

'You wouldn't think he was only nineteen, would you?' said Fred proudly.

'Nice noise to kick up in the middle of the night,' Hubert grumbled. 'I dreamt the house was falling down on top of me.'

'And it will too,' Fred prophesied, 'if I can't soon scrape together some money for repairs. There's a crack as wide as the Strand down the back.'

Sylvia wondered how so rickety a house was able to withstand the wear and tear of such a fat family, when they all with the exception of Arthur, who lay down on the kitchen table, went creaking upstairs to bed.

The examination of Monkley's cash-box produced £35; Sylvia felt ineffably rich, so rich that she offered to lend Fred Organ the money he wanted to repair his property. He accepted the offer in the spirit in which it was made, as he said, and Sylvia, whom contact with Monkley had left curiously uncynical, felt that she had endeared herself to Fred Organ for a long time to come. She was given a room of her own at Number

Fifty-three, for which she was glad, because sleeping with Edith had been rather like eating scented cornflour-pudding, a combination of the flabby with the stuffy that had never appealed to her taste. Arthur was given the choice of sleeping with Hubert or in the bath, and he chose the bath without a moment's hesitation.

Relations between Arthur and Hubert had been strained ever since Hubert had offered Arthur a bite from an apple he was munching, which had been refused with a too obvious disgust.

'Go on, what do you take me for? Eve?' Hubert had asked indignantly. 'It won't poison you.'

The strain was not relaxed by Hubert's obvious fondness for Sylvia.

'I thought when I came away with you,' Arthur grumbled, 'that we were going to live by ourselves and earn our own living; instead of which you let that fat brute hang around you all day.'

'I can't be always rude to him,' Sylvia explained. 'He's very good-natured.'

'Do you call it good natured to turn the tap on me when I'm lying in bed?' Arthur demanded.

'I expect he only did it for fun.'

'Fun!' said Arthur darkly. 'I shall hit him one of these days.'

Arthur did hit him: but Hubert with all his fat hit harder than Arthur, and he never tried it again. Sylvia found herself growing very tired of Arthur; the universal censure upon his namby-pambiness was beginning to react upon her, and the poetical youth of Hampstead Heath seemed no longer so poetical in Colonial Terrace. Yet she did not want to quarrel with him finally, for in a curious way he represented to her a link with what she still paradoxically spoke of as home. Sylvia had really had a great affection for Monkley, which made her hate him all the more for what he had tried to do; but though she hated him and though the notion of being with him again made her shudder, she could not forget that he had known her father, and was thus bound up with the memory of her mother and of all the past that being so irreparably over was now strangely cherished. Sylvia felt that, were Arthur to go, she should indeed find herself alone, in that state which first she had dreaded, then desired, and now once again dreaded, notwithstanding her bold conceptions of independence and belief in her own ability to determine the manner of life she wished. There were times when she felt what almost amounted to a passionate hatred of Colonial Terrace, which had brought her freedom indeed, but the freedom of a world too grey to make freedom worth possessing. She was fond of Fred Organ, and she fancied that he would have liked formally to adopt her; yet the idea of being adopted by him somehow repelled her. She was fond of Edith Organ too, but no fonder than she had been of Clara; Edith seemed to have less to tell her about life than Clara, perhaps because she herself was older now and had read so many books. As for Hubert, who claimed to be in love with her, he existed about the house like a large overfed dog: that was all, that and his capacity for teasing Arthur, which amused her.

Everything about this escapade was so different from what she had planned. Always in her dreams there had been a room with a green view over trees or a silver view over water, and herself encouraging someone (she supposed it must have been Arthur, though she could hardly believe this when she looked at him now) to perform the kind of fantastic deeds that people performed in books; for surely some books were true. Looking back on her old fancies, Sylvia came to the conclusion that she had always pictured herself married to Arthur: yet how ridiculous such an idea now seemed. He had always talked with regret of the adventures that were no longer possible in dull modern days; but when the very small adventure of being in a runaway cab had happened, how miserably Arthur had failed to rise to the occasion, and now here he was loafing in Colonial Terrace. Hubert had secured a position in a bookshop near Finsbury Park railway station, which he had forfeited very soon afterwards, but only because he had made a habit of borrowing for Sylvia's perusal the books that customers had bought and of sending them on to their owners two or three days later. To be sure, they had nearly all been very dull books of a religious bent, but in such a district as Finsbury Park what else could be expected? At least Hubert had sacrificed something for her; whereas Arthur had done nothing; for even when Fred Organ to please Sylvia had offered to teach him to drive a hansom, he had refused to learn.

One day, Edith Organ announced that there was to be a supper party at a public-house in Harringay where one of the barmaids was a friend of hers. It seemed that Mrs. Hartle, the proprietress, had recently had cause to rejoice over a victory, but whether it was domestic, political, or professional Edith was unable to remember; at any rate, a jolly evening could be counted upon.

'You must wear that new white dress, Syl; it suits you a treat,' Edith advised. 'I was told only to bring one gentleman, and I think it's Artie's turn.'

'Why?' Hubert demanded fiercely.

'Oh, Hube, you know you don't like parties. You always want to go home early, and I'm out to enjoy myself and I don't care who knows it.'

Sylvia suspected that Edith's real reason for wishing Arthur to be the guest was his greater presentableness, for she had often heard her praise Arthur's appearance while deprecating his namby-pamby manner; however, for a party like this, of which Edith was proclaiming the extreme selectness, that might be considered an advantage. Mrs. Hartle was reputed to be a woman to whom the least vulgarity was disgusting.

'She's highly particular, they tell me, not to say standoffish. You know: doesn't like to make herself cheap. Well, I don't blame her. She's thought a lot of round here. She had some trouble with her husband – her second husband that is – and everybody speaks very highly of the dignified way in which she made him sling his hook out of it.'

'I don't think so much of her,' Hubert grunted. 'I went into the saloon-bar once, and she said, "Here, my man, the public bar is the hother side." "Oh! his it," I said. "Well, I can't get round the corner for the crowd," I said, "listening to your old man singing *At Trinity Church I met my doom* on the pavement outside." She didn't half colour up, I can tell you. So he was singing too, fit to give anyone the ear ache to listen to him. I don't want to go to her supper party.'

'Well, if you're not going, you needn't be so nasty about it, Hube. I'd take you if I could.'

'I wouldn't come,' Hubert declared. 'Not if Mrs. Hartle was to go down on her knees and ask me to come. So shut your mouth.'

The chief event of the party for Sylvia was the meeting with Danny Lewis, who paid her a good deal of attention at supper and danced with her all the time afterwards. Sylvia was grateful to him for his patience with her bad dancing at first, and she learnt so quickly under his direction that when it was time to go she really danced rather well. Sylvia's new friend saw them back to Colonial Terrace and invited himself to tea the following afternoon. Edith, who could never bear the suggestion of impoliteness, assured him that he would be most welcome, though she confided in Sylvia as they went up to bed that she could not feel quite sure about him. Sylvia insisted he was everything he should be and praised his manners so highly that Edith humbly promised to believe in his perfection. Arthur went upstairs and slammed his door without saying good night.

The next morning, a morning of east wind, Arthur attacked Sylvia on the subject of her behaviour the night before.

'Look here,' he opened very grandly. 'If you prefer to spend the evenings waltzing with dirty little Jews, I won't stand it.'

Sylvia regarded him disdainfully.

'Do you hear?' repeated Arthur. 'I won't stand it. It's bad enough with that great hulking lout here, but when it comes to a greasy Jew I've had enough.'

'So have I,' Sylvia said. 'You'd better go back to Hampstead.'

'I'm going to-day,' Arthur declared, and waited pathetically for Sylvia to protest; she was silent. Then he tried to be affectionate, and vowed he had not meant a word he said, but she brushed away his tentative caress and meek apology.

'I don't want to talk to you any more,' she said. 'There are lots of things I could tell you; but you'll always be unhappy anyway, because you're soft and silly, so I won't. You'll be at home for dinner,' she added.

When Arthur was ready to start, he looked so forlorn that Sylvia was sorry for him.

'Here, take Maria,' she offered impulsively. 'He'll remind you of me.'

'I don't want anything to remind me of you,' said Arthur in a hollow voice. 'But I'll take Maria.'

That afternoon Danny Lewis, wearing a bright orange tie and a flashing ring, came to visit Sylvia. She had already told him a good deal about herself the night before, and when now she told him how she had dismissed Arthur, he suggested that Monkley would probably find out where she was and come to take her back. Sylvia turned pale: the possibility of Arthur's betrayal of her address had never struck her. She cried in a panic that she must leave Finsbury Park at once; and Danny promised to find her a room.

'I've got no money. I spent all I had left on new frocks,' she bewailed.

'That's all right, kid, bring the frocks along with you. I've got plenty of money.'

Sylvia packed in a frenzy of haste, expecting every moment to hear the bell ring and see Monkley waiting grimly outside: his cold eyes, as her imagination recalled them, made her shiver with fear. When they got downstairs Hubert, who was in the passage, asked where she was going, and she told him that she was going away.

'Not with that—' Hubert swore, barring the way to the front door.

Danny did not hesitate: his arm shot out, and Hubert went over, bringing down the hatstand with a crash.

'Quick, quick,' cried Sylvia in exultation at being with someone who could act. 'Edie's gone round to the baker's to fetch some crumpets for tea. Let's go before she gets back.'

They hurried out. The wind had fallen: Colonial Terrace looked very grey, very quiet, very long in the bitter March air. Danny Lewis with his orange tie promised a richer, warmer life beyond these ridiculous little houses that imitated each other.

V

Danny Lewis took Sylvia to an eating house in Euston Road kept by a married couple called Gonner. Here everything – the meat, the pies, the butter, the streaky slabs of marble, the fly-blown face of the weary clock, the sawdust sprinkled on the floor, the cane-seated chairs – combined to create an effect of greasy pallor that extended even to Mr. and Mrs. Gonner themselves, who seemed to have acquired the nature of their environment. Sylvia shrank from their whitish arms bare to the elbow and glistening with fats, and from their faces, which seemed to her like bladders of lard, especially Mrs. Gonner's, who wore on the top of her head a knob of dank etiolated hair. In such an atmosphere Danny Lewis with his brilliant tie and green beaver hat acquired a fullness of personality that quite overpowered Sylvia's judgment and preserved the condition of abnormal excitement set up by the rapidity and completeness with which this time she had abandoned herself to independence.

There was a brief conversation between Danny and the Gonners, after which Mr. Gonner returned to his task of cutting some very fat bacon into rashers and Mrs. Gonner held up the flap of the counter for Sylvia and Danny to pass upstairs through the back of the shop. For one moment Sylvia hesitated when the flap dropped back into its place, for it seemed to make dangerously irrevocable her admittance to the unknown house above; Danny saw her hesitation and with a word or two of encouragement checked her impulse to go no farther. Mrs. Gonner led the way upstairs and showed them into a bedroom prematurely darkened by coarse lace curtains that shut out the fading daylight. Sylvia had a vague impression of too much furniture, which was confirmed when Mrs. Gonner lit a gas-jet over the mantelpiece; she looked round distastefully at the double-bed pushed against the wall, at the crimson vases painted with butterflies, at the faded oleograph of two children on the edge of a precipice with a guardian angel behind them, whose face had at some time been eaten away by mice. There was a short silence, only broken by Mrs. Gonner's whispering breath.

'We shall be all right here, kid, eh?' exclaimed Danny in a tone that was at once suave and boisterous.

'What's your room like?' Sylvia asked.

He looked at her a moment, seemed about to speak, thought better of it, and turned to Mrs. Gonner, who told Danny that he could have the front room as well if he wanted it; they moved along the passage to inspect this room, which was much larger and better lighted than the other and was pleasantly filled with the noise of traffic; Sylvia immediately declared that she preferred to be here.

'So I'm to have the rabbit-hutch,' said Danny laughing easily. 'Trust a woman to have her own way! That's right, isn't it, Mrs. Gonner?'

Mrs. Gonner stared at Sylvia a moment, and murmured that she had long ago forgotten what she wanted, but that, anyway, for her one thing was the same as another, which Sylvia was very ready to believe.

When Mrs. Gonner had left the room, Danny told Sylvia that he must go and get a few things together from his flat in Shaftesbury Avenue, and asked her if she would wait till he came back.

'Of course I'll wait,' she told him. 'Do you think I want to run away twice in one day?'

Danny still hesitated, and she wondered why he should expect her, who was so much used to being left alone, to mind waiting for him an hour or two.

'We might go to the Mo to-night,' he suggested.

She looked blank.

'The Middlesex,' he explained. 'It's a music-hall. Be a good girl while I'm out. I'll bring you back some chocolates.'

He seemed anxious to retain her with the hint of pleasures that were in his power to confer: it made Sylvia impatient that he should rely on them rather than upon her capacity for knowing her own mind.

'I may be young,' she said, 'but I do know what I want. I'm not like that woman downstairs.'

'And you know how to make other people want, eh?' Danny muttered. He took a step forward, and Sylvia hoped he was not going to try to kiss her; she felt disinclined at this moment for a long explanation; but he went off, whistling.

For a long time Sylvia stood by the window, looking down at the traffic and the lights coming out one by one in the windows opposite. She hoped that Danny would not end like Monkley, and she determined to be prompt in checking the first signs of his doing so. Standing here in this room that was now dark except for the faint transitory shadows upon the walls and ceiling of lighted vehicles below, Sylvia's thoughts went back to the time she had spent with Blanche. It seemed to her that then she had been wiser than she was now, in spite of all the books she had read since; or was it that she was growing up and becoming an actress in scenes that formerly she had regarded with the secure aloofness of a child?

'I'm not innocent,' she said to herself. 'I know everything that can be known. But when Monkley tried to do that, I was horrified. I felt sick and frightened and angry, oh, dreadfully angry. Yet when Blanche behaved as she did I did not mind at all; I used to encourage her. Oh, why aren't I a boy? If I were a boy, I would show people that making love isn't really a bit necessary. Yet sometimes I liked Arthur to make love to me. I can't make myself out. I think I must be what people call an exceptional person. I hope Danny won't make love to me. But I feel he will; and if he does, I shall kill myself; I can't go on living like this with everybody making love to me. I'm not like Blanche or Mabel: I don't care for it. How I used to hate Mabel! Shall I ever get like her? Oh, I wish, I wish, I wish I were a boy. I don't believe Danny will be any better than Jimmy was. Yet he doesn't frighten me so much. He doesn't seem so much there as Jimmy was. But if he does make love to me, it will be more dangerous. How shall I ever escape from here? I'm sure Mrs. Gonner will never lift the flap.'

Sylvia began to be obsessed by that flap; and the notion of it wrought upon her fancy to such an extent that she was impelled to go downstairs and see if the way out was open or shut, excusing her abrupt appearance by asking for a box of matches. There were two or three people eating at the white tables, who eyed her curiously; she wondered what they would have done if she had suddenly begged their help. Being vexed with herself for giving way to her nerves like this, she went upstairs again with a grand resolve to be very brave; and she even challenged her terrors by going into that bedroom behind and contending with its oppressiveness. So successful was she in calming her overwrought nerves that, when Danny suddenly came back and found her in his bedroom, she was no longer afraid; she looked at him there in the doorway wearing now a large tie of pale blue silk, as she would have looked at any brigand in an opera. When he presented her with a large box of chocolates she laughed, and when he wondered why, she said it was she who ought to give *him* chocolates, which left him blank. She tried to explain her impression of him as a brigand, and he asked her if she meant that he looked like an actor.

'Yes, that's what I mean,' she agreed impatiently, though she meant nothing of the kind. Danny seemed gratified as by a compliment and admitted that he was often mistaken for an actor: he supposed it was his hair.

They dined at a restaurant in Soho, where Sylvia was conscious of arousing a good deal of attention; afterwards they went to the Middlesex music-hall, but she felt very tired, and did not enjoy it as much as she expected. Moreover, Danny irritated her by sucking his teeth with an air of importance all through the evening.

For a fortnight Danny treated Sylvia with what was almost a

94

luxurious consideration. She was never really taken in by it, but she submitted so willingly to being spoiled that, as she told herself, she could hardly blame Danny for thinking he was fast making himself indispensable to her happiness. He was very anxious for her to lead a lazy existence, encouraged her to lie in bed the whole morning, fed her with chocolates, and tried to cultivate in her a habit of supposing that it was impossible to go anywhere without driving in a hansom; he also used to buy her brightly coloured blouses and scarves, which she used to wear out of politeness, for they gave her very little pleasure. He flattered her consistently, praising her cleverness and comparing her sense of humour with that of other women always to their disadvantage. He told stories very well, particularly those against his own race; and though Sylvia was a little scornful of this truckling self-mockery, she could not help laughing at the stories. She understood by the contempt with which Danny referred to women that his victories had usually been gained very easily, and she was much on her guard. Encouraged, however, by the way in which Sylvia seemed to enjoy the superficial pleasures he provided for her, he soon attempted to bestow his favours as he bestowed his chocolates. Sylvia, who never feared Danny personally as she had feared Monkley, repulsed him, yet not so firmly as she would have done, had not her first impression of the house still affected her imagination. Danny, who divined her malaise but mistook it for the terror he was used to inspiring, began to play the bully.

It was twilight, one of those sapphire twilights of early spring: the gas had not been lighted, and the fire had died away to a glow. Sylvia had thrown off his caressing arm three times, when Danny suddenly jumped up, pulled out a clasp knife and, standing over her, threatened her with death, if she would not immediately consent to be his. Sylvia's heart beat a little faster at such a threat delivered with all the additional force that vile language could give to it, but she saw two things quite clearly: first that, if Danny were really to kill her, death would be far preferable to surrender; secondly that the surest way of avoiding either would be to assume he would turn out a coward in the face of the unexpected. She rose from the arm-chair; Danny rushed to the door, flourishing his knife and forbidding her to think of escape.

'Who wants to escape?' she asked in so cool a tone that Danny, who had naturally anticipated a more feminine reception of his violence, failed to sustain his part by letting her see that he was puzzled. She strolled across the room to the washstand: then she strolled up to the brigand.

'Put that knife away,' she said. 'I want to tell you something, darling Danny.'

In the gloom she could see that he threw a suspicious glance at her for the endearing epithet, but he put away the knife.

'What did you want to say?' he growled.

'Only this.' She brought her arm swiftly round and emptied the water-bottle over him. 'Though I ought to smash it on your greasy head. I read in a book once that the Jews were a subject race. You'd better light the gas.'

He spluttered that he was all wet, and she turned away from him, horribly scared that in a moment his fingers would be tightening around her neck; but he had taken off his coat and was shaking it.

Sylvia poked the fire and sat down again in the arm-chair.

'Listen,' she began.

He came across the room in his shirt-sleeves, his tie hanging in a cascade of amber silk over his waistcoat.

'No, don't pull down the blinds,' she added. 'I want to be quite sure you really have cooled down and aren't going to play with that knife again. Listen. It's no good your trying to make love to me. I don't want to be made love to by anybody, least of all by you.'

Danny looked more cheerful when she assured him of her indifference to other men.

'It's no use your killing me, because you'll only be hanged. It's no use your stabbing me, because you'll go to prison. If you hit me, I shall hit you back. You thought I was afraid of you. I wasn't. I'm more afraid of a bug than I am of you. I saw a bug today; so I'm going to leave this house. The weather's getting warmer. You and the bugs have come out together. Come along, Danny, dry your coat and tell me a story that will make me laugh. Tell me the story of the Jew who died of grief because he bought his wife a new hat and found his best friend had bought her one that day and he might have saved his money. Do make me laugh, Danny.'

They went to the Middlesex music-hall that evening, and Danny did not suck his teeth once. The next morning he told Sylvia that he had been to visit a friend who wished very much to meet her, and that he proposed to introduce him that afternoon, if she agreed. He was a fellow in a good way of business, the son of a bootmaker in Drury Lane, quite a superior sort of fellow and one by whom she could not fail to be impressed: his name was Jay Cohen. The friend arrived towards four o'clock, and Danny on some excuse left him with Sylvia. He had big teeth and round prominent eyes: his boots were very glossy and sharply pointed at the toes with uppers of what looked like leopard-skin. Observing Sylvia's glances directed to his boots, he asked with a smile if she admired the latest thing. She confessed they were rather too late for her taste, and Mr.

Cohen excused them as a pair sent back to his father by a well-known music-hall comedian, who complained of their pinching him. Sylvia said it was lucky they only pinched him; she should not have been astonished if they had bitten him.

'You are a Miss Smartie, aren't you?' said Jay Cohen.

The conversation languished for a while, but presently he asked Sylvia why she was so unkind to his friend Danny.

'What do you mean, "unkind"?' she repeated. 'Unkind what about?'

Mr. Cohen smiled in a deprecating way.

'He's a good boy, is Danny. Really good. He is really. All the girls are mad about Danny. You know, smart girls, girls that get around. He's very free too. Money's nothing to Danny when he's out to spend. His father's got a tobacconist's shop in the Caledonian Road. A good business – a very good business. Danny told me what the turnover was once, and I was surprised. I remember I thought what a rare good business it was. Well, Danny's feeling a bit upset to-day, and he came round to see me early this morning. He must have been very upset, because it was very early, and he said to me that he was mad over a girl and would I speak for him? He reckoned he'd made a big mistake and he wanted to put it right, but he was afraid of being laughed at, because the young lady in question was a bit high-handed. He wants to marry you. There it is right out. He'd like to marry you at once, but he's afraid of his father, and he thought . . .'

Mr. Cohen broke off suddenly in his proposal and listened:

'What's that?'

'It sounds like someone shouting downstairs,' Sylvia said. 'But you often hear rows going on down there. There was a row yesterday because a woman bit on a stone in a pie and broke her tooth.'

'That's Jubie's voice,' said Mr. Cohen, blinking his eyes and running his hands nervously through his sleek hair.

'Who's Jubie?'

Before he could explain, there was a sound of impassioned footsteps on the stairs: in a moment the door was flung open, and a handsome young Jewess with flashing eyes and earrings slammed it behind her.

'Where's Danny?' she demanded.

'Is that you, Jubie?' said Mr. Cohen. 'Danny's gone over to see his dad. He won't be here to-day.'

'You liar, he's here this moment. I followed him into the shop, and he ran upstairs. So you're the kid he's been trailing around with him,' she said, eyeing Sylvia. 'The dirty rotter!'

Sylvia resented the notion of being trailed by such an one as Danny

97

Lewis, but feeling undecided how to appease this tropical creature she took the insult without reply.

'He thinks to put it across Jubie Myers! Wait till my brother Sam knows where he is.'

Mr. Cohen had retired to the window and was studying the traffic of Euston Road; one of his large ears was twitching nervously toward the threats of the outraged Miss Myers, who, after much breathless abuse of Sylvia, at last retired to fetch her brother Sam. When she was gone, Mr. Cohen said he thought he should go too, because he did not feel inclined to meet Sam Myers, who was a pugilist with many victories to his credit at Wonderland; just as he reached the door, Danny entered and with a snarl accused him of trying to round on him.

'You know you fetched Jubie here on purpose, so as you could do me in with the kid,' said Danny. 'I know you, Jay Cohen.'

They wrangled for some time over this, until suddenly Danny landed his friend a blow between the eyes. Sylvia, recognizing the Danny who had so neatly knocked out Hubert Organ in Colonial Terrace, became pleasantly enthusiastic on his behalf, and cried 'Bravo.'

The encouragement put a fine spirit into Danny's blows; he hammered the unfortunate Cohen round and round the room, upsetting tables and chairs and washstand until with a stinging blow he knocked him backwards into the slop-pail, in which he sat so heavily that when he tried to rise the slop-pail stuck and gave him the appearance of a large baboon crawling with elevated rump on all fours. Danny kicked off the slop-pail, and invited Cohen to stand up to him; but when he did get on his feet, he ran to the door and reached the stairs just as Mrs. Gonner was wearily ascending to find out what was happening. He tried to stop himself by clutching the knob of the baluster, which broke; the result was that he dragged Mrs. Gonner with him in a glissade which ended behind the counter. The confusion in the shop became general: Mr. Gonner cut his thumb, and the sight of the blood caused a woman who was eating a sausage to choke; another customer took advantage of the row to snatch a side of bacon and try to escape, but another customer with a finer moral sense prevented him; a dog, who was sniffing in the entrance, saw the bacon on the floor and tried to seize it, but getting his tail trodden upon by somebody he took fright and bit a small boy, who was waiting to change a shilling into coppers. Meanwhile Sylvia, who expected every moment that Jubie and her pugilistic brother would come back and increase the confusion with possibly unpleasant consequences for herself, took advantage of Danny's being occupied in an argument with Cohen and the two Gonners to put on her hat and coat and escape from the shop. She jumped on the first omnibus and congratulated herself when she looked round and saw a policeman entering the eating-house.

Presently the conductor came up for her fare: she found she had fivepence in the world. She asked him where the omnibus went, and was told to the Cedars Hotel, West Kensington.

'Past Lillie Road?'

He nodded, and she paid away her last penny. After all, even if Monkley and her father did owe Mrs. Meares a good deal of money, Sylvia did not believe she would have her arrested. She would surely be too much interested to find that she was a girl and not a boy. Sylvia laughed when she thought of Jay Cohen in the slop-pail, for she remembered the baboon in Lillie Road, and she wondered if Clara was still there. What a lot she should have to tell Mrs. Meares, and if the Baron had not left, she should ask him why he had attacked her in that extraordinary way when she went to the party in Redcliffe Gardens: that was more than two years ago now. Sylvia wished she had gone to Lillie Road with Arthur Madden when she had some money and could have paid Mrs. Meares what was owing to her. Now she had not a penny in the world: she had not even any clothes. The omnibus jogged on, and Sylvia's thoughts jogged with it.

'I wonder if I shall always have adventures,' she said to herself. 'But I wish I could sometimes have adventures that have nothing to do with love. It's such a nuisance to be always running away for the same reason. It's such a stupid reason. But it's rather jolly to run away. It's more fun than being like that girl in front.' She contemplated a girl of about her own age, to whom an elderly woman was pointing out the St. James's Hall with a kind of suppressed excitement, a fever of unsatisfied pleasure.

'You've never been to the Moore and Burgess minstrels, have you, dear?' she was saying. 'We *must* get your father to take us some afternoon. Look at the people coming out.'

The girl looked dutifully, but Sylvia thought it was more amusing to look at the people struggling to mount omnibuses already full. She wondered what that girl would have done with somebody like Danny Lewis, and she felt sorry for the prim and dutiful young creature, who could never see Jay Cohen sitting in a slop-pail. Sylvia burst into a loud laugh, and a stout woman who was occupying three-quarters of her seat edged away from her a little.

'We shall be late for tea,' said the elderly woman in an ecstasy of dissipation, when she saw the clock at Hyde Park Corner. 'We shan't be home till after six. We ought to have had tea at King's Cross.'

The elderly woman was still talking about tea, when they stopped at

Sloane Street, and Sylvia's counterpart was still returning polite answers to her speculation; when they got down at South Kensington Station, the last thing Sylvia heard was a suggestion that perhaps it might be possible to arrange for dinner to be a quarter of an hour earlier.

It was dark when Sylvia reached the house in Lillie Road, and she hoped very much that Clara would open the door; but another servant came, and when she asked for Mrs. Meares, a sudden alarm caught her that Mrs. Meares might no longer be here and that she should be left alone in the night without a penny in the world. But Mrs. Meares was in.

'Have you come about the place?' whispered the new servant. 'Because if you have you'll take my advice and have nothing to do with it.'

Sylvia asked why.

'Why, it's nothing but a common lodging-house in my opinion. The woman who keeps it, lady *she* calls herself, tries to kid you as they're all paying guests: and the cats! You may like cats. I don't. Besides I've been used to company, where I've been in service: and the only company you get here is beetles. If anyone goes down into the kitchen at night, it's like walking on nutshells, they're so thick.'

'I haven't come about the place,' Sylvia explained. 'I want to see Mrs. Meares herself.'

'Oh, a friend of hers. I'm sorry I'm shaw,' said the servant, 'but I haven't said nothing but what is gospel truth, and I told her the same. You'd better come up to the droring-room – well, droring-room! You'll have to excuse the laundry which is all over the chairs because we had the sweep in this morning. A nice hullabaloo there was yesterday! Fire-engines and all. Mrs. Meares was very upset. She's in her bedroom, I expect.'

The servant lit the gas in the drawing-room and, leaving Sylvia among the outspread linen, went upstairs to fetch Mrs. Meares, who shortly afterwards descended in a condition of dignified bewilderment and entered the room with one arm arched like a note of interrogation in cautious welcome.

'Miss Scarlett? The name is familiar, but—?'

Sylvia poured out her story, and at the end of it Mrs. Meares dreamily smoothed her brow.

'I don't quite understand. Were you a girl dressed as a boy then, or are you a boy dressed as a girl now?'

Sylvia explained, and while she was giving the explanation she became aware of a profound change in Mrs. Meares' attitude towards her, an alteration of standpoint much more radical than could have been caused by any resentment at the behaviour of Monkley and her father.

Suddenly Sylvia regarded Mrs. Meares with the eyes of Clara, or of that new servant who had whispered to her in the hall: she was no longer the bland and futile Irish-woman of regal blood, the good-natured and feckless creature with open placket and draperies trailing in the dust of her ill-swept house, the soft-voiced, soft-hearted Hibernian with a gentle smile for man's failings and foibles, and a tear ever welling from that moist grey eye in memory of her husband's defection and the death of her infant son. Sylvia felt that now she was being sized up by someone who would never be indulgent again, who would exact from her the uttermost her girlhood could give, who would never forget the advantage she had gained in learning how desperate was the state of Sylvia Scarlett, and who would profit by it accordingly.

'It seems so peculiar to resort to me,' Mrs. Meares was saying, 'after the way your father treated me, but I'm not the woman to bear a grudge. Thank God, I can meet the blows of fortune with nobility and forgive an injury with anyone in the world. It's lucky indeed that I can show my true character and offer you assistance. The servant is leaving to-morrow, and though I will not take advantage of your position to ask you to do anything in the nature of menial labour, though to be sure it's myself knows too well the word – to put it shortly, I can offer you board and lodging in return for any little help you may give me until I will get a new servant. And it's not easy to get servants these days. Such grand ideas have they.'

Sylvia felt that she ought to accept this offer; she was destitute and she wished to avoid charity, having grasped that, though it was a great thing to make oneself indispensable, it was equally important not to put oneself under an obligation; finally it would be a satisfaction to pay back what her father owed. Not that she fancied his ghost would be disturbed by the recollection of any earthly debts: it would be purely a personal satisfaction, and she told Mrs. Meares that she was willing to help under the proposed arrangement.

Somewhere about nine o'clock Sylvia sat down with Mrs. Meares in the breakfast-room to supper, which was served by Amelia as if she had been unwillingly dragged into a game of cards and was showing her displeasure in the way she dealt the hand. The incandescent gas jigged up and down, and Mrs. Meares' sleeve swept her plate every time she languorously flung morsels to the numerous cats, some of which they did not like and left to be trodden into the threadbare carpet by Amelia. Sylvia made enquiries about Mr. Morgan and the Baron, but they had both left; the guests at present were a young actor who hoped to walk on in the new production at the St. James's, a Non-conformist minister who had been persecuted by his congregation into resigning, and an elderly clerk threatened with locomotor ataxia who had a theory contrary to the advice of his doctor that it was beneficial to walk to the City every morning. His symptoms were described with many details, but owing to Mrs. Meares' diving under the table to show the cats where a morsel of meat had escaped their notice, it was difficult to distinguish between the symptoms of the disease, the topography of the meat, and the names of the cats.

Next day Sylvia watched Amelia put on the plumage of departure and leave with her yellow tin trunk; then she set to work to help Mrs. Meares make the beds of Mr. Leslie Warburton the actor, Mr. Croasdale the minister, and Mr. Witherwick the clerk: her companion's share was entirely verbal and she disliked the task immensely. When the beds were finished, she made an attempt with Mrs. Meares to put away the clean linen, but Mrs. Meares went off in the middle to find the words of a poem she could not remember, leaving towels to mark her wake, as boys in paper-chases strew paper on Hampstead Heath. She did not find the words of the poem, or if she did, she had forgotten them when Sylvia discovered her; but she had decided instead to alter the arrangement of the drawing-room curtains; so that to the unsorted unburied linen were added long strips of faded green silk which hung about the house for some days. Mrs. Meares asked Sylvia if she would like to try her hand at an omelette; the result was a failure, whether on account of the butter or the eggs was not quite certain; indeed the cat to which it was given was sick.

The three lodgers made no impression on Sylvia; each of them in turn tried to kiss her when she first went into his room; each of them after-wards complained bitterly of the way the eggs were poached at breakfast and asked Mrs. Meares why she had got rid of Amelia. Gradually Sylvia found that she was working as hard as Clara used to work, that slowly and gently she was being smothered by Mrs. Meares, and that the process was regarded by Mrs. Meares as an act of holy charity, upon which she frequently congratulated herself.

Early one afternoon at the end of April, Sylvia went out shopping for Mrs. Meares, which was not such a simple matter, because a good deal of persuasiveness had to be employed with the tradesmen on account of unpaid books. As she passed the entrance to the Earl's Court Exhibition, she saw Mabel Bannerman coming out: though she had hated Mabel and had always blamed her for her father's death, past enmity fled away in the pleasure of seeing somebody who belonged to a life that a month of Mrs. Meares had wonderfully enchanted. She called after her; Mabel, only slightly more flaccid nowadays, welcomed her without hesitation.

'Why, if it isn't Sylvia. Well, I declare. You are a stranger.'

They talked for a while on the pavement, until Mabel, who disliked such publicity except in a love affair, and who was frankly eager for a full account of what had happened after she left Swanage, invited Sylvia to 'have one' at the familiar public-house to which her father in the old days used to invite Jimmy and where once he had been surprised by Sylvia's arrival with his friend.

Mabel was shocked to think that Henry had perhaps died on her account, but she assured Sylvia that for any wrong she had done him she had paid ten times over in the life she had led with the other man.

'Oh, he was a brute. Your dad was an angel beside him, dear. Oh, I was a stupid girl. But there, it's no good crying over spilt milk. What's done can't be undone, and I've paid. My voice is quite gone. I can't sing a note. What do you think I'm doing now? Working at the Exhibition. It opens next week, you know.'

'Acting?' Sylvia asked.

'Acting? No! I'm in Open Sesame, the Hall of a Thousand and One Marvels. Well, I suppose it is acting in a way, because I'm supposed to be a Turkish woman. You know, sequins and trousers and a what d'ye call it – round my face. You know, oh dear, whatever is it called? A hookah!'

'But a hookah's a pipe,' Sylvia objected. 'You mean a yashmak.'

'That's it. Well, I sell Turkish-delight, but some of the girls sell coffee, and for an extra threepence you can see the Sultan's harem. It ought to go well. There's a couple of real Turks and a black eunuch who gives me the creeps. The manager's very hopeful. Which reminds me. He's looking out for some more girls. Why don't you apply? It isn't like you, Sylvia, to be doing what's nothing better than a servant's job. I'm so afraid I shall get a varicose vein through standing about so much, and an elastic stocking makes one look so old. Oh dear, don't let's talk about age. Drink up and have another.'

Sylvia explained to Mabel about her lack of money and clothes, and it was curious to discover how pleasant and sympathetic Mabel was now – another instance of the degrading effect of love, for Sylvia could hardly believe that this was the hysterical creature who used to keep her awake in Fitzroy Street.

'I'd lend you the money,' said Mabel, 'but really, dear, until we open I haven't got very much. In fact,' she added, looking at the empty glasses, 'when I've paid for these two, I shall be quite stony. Still, I live quite close. Finborough Road. Why don't you come and stay with me? I'll take you round to the manager to-morrow morning. He's sure to engage you. Of course, the salary is small. I don't suppose he'll offer more than fifteen shillings. Still, there's tips, and anything would be better than slaving for that woman. I live at 320. I've got a nice room with a view over Brompton Cemetery. One might be in the country. It's beautifully quiet except for the cats, and you hardly notice the trains.'

Sylvia promised Mabel that she would think it over and let her know that evening.

'That's right, dear. The landlady's name is Gowndry.'

They parted with much cordiality and good wishes, and Sylvia went back to Lillie Road. Mrs. Meares was deeply injured when she was informed that her lady-help proposed to desert her.

'But surely you shall wait till I've got a servant,' she said. 'And what will poor Mr. Witherwick do? He's so fond of you, Sylvia. I'm sure your poor father would be much distressed to think of you at Earl's Court. Such temptations for a young girl. I look upon myself as your guardian, you know. I would feel a big responsibility if anything came to you.'

Sylvia, however, declined to stay.

'And I wanted to give you a little kitten. Mavourneen will be having kittens next month, and May cats are so lucky. When you told me about your black cat Maria, I said to myself that I would be giving you one. And dear Parnell is the father, and if it's not Parnell, it's my darling Brian Boru. You beauty! Was you the father of some sweet little kitties? Clever man!'

When Mrs. Meares turned away to congratulate Brian Boru upon his imminent if ambiguous paternity, Sylvia went upstairs to get her only possession – a coat with a fur-trimmed collar and cuffs, which she had worn alternately with underclothing for a month: this week the underclothing was luckily not at the wash. Sylvia shook off Mrs. Meares' last remonstrances and departed into the balmy April afternoon. The weather was so fine that she pawned her overcoat and bought a hat; then she pawned her fur cap, bought a pair of stockings – the pair in the wash belonged to Mrs. Meares – and went to Finborough Road.

Mrs. Gowndry asked if she was the young lady who was going to share Miss Bannerman's room; when Sylvia said she was, Mrs. Gowndry argued that the bed would not hold two and that she had not bargained for the sofa's being used for anything but sitting on.

'That sofa's never been slept on in its life,' she protested. 'And if I start in letting people sleep anywhere, I might as well turn my house into a public convenience and have done with it, but there, it's no good grumbling. Such is life. It's the back room. Second floor up. The last lodger burnt his name on the door with a poker, so you can't make no mistake.'

Mrs. Gowndry dived abruptly into the basement and left Sylvia to find her way up to Mabel's room above. Her hostess was in a kimono, oriental even away from the Hall of a Thousand and One Marvels; she had tied pink bows to every projection, and there was a strong smell of cheap scent. Sylvia welcomed the prettiness and sweetness after Lillie Road; her former dislike of Mabel's domestic habits no longer existed; and when she told her of the meeting with Mrs. Gowndry she was quite afraid that the plan of living here might not be allowed.

'Oh, she's always like that,' Mabel explained. 'She's a silly old crow, but she's very nice really. Her husband's a lavatory attendant, and being shut up all day underground he grumbles a lot when he comes home, and of course his wife has to suffer for it. Where's your luggage?'

'I told you I hadn't got any.'

'You really are a caution, Sylvia. Fancy! Never mind. I expect I'll be able to fit you out.'

'I shan't want much,' Sylvia said, 'with the warm weather coming.'

'But you'll have to change when you go to the Exhibition, and you don't want the other girls to stare.'

They spent the evening in cutting down some of Mabel's underclothes, and Sylvia wondered more than ever how she could have once found her so objectionable. In an access of affection she hugged Mabel and thanked her warmly for her kindness.

'Go on,' said Mabel. 'There's nothing to thank me for. You'd do the same for me.'

'But I used to be so beastly to you.'

'Oh, well, you were only a kid. You didn't understand about love. Besides, I was very nervous in those days. I expect there were faults on both sides. I spoke to the manager about you, and I'm sure it'll be all right.'

The following morning Sylvia accompanied Mabel to the Exhibition and, after being presented to Mr. Woolfe, the manager, she was engaged to sell cigarettes and serve coffee in the Hall of a Thousand and One Marvels from eleven in the morning till eleven at night on a salary of fourteen shillings a week, all extras to be shared with seven other young ladies similarly engaged.

'You'll be Ammathyst,' said Mr. Woolfe. 'You'd better go and try on your dress. The idea is that there are eight beautiful oddilisques dressed like precious stones. Pretty fancy, isn't it? Now don't grumble and say you'd rather be Dimond or Turquoys, because all the other jools are taken.'

Sylvia passed through an arched doorway hung with a heavy curtain into the dressing-room of the eight odalisques, which was lacking in Eastern splendour and very draughty. Seven girls, all older than herself, were wrestling with veils and brocades.

'He said we was to cover up our faces with this. Is it chiffong or tool, dear?'

'Oh, Daisy, you are silly to let him make you Rewby. Why don't you ask him to let you be Saffer? You don't mind, do you, kiddie? You're dark. You take Daisy's Rewby, and let her be Saffer.'

'Aren't we going to wear anything over these drawers? Oh girls, I will feel shy.'

Sylvia did not think that any of them would feel half as shy as she felt at the present moment in being plunged into the company of girls of whose thoughts and habits and sensations and manners she was utterly ignorant. She felt more at ease when she had put on her mauve dress and had veiled her face. When they were all ready, they paraded before Mr. Woolfe.

'Very good. Very good,' he said. 'Quite a lot of atmosphere. Here you, my dear, Emruld, put your yashmak up a bit higher. You look as if you'd got mumps like that. Now then, here's the henna to paint your finger-nails and the kohl for your eyes.'

'Coal for our eyes,' echoed all the girls. 'Why can't we use liquid black the same as we always do? Coal! What a liberty! Whatever next?'

'That shows you don't know anything about the East. K-O-H-L, not C-O-A-L, you silly girls. And don't you get hennering your hair. It's only to be used for the nails.'

When the Exhibition opened on the first of May, the Hall of a Thousand and One Marvels was the only side-show that was in full working order. The negro eunuch stood outside and somewhat inappropriately bellowed his invitation to the passing crowds to visit Sesame, where all the glamour of the East was to be had for sixpence, including a cup of delicious Turkish coffee specially made by the Sultan's own coffee-maker. Once inside, visitors could for a further sum of threepence view an exact reproduction of a Turkish harem, where real Turkish ladies in all the abandonment of languorous poses offered a spectacle of luxury that could only be surpassed by paying another threepence to see a faithless wife tied up in a sack and flung into the Bosphorus once every hour. Other threepennies secured admission to Aladdin's Cave, where the Genie of the Lamp told fortunes, or to the Cave of the Forty Thieves, where a lucky ticket entitled the owner to draw a souvenir from Ali Baba's sack of treasure and see Morgiana dance a voluptuous *pas seul* once every hour. Visitors to the Hall could also buy attar of roses, cigarettes, seraglio pastilles, and Turkish-delight. It was very oriental: even Mr. Woolfe wore a fez.

Either because Sylvia moved in a way that seemed to Mr. Woolfe more oriental than the others or because she got on very well with him personally, she was promoted to a small inner room more richly draped and lighted by a jewelled lamp hanging from the ceiling of gilded arabesques: here Mr. Woolfe as a mark of his esteem introduced regular customers who could appreciate the softer carpet and deeper divans. At one end was a lattice, beyond which might be seen two favourites of the harem who, slowly fanning themselves, reclined eternally amid perfumed airs, except during the intervals for dinner and tea, which lasted half an hour and exposed them to the unrest of European civilization. One of these favourites was Mabel, whom Mr. Woolfe had been heard to describe as his 'boo ideel' of a sultana, and whom he had taken from the sale of Turkish-delight to illustrate his conception. Mabel was paid a higher salary in consequence, because enclosed in the harem she was no longer able to profit by the male admirers who had bought Turkish-delight at her plump hands. The life was well suited to her natural laziness; though she dreaded getting fat, she was glad to be relieved of the menace from her varicose vein. Sylvia was the only odalisque that waited in this inner room; but her salary was not raised, since she now had the sole right to all the extras: she certainly preferred this darkened chamber to the other, and when there were no intruders from the world outside she could gossip through the lattice with the two favourites.

Mrs. Gowndry had let Sylvia a small room at the very top of the house; notwithstanding Mabel's good nature she might have grown tired of being always at close quarters with her. Sylvia's imagination was captured by the life she led at Earl's Court; and she made up her mind that one day she would somehow visit the real East. When Mr. Woolfe found out her deep interest in the part she was playing and her fondness for reading, he lent her various books that had inspired his creation at Earl's Court: she had long ago read the *Arabian Nights*, but there were several volumes of travels which fed her ambition to leave this dull Western world.

On Sunday mornings she used to lean out of her window and fancy the innumerable tombs of Brompton Cemetery were the minarets of an Eastern town; and later on, when June made every hour in the open air desirable after being shut up so long at Earl's Court, Sylvia used to spend her Sunday afternoons in wandering about the cemetery, in reading upon the tombs the exalted claims they put forward for poor mortality, and in puzzling over the broken columns, the urns and anchors and weeping angels that commemorated the wealthy dead. Everyone buried here had lived on earth a perfect life of perfect virtue, it seemed: everyone buried here had been confident of another life after the grave. Long ago at Lille she had been taught something about the future these dead people seemed to have counted upon; but there had been so much to do on Sunday mornings, and she could not remember that she had ever gone to church after she was nine. Perhaps she had made a mistake in abandoning so early the chance of finding out more about religion: it was difficult not to be impressed by the universal testimony of these countless tombs. Religion had evidently a great influence upon humanity, though in her reading she had never been struck by the importance of it. People in books attended church just as they wore fine clothes, or fought duels, or went to dinner parties: the habit belonged to the observances of polite society and if she ever found herself in such society she should doubtless behave like her peers. She had not belonged to a society with leisure for church-going. Yet in none of the books that she had read had religion seemed anything like so important as love or money. She herself thought that the pleasures of both these were much exaggerated, though in her own actual experience their power of seriously disturbing some people was undeniable. But who was ever disturbed by religion? Probably all these tombs were a luxury of the rich rather like visiting cards, which as everyone knew must be properly inscribed and follow a certain pattern. She remembered that old Mr. Gustard, who was not rich, had been very doubtful of another life, and she was consoled by this reflection, for she had been rendered faintly anxious by the pious repetitions of faith in a future life, practical comfort in which could apparently only be secured by the strictest behaviour on earth. She had the fancy to invent her own epitaph: HERE LIES SYLVIA SCARLETT WHO WAS ALWAYS RUNNING AWAY. IF SHE HAS TO LIVE ALL OVER AGAIN AND BE THE SAME GIRL SHE ACCEPTS NO RESPONSIBILITY FOR ANYTHING THAT MAY OCCUR. She printed this on a piece of paper, fastened it to a twig, and stuck it into the earth to judge the effect. Sylvia was so deeply engrossed in her task that she did not see that somebody was watching her, until she had stepped back to admire her handiwork.

'You extraordinary girl,' said a pleasant voice; looking round, Sylvia saw a thin, clean-shaven man of about thirty, who was leaning on a cane with an ivory crook and looking at her epitaph through gold-rimmed glasses. She blushed to her annoyance and snatched up the twig.

'What are you always running away from?' the stranger asked. 'Or is that an indiscreet question?'

Sylvia could have shaken herself for not giving a ready answer, but this newcomer seemed entitled to something better than rudeness, and her ready answers were usually rude.

'Now don't go away,' the stranger begged. 'It's so refreshing to meet something alive in this wilderness of death. I've been inspecting a grave for a friend who is abroad, and I'm feeling thoroughly depressed. One can't avoid reading epitaphs in a cemetery, can one? Or writing them?' he added with a pleasant laugh. 'I like yours much the best of any I've read so far. What a charming name. Sylvia Scarlett. Balzac said the best epitaphs were single names. If I saw Sylvia Scarlett on a tomb with nothing else, my appetite for romance would be perfectly satisfied.'

'Have you read many books of Balzac?' Sylvia asked.

The stranger's conversation had detained her; she could ask the question quite simply.

'I've read most of them, I think.'

'I've read some,' Sylvia said. 'But he's not my favourite writer. I like Scott better. But now I only read books about the Orient.'

She was rather proud of the last word and hoped the stranger would notice it.

'What part attracts you most?'

'I think Japan,' Sylvia said. 'But I like Turkey rather. Only I wouldn't ever let myself be shut up in a harem.'

'I suppose you'd run away?' said the stranger with a smile. 'Which reminds me that you haven't answered my first question. Please do, if it's not impertinent.'

They wandered along the paths shaded by yews and willows, and Sylvia told him many things about her life: he was the easiest person to talk to that she had ever met.

'And so this passion for the East has been inspired by the Hall of a Thousand and One Marvels. Dear me, what an unexpected consequence. And this Hall of a Thousand and One Marbles,' he indicated the cemetery with a sweep of his cane, 'this inspires you to write an epitaph? Well, my dear, such an early essay in mortuary literature may end in a famous elegy. You evidently possess the poetic temperament.'

'I don't like poetry,' Sylvia interrupted. 'I don't believe it ever. Nobody really talks like that when they're in love.'

'Quite true,' said the stranger. 'Poets have often ere this been charged with exaggeration. Perhaps I wrong you in attributing to you the poetic temperament. Yes, on second thoughts, I'm sure I do. You are an eminently practical young lady. I won't say prosaic, because the word has been debased – I suspect by the poets who are always uttering base currency of thoughts and words and emotions. Dear me, this is a most delightful adventure.'

'Adventure?' repeated Sylvia.

'Our meeting,' the stranger explained.

'Do you call that an adventure?' said Sylvia contemptuously. 'Why, I've had adventures much more exciting than this.'

'I told you that your temperament was anti-poetic,' said the stranger. 'How severe you are with my poor gossamers. You are like the Red Queen. You've seen adventures compared with which this is really an ordinary afternoon walk.'

'I don't understand half you're saying,' said Sylvia. 'Who's the Red Queen? Why was she red?'

'Why was Sylvia Scarlett?' the stranger laughed.

'I don't think that's a very good joke,' said Sylvia solemnly.

'It wasn't, and to mark my penitence, if you'll let me, I'll visit you at Earl's Court and present you with copies of *Alice's Adventures in Wonderland* and *Alice through the Looking-glass*.'

'Books,' said Sylvia in a satisfied tone. 'All right. When will you come? To-morrow?'

The stranger nodded.

'What are you?' Sylvia asked abruptly.

'My name is Iredale – Philip Iredale. No profession.'

'Are you what's called a gentleman?' Sylvia went on.

'I hope most people would so describe me,' said Mr. Iredale.

'I asked you that,' Sylvia explained, 'because I never met a gentleman before. I don't think Jimmy Monkley was a gentleman, and Arthur Madden was too young. Perhaps the Emperor of Byzantium was a gentleman.'

'I hope so indeed,' said Mr. Iredale. 'The Palaeologos family is an old one. Did you meet the Emperor in the course of your Oriental studies? Shall I meet him in the Hall of a Thousand and One Marvels?'

Sylvia told him the story of the Emperor's reception, which seemed to amuse him very much.

'Where do you live?' Sylvia asked.

'Well, I live in Hampshire generally, but I have rooms in the Temple.'

'The Temple of who?' Sylvia asked grandly.

'Mammon is probably the dedication, but by a legal fiction the titular god is suppressed.'

'Do you believe in God?' Sylvia asked.

'My dear Miss Scarlett, I protest that such a question so abruptly put in a cemetery is most unfair.'

'Don't call me Miss Scarlett. It makes me feel like a girl in a shop. Call me Sylvia. That's my name.'

'Dear me, how very refreshing you are,' said Mr. Iredale. 'Do you know I'm positively longing for to-morrow. But meanwhile, dear child, dear girl, we have to-day. What shall we do with the rest of it? Let's get on top of a bus and ride to Kensington Gardens. Hallowed as this spot is both by the mighty dead and the dear living, I'm tired of tombs.'

'I can't go on the top of a bus,' Sylvia said. 'Because I've not got any petticoats underneath my frock. I haven't saved up enough money to buy petticoats yet. I had to begin with chemises.'

'Then we must find a hansom,' said Mr. Iredale gravely.

They drove to Kensington Gardens and walked under the trees to Hyde Park Corner; there they took another hansom and drove to a restaurant with very comfortable chairs and delicious things to eat. Mr. Iredale and Sylvia talked hard all the time; after dinner he drove her back to Finborough Road and lifted his hat when she waved goodbye to him from the steps.

Mabel was furiously interested by Sylvia's account of her day, and gave her much advice.

'Now don't let everything be too easy,' she said. 'Remember he's rich, and can afford to spend a little money. Don't encourage him to make love to you at the very commencement, or he'll get tired and then you'll be sorry.'

'Oh, who's thinking about making love?' Sylvia exclaimed. 'That's just why I've enjoyed myself to-day. There wasn't a sign of love-making. He told me I was the most interesting person he'd ever met.'

'There you are,' Mabel said. 'There's only one way a girl can interest a man, is there?'

Sylvia burst into tears and stamped her foot on the floor.

'I won't believe you,' she cried. 'I don't want to believe you.'

'Well, there's no need to cry about it,' Mabel said. 'Only he'd be a funny sort of man if he didn't want to make love to you.'

'Well, he is a funny sort of man,' Sylvia declared. 'And I hope he's going on being funny. He's coming to the Exhibition to-morrow and you'll see for yourself how funny he is.'

Mabel was so deeply stirred by the prospect of Mr. Iredale's visit that she practised a more than usually voluptuous pose, which was frustrated by her fellow-favourite, who accused her of pushing her great legs all over the place and invited her to keep to her own cushions. Mabel got very angry and managed to drop a burning pastille on her companion's trousers, which caused a scene in the harem and necessitated the inter-vention of Mr. Woolfe.

'She did it for the purpose, the spiteful thing,' the outraged favourite declared. 'Behaves more like a performing seal than a Turkish lady, and then burns my costume. No, it's no good trying to "my dear" me. I've stood it long enough and I'm not going to stand it no longer.'

Mabel expressed an opinion that the rival favourite was a vulgar person; luckily before Mr. Iredale arrived the quarrel had been adjusted, and when he sat down on the divan and received a cup of coffee from Sylvia, whose brown eyes twinkled merry recognition above her yashmak, the two favourites were languorously fanning the perfumed airs of their seclusion, once again in drowsy accord.

Mr. Iredale came often to the Hall of a Thousand and One Marvels: he never failed to bring with him books for Sylvia and he was always eager to discuss with her what she had last read. On Sundays he used to take her out to Richmond or Kew, but he never invited her to visit him at his rooms.

'He's awfully gone on you,' said Mabel. 'Well, I wish you the best of luck, I'm sure, for he's a very nice fellow.'

Mr. Iredale was not quite so enthusiastic over Mabel; he often questioned Sylvia about her friend's conduct and seemed much disturbed by the materialism and looseness of her attitude towards life.

'It seems dreadful,' he used to say to her, 'that you can't find a worthier friend than that blonde enormity. I hope she never introduces you to any of her men.'

Sylvia assured him that Mabel was much too jealous to do anything of the sort.

'Jealous!' he ejaculated. 'How monstrous that a child like you should already be established in competition with that. Ugh!'

June passed away to July; Mr. Iredale told Sylvia that he ought to be in the country by now and that he could not understand himself. One day he asked her if she would like to live in the country, and became lost in meditation when she said she might. Sylvia delighted in his company and had a deep affection for this man who had so wonderfully entered into her life without once shocking her sensibility or her pride. She understood, however, that it was easy for him to behave himself, because he had all he wanted; nevertheless the companionship of a man of leisure had for herself such charm that she did not feel attracted to any deeper reflection upon moral causes; he was lucky to be what he was, but she was equally lucky to have found him for a friend.

Sometimes when he inveighed against her past associates and what he called her unhappy bringing up, she felt impelled to defend them.

'You see, you have all you want, Philip.'

Sylvia had learnt with considerable difficulty to call him Philip; she could never get rid of the idea that he was much older than herself and that people who heard her call him by his Christian name would laugh. Even now she could only call him Philip when the importance of the remark was enough to hide what still seemed an unpardonable kind of pertness.

'You think I have all I want, do you?' he answered a little bitterly. 'My dear child, I'm in the most humiliating position in which a man can find himself. There is only one thing I want, but I'm afraid to make the effort to secure it: I'm afraid of being laughed at. Sylvia dear, you were wiser than you knew, when you objected to calling me Philip for that very reason. I wish I could spread my canvas to a soldier's wind like you and sail into life, but I can't. I've been taught to tack, and I've never learnt how to reach harbour. I suppose some people in spite of our system of education succeed in learning,' he sighed.

'I don't understand a bit what you're talking about,' she said.

'Don't you? It doesn't matter. I was really talking to myself, which is very rude. Impose a penalty.'

'Admit you have everything you want,' Sylvia insisted. 'And don't be always running down poor Jimmy and my father and everyone I've ever known.'

'From their point of view I confess I have everything I want,' he agreed.

On another occasion Sylvia asked him if he did not think she ought to consider religion more than she had done. Being so much in Philip's company was giving her a desire to experiment with the habits of well-regulated people, and she was perplexed to find that he paid no attention to church-going.

'Ah, there you can congratulate yourself,' he said emphatically. 'Whatever was deplorable in your bringing up, at least you escaped that damnable imposition, that fraudulent attempt to flatter man beyond his deserts.'

'Oh, don't use so many long words all at once,' Sylvia begged. 'I like a long word now and then, because I'm collecting long words, but I can't collect them and understand what you're talking about at the same time. Do you think I ought to go to church?'

'No, no, a thousand times no,' Philip replied. 'You've luckily escaped from religion as a social observance. Do you feel the need for it? Have you ineffable longings?'

'I know that word,' Sylvia said. 'It means something that can't be said in words, doesn't it? Well, I've often had longings like that, especially in Hampstead, but no longings that had anything to do with going to church. How could they have, if they were ineffable?'

'Quite true,' Philip agreed. 'And therefore be grateful that you're a pagan. If ever a confounded priest gets hold of you and tries to bewitch you with his mumbo-jumbo, send for me and I'll settle him. No, no, going to church of one's own free will is either a drug (sometimes a stimulant, sometimes a narcotic), or it's mere snobbery. In either case it is a futile waste of time, because there are so many problems in this world – you're one of the most urgent – that it's criminal to avoid their solution by speculating upon the problem of the next world, which is insoluble.'

'But is there another world?' she asked.

'I don't think so.'

'And all those announcements in the cemetery meant nothing?'

'Nothing but human vanity – the vanity of the dead and the vanity of the living.'

'Thanks,' Sylvia said. 'I thought that was probably the explanation.'

Mabel, who had long ago admitted that Philip was just as funny as Sylvia had described him, often used to ask her what they found to talk about.

'He can't be interested in Earl's Court, and you're such a kid. I can't understand it.'

'Well, we talked about religion to-day,' Sylvia told her.

'Oh, that's it, is it?' Mabel said very knowingly. 'He's one of those fellows who ought to have been a clergyman, is he? I knew he reminded me of someone. He's the walking image of the clergyman where we used to live in Clapham. But you be careful, Sylvia. It's an old trick, that.'

'You're quite wrong. He hates clergymen.'

'Oh,' Mabel exclaimed, taken aback for a moment, but quickly recovering herself. 'Oh well, people always pretend to hate what they can't get. And I daresay he wanted to be a clergyman. But don't let him try to convert you. It's an old trick to get something for nothing. And I know, my dear.'

July passed away into August, and Sylvia buried for so many hours in the airless Hall of a Thousand and One Marvels was flagging visibly. Philip used to spend nearly every afternoon and evening in the inner room where she worked, so many indeed that Mr. Woolfe protested and told her he would really have to put her back into the outer hall, because good customers were being annoyed by her admirer's glaring at them through his glasses.

Philip was very much worried by Sylvia's wan looks, and urged her more insistently to leave her job and let him provide for her. But having

vowed to herself that never again would she put herself under an obligation to anybody, she would not hear of leaving the Exhibition.

One Sunday in the middle of August Philip took Sylvia to Oxford,
of which he had often talked to her. She enjoyed the day very much and
delighted him by the interest she took in all the colleges they visited: but
he was much worried, so he said, by the approach of age.

'You aren't so very old,' Sylvia reassured him. 'Old, but not very old.'

'Fifteen years older than you,' he sighed.

'Still, you're not old enough to be my father,' she added encouragingly.

In the afternoon they went to St. Mary's Walks and sat upon a bench
by the Cherwell: close at hand a Sabbath bell chimed a golden monotone:
Philip took Sylvia's hand and looked right into her face, as he always did
when he was not wearing his glasses.

'Little delightful thing, if you won't let me take you away from that
inferno of Earl's Court, will you marry me? Not at once, because it
wouldn't be fair to you and it wouldn't be fair to myself. I'm going to
make a suggestion that will make you laugh, but it is quite a serious
suggestion: I want you to go to school.'

Sylvia drew back and stared at him over her shoulder.

'To school?' she echoed. 'But I'm sixteen.'

'Lots of girls – most girls in the position I want you to take – are
still at school then. Only a year, dear child, and then if you will have
me, we'll be married. I don't think you'd be bored down in Hampshire.
I have thousands of books and you shall read them all. Don't get into
your head that I'm asking you to marry me because I'm sorry for
you—'

'There's nothing to be sorry for,' Sylvia interrupted sharply.

'I know there's not, and I want you terribly. You fascinate me to an
extent I never could have thought possible for any woman – I really
haven't cared much about women: they always seemed in the way. I do
believe you would be happy with me. We'll travel to the East together.
You shall visit Japan and Turkey. I love you so much, Sylvia. Tell me,
don't you love me a little?'

'I like you very much indeed,' she answered gently. 'Oh, very very very
much. Perhaps I love you. I don't think I love you, because if I loved you I
think my heart would beat much faster when you asked me to marry you,
and it isn't beating at all. Feel.'

She put his hand upon her heart.

'It certainly doesn't seem to be unusually rapid,' he agreed.

Sylvia looked at him in perplexity: his thin face was flushed, and the
golden light of the afternoon gave it a warmer glow: his very blue eyes

without their glasses had such a wide-open pleading expression that she was touched by his kindness.

'If you think I ought to go to school,' she offered, 'I will go to school.'

He looked at her with a question in his eyes. She saw that he wanted to kiss her, and she pretended to think he was dissatisfied with her answer about school.

'I won't promise to marry you,' she said. 'Because I always want to keep promises and I can't say now what I shall be like in a year, can I? I'm changing all the time. Only I do like you very very very much. Don't forget that.'

He took her hand and kissed it with the courtesy that for her was almost his greatest charm: manners seemed to Sylvia the chief difference between Philip and all the other people she had known. Once he had told her she had very bad manners; and she had lain awake half the night in her chagrin. She divined that the real reason of his wanting her to go to school was his wish to correct her manners. How little she knew about him, and yet she had been asked to marry him: his father and mother were dead, but he had a sister whom she would have to meet.

'Have you told your sister about me?' she asked.

'Not yet,' he confessed. 'I think I won't tell anybody about you except the lady to whose care I am going to entrust you.'

Sylvia asked him how long he had made up his mind to ask her to marry him, and he told her he had been thinking about it for a long time, but that he had always been afraid at the last moment.

'Afraid I should disgrace you, I suppose?' Sylvia said.

He put on his glasses and coughed, a sure sign he was embarrassed: she laughed.

'And of course there's no doubt that I *should* disgrace you. I probably shall now as a matter of fact. Mabel will be rather sorry,' she went on pensively. 'She likes me to be there at night in case she gets frightened. She told me once that the only reason she ever went wrong was because she was frightened to sleep alone. She was married to a commercial traveller, who of course was just the worst person she could have married, because he was always leaving her alone. Poor Mabel!'

Philip took her hand again and said in a tone of voice which she resented as adumbrating already, however faintly, a hint of ownership:

'Sylvia dear, you won't talk so freely as that in the school, will you? Promise me that you won't.'

'But it used to amuse you when I talked like that,' she said. 'You mustn't think now that you've got the right to lecture me.'

'My dear child, it doesn't matter what you say to me; I understand. But some people might not.'

'Well, don't say I didn't warn you,' she almost sighed.

VI

Miss Ashley's school for young ladies, situated in its own grounds on Campden Hill, was considered one of the best in England; a day or two after they got back from Oxford, Philip announced to Sylvia that he was glad to say Miss Ashley would take her as a pupil. She was a friend of his family; but he had sworn her to secrecy, and it had been decided between them that Sylvia should be supposed to be an orphan educated until now in France.

'Mayn't I tell the other girls that I've been an odalisque?' Sylvia asked.

'Good heavens, no,' said Philip earnestly.

'But I was looking forward to telling them,' she explained. 'Because I'm sure it would amuse them.'

Philip smiled indulgently and thought she would find lots of other ways of amusing them. He had told Miss Ashley, who by the way was an enthusiastic rationalist, that he did not want her to attend the outward shows of religion, and Miss Ashley had assented, though as a schoolmistress she was bound to see that her pupils went to church at least once every Sunday. He had reassured her about the bad example Sylvia would set by promising to come himself and take her out every Sunday in his capacity as guardian.

'You'll be glad of that, won't you?' he asked anxiously.

'I expect so,' Sylvia said. 'But of course I may find being at school such fun that I shan't want to leave it.'

Again Philip smiled indulgently and hoped she would. Of course, it was now holiday time, but Miss Ashley had quite agreed with him in the desirableness of Sylvia's going to Hornton House before the term began. She would be able to help her to equip herself with all the things a schoolgirl required. He knew for instance that she was short of various articles of clothing. Sylvia could take Miss Ashley completely into her confidence, but even with her he advised a certain reticence with regard to some of her adventures. She was of course a woman of infinite experience and extremely broadminded, but many years as a schoolmistress might have made her consider some things were better left unsaid: there were some people, particularly English people, who were much upset by details. Perhaps Sylvia would spare her the details?

'You see, my dear child, you've had an extraordinary number of odd adventures for your age, and they've made you what you are, my dear. But now is the chance of setting them in their right relation to your future life. You know, I'm tremendously keen about this one year's formal education. You're just the material that can be perfected by academic methods, which with ordinary material end in mere barren decoration.'

'I don't understand. I don't understand,' Sylvia interrupted.

'Sorry! My hobby horse has bolted with me and left you behind. But I won't try to explain or even to advise. I leave everything to you. After all, you are you; and I'm the last person to wish you to be anyone else.'

Philip was humming excitedly when they drove up to Hornton House, and Sylvia was certainly much impressed by its Palladian grandeur and the garden that seemed to spread illimitably behind it. She felt rather shy of Miss Ashley herself, who was apparently still in her dressing-gown, a green linen dressing-gown worked in front with what Sylvia considered were very bad reproductions of flowers in brownish silk. She was astonished at seeing a woman of Miss Ashley's dignity still in her dressing-gown at three o'clock in the afternoon, but she was still more astonished to see her in a battered straw hat apparently ready to go shopping in Kensington High Street without changing her attire: she looked at Philip, who seemed quite unaware of anything unusual. A carriage was waiting for them when they went out, and Philip left her with Miss Ashley, promising to dine at Hornton House that night.

The afternoon passed away rapidly in making all sorts of purchases, even of trunks: it seemed to Sylvia that thousands of pounds must have been spent upon her outfit, and she felt a thrill of pride. Everybody behind the various counters treated Miss Ashley with great deference; Sylvia was bound to admit that, however careless she might be of her own appearance, she was splendidly able to help other people to choose jolly things. They drove back to Hornton House in a carriage that seemed full of parcels, though they only took with them what Miss Ashley considered immediately important. Tea was waiting in the garden under a great cedar; and by the time tea was finished Sylvia was sure that she should like Miss Ashley and that she should not run away that night, which she had made up her mind to do unless she was absolutely contented with the prospect of her new existence. She liked her bedroom very much, and the noise of the sparrows in the creeper outside her window. The starched maid-servant who came to help her dress for dinner rather frightened her, but she decided to be very French in order to take away the least excuse for ridicule.

Sylvia thought at dinner that the prospect of marriage had made

Philip seem even older, or perhaps it was his assumption of guardianship which gave him this added seriousness.

'Of course, French she already knows,' he was saying, 'though it might be as well to revise her grammar a little. History she has a queer disjointed knowledge of – it would be as well to fill in the gaps. I should like her to learn a little Latin. Then there are mathematics and what is called science. Of course, one would like her to have a general acquaintance with both, but I don't want to waste time with too much elementary stuff. It would be almost better for her to be completely ignorant of either.'

'I think you will have to leave the decision to me, Philip,' said Miss Ashley in that almost too deliberately tranquil voice, which Sylvia felt might so easily become in certain circumstances exasperating. 'I think you may rely on my judgment where girls are concerned.'

Philip hastened to assure Miss Ashley that he was not presuming to dictate to her greater experience of education; he only wished to lay stress on the subjects that he considered would be most valuable for the life Sylvia was likely to lead.

'I have a class,' said Miss Ashley, 'which is composed of older girls and of which the routine is sufficiently elastic to fit any individual case: I take that class myself.'

Sylvia half expected that Miss Ashley would suggest including Philip in it, if he went on talking any longer: perhaps Philip himself expected as much, for he said no more about Sylvia's education and talked instead about the gravity of the situation in South Africa.

Sylvia was vividly aware of the comfort of her bedroom and of the extraordinary freshness of it in comparison with all the other rooms she had so far inhabited. Miss Ashley faintly reminded her of her mother, not that there was the least outward resemblance except in height, for Miss Ashley's hair was grey, whereas her mother's until the day of her death had kept all its lustrous darkness. Yet both wore their hair in similar fashion combed up high from the forehead so as to give them a majestic appearance. Her mother's eyes had been of a deep and glowing brown set in that pale face: Miss Ashley's eyes were small and grey, and her complexion had the hard rosiness of an apple. The likeness between the two women lay rather in the possession of a natural authority which warned one that disobedience would be an undertaking and defiance an impossibility. Sylvia rejoiced in the idea of being under control: it was invigorating like the delicious torment of a cold bath: of course she had no intention of being controlled in big things, but she was determined to submit over little things for the sheer pleasure of submitting to Miss

Ashley, who was, moreover, likely to be often right. In the morning, when she came down in one of her new frocks, her hair tied back with a big brown bow, and found Miss Ashley sitting in the sunny green window of the dining-room with the *Morning Post*, she congratulated herself upon the positive pleasure that such a getting up was able to give her and upon this new sense of spaciousness that such a beginning of the day was able to provide.

'You're looking at my dress,' said Miss Ashley pleasantly. 'When you're my age you'll abandon fashion and adopt what is comfortable and becoming.'

'I thought it was a dressing-gown yesterday,' Sylvia admitted.

'Rather an elaborate dressing-gown,' Miss Ashley laughed. 'I'm not so vain as all that.'

Sylvia wondered what she would have said to some of Mabel's dressing-gowns. Now that she was growing used to Miss Ashley's attire, she began to think she rather liked it. This gown of peacock-blue linen was certainly attractive, and the flowers embroidered upon its front were clearly recognizable as daisies.

During the fortnight before school reopened Sylvia gave Miss Ashley a good deal of her confidence, and found her much less shocked by her experiences than Philip had been. She told her that she felt rather ungrateful in so abruptly cutting herself off from Mabel, who had been very kind to her, but on this point Miss Ashley was firm in her agreement with Philip and would not hear of Sylvia's making any attempt to see Mabel again.

'You are lucky, my dear, in having only one person whose friendship you are forced to give up, as it seems to you, a little harshly. Great changes are rarely made with so slight an effort of separation. I am not in favour personally of violent uprootings and replantings, and it was only because you were in such a solitary position that I consented to do what Philip asked. Your friend Mabel was, I am sure, exceedingly kind to you; but you are much too young to repay her kindness. It is the privilege of the very young to be heartless. From what you have told me, you have often been heartless about other people, so I don't think you need worry about Mabel. Besides, let me assure you that Mabel herself would be far from enjoying any association with you that included Hornton House.'

Sylvia had no arguments to bring forward against Miss Ashley; nevertheless she felt guilty of treating Mabel shabbily, and wished that she could have explained to her that it was not really her fault.

Miss Ashley took her once or twice to the play, which Sylvia enjoyed more than music-halls. In the library at Hornton House she found plenty of books to read, and Miss Ashley was willing to talk about them in a very interesting way. Philip came often to see her and told her how much Miss Ashley liked her and how pleased they both were to see her settling down so easily and quickly.

The night before term began, the four assistant mistresses arrived: their names were Miss Pinck, Miss Primer, Miss Hossack, and Miss Lee; Sylvia was by this time sufficiently at home in Hornton House to survive the ordeal of introduction without undue embarrassment, though, to Miss Ashley's amusement, she strengthened her French accent. Miss Pinck, the senior assistant mistress, was a very small woman with a sharp chin and knotted fingers, two features which contrasted noticeably with her general plumpness: she taught History and English Literature and had an odd habit when she was speaking of suddenly putting her hands behind her back, shooting her chin forward and screwing up her eyes so fiercely that the person addressed involuntarily drew back in alarm. Sylvia, to whom this gesture became very familiar, used to wonder if in the days of her vanity Miss Pinck had cultivated it to avoid displaying her fingers, so that from long practice her chin had learnt to replace the forefinger in impressing a fact.

'The date is 1689,' Miss Pinck would say, and one half expected to see a pencil screwed into her chin which would actually write the figures upon somebody's notebook.

Miss Primer was a thin, melancholy, and sandy-haired woman, who must have been very pretty before her face was netted with innumerable small lines that made her look as if birds had been scratching on it when she was asleep. Miss Primer took an extremely gloomy view of everything, and with the prospect of war in South Africa she arrived in a condition of exalted, almost ecstatic depression: she taught Art, which at Hornton House was no cure for pessimism. Miss Hossack, the Mathematical and Scientific mistress, did not have much to do with Sylvia: she was a robust woman with a loud voice who liked to be asked questions. Finally there was Miss Lee who taught music and was the particular adoration of every girl in the school, including Sylvia. She was usually described as 'ethereal,' 'angelic,' or 'divine': one girl with a taste for painting discovered that she was her ideal conception of St. Cecilia; this naturally roused the jealousy of rival adorers that would not be 'copy-cats,' until one of them discovered that Miss Lee, whose first name was Mary, had Annabel for a second name, the very mixture of the poetic and the intimate that was required. Sylvia belonged neither to the Cecilias nor the Annabels, but she loved dear Miss Lee none the less deeply and passed exquisite moments in trying to play the Clementi her mistress wanted her to learn.

'What a strange girl you are, Sylvia,' Miss Lee used to say. 'Anybody would think you had been taught music by an accompanist. You don't seem to have any notion of a piece, but you really play accompaniments wonderfully. It's not mere vamping.'

Sylvia wondered what Miss Lee would have thought of Jimmy Monkley and the Pink Pierrots.

The afternoon that the girls arrived at Hornton House, Sylvia was sure that nothing could keep her from running away that night: the prospect of facing the chattering, giggling mob that thronged the hitherto quiet hall was overwhelming. From the landing above she leaned over to watch them, unable to imagine what she should talk about to them or what they would talk about to her. It was Miss Lee who saved the situation by inviting Sylvia to meet four of the girls at tea in her room and cleverly choosing, as Sylvia realized afterwards, the four leaders of the four chief sets. Who would not adore Miss Lee?

'Oh, Miss Lee, *did* you notice Gladys and Enid Worstley?' Muriel ejaculated, accentuating some of her words like the notes of an unevenly blown harmonium, and explaining to Sylvia in a sustained tremolo that these twins whose real name was Worsley, were always called Worstley because it was impossible to decide which was more wicked. 'Oh, Miss Lee, they've got the most *lovely* dresses,' she went on, releasing every stop in a diapason of envy. 'Simply *gorgeously* beautiful. I do think it's a shame to dress them up like that. I do *really*.'

Sylvia made a mental note to cultivate this pair not for their dresses, but for their behaviour: Muriel was all very well, but those eyebrows eternally arched and those eyes eternally staring out of her head would sooner or later have most irresistibly to be given real cause for amazement.

'Their mother likes them to be prettily dressed,' said Miss Lee.

'Of course she does,' Gwendyr put in primly. 'She was an actress.'

'To hell with Gwendyr,' thought Sylvia. 'Why shouldn't their mother have been an actress?'

'Oh, but they're so conceited,' said Dorothy. 'Enid Worsley *never* can pass a glass, and their frocks are most frightfully short. *Don't* you remember when they danced at last breaking up?'

'This is getting unbearable,' Sylvia thought.

'I think they're rather dears,' Phyllis drawled. 'They're jolly pretty, anyway.'

Sylvia looked at Phyllis and decided that she was jolly pretty too, with her golden hair and smocked linen frock of old rose: she would like to be friends with Phyllis. The moment had come, however, when she must venture all her future on a single throw: she must either shock Miss Lee and the four girls irretrievably or she must be henceforth accepted at Hornton House as herself: there must be none of these critical sessions about Sylvia Scarlett. She pondered for a minute or two the various episodes of her past: then suddenly she told them how she had run away from school in France, arrived in England without a penny, and earned her living as an odalisque at the Exhibition. Which would she be, she asked, when she saw the girls staring at her open-mouthed now with real amazement: villain or heroine? She became a heroine, especially to Gladys and Enid, with whom she made friends that night, and who showed her in strictest secrecy two powder puffs and a tin of Turkish cigarettes.

There were moments when Sylvia was sad, especially when war broke out and so many of the girls had photographs of brothers and cousins and friends in uniform, not to mention various generals whose ability was as yet unquestioned: she did not consider the photograph of Philip a worthy competitor with these and begged him to enlist, which hurt his feelings. Nevertheless, her adventures as an odalisque were proof in the eyes of the girls against martial relatives; their only regret was that the Exhibition closed before they had time to devise a plot to visit the Hall of a Thousand and One Marvels, and be introduced by Sylvia to the favourites of the harem.

Miss Ashley was rather cross with Sylvia for her revelations and urged her as a personal favour to herself not to make any more. Sylvia explained the circumstances quite frankly and promised that she would not offend again; but she pointed out that the girls were all very inquisitive about Philip and asked how she was to account for his taking her out every Sunday.

'He's your guardian, my dear. What could be more natural?'

'Then you must warn him not to blush and drop his glasses when the girls tell him I'm nearly ready. They *all* think he's in love with me.'

'Well, it doesn't matter,' said Miss Ashley impatiently.

'But it does matter,' Sylvia contradicted. 'Because even if he is going to marry me, he's not the sort of lover one wants to put in a frame, now is he? That's why I bought that photograph of George Alexander which Miss Pinck made such a fuss about. I *must* have a secret sorrow. All the girls have secret sorrows this term.'

Miss Ashley shook her head gravely, but Sylvia was sure she was laughing like herself.

Sylvia's chief friend was Phyllis Markham – the twins were only fourteen – and the two of them headed a society for toleration, which was designed to contend with stupid and ill-natured criticism. The society became so influential and so tolerant that the tone of the school was considered in danger, especially by Miss Primer, who lamented it much together with the reverses in South Africa: and when after the Christmas holidays, which Sylvia spent with Miss Ashley at Bournemouth, a grave defeat coincided with the discovery that the Worsleys were signalling from their window to some boys in a house opposite, Miss Primer in a transport of woe took up the matter with the head-mistress. Miss Ashley called a conference of the most influential girls, at which Sylvia was present, and with the support of Phyllis maintained that the behaviour of the twins had been much exaggerated.

'But in their nightgowns,' Miss Primer wailed. 'The policeman at the corner must have seen them. At such a time too, with these dreadful Boers winning everywhere. And their hair streaming over their shoulders.'

'It always is,' said Sylvia.

Miss Ashley rebuked her rather sharply for interrupting.

'A bull's-eye lantern. The room reeked of hot metal. I could not read the code. I took it upon myself to punish them with an extra hour's free-hand to-day. But the punishment is most inadequate. I detect a disturbing influence right through the school.'

Miss Ashley made a short speech in which she pointed out the responsibility of the older girls in such matters and emphasized the vulgarity of the twins' conduct. No one wished to impute nasty motives to them, but it must be clearly understood that the girls of Hornton House could not and should not be allowed to behave like servants. She relied upon Muriel Battersby, Dorothy Hearne, Gwendyr Jones, Phyllis Markham, Georgina Roe, Helen Macdonald, and Sylvia Scarlett to prevent in future such unfortunate incidents as this that had been brought to her notice by Miss Primer, she was sure much against Miss Primer's will.

Miss Primer at these words threw up her eyes to indicate the misery she had suffered before she had been able to bring herself to the point of reporting the twins. Phyllis whispered to Sylvia that Miss Primer looked like a dying duck in a thunderstorm, a phrase which she now heard for the first time and at which she laughed aloud.

Miss Ashley paused in her discourse and fixed Sylvia with her grey eyes in pained interrogation: Miss Pinck's chin shot out: Miss Lee bit her underlip and tenderly shook her head: the other girls stared at their laps and tried to look at one another without moving their heads. Phyllis quickly explained that it was she who had made Sylvia laugh.

'I'm awfully sorry, Miss Ashley,' she drawled.

'I'm glad to hear that you are *very* sorry,' said Miss Ashley, 'but Sylvia must realize when it is permissible and when it is not permissible to laugh. I'm afraid I must ask her to leave the room.'

'I ought to go too,' Phyllis declared. 'I made her laugh.'

'I'm sure, Phyllis, that to yourself your wit seems irresistible. Pray let us have the opportunity of judging.'

'Well, I said that Miss Primer looked like a dying duck in a thunderstorm.'

The horrified amazement of everybody in the room expressed itself in a gasp that sounded like a ghostly, an infinitely attenuated scream of dismay. Sylvia partly from nervousness, partly because the simile even on repetition appealed to her sense of the ridiculous, laughed aloud for a second time, laughed indeed with a kind of guffaw, the sacrilegious echoes of which were stifled in an appalled silence.

'Sylvia Scarlett and Phyllis Markham will both leave the room immediately,' said Miss Ashley. 'I will speak to them later.'

Outside the study of the head-mistress, Sylvia and Phyllis looked at one another like people who have jointly managed to break a mirror.

'What will she do?'

'Sylvia, I simply couldn't help it. I simply couldn't bear them all any longer.'

'My dear, I know. Oh, I think it was wonderful of you.'

Sylvia laughed heartily for the third time, and just at this moment the twins who were the original cause of all the commotion came sidling up to know what everybody had said.

'You little beasts with your bull's-eye lamps and your naughtiness,' Phyllis cried. 'I expect we shall all be expelled. What fun! I shall get some hunting. Oh, three cheers, I say.'

'Of course you know why Miss Primer was really in such a wax?' Gladys asked with the eyes of an angel and the laugh of a fairy.

'No, let me tell, Gladys,' Enid burst in. 'You know I won the toss. We tossed up which should tell and I won. You *are* a chiseller. You see, when Miss Primer came tearing up into our room, we turned the lamps on to her, and she was simply furious because she thought everybody in the street could see her in that blue flannel wrapper.'

'Which of course they could,' Sylvia observed.

'Of course,' the twins shrieked together. 'And the boys opposite clapped, and she heard them and tried to pull down the blind and her wrapper came open and she was wearing a chest-protector!'

The interview with Miss Ashley was rather distressing, because she took from the start the altogether unexpected line of blaming Phyllis and Sylvia not for the breach of discipline, but for the wound they had inflicted upon Miss Primer. All that had seemed fine and honest and brave and noble collapsed immediately; it was impossible after Miss Ashley's words not to feel ashamed, and both the girls offered to beg Miss Primer's pardon. Miss Ashley said no more about the incident after this, though she took rather an unfair advantage of their chastened spirits by exacting a promise that they would in common with the rest of the school leaders set their faces against the encouragement of such behaviour as that of the twins last night.

The news from South Africa was so bad that Miss Primer's luxury of grief could scarcely have been heightened by Phyllis's and Sylvia's rudeness: however, she wept a few tears, patted their hands and forgave them. A few days afterwards she was granted the boon of another woe, which she shared with the whole school, in the news of Miss Lee's approaching marriage. Any wedding would have upset Miss Primer, but in this case the sorrow was rendered three times as poignant by the fact that Miss Lee was going to marry a soldier under orders for the front. This romantic accessory could not fail to thrill the girls, though it was not enough to compensate for the loss of their beloved Miss Lee. Rivalries between the Cecilias and Annabels were for ever finished; several girls had been learning Beethoven's Pathetic Sonata, and the amount of expression put into it would, they hoped, show Miss Lee the depth of their emotion when for the last time these frail fingers so lightly corrected their touch, when for the last time that delicate pencil inscribed her directions upon their music.

'Of course the school will *never* be the same without her,' said Muriel.

'I shall write home and ask if I can't take up Italian instead of music,' said Dorothy.

'Fancy playing duets with anyone but Miss Lee,' said Gwendyr. 'The very idea makes me shudder.'

'Perhaps we shall have a music master now,' said Gladys.

Whereupon everybody told her she was a heartless thing: poor Gladys who really loved Miss Lee as much as anybody retired to her room and cried for the rest of the evening, until she was consoled by Enid, who pointed out that now she *must* use her powder-puff.

For Sylvia the idea of Miss Lee's departure and marriage was desolating: it was an abrupt rending of half the ties that bound her to Hornton House. Phyllis, Miss Ashley, and the twins were all that really remained, and Phyllis was always threatening to persuade her people to take her away when the weather was tolerably warm, so deeply did she resent the loss of hunting. It was curious how much more Phyllis meant to her than

Philip, so much indeed that she had never confided in her that she was going to marry Philip. How absurd that two names so nearly alike could be in the one case so beautiful, in the other so ugly. Yet she was still very fond of Philip and she still enjoyed going out with him on Sundays, even though it meant being deprived of pleasant times with Phyllis. She had warned Philip that she might get too fond of school, and he had smiled in that superior way of his. Ought she to marry him at all? He had been so kind to her that if she refused to marry him she should have to run away, for she could not continue under an obligation. Why did people want to marry? Why must she marry? Worst of all, why must Miss Lee marry? But these were questions that not even Miss Hossack would be able to answer. Ah, if it had only been Miss Hossack who had been going to marry. Sylvia began to make up a rhyme about Miss Hossack marrying a Cossack and going for her honeymoon to the Trossachs, where Helen Macdonald lived.

All the girls had subscribed to buy Miss Lee a dressing-case, which they presented to her one evening after tea with a kind of dismal beneficence, as if they were laying a wreath upon her tomb. Next morning she went away by an early train to the North of England, and after lunch every girl retired with the secret sorrow that now had more than fashion to commend it. Sylvia's sorrow was an aching regret that she had not told Miss Lee more about herself and her life and Philip: now it was too late. She met the twins wandering disconsolately enlaced along the corridor outside her room.

'Oh, Sylvia, dearest Sylvia,' they moaned. 'We've lost our duet with Miss Lee's fingering.'

'I'll help you to look for it.'

'Oh, but we lost it on purpose, because we didn't like it, and the next day Miss Lee said she was going to be married.'

Sylvia asked where they lost it.

'Oh, we put it in an envelope and posted it to the Bishop of London.'

Sylvia suggested they should write to the Bishop and explain the circumstances in which the duet was sent to him: he would no doubt return it.

'Oh, no,' said the twins mournfully. 'We never put a stamp on and we wrote inside, *A token of esteem and regard from two sinners who you confirmed*. How can we ask for it back?'

Sylvia embraced the twins, and the three of them wandered in the sad and wintry garden until it was time for afternoon school.

The next day happened to be Sunday, and Philip came as usual to take Sylvia out. He had sent her on the evening before an overcoat trimmed with grey squirrel, which if it had not arrived after Miss Lee's departure would have been so much more joyfully welcomed. Philip asked her why she was so sad and if the coat did not please her. She told him about its coming after Miss Lee had gone, and as usual he had a lot to say:

'You strange child, how quickly you have adopted the outlook and manners of the English schoolgirl. One would say that you had never been anything else. How absurd I was to be afraid that you were a wild bird whom I had caught too late. I'm quite positive now that you'll be happy with me down in Hampshire. I'm sorry you've lost Miss Lee. A charming woman, I thought, and very cultivated. Miss Ashley will miss her greatly, but she herself will be glad to get away from music-teaching. It must be an atrocious existence.'

Here was a new point of view altogether. Could it really be possible that those delicious hours with Miss Lee were a penance to the mistress? Sylvia looked at Philip angrily, for she found it unforgivable in him to destroy her illusions like this. He did not observe her expression and continued his monologue.

'Really atrocious. Exercises! Scales! Other people's chilblains! A creaking piano-stool! What a purgatory! And all to teach a number of young women to inflict an objectionable noise upon their friends and relations.'

'Thanks,' Sylvia broke in. 'You won't catch me playing again.'

'I'm not talking about you,' Philip said. 'You have temperament. You're different from the ordinary schoolgirl.' He took her arm affectionately. 'You're you, dear Sylvia.'

'And yours,' she added sullenly. 'I thought you said just now that I was just like any other English schoolgirl and that you were so happy about it.'

'I said you'd wonderfully adopted the outlook,' Philip corrected. 'Not quite the same thing.'

'Oh, well, take your horrible coat because I don't want it,' Sylvia exclaimed, and rapidly unbuttoning her new overcoat, she flung it on the pavement at his feet.

Nobody was in sight at the moment, so Philip did not get angry.

'Now don't tell me it's illogical to throw away only the coat and not undress myself completely. I know quite well that everything I've got on is yours.'

'Oh, no, it's not,' Philip said gently. 'It's yours.'

'But you paid for everything.'

'No, you paid yourself,' he insisted.

'How?'

'By being Sylvia. Come along, don't trample on your poor coat. There's a most detestable wind blowing.'

He picked up the offending overcoat and helped her into it again with so much sympathy half humorous, half grave in his demeanour that she could not help being sorry for her outburst.

Nevertheless the fact of her complete dependence upon Philip for everything, even before marriage, was always an oppression to Sylvia's mind, which was increased by the continual reminders of her loneliness that intercourse with other girls forced upon her. They, when they married, would be married from a background: the lovers when they came for them would have to fight for their love by breaking down the barriers of old associations, old friendships, and old affections; in a word they would have to win the brides. What was her own background? Nothing but a panorama of streets, which offered no opposition to Philip's choice, except in so far as it was an ugly background for a possession of his own and therefore fit to be destroyed. It was all very well for Philip to tell her that she was herself and that he loved her accordingly. If that were true, why was he taking so much trouble to turn her into something different? Other girls at Hornton House, when they married, would not begin with ugly backgrounds to be obliterated; their pasts would merge beautifully with the pasts of their husbands; they were not being transformed by Miss Pinck and Miss Primer; they were merely being supplied by them with value for their parents' money.

It was a visit to Phyllis Markham's home in Leicestershire during the Easter holidays that had branded with the iron of jealousy these facts upon her meditation. Phyllis used to lament that she had no brothers; and Sylvia used to wonder what she would have said if she had been like herself, without mother, without father, without brothers, without sisters, without relations, without friends, without letters, without photographs, with nothing in the whole world between herself and the shifting panorama from which she had been snatched but the love of a timid man inspired by an unusual encounter in Brompton Cemetery. This visit to Phyllis Markham was the doom upon their friendship; however sweet, however sympathetic, however loyal Phyllis might be, she must ultimately despise her friend's past: every word Sylvia listened to during those Easter holidays seemed to cry out the certain fulfilment of this conjecture.

'I expect I'm too sensitive,' Sylvia said to herself. 'I expect I really am common, because apparently common people are always looking out for slights. I don't look out for them now, but if I were to tell Phyllis all about myself, I'm sure I should begin to look out for them. No, I'll just be friends with her up to a point, for so long as I stay at Hornton House; then we'll separate for ever. I'm really an absolute fraud. I'm just as much of a fraud now as when I was dressed up as a boy. I'm not real in this life. I haven't been real since I came down to breakfast with Miss Ashley that first morning. I'm simply a very good impostor. I must inherit the talent from father. Another reason against telling Phyllis about myself is that, if I do, I shall become her property; Miss Ashley knows all about me, but I'm not her property, because it's part of her profession to be told secrets. Phyllis would love me more than ever, as long as she was the only person that owned the secret; but if anybody else ever knew, even if it were only Philip, she would be jealous and she would have to make a secret of it with someone else. Then she would be ashamed of herself and would begin to hate and despise me in self-defence. No, I must never tell any of the girls.'

Apart from these morbid fits, which were not frequent, Sylvia enjoyed her stay at Markham Grange: in a way it encouraged the idea of marrying Philip; for the country life appealed to her not as a Cockney by the strangeness of its inhabitants and the mere quantity of grass in sight, but more deeply with those old ineffable longings of Hampstead.

At the end of the summer term the twins invited Sylvia to stay with them in Hertfordshire: she refused at first, because she felt that she could not bear the idea of being jealously disturbed by a second home. The twins were inconsolable at her refusal and sent a telegram to their mother, who had already written one charming letter of invitation, and who now wrote another in which she told Sylvia of her children's bitter disappointment and begged her to come. Miss Ashley also was anxious that Sylvia should go, and told her frankly that it seemed an excellent chance to think over seriously her marriage with Philip in the autumn. Philip, now that the date of her final decision was drawing near, wished her to remain with Miss Ashley in London. His opposition was enough to make Sylvia insist upon going; so, when at the end of July the school was swept by a tornado of relatives and friends, Sylvia was swept away with the twins to Hertfordshire, and Philip was left to wait till the end of September to know whether she would marry him or not in October.

The Worsleys' home at Arbour End made an altogether different impression upon Sylvia from Markham Grange. She divined in some way that the background here was not immemorial, but that the Worsleys had created it themselves. And a perfect background it was – a very comfortable red brick house with a garden full of flowers, an orchard loaded with fruit, fields promenaded by neat cows, pigstyes inhabited by clean pigs, a shining dog-cart and a shining horse, all put together with the satisfying completeness of a picture-puzzle. Mr. Worsley was a handsome man, tall and fair with a boyish face and a quantity of clothes: Mrs. Worsley was slim and fair with a roseleaf complexion and as many clothes as her husband. The twins were even naughtier and more charming than they were at Hornton House; there was a small brother called Hercules aged six, who was as charming as his sisters and surpassed them in wickedness. The maids were trim and tolerant: the gardener was never grumpy: Hercules' governess disapproved of holiday tasks: the dogs wagged their tails at the least sound.

'I love these people,' Sylvia said to herself, when she was undressing on the first night of her stay. 'I love them. I love them. I feel at home – at home – at home!' She leapt into bed and hugged the pillow in a triumph of good-fellowship.

At Arbour End Sylvia banished the future and gave herself to the present. One seemed to have nothing to do but to amuse oneself there, and it was so easy to amuse oneself that one never grew tired of doing so. As the twins pointed out, their father was so much nicer than any other father, because whatever was suggested he always enjoyed. If it was a question of learning golf, Mr. Worsley took the keenest interest in teaching it. When Gladys drove a ball through the drawing-room window, no one was more delighted than Mr. Worley himself; he infected everybody with his pleasure; so that the gardener beamed at the notion of going to fetch the glazier from the village, and the glazier beamed when he mended the window, and the maids beamed while they watched him at work, and the dogs sat down in a loose semicircle, thumping the lawn with appreciative tails. The next day, when Hercules, who standing solemnly apart from the rest had observed all that happened on the previous occasion, threw a large stone through the mended window, there was the same scene of pleasure slightly intensified.

Mrs. Worsley flitted through the house, making every room she entered more beautiful and more gay for her presence. She had only one regret, which was that the twins were getting so big, and this not as with most mothers because it made her feel old, but because she should no more see their black legs and their tumbled hair. Sylvia once asked her how she could bear to let them go to school, and Mrs. Worsley's eyes filled with tears.

'I had to send them to school,' she whispered sadly. 'Because they *would* fall in love with the village boys, and they were getting Hertfordshire accents. Perhaps you've noticed that I myself speak with a slight Cockney accent. Do you understand, dear?'

The August days fled past and in the last week came a letter from Miss Ashley:

Murren,

August 26th, 1900.

My dear Sylvia,

I shall be back from Switzerland by September 3rd, and I shall be delighted to see you at Hornton House again. Philip nearly followed me here in order to talk about you, but I declined his company. I want you to think very seriously about your future, as no doubt you have been doing all this month. If you have the least hesitation about marrying Philip, let me advise you not to do it. I shall be glad to offer you a place at Hornton House, not as a schoolmistress, but as a kind of director of the girls' leisure time. I have grown very fond of you during this year and have admired the way in which you settled down here more than I can express. We will talk this over more fully when we meet, but I want you to know that, if you feel you ought not to marry, you have a certain amount of security for the future while you are deciding what you will ultimately do. Give my love to the twins. I shall be glad to see you again.

Your affectionate

Caroline Ashley

The effect of Miss Ashley's letter was the exact contrary of what she had probably intended: it made Sylvia feel that she was not bound to marry Philip and from the moment she was not bound that she was willing, even anxious, to marry him. The aspects of his character which she had criticized to herself vanished and left only the first impression of him, when she was absolutely free and was finding his company such a relief from the Exhibition. Another result of the letter was that by removing the shame of dependence and by providing an alternative it opened a way to discussion, for which Sylvia fixed upon Mrs. Worsley, divining that she certainly would look at her case unprejudiced by anything but her own experience.

Sylvia never pretended to herself that she should be at all influenced by advice: listening to advice from Mrs. Worsley would be like looking into a shop-window with money in one's pocket but with no intention of entering the shop to make a purchase; listening to her advice before Miss Ashley's offer would have been like looking at a shop-window without a penny in the world, a luxury of fancy to which Sylvia had never given way. So at the first opportunity Sylvia talked to Mrs. Worsley about Philip, going back for her opinion of him and feeling towards him to those first days together, and thereby giving her listener an impression that she liked him a very great deal, which was true, as Sylvia assured herself, yet not without some misgivings about her presentation of the state of affairs.

'He sounds most fascinating,' said Mrs. Worsley. 'Of course Lennie was never at all clever. I don't think he ever read a book in his life. When I met him first I was acting in burlesque, and I had to make up my mind between him and my profession; I'm so glad I chose him. But at first I was rather miserable. His parents were still alive, and though they were very kind to me, I was always an intruder and of course Lennie was dependent on them, for he was much too stupid an old darling to earn his own living. He really has nothing but his niceness. Then his parents died, and being an only son Lennie had all the money. We lived for a time in his father's house, but it became impossible. We had my poor old mother down to stay with us, and the neighbours called, as if she were a curiosity. When she didn't appear at tea, you could feel they were staying on, hoping against hope to get a glimpse of her. I expect I was sensitive and rather silly, but I was miserable. And then Lennie, who is not clever, but so nice that it always leads him to do exactly the right thing, went away suddenly and bought this house, where life has been one long dream of happiness. You've seen how utterly self-contained we are. Nobody comes to visit us very much, because when we first came here we used to hide when people called. And then the twins have always been such a joy – oh dear, I wish they would never grow up – but there's still Hercules, and you never know, there might be another baby. Oh, my dear Sylvia, I'm sure you ought to get married. And you say his parents are dead?'

'But he has a sister.'

'Oh, a sister doesn't matter. And it doesn't matter his being clever and fond of books, because you're fond of books yourself. The twins tell me you've read everything in the world and there's nothing you don't know. I'm sure you'd soon get tired of Hornton House – oh yes, I strongly advise you to get married.'

When Sylvia got back to London the memory of Arbour End rested in her thoughts like a pleasant dream of the night that one ponders in a summer dawn. She assured Miss Ashley that she was longing to marry Philip: and when she seemed to express in her reception of the announcement a kind of puzzled approval, Sylvia spoke with real enthusiasm of the marriage. Miss Ashley never knew that the real inspiration of such enthusiasm was Arbour End and not at all Philip himself: as for Sylvia, because she would by no means admit even to herself that she had taken Mrs. Worsley's advice, she passed over the advice and remarked only the signs of happiness at Arbour End.

Sylvia and Philip were married at a registry-office early in October: the honeymoon was spent in the Italian lakes, where Philip denounced the theatrical scenery, but crowned Sylvia with vine-leaves and wrote Latin poetry to her, which he translated aloud in the evenings as well as the mosquitoes would let him.

VII

Green Lanes lay midway between the market town of Galton and the large village of Newton Candover: it was a small tumbledown hamlet remote from any high road, and the confluence of four deserted byeways leading to other hamlets upon the wooded downland of which Green Lanes was the highest point. Will Hall, the family mansion of the Iredales, was quite two miles away in the direction of Newton Candover and was let for a long term of years to a rich stockbroker. Philip himself lived at The Old Farm, an Elizabethan farmhouse which he had filled with books. The only other 'gentleman' in Green Lanes was the Vicar, Mr. Dorward, with whom Philip had quarrelled. The Squire as Lay Rector drew a yearly revenue of £300, but he refused to allow the living more than £90, until the Vicar gave up his ritualistic fads to which, though he never went inside the church, he strongly objected.

Sylvia's first quarrel with Philip was over the Vicar, whom she met through her puppy's wandering into his cottage while he was at tea and refusing to come out. She might never have visited him again, if Philip had not objected, for he was very shy and eccentric; but after two more visits to annoy Philip, she began to like Mr. Dorward and her friendship with him became a standing source of irritation to her husband and a pleasure to herself that she declined to give up. Her second quarrel with Philip was over his sister Gertrude, who came down for a visit soon after they got back from Como. Gertrude having until her brother's marriage always lived at The Old Farm could not refrain from making Sylvia very much aware of this; her conversation was one long supercilious narrative of what she used to do at Green Lanes, with which were mingled fears for what might be done there in the future. Philip was quite ready to admit that his sister could be very irritating, but he thought Sylvia's demand for her complete exclusion from The Old Farm for at least a year was unreasonable.

'Well, if she comes, I shall go,' Sylvia said sullenly.

'My dear child, do remember that you're married and that you can't go and come as you like,' Philip answered. 'However, I quite see your point of view about poor Gertrude and I quite agree with you that for a time it will be wiser to keep ourselves rather strictly to ourselves.'

Why could he not have said that at first, Sylvia thought: she would have been so quickly generous if he had, but the preface about her being married had spoilt his concession. He was a curious creature this husband of hers. When they were alone, he would encourage her to be as she used to be: he would laugh with her, show the keenest interest in what she was reading, search for a morning to find some book that would please her, listen with delight to her stories of Jimmy Monkley or of her father or of Blanche, and be always in fact the sympathetic friend, never obtruding himself as lover or monitor, two aspects of him equally repugnant to Sylvia. Yet when there was the least likelihood let alone of a third person's presence, but even of a third person's hearing any roundabout gossip of her real self, Philip would shrivel her up with interminable corrections, and what was far worse try to sweeten the process by what she considered fatuous demonstrations of affection. For a time there was no great tension between them, because Sylvia's adventurous spirit was occupied by her passion for knowledge: she felt vaguely that at any time the moment might arrive when mere knowledge without experience would not be enough; at present the freedom of Philip's library was adventure enough. He was eager to assist her progress, and almost reckless in the way he spurred her into every liberty of thought, maintaining the stupidity of all conventional beliefs – moral, religious, or political. He warned her that the expression of such opinions, or, still worse, action under the influence of them would be for her or for anyone else in the present state of society quite impossible; Sylvia used to think at the time that it was only herself as his wife whom he wished to keep in check, and resented his reasons accordingly; afterwards looking back to this period, she came to the conclusion that Philip was literally a theorist, and that his fierce denunciations of all conventional opinions could never in any circumstances have gone further than quarrelling with the Vicar and getting married in a registry-office. Once when she attacked him for his cowardice she retorted by citing his marriage with her, and immediately afterwards apologized for what he characterized as 'caddishness.'

'If you had married me and been content to let me remain myself,' Sylvia said, 'you might have used that argument. But you showed you were frightened of what you'd done when you sent me to Hornton House.'

'My dear child, I wanted you to go there for your own comfort, not for mine. After all, it was only like reading a book: it gave you a certain amount of academic theory that you could not prove or disprove by experience.'

'A devil of a lot of experience I get here,' Sylvia exclaimed.

'You're still only seventeen,' Philip answered. 'The time will come.'

'It will come,' Sylvia murmured darkly.

'You're not threatening to run away from me already?' Philip asked with a smile.

'I might do anything,' she owned. 'I might poison you.'

Philip laughed heartily at this; and just then Mr. Dorward passed over the village green, which gave him an opportunity to rail at his cassock.

'It's ridiculous for a man to go about dressed up like that. Of course, nobody attends his church. I can't think why my father gave him the living. He's a ritualist, and his manners are abominable.'

'But he looks like a Roman Emperor,' said Sylvia.

Philip spluttered with indignation.

'Oh, he's Roman enough, my dear child, but an Emperor! Which Emperor!'

'I'm not sure which it is, but I think it's Nero.'

'Yes, I see what you mean,' Philip assented after a pause. 'You're amazingly observant. Yes, there is that kind of mixture of sensual strength and fineness about his face. But it's not surprising. The line between degeneracy and the "twopence coloured" type of religion is not very clearly drawn.'

It was after this conversation that in searching for a picture of Nero's head to compare with Mr. Dorward's, Sylvia came across the Satyricon of Petronius in a French translation. She read it through without skipping a word, applied it to the test of recognition, and decided that she found more satisfactorily than in any book she had yet read a distorting mirror of her life from the time she left France until she met Philip – a mirror, however, that never distorted so wildly as to preclude recognition. Having made this discovery, she announced it to him, who applauded her sense of humour and of literature, but begged her to keep it to herself: people might get a wrong idea of her: he knew what she meant and appreciated the reflection, but it was a book that generally speaking no woman would read, still less talk about, and least of all claim kinship with. It was of course an immortal work of art, humorous, witty, fantastic.

'And true,' Sylvia added.

'And no doubt true to its period and its place, which was Southern Italy in the time of Nero.'

'And true to Southern England in the time of Victoria,' Sylvia insisted. 'I don't mean that it's exactly the same,' she went on, striving almost painfully to express her thoughts. 'The same, though. I *feel* it's true: I don't *know* it's true. Oh, can't you understand?'

'I fancy you're trying to voice your æsthetic consciousness of great art that, however time may change its accessories, remains inherently changeless. Realism in fact as opposed to what is wrongly called realism. Lots of critics, Sylvia, have tried to define what is worrying you, and lots of long words have been enlisted on their behalf. A better and more ancient word for realism was "poetry"; but the word has been debased by the versifiers who call themselves poets just as painters call themselves artists: both are titles that only posterity can award. Great art is something that is made and that lives in itself: like that stuff radium, which was discovered the year before last, it eternally gives out energy without consuming itself. Radium, however, does not solve the riddle of life, and until we solve that, great art will remain undefinable. Which reminds me of a mistake that so-called believers make. I've often heard Christians maintain the truth of Christianity, because it is still alive. What nonsense! The words of Christ are still alive, because Christ Himself was a great poet, and therefore expressed humanity as perhaps no one else ever expressed humanity before. But the lying romantic, the bad poet in fact, who tickles the vain and credulous mob with miracles and theogonies, expresses nothing. It is a proof of nothing but the vitality of great art that the words of Christ can exist and continue to affect humanity notwithstanding the mountebank behaviour attributed to Him, out of which priests have manufactured a religion. It is equally surprising that Cervantes could hold his own against the romances of chivalry he tried to kill. He may have killed one mode of expression, but he did not prevent *East Lynne* from being written: yet he endures, because Don Quixote, whom he made, has life. By the way, you never got on with Don Quixote, did you?'

Sylvia shook her head.

'I think it's a failure on your part, dear Sylvia.'

'He was so stupid,' she said.

'But he realised how stupid he was before he died.'

She shrugged her shoulders.

'I can't help my bad taste, as you call it. He annoys me.'

'You think the Yanguesian carriers dealt with him in the proper way?'

'I don't remember them.'

'They beat him.'

'I think I could beat a person who annoyed me very much,' Sylvia said. 'I don't mean with sticks, of course, but with my behaviour.'

'Is that another warning?'

'Perhaps.'

'Anyway you think Petronius is good?'

She nodded her head emphatically.

'Come, you shall give a judgment on Aristophanes. I commend him to you in the same series of French translations.'

'I think Lysistrata is simply splendid,' Sylvia said a week or so later. 'And I like the Thesmos-something and the Eck-something.'

'I thought you might,' Philip laughed. 'But don't quote from them when my millionaire tenant comes to tea.'

'Don't be always harping upon the dangers of my conversation,' she exhorted.

'Mayn't I even tease you?' Philip asked in mock humility.

'I don't mind being teased, but it isn't teasing. It's serious.'

'Your sense of humour plays you tricks sometimes,' he said.

'Oh, don't talk about my sense of humour like that. My sense of humour isn't a watch that you can take out and tap and regulate and wind up and shake your head over. I hate people who talk about a sense of humour as you do. Are you so sure you have one yourself?'

'Perhaps I haven't,' Philip agreed, but by the way in which he spoke Sylvia knew that he would maintain he had a sense of humour, and that the rest of humanity had none, if it combined to contradict him. 'I always distrust people who are too confidently the possessors of one,' he added.

'You don't understand in the least what I mean,' Sylvia cried out in exasperation. 'You couldn't distrust anybody else's sense of humour, if you had one yourself.'

'That's what I said,' Philip pointed out in an aggrieved voice.

'Don't go on, you'll make me scream,' she adjured him. 'I won't talk about a sense of humour, because if there is such a thing it obviously can't be talked about.'

Lest Philip should pursue the argument, Sylvia left him and went for a long muddy walk by herself half-way to Galton. She had never before walked beyond the village of Medworth, but she was still in such a state of nervous exasperation that she continued down the hill beyond it without noticing how far it was taking her. The country on either side of the road ascended in uncultivated fields toward dense oak woods. In many of these fields were habitations with grandiose names, mostly built of corrugated iron. Sylvia thought at first that she was approaching the outskirts of Galton and pressed on to explore the town, the name of which was familiar from the rickety tradesmen's carts that jogged through Green Lanes. There was no sign of a town, however, and after walking about two miles through a landscape that recalled the pictures she had seen of primitive settlements in the Far West, she began to feel tired and turned round upon her tracks, wishing she had not come quite so far. Suddenly a rustic gate that was almost buried in the unclipped hazel hedge on one side of the road was flung open, and an elderly lady with a hooked nose and fierce bright eyes, dressed in what looked at first glance like a pair of soiled lace window-curtains, asked Sylvia with some abruptness if she had met a turkey going in her direction. Sylvia shook her head, and the elderly lady (Sylvia would have called her an old lady from her wrinkled countenance, had she not been so astonishingly vivacious in her movements) called in a high harsh voice:

'Emmie! There's a girl here coming from Galton way and *she* hasn't seen Major Kettlewell.'

In the distance a female voice answered shrilly:

'Perhaps he's crossed over to the Pluepotts!'

Sylvia explained that she had misunderstood the first enquiry, but that nobody had passed her since she turned back five minutes ago.

'We call the turkey Major Kettlewell because he looks like Major Kettlewell, but Major Kettlewell himself lives over there.'

The elderly lady indicated the other side of the road with a vague gesture and went on:

'Where can that dratted bird have got to? Major! Major! Major! Chuck – chuck – chilly – chilly – chuck – chuck,' she called.

Sylvia hoped that the real Major lived far enough away to be out of hearing.

'Never keep a turkey,' the elderly lady went on, addressing Sylvia. 'We didn't kill him for Christmas, because we'd grown fond of him, even though he is like that old ruffian of a Major. And ever since, he's gone on the wander. It's the springtime coming, I suppose.'

The elderly lady's companion had by this time reached the gate, and Sylvia saw that she was considerably younger but with the same hallmark of old-maidishness.

'Don't worry any more about the bird, Adelaide,' said the newcomer. 'It's tea-time. Depend upon it, he's crossed over to the Pluepotts. This time I really will wring his neck.'

Sylvia prepared to move along, but the first lady asked her where she was going and when she heard Green Lanes exclaimed:

'Gemini! That's beyond Medworth, isn't it? You'd better come in and have a cup of tea with us. I'm Miss Horne, and my friend here is Miss Hobart.'

Sunny Bank, as this particular tin house was named not altogether inappropriately, although it happened to be on the less sunny side of the road, was built half-way up a steepish slope of very rough ground from which enough flints had been extracted to pave a zigzag of ascending paths, and to vary the contour of the slope with a miniature mountain range of unused material without apparently smoothing the areas of proposed cultivation.

'These paths are something dreadful, Emmie,' said Miss Horne, as the three of them scrambled up through the garden. 'Never mind, we'll get the roller out of the hedge when Mr. Pluepott comes in on Wednesday. Miss Hobart nearly got carried away by the roller yesterday,' she explained to Sylvia.

A trellised porch outside the bungalow – such apparently was the correct name for these habitations – afforded a view of the opposite slope, which was sprinkled with bungalows surrounded like Sunny Bank by heaps of stones; there were also one or two more pretentious buildings of red brick and one or two stony gardens without any dwelling-place at all as yet.

'I suppose you're wondering why the name over the door isn't the same as the one on the gate? Mr. Pluepott is always going to take it out, but he never remembers to bring the paint. It's the name the man from whom we bought it gave the bungalow,' said Miss Hobart resentfully.

Sylvia read in gothic characters over the door Floral Nook, and agreed with the two ladies that Sunny Bank was much more suitable.

'For whatever else it may be, it certainly isn't damp,' Miss Horne declared. 'But, dear me, talking of names, you haven't told us yours.'

Sylvia felt shy: it was actually the first time she had been called upon to announce herself since she was married. The two ladies exclaimed on hearing she was Mrs. Iredale, and Sylvia felt that there was a kind of impropriety in her being married, when Miss Horne and Miss Hobart, who were so very much older than she, were still spinsters.

The four small rooms of which the bungalow consisted, were lined with varnished match-boarding; everything was tied up with brightly coloured bows of silk, and most of the pictures were draped with small curtains; the rooms were full of knick-knacks and shivery furniture, but not full enough to satisfy the owners' passion for prettiness, so that wherever there was a little space on the walls silk bows had been nailed about like political favours. Sylvia thought it would have been simpler to tie one wide sash of pink silk round the house and call it The Chocolate Box. Tea, though even the spoons were tied up with silk, was a varied and satisfying meal; the conversation of the two ladies was remarkably entertaining if ever it touched upon their neighbours; and when twilight warned Sylvia that she must hurry away she was sorry to leave them.

While she was making her farewells, there was a loud tap at the door, followed immediately by the entrance of a small bullet-headed man with quick black eyes.

'I've brought back your turkey, Miss Horne.'

'Oh, thank you, Mr. Pluepott. There you are, Emmie. You were right.'

At this moment the bird began to flap its wings as violently as its position head downwards would allow; nor, not being a horse, did it pay any attention to Mr. Pluepott's repeated shouts of 'Woa! Woa back, will you!'

'I think you'd better let him flap outside, Mr. Pluepott,' Miss Hobart advised.

Sylvia thought so too when she looked at the floor.

'Shall I wring its neck now or would you rather I waited till I come in on Wednesday?'

'Oh, I think we'll wait, thank you, Mr. Pluepott,' Miss Horne said. 'Perhaps you wouldn't mind shutting him up in the coop? He does wander so. Are you going into Galton?'

Mr. Pluepott replied, as he confined Major Kettlewell to his barracks, that on the contrary he was driving up to Medworth to see about some beehives for sale there; whereupon Miss Horne and Miss Hobart asked if he would mind taking Mrs. Iredale that far upon her way.

A few minutes later Sylvia on a splintery seat was jolting along beside Mr. Pluepott toward Medworth.

'Rum lot of people hereabouts,' he said by way of opening the conversation. 'Some of the rummest people it's ever been my luck to meet. I came here because my wife had to leave the Midlands. Chest was bad. I used to be a cobbler at Bedford. Since I've been here, I've become everything – carpenter, painter, decorator, gardener, mason, bee-expert, poultry-keeper, blacksmith, livery-stables, furniture-remover, house-agent, common carrier, bricklayer, dairyman, horse-breaker. The only thing I don't do now is make boots. Funny thing, and you won't believe it, but last week I had to buy myself the first pair of boots I ever bought since I was a lad of fifteen. Oh well, I like the latest better than the last, as I jokingly told my missus the other night. It made her laugh,' said Mr. Pluepott, looking at Sylvia rather anxiously: she managed to laugh too, and he seemed relieved.

'I often make jokes for my missus. She's apt to get very melancholy with her chest. But, as I was saying, the folk round here they beat the band. It just shows what advertisement will do.'

Sylvia asked why.

'Well, when I first came here – and I was one of the three first – I came because I read an advertisement in the paper: LAND FOR THE MILLION IN LOTS FROM A QUARTER OF AN ACRE. Some fellow had bought an old farm that was no use to nobody and had the idea of splitting it up into lots. Originally this was the Oak Farm Estate and belonged to St. Mary's College, Oxford. Now we call it Oaktown, the residents that is, but when we applied the other day to the Galton Rural District Council, so as we could have the name properly recognized – went in we did with the Major, half a dozen of us, as smart as a funeral – one of the wise men of Gotham, which is what I jokingly calls Galton nowadays, said he thought Tintown would be a better name. The Major got rare and angry, but his teeth slipped just as he was giving it 'em hot and strong, which is a trick they have. He nearly swallowed 'em last November, when he was taking the chair at a Conservative meeting, in an argument with a Radical about the war. They had to lead him outside and pat his back. It's a pity the old ladies can't get on with him. They fell out over black-berrying in his copse last Michaelmas. Well, the fact is the Major's a bit close, and I think he meant to sell the blackberries. He's put up a notice now *Beware of Dangerous Explosives*, though there's nothing more dangerous than a broken air-gun in the whole house. Miss Horne was very bitter about it, oh, very bitter she was. Said she always knew the Major was a guy, and he only wanted to put gunpowder in his boots to give the boys a rare set out on the Fifth.'

'How did Miss Horne and Miss Hobart come here?' Sylvia asked.

'Advertisement. They lived somewhere near London, I believe; came into a bit of money, I've heard, and thought they'd settle in the country. I give them a morning a week on Wednesdays. The man they bought it off had been a tax-collector somewhere in the West Indies. He swindled them properly, but they were sorry for him because he had a floating kidney – floating in alcohol, I should think, by the amount he drank. But they won't hear a word against him even now. He's living in Galton, and they send him cabbages every week which he gives to his rabbits when he's sober and throws at his house-keeper when he's drunk. Sunny Bank! I'm glad it's not my bank. As I jokingly said to my missus, I should soon be stony. Ah, well, there's all sorts here and that's a fact,' Mr. Pluepott continued with a pensive flick at his pony. 'That man over there, for instance,' he pointed with his whip through the gathering darkness to a particularly small tin cottage. 'He used to play the trombone in a theatre, till he played his inside out; now he thinks he's going to make a fortune growing early tomatoes for Covent Garden market. You get him with a pencil in his hand of an evening and you'd think about borrowing money from him next year; but when you see him next morning trying to cover a five by four packing-case with a broken sashlight, you'd be more afraid of his trying to borrow from you.'

With such conversation did Mr. Pluepott beguile the way to Medworth, and when he heard that Sylvia intended to walk in the dusk to Green Lanes he insisted on driving her the extra two miles.

'The hives won't fly away,' he said cheerfully, 'and I like to make a good job of a thing. Well, now you've found your way to Oaktown, I hope you'll visit us again. Mrs. Pluepott will be very glad to see you drop in for a cup of tea any day, and if you've got any comical reading matter, she'd be glad to borrow from you; for her chest does make her very melancholy and, being accustomed to having me always about the house when I was cobbling, she doesn't seem to get used to being alone. Only the other day she said if she'd known I was going to turn into a Buffalo Bill she'd rather have stayed in Bedford. "Land for the millions," she said. "I reckon you'd call it Land for the millions, if you had to sweep the house clean of the mud you bring into it." Well, good night to you. Very glad I was able to oblige, I'm sure.'

Philip was relieved when Sylvia got back: she had never been out for so long before, and she teased him about the running away that he had evidently imagined. She felt in a good humour after her expedition and was glad to be back in this dignified and ancient house with its books and lamplight and not a silken bow anywhere to be seen.

'So you've been down to that abomination of tin houses? It's an absolute blot on the countryside. I don't recommend too close an acquaintanceship. I'm told it's inhabited by an appalling set of rascals. Poor Melville who owns the land all round says he can't keep a hare.'

Sylvia said the people seemed rather amusing and was not at all inclined to accept Philip's condemnation of them: he surely did not suggest that Miss Horne and Miss Hobart, for instance, were poachers?

'My dear child, people who come and live in a place like the Oak Farm Estate – Oaktown as they have the impudence to call it – are there for no good. They've either done something discreditable in town or they hope to do something discreditable in the country. Oh yes, I've heard all about our neighbours. There's a ridiculous fellow who calls himself a Major – I believe he used to be in the volunteers – and can't understand why he's not made a magistrate. I'm told he's the little tin god of Tintown. No, no, I prefer even your friendship with our Vicar. Don't be cross with me, Sylvia, for laughing at your new friends, but you mustn't take them too seriously. I shall have finished the text I'm working on this month, and we'll go up to London for a bit, shall we? I'm afraid you're getting dull down here.'

The spring wore away, but the text showed no signs of being finished: Sylvia suggested that she might invite Gladys and Enid Worsley to stay with her, but Philip begged her to postpone the invitation while he was working and thought in any case it would be better to have them down in summer. Sylvia went to Oaktown once or twice, but said nothing about it to Philip, because from a sort of charitableness she did not want him to diminish himself further in her eyes by airing his prejudices with a complacency that seemed to increase all the time they stayed in the country.

One day at the end of April, Miss Horne and Miss Hobart announced they had bought a governess-car and a pony, built a stable, and intended to celebrate their first drive by calling on Sylvia at Green Lanes. Mr. Pluepott had promised, even if it should not be on a Wednesday, to superintend the first expedition and give his opinion of the boy whom it was proposed to employ as coachman. The boy in question, whom Mr. Pluepott called Jehuselah whether from an attempt to combine a satirical expression of his driving and his age or from a too slight acquaintance with Biblical personalities was uncertain, was known as Ernie to Miss Horne and Miss Hobart when he was quick and good, but as Ernest when he was slow and bad: his real name all the time was Herbert.

'Good heavens,' Philip ejaculated, when he beheld the governess-car from his window. 'Who on earth is this?'

'Friends of mine,' said Sylvia. 'Miss Horne and Miss Hobart. I told you about them.'

'But they're getting out,' Philip gasped in horror. 'They're coming here.'

'I know,' Sylvia said. 'I hope there's plenty for tea. They always give me the most enormous teas,' and without waiting for any more of Philip's protests, she hurried downstairs and out into the road to welcome the two ladies. They were both of them dressed in pigeon's-throat silk under more lace even than usual, and they arrived in a state of enthusiasm over Ernie's driving and thankfulness for the company of Mr. Pluepott, who also was extremely pleased with the whole turn-out.

'A baby in arms couldn't have handled that pony more carefully,' he declared, looking at Ernie with as much pride as if he had begotten him.

'We're so looking forward to meeting Mr. Iredale,' said Miss Horne.

'We hear he's a great scholar,' said Miss Hobart.

Sylvia took them into the dining-room, where she was glad to see that a gigantic tea had been prepared – a match even for the most profuse of Sunny Bank's.

Then she went upstairs to fetch Philip, who flatly refused to come down.

'You must come,' Sylvia urged. 'I'll never forgive you if you don't.'

'My dearest Sylvia, I really cannot entertain the eccentricities of Tintown here. You invited them. You must look after them. I'm busy.'

'Are you coming?' Sylvia asked, biting her lips.

'No I really can't. It's absurd. I don't want this kind of people here. Besides I must work.'

'You shan't work,' Sylvia cried in a fury, and she swept all his books and papers on the floor.

'I certainly shan't come now,' he said in the prim voice that was so maddening.

'Did you mean to come before I upset your books?'

'Yes, I probably should have come,' he answered.

'All right. I'm sorry. I'll pick everything up,' and she plunged down on the floor. 'There you are,' she said when everything was put back in its place. 'Now will you come?'

'No, my dear. I told you I wouldn't after you upset my things.'

'Philip,' she cried, her eyes bright with rage. 'You're making me begin to hate you sometimes.'

Then she left him and went back to her guests, to whom she explained that her husband had a headache and was lying down. The ladies were disappointed, but consoled themselves by recommending a number of remedies, which Miss Horne insisted that Sylvia should write down. When tea was finished, Miss Hobart said that their first visit to Green Lanes had been most enjoyable, and that there was only one thing they should like to do before going home, which would be to visit the church. Sylvia jumped at an excuse for not showing them over the house, and they set out immediately to walk through the garden to the little church that stood in a graveyard grass-grown like the green lanes of the hamlet whose dead were buried there. The sun was westering, and in the golden air they lowered their voices for a thrush that was singing his vespers upon a mouldering wooden cross.

'Nobody ever comes here,' Sylvia murmured. 'Hardly anybody comes to church ever. The people don't like Mr. Dorward's services. They say he can't be heard.'

Suddenly the Vicar himself appeared and seemed greatly pleased to see Sylvia and her visitors: she felt a little guilty, because, though she was great friends with Mr. Dorward, she had never been inside the church, nor had he ever hinted he would like her to come. It would seem so unkind for her to come like this for the first time with strangers, as if the church which she knew he deeply loved were nothing but a tea-time entertainment. There was no trace of reproachfulness in his manner, as he showed

Miss Horne and Miss Hobart the vestments and a little image of the Virgin in peach-blow glaze which he moved caressingly into the sunlight, as a child might fondle reverently a favourite doll. He spoke of his plans for restoration and unrolled the design of a famous architect, adding with a smile for Sylvia that the Lay Rector disapproved of it thoroughly. They left him arranging the candlesticks on the altar, a half-pathetic, half-humorous figure that seemed to be playing a solitary game.

'And you say nobody goes to his church,' Miss Horne exclaimed. 'But he's most polite and charming.'

'Scarcely anybody goes,' Sylvia said.

'Emmie,' said Miss Horne, standing upright and flashing forth an eagle's glance. '*We* will attend his service.'

'That is a very good idea of yours, Adelaide,' Miss Hobart replied.

Then they mounted the governess-car with much determination, and with friendly waves of the hand to Sylvia set out back to Oaktown.

When Miss Horne and Miss Hobart had left, Sylvia went upstairs to have it out with Philip. At this rate there would very soon be a crisis in their married life. She was a little disconcerted by his getting up the moment she entered his room and coming to meet her with an apology.

'Dearest Sylvia, you can call me what you will: I shall deserve the worst. I can't understand my behaviour this afternoon; I think I must have been working so hard that my nerves are hopelessly jangled. I very nearly followed you into the churchyard to make myself most humbly pleasant, but I saw Dorward go round almost immediately afterwards, and I could not have met him in the mood I was in without being unpardonably rude.'

He waited for her with an arm stretched out in reconciliation, but Sylvia hesitated.

'It's all very well to hurt my feelings like that, because you happened to be feeling in a bad temper,' she said, 'and then think you've only got to make a pleasant little speech to put everything right again. Besides, it isn't only to-day: it's day after day since we've been married. I feel like Gulliver when he was being tied up by the Lilliputians: I can't find any one big rope that's destroying my freedom, but somehow or other my freedom is being destroyed. Did you marry me casually, as people buy birds, to put me in a cage?'

'My dear, I married you because I loved you. You know I fought against the idea of marrying you for a long time, but I loved you too much.'

'Are you afraid of my loyalty?' she demanded. 'Do you think I go to Oaktown to be made love to?'

'Sylvia!' he protested.

'I go there because I'm bored, bored, endlessly, hopelessly, paralyzingly bored. It's my own fault. I never ought to have married you. I can't think why I did, but at least it wasn't for any mercenary reason. You're not to believe that. Philip, I do like you, but why will you always upset me?'

He thought for a moment and asked her presently what greater freedom she wanted, what kind of freedom.

'That's it,' she went on. 'I told you I couldn't find any one big rope that bound me. There isn't a single thread I can't snap with perfect ease, but it's the multitude of insignificant little threads that almost choke me.'

'You told me you thought you would like to live in the country,' he reminded her.

'I do, but Philip, do remember that I really am still a child. I've got a deep voice and I can talk like a professor, but I'm still a hopeless kid. I oughtn't to have to tell you this. You ought to see it for yourself, if you love me.'

'Dearest Sylvia, I'm always telling you how young you are, and there's nothing that annoys you more,' he said.

'Oh, Philip, Philip, you really are pathetic. When did you ever meet a young person who liked to have her youth called attention to? You're so remote from beginning to understand how to manage me, and I'm still manageable. Very soon I shan't be, though; and there'll be such a dismal smash up.'

'If you'd only explain exactly,' he began; but she interrupted him at once.

'My dear man, if I explain and you take notes and consult them for your future behaviour to me, do you think that's going to please me? It can all be said in two words. I'm human. For heaven's sake be human yourself.'

'Look here, let's go away for a spell,' said Philip brightly.

'The cat's miaowing: let's open the door. No, seriously, I think I should like to go away from here for a while.'

'By yourself?' he asked in a frightened voice.

'Oh no, not by myself. I'm perfectly content with you. Only don't suggest the Italian Lakes and try to revive the early sweets of our eight months of married life. Don't let's have a sentimental rebuilding. It will be so much more practical to build up something quite new.'

Philip really seemed to have been shaken by this conversation: Sylvia knew he had not finished his text, but he put everything aside in order not to keep her waiting; and before May was half-way through, they had reached the island of Sirene. Here they stayed two months in a crumbling pension upon the cliff's edge until Sylvia was sun-dried without and within; she was enthralled by the evidences of imperial Rome, and her only regret was that she did not meet an eccentric Englishman who was reputed to have found when digging a cistern at least one of the lost books of Elephantis, which he read in olive groves by the light of the moon. However, she met several other eccentrics of different nationalities and was pleased to find that Philip's humanism was with Sirene as a background strong enough to lend him an appearance of humanity. They planned like all other visitors to Sirene to build a big villa there; they listened like all other visitors to the Italian and foreign inhabitants' depreciation of every villa but the one in which they lived, either because they liked it or because they wanted to let it or because they wished newcomers to fall into snares laid for themselves when they were newcomers.

At last they tore themselves from all these dreams and schemes, chiefly because Sylvia had accepted an invitation to stay at Arbour End. They lingered for a while at Naples on the way home, where Sylvia looked about her with Petronian eyes, so much so indeed that a guide mistook what was merely academic curiosity for something more practical: it cost Philip fifty liras and nearly all the Italian he knew to get rid of the pertinacious and ingenious fellow.

Arbour End had not changed at all in a year; Sylvia when she thought of Green Lanes laughed a little bitterly at herself (but not so bitterly as she would have laughed before the benevolent sunshine of Sirene) for ever supposing that she and Philip could create anything like it. Gladys and Enid, though they were now fifteen, had not yet lengthened their frocks; their mother could not bring herself to contemplate the disappearance of those slim black legs.

'But we shall have to next term,' Gladys said, 'because Miss Ashley's written home about them.'

'And that stuck-up thing Gwendyr Jones said they were positively disgusting,' Enid went on.

'Yes,' added Gladys, 'and I told her they weren't half as disgusting as her ankles. And they aren't, are they, Sylvia?'

'Some of the girls call her Marrow-bones,' said Enid.

Sylvia would have preferred to avoid any intimate talks with Mrs. Worsley, but it was scarcely to be expected that she would succeed, and one night, looking ridiculously young with her fair hair hanging down her back, she came to Sylvia's bedroom and, sitting down at the end of her bed, began:

'Well, are you glad you got married?'

At any rate, Sylvia thought, she had the tact not to ask if she was glad she had taken her advice.

'I'm not so sorry I was,' Sylvia told her.

'Ah, didn't I warn you against the first year? You'll see that I was right.'

'But I was not sorry in the way you prophesied. I've never had any bothers with the county. Philip's sister was rather a bore, always wondering about his clothes for the year after next; but we made a treaty, and she's been excluded from The Old Farm – wait a bit, only till next October. By Jove! I say, the treaty'll have to be renewed. I don't believe even memories of Sirene would enable me to deal with Gertrude this winter. No, what worries me most in marriage is not other people, but our two selves. I hate writing Sylvia Iredale instead of Sylvia Scarlett. Quite unreasonable of me, but most worries are unreasonable. I don't want to be owned. I'm a book to Philip: he bought me for my binding and never intended to read me, even if he could: I don't mean to say I was beautiful, but I was what an American girl at Hornton House used to call cunning: the pattern was unusual, and he couldn't resist it. But now that he's bought me, he expects me to stay quite happily on a shelf in a glass-case; one day he may perhaps try to read me, but at present as long as I'm taken out and dusted – our holiday at Sirene was a dusting – he thinks that's enough. But the worm that flies in the heart of the storm has got in, Victoria, and is making a much more unusual pattern across my inside – I say, I think it's about time to drop this metaphor, don't you?'

'I don't think I quite understand all you're saying,' said Victoria Worsley.

Sylvia brought her hand from beneath the bed-clothes and took her friend's.

'Does it matter?'

'Oh, but I like to understand what people are saying,' Mrs. Worsley insisted. 'That's why we never go abroad for our holidays. But, Sylvia, about being owned, which is where I stopped understanding: Lennie doesn't own me.'

'No, you own *him*, but I don't own Philip.'

'I expect you will, my dear, after you've been married a little longer.'

'You think I shall acquire him in monthly instalments. I should find at the end he cost too much in repairs, like Fred Organ.'

'Who's he?'

'Hube's brother, the cabman. Don't you remember?'

'Oh, of course, how silly of me. I thought it might be an Italian you met at Sirene. You've made me feel quite sad, Sylvia. I always want

149

everybody to be happy,' she sighed. 'I am happy – perfectly happy – in spite of being married.'

'Nobody's happy because of being married,' Sylvia enunciated rather sententiously.

'What nonsense you talk, and you're only just eighteen.'

'That's why I talk nonsense,' Sylvia said, 'but all the same it's very true nonsense. You and Lennie couldn't have ever been anything but happy.'

'Darling Lennie, I think it must be because he's so stupid. I wonder if he's smoking in bed. He always does if I leave him to go and talk to anybody. Good night, dear.'

Sylvia returned to her book, wondering more than ever how she could have supposed a year ago that she could follow Victoria Worsley along the pathway of her simple and happy life.

The whole family from Arbour End came to London for the ten days before term began, and Sylvia stayed with them at an hotel. Gladys and Enid had to get their new frocks, and certain gaps in Hercules' education had to be filled up, such as visiting the Zoo and the Tower of London and the Great Wheel at Earl's Court. Sylvia and the twins searched in vain for the Hall of a Thousand and One Marvels, but they found Mabel selling Turkish-delight by herself at a small stall in another part of the Exhibition. Sylvia thought the best way of showing her penitence for the way she had treated her was to buy as much Turkish-delight as could possibly be carried away, since she probably received a percentage on the takings. Mabel seemed to bear no resentment, but she was rather shy, because she mistook the twins for Sylvia's sisters-in-law and therefore avoided the only topic upon which she could talk freely, which was men. They left the florid and accommodating creature with a callow youth who was leaning familiarly across the counter and smacking with a cane his banana-coloured boots: then they ate as much Turkish-delight as they could and divided the rest among some ducks and the Kaffirs in the kraal.

Sylvia also visited Hornton House and explained to Miss Ashley why she had demanded the banishment of Gertrude from Green Lanes.

'Poor Gertrude, she was very much upset,' Miss Ashley said.

Sylvia, softened by the memories of a so happy year that her old school evoked, made up her mind not to carry on the war against Gertrude. She felt, too, a greater charity toward Philip who, after all, had been the cause of her being given that so happy year, and she went back to Hampshire with the firm intention of encouraging this new mood that the last four months had created in her. Philip was waiting on the platform and was so glad to see her again that he drove even more absent-mindedly than usual, until she took the reins from him and whipped up the horse with a quite positive anticipation of home.

Sylvia learned from Philip that the visit of Miss Horne and Miss Hobart had influenced other lives than their own, for it seemed that Miss Horne's announcement of their attendance in future at Mr. Dorward's empty church had been fully carried out. Not a Sunday passed without their driving up in the governess-car to Mass, so Philip told her with a wry face for the word; what was more, they stayed to lunch with the Vicar, presided at the Sunday school and attended the evening service, which had been put forward half an hour to suit their supper.

'They absolutely rule Green Lanes ecclesiastically,' Philip said. 'And some of the mercenary bumpkins and boobies round here have taken to going to church for what they can get out of the two old ladies. I'm glad to say, however, that the farmers and their families haven't come round yet.'

Sylvia said she was glad for Mr. Dorward's sake, and she wondered why Philip made such a fuss about the form of a service in the reality of which, whatever way it was presented, he had no belief.

'I suppose you're right,' he agreed. 'Perhaps what I'm really afraid of is that our fanatical Vicar will really convert the parish to his childish religion. Upon my soul, I believe Miss Horne has her eye upon me. I know she's been holding forth upon my iniquitous position as Lay Rector, and these confounded Radicals will snatch hold of anything to create prejudice against land-owners.'

'Why don't you make friends with Mr. Dorward?' Sylvia suggested. 'You could surely put aside your religious differences and talk about the classics.'

'I daresay I'm bigoted in my own way,' Philip answered. 'But I can't stand a priest, just as some people can't stand cats or snakes. It's a positively physical repulsion that I can't get over. No, I'm afraid I must leave Dorward to you, Sylvia. I don't think there's much danger of your falling a victim to man-millinery. It'll take all your strength of mind, however, to resist the malice of these two old witches, and I wager you'll be excommunicated from the society of Tintown in next to no time.'

Sylvia found that Philip had by no means magnified the activities of Miss Horne and Miss Hobart, and for the first time on a Sunday morning at Green Lanes she saw a thin black stream of worshippers flow past the windows of The Old Farm after service; it was more than curiosity could bear, and without saying a word to anybody she attended the evening service herself. The church was very small, and her entrance would have attracted much more attention than it did, if Ernie, who was holding the thurible for Mr. Dorward to put in the incense, had not given at that moment a mighty sneeze, scattering incense and charcoal upon the altar steps and frightening the woman at the harmonium into a violent discord, from which the choir was rescued by Miss Horne's unmoved and harsh soprano that positively twisted back the craning necks of the congregation into their accustomed apathy. Sylvia wondered whether fear, conversion, or extra wages had induced Ernie to put on that romantic costume which gave him the appearance of a rustic table covered with a tea-cloth, as he waited while the priest tried to evoke a few threads of smoke from the ruin caused by his sneeze. Sylvia was so much occupied in watching Ernie that she did not notice the rest of the congregation had sat down. Mr. Dorward must have seen her, for he had thrown off the heavy vestment he was wearing and was advancing apparently to say how d'ye do. No, he seemed to think better of it, and had turned aside to read from a large book; but what he read neither Sylvia nor the congregation had any idea. She decided that all this standing up and kneeling and sitting down again was too confusing for a novice, and during the rest of the service she remained seated, which was at once the most comfortable and least conspicuous attitude. Sylvia had intended to slip out before the service was over, because she did not want Miss Horne and Miss Hobart to exult over her imaginary conversion; but the finale came sooner than she expected in a fierce hymnal outburst during which Mr. Dorward hurriedly divested himself and reached the entrance. Miss Horne had scarcely thumped the last beat on the choir-boy's head in front of her and the echoes of the last amen had scarcely died away, before the female sexton, an old woman called Cassandra Batt, was turning out the oil-lamps and the little congregation had gathered round the Vicar by the west door to hear Miss Horne's estimate of its behaviour. There was no chance for Sylvia to escape.

'Ernest,' said Miss Horne. 'What did you sneeze for during the Magnificat? Father Dorward never got through with censing the altar, you bad boy.'

'The stoff got all op me nose,' said Ernie. 'Oi couldn't help meself.'

'Next time you want to sneeze,' said Miss Hobart kindly, 'press your top lip below the nose, and you'll keep it back.'

'I got too moch to do,' Ernie muttered, 'and too moch to think on.'

'Jane Frost,' said Miss Horne, quickly turning the direction of her attack, 'you must practise all this week. Suppose Father Dorward gets a new organ? You wouldn't like not to be allowed to play on it. Some of your notes to-night weren't like a musical instrument at all. The Nunc Dimittis was more like water running out of a bath. *Lord, now lettest thou thy servant depart in peace* are the words, not in pieces, which was what it sounded like the way you played it.'

Miss Jane Frost, a daughter of the woman who kept the Green Lanes shop, blushed as deeply as her anæmia would let her, and promised she would do better next week.

'That's right, Jane,' said Miss Hobart, whose part seemed to be the consolation of Miss Horne's victims. 'I daresay the pedal is a bit obstinate.'

'Oh, it's turble obstinate,' proclaimed Cassandra the sexton, who having extinguished all the lamps now elbowed her way through the clustered congregation, a lighted taper in her hand. 'I jumped on 'un once or twice this morning to make 'un a bit easier like, but a' groaned at me like a wicked old toad. It's ile that 'a wants.'

The congregation, on which a good deal of grease was being scattered by Cassandra's taper in her excitement, hastened to support her diagnosis:

'Oh, yass, yass, 'tis ile that 'a wants.'

'I will bring a bottle of oil up during the week,' Miss Horne proclaimed. 'Good night, everybody, and remember to be punctual next Sunday.'

The congregation murmured its good night, and Sylvia, to whom it probably owed such a speedy dismissal, was warmly greeted by Miss Horne.

'So glad you've come, Mrs. Iredale, though I wish you'd brought the Lay Rector. Lay Rector indeed! Sakes alive, what will they invent next?'

'Yes, we're so glad you've come, dear,' Miss Hobart added.

Mr. Dorward came up in his funny quick way; when they were all walking across the churchyard, he whispered to Sylvia in his funny quick voice:

'Church fowls, church fowls, you know! Mustn't discourage them. Pious fowls! Godly fowls! An example for the parish. Better attendance lately.'

Then he caught up the two ladies and helped them into the vehicle, wishing them a pleasant drive and promising a nearly full moon shortly after Medworth very much as if the moon was really made of cheese and would be eaten for supper by Miss Horne and Miss Hobart.

When Sylvia got back to The Old Farm she amused Philip so much by her account of the service that he forgot to be angry with her for doing what at first he maintained put him in a false position.

All that autumn and winter, Miss Horne and Miss Hobart wrestled with Satan for the souls of the hamlet; incidentally they wrestled with him for Sylvia's soul, but she scratched the event by ceasing to appear at all in church, and intercourse between them became less frequent: the friends of Miss Horne and Miss Hobart had to be all or nothing, and not the least divergence of belief or opinion, manners or policy was tolerated by these two bigoted old ladies. The congregation notwithstanding their efforts remained stationary, much to Philip's satisfaction.

'The truth is,' he said, 'that the measure of their power is the pocket. Every scamp in the parish who thinks it will pay him to go to church is going to church already. The others don't go at all or walk over to Medworth.'

Her contemplation of the progress of religion in Green Lanes which, however much she affected to laugh at it, could not help interesting Sylvia on account of her eccentric friend the Vicar, was temporarily interrupted by a visit from Gertrude Iredale. Remembering what Miss Ashley had told her, Sylvia had insisted upon Philip's asking his sister to stay, and he had obviously been touched by her suggestion. Gertrude perhaps had also taken some advice from Miss Ashley, for she was certainly less inclined to wonder what her brother would do about his clothes the year after next. Yet she could not quite keep to herself her criticism of the housewifery at The Old Farm, a simple business in Sylvia's eyes, which consisted of letting the cook do exactly as she liked, with what she decided were very satisfactory results.

'But it's so extravagant,' Gertrude objected.

'Well, Philip doesn't grumble. We can afford to pay a little extra every week to have the house comfortably run.'

'But the principle is so bad,' Gertrude insisted.

'Oh, principle,' said Sylvia in an airy way, which must have been galling to her sister-in-law. 'I don't believe in principles. Principles are only excuses for what we want to think or what we want to do.'

'Don't you believe in abstract morality?' Gertrude asked, taking off her glasses and gazing with weak and earnest eyes at Sylvia.

'I don't believe in anything abstract,' Sylvia replied.

'How strange,' the other murmured. 'Goodness me, if I didn't believe in abstract morality I don't know where I should be – or what I should do.'

Sylvia regarded the potential sinner with amused curiosity.

'Do tell me what you might do,' she begged. 'Would you live with a man without marrying him?'

'Please don't be coarse,' said Gertrude. 'I don't like it.'

'I could put it much more coarsely,' Sylvia said with a laugh. 'Would you—?'

'Sylvia!' Gertrude whistled through her teeth in an agony of apprehensive modesty. 'I entreat you not to continue.'

'There you are,' said Sylvia. 'That shows what rubbish all your scruples are. You're shocked at what you thought I was going to say. Therefore you ought to be shocked at yourself. As a matter of fact I was going to ask if you would marry a man without loving him.'

'If I were to marry,' Gertrude said primly, 'I should certainly want to love my husband.'

'Yes, but what do you understand by love? Do you mean by love the emotion that makes people go mad to possess—'

Gertrude rose from her chair.

'Sylvia, the whole conversation is becoming extremely unpleasant. I must ask you either to stop or to let me go out of the room.'

'You needn't be afraid of any personal revelations,' Sylvia assured her. 'I've never been in love that way. I only wanted to find out if you had been and ask you about it.'

'Never,' said Gertrude decidedly. 'I've certainly never been in love like that, and I hope I never shall.'

'I think you're quite safe. And I'm beginning to think I'm quite safe too,' Sylvia added. 'However, if you won't discuss abstract morality in an abstract way, you mustn't expect me to do so, and the problem of house-keeping returns to the domain of practical morality, where principles don't count.'

Sylvia decided after this conversation to accept Gertrude as a joke, and she ceased to be irritated by her any longer, though her sister-in-law stayed from Christmas till the end of February. In one way her presence was of positive utility, because Philip, who was very much on the look-out for criticism of his married life, was careful not to find fault with Sylvia while she remained at Green Lanes: it also acted as a stimulus to Sylvia herself, who used her like a grindstone on which to sharpen her wits. Another advantage from Gertrude's visit was that Philip was able to finish his text, thanks to her industrious docketing and indexing and generally fussing about in his study: therefore when Sylvia proposed that the twins should spend their Easter holidays at The Old Farm, he had no objection to offer.

The prospect of the twins' visit kept Sylvia at the peak of pleasurable expectation throughout the month of March, and when at last on a budding morn in early April she drove through sky-enchanted puddles to meet them, she sang for the first time in months about the raggle-taggle gipsies, and reached the railway station fully half an hour before the train was due. Nobody got out but the twins; yet they laughed and talked so much, the three of them, in the first triumph of meeting that several passengers thought the wayside station must be more important that it was, and asked anxiously if this was Galton.

Gladys and Enid had grown a good deal in six months, and now with their lengthened frocks and tied-back hair they looked perhaps older than sixteen; their faces, however, had not grown longer with their frocks, and they themselves were as full of spirits as formerly; Sylvia found that, while they still charmed her as of old with that quality of demanding to be loved for the sheer grace of their youth, they were now capable of giving her the intimate friendship she so greatly desired.

'You darlings,' she cried. 'You're like champagne-cup in two beautiful crystal glasses with rose-leaves floating about on top.'

The twins with all the zest in their own beauty that is the prerogative of a youth unhampered by parental jealousy frankly loved to be admired; Sylvia's admiration never made them self-conscious, because it seemed a natural expression of affection. Their attitude towards Philip was entirely free from any conventional respect; as Sylvia's husband he was candidate for all the love they had for her, but when they found that Philip treated them as Sylvia's toys they withheld the honour of election and began to criticize him; when he seemed shocked at their criticism they began to tease him, explaining to Sylvia that he had obviously never been teased in his life. Philip for his part found them precocious and vain, which annoyed Sylvia and led to her seeking diversions and entertainment for the twins' holidays outside The Old Farm. As a matter of fact she had no need to search far, because they both took a great fancy to Mr. Dorward, who turned out to have an altogether unusual gift for drawing nonsensical pictures which were almost as funny as his own behaviour, that behaviour which irritated so many more people than it amused.

The twins teased Mr. Dorward a good deal about his love affair with Miss Horne and Miss Hobart, and though this teasing may only have coincided with Mr. Dorward's previous conviction that the two ladies were managing him and his parish rather too much for his dignity and certainly too much for his independence, there was no doubt that the quarrel between them was prepared during the time that Gladys and Enid were staying at Green Lanes; indeed Gladys thought she could name the actual afternoon.

Sylvia's intercourse with Miss Horne and Miss Hobart was still friendly enough to necessitate an early visit to Sunny Bank to present the twins. The two ladies were very fond of what they called 'young people,' and at first they were enraptured by Gladys and Enid, particularly when they played some absurd schoolgirls' trick upon Major Kettlewell. Sylvia too had by her tales of the island of Sirene inspired them with a longing to go there: they liked nothing better than to make her describe the various houses and villas that were for sale or to let, in every one of which in turn Miss Horne and Miss Hobart saw themselves installed.

On the particular afternoon from which Sylvia dated the preparation of the quarrel, they were all at tea with Mr. Dorward in his cottage. The conversation came round to Sirene, and Sylvia told how she had always thought that the Vicar resembled a Roman Emperor. Was it Nero? He was perhaps flattered by the comparison, notwithstanding the ladies' loud exclamations of dissent, and was anxious to test the likeness from a volume of engraved heads which he produced. With Gladys sitting on one arm of his chair and Enid on the other, the pages were turned over slowly to allow time for a careful examination of each head, which involved a good deal of attention to Mr. Dorward's own. In the end Nero was ruled out, and a more obscure Emperor was hailed as his prototype, after which the twins rushed out into the garden and gathered strands of ivy to encircle his imperial brow; Miss Horne and Miss Hobart, who had taken no part in the discussion, left immediately after the coronation, and though it was a perfectly fine evening, they announced as they got into their vehicle that it looked very much like rain.

Next Sunday the ladies came to church as usual, but Mr. Dorward kept them waiting half an hour for lunch while he showed the twins his ornaments and vestments, which they looked at solemnly as a penance for having spent most of the service with their handkerchiefs in their mouths. What Miss Horne and Miss Hobart said at lunch Sylvia never found out, but they drove away before Sunday school and never came back to Green Lanes, either on that Sunday or on any Sunday afterwards.

All that Mr. Dorward would say about the incident was:

'Church fowls! Chaste fowls! Chaste and holy, but tiresome. The Vicar mustn't be managed. Doesn't like it. Gets frightened. Felt remote at lunch. That was all. Would keep on talking. Got bored and more remote. Vicar got so remote that he had to finish his lunch under the table.'

'Oh, no, you didn't really?' cried the twins in an ecstasy of pleasure. 'You didn't really get under the table, Mr. Dorward?'

'Of course, of course, of course. Vicar always speaks the truth. Delicious lunch.'

Sylvia had to tell Philip about this absurd incident, but he would only say that the man was evidently a buffoon in private as well as in public.

'But, Philip, don't you think it's a glorious picture? We laughed till we were tired.'

'Gladys and Enid laugh very easily,' he answered. 'Personally I see nothing funny in a man, especially a clergyman, behaving like a clown.'

'Oh, Philip, you're impossible,' Sylvia cried.

'Thanks,' he said dryly. 'I've noticed that ever since the arrival of our young guests you've found more to complain of in my personality even than formerly.'

'Young guests!' Sylvia echoed scornfully. 'Who would think to hear you talk now that you married a child? Really you're incomprehensible.'

'Impossible! Incomprehensible! In fact thoroughly negative,' Philip said.

Sylvia shrugged her shoulders and left him.

The twins went back to school at the beginning of May, and Sylvia, who missed them very much, had to fall back on Mr. Dorward to remind her of their jolly company. Their intercourse, which the twins had established upon a certain plane, continued now upon the same plane. Life had to be regarded as Alice saw it in Wonderland or Through the Looking-glass. Sylvia remembered with irony that it was Philip who first introduced her to those two books; she decided he had only liked them because it was correct to like them. Mr. Dorward, however, actually was somebody in that fantastic world, not like anybody Alice met there, but another inhabitant whom she just happened to miss.

To whom else but Mr. Dorward could have occurred that ludicrous adventure when he was staying with a brother priest in a remote part of Devonshire?

'I always heard he was a little odd. However, we had dinner together in the kitchen. He only dined in the drawing-room on Thursdays.'

'When did he dine in the dining-room?' Sylvia asked.

'Never. There wasn't a dining-room. There were a lot of rooms that were going to be the dining-room, but it was never decided which. And that cast a gloom over the whole house. My host behaved in the most evangelical way at dinner and only once threw the salad at the cook. After dinner we sat comfortably before the kitchen fire and discussed the Mozarabic rite and why yellow was no longer a liturgical colour for confessors. At half-past eleven my host suggested it was time to go to bed. He showed me upstairs to a nice bedroom and said good night, advising me to lock the door. I locked the door, undressed, said my prayers and got into bed. I was just dozing off when I heard a loud tap at the door. I felt rather frightened. Rather frightened I felt. But I went to the door and opened it. Outside in the passage was my host in his nightgown with a candlestick.

' "Past twelve o'clock," he shouted. "Time to change beds!" and before I knew where I was he had rushed past me and shut me out into the passage."

'Did you change beds?'

'There wasn't another bed in the house. I had to sleep in one of the rooms that might one day be a dining-room, and the next morning a Rural Dean arrived, which drove me away.'

Gradually from underneath what Philip called 'a mass of affectation,' but what Sylvia divined as an armour assumed against the unsympathetic majority by a shy, sensitive, and lovable spirit, there emerged for her the reality of Mr. Dorward. She began to apprehend his faith, which was as simple as a little child's; she began to grasp also that he was impelled to guard against the jeers of unbelievers what he held to be most holy by diverting towards his own eccentricity the world's mockery. He was a man of the deepest humility who considered himself incapable of pros-elytizing. Sylvia used to put before him sometimes the point of view of the outside world and try to show how he could avoid criticism and gain adherents. He used always to reply that if God had intended him to be a missionary he should not have been placed in this lowly parish, that here he was unable to do much harm, and that any who found faith in his church must find it through the grace of God, since it was impossible to suppose they would ever find it through his own poor ministrations. He insisted that people who stayed away from church because he read the service badly or burned too many candles or wore vestments were only ostentatious worshippers who looked upon the church as the waxworks must regard Madame Tussaud's. He explained that he had been driven to discourage the work of Miss Horne and Miss Hobart, because he had detected in himself a tendency toward spiritual pride in the growth of a congregation that did not belong either to him or to God: if he had toler-ated Miss Horne's methods for a time it was because he feared to oppose the Divine intention. However, as soon as he found that he was thinking complacently of a congregation of twenty-four, every member of which was a pensioner of Miss Horne, he realized that the two ladies were instruments of the Devil, particularly when at lunch they suggested . . .

'What?' Sylvia asked, when he paused.

'The only thing to do was to finish my lunch under the table,' he snapped; nor could he be persuaded to discuss the quarrel further.

Sylvia, who felt that the poor ladies had after all been treated in rather a cavalier fashion and was reproaching herself for having deserted them, went down to Oaktown shortly after this to call at Sunny Bank. They received her with freezing coldness, particularly Miss Hobart, whose eyes under lowering eyelids were sullen with hate: she said much less than Miss Horne, who walked in and out of the shivery furniture, fanning herself in her agitation and declaiming against Mr. Dorward at the top of her voice.

'And your little friends?' Miss Hobart put in with a smile that was not a smile. 'We thought them just a little badly brought up.'

'You liked them very much at first,' Sylvia said.

'Yes, one often likes people at first.'

And as Sylvia looked at her, she realized that Miss Hobart was not nearly so old as she had thought her, perhaps not yet fifty. Still, at fifty one had no right to be jealous.

'In fact,' said Sylvia brutally, 'you liked them very much till you thought Mr. Dorward liked them too.'

Miss Hobart's eyelids almost closed over her eyes, and her thin lips disappeared. Miss Horne stopped in her restless parade and, pointing with her fan to the door, bade Sylvia be gone and never come to Sunny Bank again.

'The old witch,' thought Sylvia, when she was toiling up the hill to Medworth in the midsummer heat. 'I believe he's right and that she is the Devil.'

She did not tell Philip about her quarrel, because she knew that he would have reminded her one by one of every occasion he had taken to warn Sylvia against being friendly with any inhabitants of Tintown. A week or two later, Philip announced with an air of satisfaction that a van of Treacherites had arrived in Newton Candover and might be expected at Green Lanes next Sunday.

Sylvia asked what on earth Treacherites were, and he explained that they were the followers of a certain Mr. John Treacher who regarded himself as chosen by God to purify the Church of England of popish abuses.

'A dreadful little cad, I believe,' he added. 'But it will be fun to see what they make of Dorward. It's a pity the old ladies have been kept away by the heat, or we might have had a free fight.'

Sylvia warned Mr. Dorward of the Treacherites' advent, and he seemed rather worried by the news: she had a notion he was afraid of them, which made her impatient, as she frankly told him.

'Not many of us. Not many of us,' said Mr. Dorward. 'Hope they won't try to break up the church.'

The Treacherites arrived on Saturday evening and addressed a meeting by The Old Farm, which fetched Philip out into the road with threats of having them put in jail for creating a disturbance.

'If you want to annoy people, go to church to-morrow and annoy the Vicar,' he said grimly.

Sylvia, who had heard Philip's last remark, turned on him in a rage: 'What a mean and cowardly thing to say, when you know Mr. Dorward can't defend himself as you can. Let them come to church to-morrow and annoy the Vicar. You see what they'll get.'

'Come, come, Sylvia,' Philip said with an attempt at pacification and evidently rather ashamed of himself. 'Let these Christians fight it out among themselves. It's nothing to do with us, as long as they don't . . .'

'Thank you, it's everything to do with me,' she interrupted. He looked at her in surprise.

Next morning Sylvia took up her position in the front of the church and threatened with her eye as fiercely as Miss Horne and Miss Hobart might have done the larger congregation that had gathered in the hope of a row. The Treacherites were two young men with pimply faces who swaggered into church and talked to one another loudly before the service began, commenting upon the ornaments with cockney facetiousness. Cassandra Batt came over to Sylvia and whispered hoarsely in her ear that she was afraid there would be trouble, because some of the village lads had looked in for a bit of fun. The service was carried through with constant interruptions, and Sylvia felt her heart beating faster and faster with suppressed rage. When it was over, the congregation dispersed into the churchyard, where the yokels hung about waiting for the Vicar to come out. As he appeared in the west door a loud booing was set up, and one of the Treacherites shouted:

'Follow me, loyal members of the Protestant Established Church and destroy the idols of the Pope.'

Whereupon the iconoclast tried to push past the priest, who was fumbling in his vague way with the lock of the door: he turned white with rage and seizing the Treacherite by the scruff of his neck flung him head over heels across two mounds. At this the yokels began to boo more vehemently, but he managed to shut the door and lock it, after which he walked across to the discomfited Treacherite and holding out his hand apologized for his violence. The yokels, who mistook generosity for weakness, began to throw stones at the Vicar, one of which cut his face. Sylvia, who had been standing motionless in a trance of fury, was roused by the blood to action. With a bound she sprang at the first Treacherite and pushed him into a half-dug grave; then turning swiftly she advanced against his companion with upraised stick.

The youth just had time to gasp a notification to the surrounding witnesses that Sylvia assaulted him first, before he ran: but the yokels, seeing that the squire's wife was on the side of the parson and fearing for the renewal of their leases and the repairs to their cottages, turned round upon the Treacherites and dragged them off toward the village pond.

'Come on, Cassandra,' Sylvia cried. 'Let's go and break up the van.'

Cassandra seized her pickaxe and followed Sylvia who with hair streaming over her shoulders and elation in her aspect charged past The Old Farm just when Philip was coming out of the gate.

'Come on, Philip,' she cried. 'Come on and help me break up their damned van.'

By this time the attack had brought most of the village out of doors: dogs were barking; geese and ducks were flapping in all directions; Sylvia kept turning round to urge the sexton whose progress was hampered by a petticoat's slipping down not to bother about her clothes, but to come on. A grand-nephew of the old woman picked up the crimson garment and, as he pursued his grand-aunt to restore it to her, waved it in the air like a standard. The yokels, who saw the squire watching from his gate, assumed his complete approval of what was passing (as a matter of fact he was petrified with dismay) and paid no attention to the Vicar's efforts to rescue the Treacherites from their doom in the fast-nearing pond. The van of the iconoclasts was named Ridley: *We shall this day light such a candle by God's grace in England as I trust shall never be put out was* printed on one side: on the other was inscribed *John Treacher's Poor Preachers. Supported by Voluntary Contributions.* By the time Sylvia, Cassandra, and the rest had finished with the van it was neither legible without nor habitable within.

Naturally there was a violent quarrel between Sylvia and Philip over her behaviour, a quarrel that was not mended by her being summoned later on by the outraged Treacherites, together with Mr. Dorward and several yokels.

'You've made a fool of me from one end of the county to the other,' Philip told her. 'Understand once and for all that I don't intend to put up with this sort of thing.'

'It was your fault,' she replied. 'You began it by egging on those brutes to attack Mr. Dorward. You could easily have averted any trouble if you'd wanted to. It serves you jolly well right.'

'There's no excuse for your conduct,' Philip insisted. 'A stranger passing through the village would have thought a lunatic asylum had broken loose.'

'Oh, well, it's a jolly good thing to break loose sometimes – even for lunatics,' Sylvia retorted. 'If you could break loose yourself sometimes, you'd be much easier to live with.'

'The next time you feel repressed,' he said, 'all I ask is that you'll choose a place where we're not quite so well-known in which to give vent to your feelings.'

The argument went on endlessly, for neither Sylvia nor Philip would yield an inch; it became indeed one of those eternal disputes that reassert themselves at the least excuse. If Philip's egg were not cooked long enough, the cause would finally be referred back to that Sunday morning: if Sylvia were late for lunch, her unpunctuality would ultimately be dated from the arrival of the Treacherites.

Luckily the Vicar, with whom the events of that Sunday had grown into a comic myth that was continually being added to, was able to give Sylvia relief from Philip's exaggerated disapproval. Moreover, the Treacherites had done him a service by advertising his church and bringing a certain number of strangers there every Sunday out of curiosity: these pilgrims inflated with a sense of their own importance the natives of Green Lanes, who now filled the church, taking pride and pleasure in the ownership of an attraction and boasting to the natives of the villages round about the size of the offertory. Mr. Dorward's popery and ritualism were admired now as commercial smartness, and if he had chosen to ride into church on Palm Sunday or any other Sunday on a donkey (a legendary ceremony invariably attributed to High Church vicars) there was not a man, woman or child in the parish of Green Lanes that would not have given a prod of encouragement to the sacred animal.

One hot September afternoon, Sylvia was walking back from Medworth when she was overtaken by Mr. Pluepott in his cart; they stopped to exchange the usual country greetings, at which by now Sylvia was an adept; and when presently Mr. Pluepott invited her to take advantage of a lift home, she climbed up beside him. For a while they jogged along in silence; suddenly Mr. Pluepott delivered himself of what was evidently much upon his mind:

'Mrs. Iredale,' he began. 'You and me has known each other the best part of two years, and your coming and having a cup of tea with Mrs. Pluepott once or twice and Mrs. Pluepott having a big opinion of you makes me so bold.'

He paused and reined in his pony to a walk that would suit the gravity of his communication.

'I'd like to give you a bit of a warning as from a friend and, with all due respect, an admirer. Being a married man myself and you a young lady, you won't go for to mistake my meaning when I says to you right out that Women is Worse than the Devil. Miss Horne! As I jokingly said to Mrs. Pluepott, though being a sacred subject she wouldn't laugh, "Miss Horne," I said. "Miss Horns! That's what she ought to be called." Mrs. Iredale,' he went on, pulling up the pony to a dead stop and turning round with a very serious countenance to Sylvia. 'Mrs. Iredale, you've got a wicked bad enemy in that old woman.'

'I know,' she agreed. 'We quarrelled over something.'

'If you quarrelled, and whether it was your fault or whether it was hers, isn't nothing to do with me; but the lies she's spreading around about you and the Reverend Dorward beat the band. I'm not speaking gossip. I'm not going by hearsay. I've heard her myself, and Miss Hobart's as bad, if not worse. There, now I've told you, and I hope you'll pardon the liberty, but I couldn't help it.'

With which Mr. Pluepott whipped up his pony to a frantic gallop and very soon they reached the outskirts of Green Lanes, where Sylvia got down.

'Thanks,' she said, offering her hand. 'I don't think I need bother about Miss Horne, but it was very kind of you to tell me. Thanks very much,' and with a wave of her stick Sylvia walked pensively along into the village: as she passed Mr. Dorward's cottage she rattled her stick on his gate till he looked out from a window in the thatch, like a bird disturbed on its nest.

'Hullo, old owl,' Sylvia cried. 'Come down a minute. I want to say something to you.'

The Vicar presently came blinking out into the sunlight of the garden.

'Look here,' she said, 'do you know that those two old villains in Oaktown are spreading it about that you and I are having a love affair? Haven't you got a prescription for that sort of thing in your church business? Can't you curse them with bell, book, and candle or something? I'll supply the bell, if you'll supply the rest of the paraphernalia.'

Dorward shook his head.

'Can't be done. Cursing is the prerogative of bishops. Not on the best terms with my bishop, I'm afraid. Last time he sent for me I had to spend the night and I left a rosary under my pillow. He was much pained, so my spies at the Palace tell me.'

'Well, if *you* don't mind, *I* don't mind,' she said. 'All right. So long.'

Three days later, an anonymous postcard was sent to Sylvia, a vulgar Temptation of St. Anthony; and a week afterwards Philip suddenly flung down a letter before her which he told her to read. It was an ill-spelt ungrammatical screed, purporting to warn Philip of his wife's behaviour, enumerating the hours she had spent alone with Dorward either in his cottage or in the church, and winding up with the old proverb of there being none so blind as he who won't see. Sylvia blushed while she read it, not for what it said about herself, but for the vile impulse that launched this smudged and scrabbled impurity.

'That's a jolly thing to get at breakfast,' Philip said.

'Beastly,' she agreed. 'And your showing it to me puts you on a level with the sender.'

'I thought it would be a good lesson for you,' he said.

'A lesson?' she repeated.

'Yes, a lesson that one can't behave exactly as one likes, particularly in the country among a lot of uneducated peasants.'

'But I don't understand,' Sylvia went on. 'Did you show me this filthy piece of paper with the idea of asking me to change my manner of life?'

'I showed it to you in order to impress upon you that people talk, and that you owe it to me to keep their tongues quiet.'

'What do you want me to do?'

'Something perfectly simple,' Philip said. 'I want you to give up visiting Dorward in his cottage, and, as you have no religious inclinations, I should like you to avoid his church.'

'And that's why you showed me this anonymous letter?'

He nodded.

'In fact you're going to give it your serious attention?' she went on.

'Not at all,' he contradicted. 'For a long time I've objected to your friendship with Dorward, but knowing you were too headstrong to listen to my advice, I said nothing. This letter makes it impossible to keep silent any longer about my wishes.'

'But you don't really believe that Dorward and I are having an affair?' she gasped.

Philip made an impatient gesture.

'What a foolish question! Do you suppose that if I had for one moment thought such a thing I shouldn't have spoken before? No, no, my dear, it's all very unpleasant, but you must see that as soon as I am made aware, however crude the method of bringing it to my knowledge, that people are talking about you and my Vicar, I have no alternative but to forbid you to do anything that will make these tongues go on wagging.'

'To forbid me?' she repeated.

Philip bowed ironically, Sylvia thought; the gesture, infinitely slight and unimportant as it was, cut the last knot.

'I shall have to tell Mr. Dorward about this letter and explain to him,' she said.

Philip hesitated for a moment.

'Yes, I think that would be the best thing to do,' he agreed.

Sylvia regarded him curiously.

'You don't mind his knowing that you showed it to me?' she asked.

'Not at all,' said Philip.

She laughed, and he took alarm at the tone.

'I thought you were going to be sensible,' he began; but she cut him short.

'Oh, I am, my dear man. Don't worry.'

Now that the unpleasant scene was over, he seemed anxious for her sympathy.

'I'm sorry this miserable business has occurred, but you understand, don't you, that it's been just as bad for me as for you?'

'Do you want me to apologize?' Sylvia demanded in her brutal way.

'No, of course not. Only I thought perhaps you might have shown a little more appreciation of my feelings.'

'Ah, Philip, if you want that, you'll have to let me really go wrong with Dorward.'

'Personally I consider that last remark of yours in very bad taste; but I know we have different standards of humour.'

Sylvia found Dorward in the church, engaged in an argument with Cassandra about the arrangement of the chrysanthemums for Michaelmas.

'I will not have them like this,' he was saying.

'But we always putts them fan-shaped like that.'

'Take them away,' he shouted; since Cassandra still hesitated, he flung the flowers all over the church.

The short conversation that followed always remained associated in Sylvia's mind with Cassandra's grunts and her large base elevated above the pews, while she browsed hither and thither, bending over to pick up the scattered chrysanthemums.

'Mr. Dorward, I want to ask you something very serious.'

He looked at her sharply, almost suspiciously.

'Does it make you very much happier to have faith?'

'Yes, yes, yes, yes, yes,' he said, brushing petals from his cassock.

'But would it make me?'

'I expect so – I expect so,' he said, still brushing and trying with shy curtness to avoid the contact of reality.

'Well, how can I get faith?'

'You must pray, dear lady, you must pray.'

'You'll have to pray for me,' Sylvia said.

'Always do. Always pray for you. Never less than three prayers every day. Mass once a week.'

Sylvia felt a lump in her throat: it seemed to her that this friend, accounted mad by the world, had paid her the tenderest and most exquisite courtesy she had ever known.

'Come along now, Cassandra,' cried the Vicar, clapping his hands impatiently to cover his embarrassment. 'Where are the flowers? Where are the flowers, you miserable old woman?'

Cassandra came up to him, breathing heavily with exertion.

'You know, Mr. Dorward, you're enough to try the patience of an angel on a tomb, you are indeed.'

Sylvia left them arguing all over again about the chrysanthemums. That afternoon she went away from Green Lanes to London.

Three months later, she obtained an engagement in a musical comedy company on tour and sent back to Philip the last shred of clothing that she had possessed through him, with a letter and ten pounds in bank notes:

You must *divorce me now. I've not been able to earn enough to pay you back more than this for your bad bargain. I don't think I've given any more pleasure to the men who have paid less for me than you did, if that's any consolation.*

Sylvia Scarlett

BOOK II

Sylvia and Arthur

I

Sylvia stood before the looking-glass in the Birmingham lodgings and made a speech to herself:

'Humph! You look older, my dear. You look more than nineteen and a half. You're rather glad though, aren't you, to have finished with the last three months? You feel degraded, don't you? What's that you say? You don't feel degraded any more by what you've done now than by what you did when you were married? You consider the net result of the last three months has simply been to prove what you'd suspected for a long time – the wrong you did yourself in marrying Philip Iredale? Wait a minute: don't go so fast: there's something wrong with your moral sense. You know perfectly well your contention is impossible; or do you accuse every woman who marries to have a position and a home of being a prostitute? Ah, but you didn't marry Philip for either of those reasons, you say? Yes, you did – you married him to make something like Arbour End.'

Tears welled up in Sylvia's eyes: she thought she had driven Arbour End from her mind for ever.

'Come, come, we don't want any tears. What are you crying for? You knew when you left Green Lanes that everything which had come into your life through Philip Iredale must be given up. You were rather proud of your ruthlessness; don't spoil it now. That's right: no more tears. You're feeling a bit *abrutie*, aren't you? My advice to you is to obliterate the last three months from your imagination. I quite understand that you suffered a good deal, but novices must be prepared to suffer. In my opinion you can congratulate yourself on having come through so easily. Here you are, a jolly little *cabotine* with a complete contempt for men. You're not yet twenty: you're not likely to fall in love, for you must admit that after those three months the word sounds more than usually idiotic: from what I've seen of you I should say that for the future you'll be very well able to look after yourself: you might even become a famous actress. Ah, that makes you smile, eh?'

Sylvia dabbed her face with the powder-puff and went downstairs to dinner. Her two companions had not yet begun; for this was the first meal at which they would all sit down together, and an atmosphere of

169

politeness hung over life at present. Lily Haden and Dorothy Lonsdale had joined the *Miss Elsie of Chelsea* company at the same time as Sylvia, and were making their first appearance on any stage, having known each other in the dullness of West Kensington. For a fortnight they had clung together, but, having been given an address for rooms in Birmingham that required a third's person's contribution, they had invited Sylvia to join them. Lily was a tall slim girl with light golden hair, who had an aura of romantic mystery that was due to indolence of mind and body. Dorothy also was fair with a mass of light brown hair, a perfect complexion, profile, and figure, and what finally gave her a really distinguished beauty in such a setting – brown eyes instead of blue. Lily's languorous grace of manner and body was so remarkable that in a room it was difficult to choose between her and Dorothy, but behind the footlights there was no comparison: there Dorothy had everybody's glances, and Lily's less definite features went for nothing.

Each girl was prompt to take Sylvia into her confidence about the other. Thus from Lily she learnt that Dorothy's real name was Norah Caffyn; that she was the eldest of a very large family; that Lily had known her at school; that she had been engaged to a journalist who was disapproved of by her family; that she had offered to break with Wilfred Curlew, if she were allowed to go on the stage; and that she had taken the name of Lonsdale from the road where she lived, and Dorothy from the sister next to her.

'I suppose in the same way as she used to take her dolls?' Sylvia suggested.

Lily looked embarrassed: she was evidently not sure whether a joke was intended, and when Sylvia encouraged her to suppose it was, she laughed a little timidly, being rather doubtful if it was not a pun.

'Her sister was awfully annoyed about it, because she hasn't got a second name. She's the only one in the family who hasn't.'

Lily also told Sylvia something about herself, how her mother had lately died and how she could not get on with her sister, who had married an actor and was called Doris. Her mother had been a reciter, and there had always been lots of theatrical people at their house; so it had been easy for her to get an introduction to Mr. Walter Keal, who had the touring rights of all John Richards' great Vanity Theatre productions.

From Dorothy Sylvia learned that she had known Lily at school, but not for long, because Mrs. Haden never paid her daughters' fees; that Mr. Haden had always been supposed to live in Burma, but that people who knew Mrs. Haden declared he had never existed; and finally that Lily had been 'awfully nice' to herself and helped her to get an introduction to Mr. Walter Keal.

The association of Sylvia with the two girls begun at Birmingham was not interrupted until the end of the tour. Lily and Dorothy depended upon it, Lily because Sylvia saved her the trouble of thinking for herself, Dorothy because she found in Sylvia someone that could deflect all the difficulties of life on tour and leave her free to occupy herself with her own prosperity and her own comforts. Dorothy possessed a selfishness that almost attained to the dignity of ambition, though never quite, because her conceit would not allow her to state an object in her career for fear of failure; her method was invariably to seize the best of any situation that came along, whether it was a bed, a chair, a potato, or a man: this method with ordinary good luck should ensure success through life. Lily was too lazy to minister to Dorothy's selfishness; moreover, she often managed by taking the nearest and the easiest to rob Dorothy of the best.

Sylvia was perfectly aware of their respective characters, but she was always willing to give herself any amount of trouble to preserve beauty around her; Lily and Dorothy were not really more troublesome than two cats would have been, in fact rather less, because at any rate they could carry themselves, if not their luggage.

Life on tour went its course with the world divided into three categories – the members of the company, the public expressing its personality in different audiences, and for the actors saloon-bars and the drinks they were stood, for the actresses admirers and the presents they were worth. Sometimes when the saloon-bars and the admirers were alike unprofitable, the members of the company mixed among themselves whether in a walk round a new town or at tea in rooms where a landlady possessed hospitable virtues. Sylvia had a special gift for getting the best out of landladies, and the men of the company came more often to tea with herself and her friends than with the other ladies. They came indeed too often to please Dorothy, who disapproved of Lily's easy-going acceptance of the sort of love that is made because at the moment there is nothing else to do. She spoke to Sylvia about this, who agreed with her, but thought that with Lily it was inevitable.

'Still, not with boys in the company,' Dorothy urged disdainfully. 'It makes us all so cheap. I don't want to put on side, but after all we are a little different from the other girls.'

Sylvia found this belief universal in the chorus; she could not think of any girl, who had not at one time or another taken her aside and claimed for herself, and by the politeness owed to present company for Sylvia, this 'little difference.'

'Personally,' Sylvia said, 'I think we're all much the same. Some of us drop our aitches, others our p's and q's: some of us sing flat, the rest sing sharp: and we all look just alike when we're waiting for the train on Sunday morning.'

Notwithstanding her prevision of a fate upon Lily's conduct, Sylvia did speak to her about the way in which she tolerated the familiarity of the men in the company.

'I suppose you're thinking of Tom,' Lily said.

'Tom, Dick, and Harry,' Sylvia put in.

'Well, I don't like to seem stuck up,' Lily exclaimed. 'Tom's always very nice about carrying my bag and getting me tea when we're travelling.'

'If I promise to look after the bag,' Sylvia asked, 'will you promise to discourage Tom?'

'But, my dear, why should you carry my bag, when I can get Tom to do it?'

'It bores me to see you and him together,' Sylvia explained. 'These boys in the company are all very well, but they aren't really men at all.'

'I know,' Lily assented eagerly. 'That's what I feel. They don't seem real to me. Of course, I shouldn't let anybody make love to me seriously.'

'What do you call serious love-making?'

'Oh, Sylvia, how you do go on asking questions. You know perfectly well what I mean. You only ask questions to make me feel uncomfortable.'

'Just as I might disarrange the cushions of your chair?'

'I know quite well who's been at you to worry me,' Lily went on. 'I know it's Dorothy. She's always been used to being the eldest and finding fault with everybody else. She doesn't really mind Tom's kissing me: she's perfectly ready to make use of him herself, but she's always thinking about other people and she's so afraid that some of the men she goes out with will laugh at his waistcoat. I'm used to actors: she isn't. I never bother about her. I don't complain about her practising her singing or talking for hours and hours about whether I think she looks better with a teardrop or without. Why can't she let me alone? Nobody ever lets me alone. It's all I've ever asked all my life.'

The feeling between Lily and Dorothy was reaching the point of tension; Sylvia commented on it one evening to Fay Onslow, the oldest member of the chorus, a fat woman wise and genial, universally known as Onzie except by her best boy of the moment, who had to call her Fay: however, she cost him very little else, and was generally considered to throw herself away, though, of course, as her friends never failed to add, she was getting on and could no longer afford to be too particular.

'Well, between you and I, Sylvia, I've often wondered you've kept your little family together for so long. I've been on the stage now for

172

twenty-five years. I'm not far off forty, dear; I used to be in burlesque at the old Frivolity.'

'Do you remember Victoria Deane?' Sylvia asked.

'Of course I do. She made a big hit and then got married and left the stage. A sweetly pretty little thing, she was. But, as I was saying, dear, in all my experience I never knew two fair girls get through a tour together without falling out, two girls naturally fair that is, and you mark my words: Lily Haden and Dolly Lonsdale will have a row.'

Sylvia was anxious to avert this, because she would have found it hard to choose between their rival claims upon her. She was fonder of Lily, but she was very fond of Dorothy, and she believed that Dorothy might attain real success in her profession. It seemed more worth while to take trouble over Dorothy: yet something warned her that an expense of devotion in that direction would ultimately be from a selfish point of view wasted. Dorothy would never consider affection where advancement was concerned; yet was it not just this quality in her that she admired? There would certainly be an unusual exhilaration in standing behind Dorothy and in helping her to rise and rise, whereas with Lily the best that could be expected was to prevent her falling infinitely low.

'How I've changed since I left Philip,' she said to herself. 'I seem to have lost myself somehow and to have transferred all my interest in life to other people. I suppose it won't last. God forbid I should become a problem to myself like a woman in a damned novel. Down with introspection! Though, heaven knows, observation in *Miss Elsie of Chelsea* is not a profitable pastime.'

Sylvia bought an eyeglass next day, and while all agreed with one another in private that it was an affectation, everybody assured her that she was a girl who could wear an eyeglass with advantage. Lily thought the cord must be rather a bother.

'It's symbolic,' Sylvia declared to the dressing-room.

'I think I'll have *my* eyes looked at in Sheffield,' said Onzie. 'There's a doctor there who's very good to pros. I often feel my eyes are getting a bit funny. It may be the same as Sylvia's got.'

The tour was coming to an end: the last three nights would be played at Oxford, to which everybody looked forward. All the girls who had been to Oxford before told wonderful tales of the pleasures that might be anticipated; and some of the men were heard to speculate if such or such a friend were still there, which annoyed those who could not even boast of having had a friend there two years ago; the jealous ones revenged themselves by criticizing the theatrical manners of the undergraduate, especially upon the last night of a musical comedy. One heard a great deal of talk, they said, about a college career, but personally and without offence to anybody present who had friends at College they considered that a college career in nine cases out of ten meant rowdiness and a habit of thinking oneself better than other people.

Sylvia, Lily, and Dorothy had rooms in Eden Square, which was the recognized domain of theatrical companies playing in Oxford. Numerous invitations to lunch and tea arrived, and Sylvia who possessed a preconceived idea of Oxford based upon Philip was astonished how little the undergraduates she met resembled him. Dorothy managed with her usual instinct for the best to secure as an admirer Lord Clarehaven, or as the other girls preferred to call him with a nicer formality the Earl of Clarehaven. He invited her with a friend to lunch at Christ Church on the last day. Dorothy naturally chose Sylvia, and as Lily was already engaged elsewhere Sylvia accepted. Later in the afternoon, Dorothy proposed that the young men should come back and have tea in Eden Square, and Sylvia divined Dorothy's intention of proving to these young men that the actress in her own home would be as capable of maintaining propriety as she had been at lunch.

'We'll buy the cakes on the way,' said Dorothy, which was another example of her infallible instinct for the best and the most economical.

Loaded with éclairs, meringues, and chocolates, the party reached Eden Square.

'You'll have to excuse the general untidiness,' Dorothy said with an affected little laugh, flinging open the door of the sitting-room. She would probably have found another way of describing the picture of Lily sitting on Tom's knee in the worn leather-backed arm-chair, if she had entered first: unfortunately Lord Clarehaven was accorded that privilege, and the damage was done. Sylvia quickly introduced everybody, and nobody could have complained of the skill with which the undergraduates sailed over an awkward situation; nor could much have been urged against Tom, who left immediately. As for Lily she was a great success with the young men, and seemed quite undisturbed by the turn of events.

As soon as the three girls were alone together, Dorothy broke out:

'I hope you don't think I'll ever live with you again after that disgusting exhibition. I suppose you think just because you gave me an introduction to a manager that you can do as you like. I don't know what Sylvia thinks of you, but I can tell you what I think. You make me feel absolutely sick. That beastly chorus-boy! The idea of letting anybody like that even look at you. Thank heaven, the tour's over. I'm going down to the theatre. I can't stay in this room. It makes me blush to think of it. I'll take jolly good care who I live with in future.'

Then suddenly to Sylvia's immense astonishment Dorothy slapped Lily's face: what torments of mortification must be raging in that small soul to provoke such an unladylike outburst!

'I should hit her back if I were you, my lass,' Sylvia advised, putting up her eyeglass for the fray; but Lily began to cry, and Dorothy flounced out of the room.

Sylvia bent over Lily in consolation; though her sense of justice made her partly excuse Dorothy's rage.

'How did I know she would bring her beastly men back to tea? She only did it to brag about having a lord to our digs. After all they're just as much mine as hers. I was sorry for Tom. He doesn't know anybody in Oxford, and he felt out of it with all the other boys going out. He asked me if I was going to turn him down because I'd got such fine friends. I was sorry for him, Sylvia, and so I asked him to tea. I don't see why Dorothy should turn round and say nasty things to me. I've always been decent to her. Oh, Sylvia, you don't know how lonely I feel sometimes.'

This appeal was too much for Sylvia, who clasped Lily to her and let her sob forth her griefs upon her shoulder.

'Sylvia, I've got nobody. I hate my sister Doris. Mother's dead. Everybody ran her down, but she had a terrible life. Father used to take drugs, and then he stole and was put in prison. People used to say mother wasn't married, but she was. Only the truth was so terrible, she could never explain. You don't know how she worked. She brought up Doris and me entirely. She used to recite, and she used to be always hard up. She died of heart failure, and that comes from worry. Nobody understands me. I don't know what will become of me.'

'My dear,' Sylvia said. 'You know I'm your pal.'

'Oh, Sylvia, you're a darling. I'd do anything for you.'

'Even carry your own bag at the station to-morrow?'

'No, don't tease me,' Lily begged. 'If you won't tease me, I'll do anything.'

That evening Mr. Keal with the mighty Mr. Richards himself came up from London to see the show. The members of the chorus were much agitated: it could only mean that girls were to be chosen for the Vanity production in the autumn: every one of them put on rather more make-up than usual, acted hard all the time she was on the stage, and tried to study Mr. Richards' face from the wings.

'You and I are one of the "also rans," ' Sylvia told Lily. 'The great man eyed me with positive dislike.'

In the end it was Dorothy Lonsdale who was engaged for the Vanity; she was so much elated that she was reconciled with Lily and told

175

everybody in the dressing-room that she had met a cousin at Oxford, Arthur Lonsdale, Lord Cleveden's son.

'Which side of the road are you related to him?' Sylvia asked. Dorothy blushed, but she pretended not to understand what Sylvia meant, and said quite calmly that it was on her mother's side. She parted with Sylvia and Lily very cordially at Paddington, but she did not invite either of them to come and see her at Lonsdale Road.

Sylvia and Lily stayed together at Mrs. Gowndry's in Finborough Road, for it happened that the final negotiations for Sylvia's divorce from Philip were being concluded, and she took pleasure in addressing her communications from the house where she had been living when he first met her. Philip was anxious to make her an allowance, but she declined it: her case was undefended. Lily and she managed to get an engagement in another touring company which opened in August somewhere on the south coast. About this time Sylvia read in a paper that Jimmy Monkley had been sentenced to three years' penal servitude for fraud, and by an odd coincidence in the same paper she read of the decree nisi made absolute that set Philip and herself free. Old associations seemed to be getting wound up; unfortunately the new ones were not promising; no duller collection of people had surely ever been gathered together than the company in which she was working at present. Not only was the company tiresome, but they failed to meet anywhere on the tour one amusing person. To be sure, Lily thought that Sylvia was too critical and therefore so alarming that several 'nice boys' were discouraged too early in their acquaintanceship for a final judgment to be passed upon them.

'The trouble is,' said Sylvia, 'that at this rate we shall never make our fortunes. I stipulate that if we adopt a gay life it really will be a gay life. I don't want to have soul-spasms and internal wrestles merely for the sake of being bored.'

Sylvia tried to produce Lily as a dancer; for a week or two they worked hard at imitations of the classical school, but very soon they both grew tired of it.

'The nearest we shall ever get to jingling our money at this game,' Sylvia said, 'is jingling our landlady's ornaments on the mantelpiece. Lily, I think we're not meant for the stage. And yet, if I could only find my line, I believe . . . I believe . . . oh, well, I can't, and so there's an end of it. But look here, winter's coming on. We've got nothing to wear. We haven't saved a penny. Ruin stares us in the face. Say something, Lily; do say something, or I shall scream.'

'I don't think we ought to have eaten those plums at dinner. They weren't really ripe,' Lily said.

'Well, anyhow that solves the problem of the moment. Put your things on. You'd better come out and walk them off.'

They were playing in Eastbourne that week, where a sudden hot spell had prolonged the season farther into September than usual; a new company of entertainers known as The Highwaymen was attracting audiences almost as large as in the prime of summer. Sylvia and Lily paused to watch them from the tamarisks below the Marina.

Suddenly Sylvia gave an exclamation.

'I do believe that's Claude Raglan who's singing now. Do you remember, Lily, I told you about the Pink Pierrots? I'm sure it is.'

Presently the singer came round with the bag and a packet of his picture-postcards: Sylvia asked if he had a photograph of Claude Raglan; when he produced one she dug him in the ribs and cried:

'Claude, you consumptive ass, don't you recognize me? Sylvia.'

He was delighted to see her again, and willingly accepted an invitation to supper after the show, if he might bring a friend with him.

'Jack Airdale – an awfully decent fellow. Quite a good voice too, though I think from the point of view of the show it's a mistake to have a high barytone when they've already got a tenor. However, he does a good deal of accompanying. In fact, he's a much better accompanist than he is a singer.'

'I suppose you've got more girls than ever in love with you, now you wear a mask?' said Sylvia.

Claude seemed doubtful whether to take this remark as a compliment to his voice or as an insult to his face: finally he took it as a joke and laughed.

'Just the same, I see,' he said. 'Always chaffing a fellow.'

Claude Raglan and Jack Airdale came to supper in due course. Sylvia liked Jack; he was a round-faced young man in the early twenties with longish light hair that flopped all over his face when he became excited. Sylvia and he were good friends immediately and made a great deal of noise over supper, while Claude and Lily looked at one another.

'How's the consumption, Claudie?' Sylvia asked.

Claude sighed with a soulful glance at Lily's delicate form.

'Don't imagine she's sympathizing with you,' Sylvia cried. 'She's only thinking about plums.'

'He's grown out of it,' Airdale said. 'Look at the length of his neck.'

'I have to wear these high collars. My throat . . .' Claude began.

'Oh, shut up with your ailments,' Sylvia interrupted.

'Hear, hear,' Airdale shouted. 'Down with ailments,' and he threw a cushion at Claude.

'I wish you wouldn't behave like a clown,' said Claude, smoothing his ruffled hair and looking to see if Lily was joining in the laugh against him.

Presently the conversation turned upon the prospects of the two girls for next winter, about which Sylvia was pessimistic.

'Why don't we join together and run a street show – Pierrot, Pierrette, Harlequin and Columbine?' Airdale suggested. 'I'll swear there's money in it.'

'About enough to pay for our coffins,' said Claude. 'Sing out of doors in the winter? My dear Jack, you're mad.'

Sylvia thought the idea was splendid, and had sketched out Lily's Columbine dress before Lily herself had grasped that the conversation had taken a twist.

'Light blue crêpe de Chine with bunches of cornflowers for Columbine. Pierrette in dark blue with bunches of forget-me-nots, Pierrot in light blue. Silver and dark blue lozenges for Harlequin.'

'Paregoric lozenges would suit Claude better,' said Airdale. 'O Pagliacci! Can't you hear him? No, joking apart, I think it would be a great effort. We shan't have to sing much outside. We shall get invited into people's houses!'

'Shall we?' Claude muttered.

'And if the show goes,' Airdale went on, 'we might vary our costumes. For instance we might be Bacchanals in pink fleshings and vine leaves.'

'Vine leaves,' Claude ejaculated. 'Vine Street more likely.'

'Don't laugh, old boy, with that lung of yours,' Airdale earnestly advised.

In the end, before the company left Eastbourne, it was decided notwithstanding Claude's lugubrious prophecies to launch the enterprise; when the tour broke up in December, Sylvia had made dresses for both Lily and herself as she had first planned them with an eye only for what became Lily. Claude's hypochondria was appeased by letting him wear a big patchwork cloak over his harlequin's dress in which white lozenges had been substituted for silver ones owing to lack of money. They hired a small piano like the one that belonged to the Pink Pierrots; and on Christmas Eve they set out from Finborough Road, where Claude and Jack had taken rooms near Mrs. Gowndry's. They came into collision with a party of carol singers who seemed to resent their profane competition, and much to Jack Airdale's disappointment they were not invited into a single house; the money taken after three hours of wandering music was one shilling and fivepence in coppers.

'Never mind,' said Jack. 'We aren't known yet. It's a pity we didn't start singing last Christmas Eve. We should have had more engagements this year than we should have known what to do with.'

'We must build up the show for next year,' Sylvia agreed enthusiastically.

'I shall sing the *Lost Chord* next year,' Claude answered. 'If I cough loud enough outside Heaven's gates, they may let me in to hear that last amen.'

Jack and Sylvia were justified in their optimism, for gradually the Carnival Quartet, as they called themselves, became known in South Kensington, and they began to get engagements to appear in other parts of London. Jack taught Sylvia to vamp well enough on the guitar to accompany herself in duets with him; Claude looked handsome in his harlequin's dress, to which prosperity soon added the silver lozenges; Lily danced actively enough for the drawing-rooms in which they performed. Sylvia, inspired by the romantic exterior of herself and her companions, invented a mime to the music of Schumann's *Carneval* which Jack Airdale played, or as Claude said maltreated.

The Quartet showed signs of increasing vitality with the approach of spring, and there was no need to think any more of touring in musical comedy, which was a relief to Sylvia: when summer came, they agreed to keep together and work the south coast.

However, all these fine plans came suddenly to nothing, because one misty night in March, Harlequin and Columbine lost Pierrot and Pierrette on the way home from a party in Chelsea; a brief note from Harlequin to Pierrot, which he found when he got home, indicated that the loss should be considered permanent.

This treachery was a shock to Sylvia, and she was horrified at herself for feeling it so deeply. Ever since that day in Oxford when Lily had sobbed out her griefs, Sylvia had concentrated upon her all the capacity for affection which had begun to blossom during the time she was with Philip and which had been cut off ruthlessly with everything else that belonged to life with him. She knew that she should have foreseen the possibility, nay the probability of this happening, but she had charmed herself with the romantic setting of their musical adventure and let all else go.

'I'm awfully sorry, Sylvia,' said Jack. 'I ought to have kept a better look out on Claude.'

'It's not your fault, old son. But, oh god, why can't four people stay friends without muddling everything up with this accursed love?'

Jack was sympathetic, but it was useless to confide in him her feeling for Lily: he would never understand: she would seem to him so little worth while: for him the behaviour of such a one meant less than the breaking of a porcelain figure.

'It did seem worth while,' Sylvia said to herself that night, 'to keep that frail and lovely thing from this. It was my fault, of course, for I knew both Lily and Claude through and through. Yet what does it matter? What a fool I am. It was absurd of me to imagine we could go on for ever as we were. I don't really mind about Lily; I'm angry because my conceit has been wounded. It serves me right. But that dirty little actor won't appreciate her. He's probably sick of her easiness already. Oh, why the hell aren't I a man?'

Presently, however, Sylvia's mood of indignation burnt itself out: she began to attribute the elopement of Claude and Lily to the characters they had assumed of Harlequin and Columbine, and to regard the whole affair as a scene from a play, which must not be taken more deeply to heart than with the pensive melancholy that succeeds the fall of a curtain on mimic emotions. After all, what had Lily been to her more than a puppet whose actions she had always controlled for her own pleasure until she was stolen from her? Without Lily she was once more at a loose end; there was the whole history of her sorrow.

'I can't think what they wanted to run away for,' said Jack.

Sylvia fancied the flight was the compliment both Harlequin and Columbine had paid to her authority.

'I don't find you so alarming,' he said.

'No, old son, because you and I have always regarded the Quartet from a strictly professional point of view, and consequently each other. Meanwhile the poor old Quartet is done in. We two can't sustain a programme alone.'

Airdale gloomily assented, but thought it would be well to continue for a week or so, in case Claude and Lily came back.

'I notice you take it for granted that I'll be willing to continue busking with them,' Sylvia remarked.

That evening, Airdale and she went out as usual; but the loss of the other two seemed somehow to have robbed the entertainment of its romantic distinction, and Sylvia was dismayed to find with what a shameful timidity she now took herself and her guitar into saloon-bars; she felt like a beggar and was humiliated by Jack's apologetic manner, and still more by her own instinctive support of such cringing to the benevolence of potmen and barmaids.

One evening, after about a week of these distasteful peregrinations, the two mountebanks came out of a public-house in Fulham Road where they had been forced to endure a more than usually intolerable patronage. Sylvia vowed she would not perform again under such conditions, and they turned up Tinderbox Lane to wander home. This thoroughfare, only used by pedestrians, was very still, and the trees planted down the middle of the pavement gave to the mild March evening an effluence of spring. Sylvia began to strum upon her guitar the tune that Arthur Madden and she whistled together from the windows of Hampstead on the night she met him first; her companion soon caught hold of the air, and they strolled slowly along dreaming, she looking downwards of the past, he of the future with his eyes fixed on the chimneys of the high flats that encircled the little houses and long gardens of Tinderbox Lane. They were passing a wall on their right in which numbered doors were set at intervals: from one of these a tall figure emerged, and stopped a moment to say good-bye to somebody standing in the entrance. The two musicians with a simultaneous instinct for an audience that might appreciate them stopped and addressed their song to the parting pair – a tall old gentleman with drooping grey whiskers, very much muffled up, and an exceedingly stout woman of ripe middle age.

'Bravo!' said the old gentleman in a tremulous voice, as he tapped his cane on the pavement. 'Polly, this is devilish appropriate. By gad, it makes me feel inclined to dance again, Polly,' and the old gentleman forthwith postured with his thin legs like a cardboard antic at the end of a string. The fat woman standing in the doorway came out into the lamplight and, clasping her hands in alarm, begged him not to take cold; but the old gentleman would not stop until Polly had made a pretence of dancing a few steps with him, after which he again piped 'bravo,' vowed he must have a whisky, and invited Sylvia and Jack to come inside and join them.

'Dashwood is my name, Major-General Dashwood, and this is Mrs. Gainsborough.'

'Come along,' said Mrs. Gainsborough. 'The Captain—'

'She will call me Captain,' said the General with a chuckle. 'Obstinate gal! Knew me first when I was a captain thirty-six years ago and has never called me anything since. What a woman though!'

'He's very gay to-night. We've been celebrating our anniversary,' Mrs. Gainsborough explained, while the four of them walked along a gravel path towards a small square creeper-covered house at the end of a long garden.

'We met first at the Argyll Rooms in March, 1867; and in September, 1869, Mulberry Cottage was finished. I planted those mulberry trees myself, and they'll outlive us both,' said the General.

'Now don't let's have any more dismals,' Mrs. Gainsborough begged. 'We've had quite enough to-night, talking over old times.'

Mulberry Cottage was comfortable inside, full of mid-Victorian furniture and ornaments that suited its owner, who Sylvia now perceived by the orange lamplight was even fatter than she had seemed at first. Her hair worn in a chignon was black; her face was rosy and large, monumental almost with its plinth of chins.

The General so much enjoyed having a fresh audience for his tales and sat so long over the whisky that Mrs. Gainsborough became worried.

'Bob, you ought to go. You know I don't like to argue before strangers, but your sister will be getting anxious. Miss Dashwood's quite alone,' she explained to her guests. 'I wonder if you'd mind walking back with him?' she whispered to Sylvia. 'He lives in Redcliffe Gardens. That's close to you, isn't it?'

'If we can have music all the way, by gad, of course,' said the General, standing up so straight that Sylvia was afraid he would bump his head on the ceiling.

'Now, Bob dear, don't get too excited and do keep your muffler well wrapped round your throat.'

The General insisted on having one more glass for the sake of old times, and there was a short delay in the garden, because he stuck his cane fast in the ground to show the size of the mulberry trees when he planted them; but ultimately they said good night to Mrs. Gainsborough, upon whom Sylvia promised to call next day, and set out for Redcliffe Gardens to the music of guitars.

General Dashwood turned round from time to time to shake his cane at passers-by that presumed to stare at the unusual sight of an old gentleman respectable in his dress and demeanour escorted down Fulham Road by two musicians.

'Do you see anything so damned odd in our appearance?' he asked Sylvia.

'Nothing at all,' she assured him.

'Sensible gal! I've a very good mind to knock down the next scoundrel who stares at us.'

Presently the General, on whom the fresh air was having an effect, took Sylvia's arm and grew confidential.

'Go on playing,' he commanded Jack Airdale; 'I'm only talking business. The fact is,' he said to Sylvia, 'I'm worried about Polly. Hope I shall live another twenty years, but fact is, my dear, I've never really got over that wound of mine at Balaclava. Damme, I've never been the same man since.'

Sylvia wondered what he could have been before.

'Naturally she's well provided for. Bob Dashwood always knew how to treat a woman. No wife, no children, you understand me? But it's the loneliness. She ought to have somebody with her. She's a wonderful woman, and she was a handsome gal. Damme, she's still handsome, what? Fifty-five you know. By gad, yes. And I'm seventy. But it's the loneliness. Ah dear, if the gods had been kind, but then she'd have probably been married by now.'

The General blew his nose, sighed, and shook his head: Sylvia asked tenderly how long the daughter had lived.

'Never lived at all,' said the General, stopping dead and opening his eyes very wide, as he looked at Sylvia. 'Never was born. Never was going to be born. Hale and hearty, but too late now, damme! I've taken a fancy to you. Sensible gal! Damned sensible. Why don't you go and live with Polly?'

In order to give Sylvia time to reflect upon her answer, the General skipped along for a moment to the tune that Jack was playing.

'Nothing between you and him?' he asked presently, indicating Jack with his cane.

Sylvia shook her head.

'Thought not. Very well then, why don't you go and live with Polly? Give you time to look round a bit. Understand what you feel about playing for your bread and butter like this. Finest thing in the world music, if you haven't got to do it. Go and see Polly to-morrow. I spoke to her about it to-night. She'll be delighted. So shall I. Here we are in Redcliffe Gardens. Damned big house and only myself and my sister to live in it. Live there like two needles in a haystack. Won't ask you in. Damned inhospitable, but no good because I shall have to go to bed at once. Perhaps you wouldn't mind pressing the bell? Left my latchkey in me sister's work-basket.'

The door opened, and the General after bidding Sylvia and Jack a courteous good-night marched up his front-door steps with as much martial rigidity as he could command.

On the way back to Finborough Road, Sylvia who had been attracted to the General's suggestion postponed raising the question with Jack by telling him about her adventure in Redcliffe Gardens when she threw the bag of chestnuts through the window. She did not think it fair, however, to make any other arrangement without letting him know, and before she went to see Mrs. Gainsborough the next day she announced her idea and asked him if he would be much hurt by her backing out.

'My dear girl, of course not,' said Jack. 'As a matter of fact I've had rather a decent offer to tour in a show through the East. I should rather like to see India and all that. I didn't say anything about it, because I didn't want to let you down. However, if you're all right, I'm all right.'

Mrs. Gainsborough by daylight appealed to Sylvia as much as ever;

she told her what the General had said, and Mrs. Gainsborough begged her to come that very afternoon.

'The only thing is,' Sylvia objected, 'I've got a friend, a girl, who's away at present, and she might want to go on living with me.'

'Let her come too,' Mrs. Gainsborough cried. 'The more the merrier. Good Land! What a set out we shall have. The Captain won't know himself. He's very fond of me, you know; but it would be more jolly for him to have some youngsters about. He's that young. Upon my word, you'd think he was a boy. And he was always the same. Oh, dearie me, the times we've had, you'd hardly believe. Life with him was a regular circus.'

So it was arranged that Sylvia should come at once to live with Mrs. Gainsborough in Tinderbox Lane, and Jack went off to the East.

The General used to visit them nearly every afternoon, but never in the evening.

'Depend upon it, Sylvia,' Mrs. Gainsborough said, 'he got into rare hot water with his sister the other night. Of course it was an exception, being our anniversary, and I daresay next March, if we're all spared, he'll be allowed another evening. It's a great pity though that we didn't meet first in June. So much more seasonable for jollifications. But there, we were young and never looked forward to being old.'

The General was not spared for another anniversary: scarcely a month after Sylvia had gone to live with Mrs. Gainsborough, he died very quietly in the night. His sister came herself to break the news, a frail old lady who seemed very near to joining her brother upon the longest journey.

'She'll never be able to keep away from him,' Mrs. Gainsborough sobbed. 'She'll worry and fret herself for fear he might catch cold in his coffin. And look at me! As healthy and rosy as a great radish!'

The etiquette of the funeral caused Mrs. Gainsborough considerable perplexity.

'Now tell me, Sylvia, ought I or ought I not to wear a widow's veil? Miss Dashwood inviting me in that friendly way, I do want to show that I appreciate her kindness. I know that strictly we weren't married. I daresay nowadays it would be different, but people was much more old-fashioned about marrying ballet girls when I was young. Still it doesn't seem hardly decent for me to go gallivanting to his funeral in me black watered silk, the same as if I was going to the Upper Boxes of a theatre with Mrs. Marsham or Mrs. Beardmore.'

Sylvia told Mrs. Gainsborough that in her opinion a widow's cap at the General's funeral would be like the dash of mauve in the story. She suggested as the appropriate garb a new black dress unprofaned by visits to the Upper Boxes.

'If I can get such an outsize in the time,' Mrs. Gainsborough sighed, 'which is highly doubtful.'

However the new dress was obtained, and Mrs. Gainsborough went off to the funeral at Brompton.

'Oh, it was a beautiful ceremony,' she sobbed when she got home. 'And really Miss Dashwood, well, she couldn't have been nicer. Oh, my poor dear Captain, if only all the clergyman said was true. And yet I should feel more comfortable somehow if it wasn't. Though I suppose if it was true, there'd be no objection to our meeting in heaven as friends only. Dear me, it all sounded so real when I heard the clergyman talking about it. Just as if he was going up in a lift, as you might say. So natural it sounded. "A gallant soldier," he said, "a veteran of the Crimea." So he was gallant, the dear Captain. You should have seen him lay out two roughs who tried to snatch me watch and chain once at the Epsom Derby. He was a gentleman too. I'm sure nobody ever treated any woman kinder than he treated me. Seventy years old he was. Captain Bob Dashwood of the Seventeenth Hussars. I can see him now as he used to be. He liked to come stamping up the garden. Oh, he was a stamper, and "Polly," he hollered out, "get on your frills. Here's Dick Avon" – the Markiss of Avon *that* was – oh, he was a wild thing – "and Jenny Ward" – you know, she threw herself off Westminster Bridge and caused such a stir in Jubilee year. People talked a lot about it at the time. I remember we drove to the Star and Garter at Richmond that day – a lovely June day it was – and caused quite a sensation, because we all looked so smart. Oh, my Bob, my Bob, it only seems yesterday.'

Sylvia consoled Mrs. Gainsborough and rejoiced in her assurance that she did not know what she should have done without her.

'Fancy him thinking about me being so lonely and wanting you to come and live with me. Depend upon it he knew he was going to die all of a sudden,' said Mrs. Gainsborough. 'Oh, there's no doubt he was clever enough to have been a doctor. Only of course with his family he had to be a soldier.'

Sylvia mostly spent these spring days in the garden with Mrs. Gainsborough, listening to her tales about the past and helping her to overlook the labours of the jobbing gardener who came in twice a week. Her landlady or hostess (for the exact relation was not yet determined) was very strict in this regard, because her father had been a nursery gardener and she insisted upon a peculiar knowledge of the various ways in which horticultural obligations could be evaded. When Sylvia raised the question of her status at Mulberry Cottage, Mrs. Gainsborough always begged her not to be in a hurry to settle anything; later on, when Sylvia was able to earn some money, she should pay for her board, but payment for her lodging, so long as Mrs. Gainsborough was alive and the house not burnt to the ground, was never to be mentioned. That was certainly the Captain's intention and it must be respected.

Sylvia often went to see Mrs. Gowndry in Finborough Road in case there should be news of Lily. Her old landlady was always good enough to say that she missed her, and in her broken-up existence the affection even of Mrs. Gowndry was very grateful.

'I've told my old man to keep a good look out for her,' said the wife of the lavatory attendant.

'He's hardly likely to meet her at his work,' Sylvia said.

'Certainly not. No. But he often goes up to get a breath of air – well – it isn't to be expected that he wouldn't. I often say to him when he comes home a bit grumblified that his profession is as bad as a miner's, and *they* only does eight hours whereas in his lavatory they does twelve. Too long, too long, and it must be fidgety work, with people bobbing in and out all the time and always in a hurry, as you might say. Of course now and again you get a lodger who makes himself unpleasant, but year in year out, looking after lodgers is a more peaceful sort of life than looking after a lavatory. Don't you be afraid, Miss Scarlett. If ever a letter comes for you, our Tommy shall bring it straight round, and he's a boy as can be trusted not to lose anything he's given. You wouldn't lose the pretty lady's letter, would you, Tommy? You never lose nothing, do you?'

'I lost a acid drop once.'

'There, fancy him remembering. That's a hit for his ma, that is. He'd only half sucked this here acid drop and laid it aside to finish sucking it when he went up to bed, and I must have swept it up not thinking what it was. Fancy him remembering! He don't talk much, but he's a artful one.'

Tommy had a bagful of acid drops soon after this, for he brought a letter to Sylvia from Lily:

Dear Sylvia,

I suppose you're awfully angry with me, but Claude went on tour a month ago, and I hate being alone. I wonder if this will find you. I'm staying in rotten rooms in Camden Town. 14 Winchester Terrace. Send me a card if you're in London.

Loving

Lily

Sylvia immediately went over to Camden Town and brought Lily away from the rooms, which were indeed 'rotten'. When she had installed her at Mulberry Cottage, she worked herself up to having a clear understanding with Lily, but when it came to the point she felt it was useless to scold her except in fun, as a child scolds her doll. She did, however, treat her henceforth in what Mrs. Gainsborough called a 'highly dictatorial way'. Sylvia thought that she might give Lily the appearance of moral or immoral energy, however impossible it might be to give her the reality; with this end in view she made Lily's will entirely subordinate to her own, which was not difficult. The affection that Sylvia now had for her was not so much tender as careful, the affection one might feel for a bicycle rather than for a horse. She was always brutally frank with herself about their relation to one another, and because she never congratulated herself upon her kindness she was able to sustain her affection.

'There is nothing so fickle as a virtuous impulse,' Sylvia declared to herself. 'It's a kind of moral usury which is always looking for a return on the investment. The moment the object fails to pay an exorbitant interest in gratitude, the impulse to speculate withers up. The lowest circle in hell should be reserved for people who try to help others and cannot understand why their kindness is not appreciated. Really that was Philip's trouble. He never got over being hurt that I didn't perpetually remind him of his splendid behaviour towards me. I suppose I'm damned inhuman. Well, well, I couldn't have stood those three months after I left him, if I hadn't been.'

The affair between Lily and Claude Raglan was not much discussed; he had, it seemed, only left her because his career was at stake; he had received a good offer and she had not wished to detain him.

'But is it over between you?' Sylvia demanded.

'Yes, of course it's over, at any rate for a long time to come,' Lily answered. 'He cried when he left me. He really was a nice boy. If he lives, he thinks he will be a success – a real success. He introduced me to a lot of nice boys.'

'That was rash of him,' Sylvia laughed. 'Were they as nice as the lodgings he introduced you to?'

'No, don't laugh at him. He couldn't afford anything better.'

'But why in heaven's name, if you wanted to play around together, had you got to leave Finborough Road?'

Lily blushed faintly.

'You won't be angry if I tell you?'

Sylvia shook her head.

'Claude said he couldn't bear the idea that you were looking at us. He said it spoilt everything.'

'What did he think I was going to do?' Sylvia snapped. 'Put pepper on the hymeneal pillow?'

'You said you wouldn't be angry.'

'I'm not.'

'Well, don't use long words, because it makes me think you are.'

Soon after Lily came to Tinderbox Lane, Sylvia met Dorothy Lonsdale with a very lovely dark girl called Olive Fanshawe, a fellow member of the Vanity Chorus. Dorothy was glad to see her principally, Sylvia thought, because she was able to talk about lunch at Romano's and supper at the Savoy.

'Look here,' Sylvia said. 'A little less of the Queen of Sheba, if you don't mind. Don't forget I'm one of the blokes as is glad to smell the gratings outside a baker's.'

Miss Fanshawe laughed, and Sylvia looked at her quickly, wondering if she were worth while cultivating.

Dorothy was concerned to hear she was still with Lily.

'That dreadful girl,' she simpered.

'Oh, go to hell,' said Sylvia sharply, and walked off.

Next day a note came from Dorothy, to invite her and Lily to tea at the flat she shared with Olive.

'Wonderful how attractive rudeness is,' Sylvia commented.

'Oh, do let's go. Look, she lives in Half Moon Street,' Lily said.

'And a damned good address for the *demi-monde*,' Sylvia added.

However, the tea-party was definitely a success, and for the rest of the summer Sylvia and Lily spent a lot of time on the river with what Sylvia called the semicircle of intimate friends they had brought away from Half Moon Street. She grew very fond of Olive Fanshawe and warned her against her romantic adoration of Dorothy.

'But you're just as romantic over Lily,' Olive argued.

'Not a single illusion left, my dear,' Sylvia assured her. 'Besides, I should never compare Lily with Dorothy. Dorothy is more beautiful, more ambitious, more mercenary: she'll probably marry a lord. She's brought the art of getting a lot for nothing to a perfection that could only be matched by a politician, or by a girl with the same brown eyes in the same glory of light brown hair. And when it suits her she'll go back on her word just as gracefully, and sell her best friend as readily as a politician will sell his country.'

'You're very down on politicians. I think there's something so romantic about them,' Olive declared. 'Young politicians, of course.'

'My dear, you'd think a Bradshaw romantic.'

'It is sometimes,' said Olive.

'Well, I know two young politicians,' Sylvia continued. 'A Liberal and a Conservative. They both spend their whole time in hoping I shan't suggest walking down Bond Street with them, the Liberal because I may see a frock and the Conservative because he may meet a friend. They both make love to me, as if they were addressing their future constituents, with a mixture of flattery, condescension, and best clothes; but they reserve all their affection for the constituency. As I tell them, if they'd fondle the constituency and nurse me, I should endure their company more easily. Unhappily they both think I'm intelligent, and a man who admires a woman's intelligence is like a woman who admires her friend's looking-glass – each one is granting an audience to himself.'

'At any rate,' said Olive, 'you've managed to make yourself quite a mystery. All the men we know are puzzled by you.'

'Tell them, my dear, I'm quite simple. I represent the original conception of the Hetæra – the companion. I don't want to be made love to, and every man who makes love to me I dislike. If I ever do fall in love, I'll be a man's slave. Of that I'm sure. So don't utter dark warnings, for I've warned myself already. I do want a certain number of things – nice dresses, because I owe them to myself, good books, and – well really, I think that's all. In return for the dresses and the books – I suppose one ought to add an occasional fiver just to show there's no ill feeling about preferring to sleep in my own room – in return for very little I'm ready to talk, laugh, sing, dance, tell incomparably bawdy stories and, what is after all the most valuable return of all, I'm ready to sit perfectly still and let myself be bored to death while giving him an idea that I'm listening intelligently. Of course, sometimes I do listen intelligently without being bored. In that case I let him off with books only.'

'You really are an extraordinary girl,' said Olive.

'You, on the other hand, my dear,' Sylvia went on, 'always give every man the hope that if he's wise and tender, and of course lavish – ultimately all men believe in the pocket – he will be able to cry Open Sesame to the mysterious treasure of romantic love that he discerns in your dark eyes, in your caressing voice, and in your fervid aspirations. In the end you'll give it all to a curly-headed actor, and live happily ever afterwards at Ravenscourt Park. Farewell to Coriolanus in his smart waistcoat: farewell to Julius Cæsar and his amber cigarette-holder: farewell to every nincompoop with a top-hat as bright as a halo; farewell incidentally to Dolly Lonsdale, who'll discover that Ravenscourt Park is too difficult for the chauffeur to find.'

'Oh, Sylvia, shut up,' Olive said. 'I believe you drank too much champagne at lunch.'

'I'm glad you reminded me,' Sylvia cried. 'By Jove, I'd forgotten the fizz. That's where we all meet on common ground – or rather I should say in common liquid. It sounds like mixed bathing. It is a kind of mixed bathing after all. You're quite right, Olive, whatever our different tastes in men, clothes, and behaviour, we all must have champagne. Champagne is our element.'

Gradually Sylvia did succeed in sorting out from the various men a few who were content to accept the terms of friendship she offered. She had to admit that most of them fell soon or late, and with each new man she gave less and took more. As regards Lily she tried to keep her as unapproachable as herself, but it was not always possible; sometimes with a shrug of the shoulders she let Lily go her own way, though she was always as hard as steel with the fortunate suitor. Once a rich young financier called Hausberg, who had found Lily somewhat expensive, started a theory that Sylvia was living on her friend; she heard of the slander and dealt with it very directly. The young man in question was anxious to set Lily up in a flat of her own. Sylvia let Lily appear to view the plan with favour. The flat was taken and furnished; a date was fixed for Lily's entrance; the young man was given the latchkey and told to come at midnight. When he arrived, there was nobody in the flat but a chimpanzee that Sylvia had bought at Jamrack's. She and Lily were at Brighton with Arthur Lonsdale and Tony Clarehaven whom they had recently met again at a Covent Garden ball.

They were both just down from Oxford, and Lonsdale had taken a great fancy to Lily. He was a jolly youth, whose father Lord Cleveden had consented after a struggle to let him go into partnership with a distinguished professional motorist: it was with him that Dorothy Lonsdale claimed distant kinship. Clarehaven's admiration for Dorothy had not diminished; somebody had told him that the best way to get hold of her would be to make her jealous; this was his object in inviting Sylvia to Brighton. Sylvia agreed to go partly to tease Dorothy, partly to disappoint Clarehaven. Lonsdale had helped her to get the chimpanzee into the flat, and all the way down to Brighton they laughed.

'My word, you know,' Lonsdale chuckled, 'the jolly old chimpanzee will probably eat the wall-paper. What do you think Hausberg will say when he opens the door?'

'I expect he'll say "Are you there, Lily?" ' Sylvia suggested.

'What do you think the jolly old chimpanzee will do? Probably bite his ear off, what? Topping. Good engine this. We're doing fifty-nine or an unripe sixty. Why does a chicken cross the road? No answer, thank you, this time. Must slow down a bit. There's a trap somewhere along here. I say, you know, I've got a sister called Sylvia. Hullo! hullo! mind your hoop, Tommy! Too late. Funeral on Friday. Colonial papers please copy. I wonder how they'll get the chimpanzee out again. I told the hall-porter, when he cast a cold and glassy eye on the crate, it was a marble Venus that Mr. Hausberg was going to use as a hatstand. My word, I expect the jolly old flat looks like the last days of Pompeii by now. When I undid the door of the crate, the brute was making a noise like a discontented cistern. I rapidly scattered nuts and bananas on the floor to occupy his mind and melted away like a strawberry ice on a grill. Hullo, we're getting into Brighton.'

Clarehaven did not enjoy his week-end, for it consisted entirely of a lecture by Sylvia on his behaviour; this caused him to drink many more whiskies and sodas than usual, and he came back to London on Monday with a bad headache which he attributed to Sylvia's talking.

'My dear man, I haven't got a mouth; you have,' she said.

This week-end caused a quarrel between Sylvia and Dorothy, for which she was not sorry; she had recently met a young painter, Ronald Walker, who wanted Lily to sit for him; he had taken them once or twice to the Café Royal, which Sylvia had found a pleasant change from the society of Half Moon Street. Soon after this Lonsdale began a liaison with Queenie Molyneux of the Frivolity Theatre; and the only member of the Half Moon Street set with whom Sylvia kept up a friendship was Olive Fanshawe.

II

During her second year at Mulberry Cottage Sylvia achieved an existence that save for the absence of any one great motive like art or love was complete. She had also one real friend in Jack Airdale who had returned from his tour. Apart from the pleasant security of knowing that he would always be content with good fellowship only, he encouraged her to suppose that somewhere, could she but find the first step, a career lay before her. Sylvia did not in her heart believe in this career; but in moments of depression Jack's confidence was of the greatest comfort, and she was always ready to play with the notion, particularly as it seemed to provide a background for her present existence and to cover the futility of its perfection. Jack was anxious that she should try to get on the proper stage; but Sylvia feared to destroy by premature failure a part of the illusion of ultimate success she continued to allow herself, to which the theatre was a possible channel.

In the summer, Lily became friendly with one or two men whom Sylvia could not endure, but a lassitude had descended upon her and she lacked any energy to stop the association. As a matter of fact she was sickening for diphtheria at the time, and while she was in the hospital, Lily took to frequenting the Orient promenade with these new friends. As soon as Sylvia came out, they were banished; but each time that she intervened on Lily's behalf it seemed to her a little less worth while. Nevertheless, finding that Lily was bored by her own habit of staying in at night, she used much against her will to accompany her very often to various places of amusement without a definite invitation from a man to escort them.

One day at the end of December, Mrs. Gainsborough came home from shopping with two tickets for a fancy-dress dance at the Redcliffe Hall in Fulham Road. When the evening arrived, Sylvia did not want to go, for the weather was raw and foggy; but Mrs. Gainsborough was so much disappointed at her tickets not being used that to please her Sylvia agreed to go. It seemed unlikely to be an amusing affair, so she and Lily went in the most ordinary of their fancy dresses as masked Pierrettes: the company, as they had anticipated, was exceptionally dull.

'My dear, it's like a skating-rink on Saturday afternoon,' Sylvia declared. 'We'll have one more dance together and then go home.'

They were standing at the far end of the hall near the orchestra, and Sylvia was making disdainful comments upon the various couples that were passing out to refresh themselves, or to flirt in the draughty corridors.

Suddenly Sylvia saw a man in evening dress pushing his way in their direction, regardless of what ribbons he tore or toes he outraged in his transit. He was a young man of about twenty-three or twenty-four with a countenance in which eagerness was curiously mixed with impassivity. Sylvia saw him as one sees a picture on first entering a gallery, which one postpones visiting with a scarcely conscious and yet perfectly deliberate anticipation of pleasure later on. She continued talking to Lily who had her back to the newcomer; while she talked she was aware that all her own attention was fixed upon this newcomer and that she was asking herself the cause of the contradictions in his face and deciding that it was due to the finely carved immobile mouth beneath such eager dark eyes. Were they brown or blue? The young man had reached them, and from that immobile mouth came in accents that were almost like despair a salutation to Lily. Sylvia felt for a moment as if she had been wounded;

she saw that Lily was looking at her with that expression she always put on when she thought Sylvia was angry with her; then after what seemed an age she turned round slowly to the young man and, lifting her mask, engaged in conversation with him. Sylvia felt that she was trespassing upon the borders of great emotion and withdrew out of hearing, until Lily beckoned her forward to introduce the young man as Mr. Michael Fane. Sylvia did not raise her mask and after nodding to him again retired from the conversation.

'But this is absurd,' she said to herself after a while, and abruptly raising her mask she broke in upon the duologue. The music had begun; he was asking Lily to dance and she, waiting for Sylvia's leave in a way that made Sylvia want to slap her, was hesitating.

'What rot, Lily,' she exclaimed impatiently. 'Of course you can dance.'

The young man turned towards Sylvia and smiled; a moment later he and Lily had waltzed away.

'Good god,' said Sylvia to herself. 'Am I going mad? A youth smiles at me and I feel inclined to cry. What is this waltz they're playing?'

She looked at one of the sheets of music, but the name was nowhere legible, and she nearly snatched it away from the player in exasperation. Nothing seemed to matter in the world except that she should know the name of this waltz; without thinking what she was doing she thumped the clarinet player on the shoulder, who stopped indignantly and asked if she was trying to knock his teeth out.

'What waltz are you playing? What waltz are you playing?'

'Waltz Amarousse. Perhaps you'll punch one of the strings next time, miss?'

'Happy New Year,' Sylvia laughed, and the clarinet player with a disgusted glance turned round to his music again.

By the time the dance was over and the other two had rejoined her, Sylvia was laughing at herself; but they thought she was laughing at them. Fane and Lily danced several more dances together; and gradually Sylvia made up her mind that she disapproved of this new intimacy, this sudden invasion of Lily's life out of a past from which she should have cut herself off as completely as Sylvia had done from her own. What right had Lily to complicate their existence in this fashion? How unutterably dull this masquerade was; she whispered to Lily in the next interval that she was tired and wanted to go home.

The fog outside was very dense; Fane took their arms to cross the road, and Sylvia, though he caught her arm close to him, felt drearily how mechanical its gesture was towards her, how vital towards Lily. Neither of her companions spoke to one another, and she asked them questions about their former friendship, which Lily did not answer because she was evidently afraid of her annoyance, and which he did not answer because he did not hear. Sylvia had made up her mind that Fane should not enter Mulberry Cottage when Lily whispered to her that she should ask him; but at the last moment she remembered his smile and invited him to supper. A strange shyness took possession of her, which she tried to cover by exaggerated, almost, she thought, hysterical fooling with Mrs. Gainsborough that lasted until two o'clock in the morning of New Year's Day, when Michael Fane went home after exacting a promise from the two girls to lunch with him at Kettner's that afternoon. Lily was so sleepy that she did not rise to see him out; Sylvia was glad of the indifference.

Next morning Sylvia found out that Michael was a 'nice boy' whom Lily had known in West Kensington when she was seventeen. He had been awfully in love with her, and her mother had been annoyed because he wanted to marry her. He had only been seventeen himself, and like many other schoolboy-loves of those days this one had just ended somehow, but exactly how Lily could not recall. She wished that Sylvia would not go on asking so many questions; she really could not remember anything more about it; they had once gone for a long drive in a cab, and there had been a row about that at home.

'Are you in love with him now?' Sylvia demanded.

'No, of course not. How could I be?'

Sylvia was determined that she never should be either: there should be no more Claude Raglans to interfere with their well-devised existence.

During the next fortnight, Sylvia took care that Lily and Fane should never be alone together, and she tried very often, after she discovered that Fane was sensitive, to shock him by references to their life and with an odd perversity to try particularly to shock him about herself by making brutally coarse remarks in front of Lily, taking pleasure in his embarrassment. Yet there was in the end little pleasure in shocking him, for he had no conventional niceness; yet there was a pleasure in hurting him, a fierce pleasure.

'Though why on earth I bother about his feelings, I can't imagine,' Sylvia said to herself. 'All I know is that he's an awful bore and makes us break all sorts of engagements with other people. You liar! You know he's not a bore, and you know that you don't care a damn how many engagements you break. Don't pose to yourself. You're jealous of him because you think that Lily may get really fond of him. You don't want her to get fond of him, because you don't think she's good enough for him. You don't want *him* to get fond of *her*.'

The boldness of this thought, the way in which it had attacked the secret recesses of her being startled Sylvia. It was almost a sensation of turning pale at herself, of fearing to understand herself, that made her positively stifle the mood and flee from these thoughts, the violators of her personality.

Downstairs, there was a telegram from Olive Fanshawe at Brighton begging Sylvia to come at once; she was terribly unhappy. Sylvia could scarcely tear herself away from Mulberry Cottage at such a moment even for Olive; but, knowing that if she did not go she would be sorry, she went.

Sylvia found Olive in a state of collapse. Dorothy Lonsdale and she had been staying in Brighton for a week's holiday, and yesterday Dorothy had married Clarehaven. Sylvia laughed.

'Oh, Sylvia, don't laugh,' Olive begged. 'It was perfectly dreadful. Of course, it was a great shock to me, though I did not show it. I told her she could count on me as a pal to help her in every way. And what do you think she said? Sylvia, you'll never guess. It was too cruel. She said to me in a voice of ice, dear, really a voice of ice, she said the best way I could help her was by not seeing her any more: she did not intend to go near the stage-door of a theatre again: she did not want to know any of her stage friends any more. She didn't even say she was sorry; she was quite calm. She was like ice, Sylvia dear. Clarehaven came in, and she asked if he'd telegraphed to his mother and, when he said he had, she got up as if she'd been calling on me quite formally and shook hands, and said "Good-bye, Olive, we're going down to Clare Court to-morrow, and I don't expect we shall see each other again for a long time." Clarehaven said what rot and that I must come down to Devonshire and stay with them, and Dolly froze him, my dear; she froze him with one look. I never slept all night, and the book I was reading began to repeat itself, and I thought I was going mad; but this morning I found the printers had made some mistake and put sixteen pages twice over. But I really thought I was going mad, so I wired for you. Oh, Sylvia, say something to console me. She was like ice, dear, really like a block of ice.'

'If she'd only waited till you had found the curly-headed actor, it wouldn't have mattered so much,' Sylvia said.

Poor Olive really was on the verge of a nervous collapse, and Sylvia stayed with her three days, though it was agony to leave Lily in London with Michael Fane. Nor could she talk of her own case to Olive: it would seem like a competitive sorrow, a vulgar bit of egotistic assumption to suit the occasion.

When Sylvia got back to Mulberry Cottage, she found an invitation from Jack Airdale to dine at Richmond and go to a dance with him afterwards. Conscious from something in Michael's watchful demeanour of a development in the situation, she was pleased to be able to disquiet him by insisting that Lily should go with her.

On the way, Sylvia extracted from Lily that Michael had asked her to marry him. it took all Jack Airdale's good nature not to be angry with Sylvia that night – as she tore the world to shreds. At the moment when Lily had told her, she had felt with a despair that was not communicable, as Olive's despair had been, how urgent it was to stop Michael from marrying Lily. She was not good enough for him. The knowledge rang in her brain like a discordant clangour of bells, and Sylvia knew in that moment that the real reason of her thinking this was jealousy of Lily. The admission tortured her pride, and she spent a terrible night in which the memory of Olive's grief interminably dwelt upon and absorbed helped her to substitute the pretence, so passionately invoked that it almost ceased to be a pretence, that she was opposing the marriage, partly because Michael would never keep Lily faithful, partly because she could not bear the idea of losing her friend.

When the next day Sylvia faced Michael for the discussion of the marriage, she was quite sure not merely that he had never attracted her, but even that she hated him and, what was more deadly, despised him. She taunted him with wishing to marry Lily for purely sentimental reasons, for the gratification of a morbid desire to redeem her. She remembered Philip, and all the hatred she had felt for Philip's superiority was transferred to Michael. She called him a prig, and made him wince by speaking of Lily and herself as 'tarts,' exacting from the word the uttermost tribute of its vulgarity. She dwelt on Lily's character and evolved a theory of woman's ownership by man that drove her into such illogical arguments and exaggerated pretensions that Michael had some excuse for calling her hysterical. The dispute left Lily on one side for a time and became personal to herself and him. He told her she was jealous; in an access of outraged pride she forgot that he was referring to her jealousy about Lily, and to anyone less obsessed by an idea than he was she would have revealed her secret. Suddenly he seemed to give way; when he was going, he told her that she hated him because he loved Lily and hated him twice as much because his love was returned.

Sylvia felt she should go mad, when Michael said that he loved Lily; but he was thinking it was because Lily loved him that Sylvia was biting her nails and glaring at him. Then he asked her what college at Oxford her husband had been at: she had spoken of Philip during their quarrel. This abrupt linking of himself with Philip restored her balance, and coolly she began to arrange in her mind for Lily's withdrawal from London for

a while. Of passion and fury there was nothing left except a calm determination to disappoint him. She remembered Olive Fanshawe's *Like ice,
dear, she was like a block of ice:* she, too, was like a block of ice, when
she watched him walking away down the long garden.

After Michael had gone, Sylvia told Lily that marriage with him was
impossible.

'Why do you want to be married?' she demanded. 'Was your mother
so happy in her marriage? I tell you, child, that marriage is almost
inconceivably dull. What have you got in common with him? Nothing,
absolutely nothing.'

'I'm not a bit anxious to be married,' Lily protested. 'But when somebody goes on and on asking, it's so difficult to refuse. I liked Claude
better than I like Michael. But Claude had to think about his future.'

'And what about your future?' Sylvia exclaimed.

'Oh, I expect it'll be all right. Michael has money.'

'I say you shall not marry him,' Sylvia almost shouted.

'Oh, don't keep on so,' Lily fretfully implored. 'It gives me a headache.
I won't marry him, if it's going to upset you so much. But you mustn't
leave me alone with him again; because he worries me just as much as
you do.'

'We'll go away to-morrow,' Sylvia announced abruptly. It flashed upon
her that she would like to go to Sirene with Lily, but, alas, there was not
enough money for such a long journey, and Bournemouth or Brighton
must be the colourless substitute.

Lily cheered up at the idea of going away, and Sylvia was half-resentful
that she could accept so easily parting from Michael. Lily's frocks were
not ready the next day, and in the morning Michael's ring was heard.

'Oh, now I suppose we shall have more scenes,' Lily complained.

Sylvia ran after Mrs. Gainsborough, who was waddling down the
garden-path to open the door.

'Come back, come back at once,' she cried. 'You're not to open the
door.'

'Well, there's a nice thing. But it may be the butcher.'

'We don't want any meat. It's not the butcher. It's Fane. You're not to
open the door. We've all gone away.'

'Well, don't snap my head off,' said Mrs. Gainsborough, turning back
unwillingly to the house.

All day long at intervals the bell rang.

'The neighbours'll think the house is on fire,' Mrs. Gainsborough
bewailed.

'Nobody hears it except ourselves, you silly old thing,' Sylvia said.

'And what'll the passers-by think?' Mrs. Gainsborough asked. 'It looks so funny to see anyone standing outside a door, ringing all day long like a chimney sweep who's come on Monday instead of Tuesday. Let me go out and tell him you've gone away. I'll hold the door on the jar, the same as if I was arguing with a hawker. Now be sensible, Sylvia. I'll just pop out, pop my head round the door, and pop back in again.'

'You're not to go. Sit down.'

'You do order anyone about so. I might be a serviette the way you crumple me up. Sylvia, don't keep prodding into me. I may be fat, but I have some feelings left. You're a regular young spiteful. A porter wouldn't treat luggage so rough. Give over, Sylvia.'

'What a fuss you make about nothing,' Sylvia exclaimed.

'Well, that ping-ping-pinging gets on my nerves. I feel as if I were coming out in black spots like a domino. Why don't the young fellow give over? It's a wonder his fingers aren't worn out.'

The ringing continued until nearly midnight in bursts of half an hour at a stretch. Next morning Sylvia received a note from Fane in which he invited her to be sporting and let him see Lily.

'How I hate that kind of gentlemanly attitude,' she scoffed to herself.

Sylvia wrote as unpleasant letter as she could invent, which she left with Mrs. Gainsborough to be given to Michael when he should call in answer to an invitation she had posted for the following day at twelve o'clock. Then Lily and she left for Brighton. All the way down in the train she kept wondering why she had ended her letter to Michael by calling him *my little Vandyck*; suddenly she flew into a rage with herself, because she knew that she was making such speculation an excuse to conjure his image to her mind.

Towards the end of February Sylvia and Lily came back to Mulberry Cottage. Sylvia had woken up one morning with the conviction that it was beneath her dignity to interfere further between Lily and Michael. She determined to leave everything to fate: she would go and stay with Olive for a while, and if Lily went away with Michael, so much the better: to hell with both of them. This resolution once taken, Sylvia, who had been rather charming to Lily all the time at Brighton, began now to treat her with a contempt that was really an expression of the contempt she felt for Michael. A week after their return to London she spent the whole of one day in ridiculing him so cruelly that even Mrs. Gainsborough protested. Then she was seized with an access of penitence and, clasping Lily to her, she almost entreated her to vow that she loved her better than anyone else in the world. Lily, however, was by this time thoroughly sulky and would have nothing to do with Sylvia's tardy sweetness. The petulant way in which she shook herself free from the embrace at last brought Sylvia up to the point of leaving Lily to herself. She should go and stay with Olive Fanshawe and if when she came back Lily were still at Mulberry Cottage, she would atone for the way she had treated her lately; if she were gone, it would be only one more person ruthlessly cut out of her life. It was curious to think of everybody – Monkley, Philip, the Organs, Mabel, the twins, Miss Ashley, Dorward, all going on with their lives at this moment regardless of her.

'I might just as well be dead,' she told herself. 'What a fuss people make about death.'

Sylvia was shocked to find how much Olive had suffered from Dorothy's treatment of her. For the first time in her life she was unable to dispose of emotion as mere romantic or sentimental rubbish: there was indeed something deeper than the luxury of grief that could thus ennoble even a Vanity girl.

'I do try, Sylvia, not to mope all the time. I keep on telling myself that, if I really loved Dorothy, I should be glad for her to be Countess of Clarehaven, with everything that she wants. She was always a good girl. I lived with her more than two years, and she was *frightfully* strict about men. She deserved to be a countess. And I'm sure she's quite right in wanting to cut herself off altogether from the theatre. I think, you know, she may have meant to be kind in telling me at once like that, instead of gradually dropping me, which would have been worse, wouldn't it? Only I do miss her. She was such a lovely thing to look at.'

'So are you,' Sylvia said.

'Ah, but I'm dark, dear: and a dark girl never has that almost unearthly beauty Dolly had.'

'Dark girls have often something better than unearthly and seraphic beauty,' Sylvia said. 'They often have a gloriously earthly and human faithfulness.'

'Ah, you used to tease me about being romantic, but I think it's you that's being romantic now. You were quite right, dear; I used to be stupidly romantic over foolish little things without any importance, and now it all seems such a waste of time. That's really what I feel most of all, now that I've lost my friend. It seems to me that every time I patted a dog I was wasting time.'

Sylvia had a fleeting thought that perhaps Gladys and Enid Worsley might have felt like that about her, but in a moment she quenched the fire it kindled in her heart. She was not going to bask in the warmth of self-pity like a spoilt little girl that hopes she may die to punish her brother for teasing her.

'I think, you know,' Olive went on, 'that girls like us aren't prepared to stand sorrow. We've absolutely nothing to fall back upon. I've been thinking all these days what an utterly unsatisfactory thing lunch at Romano's really is. The only period in my life that I can look back to for comfort is summer at the Convent in Belgium. Of course we giggled all the time; but all the noise of talking has died away, and I can only see a most extraordinary peacefulness. I wonder if the nuns would have me as a boarder for a little while this summer. I feel I absolutely must go there. It isn't being sentimental, because I never knew Dorothy in those days.'

Perhaps Olive's regret for her lost friend affected Sylvia; when she went back to Mulberry Cottage and found that Lily had gone away, notwithstanding her own deliberate provocation of the elopement, she was dismayed. There was nothing left of Lily but two old frocks in the wardrobe, two old frocks the colour of dead leaves; and this poignant reminder of a physical loss drove out all the other emotions. She told herself that it was ridiculous to be moved like this, and she jeered at herself for imitating Olive's grief. But it was no use; those two frocks affrighted her courage with their deadness; no kind of communion after marriage would compensate for the loss of Lily's presence: it was like the fading of a flower in the completeness of its death. Even if she had been able to achieve the selflessness of Olive and take delight in Lily's good fortune, how impossible it was to believe in the fitness of this marriage. Lily would either be bored or she would become actively miserable – Sylvia scoffed at the adverb – and run away, or rather slowly melt to damnation: it would not even be necessary for her to be miserable – any unscrupulous friend of her husband's would have his way with her. For an instant Sylvia had a tremor of compassion for Michael, but it died in the thought of how such a disillusion would serve him right. He had built up this passion out of sentimentality: he was like Don Quixote: he was stupid. No doubt he had managed by now to fall in love with Lily, but it had never been an inevitable passion, and no pity should be shown to lovers that did not love wildly at first sight: they alone could plead fate's decrees.

Jack Airdale came to see Sylvia, and he took advantage of her dejection to press his desire for her to go upon the stage. He was positive that she had in her the makings of a great actress. He did not want to talk about himself, but he must tell Sylvia that there was a wonderful joy in getting on: he should never of course do anything very great, but he was understudy to someone or other at some theatre or other, and there was always a chance of really showing what he could do one night, or at any rate one afternoon. Even Claude was getting on: he had met him the other day in a tail coat and a top-hat. Since there had been such an outcry against tubercular infection, he had been definitely cured of his tendency toward consumption: he had nothing but neurasthenia to contend with now.

But Sylvia would not let Jack 'speak about her' to the managers he knew. She had no intention of continuing as she was at present, but she should wait till she was twenty-three before she took any step that would involve anything more energetic than turning over the pages of a book: she intended to dream away the three months that were left to twenty-two. Jack Airdale went away discouraged.

Sylvia met Ronald Walker who had painted Lily; from him she learnt that Fane had taken a house for her somewhere near Regent's Park. By a curious coincidence, a great friend of his who was also a friend of Fane's had helped to acquire the house. Ronald understood that there was considerable feeling against the marriage among Fane's friends. What was Fane like? He knew several men who knew him, and he seemed to be one of those people about whose affairs everybody talked.

'Thank heaven, nobody bothers about me,' said Ronald. 'This man Fane seems to have money to throw about. I wish he'd buy my picture of Lily. You're looking rather down, Sylvia. I suppose you miss her? By Jove, what an amazing sitter. She wasn't really beautiful, you know – I mean to say with the kind of beauty that lives outside its setting. I don't quite mean that, but in my picture of her, which most people consider the best thing I've done, she never gave me what I ought to have had from such a model. I felt cheated somehow, as if I'd cut a bough from a tree and in doing so destroyed all its grace. It was her gracefulness really; and dancing's the only art for that. I can't think why I didn't paint you.'

'You're not going to begin now,' Sylvia assured him.

'Well, of course, now you challenge me,' he laughed. 'The fact is, Sylvia, I've never really seen you in repose till this moment. You were always tearing around and talking. Look here, I do want to paint you. I say, let me paint you in this room with Mrs. Gainsborough. By Jove, I see exactly what I want.'

'It sounds as if you wanted an illustration for the Old and New Year,' Sylvia said.

In the end, however, she gave way; and really it passed the time, sitting for Ronald Walker with Mrs. Gainsborough in that room where nothing of Lily remained.

'Well,' Mrs. Gainsborough declared, when the painter had finished. 'I knew I was fat, but really it's enough to make anyone get out of breath just to look at anyone so fat as you've made me. He hasn't been stingy with his paint, I'll say that. But really, you know, it looks like a picture of the Fat Woman in a fair. Now Sylvia's very good. Just the way she looks at you with her chin stuck out like a step-ladder. Your eyes are very good too. He's just got that nasty glitter you get in them sometimes.'

One day in early June without any warning Michael Fane revisited Mulberry Cottage. Sylvia had often declaimed against him to Mrs. Gainsborough, and now while they walked up the garden, she could see that Mrs. Gainsborough was nervous, and by the way that Michael walked either that he was nervous or that something had happened. Sylvia came down the steps from the balcony to meet them, and reading in his countenance that he had come to ask her help, she was aware of an immense relief, which she hid under an attitude of cold hostility. They sat on the garden-seat under the budding mulberry tree, and without any preliminaries of conversation Michael told her that he and Lily had parted. Sylvia resented an implication in his tone that she would somehow be awed by this announcement; she felt bitterly anxious to disappoint and humiliate him by her indifference, hoping that he would beg her to get Lily back for him. Instead of this he spoke of putting her out of his life, and Sylvia perceived that it was not at all to get Lily back that he had come to her. She was angry at missing her opportunity and she jeered at the stately way in which he confessed his failure and his loss: nor would he wince when she mocked his romantic manner of speech. At last she was nearly driven into the brutality of picturing in unforgivable words the details of Lily's infidelity, but from this he flinched, stopping her with a gesture. He went on to give Sylvia full credit for her victory, to grant that she had been right from the first, and gradually by dwelling on the one aspect of Lily that was common to both of them, her beauty, he asked her very gently to take Lily back to live with her again. Sylvia could not refrain from sneers, and he was stung into another allusion to her jealousy, which Sylvia set out to disprove almost mathematically, though all the time she was afraid of what clear perception he might not have attained through sorrow. But he was still obsessed by the salvation of Lily; and Sylvia, because she could forgive him for his indifference to her own future except so far as it might help Lily, began to mock at herself, to accuse herself for those three months after she left Philip, to rake up that corpse from its burial-place so that this youth who troubled her very soul might turn his face from her in irremediable disgust and set her free from the spell he was unaware of casting.

When she had worn herself out with the force of her denunciation both of herself and of mankind, he came back to his original request; Sylvia incapable of struggling further yielded to his perseverance, but with a final flicker of self-assertion she begged him not to suppose that she was agreeing to take Lily back for any other reason than because she wanted to please herself.

Michael began to ask her about Lily's relation to certain men with whom he had heard her name linked, with Ronald Walker, and with Lonsdale whom he had known at Oxford. Sylvia told him the facts quite simply; and then because she could not bear this kind of self-torture he was inflicting on himself, she tried to put out of its agony his last sentimental regret for Lily by denying to her and by implication to herself also the justification even of a free choice.

'Money is necessary sometimes, you know,' she said.

Sylvia expected he would recoil from this, but he accepted it as the statement of a natural fact, agreed with its truth, and begged that in the future if ever money were necessary that he might be given the privilege of helping. So long as it was apparently only Lily whom he desired to help thus, Michael had put forward his claims easily enough: then in a flash Sylvia felt that now he was transferring half his interest in Lily to her. He was stumbling hopelessly over that: he was speaking in a shy way of sending her books that she would enjoy: then abruptly he had turned from her, and the garden door had slammed behind him. It was with a positive exultation that Sylvia realized that he had forgotten to give her Lily's address and that it was the dread of seeming to intrude upon *her* which had driven him away like that. She ran after him and called him back. He gave her a visiting-card on which his name was printed above the address: it was like a little tombstone of his dead love. He was talking now about selling the furniture and sending money to Lily; Sylvia all the time was wondering why the first man that had ever appealed to her in the least should be in the same category as the hero of literature that had always most bored her. With an impulse to avenge Michael she asked the name of the man for whom Lily had betrayed him. But he had never known: he had only seen his hat.

Sylvia pulled Michael to her and kissed him with the first kiss she had given to any man that was not contemptuous either of him or of herself.

'How many women have kissed you suddenly like that?' she asked.

'One – well, perhaps two,' he answered.

Even this kiss of hers was not hers alone, but because she might never see him again Sylvia broke the barrier of jealousy and in a sudden longing to be prodigal of herself for once she gave him all she could – her pride – by letting him know that she for her part had never kissed any man like that before.

Sylvia went back to the seat under the mulberry tree and made up her mind that the time was ripe for activity again. She had allowed herself to become the prey of emotion by leading this indeterminate life in which sensation was cultivated at the expense of incident. It was a pity that Michael had entrusted her with Lily, for at this moment she would have liked to be away out of it at once; any adventure embarked upon with Lily would always be bounded by her ability to pack in time. Sylvia could imagine how those two dresses she had left behind must have been the most insuperable difficulty of the elopement: another objection to Lily's company now was the way in which it would repeatedly remind her of Michael.

'Of course it won't remind me sentimentally,' Sylvia assured herself. 'I'm not such a fool as to suppose that I'm going to suffer from a sense of personal loss. On the other hand I shan't ever be able to forget what an exaggerated impression I gave him. It's really perfectly damnable to divine one's sympathy with a person, to know that one could laugh together through life, and by circumstances to have been placed in an utterly abnormal relation to him. It really is damnable. He'll think of me, if he ever thinks of me at all, as one of the great multitude of wronged women. I shall think of him, though as a matter of fact I shall avoid thinking of him, either as what might have been – a false concept, for of course what might have been is fundamentally inconceivable – or as what he was – a sentimental fool. However, the mere fact that I'm sitting here bothering my head about what either of us thinks shows that I need a change of air.'

That afternoon a parcel of books arrived for Sylvia from Michael Fane: among them was Skelton's *Don Quixote* and Aldington's *Apuleius*, in the fly leaf of which he had written: *I've eaten rose leaves and I am no longer a golden ass.*

'No, damn his eyes,' said Sylvia. 'I'm the ass now. And how odd that he should send me *Don Quixote*.'

At twilight Sylvia went to see Lily at Ararat House. She found her in a strange rococo room that opened on a garden bordered by the Regent's Canal; here amid candles and mirrors she was sitting in conversation with her housekeeper. Each of them existed from every point of view and infinitely reduplicated in the mirrors, which was not favourable to toleration of the housekeeper's figure that was like an hour-glass. Sylvia waited coldly for her withdrawal before she acknowledged Lily's greeting. At last the objectionable creature rose and accompanied by a crowd of reflections, left the room.

'Don't lecture me,' Lily pleaded. 'I had the most awful time yesterday.'
'But Michael said he had not seen you.'
'Oh, not with Michael,' Lily exclaimed. 'With Claude.'

'With Claude?' Sylvia echoed.

'Yes, he came to see me and left his hat in the hall and Michael took it away with him in his rage. It was the only top-hat he'd got, and he had an engagement for an At Home, and he couldn't go out in the sun, and oh, dear, you never heard such a fuss, and when Mabel . . .'

'Mabel?'

'Miss Harper, my housekeeper, offered to go out and buy him another, he was livid with fury. He asked if I thought he was made of money and could buy top-hats like matches. I'm glad you've come. Michael has broken off the engagement, and I expected you rather. A friend of his – rather a nice boy called Maurice Avery – is coming round this evening to arrange about selling everything. I shall have quite a lot of money. Let's go away and be quiet after all this bother and fuss.'

'Look here,' Sylvia said. 'Before we go any further I want to know one thing: is Claude going to drop in and out of your life at critical moments for the rest of time?'

'Oh, no, we've quarrelled now. He'll never forgive me over the hat. Besides he puts some stuff on his hair now that I don't like. Sylvia, do come and look at my frocks. I've got some really lovely frocks.'

Maurice Avery, to whom Sylvia took an instant dislike, came in presently. He seemed to attribute the ruin of his friend's hopes entirely to a failure to take his advice:

'Of course this was the wrong house to start with. I advised him to take one at Hampstead, but he wouldn't listen to me. The fact is Michael doesn't understand women.'

'Do you?' Sylvia snapped.

Avery looked at her a moment, and said he understood them better than Michael.

'Of course nobody can ever really understand a woman,' he added with an instinct of self-protection. 'But I advised him not to leave Lily alone. I told him it wasn't fair to her or to himself.'

'Did you give him any advice about disposing of the furniture?' Sylvia asked.

'Well, I'm arranging about that now.'

'Sorry,' said Sylvia. 'I thought you were paving Michael's past with your own good intentions.'

'You mustn't take any notice of her,' Lily told Avery, who was looking rather mortified. 'She's rude to everybody.'

'Well, shall I tell you my scheme for clearing up here?' he asked.

'If it will bring us any nearer to business,' Sylvia answered, 'we'll manage to support the preliminary speech.'

A week or two later Avery handed Lily £270, which she immediately transferred to Sylvia's keeping.

'I kept the Venetian mirror for myself,' Avery said. 'You know, the one with the jolly little Cupids in pink and blue glass. I shall always think of you and Ararat House when I look at myself in it.'

'I suppose all your friends wear their hearts on your sleeve,' Sylvia said. 'That must add a spice to vanity.'

Mrs. Gainsborough was very much upset at the prospect of the girls' going away.

'That comes of having me picture painted. I felt it was unlucky when he was doing it. Oh, dearie me, whatever shall I do?'

'Come with us,' Sylvia suggested. 'We're going to France. Lock up your house, give the key to the copper on the beat, put on your gingham gown, and come with us, you old sea-elephant.'

'Come with you?' Mrs. Gainsborough gasped. 'But there, why shouldn't I?'

'No reason at all.'

'Why then I will. I believe the Captain would have liked me to get a bit of a blow.'

'Anything to declare?' the customs official asked at Boulogne.

'I declare I'm enjoying myself,' said Mrs. Gainsborough, looking round her and beaming at France.

III

When she once more landed on French soil, Sylvia actuated by a classic piety desired to visit her mother's grave. She would have preferred to go to Lille by herself, for she lacked the showman's instinct, but her companions were so horrified at the notion of being left to themselves in Paris until she rejoined them, that in the end she had to take them with her.

The sight of the old house and the faces of some of the older women in the *quartier* conjured up the past so vividly for Sylvia that she could not bring herself to make any enquiries about the rest of her family: it seemed as if she must once more look at Lille from her mother's point of view and maintain the sanctity of private life against the curiosity or criticism of neighbours. She did not wish to hear the details of her father's misdoing or perhaps be condoled with over Valentine. The simplest procedure would have been to lay a wreath upon the grave and depart again; this she might have done, if Mrs. Gainsborough's genial inquisitiveness about her relatives had not roused in herself a wish to learn something about them. She decided to visit her eldest sister in Brussels, leaving it to chance if she still lived where Sylvia had visited her twelve years ago.

'Brussels,' said Mrs. Gainsborough. 'Well, that sounds familiar anyway. Though I suppose the sprout gardens are all built over nowadays. Ah dear!'

The building over of her father's nursery-garden and of many other green spots she had known in London always drew a tear from Mrs. Gainsborough, who was inclined to attribute most of human sorrow to the utilitarian schemes of builders.

'Yes, they found the Belgian hares ate up all the sprouts,' Sylvia said. 'And talking of hair,' she went on, 'what's the matter with yours?'

'Ah, well, there! Now I meant to say nothing about it. But I've left me mahogany wash at home. There's a calamity!'

'You'd better come out with me and buy another bottle,' Sylvia advised.

'You'll never get one here,' said Mrs. Gainsborough. 'This is a wash, not a dye, you must remember. It doesn't tint the hair: it just brings up the colour and gives it a nice gloss.'

'If that's all it does, I'll lend you my shoe-polish. Go along, you wicked old fraud, and don't talk to me about washes. I can see the white hairs glistening like minnows.'

Sylvia found Elène in Brussels, and was astonished to see how much she resembled her mother nowadays. M. Durand, her husband, had prospered and he now owned a large confectioner's shop in the heart of the city, above which Madame Durand had started a pension for economical tourists. Mrs. Gainsborough could not get over the fact that her hostess did not speak English: it struck her as unnatural that Sylvia should have a sister who could only speak French. The little Durands were a more difficult problem: she did not so much mind feeling awkward with grown-up people through having to sit dumb, but children stared at her so, if she said nothing; and if she talked, they stared at her still more; she kept feeling that she ought to stroke them or pat them, which might offend their mother. She found ultimately that they were best amused by her taking out two false teeth she had, one of which was lost, because the eldest boy would play dice with them.

Elène gave Sylvia news of the rest of the family, though since all the four married sisters were in different towns in France and she had seen none of them for ten years, it was not very fresh news. Valentine, in whose career Sylvia was most interested, was being well *entretenue* by a *Marseillais* who had bought her an apartment that included a porcelain-tiled bathroom: she might be considered lucky, for the man with whom she had left Lille had been a rascal. It happened that her news of Valentine was fresh and authentic, because a *Lilleoise* who lived in Bruxelles had recently been obliged to go to Marseilles over some legal dispute and, meeting Valentine, had been invited to see her apartment. It was a pity that she was not married, but her position was the next best thing to marriage. Of the Bassompierrres Elène had heard nothing for years, but what would interest Sylvia were some family papers and photographs that Sylvia's father had sent to her as the eldest daughter when their mother died, together with an old-fashioned photograph of their grandmother. From these papers it seemed that an English *milord* and not Bassompierre had really been their grandfather. Sylvia being half English already it might not interest her so much, but for herself to know she had English blood *l'avait beaucoup impressionée:* so many English tourists came to her pension.

Sylvia looked at the daguerreotype of her grandmother, a glass faintly bloomed, the likeness of a ghost indeed. She then had loved an Englishman: her mother, too: herself? . . . Sylvia packed the daguerreotype out of sight, and turned to look at a golden shawl of a material rather like crêpe de Chine, which had been used to wrap up their mother when she was a baby. Would Sylvia like it? It was no use to Elène, too old and frail and faded. Sylvia stayed in Brussels for a week and left with many promises to return soon. She was glad she had paid the visit; for it had given back to her the sense of continuity which in the shifting panorama of her life she had lost, so that she had come to regard herself as an unreal person, an exception in humanity, an emotional freak; this separation from the rest of the world had been irksome to Sylvia since she had discovered the possibility of her falling in love, because it was seeming the cause of her not being loved. Henceforth she would meet man otherwise than with defiance or accusation in her eyes: she, too, perhaps should meet a lover thus.

Sylvia folded up the golden shawl to put it at the bottom of her trunk; figuratively she wrapped up in it her memories, tender, gay, sorrowful, vile – all together.

'Soon be in Paris, shall we?' said Mrs. Gainsborough, when the train reached the eastern suburbs. 'It makes one feel quite naughty, doesn't it? The Captain was always going to take me, but we never went somehow. What's that? There's the Eiffel Tower? So it is, upon my word, and just what it looks like in pictures. Not a bit different. I hope it won't fall down while we're still in Paris. Nice set out that would be. I've always been afraid of sky accidents since a friend of mine, a Mrs. Ewings, got stuck in the Great Wheel at Earl's Court with a man who started undressing himself. It was all right, as it happened, because he only wanted to wave his shirt to his wife, who was waiting for him down below, so as she shouldn't get anxious, but it gave Mrs. Ewings a nasty turn. Two hours she was stuck with nothing in her bag but a box of Little Liver Pills, which made her mouth water, she said, she was that hungry. She *thinks* she'd have eaten them, if she'd have been alone; but the man, who was an undertaker from Wandsworth, told her a lot of interesting stories about corpses, and that kept her mind occupied till the Wheel started going round again, and the Exhibition gave her soup and ten shillings compensation, which made a lot of people go up in it on the chance of being stuck.'

It was strange, Sylvia thought, that she should be as ignorant of Paris as Mrs. Gainsborough, but somehow the three of them would manage to enjoy themselves: Lily was more nearly vivacious than she had ever known her.

'Quite saucy,' Mrs. Gainsborough vowed. 'But there, we're all young, and you soon get used to the funny people you see in France. After all, they're foreigners. We ought to feel sorry for them.'

'I say steady, Mrs. Gainsborough,' Lily murmured with a frown. 'Some of these people in the carriage may speak English.'

'Speak English?' Mrs. Gainsborough repeated. 'You don't mean to tell me they'd go on jabbering to one another in French if they could speak English. What an idea!'

A young man who had got into the compartment at Chantilly had been casting glances of admiration at Lily ever since, and it was on account of him that she had warned Mrs. Gainsborough. He was a slim dark young man dressed by an English tailor, diffident for a Frenchman, but when Sylvia began to speculate upon the choice of an hotel, he could no longer keep silence and asked in English if he could be of any help; when Sylvia replied to him in French, he was much surprised:

'*Mais vous êtes française!*'

'*Je suis du pays de la lune,*' Sylvia said.

'Now don't encourage the young fellow to gabble in French,' Mrs. Gainsborough protested. 'It gives me the pins and needles to hear you. You ought to encourage people to speak English, if they want to, I'm sure.'

The young Frenchman smiled at this and offered his card to Sylvia, whom he evidently accepted as the head of the party. She read *Hector Ozanne*, and smiled for the heroic first name; somehow he did not look like Hector, and because he was so modest she presented him to Lily to make him happy.

'I am enchanted to meet a type of English beauty,' he said. 'You must forgive my sincerity which arises only from admiration. Madame,' he went on, turning to Mrs. Gainsborough, 'I am very honoured to meet you.'

Mrs. Gainsborough, who was not quite sure how to deal with such politeness, became flustered and dropped her bag. Ozanne and she both plunged for it simultaneously and bumped their heads; upon this painful salute a general friendliness was established.

'I am a bachelor,' said Ozanne. 'I have nothing to occupy myself, and if I might be permitted to assist you in a research for an apartment I shall be very elated.'

Sylvia decided in favour of rooms on the *rive gauche*: she felt it was a conventional taste, but held her opinion against Ozanne's objections.

'But I have an apartment in the Rue Montpensier with a view of the Palais Royal. I do not live there now myself. I beseech you to make me the pleasure to occupy it. It is so very good, the view of the garden. And if you like an ancient house, it is very ancient. Do you concur?'

'And where will you go?' Sylvia asked.

'I live always in my Club. For me it would be a big advantage, I assure you.'

'We should have to pay rent,' said Sylvia quickly.

'The rent will be one thousand a year.'

'God have mercy upon us!' Mrs. Gainsborough gasped. 'A thousand a year? Why the man must think that we're the Royal Family broken out from Windsor Castle on the randan.'

'Shut up, you silly old thing,' said Sylvia. 'He's asking nothing at all. Francs not pounds. *Vous êtes trop gentil pour nous, monsieur.*'

'*Alors, c'est entendu?*'

'*Mais oui.*'

'*Bon! Nous y irons ensemble tout de suite, n'est-ce pas?*'

The apartment was really charming: from the window one could see the priests with their breviaries muttering up and down the old garden of the Palais Royal; and as in all gardens in the heart of a great city many sorts of men and women were resting there in the sunlight. Ozanne invited them to dine with him that night and left them to unpack.

'Well, I'm bound to say we seem to have fallen on our feet right off,' Mrs. Gainsborough said. 'I shall quite enjoy myself here; I can see that already.'

The acquaintance with Hector Ozanne ripened into friendship and from friendship his passion for Lily became obvious, not that really it had ever been anything else, Sylvia thought: the question was whether it should be allowed to continue. Sylvia asked Ozanne his intentions; he declared his desperate affection, exclaimed against the iniquity of not being able to marry on account of a mother from whom he derived his entire income, stammered, and was silent.

'I suppose you'd like me and Mrs. Gainsborough to clear out of this?' Sylvia suggested.

No, he would like nothing of the kind: he greatly preferred that they should all stay where they were as they were, save only that of course they must pay no rent in future and that he must be allowed to maintain entirely the upkeep of the apartment. He wished it to be essentially their own, and he had no intention of intruding there except as a guest. From time to time no doubt Lily would like to see something of the French countryside and of the *plages*, and no doubt equally Sylvia would not be lonely in Paris with Mrs. Gainsborough. He believed that Lily loved him: she was of course like all English girls cold, but for his part he admired such coldness, in fact he admired everything English. He knew that his happiness depended upon Sylvia, and he begged her to be kind.

Hector Ozanne was the only son of a rich manufacturer, who had died about five years ago: the business had for some time been a limited company of which Madame Ozanne held the greater number of shares. Hector himself was now twenty-five and would within a year be found a wife by his mother: until then he might be allowed to choose a mistress by himself. He was kind-hearted, simple, and immensely devoted to Lily: she liked lunching and dining with him, and would like still better dressing herself at his expense: she certainly cared for him as much now as his future wife would care for him on the wedding-day: there seemed no reason to oppose the intimacy. If it should happen that Hector should fail to treat Lily properly, Sylvia would know how to deal with him, or rather with his mother. Amen.

July was burning fiercely, and Hector was unwilling to lose delightful days with Lily: they drove away together one morning in a big motor-car, which Mrs. Gainsborough blessed with as much fervour as she would have blessed a hired brougham at a suburban wedding. She and Sylvia were left together either to visit some *plage* or amuse themselves in Paris.

'Paris I think, you uncommendable mammoth, you phosphor-eyed hippotamus, Paris I *think*.'

'Well, I should like to see a bit of life, I must say. We've led a very quiet existence so far. I don't want to go back to England and tell my friend Mrs. Marsham that I've seen nothing. She's a most enterprising woman herself. I don't think you ever saw her, did you? Before she was going to have her youngest she had a regular craving to ride on a camel. She used to dream of camels all night long, and at last, being as I said a very enterprising woman and being afraid when her youngest was born he might be a humpback through her dreaming of camels all the time, she couldn't stand it no longer and one Monday morning, which is a sixpenny day, she went off to the Zoo by herself, being seven months gone at the time, and took six rides on the camel right off the reel, as they say.'

'That must have been the last straw,' Sylvia said.

'Have I told you this story before then?'

Sylvia shook her head.

'Well, that's a queer thing. I was just about to say that when she'd finished her rides she went to look at the giraffes, and one of them got hold of her straw hat in his mouth and nearly tore it off her head. She hollered out, and the keeper asked her if she couldn't read the notice that visitors was requested not to feed these animals. This annoyed Mrs. Marsham very much, and she told the keeper he wasn't fit to manage performing fleas, let alone giraffes, which annoyed *him* very much. It's a pity you never met her. I sent her a postcard the other day, as vulgar a one as I could find, but you can buy them just as vulgar in London.'

Sylvia did so far gratify Mrs. Gainsborough's desire to impress Mrs. Marsham as to take her to one or two Montmartre ball-rooms; but she declared they did not come up to her expectations, and decided that she should have to fall back on her own imagination to thrill Mrs. Marsham.

'As most travellers do,' Sylvia added.

They also went together to several plays, at which Sylvia laughed very heartily, much to Mrs. Gainsborough's chagrin.

'I'm bothered if I know what you're laughing at,' she said finally. 'I can't understand a word of what they're saying.'

'Just as well you can't,' Sylvia told her.

'Now there's a tantalizing hussy for you. But I can guess, you great tomboy.'

Whereupon Mrs. Gainsborough laughed as heartily as anybody in the audience at her own particular thoughts: she attracted a good deal of attention by this, because she often laughed at them without reference to what was happening on the stage. When Sylvia dug her in the ribs to make her keep quiet, she protested that, if she could only tell the audience what she was thinking, they would not bother any more about the stage.

'A penny for your thoughts, they say. I reckon mine are worth the price of a seat in the circle anyway.'

It was after this performance that Sylvia and Mrs. Gainsborough went to the Café de la Chouette, which was frequented mostly by the performers, poets, and composers of the music-hall world. The place was crowded, and they were forced to sit at a table already occupied by one of those figures that only in Paris seem to have the right to live on an equality with the rest of mankind merely on account of their eccentric appearance. He was probably not more than forty years old, but his gauntness made him look older: he wore blue and white checked trousers, a tail coat from which he or somebody else had clipped off the tails, a red velvet waistcoat, and a yachting-cap: his eyes were cavernous, his cheeks were rouged rather than flushed with fever: he carried a leather bag slung round his middle filled with waste paper, from which he occasionally took out a piece and wrote upon it a few words: he was drinking an unrecognizable liqueur.

Mrs. Gainsborough was rather nervous of sitting down beside so strange a creature, but Sylvia insisted. The man made no gesture at their approach, but turned his eyes upon them with the impassivity of a cat.

'Look here, Sylvia, in two twos he's going to give me an attack of the horrors,' Mrs. Gainsborough whispered. 'He's staring at me and twitching his nose like a hungry child at a jam roll. It's no good you telling me to give over. I can't help it. Look at his eyes. More like coal-cellars than eyes. I've never been able to abide being stared at since I sat down beside a waxwork at Louis Tussaud's and asked it where the ladies' cloakroom was.'

'He amuses me,' Sylvia said. 'What are you going to have?'

'Well, I *was* going to have a Grenadier, but really if that skelington opposite is going to look at me all night, I think I'll have to take something stronger.'

'Try a Cuirassier,' Sylvia suggested.

'Whatever's that?'

'It's the same relation to a curaçao that a grenadier is to a grenadine.'

'What I should really like is a nice little drop of whisky with a little tiddly bit of lemon, but there, I've noticed if you ask for whisky in Paris, it causes a regular commotion. The waiter holds the bottle as if it was going to bite him, and the proprietor winks at him that he's pouring out too much, and I can't abide those blue syphons. Sells they call them, and sells they are.'

'I shall order you a bock in a moment,' Sylvia threatened.

'Now don't be unkind just because I made a slight complaint about being stared at. Perhaps they won't make such a bother, if I *do* have a little whisky. But there, I can't resist it. It's got a regular taste of London, whisky has.'

The man at the table leaned over suddenly and asked in a tense voice: 'Scotch or Irish?'

'Oh, good Land, what a turn you gave me! I couldn't have jumped more,' Mrs. Gainsborough exclaimed, 'not if one of the lions in Trafalgar Square had said "pip-ip" as I passed.'

'You didn't think I was English, did you?' said the stranger. 'I forget it myself sometimes. I'm a terrible warning to the world. I'm a pose that's become a reality.'

'Pose?' Mrs. Gainsborough echoed. 'Oh, I didn't understand you for a moment. You mean you're an artist's model?'

The stranger turned his eyes upon Sylvia and whether from sympathy or curiosity she made friends with him, so that when they were ready to go home, the eccentric Englishman whom everyone called Milord, and who did not offer any alternative name to his new friends, said he would walk with them a bit of the way, much to Mrs. Gainsborough's embarrassment.

'I'm the first of the English decadents,' he proclaimed to Sylvia. 'Twenty years ago, I came to Paris to study art. I hadn't a penny to spend on drugs. I hadn't enough money to lead a life of sin. There's a tragedy! For five years I starved myself instead. I thought I should make myself interesting. I did. I became a figure. I learned the raptures of hunger. Nothing surpasses them – opium, morphine, ether, cocaine, hemp. What are they beside hunger? Have you got any coco with you? Just a little pinch? No? Never mind. I don't really like it. Not really. Some people like it, though. Who's the old woman with you? A procuress? Last night I had a dream in which I proved the non-existence of God by the Least Common Multiple. I can't exactly remember how I did it now. That's why I was so worried this evening; I can't remember if the figures were two, four, sixteen, and thirty-two. I worked it out last night in my dream. I obtained a view of the universe as a geometrical abstraction. It's perfectly simple, but I cannot get it right now. There's a crack in my ceiling which indicates the way. Unless I can walk along that crack, I can't reach the centre of the universe, and of course it's hopeless to try to obtain a view of the universe as a geometrical abstraction, if one can't reach the centre. I take it you agree with me on that point? That point! Wait a minute. I'm almost there. That point. Don't let me forget. That point? That *is* the point. Ah!'

The abstraction eluded him and he groaned aloud.

'The more I listen to him,' said Mrs. Gainsborough, 'the more certain sure I am he ought to see a doctor.'

'I must say good-night,' the stranger murmured sadly. 'I see that

I must start again at the beginning of that crack in my ceiling. I was lucky to find a room that had such a crack, though in a way it's rather a nuisance. It branches off so, and I very often lose the direction. There's one particular branch that always leads away from the point. I'm afraid to do anything about it in the morning. Of course, I might put up a notice to say *this is the wrong way*; but supposing it were really the right way? It's a great responsibility to own such a crack. Sometimes I almost go mad with the burden of responsibility. Why by playing about with that ceiling when my brain isn't perfectly clear, I might upset the whole universe. We'll meet again one night at the Chouette. I think I'll cross the boulevard now. There's no traffic, and I have to take a certain course not to confuse my line of thought.'

The eccentric stranger left them and, crossing the road in a series of diagonal tacks, disappeared.

'Coco,' said Sylvia.

'Cocoa?' echoed Mrs. Gainsborough. 'Brandy more like.'

'Or hashish.'

'Ashes? Well, I had a fox-terrier once that died in convulsions from eating coke, so perhaps it is ashes.'

'We must meet him again,' said Sylvia. 'These queer people outside ordinary life interest me.'

'Well, it's interesting to visit a hospital,' Mrs. Gainsborough agreed. 'But that doesn't say you want to go twice. Once is enough for that fellow to my thinking. He's interesting but uncomfortable, like the top of a 'bus.'

Sylvia, however, was determined to pursue her acquaintance with the outcast Englishman. She soon discovered that for years he had been taking drugs and that nothing but drugs had brought him to his present state of abject buffoonery. Shortly before he became friends with Sylvia he had been taken up as a week's amusement by some young men who were under the impression that they were seeing Parisian life in his company. They had been generous to him, and latterly he had been able to drug himself as much as he wanted. The result had been to hasten his supreme collapse. Even in his last illness he would not talk to Sylvia about his youth before he came to Paris, and in the end she was inclined to accept him at his own estimate, a pose that was become a reality.

One evening, he seemed more haggard than usual and talked much less: by the twitching of his nostrils he had been dosing himself hard with cocaine. Suddenly he stretched his thin hand across the marble table and seized hers feverishly:

'Tell me,' he asked. 'Are you sorry for me?'

'I think it's an impertinence to be sorry for anybody,' she answered.

'But if you mean do I wish you well? Why, yes, old son, I wish you very well.'

'What I told you once about my coming to Paris to work at art was all lies. I came here because I had to leave England. Perhaps you can guess more or less what for? I was a schoolmaster once. I only tell you this so that you may understand that the poems I am going to give you to-night are not sham. I leave nothing else behind, not even a name. You said one evening when we were arguing about ambition that, if you could only find your line, you might do something on the stage. Why don't you recite my poems? Read them through. One or two are in English, but most of them are in French. They are really more sighs than poems. They require no acting. They want just a voice.'

He undid the leather strap that supported his satchel, and handed it to Sylvia.

'To-morrow,' he said, 'if I'm still alive, I'll come here and find out what you think of them. But you've no idea how threatening that "if" is. It gets longer and longer. I can't see the end of it anywhere. It was very long last night. The dot of the "i" was already out of sight. It's the longest "if" that was ever imagined.'

He rose hurriedly and left the café; Sylvia never saw him again.

The poems of this strange and unhappy creature formed a record of many years' slow debasement. Many of them seemed to her too personal and too poignant to be repeated aloud, almost even to be read to oneself: there was nothing indeed to do but burn them that no one else might comprehend a man's degradation. Some of the poems, however, were objective and in their complete absence of any effort to impress or rend or horrify, they seemed not so much poems as actual glimpses into human hearts. Nor was that a satisfactory definition, for there was no attempt to explain any of the people described in these poems; they were ordinary people of the streets that lived in a few lines: this could only be said of the poems written in French; those in English seemed to her not very remarkable. She wondered if perhaps the less familiar tongue had exacted from him an achievement that was largely fortuitous.

'I've got an idea for a show,' Sylvia said to Mrs. Gainsborough. 'One or two old folk-songs, and then one of these poems half sung, half recited to an improvised accompaniment. Not more than one each evening.'

Sylvia was convinced of her ability to make a success, and spent a couple of weeks in searching for the folk-songs she required.

Lily and Hector came back in the middle of this new idea, and Hector was sure that Sylvia would be successful. She felt that he was too well pleased with himself at the moment not to be uncritically content with the rest of the world, but he was useful to Sylvia in securing an *audition* for her. The agent was convinced of the inevitable failure of Sylvia's performance with the public, and said he thought it was a pity to waste such real talent on antique rubbish like the songs she had chosen. As for the poems, they were no doubt all very well in their way: he was not going to say that he had not been able to listen to them, but the public did not expect that kind of thing. He did not wish to discourage a friend of M. Ozanne: he had by him the rights for what would be three of the most popular songs in Europe, if they were well sung. Sylvia read them through and then sang them. The agent was delighted; she knew he was really pleased because he gave up referring to her as a friend of M. Ozanne and addressed her directly. Hector advised her to begin with the ordinary stuff, and when she was well enough known to experiment upon the public with her own ideas. Sylvia, who was feeling the need to do something at once, decided to risk an *audition* at one of the outlying music-halls. She herself declared that the songs were so good in their own way that she could not help making a hit, but the others insisted that the triumph belonged to her.

'*Vous avez vraiment de l'espièglerie*,' said Hector.

'You really were awfully jolly,' said Lily.

'I didn't understand a word of course,' said Mrs. Gainsborough; 'but you looked that wicked – well, really – I thoroughly enjoyed myself.'

During the autumn Sylvia had secured engagements in music-halls of the *quartier*, but the agent advised her to take a tour before she ventured to attack the real Paris. It seemed to her a good way of passing the winter. Lily and Hector were very much together, and though Hector was always anxious for Sylvia to make a third, she found that the kind of amusement that appealed to him was much the same as that which had appealed to the young men who frequented Half Moon Street. It was a life of going to races, at which Hector would pass ladies without saluting or being saluted, who he informed Sylvia and Lily afterwards were his aunts or his cousins and actually on one occasion his mother. Sylvia began to feel the strain of being in the *demi-monde* but not of it: it was an existence that suited Lily perfectly, who could not understand why Sylvia should rail at their seclusion from the world. Mrs. Gainsborough began to grow restless for the peace of Mulberry Cottage and the safety of her furniture.

'You never know what will happen. I had a friend once – a Mrs. Beardmore. She was housekeeper to two maiden ladies in Portman Square – well, housekeeper – she was really more of a companion because one of them was stone deaf. One summer they went away to Scarborough, and when they came back some burglars had brought a furniture-van three days running and emptied the whole house, all but the bell-pulls. Drove back they did from King's Cross in a four-wheeler, and the first thing they saw was a large board up – TO BE LET OR SOLD. A fine set out there was in Portman Square, I can tell you; and the sister that was deaf had left her ear-trumpet in the train and nobody couldn't explain to her what had happened.'

So Mrs. Gainsborough, whose fears had been heightened by the repetition of this tale, went back to London with what she described as a collection of vulgarities for Mrs. Marsham; Sylvia went away on tour.

Sylvia found the life of a music-hall singer on tour very solitary: her fellow-vagabonds were so much more essentially mountebanks than in England and so far away from normal existence that even when she travelled in company, because her next town coincided with the next town of other players, she was never able to identify herself with them, as in England she had managed to identify herself with the other members of the chorus. She found that it paid her best to be English, and to affect in her songs an almost excessive English. She rather resented the exploitation of her nationality, because it seemed to her the same kind of appeal that would have been made by a double-headed woman or a performing seal. Nobody wanted her songs to be well rendered so much as unusually rendered; everybody wanted to be surprised by her ability to sing at all in French. But if the audiences wished her to be English, she found that being English off the stage was a disadvantage among these continental mountebanks. Sylvia discovered the existence of a universal prejudice against English actresses, partly on account of their alleged personal uncleanliness, partly on account of their alleged insincerity. On several occasions astonishment was expressed at the trouble she took with her hair, and at her capacity for being a good pal: when, later on, it would transpire that she was half French, everybody would find almost with relief an explanation of her apparent unconformity to rule.

Sylvia grew weary of the monotonous life in which everybody's interest was bounded by the psychology of an audience. Interest in the individual never extended beyond the question of whether she would or would not, if she were a woman: of whether he desired or did not desire, if he were a man. When either of these questions was answered the interest reverted to the audience. It seemed maddeningly unimportant to Sylvia that the audience on Monday night should have failed to appreciate a point which the audience of Tuesday night would probably hail with enthusiasm; yet often she had to admit to herself that it was just her own inability or unwillingness to treat an audience as an individual that prevented her from gaining real success. She decided that every interpretative artist must pander his emotion, his humour, his wit, his movements nightly, and that somehow he must charm each audience into the complacency with which a sophisticated libertine seeks an admission of enduring love from the woman he has paid to satisfy a momentary desire. Assuredly the most successful performers in the grand style were those who could conceal even from the most intelligent audiences their professional relation to them. A performer of acknowledged reputation would not play to the gallery with battered wiles and manifest allurements, but it was unquestionable that the foundation of success was playing to the gallery, and that the third-rate performer who flattered these provincial audiences with the personal relation could gain louder applause than Sylvia, who wanted no audience but herself. It was significant how a word of *argot* that meant a fraud of apparent brilliancy executed by an artist upon the public had extended itself into daily use. Everything was *chiqué*. It was *chiqué* to wear a hat of the latest fashion: it was *chiqué* to impress one's lover by a jealous outburst: it was *chiqué* to refuse a man one's favours. Everything was *chiqué*: it was impossible to think or act or speak in this world of vagabonds without *chiqué*.

The individualistic life that Sylvia had always led both in private and in public seemed to her, notwithstanding the various disasters of her career, infinitely worthier than this dependency upon the herd that found its most obvious expression in the theatre. It was revolting to witness human nature's lust for the unexceptionable or its cruel pleasure in the exception. Yet now, looking back at her past, she could see that it had always been her unwillingness to conform that had kept her apart from so much human enjoyment and human gain, though equally she might claim apart from such human sorrow and human loss.

'The struggle, of course, would be terrible for a long while,' Sylvia said to herself, 'if everybody renounced entirely any kind of co-operation or interference with or imitation of or help from anybody else, but out of that struggle might arise the true immortals. A cat with a complete personality is surely higher than a man with an incomplete personality. Anyway it's quite certain that this *cabotinage* is for me impossible. I believe that if I pricked a vein sawdust would trickle out of me now.'

In such a mood of cheated hope did Sylvia return to Paris in the early spring; she was about to comment on Lily's usual state of molluscry – by yielding to which in abandoning the will she had lost the power to develop – when Lily herself proceeded to surprise her.

The affection between Hector and Lily had apparently made a steady growth and had floated in an undisturbed and equable depth of water for so long that Lily, like an ambitious water-lily, began to be ambitious of becoming a terrestrial plant. While for nearly a year she had been blossoming apparently without regard for anything but the beauty of the moment, she had all the time been sending out long roots beneath the water, long roots that were growing more and more deeply into the warm and respectable mud.

'You mean you'd like to marry Hector?' Sylvia asked.

'Why yes, I think I should rather. I'm getting tired of never being settled.'

'But does he want to marry you?'

'We've talked about it often. He hates the idea of not marrying me.'

'He'd like to go away with you and live on the top of a mountain remote from mankind or upon a coral island in the Pacific with nothing but the sound of the surf and the cocoanuts dropping idly one by one, wouldn't he?'

'Well, he did say he wished we could go away somewhere all alone. How did you guess? How clever you are, Sylvia,' Lily exclaimed, opening wide her deep blue eyes.

'My dear girl, when a man knows that it's impossible to be married either because he's married already or for any other reason, he always hymns a solitude for two. You never heard any man with serious intentions propose to live with his bride elect in an Alpine hut or under a lonely palm. The man with serious intentions tries to reconcile his purse, not his person, with poetic aspirations. He's in a quandary between Hampstead and Kensington, not between mountain-tops and lagoons. I suppose he has also talked of a dream-child – a fairy miniature of his Lily?' Sylvia went on.

'We have talked about a baby,' Lily admitted.

'The man with serious intentions talks about the aspect of the nursery and makes reluctant plans to yield, if compelled to, the room he had chosen for his study.'

'You make fun of everything,' Lily murmured rather sulkily.

'But, my dear,' Sylvia argued, 'for me to be able to reproduce Hector's dream so accurately proves that I'm building to the type. I'll speculate farther. I'm sure he has regretted the irregular union and vowed that, had he but known at first what an angel of purity you were, he would have died rather than propose it.'

Lily sat silent, frowning. Presently she jumped up, and the sudden activity of movement brought home to Sylvia more than anything else the change in her.

'If you promise not to laugh, here are his letters,' Lily said, flinging into Sylvia's lap a bundle tied up with ribbon.

'Letters,' Sylvia snapped. 'Who cares about letters? The love-letters of a successful lover have no value. When he has something to write that he cannot say to your face, then I'll read his letter. All public blandishments shock me.'

Hector was called away from Paris to go and stay with his mother at Aix-les-Bains: for a fortnight two letters arrived every day.

'The snow in Savoy will melt early this year,' Sylvia mocked. 'It's lucky he's not staying at St. Moritz. Winter sports could never survive such a furnace.'

Then followed a week's silence.

'The Alpine Club must have protested,' Sylvia mocked. 'Avalanches are not expected in March.'

'He's probably motoring with his mother,' Lily explained.

The next day a letter arrived from Hector.

> *Hotel Superbe,*
> *Aix-les-Bains*

My dear Lily,

I do not know how to express myself. You have known always the great difficulties of my position opposite to my mother. She has found that I owe to marry myself, and I have demanded the hand of Mademoiselle Arpenteur-Legage. I dare not ask your pardon, but I have written to make an arrangement for you, and from now please use the apartment which has for me memories the most sacred. It is useless to fight against circumstances.

> *Hector*

'I think he might have used black-edged note-paper,' Sylvia said. 'They always have plenty at health resorts.'

'Don't be so unkind, Sylvia,' Lily cried. 'How can you be so unkind, when you see that my heart is broken?' She burst into tears.

In a moment Sylvia was on her knees beside her.

'Lily, my dearest Lily, you did not really love him? Oh, no, my dear, not really. If you really loved him, I'll go now to Aix myself and arrange matters over the head of his stuffy old mother. But you didn't really love him. You're simply upset at the breaking of a habit. Oh, my dear, you couldn't really have loved him.'

'He shan't marry this girl,' Lily declared, standing up in a rage. 'I'll go to Aix-les-Bains myself, and I'll see this Mademoiselle,' she snatched the letter from the floor to read the odious name of her rival. 'I'll send her all his letters. You mightn't want to read them, but she'll want to read them. She'll read every word. She'll read how, when he was thinking of proposing to her, he was calling me his angel, his life, his soul, how he was – oh – she'll read every word, and I'll send them to her by registered post, and then I'll know she gets them. How dare a Frenchman treat an English girl like that? How dare he? How dare he? French people think English girls have no passion. They think we're cold. Are we cold? We may not like being kissed all the time like French girls, but we're not cold – oh, I feel I could kill him.'

Sylvia interrupted her rage.

'My dear, if all this fire and fury is because you're disappointed at not being married, twist him for fifty thousand francs, buy a silver casket, put his letters inside, and send them to him for a wedding-present with your good wishes. But if you love him, darling Lily, let me go and tell him the truth; if I think he's not worth it, then come away with me and be lonely with me somewhere. My beautiful thing, I can't promise you a coral island, but you shall have all my heart if you will.'

'Love him?' echoed Lily. 'I hate him. I despise him after this, but why should he marry her?'

'If you feel like that about him, I should have thought the best way to punish him would be to let the marriage proceed; to punish him further you've only to refuse yourself to him when he's married, for I'm quite sure that within six months he'll be writing to say what a mistake he made, how cold his wife is, and how much he longs to come back to you, *la jolie maîtresse de sa jeunesse, le souvenir du bon temps jadis*, and so on with the sentimental eternities of reconstructed passion.'

'Live with him after he's married?' Lily exclaimed. 'Why, I've never even kissed a married man. I should never forgive myself.'

'You don't love him at all, do you?' Sylvia asked, pressing her hands down on Lily's shoulders and forcing her to look straight at her. 'Laugh, my dear, laugh! Hurrah! you can't pretend you care a bit about him. Fifty thousand francs and freedom! And just when I was getting bored with Paris.'

'It's all very well for you, Sylvia,' Lily said resentfully, as she tried to shake off Sylvia's exuberance. 'You don't want to be married: I do. I really looked forward to marrying Michael.'

Sylvia's face hardened.

'Oh, I know you blame me entirely for that,' she continued. 'But it wasn't my fault really. It was bad luck. It's no good pretending I wasn't fond of Claude. I was, and when I met him—'

'Look here, don't let's live that episode over again in discussion,' Sylvia said. 'It belongs to the past, and I've always had a great objection to body-snatching.'

'What I was going to explain,' Lily went on, 'was that Michael put the idea of marriage into my head. Then being always with Hector, I got used to being with somebody. I was always treated like a married woman when we went to the seaside or on motoring tours. You always think that because I sit still and say nothing my mind's an absolute blank, but it isn't. I've been thinking for a long time about marriage. After all, there must be something in marriage, or so many people wouldn't get married. You married the wrong man, but I don't believe you'll ever find the right man. You're much, much, much too critical. I *will* get married.'

'And now,' Sylvia said with a laugh, 'to all the other riddles that torment my poor brain I must add you.'

Hector Ozanne tried to stanch Lily's wounded ideals with a generous compress of notes; he succeeded.

'After all,' she admitted, twanging the elastic round the bundle. 'I'm not so badly off.'

'We must buy that silver casket for the letters,' Sylvia said. 'His wedding day draws near. I think I shall dress up like the Ancient Mariner and give them to him myself.'

'How much will a silver casket cost?' Lily asked.

Sylvia estimated roughly.

'It seems a good deal,' said Lily thoughtfully. 'I think I shall just send them to him in a cardboard-box. I finished those chocolates after dinner. Yes, that will do quite well. After all, he treated me very badly and to get his letters back safely will be quite a good enough present. What could he do with a silver casket? He'd probably use it for visiting-cards.'

That evening Sylvia, greatly content to have Lily to herself again, took her to the Café de la Chouette.

Her agent, who was drinking in a corner, came across to speak to her.

'Brazil?' she repeated doubtfully.

'Thirty francs for three songs and you can go home at twelve. It isn't as if you had to sit drinking champagne and dancing all night.'

Sylvia looked at Lily.

'Would you like a voyage?'

'We might as well go.'

The contract was arranged.

IV

One of the habits that Sylvia had acquired on tour in France was card-playing: perhaps she inherited her skill from Henry, for she was a very good player. The game on the voyage was poker; before they had passed Teneriffe Sylvia had lost five hundred francs; she borrowed five hundred francs from Lily and set herself to win them back. The sea became very rough in the Atlantic; all the passengers were sea-sick; the other four poker-players, who were theatrical folk, wanted to stop, but Sylvia would not hear of it; she was much too anxious about her five hundred francs to feel sea-sick. She lost Lily's first five hundred francs and borrowed five hundred more. Lily began to feel less sea-sick now, and she watched the struggle with a personal interest; the other players with the hope that Sylvia's bad luck would hold were so deeply concentrated upon maintaining their advantage that they too forgot to be sea-sick. The ship rolled, but the poker-players only left the card-room for meals in the deserted saloon. Sylvia began to win again; blue skies and calmer weather appeared; the other poker-players had no excuse for not continuing, especially now that it was possible to play on deck. Sylvia had won back all she had lost and two hundred francs besides, when the ship entered the harbour of Rio de Janeiro.

'I think I should like gambling,' Lily said, 'if only one didn't have to shuffle and cut all the time.'

The place where Sylvia was engaged to sing was one of those centres of aggregated amusement that exist all over the world without any particular characteristic to distinguish one from another, like the dinners in what are known as first class hotels on the Continent. Everything here was more expensive than in Europe: even the roulette boards had zero and double zero to help the bank. The tradition of Brazil for supplying gold and diamonds to the world had bred a familiarity with the external signs of wealth that expressed itself in over-jewelled men and women, whose display one forgave more easily on account of the natural splendour of the scene with which they had to compete.

Lily with the unerring bad taste that nearly always is to be found in sensuous and indolent women, to whom the obvious makes the quickest and easiest appeal, admired the flashing stones and stars and fireflies with an energy that astonished Sylvia, notwithstanding the novel glimpse she had been given of Lily's character in the affair with Hector Ozanne. The climate was hot, but a sea breeze freshened the city after sunset; the enforced day-long inactivity with the luxurious cool baths and competent negresses who attended upon her lightest movement satisfied Lily's conception of existence, and when they drove along the margin of the bay before dinner her only complaint was that she could not coruscate like other women in the carriages they passed.

With the money they had in hand Sylvia felt justified in avoiding a *pension d'artistes*, and they had taken a flat together. This meant that when Sylvia went to work at the cabaret, Lily unless she came with her was left alone, which did not at all suit her. Sylvia therefore suggested that she should accept an engagement to dance at midnight with the stipulation that she should not be compelled to stay until three a.m. unless she wanted to, and that by forgoing any salary she should not be expected to drink gooseberry wine at 8000 reis a bottle, on which she would receive a commission of 1000 reis. The management knew what a charm the tall fair English girl would exercise over the swart Brazilians and was glad to engage her at her own terms. Sylvia had not counted upon Lily's enjoying the cabaret life so much: the heat was affecting her much more than Lily, and she began to complain of the long hours of what for her was a so false gaiety. Nothing, however, would persuade Lily to go home before three o'clock at the earliest, and Sylvia on whom a great lassitude and indifference had settled, used to wait for her, sitting alone while Lily danced.

One night, when Sylvia had sung two of her songs with such a sense of hopeless depression weighing her down that the applause which followed each of them seemed to her a mockery, she had a sudden vertigo from which she pulled herself together with a conviction that nothing would induce her to sing the third song. She went on the scene, seated herself at the piano, and to the astonishment and discomfort of the audience and her fellow-players half chanted, half recited one of the eccentric Englishman's poems about a body in the Morgue. Such a performance in such a place created consternation, but in the silence that followed Sylvia fainted. When she came to herself, she was back in her own bedroom with a Brazilian doctor jabbering and mouthing over her symptoms. Presently she was taken to a clinic and, when she was well enough to know what had happened, she learnt that she had yellow fever, but that the crisis had passed. At first Lily came to see her every day, but when convalescence was further advanced, she gave up coming, which worried Sylvia intensely and hampered her progress. She insisted that something terrible had happened to Lily and worked herself up into such a state that the doctor feared a relapse. She was too weak to walk; realizing at last that the only way of escaping from the clinic would be to get well, she fought against her apprehensions for Lily's safety, and after a fortnight of repressed torments was allowed out. When Sylvia reached the flat she was met by the grinning negresses who told her that Lily had gone to live elsewhere and let her understand that it was with a man.

Sylvia was not nearly well enough to reappear at the cabaret, but she went down that evening and was told by the other girls that Lily was at the tables. They were duly shocked at Sylvia's altered appearance, congratulated her upon having been lucky enough to escape the necessity of shaving her head, and expressed their regrets at not knowing in which clinic she had been staying so that they might have brought her the news of their world. Sylvia lacked the energy to resent their hypocrisy, and went to look for Lily, whom she found blazing with jewels at one of the roulette tables.

There was something so fantastic in Lily's appearance thus bedecked, that Sylvia thought for a moment it was a feverish vision such as had haunted her brain at the beginning of the illness. Lily wore suspended from a fine chain round her neck a large diamond, one of those so-called blue diamonds of Brazil that in the moonlight seem like sapphires, her fingers flashed fire; and a large brooch of rubies in the likeness of a butterfly winked sombrely from her black corsage.

Sylvia made her way through the press of gamblers and touched Lily's arm: so intent was she upon the tables that she brushed away the hand as if it had been a mosquito.

'Lily! Lily!' Sylvia called sharply. 'Where have you been? Where have you gone?'

At that moment the wheel stopped, and the croupier cried the number and the colour in all their combinations; Sylvia was sure that he exchanged glances with Lily and that the gold piece upon the 33 on which he was paying had not been there before the wheel had stopped.

'Lily! Lily! Where have you been?' Sylvia called again. Lily gathered in her winnings and turned round. It was curious how changed her eyes were; they seemed merely now like two more rich jewels that she was wearing.

'I'm sorry I've not been to see you,' she said. 'My dear, I've won nearly £2000.'

'You have, have you?' Sylvia exclaimed. 'Then the sooner you leave Brazil the better.'

Lily threw a swift glance of alarm towards the croupier, a man of unnatural thinness, who, while he intoned the invitation to place the stakes, fixed his eyes upon her.

'I can't leave Brazil,' she said in a whisper. 'I'm living with him.'

'Living with a croupier?' Sylvia gasped.

'Hush, he belongs to quite a good family. He ruined himself. His name is Manuel Camacho. Don't talk to me any more, Sylvia. He's madly jealous. He wants to marry me.'

'Like Hector, I suppose,' Sylvia scoffed.

'Not a bit like Hector. He brings a priest every morning and says he'll kill me and himself and the priest too, if I don't marry him. But I want to make more money, and then I will marry him. I must. I'm afraid of what he'll do, if I refuse. Go away from me, Sylvia, go away. There'll be a fearful scene to-night, if you will go on talking to me. Last night a man threw a flower into our carriage when we were driving home, and Manuel jumped out and beat him insensible with his cane. Go away.'

Sylvia demanded where she was living, but Lily would not tell her, because she was afraid of what her lover might do.

'He doesn't even let me look out of the window. If I look out of the window, he tears his clothes with rage and digs his finger-nails into the palms of his hands. He's very violent. Sometimes he shoots at the chandelier.'

Sylvia began to laugh: there was something ridiculous in the notion of Lily's leading this kind of lion-tamer's existence. Suddenly the croupier with an angry movement swept a pile of money from the table.

'Go away, Sylvia, go away. I know he'll break out in a moment. That was meant for a warning.'

Sylvia understood that it was hopeless to persist for the moment, and she made her way back to the cabaret. The girls were eager to know what she thought of Lily's protector:

'*Elle a de la veine, tu sais, la petite Lili. Elle l'a pris comme ça, et il l'aime à la folie. Et elle gagne! mon dieu, comme elle gagne! Tout va pour elle. Tu sais, elle a des brillants merveilleux. Ça fait riche, pas vrai? Y'a pas de chiqué. Mais, il est jaloux! Il se porte comme un loufouque. Ça me raserait, tu sais, être collée avec un homme pareil. Pourtant, elle est bisenesseuse, la petite Lili! elle ne lui donne pas un rond. C'qu'elle est le type anglais sans blague! Et le mec, dis, n'est-ce pas qu'il est maigre comme tout? On dirait un squelette.*'

With all their depreciation of the croupier, it seemed to Sylvia that most of the girls would have been well pleased to change places with Lily. But how was she herself to regard the affair? During those long days of illness, when she had lain hour after hour with her thoughts, to what a failure her life had seemed to be turning, and what a haphazard harbour-less course hers had seemed to be. Now she must perhaps jettison the little cargo she carried, or would it be fairer to say that she must decide whether she should disembark it? It was absurd to pretend that Michael would have viewed with anything but dismay the surrender of Lily to such a one as that croupier, and if she made that surrender, she should be violating the trust that counted for so much in her aimless career. Yet was she not attributing to Michael the sentiment he felt before Lily's betrayal of him? He had only demanded of Sylvia that she should prevent Lily from drifting downwards along the dull road of undistinguished ruin. If this fantastic Brazilian wished to marry her, why should he not do so? Then she herself should be alone indeed and, unless a miracle happened, should be lost in the eternal whirl of vagabonds to and fro across the face of the earth.

'They say one must expect to be depressed after yellow fever,' Sylvia reassured herself. 'Perhaps this mood won't last, but oh, the endlessness of it all. How even one's brush and comb seem weighed down by an interminable melancholy. As I look round me, I can see nothing that doesn't strike me as hopelessly, drearily, appallingly superfluous. The very soap in its china dish looks wistful. How pathetic the life of a piece of soap is, when one stops to contemplate it. A slow and steady diminution. I must really do something to shake off this intolerable heaviness.'

The most direct path to energy and action seemed to be an attempt to interview Camacho; and the following evening Sylvia tried to make Lily divulge her address, but she begged not to be disturbed, and Sylvia, seeing that she was utterly absorbed by the play, had to leave her alone.

'Either I am getting flaccid beyond belief,' she said to herself, 'or Lily has acquired an equally incredible determination. I think it's the latter. It just shows what passion will do even for a Lily. All her life she has remained unmoved, until roulette reveals itself to her and she finds out what she was intended for. Of course I must leave her to the fierce skeleton; he represents the corollary to the passion. Queer thing, the way she always wins. I'm sure they're cheating somehow, the two of them. There's the final link. They'll go away presently to Europe, and Lily will enjoy the sweetest respectability that exists – the one that is founded on early indiscretion and dishonesty – a paradise preceded by the fall.'

Sylvia waited by the entrance to the roulette-room on the next night until play was finished, watched Lily come out with Camacho, and saw them get into a carriage and drive away immediately. None of the attendants or the other croupiers knew where Camacho lived, or if he knew, he refused to tell Sylvia. On the fourth evening, therefore, she waited in a carriage by the entrance and ordered her driver to follow the one in which Lily was. She found that Camacho's apartment was not so far from her own; the next morning she watched at the corner of the street until she saw him come out; then she rang the bell. The negress who opened the door shook her head at the notion of letting Sylvia enter; but the waiting in the sun had irritated her, and she pushed past and ran upstairs. The negress had left the upper door open, and Sylvia was able to enter the flat. Lily was in bed, playing with her jewels as if they were toys.

'Sylvia,' she cried in alarm. 'He'll kill you if he finds you here. He's gone to fetch the priest. They'll be back in a moment. Go away.'

Sylvia said she insisted on speaking to Camacho: she had some good advice to give him.

'But he's particularly jealous of you. The first evening you spoke to me . . . look!' Lily pointed to the ceiling, which was marked like a die with five holes. 'He did that when he came home to show what he would do to you.'

'Rubbish,' said Sylvia. 'He'll be like a lamb when we meet. If he hadn't fired at the ceiling, I should have felt much more alarmed for the safety of my head.'

'But Sylvia,' Lily entreated. 'You don't know what he's like. Once, when he thought a man nudged me, he came home and tore all the towels to pieces with his teeth. The servant nearly cried when she saw the room in the morning. It was simply covered with bits of towel, and he swallowed one piece and nearly choked. You don't know what he's like. I can manage him, but nobody else could.'

Here was a new Lily indeed, who dared to claim that she could manage somebody of whom Sylvia must be afraid: she challenged Lily to say when she had ever known her flinch from an encounter with a man.

'But, my dear, Manuel isn't English. When he's in one of those rages, he's not like a human being at all. You can't soothe him by arguing with him. You have to calm him without talking.'

'What do you use? A red-hot poker?'

Lily became agitated at Sylvia's obstinacy, and regardless of her jewels, which tinkled down into a heap on the floor, she jumped out of bed and implored her not to stay.

'I want to know one or two things before I go,' Sylvia said and was conscious of taking advantage of Lily's alarm to make her speak the truth owing to the lack of time for the invention of lies. 'Do you love this man?'

'Yes, in a way I do.'

'You could be happy married to him?'

'Yes, when I've won £3000.'

'He cheats for you?'

Lily hesitated.

'Never mind,' Sylvia went on. 'I know he does.'

'Oh, my dear,' Lily murmured, biting her lip. 'Then other people might notice. Never mind. I ought to finish to-night. The boat sails the day after to-morrow.'

'And what about me?' Sylvia asked.

Lily looked shamefaced for a moment, but the natural optimism of the gambler quickly reasserted itself.

'I thought you wouldn't like to break your contract.'

'My contract,' Sylvia repeated bitterly. 'What about – oh, but how foolish I am. You dear, unimaginative creature.'

'I'm not at all unimaginative,' Lily interposed quickly. 'One of the reasons why I want to leave Brazil is because the black people here make me nervous. That's why I left our flat. I didn't know what to do. I was so frightened. I think I'm very imaginative. *You* got ill. What was I to do?'

She asked this like an accusation, and Sylvia knew that it would be impossible to make her see another point of view.

'Besides, it was your fault I started to gamble. I watched you on the boat.'

'But were you going away without a word to me?' Sylvia could not refrain from tormenting herself with this question.

'Oh, no, I was coming to say good-bye, but you don't understand how closely he watches me.'

The thought of Camacho's jealous antics recurred to Lily with the imminence of his return; she begged Sylvia, now that all her questions were answered, to escape. It was too late; there was a sound of foot-steps upon the stairs and the noise of angry voices above deep gobbles of protested innocence from the black servant.

The entrance reminded Sylvia of *Il Barbiere de Siviglia*, for when Camacho came leaping into the room, as thin and active as a grass-hopper, the priest was holding his coat-tails with one hand and with the other making the most operatic gestures of despair, like Don Basilio. In the doorway the black servant continued to gobble at everybody in turn, including the Almighty, to witness the clarity of her conscience.

'What language do you speak?' Sylvia asked sharply, while Camacho was struggling to free himself from the restraint of the priest.

'I speak English! Goddam! Hell! Five hundred hells!' the croupier shouted. 'And I have sweared a swore that you will not interrupt between me myself and my Lili.'

Camacho raised his arm to shake his fist, and the priest caught hold of it, which made Camacho turn round and open on him with Portuguese expletives.

'When you've quite done cracking Brazil nuts with your teeth, perhaps you'll listen to me,' Sylvia began.

'No, you hear me, no, no, no, no, no, no!' Camacho shouted. 'And I will not hear you. I have heard you enough. You shall not take her away. *Putain!*'

'If you want to be polite in French,' Sylvia said. 'Come along!

> *Ce marloupatte pâle et mince*
> *Se nommait simplement Navet;*
> *Mais il vivait ainsi qu'un prince . . .*
> *Il aimait les femmes qu'on rince.*

T'as compris? Mais moi, je ne suis pas une femme qu'on rince.'

It was certainly improbable, Sylvia thought, that the croupier had understood much of Richepin's verse, but the effect of the little recitation was excellent, because it made him choke. Lily now intervened, and when Sylvia beheld her soothing the inarticulate Camacho by stroking his head, she abandoned the last faint inclination to break off this match and called upon the priest to marry them at once. No doubt the priest would have been willing to begin the ceremony, if he had been able to understand a word of what Sylvia said; but he evidently thought she was appealing to him against Camacho's violence and with a view to affording the ultimate assistance of which he was capable he crossed himself and turned up his eyes to Heaven.

'What an awful noise there is,' Sylvia cried and, looking round her with a sudden awareness of its volume, she perceived that the negress in the doorway had been reinforced by what was presumably the cook – another negress who was joining in her fellow-servant's protestations. At the same time the priest was talking incessantly in rapid Portuguese; Camacho was probably swearing in the same language; and Lily was making a noise that was exactly half-way between a dove cooing and an ostler grooming a horse.

'Look here, Mr. Camacho,' Sylvia began.

'Oh, don't speak to him, Sylvia,' Lily implored. 'He can't be spoken to when he's like this. It's a kind of illness really.'

Sylvia paid no attention to her, but continued to address the croupier.

'If you'll listen to me, Mr. Camacho, instead of behaving like an exasperated toy-terrier, you'll find that we both want the same thing.'

'You shall not have her,' the croupier chattered. 'I will shoot everybody before you shall have her.'

'I don't want her,' Sylvia screamed. 'I've come here to be a bridesmaid

231

or a godmother or any other human accessory to a wedding you like to mention. Take her, my dear man, she's yours.'

At last Sylvia was able to persuade him that she was not to be regarded as an enemy to his matrimonial intentions, and after a final burst of rage directed against the negresses, whom he ejected from the room as a housemaid turns a mattress, he made a speech:

'I am to marry Lily. We go to Portugal, where I am not to be a croupier, but a gentleman. I excuse my furage. You grant excusals, yes? It is a decomprehence.'

'He's apologizing,' Lily explained in the kind of way one might call attention to the tricks of an intelligent puppy.

'She's actually proud of him,' Sylvia thought. 'But, of course, to her he represents gold and diamonds.'

The priest, who had grasped that the strain was being relaxed, began to exude smiles and to rub his hands: he sniffed the prospect of a fee so richly that one seemed to hear the notes crackle like pork. Camacho produced the wedding-ring that was even more outshone than wedding-rings usually are by the diamonds of betrothal.

'But I can't be married in my dressing-gown,' Lily protested.

Sylvia felt inclined to say it was the most suitable garment except a nightgown that she could have chosen, but in the end after another discussion it was decided that the ecclesiastical ceremony should be performed to-morrow in church and that to-day should be devoted to the civil rite. Sylvia promised not to say a word about the departure to Europe.

Three days later, Sylvia went on board the steamer to make her farewells. She gave Lily a delicate little pistol for a wedding present: from Lily in memory of her marriage she received a box of chocolates.

It was impossible not to feel lonely, when Lily had gone: in three and a half years they had been much together. For a while Sylvia tried to content herself with the company of the girls in the *pension d'artistes*, to which she had been forced to go because the flat was too expensive for her to live in now. Her illness had swallowed up any money she had saved, and the manager took advantage of it to lower her salary. When she protested, the manager told her he should be willing to pay the original salary, if she would go to São Paulo. Though Sylvia understood that the management was trying to get the best of a bargain, she was too listless to care much and she agreed to go. The voyage to Santos was like a nightmare. The boat was full of gaudy negroes who sang endlessly their mysterious songs; the smell was vile; the food was worse; cockroaches swarmed. São Paulo was a squalid reproduction of Rio de Janeiro, and the women who sang in the cabaret were all seamed with ten years' longer vagabondage than those at Rio. The men of São Paulo treated them with the insolence of the half-breeds they all seemed. On the third night a big man with teeth like an ancient fence and a diamond in his shirt-front like a crystal stopper leaned over from a box and shouted to Sylvia to come up and join him, when she had finished her songs: he said other things that made her shake with anger. When she left the scene, the grand pimp, who was politely known as the manager, congratulated Sylvia upon her luck: she had caught the fancy of the richest patron.

'You don't suppose I'm going to see that *goujat* in his box?' she growled.

The grand pimp was in despair. Did she wish to drive away their richest patron? He would probably open a dozen bottles of champagne; he might . . . the grand pimp waved his arms in mental inability to express all the splendours within her grasp. Presently the impatient suitor came behind the scene to know the reason of Sylvia's delay. He grasped her by the wrist and tried to drag her up to his box; she seized the only weapon in reach – a hand-glass, and smashed it against his face. The suitor roared; the grand pimp squealed; Sylvia escaped to the stage which was almost flush with the main dancing hall. She forced her way through the orchestra, kicking the instruments right and left, and fell into the arms of a man resplendent like the rest, but a *rastaquouère* of more Parisian cut, who in a dago-American accent promised to plug the first guy that tried to touch her.

Sylvia felt like Carmen on the arm of the Toreador, when she and her protector walked out of the cabaret. He was a youngish man wearing a blue serge suit and high-heeled shoes half buck-skin, half patent-leather tied with white silk laces, so excessively American in shape that one looked twice to be sure he was not wearing them on the wrong feet. His trousers after exhausting the ordinary number of buttons in front prolonged themselves into a kind of corselet that drew attention to the slimness of his waist. He wore a frilled white shirt with blue hearts and a white silk tie with a large diamond pin. The back of his neck was shaved, which gave his curly black hair the look of a wig. He was the Latin dandy after being operated upon in an American barbershop, and his name was Carlos Morera.

Sylvia noted his appearance in such detail, because the appearance of anybody after that monster in the box would have come as a relief and a diversion. Morera had led her to a bar that opened out of the cabaret and after placing two automatic pistols on the counter he ordered champagne cocktails for them both.

'He won't come after you in here. Dat stiff don't feel he would like

233

to meet Carlos Morera. Say, do you know why? Why, because Carlos Morera's ready to plug any stiff dat don't happen to suit his fancy right away. Dat's me – Carlos Morera. I'm pretty rich, I am. I'm a gentleman, I am. But dat ain't going to stop me using those,' he indicated the pistols. 'Drink up and let's have another. Don't you want to drink? See here, then!' He poured Sylvia's cocktail on the floor. 'Nothing won't stop Carlos Morera, if he wants to call another round of drinks. Two more champagne cocktails!'

'Is this going to be my Manuel?' Sylvia asked herself. She felt at the moment inclined to let him be anything rather than go back to the cabaret and face that man in the box.

'You're looking some white,' Morera commented. 'I believe he scared you. I believe I ought to have shot him. Say, you sit here and drink up; I tink I'll go back and shoot him now. I shan't be gone long.'

'Sit still, you fire-eater,' cried Sylvia, catching hold of his arm.

'Say, dat's good. Fire-eater! Yes, I believe I'd eat fire if it came to it. I believe you could make me laugh. I'm going to Buenos Aires to-morrow. Why don't you come along of me! This São Paulo is a bum Brazilian town. You want to see the Argentina. I'll show you lots of life.'

'Look here,' said Sylvia. 'I don't mind coming with you to make you laugh and to laugh myself, but that's all. Understand?'

'Dat's all right,' Carlos agreed. 'I'm a funny kind of a fellow, I am. I ain't a guy dat shakes hands with a girl's legs when he's foist introduced. As soon as I found I could buy any girl I wanted, I didn't seem to want them no more. 'Sides, I've got seven already. You come along of me. I'm good company, I am. Everybody dat goes along of me laughs and has good fun. Hear that?'

He jingled the money in his pocket with a joyful reverence, as if he were ringing a sanctus-bell. 'Now, you come back with me into the cabaret.'

Sylvia hesitated.

'Don't you worry. Nobody won't dare to look at you when you're with me.'

Morera put her arm in his, and back they walked into the cabaret again, more than ever like Carmen with her Toreador. The grand pimp, seeing that Sylvia was safely protected, came forward with obeisances and apologies.

'See here, bring two bottles of champagne,' Morera commanded. The grand pimp beckoned authoritatively to a waiter, but Morera stood up in a fury.

'I didn't tell you to bring a waiter. I told you to bring two bottles of champagne. Bring them yourself.'

The grand pimp returned very meekly with the bottles.

'Dat's more like. Draw the cork of one.'

The grand pimp asked if he should put the other on ice.

'Don't you worry about the other,' said Morera. 'The other's only there so as I can break it on your dam head in case I get tired of looking at you. See what I mean?'

The grand pimp professed the most perfect comprehension.

'Well, this is a bum place,' Morera declared, after they had sat for a while. 'I believe we shan't get no fun here. Let's quit.'

He drove her back to the pension, and two days later they took ship to Buenos Aires.

Morera insisted on Sylvia's staying at an expensive hotel and was very anxious for her to buy plenty of new evening frocks.

'I've got a fancy,' he explained, 'to show you a bit of life. You hadn't seen life before you came to Argentina.'

The change of air had made Sylvia feel much better, and when she had fitted herself out with new clothes to which Morera added a variety of expensive and gaudy jewels, she felt quite ready to examine life under his guidance.

He took her to one or two theatres, to the opera, and to the casinos; then one evening he decided upon a special entertainment of which he made a secret.

'I want you to dress yourself up fine to-night,' he said. 'We're going to some smart ball. Put on all your jewelry. I'm going to dress up smart too.'

Sylvia had found that over-dressing was the best way of returning his hospitality; this evening she determined to surpass all previous efforts.

'Heavens,' she ejaculated when she made the final survey of herself in the looking-glass. 'Do I look more like a Christmas tree or a chemist's shop?'

When she rejoined Morera in the lounge, she saw that he was in evening dress with diamonds wherever it was possible to put them.

'You're fine,' he said contentedly. 'Dat's the way I like to see a goil look. I guess we're going to have lots of fun to-night.'

They drank a good deal of champagne at dinner and about eleven o'clock went out to their carriage. When the coachman was given the address of the ballroom, he turned round in surprise and was sworn at for his insolence, so with a shrug of the shoulders he drove off. They left the ordinary centres of amusement behind them, and entered a meaner quarter along the banks of the great River Plate; at last after a long drive they pulled up before what looked like a third-rate saloon. Sylvia hesitated before she got out; it did not seem at all a suitable environment for their conspicuous attire.

'We shall have lots of fun,' Morera promised. 'This is the toughest dancing-saloon in Buenos Aires.'

'It looks it,' Sylvia agreed.

They entered a vestibule that smelt of sawdust, scent and raw spirits, and went downstairs to a crowded hall that was thick with tobacco-smoke and dust. An accordion band was playing tangos in a corner; all along one side of the hall ran a bar. The dancers composed a queer medley. The men were mostly of the Parisian Apache type, though naturally more swarthy: the women were mostly in black dresses with shawls of brilliantly coloured silk and tawdry combs in their black hair. There were one or two women dancing in coat and skirt and hat, whose lifted petticoats and pale dissolute faces shocked even Sylvia's masculine tolerance: there was something positively evil in their commonplace attire and abandoned motion: they were like anæmic shop-girls possessed with unclean spirits.

'I believe we shall make these folk mad,' said Morera with a happy chuckle; before Sylvia could refuse he had taken her in his arms and was dancing round the room at double time. The cracked mirrors caught their reflections as they swept round, and Sylvia realized with a shock the amount of diamonds they were wearing between them and the effect they must be having in this thieves' kitchen.

'Some of these guys are looking mad already,' Morera proclaimed enthusiastically.

The dance came to an end, and they leaned back against the wall exhausted. Several men walked provocatively past, looking Sylvia and her partner slowly up and down.

'Come along of me,' Morera said. 'We'll promenade right around the hall.'

He put her arm in his and swaggered up and down; the other dancers were gathering in knots and eyeing them menacingly. At last an enormous American slouched across the empty floor and stood in their path.

'Say, who the hell are you, anyway?' he asked.

'Say, what the hell's dat to you?' demanded Morera.

'Quit,' bellowed the American.

Morera fired without taking his hand from his pocket, and the American dropped.

'Hands up! *Manos arriba!*' cried Morera, pulling out his two pistols and covering the dancers while he backed with Sylvia towards the entrance. When they were upstairs in the vestibule, he told her to look if the carriage were at the door; when he heard that it was not, he gave a loud whoop of exultation.

'I said I believed we was going to have lots of fun. We got to run now and see if any of those guys can catch us.'

He seized Sylvia's arm, and they darted down the steps and out into the street. Morera looked rapidly right and left along the narrow thoroughfare. They could hear the noise of angry voices gathering in the vestibule of the saloon.

'This way and round the turning,' he cried, pulling Sylvia to the left. There was only one window alight in the narrow alley up which they had turned, a dim orange stain in the darkness. Morera hammered on the door, as their pursuers came running round the corner. Two or three shots were fired, but before they were within easy range the door had opened, and they were inside. The old hag who had opened it protested when she saw Sylvia, but Morera commanded her in Spanish to bolt it, and she seemed afraid to disobey. Somewhere in the distant part of the house there was a sound of women's crooning; outside they could hear the shuffling of their pursuers' feet.

'Say, this is fun,' Morera chuckled. 'We've arrived into a *casa moblada*.'

It was impossible for Sylvia to be angry with him, so frank was he in his enjoyment of the situation. The old woman, however, was very angry indeed, for the pursuers were banging upon her door, and she feared a visit from the police. Her clamour was silenced with a handful of notes.

'Champagne for the girls,' Morera cried.

For Sylvia the evening had already taken on the nature of a dream, and she accepted the immediate experience as only one of an inconsequent procession of events. Having attained this state of mind, she saw nothing unusual in sitting down with half a dozen women who clung to their sofas as sea-anemones to the rocks of an aquarium. She had a fleeting astonishment that they should have names, that beings so utterly indistinguishable should be called Juanilla or Belita or Tula or Lola or Maruca, but the faint shock of discerning a common humanity passed off almost at once, and she found herself enjoying a conversation with Belita who spoke a few words of broken French. With the circulation of the champagne the women achieved a kind of liveliness and examined Sylvia's jewels with murmurs of admiration. The ancient bawd who owned them proposed a dance, to which Morera loudly agreed: the women whispered and giggled among themselves, looking bashfully over their shoulders at Sylvia in a way that made the crone thump her stick on the floor with rage. She explained in Spanish the cause of their hesitation.

'They don't want to take off all their clothes in front of you,' Morera translated to Sylvia with apologies for such modesty from women who no longer had the right to possess even their own emotions: nevertheless he suggested that they might be excused to avoid spoiling a jolly evening.

'Good heavens, I should think so,' Sylvia agreed.

Morera gave a magnanimous wave of his arm in which he seemed to confer upon the women the right to keep on their clothes. They clapped their hands and laughed like children; soon to the sound of castanets they wriggled their bodies in a way that was not so much suggestive of dancing as of flea-bites; a lamp with a tin reflector jarred fretfully upon a shelf, and the floor creaked.

Suddenly Morera held up his hand for silence: the knocking on the street door was getting louder: he asked the old woman if there was any way of getting out at the back.

'Dat's all right, kid,' he told Sylvia. 'We can crawl over the door-yards at the back. Dat door in front ain't going to hold not more than five minutes.'

He tore the elastic from a bundle of notes and scattered them in the air like leaves; the women pounced upon the largesse and were fighting with one another on the floor when Sylvia and Morera followed the old woman to the back door and out into a squalid yard.

How they ever surmounted the various walls and crossed the various yards they encountered Sylvia could never understand. All she remembered was being lifted on packing cases and dustbins, of slipping once and crashing into a hen-coop, of tearing her dress on some broken glass, of riding astride walls and pricking her face against plants, and of repeating to herself all the time: *When lilacs last in the door-yard bloomed.* When at last they extricated themselves from the maze of door-yards, they wandered for a long time through a maze of narrow streets. Sylvia had managed to stuff all her jewelry out of sight into her corsage, where it scratched her most uncomfortably, but any discomfort was preferable to the covetous eyes that watched her from the shadows.

'I guess you enjoyed yourself,' said Morera in a satisfied voice, when at last they found a carriage and leaned back to breathe the gentle night air.

'I enjoyed myself thoroughly,' said Sylvia.

'Dat's the way to see a bit of life,' he declared. 'What's the good of sitting in a bum theatre all the night? Dat don't amuse me any. I plugged him in the leg,' he added in a tone of almost tender reminiscence.

Sylvia expressed surprise at his knowing where he had hit him, and Morera was very indignant at the idea of her supposing that he should shoot a man without knowing exactly at what part of him he was aiming and where he should hit him.

'Why, I might have killed him dead,' he added. 'I didn't want to kill a man just for a bit of fun. I started them guys off, see? They thought they'd got a slob. Dat's where I was laughing. I guess I'll sleep good to-night.'

Sylvia spent a month seeing life with Carlos Morera; though she never had another experience so exciting as the first, she passed a good deal of her time upon the verge of melodramatic adventure. She grew fond of this childlike creature with his spendthrift ostentation and bravado. He never showed the least sign of wanting to make love to her and demanded nothing from Sylvia but over-dressing and admiration of his exploits. At the end of the month, he told her that business called him to New York and invited her to come with him. He let her understand, however, that now he wanted her as a mistress. Even if she could have tolerated the idea, Sylvia was sure that from the moment she accepted such a position he would begin to despise her. She had heard too many of his contemptuous references to the women he had bought. She refused to accompany him on the plea of wanting to get back to Europe. Morera looked sullen, and she had a feeling that he was regretting the amount he had spent upon her; her pride finding such a sensation insupportable impelled her to return him all his jewels.

'Say, what sort of a guy do you think I am?'

He threw the jewels at her feet, and left her like a spoilt child; but an hour or two later he came back with a necklace that must have cost five thousand dollars.

'Dat's the sort of guy I am,' he said, and would take no refusal from her to accept it.

'You can't go on spending money for nothing like this,' Sylvia protested.

'I got plenty, hadn't I?' he asked.

She nodded.

'And I believe it's my money, ain't it?' he continued.

She nodded again.

'Well, dat finishes dat argument right away. Now I got another proposition. You listening? I got a proposition dat we get married. I believe I ain't met no girl like you. I know you've been a cabaret girl. Dat don't matter a cent to me. You're British. Well, I've always had a kind of notion I'd like to marry a British girl. Don't you tink I'm always the daffy guy you've bummed around with in Buenos Aires. You saw me in dat dancing-saloon? Well, I guess you know what I can do. Dat's what I am in business. Say, Sylvia, will you marry me?'

She shook her head.

'My dear old son, it wouldn't work for you or for me.'

'I don't see how you figure dat out.'

'I've figured it out to seventy times seven. It wouldn't do. Not for another mad month even. Come, let's say good-bye. I want to go to Europe. I'm going to have a good time. It'll be you that's going to give it to me. My dear old Carlos, you may have spent your money badly from your point of view, but you haven't really. You never spent any money better in all your life.'

Morera did not bother her any more; with all his exterior foolishness he had a deep perception of individual humanity. There was a boat sailing for Marseilles in a day or two, and he bought a ticket for Sylvia.

'It's a return ticket,' he told her. 'It's good for a year.'

She assured him that even if she came back, it could never be to marry him, but he insisted upon her keeping it, and to please him she yielded.

Sylvia left the Argentine worth nearly as much as Lily when she went away from Brazil, and as if her luck was bent upon an even longer run she gained heavily at poker all the way back across the Atlantic.

When she reached Marseilles, Sylvia conceived a longing to meet Valentine again, and she telegraphed to Elène at Brussels for her address. It was with a quite exceptional anticipation that Sylvia asked the *concierge* if Madame Lataille was in. While she walked upstairs to her sister's apartment she remembered how she had yearned to be friends with Valentine nearly thirteen years ago, forgetting all about the disappointment of her hope in a sudden desire to fill up a small corner of her present loneliness.

Valentine had always lingered in Sylvia's imagination as a rather wild figure, headstrong to such a pitch where passion was concerned that she herself had always felt colourless and insignificant in comparison. There was something splendidly tropical about Valentine as she appeared to Sylvia's fancy; in all the years after she quitted France she had cherished a memory of Valentine's fiery anger on the night of her departure as something nobly independent.

Like other childish memories Sylvia found Valentine much less impressive when she met her again, much less impressive for instance than Elène, who though she had married a shopkeeper and had settled down to a most uncompromising and ordinary respectability, retained a ripening outward beauty that made up for any pinching of the spirit. Here was Valentine scarcely even pretty, who achieved by neatness any effect of personality that she did. She had fine eyes – it seemed impossible for any of her mother's children to avoid them, however dull and inexpressive might have been the father's. Sylvia was thinking of Henry's eyes, but what she had heard of M. Lataille in childhood had never led her to picture him as more remarkable outwardly than her own father.

'Twelve years since we met,' Valentine was murmuring, and Sylvia was agreeing and thinking to herself all the time how very much compressed Valentine was, not uncomfortably or displeasingly, but like a new dress before it has blossomed to the individuality of the wearer. There recurred to Sylvia out of the past a likeness between Valentine and Maudie Tilt when Maudie had dressed up for the supper-party with Jimmy Monkley.

When the first reckonings of lapsed years were over, there did not seem much to talk about, but presently Sylvia described with much detail the voyage from La Plata to Marseilles, just as when one takes up a long interrupted correspondence great attention is often devoted to the weather at the moment.

'*Alors, vous êtes chanteuse?*' Valentine asked.

'*Oui, je suis chanteuse,*' Sylvia replied.

Neither of the sisters used the second person singular: the conversation, which was desultory like the conversation of travellers in a railway-carriage, ended abruptly as if the train had entered a tunnel.

'*Vous êtes très bien ici,*' said Sylvia, looking round. The train had emerged and was running through a dull cutting.

'*Oui, je suis très bien ici,*' Valentine replied.

There was no hostility between the sisters: there was merely a blank, a sundering stretch of twelve years, that dismayed both of them with its tracklessness. Presently Sylvia noticed a photograph upon the wall so conspicuously framed as to justify a supposition that it represented the man who was responsible for Valentine's well-being.

'*Oui, c'est mon amant,*' said Valentine in reply to the unspoken question.

Sylvia was faced by the problem of commenting satisfactorily upon a photograph. To begin with it was one of those photographs that preserve the individual hairs of the moustache, but eradicate every line from the face. It was impossible to comment on it, and it would have been equally impossible to comment on the original in person. The only fact emerging from the photograph was that in addition to a moustache the subject of it owned a pearl tie-pin; but even of the genuineness of the pearl it was unable to give any assurance.

'Photographs tell one nothing, do they?' Sylvia said at last. 'They're like somebody else's dreams.'

Valentine knitted her brows in perplexity.

'Or somebody else's baby,' Sylvia went on desperately.

'I don't like babies,' said Valentine.

'*Vraiment on est très bien ici,*' said Sylvia.

She felt that by flinging an accentuated compliment to the room Valentine might feel her lover was included in the approbation.

'And it's mine,' said Valentine complacently. 'He bought it for me. *C'est pour la vie.*'

Passion might be quenched in the slough of habitude: love's pinions might moult like any farmyard hen's: but the apartment was hers for life.

'How many rooms have you?' Sylvia asked.

'Besides this one, I have a bedroom, a dining-room, a kitchen, and a bathroom. Would you like to see the bathroom?'

When Valentine asked the last question, she was transformed; and a latent exultation flamed out from her immobility.

'I should love to see the bathroom,' said Sylvia. 'I think a bathroom is often the most interesting part of a house.'

'But this is an exceptional bathroom. It cost two thousand francs to instal.'

Valentine led the way to the admired chamber to which a complicated arrangement of shining pipes gave an orchestral appearance. Valentine flitted from tap to tap: Aretino himself could scarcely have imagined more methods of sprinkling water upon the human body.

'And these pipes are for warming the towels,' she explained. It was a relief to find pipes that led a comparatively passive existence amid such a convolution of fountainous activity.

'I thought while I was about it that I would have the tiles laid right up to the ceiling,' Valentine went on pensively. 'And you see, the ceiling is made of looking-glass. When the water is very hot, *ça fait drôle, tu sais, on ne se voit plus.*'

It was the first time she had used the second person singular; the bathroom had created in Valentine something that almost resembled humanity.

'Yes,' Sylvia agreed. 'I suppose that is the best way of making the ceiling useful.'

'*C'est pour la vie,*' Valentine contentedly sighed.

'But if he were to marry?' Sylvia ventured.

'It would make no difference,' Valentine answered. 'I have saved money and with a bathroom like this one can always get a good rent. Everything in the apartment is mine and the apartment is mine too.'

'*Alors, tu es contente?*' said Sylvia.

'*Oui, je suis contente,*' said Valentine.

'*Elle est jolie, ta salle de bain.*'

'*Oui, elle est jolie comme un amour,*' Valentine assented with a sweet maternal smile.

They talked of the bathroom for a while when they came back to the boudoir; Sylvia was conscious of displaying the polite enthusiasm with which one descends from the nursery at an afternoon call.

'*Enfin,*' said Sylvia. '*Je file.*'

'*Tu quittes Marseilles tout de suite?*'

'*Oui, je m'en vais ce soir.*'

She had not really intended to leave Marseilles that evening, but there seemed no reason to stay.

'*C'est dommage que tu n'as pas vu Louis.*'

'*Il s'appelle Louis?*'

'*Oui, il s'appelle Louis. Il est à Lyon pour ses affaires.*'

'*Alors, au revoir, Valentine.*'

'*Au revoir, Sylvie.*'

They hesitated, both of them, to see which would offer her cheek first: in the end they managed to be simultaneous.

'Even the farewell was a stalemate,' Sylvia said to herself on the way downstairs.

She wondered while she was walking back to her hotel what was going to be the passion of her own life. One always started out with a dim conception of perfect love, however one might scoff at it openly in self-protection; but evidently it by no means followed that love for a man, let alone perfect love would ever arrive. Lily had succeeded in inspiring at least one man with love for her; she had found her own passion in roulette with Camacho tacked to it, inherited like a husband's servant, familiar with every caprice, but jealous and irritable. Valentine had found her grand passion in a bathroom that satisfied her profoundest maternal instincts. Dorothy had loved a coronet with such fervour that she had been able to abandon everything that could smirch it. Her own mother had certainly found at thirty-four her grand passion, but she felt that it would be preferable to fall in love with a bathroom now than to wait ten years for a Henry.

Sylvia reached the hotel, packed up her things and set out to Paris without any definite plans in her head for the future, and just because she had no definite plans and nothing to keep her from sleeping, she could not sleep and tossed about on the *wagon-lit* half the night.

'It's not as if I hadn't got money. I'm amazingly lucky. It's really fantastic luck to find somebody like poor old Carlos to set me up for five years of luxurious independence. I suppose if I were wise I should buy a house in London – and yet I don't want to go back to London. The trouble with me is that, though I like to be independent, I don't like to be alone. Yet with Michael . . . but what's the use of thinking about him? Do I actually miss him? No, certainly not. He's nothing more to me than something I might have had, but failed to secure. I'm regretting a missed experience. If one loses somebody like that, it leaves a sense of incompletion. How often does one feel a quite poignant regret, because one has forgotten to finish a cup of coffee; but the regret is always for the incomplete moment; it doesn't endure. Michael in a year will have changed: I've changed also. There is nothing to suggest that if we met again now, we should meet in the same relation, with the same possibility in the background of our intercourse. Then why won't I go back to Mulberry Cottage? Obviously because I have outlived Mulberry Cottage. I don't want to stop my course by running into a backwater that's already been explored. I want to go on and on until . . . yes, until what? I can travel now, if I want to. Well, why shouldn't I travel? If I visit my agent in Paris – and I certainly shall visit him in order to tell him what I think of the management of that damned Casino at Rio – he'll offer me another contract to sing in some outlandish corner of the globe, and if I weren't temporarily independent, I should have to accept it with all its humiliations. Merely to travel would be a mistake, I think. I've got myself into the swirl of mountebanks, and somehow I must continue with them. It's a poor little loyalty, but even that is better than nothing. Really if one isn't tied down by poverty, one can have a very good time, travelling the world as a singer. Or I could live in Paris for a while. I should meet amusing people. Oh, I don't know what I want. I should rather like to get hold of Olive again. She may be married by now. She probably is married. She's bound to be married. A superfluity of romantic affection was rapidly accumulating that must have been deposited somewhere by now. I might get Mrs. Gainsborough out from England to come with me. Come with me, where? It seems a shame to uproot the poor old thing again. She's nearly sixty. But I must have somebody.'

When Sylvia reached Paris, she visited two trunks that were in a repository. Amongst other things she took out the volume of Adlington's Apuleius.

'Yes, there's no doubt I'm still an ass,' she said. 'And since the Argentine really a golden ass; but oh, when, when, when shall I eat the rose-leaves and turn into Sylvia again? One might make a joke about that, as the White Knight said, something about Golden and Silver and Argentine.'

Thinking of jokes reminded Sylvia of Mr. Pluepott, and thinking of *Alice through the Looking-glass* brought back the Vicar. What a long way off they seemed.

'I can't let go of everybody,' she cried. So she telegraphed and wrote urgently to Mrs. Gainsborough, begging her to join her in Paris. While she was waiting for a reply, she discussed projects for the future with her agent, who when he found that she had some money was anxious for her to invest a certain amount in the necessary *réclame* and appear at the Folies Bergères.

'But I don't want to make a success by singing French songs with an English accent,' Sylvia protested. 'I'd as soon make a success by singing without a roof to my mouth. You discouraged me from doing something I really wanted to do. All I want now is an excuse for roaming.'

'What about a tour in Spain?' the agent suggested. 'I can't get you more than ten francs a night though, if you only want to sing. Still Spain's much cheaper than America.'

'*Mon cher ami, j'ai besoin du travail pour me distraire.* Ten francs is the wage of a slave, but pocket-money if one is not a slave.'

'*Vous avez de la veine, vous.*'

'*Vraiment?*'

'*Mais oui.*'

'*Peut-être quelqu'un m'a plaquée.*'

He tried to look grave and sympathetic.

'*Salaud,*' she mocked. '*Crois-tu que je t'en dirais. Bigre! je crèverais plutôt.*'

She had dropped into familiarity of speech with him, but he, still hopeful of persuading her to entrust a profitable *réclame* to him, continued to treat her formally. Sylvia realized the *arrière pensée* and laughed at him.

'*Je ne suis pas encore en grande vedette, tu sais.*'

He assured her that such a triumph would ultimately come to her, and she scoffed.

'*Mon vieux, si je n'avais pas de la galette, je pourrais crever de faim devant ta porte. C'que tu me dis, c'est du chiqué.*'

'Well, will you go to Spain?'

The contract was signed.

A day or two later when she was beginning to give up hope of getting an answer from Mrs. Gainsborough, the old lady herself turned up at the hotel, looking not a minute older.

'You darling and daring old plesiosaurus,' cried Sylvia, seizing her by the hand and twirling her round the vestibule.

'Yes, I am pleased to see you and no mistake,' said Mrs. Gainsborough. 'But what a tyrant! Well really, I was in me bed when your telegram came and that boy he knocked like a tiger. Knock – knock! all the time I was trying to slip on me petticoat, which through me being in a regular fluster I put on wrong way up and got me feet all wound up with the strings. Knock – knock! "Whatever do you think you're doing?" I said when at last I was fairly decent and went to open the door. "Telegram," he says as saucy as brass. "Telegram?" I said, "I thought by the row you was making that you was building St. Paul's Cathedral." "Wait for the answer?" he said.

245

"Answer?" I said. "Certainly not." Well, there was I with your telegram in one hand and me petticoat slipping down in the other. Then on the top of that came your letter, and I couldn't resist a sight of you, my dearie. Fancy that Lily waltzing off like that. And with a Portuguese. She'll get Portuguese before he's finished with her. Portugoose is what she'll be. And the journey! Well really, I don't know how I managed. I kept on saying, "France," the same as if I was asking a policeman the way to Oxford Circus, and they bundled me about like . . . well, really, everybody was most kind. Still when I got to France, it wasn't much use going on shouting "France" to everybody. However, I met a nice young fellow in the train, and he very thoughtfully assisted me into a cab and . . . well, I am glad to see you.'

'Now you're coming with me to Spain,' Sylvia announced.

'Good land alive, where?'

'Spain.'

'Are you going chasing after Lily again?'

'No, we're going off on our own.'

'Well, I may have started on the gad late in life, but I've certainly started now,' said Mrs. Gainsborough. 'Spain? That's where the Spanish flies come from, isn't it? Well, they ought to be lively enough, so I suppose we shall enjoy ourselves. And how do we get there?'

'By train.'

'Dear land, it's wonderful what they can do nowadays. What relation then is Spain to Portugal exactly? You must excuse my ignorance, Sylvia, but really I'm still all of a fluster. Fancy being bounced out of me bed into Spain. You really are a demon. Fancy you getting yellow fever. You haven't changed colour much. Spain! Upon my word I never heard anything like it. We'd better take plenty with us to eat. I knew it reminded me of something. The Spanish Armada! I once heard a clergyman recite the Spanish Armada, though what it was all about I've completely forgotten. There was some fighting in it, though. I went with the Captain. Well, if he could see me now. You may be sure he's laughing, wherever he is. The idea of me going to Spain!'

The idea materialized; that night they drove to the Gare d'Orléans.

V

The journey to Madrid was for Mrs. Gainsborough a long revelation of human eccentricity.

'Not even Mrs. Ewings would believe it,' she assured Sylvia. 'It's got to be seen to be believed. I opened my mouth a bit wide when I first came to France, but France is Peckham Rye if you put it alongside of Spain. When that guard or whatever he calls himself opened our door and bobbed in out of the tunnel with the train going full speed and asked for our tickets, you could have knocked me down with a feather. Showing off, that's what I call it. And carrying wine inside of goats! Disgusting I should say. Nice set out there'd be in England if the brewers started sending round beer inside of sheep. Why, it would cause a regular outcry; but these Spanish seem to put up with anything. I'm not surprised they come round selling water at every station. The cheek of it though, when you come to think about it. Putting wine inside of goats so as to make people buy water. If I'd have been an enterprising woman like Mrs. Marsham, I should have got out at the last station and complained to the police about it. But really the stations aren't fit for a decent person to walk about in. I'm not considered very particular, but when a station consists of nothing but a signal-box and a lavatory and no platform, I don't call it a station. And what a childish way of starting a train – blowing a toy horn like that. More like a school-treat than a railway-journey. And the turkeys! Now I ask you, Sylvia, would you believe it? Four turkeys under the seat and three on the rack over me head. A regular Harlequinade! And every time anybody takes out a cigarette or a bit of bread they offer it all around the compartment. Fortunately I don't look hungry, or they might have been offended. No wonder England's full of aliens. I shall explain the reason of it when I get home.'

The place of entertainment where Sylvia worked was called the Teatro Japonés, for what reason it would have been difficult to say. The girls were as usual mostly French, but there were one or two Spanish dancers that, as Mrs. Gainsborough put it, kept one 'rum-tum-tumming in one's seat all the time it was going on.' Sylvia found Madrid a dull city entirely without romance of aspect, nor did the pictures in the Prado make up for the bullring's wintry desolation. Mrs. Gainsborough considered the most remarkable evidence of Spanish eccentricity was the way in which flocks of turkeys after travelling in passenger-trains actually wandered about the chief thoroughfares.

'Suppose if I was to go shooting across Piccadilly with a herd of chickens, let alone turkeys, well, it *would* be a circus, and that's a fact.'

When they first arrived, they stayed at a large hotel in the Puerta del Sol, but Mrs. Gainsborough got into trouble with the baths, partly because they cost five pesetas each and partly because she said it went to her heart to see a perfectly clean sheet floating about in the water. After that, they tried a smaller hotel where they were fairly comfortable, though Mrs. Gainsborough took a long time to get used to being brought chocolate in the morning.

'I miss my morning tea, Sylvia, and it's no use me pretending I don't. I don't feel like chocolate in the morning. I'd just as lieve have a slice of plum-pudding in a cup. Why, if you try to put a lump of sugar in, it won't sink: it keeps bobbing up like a kitten. And another thing I can't seem to get used to is having the fish after the meat. Every time it comes in like that it seems a kind of carelessness. What fish it is, too, when it does come! Well, they say a donkey can eat thistles, but it would take him all his time to get through one of those fish. No wonder they serve them after the meat. I should think they were afraid of the amount of meat anyone might eat so as to get the bones out of one's throat. I've felt like a pin-cushion ever since I got to Madrid, and how you can sing beats me. Your throat must be like a zither by now.'

It really did not seem worth while to remain any longer in Madrid; and Sylvia asked to be released from her contract. The manager, who had been wondering to all the other girls why Sylvia had ever been sent to him, discovered that she was his chief attraction when she wanted to break the contract. However, a hundred pesetas in his own pocket removed all objections, and she was free to leave Spain.

'Well, do you want to go home?' she asked Mrs. Gainsborough. 'Or will you come to Seville?'

'Now we've come so far, we may as well go on a bit farther,' Mrs. Gainsborough thought.

Seville was different from Madrid.

'Really, when you see oranges growing in the streets,' Mrs. Gainsborough said, 'you begin to understand why people ever goes abroad. Why, the flowers are really grand, Sylvia. Carnations as common as daisies. Well, I declare, I wrote home a postcard to Mrs. Beardmore and told her Seville was like being in a conservatory. She's living near Kew now, so she'll understand my meaning.'

They both much enjoyed the dancing in the cafés, where solemn men hurled their sombreros on the dancers' platform to mark their appreciation of the superb creatures who flaunted themselves so gracefully.

'But they're bold hussies with it all, aren't they?' Mrs. Gainsborough observed. 'Upon my word, *I* wouldn't care to climb up there and swing my hips about like that.'

From Seville after an idle month of exquisite weather, often so warm that Sylvia could sit in the garden of the Alcazar and read in the shade of the lemon trees, they went to Granada.

'So they've got an Alhambra here, have they?' said Mrs. Gainsborough.

'But from what I've seen of the performances in Spain it won't come up to the good old Leicester Square.'

On Sylvia the Alhambra cast an enchantment more powerful than any famous edifice she had yet seen. Her admiration of cathedrals had always been tempered by a sense of missing most of what they stood for: they were still exercising their functions in a modern world and thereby overshadowed her personal emotions in a way that she found most discouraging to the imagination. The Alhambra, which once belonged to kings, now belonged to individual dreams. Those shaded courts where even at midday the ice lay thick upon the fountains: that sudden escape from a frozen chastity of brown stone cut out on the terraces rich with sunlight: that vision of the Sierra Nevada leaping against the blue sky with all its snowy peaks: this incredible meeting of East and South and North: to know all these was to stand in the centre of the universe, oneself a king.

'What's it remind you of, Sylvia?' Mrs. Gainsborough asked.

'Everything,' Sylvia cried. She felt that it would take but the least effort of will to light in one swoop upon the Sierra Nevada and from those bastions storm . . . what?

'It reminds me just a tiddly-bit of Earl's Court,' said Mrs. Gainsborough, putting her head on one side like a meditative hen. 'If you shut one eye against those mountains, you'll see what I mean.'

Sylvia came often by herself to the Alhambra: she had no scruples in leaving Mrs. Gainsborough, who had made friends at the pension with a lonely American widower.

'He knows everything,' said Mrs. Gainsborough. 'I've learnt more in a fortnight with him than I ever learnt in my whole life. What that man doesn't know! Well, I'm sure it's not worth knowing. He's been in trade and never been able to travel till now, but he's got the world off by heart, as you might say. I sent a p.c. to Mrs. Ewings to say I'd found a masher at last. The only thing against him is the noises he makes with his throat. I gave him some lozenges at first, but he made more noise than ever sucking them, and I had to desist.'

Soon after Mrs. Gainsborough met her American, Sylvia made the acquaintance of a youthful guide of thirteen or fourteen years, who for a small wage adopted her and gave her much entertainment. Somehow or other Rodrigo had managed to pick up a good deal of English and French, which, as he pointed out, enabled him to compete with the older guides who resented his intrusion. Rodrigo did not consider that the career of a guide was worthy of real ambition: for the future he hesitated between being a gentleman's servant and a tobacconist in Gibraltar. He was a slim child with the perfect grace of the young South in movements and in manners alike.

Rodrigo was rather distressed at the beginning by Sylvia's want of appetite for mere sight-seeing; he reproved her indeed very gravely for wasting valuable time in repeating her visits to favourite spots while so many others remained unvisited. He was obsessed by the rapidity with which most tourists passed through Granada; but when he discovered that Sylvia had no intention of hurrying or being hurried, his native indolence blossomed to her sympathy and he adapted himself to her pleasure in sitting idle and dreaming in the sun.

Warmer weather came in February, and Rodrigo suggested that the Alhambra should be visited by moonlight. He did not make this suggestion because it was the custom of other English people to desire this experience; he knew that the Señorita was not influenced by what other people did; at the same time the Alhambra by moonlight could scarcely fail to please the Señorita's passion for beauty; he himself had a passion for beauty, and he pledged his word she would not regret following his advice: moreover he would bring his guitar.

On a February night, when the moon was still high, Sylvia and Rodrigo walked up the avenue that led to the Alhambra. There was nobody on the summit but themselves. Far down, lights flitted in the gipsy quarter, whence there came up a faint noise of singing and music.

It was Carnival, Rodrigo explained, and the Señorita would have enjoyed it; but, alas, there were many rascals about on such nights and, though he was armed, he did not recommend a visit. He brought out his guitar; from beneath her Spanish cloak Sylvia also brought out a guitar.

'The Señorita plays? *Maravilloso!*' Rodrigo exclaimed. 'But why the Señorita did not inform me to carry her guitar? The hill was long. The Señorita will be tired.'

Sylvia opened with one of her old French songs, after which Rodrigo, who paid her a courteous and critical attention, declared that she had a musician's soul like himself, and forthwith in a treble that was limpid as the moonlight, unpassionate as the snow, remote as the mountains, he too sang.

'Exquisite,' she sighed.

The Señorita was too kind, and as if to disclaim the compliment he went off into a mad gipsy tune. Suddenly he broke off:

'Hark, does the Señorita hear a noise of weeping?' There was indeed a sound of someone's crying, a sound that came nearer every moment.

'It is most unusual to hear a sound of weeping in the Alhambra *au clair de la lune*,' said Rodrigo. 'If the Señorita will permit me, I shall find out the cause.'

Soon he came back with a girl whose cheeks glistened with tears.

'She is a dancer,' he explained. 'She says she is Italian, but' – with a shrug of the shoulders he gave Sylvia to understand that he accepted no responsibility for her statement. It was Carnival.

Sylvia asked the newcomer in French what was the matter, but for some time she could only sob without saying a word. Rodrigo, who was regarding her with a mixture of disapproval and compassion, considered that she had reached the stage – he spoke with all possible respect for the Señorita who must not suppose herself included in his generalization – the stage of incoherence that is so much more frequent with women than with men whose feelings have been upset. If he might suggest a remedy to the Señorita, it would be to leave her alone for a few minutes and continue the interrupted music. They had come here to enjoy the Alhambra by moonlight; it seemed a pity to allow the grief of an unknown dancer to spoil the beauty of the scene, grief that probably had nothing to do with the Alhambra, but was an echo of the world below. It might be a lover's quarrel due to the discovery of a masked flirtation, a thing of no importance compared with the Alhambra by moonlight.

'I'm not such a philosopher as you, Rodrigo. I am a poor inquisitive woman.'

Certainly inquisitiveness might be laid to the charge of the feminine sex, he agreed, but not to all women. There must be exceptions, and with a gesture expressive of tolerance for the weaknesses of womankind he managed to convey his intention of excepting Sylvia from Eve's heritage. Human nature was not woven to the same pattern. Many of his friends for instance would fail to appreciate the Alhambra on such a night, and would prefer to blow horns in the streets.

By this time the grief of the stranger was less noisy, and Sylvia again asked her who she was and why she was weeping. She spoke in English this time; the fair slim child, for when one looked at her she was scarcely more than fifteen, brightened.

'I don't know where I was,' she said.

Rodrigo clicked his tongue and shook his head; he was shocked by this avowal much more deeply than in his sense of locality. Sylvia was puzzled by her accent. The 'w's' were nearly 'v's,' but the intonation was Italian.

'And you're a dancer?' she asked.

'Yes, I was dancing at the Estrella.'

Rodrigo explained that this was a cabaret, the kind of place with which the Señorita would not be familiar.

'And you're Italian?'

The girl nodded, and Sylvia seeing that it would be impossible to extract anything about her story in her present overwrought state decided to take her back to the pension.

'And I will carry the Señorita's guitar,' said Rodrigo. 'To-morrow morning at eleven o'clock?' he asked by the gate of Sylvia's pension. 'Or would the Señorita prefer that I waited to conduct the *señorita extraviada*?'

Sylvia bade him come in the morning; with a deep bow to her and to the stranger he departed, twanging his guitar.

Mrs. Gainsborough, who by this time had reached the point of thinking that her American widower existed only to be oracular, wished to ask his advice about the stranger, and was quite offended with Sylvia for telling her rather sharply that she did not want all the inmates of the pension buzzing round the frightened child.

'Chocolate would be more useful than advice,' Sylvia said.

'I know you're very down on poor Mr. Linthicum, but he's a mass of information. Only this morning he was explaining how you can keep eggs fresh for a year by putting them in a glass of water. Now I like a bit of advice. I'm not like you, you great harumscarum thing.'

Mrs. Gainsborough was unable to remain very long in a state of injured dignity; she soon came up to Sylvia's bedroom with cups of chocolate.

'And though you laugh at poor Mr. Linthicum,' she said, 'it's thanks to him you've got this chocolate so quick, for he talked to the servant himself.'

With this Mrs. Gainsborough left the room in high good humour at the successful rehabilitation of the informative widower.

The girl, whose name was Concetta, had long ceased to lament, but she was still very shy, and Sylvia found it extremely difficult at first to reach any clear comprehension of her present trouble. Gradually, however, by letting her talk in her own breathless way, and in an odd mixture of English, French, German and Italian, she was able to piece together the facts into a kind of consecutiveness.

Her father had been an Italian, who for some reason that was not at all clear had lived at Aix-la-Chapelle; her mother, to whom he had apparently never been married, had been a Fleming. The mother had died when Concetta was about four, and her father had married a German woman who had beaten her, particularly after her father had either died or abandoned his child to the stepmother – it was not clear which. At this point an elder brother appeared in the tale, who at the age of eleven had managed to steal some money and run away. Of this brother Concetta had made an ideal hero: she dreamed of him even now and never came to any town but that she expected to meet him there. Sylvia had asked her how she expected to recognize somebody who had disappeared from her life when she was only six years old, but Concetta insisted that she should know him again. When she said this, she looked round her with an expression of fear and asked if anybody could overhear them. Sylvia assured her that they were quite alone, and Concetta said in a whisper:

'Once in Milano I saw Francesco. Hush! he passed in the street, and I said "Francesco!" and he said "Concettina!"; but we could not speak together more longer.'

Sylvia would not contest this assertion, though she made up her mind that it must have been a dream.

'It was a pity you could not speak,' she said.

'Yes, nothing but Francesco and Concettina before he was gone. *Peccato! Peccato!*'

Francesco's example had illuminated his sister's life with the hope of escaping from her stepmother, and she had hoarded pennies month after month for three years. She would not speak in detail of the cruelty of her stepmother: the memory of it even at this distance of time was too much charged with horror. It was evident to Sylvia that she had suffered exceptional things and that this was no case of ordinary unkindness. There was still in Concetta's eyes the look of an animal in a trap, and Sylvia felt a rage at human cruelty hammering upon her brain: one read of these things with an idle shudder, but oh, to behold before one a child whose very soul was scarred. There was more to affright the imagination, because Concetta said that not only was her stepmother cruel, but also her school-teachers and schoolmates.

'Everybody was liking to beat me. I don't know why, but they was liking to beat me; no really, they was liking it.'

At last, and here Concetta was very vague, as if she were seeking to recapture the outlines of a dream that fades in the light of morning, somehow or other she ran away and arrived at a place with trees in a large city.

'Where at, Aix-la-Chapelle?'

'No, I got into a train and came somewhere to a big place with trees in the middle of a city.'

'Was it a park in Brussels?'

She shrugged her shoulders and came back to her tale. In this park she had met some little girls who had played with her: they had played in a game of joining hands and dancing round in a circle until they fell down on the grass. A gentleman had laughed to see them amusing themselves so much; and the little girls had asked her to come with them and the gentleman; they had danced round him and pulled his coat to make him take Concetta. He had asked her whence she came and whither she was going: he was a schoolmaster, and he was going far away with all these other little girls. Concetta had cried when they were leaving her, and the gentleman, when he found that she was really alone in this big city, had finally been persuaded to take her with him. They went far away in the train to Dantzig, where he had a school to learn dancing. She had been happy there: the master was very kind. When she was thirteen she had gone with other girls from the school to dance in the ballet at La Scala in Milan, but before that she had danced at Dresden and Munich. Then about six months ago a juggler called Zozo had wanted her and another girl to join his act. He was a young man: she had liked him, and she had left Milan with him. They had performed in Rome and Naples and Bari and Palermo. At Palermo the other girl had gone back to her home in Italy, and Concetta had travelled to Spain with this man through Tunis and Algiers and Oran. Zozo had treated her kindly until they came here to the Estrella Concert; but here he had changed and, when she did not like him to make love to her, he had beaten her. To-night before they went to the cabaret he had told her that unless she would let him love her he would throw the daggers at her heart: in their act she was tied up, and he threw daggers all round her. She had been frightened, and when he went to dress she had run away; but the streets were full of people in masks, and she had lost herself.

Sylvia looked at this child with her fair hair, who, but for the agony and fear in her blue eyes, would have been like one of those rapturous angels in old Flemish pictures. Here she sat, as ten years ago Sylvia had sat in the cab-shelter talking to Fred Organ. Her story and Concetta's met at this point in man's vileness.

'My poor little thing, you must come and live with me,' cried Sylvia, clasping Concetta to her arms. 'I too am all alone, and I should love to feel that somebody was dependent on me. You shall come with me to England. You're just what I've been looking for. Now I'm going to put you to bed, for you're worn out.'

'But he'll come to find me,' Concetta gasped in sudden affright. 'He was so clever. On the programme you can read: ZOZO EL MEJOR PRES-TIGITADOR DEL MUNDO. He knows everything.'

'We must introduce him to Mrs. Gainsborough. She likes encyclope-dias with pockets.'

'Please?'

'I was talking to myself. My dear, you'll be perfectly safe with me from the greatest magician in the world.'

In the end she was able to calm Concetta's fears: in sleep, when those frightened blue eyes were closed, she seemed younger than ever, and Sylvia brooded over her by candlelight as if she were indeed her child.

Mrs. Gainsborough, on being told next morning Concetta's story and Sylvia's resolve to adopt her, gave her blessing to the plan.

'Mulberry Cottage'll be nice for her to play about in. She'll be able to dig in the garden. We'll buy a bucket and spade. Fancy, what wicked people there are in this world! But I blame her stepmother more than I do this Shoushou.'

Mrs. Gainsborough persisted in treating Concetta as if she were about nine years old and was continually thinking of toys that might amuse her. When at last she was brought to grasp that she was fifteen, she was greatly disappointed on behalf of Mr. Linthicum, to whom she had presented Concetta as an infant prodigy.

'He commented so much on the languages she could speak, and he told her of a quick way to practise elemental American, which I always thought was the same as English, but apparently it's not. It's a much older language really, and came over with Christopher Columbus in the *Mayflower*.'

Rodrigo was informed by Sylvia that henceforth the Señorita Concetta would live with her; he expressed no surprise and accepted with a charming courtliness the new situation at the birth of which he had presided. Sylvia thought it might be prudent to take Rodrigo so far into her confidence as to give him a hint about a possible attempt by the juggler to get Concetta back into his power. Rodrigo looked very serious at the notion, and advised the Señorita to leave Granada quickly. It was against his interest to give this counsel, for he should lose his Señorita, the possession of whom had exposed him to a good deal of envy from the other guides. Besides he had grown fond of the Señorita and he should miss her; he had intended to practise much on his guitar this spring, and he had looked forward to hearing the nightingales with her; they would be singing next month in the lemon groves; many people were deaf to the song of birds, but personally he could not listen to them without . . . a shrug of the shoulders expressed the incommunicable emotion.

'You shall come with us, Rodrigo.'

'To Gibraltar?' he asked quickly with flashing eyes.

'Why not?' said Sylvia.

He seized her hand and kissed it.

'*El destino*,' he murmured. 'I shall certainly see there the tobacco-shop that one day I shall have.'

For two or three days Rodrigo guarded the pension against the conjurer and his spies; by this time between Concetta's apprehensions and Mrs. Gainsborough's exaggeration of them, Zozo had acquired a demoniac menace, lurking in the background of enjoyment like a child's fear.

The train for Algeciras would leave in the morning at four o'clock: it was advisable, Rodrigo thought, to be at the railway station by two o'clock at the latest: he should come with a carriage to meet them. Would the Señorita excuse him this evening, because his mother – he gave one of his inimitable shrugs to express the need of sometimes yielding to maternal fondness – wished him to spend his last evening with her.

At two o'clock next morning Rodrigo had not arrived, but at three a carriage drove up, and the coachman handed Sylvia a note. It was in Spanish to say that Rodrigo had met with an accident and that he was very ill: he kissed the Señorita's hand: he believed that he was going to die, which was his only consolation for not being able to go with her to Gibraltar: it was *el destino:* he had brought the accident on himself.

Sylvia drove with Mrs. Gainsborough and Concetta to the railway-station. When she arrived and found that the train would not leave till five, she kept the coachman, and after seeing her companions safely into their compartment drove to where Rodrigo lived.

He was lying in a hovel in the poorest part of the city: his mother, ragged and prematurely old, was lamenting in a corner; one or two neighbours were trying to quieten her. On Sylvia's arrival they all broke out in a loud wail of apology for the misfortune that had made Rodrigo break his engagement. Sylvia paid no attention to them, but went quickly across to the bed of the sick boy. He opened his eyes and with an effort put out a slim brown arm and caught hold of her hand to kiss it: she leant over and kissed his pale lips. In a very faint voice, hiding his head in the pillow for shame, he explained that he had brought the accident on himself by his boasting. He had boasted so much about the tobacco-shop and the favour of the Señorita that an older boy, another guide, a – he tried to shrug his shoulders in contemptuous expression of this older boy's inferior quality, but his body contracted in a spasm of pain, and he had to set criticism on one side. This older boy had hit him out of jealousy, and, alas, he had lost his temper and drawn a knife, but the other boy had stabbed first. It was *el destino* most unhappily precipitated by his own vainglory.

Sylvia turned to the women to ask what could be done; their weeping redoubled; the doctor had declared it was only a matter of hours; the priest had given Unction. Suddenly Rodrigo with a violent effort clutched at Sylvia's hand:

'Señorita, the train!'

He fell back dead.

Sylvia left money for the funeral: there was nothing more to be done. In the morning twilight she went down the foul stairs and back to the carriage that seemed now to smell of death.

When she arrived at the station a great commotion was taking place on the platform, and Mrs. Gainsborough appeared surrounded by a gesticulating crowd of porters, officials, and passengers.

'Sylvia! Well, I'm glad you've got here at last. She's gone. He's whisked her away. And can I explain what I want to these Spanish idiots? No. I've shouted as hard as I could, and they *won't* understand. They *won't* understand me. They don't want to understand, that's my opinion.'

With this Mrs. Gainsborough sailed off again along the platform, followed by the crowd, which in addition to arguing with her occasionally detached from itself small groups to argue furiously with one another about her incomprehensible desire. Sylvia extricated their luggage from the compartment for the train to go to Algeciras without them: then she extricated Mrs. Gainsborough from the general noise and confusion that was now being added to by loud whistles from the impatient train.

'I was sitting in one corner and Concertina was sitting in the other,' Mrs. Gainsborough explained to Sylvia. 'I'd just bobbed down to pick up me glasses when I saw that Shoushou beckoning to her, though for the moment I thought it was the porter. Concertina went as white as her shift. "Here," I hollered, "what are you doing?" and with that I got up from me place and tripped over *your* luggage and came down bump on the foot-warmer. When I got up, she was gone. Depend upon it, he'd been watching out for her at the station. As soon as I could get out of the carriage, I started hollering, and everyone in the station came running round to see what was the matter. I tried to tell them about Shoushou, and they pretended, for don't you tell me I can't make myself understood if people want to understand, they pretended they thought I was asking whether I was in the right train. When I hollered "Shoushou," they all started to holler "Shoushou" as well and nod their heads and point to the train. I got that aggravated, I could have killed them. And then what do you think they did? Insulting I call it. Why, they all began to laugh and beckon to me, and I, thinking that at last they'd found out me meaning, went and followed them like a silly juggins, and where do you think they took me? To the Moojeries! what *we* call the ladies' cloak-room. Well, that did make me annoyed, and I started to tell them what I thought of such behaviour. "I don't want the Moojeries," I shouted. Then I tried to explain by illustrating my meaning. I took hold of one young fellow and said "Shoushou" and then I caught hold of a hussy that was laughing, intending to make her stand for Concertina, but that silly little bitch – really it's enough to make anyone a bit unrefined – *she* thought I was going to hit her and started in to scream the station-roof down. After that you came along, but of course it was too late.'

Sylvia was very much upset by the death of Rodrigo and the loss of Concettina, but could not help laughing over Mrs. Gainsborough's woes.

'It's all very well for you to sit there and laugh, you great tomboy, but it's your own fault. If you'd have let me bring Mr. Linthicum, this wouldn't have happened. What could I do? I felt like a missionary among a lot of cannibals.'

In the end Sylvia was glad to avail herself of the widower's help; but after two days even he had to admit himself beaten.

'And if he says they can't be found,' said Mrs. Gainsborough, 'depend upon it, they can't be found – not by anybody. That man's as persistent as a beggar. When he came up to me this morning and cleared his throat and shook his head, well, then I knew we might as well give up hope.'

Sylvia stayed on for a while in Granada, because she did not like to admit defeat; but the sadness of Rodrigo's death and the disappointment over Concetta had spoilt the place for her. Here was another of these incomplete achievements that made life so bitter. She had thought for a brief space that the solitary and frightened child would provide the aim that she had so ardently desired: Concetta had responded so sweetly to her protection, had chattered with such delight of going to England and of becoming English; now she had been dragged back. *El destino!* Rodrigo's death did not affect her so much as the loss of that fair slim child; his short life had been complete; he was spared for ever from disillusionment, and by existing in her memory eternally young and joyous and wise he had spared his Señorita also the pain of disillusionment, just as when he was alive he had always assumed the little bothers upon his shoulders, the little bothers of everyday existence: his was a perfect episode, but Concetta disturbed her with vain regrets and speculations. Yet in a way the child had helped her, for she knew now that she held in her heart an inviolate treasure of love. Never again could anything happen like those three months after she had left Philip: never again could she treat anyone with the scorn with which she had treated Michael: never again could she take such a cynical attitude towards anyone as that she had once taken towards Lily. All these disappointments added a little gold tried by fire to the treasure in her heart, and firmly she must believe that it was being stored to some purpose soon to be showered prodigally, ah, how prodigally upon somebody.

That evening Sylvia had made up her mind to return to England at once, but after she had gone to bed, she was roused by Mrs. Gainsborough's coming into her room and in a choked voice asking for help. When the light was turned on, Sylvia saw that she was enmeshed in a mosquito-net and looking in her nightgown like a large turbot.

'I knew it would happen,' Mrs. Gainsborough panted. 'Every night I've said to myself, "It's bound to happen," and it has. I was dreaming how that Shoushou was chasing me with a butterfly-net, and look at me! Don't tell me dreams don't sometimes come true. Now don't stand there in fits of laughter. I can't get out of it, you unfeeling thing. I've swallowed about a pint of Keating's. I hope I shan't come out in spots. Come and help me! I daren't move a finger, or I shall start off sneezing again. And every time I sneeze, I get deeper in. It's something chronic.'

'Didn't Linthicum ever inform you how to get out of a mosquito-net that collapses in the middle of the night?' Sylvia asked, when she had disentangled the old lady.

'No, the conversation never happened to take a turn that way. But depend upon it, I shall ask him to-morrow. I won't be caught twice.'

Sylvia suddenly felt that it would be impossible to return to England yet.

'We must go on,' she told Mrs. Gainsborough. 'You must have more opportunities for practising what Linthicum has been preaching to you.'

'What you'd like is for me to make a poppy-show of myself all over the world and drag me round the continent like a performing bear.'

'We'll go to Morocco,' Sylvia cried.

'Don't shout like that. You'll set me off on the sneeze again. You're here, there and everywhere like a demon king, I do declare. Morocco? That's where the leather comes from, isn't it? Do they have mosquito-nets there too?'

Sylvia nodded.

'Well, the first thing I shall do to-morrow is to ask Mr. Linthicum what's the best way of fastening up a mosquito-net in Morocco. And now I suppose I shall wake up in the morning with a nose like a tomato. Ah, well, such is life.'

Mrs. Gainsborough went back to bed, and Sylvia lay awake thinking of Morocco.

Mr. Linthicum came to see them off on their second attempt to leave Granada: he cleared his throat rather more loudly than usual to compete with the noise of the railway, invited them to look him up if they ever came to Schenectady, pressed a book called *Five Hundred Facts for the Waistcoat Pocket* into Mrs. Gainsborough's hands, and waved them out of sight with a large bandana handkerchief.

'Well, I shall miss that man,' said Mrs. Gainsborough, settling down to the journey. 'He must have been a regular education for his customers, and I shall never forget his recipe for avoiding bunions when mountaineering.'

'How's that done?'

'Oh, I don't remember the details. I didn't pay any attention to them, because it's not to be supposed that I'm going to career up Mong Blong at my time of life. No, I was making a reference to the tone of his voice. They may be descended from Indians, but I daresay Adam wasn't much better than a Red Indian, if it comes to that.'

They travelled to Cadiz for the boat to Tangier: Mrs. Gainsborough got very worried on the long spit of land over which the train passed and insisted on piling up all the luggage at one end of the compartment in case they fell into the sea, though she was unable to explain how this would help in such an emergency. The result was that, when they stopped at a station before Cadiz and the door of the compartment was opened suddenly, all the luggage fell out on top of three priests that were preparing to climb in, one of whom was knocked flat: apart from the argument that ensued the journey was uneventful.

The boat from Tangier left in the dark; at dawn Cadiz glimmered like a rosy pearl upon the horizon.

'We're in Trafalgar Bay now,' Sylvia announced.

But Mrs. Gainsborough, who was feeling the effects of getting up so early, said she wished it was Trafalgar Square and begged to be left in peace. After an hour's doze in the sunlight she roused herself slightly:

'Where's this Trafalgar Bay you were making such a fuss about?'

'We've passed it now,' Sylvia said.

'Oh, well, I daresay it wasn't anything to look at. I'm bound to say the chocolate we had this morning does not seem to go with the sea air. They're arguing the point inside me something dreadful. I suppose this boat is safe? It seems to be jigging a good deal. Mr. Linthicum said it was a good plan to put the head between the knees when you felt a bit – well, I wouldn't say seasick – but you know . . . I'm bound to say I think he was wrong for once. I feel more like putting my knees up over my head. Can't you speak to the captain and tell him to go a bit more quietly? It's no good racing along like he's doing. Of course the boat jigs. I shall get aggravated in two twos. It's to be hoped Morocco will be worth it. I never got up so early to go anywhere. Was that sailor laughing at me when he walked past? It's no good my getting up to tell him what I think of him, because every time I try to get up, the boat gets up with me. It keeps butting into my behind like a great billy goat.'

Presently Mrs. Gainsborough was unable even to protest against the motion, and could only murmur faintly to Sylvia a request to remove her veil.

'Here we are,' cried Sylvia three or four hours later. 'And it's glorious!'

Mrs. Gainsborough sat up and looked at the row-boats filled with Moors, negroes, and Jews.

'But they're nearly all of them black,' she gasped.

'Of course they are. What colour did you expect them to be? Green like yourself?'

'But do you mean to say you've brought me to a place inhabited by blacks? Well, I never did. It's to be hoped we shan't be eaten alive. Mrs. Marsham! Mrs. Ewings! Mrs. Beardmore! Well, I don't say they haven't told me some good stories now and again, but—'

Mrs. Gainsborough shook her head to express the depth of insignificance to which henceforth the best stories of her friends would have to sink when she should tell about herself in Morocco.

'Ali Baba and the Forty Thieves,' said Mrs. Gainsborough, when they stood upon the quay. 'And I feel like the Widow Twankey myself.'

Sylvia remembered her ambition to visit the East, when she herself wore a yashmak in Open Sesame: here it was fulfilling perfectly her most daring hopes.

Mrs. Gainsborough was relieved to find a comparatively European hotel, and next morning after a long sleep she was ready for any adventure.

'Sylvia!' she suddenly screamed when they were being jostled in the crowded bazaar. 'Look, there's a camel coming towards us! Did you ever hear such a hollering and jabbering in all your life? I'm sure I never did. Mrs. Marsham and her camel at the Zoo! Tut-tut-tut. Do you suppose Mrs. Marsham ever saw a camel coming towards her in the street like a cab-horse might? Certainly not. Why, after this, there's nothing *in* her story. It's a mere anecdote.'

They wandered up to the outskirts of the prison, and saw a fat Jewess being pushed along under arrest for giving false weight. She made some resistance in the narrow entrance, and the guard planted his foot in the small of her back, so that she seemed suddenly to crumple up and fall inside.

'Well, I've often said lightly "what a heathen" or "there's a young heathen," but that brings it home to one,' said Mrs. Gainsborough gravely.

Sylvia paid no attention to her companion's outraged sympathy: she was in the East where elderly obese Jewesses who gave false weight were treated thus. She was living with every moment of rapturous reality the dreams of wonder that the Arabian Nights had brought her in youth.

Yet Tangier was only a gateway to enchantments a hundredfold more powerful. She turned suddenly to Mrs. Gainsborough and asked her if she could stay here while she rode into the interior.

'Stay here alone?' Mrs. Gainsborough exclaimed. 'Not if I know it.'

This plan of Sylvia's to explore the interior of Morocco was narrowed down ultimately into riding to Tetuan, which was apparently just feasible for Mrs. Gainsborough, though likely to be fatiguing.

A dragoman was found, a certain Don Alfonso reported to be comparatively honest: he was an undersized man rather like the stump of a tallow candle into which the wick has been pressed down by the snuffer, for he was bald and cream-coloured with a thin uneven black moustache and two nodules on his forehead; his clothes too were crinkled like a candlestick. He spoke French well, but preferred to speak English, of which he only knew two words, 'all right'; this often made his advice unduly optimistic. In addition to Don Alfonso they were accompanied by a Moorish trooper and a native called Mohammed.

'A soldier, is he?' said Mrs. Gainsborough, regarding the grave bearded man to whose care they were entrusted. 'He looks more like the outside of an ironmonger's shop. Swords, pistols, guns, spears. It's to be hoped he won't get aggravated with us on the way. I should look very funny lying in the road with a pistol through my heart.'

They rode out of Tangier before a single star had paled in the East; and when dawn broke they were in a wide valley fertile and bright with flowers; green hills rose to right and left of them and faded far away into blue mountains.

'I wish you'd tell that Mahomet not to irritate my poor mule by edging it on all the time,' Mrs. Gainsborough said to Don Alfonso, who realizing by her gestures that she wanted something done to her mount and supposing by her smile that the elation of adventure had seized her, replied 'all right,' and said something in Arabic to Mohammed: he at once caught the mule a terrific whack on the crupper, causing the animal to leap forward and leave Mrs. Gainsborough and the saddle in the path.

'Now there's a nice game to play,' said Mrs. Gainsborough indignantly. ' "All right," he says, and boomph! What's he think I'm made of? Well, of course here we shall have to sit now, until someone comes along with a step-ladder. If you'd have let me ride on a camel,' she added reproach-fully to Sylvia, 'this wouldn't have occurred. I'm not sitting on myself any more: I'm sitting on bumps like eggs: I feel like a hen. It's all very fine for Mr. Alfonso to go on gabbling "all right," but it's all wrong, and if you'll have the goodness to tell him so in his own unnatural language, I'll be highly obliged.'

The Moorish soldier sat regarding the scene from his horse with immutable gravity.

'I reckon he'd like nothing better than to get a good jab at me now,' said Mrs. Gainsborough. 'Yes, I daresay I look very inviting sitting here on the ground. Well, it's to be hoped they'll have the Forty Thieves or Aladdin for the next pantomime at Drury Lane. I shall certainly invite Mrs. Marsham and Mrs. Beardmore to come with me into the Upper Boxes so as I can explain what it's all about. Mrs. Ewings doesn't like panto, or I'd have taken her too. She likes a good cry when she goes to the theatre.'

Mrs. Gainsborough was settling down to spend the rest of the morning in amiable reminiscence and planning; but she was at last persuaded to get up and mount her mule again after the strictest assurances had been given to her of Mohammed's good behaviour for the rest of the journey.

'He's not to bellow in the poor animal's ear,' she stipulated.

Sylvia promised.

'And he's not to go screeching "*arrassy*," or whatever it is, behind, so as the poor animal thinks it's a lion galloping after him.'

Mrs. Gainsborough was transferring all consideration for herself to the mule.

'And he's to throw away that stick.'

This clause was only accepted by the other side with a good deal of protestation.

'And he's to keep his hands and feet to himself and not to throw stones or nothing at the poor beast, who's got quite enough to do to carry me.'

'And Ali Baba's to ride in front,' she indicated the trooper. 'It gets me on the blink when he's behind me, as if I was in a shooting gallery. If he's going to be any use to us, *which* I doubt, he'll be more useful in front than hiding behind me.'

'All right,' said Don Alfonso, who was anxious to get on, because they had a long way to go.

'And that's enough of "all right" from him,' said Mrs. Gainsborough. 'I don't want to hear any more "all rights." '

At midday they reached a khan, where they ate lunch and rested for two hours in the shade.

Soon after they had started again, they met a small caravan with veiled women and mules loaded with oranges.

'Quite pleasant-looking people,' Mrs. Gainsborough beamed. 'I should have waved my hand, if I could have been sure of not falling off again. Funny trick, wearing that stuff round their faces. I suppose they're ashamed of being so black.'

Mrs. Gainsborough's progress, which grew more and more leisurely as the afternoon advanced, became a source of real anxiety to Don Alfonso, who confided to Sylvia that he was afraid the gates of Tetuan would be shut. When Mrs. Gainsborough was told of his alarm, she was extremely scornful.

'He's having you on, Sylvia, so as to give Mahomet the chance of sloshing my poor mule again. Whoever heard of a town having gates? He'll tell us next that we've got to pay sixpence at the turnstile to pass in.'

They came to a high place where a white stone by the path recorded a battle between Spaniards and Moors; far below were the domes and rose-dyed minarets of Tetuan, and a shining river winding to the sea. They heard the sound of a distant gun.

'Sunset,' cried Don Alfonso much perturbed. 'In half an hour the gates will be shut.'

He told tales of brigands and of Riffs, of travellers found with their throats cut outside the city walls, and suddenly as if to give point to his fears a figure leaning on a long musket appeared in silhouette upon the edge of the hill above them. It really seemed advisable to hurry, and notwithstanding Mrs. Gainsborough's expostulations the speed of the party was doubled down a rocky descent to a dried-up water-course with high banks. Twilight came on rapidly, and the soldier prepared one of his numerous weapons for immediate use in an emergency. Mrs. Gainsborough was much too nervous about falling off to bother about brigands, and at last without any mishap they reached the great castel-lated gate of Tetuan: it was shut.

'Well, I never saw the like,' said Mrs. Gainsborough. 'It's true then. We must ring the bell, that's all.'

The soldier, Mohammed and Don Alfonso raised their voices in a loud hail, but nobody paid any attention, and the twilight deepened. Mrs. Gainsborough alighted from her mule and thumped at the iron-studded door: silence answered her.

'Do you mean to tell me seriously that they're going to keep us outside here all night? Why, it's laughable.' Suddenly she lifted her voice and cried, 'Milk-ho!'

Whether the unusual sound aroused the curiosity or the alarm of the porter within was uncertain, but he leaned his head out of a small window above the gate and shouted something at the belated party below. Immediately the dispute for which Mohammed and Don Alfonso had been waiting like terriers on a leash was begun: it lasted for ten minutes without any of the three participants drawing breath.

In the end Don Alfonso announced that the porter declined to open for less than two francs, although he had offered him as much as one franc fifty. With a determination not to be beaten that was renewed by the pause for breath, Don Alfonso flung himself into the argument again, splendidly assisted by Mohammed who seemed to be tearing out his hair in baffled fury.

'I wish I knew what they were calling each other,' said Sylvia.

'Something highly insulting, I should think,' Mrs. Gainsborough answered. 'Wonderful the way they use their hands.' She pointed to the soldier who was regarding the dispute with contemptuous gravity. 'He doesn't seem to be worrying himself so very much. I suppose he'll start in shooting at the end.'

Another window in a tower on the other side of the gate was opened, and the first porter was reinforced. Perspiration was dripping from Don Alfonso's forehead, who looked more like a candle stump than ever, when presently he stood aside from the argument to say that he had been forced to offer one franc seventy-five to enter Tetuan.

'Tetuan,' commented Mrs. Gainsborough. 'Tetuarn't, I should say.'

Sylvia asked Don Alfonso what he was calling the porter, and it appeared, though he minimized the insult with a gesture, that he had just invited forty-three dogs to devour the corpse of the porter's grand-mother. This, however, he hastened to add had not annoyed him so much as his withdrawal from one franc fifty to one franc twenty-five.

In the end the porter agreed to open the gate for one franc seventy-five.

'Which is just as well,' said Mrs. Gainsborough, 'for I'm sure Mahomet would have thrown a fit soon. He's got to banging his forehead with his fists, and that's a very bad sign.'

They rode through the darkness between double walls, disturbing every now and then a beggar who whined for alms or cursed them if the mule trod upon his outspread legs. They found an inn called the *Hotel Splendide*, a bug-ridden tumbledown place kept by Spanish Jews as voracious as the bugs. Yet out on the roof, looking at the domes and minarets glimmering under Venus setting in the West from a sky full of stars, listening to the howling of distant dogs, breathing the perfume of the East, Sylvia felt like a conqueror.

Next morning Mrs. Gainsborough, finding that the bugs had retreated with the light, decided to spend the morning in sleeping off some of her bruises. Sylvia wandered through the bazaars with Don Alfonso, and sat for a while in the garden of a French convent, where a fountain whispered in the shade of pomegranates. Suddenly walking along the path towards her she saw Maurice Avery.

Sylvia had disliked Avery when she met him in London nearly two years ago; but the worst enemy, the most flagitious bore, is transformed when encountered alone in a distant country, and now Sylvia felt well disposed towards him and eager to share with anyone who could appreciate her pleasure at the marvel of being in Tetuan. He too, by the way his face lighted up, was glad to see her, and they shook hands with a cordiality that was quite out of proportion to their earlier acquaintance.

'I say, what a queer place to meet,' he exclaimed. 'Are you alone then?'

'I've got Mrs. Gainsborough with me, that's all. I'm not married . . . or anything.'

It was absurd how eager she felt to assure Avery of this; and then in a moment the topic had been started.

'No, have you really got Mrs. Gainsborough?' he exclaimed. 'Of course I've heard about her from Michael. Poor old Michael!'

'Why, what's the matter?' Sylvia asked sharply.

'Oh, he's perfectly all right, but he's lost to his friends. At least I suppose he is – buried in a monastery. He's not actually a monk. I believe he's what's called an oblate, pursuing the Fata Morgana of faith – a sort of dream . . .'

'Yes, yes,' Sylvia interrupted. 'I understand the allusion. You needn't talk down to me.'

Avery blushed: the colour in his cheeks made him seem very young.

'Sorry. I was thinking of somebody else for the moment. That sounds very discourteous also. I must apologize again. What's happened to Lily Haden?'

Sylvia told him briefly the circumstances of Lily's marriage at Rio. 'Does Michael ever talk about her?' she asked.

'Oh, no, never,' said Avery. 'He's engaged in saving his own soul now. That sounds malicious, but seriously I don't think she was ever more to him than an intellectual landmark. To understand Michael's point of view in all that business you've got to know that he was illegitimate. His father, Lord Saxby, had a romantic passion for the daughter of a country parson – a queer cross-grained old scholar. You remember Arthur Lonsdale? Well, his father Lord Cleveden knew the whole history of the affair. Lady Saxby wouldn't divorce him: so they were never married. I suppose Michael brooded over this and magnified his early devotion to Lily in some way or other up to a vow of reparation. I'm quite sure it was a kind of indirect compliment to his own mother. Of course it was all very youthful and foolish – and yet I don't know . . .' he broke off with a sigh.

'You think one can't afford to bury the past?'

Avery looked at her quickly.

'What made you ask me that?'

'I thought you seemed to admire Michael's youthful foolishness.'

'I do really. I admire anyone that's steadfast even to a mistaken idea. It's strange to meet an Englishwoman here,' he said, looking intently at Sylvia. 'One's guard drops. I'm longing to make a confidante of you, but you might be bored. I'm rather frightened of you really. I always was.'

'I shan't exchange confidences,' she said, 'if that's what you're afraid of.'

'No, of course not,' Avery said quickly. 'Last spring I was in love with a girl . . .'

Sylvia raised her eyebrows.

'Oh yes, it's a very commonplace beginning and rather a commonplace end, I'm afraid. She was a ballet girl – the incarnation of May and London. That sounds exaggerated, for I know that lots of other Jenny Pearls have been the same to somebody, but I do believe most people agreed with me. I wanted her to live with me: she wouldn't. She had sentimental, or what I thought were sentimental ideas about her mother and family. I was called away to Spain. When my business was finished I begged her to come out to me there: that was last April. She refused, and I was piqued, I suppose, at first and did not go back to England. Then, as one does, I made up my mind to the easiest thing at the moment by letting myself be enchanted by my surroundings into thinking that I was happier as it was. For a while I was happier: in a way our love had been a great strain upon us both. I came to Morocco and gradually ever since I've been realizing that I left something unfinished. It's become a kind of obsession. Do you know what I mean?'

'Indeed I do, very well indeed,' Sylvia said.

'Thanks,' he said with a grateful look. 'Now comes the problem. If I go back to England this month, if I arrive in England on the first of May exactly a year later, there's only one thing I can do to atone for my behaviour – I must ask her to marry me. You see that, don't you? This little thing is proud, oh, but tremendously proud; I doubt very much if she'll forgive me, even if I show the sincerity of my regret by asking her to marry me now, yet it's my only chance. And yet – oh, I expect this will sound damnable to you, but it's the way we've all been moulded in England – she's common. Common! What an outrageous word to use. But then it is used by everybody. She's the most frankly cockney thing you ever saw. Can I stand her being snubbed and patronized? Can I stand my wife's being snubbed and patronized? Can love survive the sort of ambushed criticism that I shall perceive all round us? For I wouldn't try to change her. No, no, no! She must be herself. I'll have no throaty "aws" masquerading as "o's." She must keep her own clear "aou's." There must not be any "naceness" or patched-up shop-walker's English. I love her

267

more at this moment than I ever loved her, but can I stand it? And I'm not asking this egotistically: I'm asking it for both of us. That's why you meet me in Tetuan, for I dare not go back to England, lest the first cockney voice I hear may kill my determination, and I really am longing to marry her. Yet I wait here, staking what I know in my heart is all my future happiness on chance, assuring myself that presently impulse and reason will be reconciled and will send me back to her, but still I wait.'

He paused; the fountain whispered in the shade of the pomegranates; a nun was gathering flowers for the chapel; outside, the turmoil of the East sounded like the distant chattering of innumerable monkeys.

'You've so nearly reached the point at which a man has the right to approach a woman,' Sylvia said, 'that if you're asking my advice, I advise you to wait until you do actually reach that point. Of course you may lose her by waiting. She may marry somebody else.'

'Oh, I know, I've thought of that. In a way that would be a solution.'

'So long as you regard her marriage with somebody else as a solution, you're still some way from the point. It's curious she should be a ballet girl, because Mrs. Gainsborough, you know, was a ballet girl. In 1869 when she took her emotional plunge, she was able to exchange the wings of Covent Garden for the wings of love easily enough. In 1869 ballet girls never thought of marrying what were and are called "gentlemen." I think Mrs. Gainsborough would consider her life a success: she was not too much married to spoil love, and the Captain was certainly more devoted to her than most husbands would have been. The proof that her life was a success is that she has remained young. Yet if I introduce you to her, you'll see at once your own Jenny at sixty like her – that won't be at all a hard feat of imagination. But you'll still be seeing yourself at twenty-five or whatever you are: you'll never be able to see yourself at sixty: therefore I shan't introduce you. I'm too much of a woman not to hope with all my heart that you'll go home to England, marry your Jenny and live happily ever afterwards, and I think you'd better not meet Mrs. Gainsborough, in case she prejudices your resolve. Thanks for giving me your confidence.'

'Oh, no, thank *you* for listening,' said Avery.

'I'm glad you're not going to develop her. I once suffered from that kind of vivisection myself, though I never had a cockney accent. Some souls can't stand straitlacing just as some bodies revolt from stays. And so Michael is in a monastery? I suppose that means all his soul-spasms are finally allayed?'

'Oh lord, no,' said Avery. 'He's in the very middle of them.'

'What I really meant to say was heart palpitations.'

'I don't think really,' said Avery, 'that Michael ever had them.'

'What was Lily then?'

'Oh, essentially a soul-spasm,' he declared.

'Yes, I suppose she was,' Sylvia agreed pensively.

'I think, you know, I must meet Mrs. Gainsborough,' said Avery.

'Fate answers for you. Here she comes.'

Don Alfonso with the pain that every dog and dragoman feels in the separation of his charges, had taken advantage of Sylvia's talk with Avery to bring Mrs. Gainsborough triumphantly back to the fold.

'Here we are again,' said Mrs. Gainsborough, limping down the path. 'And my behind looks like a magic-lantern. Oh, I beg your pardon, I didn't see you'd met a friend. So that's what Alfonso was trying to tell me. He's being going like an alarm-clock all the way here. Pleased to meet you, I'm sure. How do you like Morocco? We got shut out last night.'

'This is a friend of Michael Fane's,' said Sylvia.

'Did you know *him*? He *was* a very nice young fellow. Very nice he was. But he wouldn't know me now. Very stay at home I was, when he used to come to Mulberry Cottage. Why, he tried to make me ride in a hansom once, and I was actually too nervous. You know, I'd got into a regular rut. But now, well, upon my word, I don't believe now I should say "no" if any one was to invite me to ride inside of a whale. It's her doing, the tartar!'

Avery had learnt a certain amount of Arabic during his stay in Morocco, and he made the bazaars of Tetuan much more interesting than Don Alfonso could have done. He also had many tales to tell of the remote cities like Fez and Mequinez and Marakeesh. Sylvia almost wished that she could pack Mrs. Gainsborough off to England and accompany him back into the real interior: some of her satisfaction in Tetuan had been rather spoilt that morning by finding a visitors' book in the hotel with the names of travelling clergymen and their daughters patronizingly inscribed therein. However, Avery decided to ride away almost at once and said that he intended to banish the twentieth century for two or three months.

They stayed a few days at Tetuan, but the bugs were too many for Mrs. Gainsborough, who began to sigh for a tranquil bed. Avery and Sylvia had a short conversation together before they left. He thanked her for her sympathy, held to his intention of spending the summer in Morocco, but was nearly sure he should return to England in the autumn with a mind serenely fixed.

'I wish if you go back to London, you'd look Jenny up,' he said.

Sylvia shook her head very decidedly.

'I can't imagine anything that would annoy her more, if she's the girl I suppose her to be.'

'But I'd like her to have a friend like you,' he urged.

Sylvia looked at him severely.

'Are you quite sure that you don't want to change her?' she asked.

'Of course. Why?'

'Choosing friends for somebody else is not very wise; it sounds uncommonly like a roundabout way of developing her. No, no, I won't meet your Jenny.'

'I see what you mean,' Avery assented. 'I'll write to Michael and tell him I've met you. Shall I tell him about Lily? Where is she now?'

'I don't know. I've never had even a postcard. My fault really. Yes, you can tell Michael that she's probably quite happy and – no, I don't think there's any other message. Oh yes, you might say I've eaten one or two rose-leaves, but not enough yet.' Avery looked puzzled.

'Apuleius,' she added.

'Strange girl. I *wish* you would go and see Jenny.'

'Oh, no, she's eaten all the rose-leaves she wants, and I'm sure she's not the least interested in Apuleius.'

Next day Sylvia and Mrs. Gainsborough set out on the return journey to Tangier, which apart from a disastrous attempt by Mrs. Gainsborough to eat a prickly pear lacked incident.

'Let sleeping pears lie,' said Sylvia. 'They're not rose-leaves.'

'Well, you don't expect a fruit to be so savage,' retorted Mrs. Gainsborough. 'I thought I must have aggravated a wapse. Talk about nettles. They're chammy-leather beside them. Prickly pears! I suppose the next thing I try to eat will be stabbing apples.'

They went home by Gibraltar, where Mrs. Gainsborough was delighted to see English soldiers.

'It's nice to know we've got our eyes open even in Spain. I reckon I'll get a good cup of tea here.'

They reached England at the end of April, and Sylvia decided to stay for a while at Mulberry Cottage. Reading through *The Stage* she found that Jack Airdale was resting at Richmond in his old rooms and went down to see him. He was looking somewhat thin and worried.

'Had rather a rotten winter,' he told her. 'I got ill with a quinsy and had to throw up a decent shop, and somehow or other I haven't managed to get another yet.'

'Look here, old son,' Sylvia said, 'I don't want any damned pride from you. I've got plenty of money at present. You've got to borrow £50. You want feeding up and fitting out. Don't be a cad now, and refuse a "lidy."'

Shut up! Shut up! Shut up! You know me by this time. Who's going to be more angry, you at being lent money or me at being refused by one of the few – the very few, mark you – good pals I've got? Don't be a beast, Jack; you've got to take it.'

He surrendered from habit. Sylvia gave him all her news, but the item that interested him most was her having half taken up the stage.

'I knew you'd make a hit,' he declared.

'But I didn't.'

'My dear girl, you don't give yourself a chance. You can't play hide and seek with the public; though, by Jove,' he added ruefully, 'I have been lately.'

'For the present I can afford to wait.'

'Yes, you're lucky in one way, and yet I'm not sure that you aren't really very unlucky. If you hadn't found some money you'd have been forced to go on.'

'My dear lad, lack of money wouldn't make me an artist.'

'What would then?'

'Oh, I don't know. Being fed up with everything. That's what drove me into self-expression, as I should call it if I were a temperamental miss with a light-boiled ego swimming in a saucepan of emotion for the public to swallow or myself to crack. But conceive my disgust! There was I yearning unattainable "isms" from a soul nurtured on tragic disillusionment, and I was applauded for singing French songs with an English accent. No, seriously, I shall try again, old Jack, when I receive another buffet. At present I'm just dimly uncomfortable. I shall blossom late like a chrysanthemum: I ain't no daffodil, I ain't. Or perhaps it would be truer to say that I was forced when young – don't giggle, you ribald ass, not that way – and I've got to give myself a rest before I bloom *en plein air*.'

'But you really have got plenty of money?' Airdale enquired anxiously.

'Masses! Cataracts! And all come by perfectly honest. No, seriously, I've got about £4000.'

'Well, I really do think you're rather lucky, you know.'

'Of course. But it's all written in the book of Fate. Listen. I've got a mulberry mark on my arm: I live at Mulberry Cottage: and Morera, that's the name of my fairy godfather, is Spanish for mulberry tree. Can you beat it?'

'I hope you've invested this money,' said Airdale.

'It's in a bank.'

He begged her to be careful of her riches, and she rallied him on his inconsistency, because a moment back he had been telling her that their possession was hindering her progress in art.

'My dear Sylvia, I haven't known you for five years not to have discovered that I might as well advise a schoolmaster as you, but what *are* you going to do?'

'Plans for this summer? A little gentle reading. A little browsing among the classics. A little theatre-going. A little lunching at Verrey's with *Mr. John Airdale. Resting. Address: 6 Rosetree Terrace, Richmond, Surrey*. A little bumming around town, as Señor Morera would say. Plans for the autumn? A visit to the island of Sirene, if I can find a nice ladylike young woman to accompany me. Mrs. Gainsborough has decided that she will travel no more. Her brain is bursting with unrelated adventure.'

'But you can't go on from month to month like that.'

'Well, if you'll tell me how to skip over December, January, and August, I'll be grateful,' Sylvia laughed.

'No, don't rag about. I mean for the future in general,' he explained. 'Are you going to get married? You can't go on for ever like this.'

'Why not?'

'Well, you're young now. But what's more gloomy than a restless old maid?'

'My dear man, don't you fret about my withering. I've got a little crystal flask of the finest undiluted strychnine. I believe strychnine quickens the action of the heart? Verdict: Death from attempted galvanization of the cardiac muscles. No flowers by request. Boomph! as dear Gainsborough would say. Ring off. The last time I wrote myself an epitaph it led me into matrimony. *Absit omen.*'

Airdale was distressed by Sylvia's joking about her death, and begged her to stop.

'Then don't ask me any more about the future in general. And now let's go and be Epicurean at Verrey's.'

After Jack Airdale the only other old friend that Sylvia took any trouble to find was Olive Fanshawe. She was away on tour when Sylvia returned to England; but she came back to London in June, was still unmarried, and had been promised a small part in the Vanity production that autumn. Sylvia found that Olive had recaptured her romantic ideals and was delighted with her proposal that they should live together at Mulberry Cottage. Olive took very seriously her small part at the Vanity, of which the most distinguished line was: *Girls, have you seen the Duke of Mayfair? He's awfully handsome*. Sylvia was not very encouraging to Olive's opportunities of being able to give an original reading of such a line, but she listened patiently to her variations in which each word was over-accentuated in turn. Luckily there was also a melodious quintet consisting of the juvenile lead and four beauties of whom Olive was to be one: this, it seemed, promised to be a hit, and indeed it was.

The most interesting event for the Vanity world that autumn, apart from the individual successes and failures in the new production, was the return of Lord and Lady Clarehaven to London, and not merely their return, but their re-entry into the Bohemian society from which Lady Clarehaven had so completely severed herself.

'I know it's perfectly ridiculous of me,' said Olive, 'but, Sylvia, do you know, I'm quite nervous at the idea of meeting her again.'

A most cordial note had arrived from Dorothy inviting Olive to lunch with her in Curzon Street.

'Write back and tell her you're living with me,' Sylvia advised. 'That'll choke off some of the friendliness.'

But to Sylvia's boundless surprise a messenger boy arrived with an urgent invitation for her to come too.

'Curiouser and curiouser,' she murmured. 'What does it mean? She surely can't be tired of being a countess already. I'm completely stumped. However, of course we'll put on our clean bibs and go. Don't look so frightened, Olive: if conversation hangs fire at lunch, we'll tickle the footmen.'

'I really feel quite faint,' said Olive. 'My heart's going pitter-pat. Isn't it silly of me?'

Lunch, to which Arthur Lonsdale had also been invited, did nothing to enlighten Sylvia about the Clarehavens' change of attitude: Dorothy, more beautiful than ever and pleasant enough superficially, seemed withal faintly resentful: Clarehaven was in exuberant spirits and evidently enjoying London tremendously. The only sign of tension – well not exactly tension, but slight disaccord, and that was too strong a word – was once when Clarehaven, having been exceptionally rowdy, lanced at Dorothy a swift look of defiance for checking him.

'She's grown as prim as a parlour-maid,' Lonsdale observed to Sylvia when after lunch they had a chance of talking together. 'You ought to have seen her on the ancestral acres. My mother who presides over our place like a Queen Turnip is without importance beside Dolly, absolutely without importance. It got on Tony's nerves, that's about the truth of it. He never could stand the land. It has the same effect on him as the sea has on some people. Black vomit, coma and death, what?'

'Dorothy, of course, played the countess in real life as seriously as she would have played her on the stage. She was the star,' Sylvia said.

'Star, my dear girl, she was a comet. And the dowager loved her. They used to drive round in a barouche and administer gruel to the village without anæsthetics.'

'I suppose they kept them for Clarehaven?' Sylvia laughed.

'That's it. Of course, I shouted when I saw the state of affairs, having first of all been called in to recover old Lady Clarehaven's reason when she heard that her only child was going to wed a Vanity girl. But they loved her. Every frump in the county adored her. It's Tony who insisted on this move to London. He stood it in Devonshire for two and a half years, but the lights of the wicked city – soft music, please – called him, and they've come back. Dolly's fed up to the wide about it. I say, we are a pair of gossips. What's your news?'

'I met Maurice Avery in Morocco.'

'What, Mossy Avery. Not really? Disguised as a slipper, I suppose. Rum bird. He got awfully keen on a little girl at the Orient and tootled her all over town for a while, but I haven't seen him for months. I used to know him rather well at the Varsity: he was one of the æsthetic push. I say, what's become of Lily? Married to a croupier? Not really. By Jove, what a time I had over her with Michael Fane's people. His sister, an awfully good sport, put me through a fearful catechism.'

'His sister?' repeated Sylvia.

'You know what Michael's doing now? Greatest scream on earth. He's a monk. Some special kind of a monk that sounds like omelette, but isn't. Nothing to be done about it. I buzzed down to see him last year, and he was awfully fed up. I asked him if he couldn't stop monking for a bit and come out for a spin on my new 45 Shooting Star. He wasn't in uniform, so there's no reason why he shouldn't have come.'

'He's in England now then?' Sylvia asked.

'No, he got fed up with everybody buzzing down to see what he looked like as a monk, and he's gone off to Chartreuse or Benedictine or some-where – I know it's the name of a liqueur – somewhere abroad. I wanted him to become a partner in our business, and promised we'd put a jolly little runabout on the market called The Jovial Monk, but he wouldn't. Look here, we'd better join the others. Dolly's got her eye on me. I say,' he chuckled in a whisper, 'I suppose you know she's a connection of mine?'

'Yes, by carriage.'

Lonsdale asked what she meant, and Sylvia told him the origin of Dorothy's name.

'Oh, I say, that's topping. What was her real name?'

'No, no,' Sylvia said. 'I've been sufficiently spiteful.'

'Probably Buggins really. I say, Cousin Dorothy,' he went on in a louder voice. 'What about bridge to-morrow night after the Empire?'

Lady Clarehaven flashed a look at Sylvia, who could not resist shaking her head and earning thereby another sharper flash. When Sylvia talked over the Clarehavens with Olive, she found that Olive had been quite oblivious of anything unusual in the sudden move to town.

'Of course, Dorothy and I can never be what we were to each other; but I thought they seemed so happy together. I'm so glad it's been such a success.'

'Well, has it?' said Sylvia doubtfully.

'Oh yes, my dear. How can you imagine anything else?'

With the deepening of winter Olive fell ill, and the doctors prescribed the Mediterranean for her. The malady was nothing to worry about; it was nothing more than fatigue; if she were to rest now and if possible not work before the following autumn, there was every reason to expect that she would be perfectly cured.

Sylvia jumped at an excuse to go abroad again and suggested a visit to Sirene. The doctor on being assured that Sirene was in the Mediterranean decided that it was exactly the place best suited to Olive's state of health. Like most English doctors he regarded the Mediterranean as a little larger than the Serpentine with a characteristic climate throughout. Olive, however, was much opposed to leaving London, and when Sylvia began to get annoyed with her obstinacy she confessed that the real reason for wishing to stay was Jack.

'Naturally, I wanted to tell you at once, my dear. But Jack wouldn't let me, until he could see his way clear to our being married. He was quite odd about you, for you know how fond he is of you – he thinks there's nobody like you – but he particularly asked me not to tell you just yet.'

'I know the reason,' Sylvia proclaimed instantly. 'The silly, scrupulous, proud ass. I'll have it out with him to-morrow at lunch. Dearest Olive, I'm so happy that I like your curly-headed actor.'

'Oh but, darling Sylvia, his hair's quite straight.'

'Yes, but it's very long and gets into his eyes. It's odd hair anyway. And when did the flaming arrow pin your two hearts together?'

'It was that evening you played baccarat at Curzon Street – about ten days ago. You didn't think we'd known long, did you? Oh, my dear, I couldn't have kept the secret any longer.'

Next day Sylvia lunched with Jack Airdale and came to the point at once.

'Look here, you detestably true-to-type, impossibly sensitive ass, because I to please me lent you fifty pounds, is that any excuse for you to keep me out in the cold over you and Olive? Seriously, Jack, I do think it was mean of you.'

Jack was abashed and mumbled many excuses. He had been afraid Sylvia would despise him for talking about marriage while he owed her money. He felt anyway that he wasn't good enough for Olive. Before Olive had known anything about it, he had been rather ashamed of himself for being in love with her: he felt he was taking advantage of Sylvia's friendship.

'All which excuses are utterly feeble,' Sylvia pronounced. 'Now listen. Olive's ill. She ought to go abroad. I very selfishly want a companion. You've got to insist on her going. The fifty pounds I lent you will pay her expenses; so that debt's wiped out, and you're standing her a holiday in the Mediterranean.'

Jack thought for a moment with a puzzled air.

'Don't be absurd, Sylvia. Really for the moment you took me in with your confounded arithmetic. Why, you're doubling the obligation.'

'Obligation! Obligation! Don't you dare to talk about obligations to me. I don't believe in obligations. Am I to understand that for the sake of your unworthy – well, it can't be dignified with the word – pride Olive is to be kept in London throughout the spring?'

Jack protested he had been talking about the loan to himself: Olive's obligation would be a different one.

'Jack, have you ever seen a respectable woman throw a Sole Mornay across a restaurant? Because you will in one moment. Amen to the whole discussion. Please! The only thing you've got to do is to insist on Olive's coming with me. Then while she's away you must be a good little actor and act away as hard as you know how so that you can be married next June as a present to me on my twenty-sixth birthday.'

'You're the greatest dear,' said Jack fervently.

'Of course I am. But I'm waiting.'

'What for?'

'Why, for an exhortation to matrimony. Haven't you noticed that people who are going to get married always try to persuade everybody else to come in with them? I'm sure human cooperation began with paleolithic bathers.'

So Olive and Sylvia left England for Sirene.

'I'd like to be coming with you,' said Mrs. Gainsborough at Charing Cross. 'But I'm just beginning to feel a tiddly-bit stiff, and well, there, after Morocco I shouldn't be satisfied with anything less than a cannibal island, and it's too late for me to start in being a Robinson Crusoe, which reminds me that when I took Mrs. Beardmore to the Fulham pantomime last night it was Dick Whittington. And upon my soul, if he didn't go to Morocco with his cat. "Well," I said to Mrs. Beardmore, "it's not a bit like it." I told her that if Dick Whittington went there now he wouldn't take his cat with him: he'd take a box of Keating's. Somebody behind said, "Hush." And I said, "Hush yourself. Perhaps *you've* been to Morocco?" Which made him look very silly, for I don't suppose he'd ever been farther east than Aldgate in his life. We had no more "hushes" from him, I can tell you; and Mrs. Beardmore looked round at him in a very ladylike way which she's got from being a housekeeper, and said, "My friend *has* been to Morocco." After that we la-la'd the chorus in peace and quiet. Good-bye, duckies, and don't gallivant about too much.'

Sylvia had brought a bagful of books about the Roman Emperors, and Olive had brought a number of anthologies that made up by the taste of the binder for the lack of it in the compiler: they were mostly about love. To satisfy Sylvia's historical passion a week was spent in Rome and another week at Naples. She told Olive of her visit to Italy with Philip over seven years ago, and much to her annoyance Olive poured out a good deal of emotion over that hapless marriage.

'Don't you feel any kind of sentimental regret?' she asked while they were watching from Posilipo the vapours of Vesuvius rose-plumed in the wintry sunset. 'Surely you feel softened towards it all now? Why, I think I should regret anything that had once happened in this divinely beautiful place.'

'The thing I remember most distinctly is Philip's having read somewhere that the best way to get rid of an importunate guide was to use the local negative and throw the head back instead of shaking it. The result was that Philip used to walk about as if he were gargling. To annoy him I used to wink behind his back at the guides and naturally with such encouragement his local negative was absolutely useless.'

'I think you must have been rather trying, Sylvia dear.'

'Oh, I was – infernally trying, but one doesn't marry a child of seventeen as a sedative.'

'I think it's all awfully sad,' Olive sighed.

Sylvia had rather a shock, a few days after they had reached Sirene, when she saw Miss Horne and Miss Hobart drive past on the road up to Anasirene, the green rival of Sirene among the clouds to the west of the island. She made enquiries at the pension and was informed that two sisters *le signorine* Hobart-Horne, English millionaires many times over, had lived at Sirene these five years. Sylvia decided that it would be quite easy to avoid meeting them, and warned Olive against making friends with any of the residents on the plea that she did not wish to meet people whom she had met here seven years ago with her husband. In the earlier part of the spring they stayed at a pension, but Sylvia found that it was difficult to escape from people there, and they moved up to Anasirene, where they took a *villino* that was cut off from all dressed-up humanity by a sea of olives. Here it was possible to roam by paths that were not frequented save by peasants, whose personalities so long attuned to earth had lost the power of detaching themselves from the landscape and did not affect the onlooker more than the movement of trees or the rustle of small beasts. Life was made up of these essentially undisturbing personalities set in a few pictures that escaped from the swift southern spring: anemones splashed out like wine upon the green corn: some girl with slanting eyes that regarded coldly a dead bird in her thin brown hand: wind over the olives and the sea, wind that shook the tresses of the broom and ruffled the scarlet poppies: then suddenly the first cicada and eternal noon, with red-beaded cherry trees that threw shadows on the tawny wheat below.

It would have been hard to say how they had spent these four months, Sylvia thought.

'Can you bear to leave your beloved trees, your namesakes?' she asked.

'Jack is getting impatient,' said Olive.

'Then we must fade out of Anasirene just as one by one the flowers have all faded.'

'I don't think I've faded much,' Olive laughed. 'I never felt so well in my life, thanks to you.'

Jack and Olive were married at the end of June: it was necessary to go down to a small Warwickshire town and meet all sorts of country people that reminded Sylvia of Green Lanes. Olive's father, who was a solicitor, was very anxious for Sylvia to stay when the wedding was over; he was cheating the gods out of half their pleasure in making him a solicitor by writing a history of Warwickshire worthies. Sylvia had so much impressed him as an intelligent observer that he would have liked to retain her at his elbow for a while; she would not stay, however. The particular song that the Sirens had sung to her during her sojourn in their territory was about writing a book: they called her back now and flattered her with a promise of inspiration. Sylvia was not much more ready to believe in Sirens than in mortals, and she resisted the impulse to return. Nevertheless with half an idea of scoring off them by writing the book somewhere else, she settled down in Mulberry Cottage to try: the form should be essays, and she drew up a list of subjects:—

1. *Obligations.*
   Judaic like the rest of our moral system: post obits on human gratitude.
2. *Friendship.*
   A flowery thing: objectionable habit of keeping pressed flowers.
3. *Marriage.*

Judaic: include this with obligations: nothing wrong with the idea of marriage: the marriage of convenience probably more honest than the English marriage of so-called affection: Levi the same as Lewis.

4. *Gambling.*

A moral occupation that brings out the worst side of everybody.

5. *Development.*

Exploiting human personality: Judaic of course.

6. *Acting.*

A low art form: oh yes, very low: being paid for what the rest of the world does for nothing.

7. *Prostitution.*

Selling one's body to keep one's soul: this is the meaning of the sins that were forgiven to the woman because she loved much: one might say of most marriages that they were selling one's soul to keep one's body.

Sylvia found that when she started to write on these and other subjects she knew nothing about them. The consequence was that summer passed into autumn and autumn into winter, while she went on reading history and philosophy: for pastime she played baccarat at Curzon Street and lost six hundred pounds. In February she decided that so much having been written on the subjects she had chosen it was useless to write any more. She went to stay with Jack and Olive, who were now living in West Kensington: Olive was expecting a baby in April.

'If it's a boy, we're going to call him Sylvius. But if it's a girl, Jack says we can't call her Sylvia, because for us there can never be more than one Sylvia.'

'Call her Argentina.'

'No, we're going to call her Sylvia Rose.'

'Well, I hope it'll be a boy,' said Sylvia. 'Anyway I hope it'll be a boy, because there are too many girls.'

Olive announced that she had taken a cottage in the country close to where her people lived, and that Sylvius or Sylvia Rose was to be born there: she thought it was right.

'I don't know why childbirth should be more moral in the country,' Sylvia said.

'Oh, it's nothing to do with morals; it's on account of baby's health. You will come and stay with me, won't you?'

In March therefore, Sylvia went down to Warwickshire with Olive, much to the gratification of Mr. Fanshawe: it was a close race whether he would be a grandfather or an author first, but in the end Mr. Fanshawe had the pleasure of placing a copy of his work on Warwickshire worthies in the hands of the monthly nurse before she could place in his arms a grandchild. Three days later, Olive brought into the world a little girl and a little boy. Jack was acting in Dundee; the problem of nomenclature was most complicated; Olive had to think it all out over again from the beginning. Jack had to be consulted by telegram about every change, and on occasions where accuracy was all-important, the post-office clerks were usually most careless. For instance, Mr. Fanshawe thought it would be charming to celebrate the forest of Arden by calling the children Orlando and Rosalind; Jack thereupon replied:

Do not like Rosebud. What will boy be called? Suggest Palestine. First name arrived Ostend. If Oswald no.

'Palestine?' exclaimed Olive.

'Obviously Valentine,' said Sylvia. 'But look here, why not Sylvius for the boy and Rose for the girl? *Rose Airdale, all were thine!*'

When several more telegrams had been exchanged to enable Olive in Warwickshire to be quite sure that Jack by this time in Aberdeen had got the names right, Sylvius and Rose were decided upon; though Mr. Fanshawe advocated Audrey for the girl with such pertinacity that he even went as far as to argue with his daughter on the steps of the font. Indeed, as Sylvia said afterwards, if the clergyman had not been so deaf, Rose would probably have been Audrey at that moment.

On the afternoon of the christening Sylvia received a telegram.

'Too late,' she said with a laugh, as she tore it open. 'He can't change his mind now.'

But the telegram was signed Beardmore and asked Sylvia to come at once to London, because Mrs. Gainsborough was very ill.

When she arrived at Mulberry Cottage on a fine morning in early June, Mrs. Beardmore, whom Sylvia had never seen, was gravely accompanying two other elderly women to the garden-door.

'She's not dead?' Sylvia cried.

The three friends shook their heads and sighed.

'Not yet, poor soul,' said the thinnest, bursting into tears.

This must be Mrs. Ewings.

'I'm just going to send another doctor,' said the most majestic, which must be Mrs. Marsham.

Mrs. Beardmore said nothing, but she sniffed and led the way towards the house. Mrs. Marsham and Mrs. Ewings went off together.

Inside the darkened room, but not so dark in the June sunshine as to obscure entirely the picture of Captain Dashwood in whiskers that hung upon the wall by her bed, Mrs. Gainsborough lay breathing heavily. The nurse made a gesture of silence, and came out on tiptoe from the room; downstairs in the parlour Sylvia listened to Mrs. Beardmore's story of the illness.

'I heard nothing till three days ago when the woman who comes in of a morning ascertained from Mrs. Gainsborough the wish she had for me to visit her. The Misses Hargreaves with who I reside was exceptionally kind and insisted upon me taking the tram from Kew that very moment. I communicated with Mrs. Marsham and Mrs. Ewings, but they both having lodgers was unable to evacuate their business, and Mrs. Gainsborough was excessively anxious as you should be communicated with on the telegraph, which I did accordingly. We have two nurses night and day, and the doctor is all that can be desired, all that can be desired notwithstanding whatever Mrs. Marsham may say to the contrary; Mrs. Marsham, who I've known for some years, has that habit of contradicting everybody else something outrageous. Mrs. Ewings and me was both entirely satisfied with Dr. Barker. I'm very glad you've come, Miss Scarlett, and Mrs. Gainsborough will be very glad you've come. If you'll permit the liberty of the observation, Mrs. Gainsborough is very fond of you. As soon as she wakes up, I shall have to get back to Kew, not wishing to trespass too much on the kindness of the two Miss Hargreaves to who I act as housekeeper. It's her heart that's the trouble. Double pneumonia through pottering in the garden. That's what the doctor diag— yes, that's what the doctor says, and though Mrs. Marsham contradicted him, taking the words out of his mouth and throwing them back in his face and saying it was nothing of the kind, but going to the King's funeral, I believe he's right.'

Mrs. Beardmore went back to Kew; Mrs. Gainsborough, who had been in a comatose state all the afternoon, began to wander in her mind about an hour before sunset.

'It's very dark. High time the curtain went up. The house will be getting impatient in a minute. It's not to be supposed they'll wait all night. Certainly not.'

Sylvia drew the curtains back, and the room was flooded with gold.

'That's better. Much better. The country smells beautiful, don't it, this morning? The Glory Die-Johns are a treat this year, but the Captain he always likes a camelia or a gardenia. Well, if they start in building over your nursery, pa . . . certainly not, certainly not. They'll build over everything. Now don't talk about dying, Bob. Don't let's be dismal on our anniversary. Certainly not.'

She suddenly recognized Sylvia, and her mind cleared.

'Oh, I *am* glad you've come. Really, you know, I hate to make a fuss, but I'm not feeling at all myself. I'm just a tiddly-bit ill, it's my belief. Sylvia, give me your hand. Sylvia, I'm joking. I really am remarkably ill. Oh, there's no doubt I'm going to die. What a beautiful evening! Yes, it's not to be supposed I'm going to live for ever, and there, after all, I'm not sorry. As soon as I began to get that stiffness, I thought it meant I was not meself. And what's the good of hanging about, if you're not yourself?'

The nurse came forward and begged her not to talk too much.

'You can't stop me talking. There was a clergyman came through Mrs. Ewings getting in a state about me, and he talked till I was sick and tired of the sound of his voice. Talked away he did about the death of Our Lord and being nailed to the cross. It made me very dismal. "Here, when did all this occur?" I asked. "Nineteen hundred and ten years ago," he said. "Oh, well," I said, "it all occurred such a long time ago and it's all so sad, let's hope it never occurred at all." '

The nurse said firmly that if Mrs. Gainsborough would not stop talking, she would have to make Sylvia go out of the room.

'There's a tyrant,' said Mrs. Gainsborough. 'Well, just sit by me quietly and hold my hand.'

The sun set behind the housetops; Mrs. Gainsborough's hand was cold when twilight came.

Sylvia felt that it was out of the question to stay longer at Mulberry Cottage, though Miss Dashwood, to whom the little property reverted, was very anxious for her to do so. After the funeral Sylvia joined Olive and Jack in Warwickshire.

They knew that she was feeling very deeply the death of Mrs. Gainsborough, and insisted that she should arrange to live with them in West Kensington.

Sylvia, however, said that she wished to remain friends with them, and declined the proposal.

'Do you remember what I told you once,' she said to Jack, 'about going back to the stage in some form or another when I was tired of things?'

Jack, who had not yet renounced his ambition for Sylvia's theatrical career, jumped at the opportunity of finding her an engagement, and when they all went back to London with the babies he rushed about the Strand to see what was going. Sylvia moved all her things from Mulberry Cottage to the Airdales' house, refusing once more Miss Dashwood's almost tearful offer to make over the cottage to her; she was sorry to withstand the old lady, who was very frail by now, but she knew that if she accepted it would mean more dreaming about writing books, and gambling at Curzon Street, and ultimately doing nothing until it was too late.

'I'm reaching the boring idle thirties. I'm twenty-seven,' she told Jack and Olive. 'I must sow a few more wild oats before my face is ploughed with wrinkles to receive the respectable seeds of a flourishing old age. By the way, as demon-godmother I've placed £1000 to the credit of Rose and Sylvius.'

The parents protested, but Sylvia would take no denial.

'I've kept lots for myself,' she assured them. As a matter of fact she had nearly another £1000 in the bank.

At the end of July Jack came in radiant to say that a piece with an English company was being sent over to New York the following month. There was a small part, for which the author required somebody whose personality seemed to recall Sylvia's. Would she read it? Sylvia said she would.

'The author was pleased, eh?' Jack asked enthusiastically when Sylvia came back from the trial.

'I don't really know. Whenever he tried to speak, the manager said, "One moment please": it was like a boxing match. However, as the important thing seemed to be that I should speak English with a French accent, I was engaged.'

Sylvia could not help being amused at herself when she found that her first essay with legitimate drama was to be the exact converse of her first essay with the variety stage, dependent as before upon a kind of infirmity: really the only time she had been able to express herself naturally in public had been when she sang *The Raggle-taggle Gipsies* with the Pink Pierrots, and that had been a failure. However, a tour in the States would give her a new glimpse of life, which at twenty-seven was the important consideration; and perhaps New York, more generous than other capitals, would give her life itself, or one of the only two things in life that mattered, success and love.

VI

The play in which Sylvia was to appear in New York was called *A Honeymoon in Europe*, and if it might be judged from the first few rehearsals, at which the performers had read their parts like half-witted school-board children, it was thin stuff: still it was not fair to pass a final opinion without the two American stars who were awaiting the English company in their native land.

The author, Mr. Marchmont Hearne, was a timid little man who between the business manager and producer looked and behaved very much like the Dormouse at the Mad Tea-party. The manager did not resemble the Hatter except in the broad brim of his top-hat, which in mid-Atlantic he reluctantly exchanged for a cloth cap. The company declared he was famous for his tact: certainly he managed to suppress the Dormouse at every point by shouting 'One minute, Mr. Stern, *please*,' or 'Please, Mr. Burns, one minute,' and apologizing at once so effusively for not calling him by his right name that the poor little Dormouse had no courage to contest the real point at issue, which had nothing to do with his name. When the manager had to exercise a finer tactfulness, as with obdurate actresses, he was wont to soften his remarks by adding that nothing 'derogatory' had been intended: this seemed to mollify everybody probably, Sylvia thought, because it was such a long word. The Hatter's name was Charles Fitzherbert. The producer, Mr. Wade Fortescue, by the length of his ears, by the way in which his electrical hair propelled itself into a peak on either side of his head, and by his wild artistic eye was really rather like the March Hare outwardly; his behaviour was not less like. Mr. Fortescue's attitude towards *A Honeymoon in Europe* was one that Beethoven might have taken up on being invited to orchestrate *Ta-ra-ra-boom-de-ay*. The author did not go so far as to resent this attitude, but on many occasions he was evidently pained by it, notwithstanding Mr. Fitzherbert's assurances that Mr. Fortescue had intended nothing 'derogatory.'

Sylvia's part was that of a French chambermaid. The author had drawn it faithfully to his experience of Paris in the course of several week-ends: as his conception coincided with that of the general public in supposing a French chambermaid to be a cross between a street-walker and a tight-rope walker, it seemed probable that the part would be a success; although Mr. Fortescue wanted to mix the strain still further by introducing the blood of a comic ventriloquist.

'You must roll your "r's" more, Miss Scarlett,' he assured her. 'That line will go for nothing as you said it.'

'I said it as a French chambermaid would say it,' Sylvia insisted.

'If I might venture,' the Dormouse began.

'One minute, please, Mr. Treherne,' interrupted the Mad Hatter. 'What Mr. Fortescue wants, Miss Scarlett, is exaggeration – a little exaggeration. I believe that is what you want, Mr. Fortescue?'

'I don't want a caricature,' snapped the March Hare. 'The play is farcical enough as it is. What I want to impart is realism. I want Miss Scarlett to say the line as a French girl would say it.'

'Precisely,' said the Hatter. 'That's precisely what I was trying to explain to Miss Scarlett. You're a bit hasty, old chap, you know, and I think you frightened her a little. That's all right, Miss Scarlett, there's nothing to be frightened about. Mr. Fortescue intended nothing derogatory.'

'I'm not in the least frightened,' said Sylvia indignantly.

'If I might make a suggestion. I think that—' the Dormouse began.

'One minute, please, please, Mr. Burns, one minute – god bless my soul, Mr. Hearne, I was confusing you with the poet. Nothing derogatory in that, eh?' he laughed jovially.

'May I ask a question?' said Sylvia, and asked it before Mr. Fitzherbert could interrupt again. 'Why do all English authors draw all French women as cocottes and all French authors draw all English women as governesses? The answer's obvious.'

The Mad Hatter and the March Hare were so much taken aback by this attack from Alice, that the Dormouse was able to emit an entire sentence.

'I should like to say that Miss Scarlett's rendering of the accent gives me every satisfaction. I have no fault to find. I shall be much obliged, Miss Scarlett, if you will correct my French whenever necessary. I am fully sensible of its deficiencies.'

Mr. Marchmont Hearne blinked after this challenge, and breathed rather heavily.

'I've had a good deal of experience,' said Mr. Fortescue grimly, 'but I never yet found that it improved a play to allow the performers of minor roles, essentially minor roles, to write their parts in at rehearsal.'

Mr. Fitzherbert was in a quandary for a moment whether he should smooth the rufflings of the author or of the actress or of the producer; deciding that the author could be more profitable to his career in the end, he took him up stage and tried to whisper away Mr. Fortescue's bad temper. In the end Sylvia was allowed to roll her 'r's' at her own pace.

'I'm glad you stood up to him, dear,' said an elderly actress like a pink cabbage-rose fading at the tips of the petals, who had been sitting throughout the rehearsal so nearly on the scene that she was continually being addressed in mistake by people that really were 'on'; the author, who had once or twice smiled at her pleasantly, was evidently under the delusion that she was interested in his play.

'Yes, I was delighted with the way you stood up to them,' continued Miss Nancy Tremayne. 'My part's wretched, dear. All feeding! Still if I'm allowed to slam the door when I go off in the third act, I may get a hand. Have you ever been to New York before? I like it myself, and you can live quite cheaply if you know the ropes. Of course, I'm drawing a very good salary, because they wanted me. I said I couldn't come for a penny under a hundred dollars and I really didn't want to come at all. However, he *would* have me, and between you and me, I'm really rather glad to have the chance of saving a little money. The managers are getting very stingy in England. Don't tell anybody what I'm getting, will you, dear? One doesn't like to create jealousy at the commencement of a tour. It seems to be quite a nice crowd, though the girls look a little old, don't you think? Amy Melhuish, who's playing the ingénue, must be at least thirty. It's wonderful how some women have the nerve to go on. I gave up playing ingénues, as soon as I was over twenty-eight, and that's four years ago now, or very nearly. Oh dear, how time flies!'

Sylvia thought that, if Miss Tremayne was only twenty-eight four years ago, time must have crawled.

'They're sending us out in the *Minneworra*. The usual economy, but really in a way it's nicer, because it's all one class. Yes, I'm glad you stood up to them, dear. Fortescue's been impossible ever since he produced one of those filthy Strindberg plays last summer for the Unknown Plays Committee. I hate this continental muck. Degenerate, I say it is. In my opinion Ibsen has spoilt the drama in England. What do you think of Charlie Fitzherbert? He's such a nice man. Always ready to smooth over any little difficulties. When Mr. Vernon said to me that Charlie would be coming with us, I felt quite safe.'

'Morally?' Sylvia asked.

'Oh go on, you know what I mean. Comfortable, and not likely to be stranded. Well, I'm always a little doubtful about American productions. I suppose I'm conservative. I like old-fashioned ways.'

Which was not surprising, Sylvia thought.

'Miss Tremayne, I can't hear myself speak. Are you on in this scene?' demanded the producer.

'I really don't know. My next cue is—'

'I don't think Miss Tremayne comes on till act three,' said the author.

'We shan't get there for another two hours,' the producer growled.

Miss Tremayne moved her chair back a yard, and turned to finish her conversation with Sylvia.

'What I was going to say when I was interrupted, dear, was that, if you're a bad sailor, you ought to make a point of making friends with the purser. Unfortunately I don't know the purser on the *Minneworra*, but the purser on the *Minnetoota* was quite a friend of mine, and gave me a beautiful deck-cabin. The other girls were very jealous.'

'Damn it, Miss Tremayne, didn't I ask you not to go on talking?' the producer shouted.

'Nice gentlemanly way of asking anybody not to whisper a few words of advice, isn't it?' said Miss Tremayne with a scathing glance at Mr. Fortescue, as she moved her chair quite six feet further away from the scene.

'Now, of course, we're in a draught,' she grumbled to Sylvia. 'But I always say that producers never have any consideration for anybody but themselves.'

By the time the s.s *Minneworra* reached New York, Sylvia had come to the conclusion that the representatives of the legitimate drama differed only from the chorus of a musical comedy in taking their temperaments and exits more seriously: Sylvia's earlier experience had led her to suppose that quantity of make-up and proximity to the footlights were the most important things in art.

Whatever hopes of individual ability to shine the company might have cherished before it reached New York were quickly dispelled by the two American stars, up to whom and not with whom they were expected to twinkle. Mr. Diomed Olver and Miss Marcia Neville regarded the rest of the company as Jupiter and Venus might regard the Milky Way. Miss Tremayne's exit upon a slammed door was forbidden the first time she tried it, because it would distract the attention of the audience from Miss Neville, who at that moment would be sustaining a dimple – which she called holding a situation. This dimple, which was famous from Boston to San Francisco, from Buffalo to New Orleans, had when Miss Neville first swam into the ken of a manager's telescope been easy enough to sustain. Of late years a slight tendency toward stoutness had made it necessary to assist the dimple with the forefinger and internal suction; the slamming of a door might disturb so nice an operation, and an appeal, which came oddly from Miss Neville, was made to Miss Tremayne's sense of natural acting.

Mr. Olver did not bother to conceal his intention of never moving from the centre of the stage, where he maintained himself with the noisy skill of a gyroscope.

'See here,' he explained to members of the company that tried to compete with his stellar supremacy. 'The public pays to see Diomed Olver and Marcia Neville: they don't care a goddamned cent for anything else in creation. Got me? That's bully. Now we'll go along together fine.'

Mr. Charles Fitzherbert assisted no more at rehearsals but occupied himself entirely with the box-office; Mr. Wade Fortescue was very fierce about two a.m. in the bar of his hotel, but very mild at rehearsals; Mr. Marchmont Hearne hibernated during this period, and when he appeared very shyly at the opening performance in Brooklyn, the company greeted him with the surprised cordiality that is displayed to some one who has broken his leg and emerges weeks later from hospital without a limp.

New York made a deep and instant impression on Sylvia: no city that she had seen was so uncompromising; so sure of its flamboyant personality; so completely an ingenious, spoilt, and precocious child; so lovable for its extravagance and mischief. To her the impression was of some Gargantuan boy in his nursery building up tall towers to knock them down, running his clockwork-engines for fun through the streets of his toy city, scattering in corners quantities of toy bricks in readiness for a new fit of destructive construction, scooping up his tin inhabitants at the end of a day's play to put them helter-skelter into their box, eking out the most novel electrical toys of that Christmas with the battered old trams of the Christmas before, cherishing old houses with a child's queer conservatism, devoting a large stretch of bright carpet to a park, and robbing his grandmother's mantelpiece of her treasures to put inside his more permanent structures. After seeing New York she sympathized very much with the remark she had heard made by a young New Yorker on board the *Minneworra*, which at the time she had thought a mere callow piece of rudeness.

A grave doctor from Toledo, Ohio, almost as grave as if he were from the original Toledo, had expressed a hope to Sylvia that she would not accept New York as representative of the United States. She must travel to the West. New York had no family life: if Miss Scarlett wished to see family life, he should be glad to show it to her in Toledo. For confirmation of his criticism he had appealed to a young man standing at his elbow.

'Well,' the young man had replied. 'I've never been fifty miles west of New York in my life, and I hope I never shall. When I want to travel, I cross over to Europe for a month.'

The Toledo doctor had afterwards spoken severely to Sylvia on the subject of this young New Yorker, citing him as a dangerous element in the national welfare. Now after seeing the Gargantuan boy's nursery she understood the spirit that wanted to enjoy his nursery and not be bothered to go for polite walks with maiden aunts in the country: equally no doubt in Toledo she should appreciate the point of view of the doctor and recognize the need for the bone that would support the vast bulk of the growing child.

Sylvia had noticed that, as she grew older, impressions became less vivid: her later and wider experience of London was already dim beside those first years with her father and Monkley. It had been the same during her travels: already even the Alhambra was no longer quite clearly imprinted upon her mind, and each year it had been growing less and less easy to be astonished. But this arrival in New York had been like an arrival in childhood, as surprising, as exciting, as terrifying, as stimulating. New York was like a rejuvenating potion, in the magic influence of which the memories of past years dissolved. Partly no doubt this effect might be ascribed to the invigorating air, and partly, Sylvia thought, to the anxiously receptive condition of herself now within sight of thirty; but neither of these explanations was wide enough to include all that New York gave of regenerative emotion, of willingness to be alive and unwillingness to go to bed, and of zest in being amused. Sylvia had supposed that she had long ago outgrown the pleasure of wandering about streets for no other reason than to be wandering about streets, of staring into shops, of staring after people, of staring at advertisements, of staring in company with a crowd of starers as well entertained as herself at a bat that was flying about in daylight outside the Plaza Hotel. Here in New York all that old youthful attitude of assuming that the world existed for one's diversion, mixed with a sharp, though always essentially contemptuous curiosity about the method it was taking to amuse one, was hers again. Sylvia had hitherto regarded England as the frivolous nation that thought of nothing but amusement, England that took its pleasure so earnestly and its business so lightly: in New York there was no question of qualifying adverbs: everything was a game. It was a game, and apparently by the enthusiasm with which it was played a novel game, to control the traffic in Fifth Avenue, a rather dangerous game like American football, in which at first the casualties to the policemen who played it were considerable; street-mending was another game, rather an elementary game that contained a large admixture of practical joking; getting a carriage after the theatre was a game played with counters; eating even could be made into a game, either mechanical like the automatic dime-lunch, or intellectual like the free lunch, or imaginative like the quick lunch.

Sylvia had already made acquaintance with the crude material of America in Carlos Morera: New York was Carlos Morera much more refined and more matured, sweetened by its own civilization, which having severed itself from other civilizations like the Anglo-Saxon or Latin was already most convincingly a civilization of its own bearing the veritable stamp of greatness. Sometimes Sylvia would be faced even in New York by a childishness that scarcely differed from the childishness of Carlos Morera. One evening for instance two of the men in the company who knew her tastes invited her to come with them to Murden's all-night saloon off Sixth Avenue: they had been told it was a sight worth seeing.

Sylvia, with visions of something like the dancing saloon in Buenos Aires, was anxious to make the experiment: it sounded exciting when she heard that the place was kept going by 'graft.' After the performance she and her companions went to Jack's for supper; thence they walked along Sixth Avenue to Murden's. It was only about two o'clock when they entered by a side door into a room exactly like the bar parlour of an English public-house, where they sat rather drearily drinking some inferior beer, until one of Sylvia's companions suggested that they had arrived too near the hours of legal closing. They left Murden's and visited a Chinese restaurant in Broadway with a cabaret attached. The prices, the entertainment, the food, and the company were in a descending scale; the prices were much the highest. Two hours later they went back to Murden's; the parlour was not less dreary; the beer was still abominable. However, just as they had decided that this could not be the right place, an enormous man slightly drunk entered under the escort of two ladies of the town. Perceiving that Sylvia and her companions had risen, the newcomer waved them back into their chairs and called for drinks all round.

'British?' he asked.

They nodded.

'Yes, I thought you were Britishers. I'm Under-Sheriff McMorris.' With this he seated himself, hugging the two nymphs on either side of him like a Bacchus in his chariot.

'Actor folk?' he asked.

They nodded.

'Yes, I thought you were actor folk. Ever read Shakespeare? Some boy, eh? Gee, I used to be able to spout Parsha without taking breath.'

Forthwith he delivered the speech about the quality of mercy.

'Well?' he demanded at the end.

The English actors congratulated him and called for another round; Mr. McMorris turned to one of the nymphs:

'Well, honey?'

'Cut it out, you fat old slob, you're tanked!' said honey.

Mr. McMorris recited several other speeches including the vision of the dagger from *Macbeth*. From Shakespeare he passed to Longfellow, and from Longfellow to Byron. After an hour of recitations, he was persuaded by the bartender to give some of his reminiscences of criminals in New York, which he did so vividly that Sylvia began to suppose that at one time or another he really had been connected with the law. Finally about six o'clock he became pathetic and wept away most of what he had drunk.

'I'm feeling bad this morning. I gart to go and arrest a man for whom I have a considerable admiration. I gart to go down town to Washington Square and arrest a prominent citizen at eight o'clock sharp. I guess they're waiting right now for me to come along and make that arrest. Where's my black-jack?'

He fumbled in his pocket for a leather-covered life-preserver, which he flourished truculently. Leaning upon the shoulders of the nymphs, he waved a farewell and staggered out.

Sylvia asked the bar-tender what he really was.

'He's Under-Sheriff McMorris. At eight o'clock he's going to arrest a prominent New York citizen for misappropriation of some fund.'

That evening in the papers Sylvia read that Under-Sheriff McMorris had burst into tears when Ex-Governor Somebody or other had walked down the steps of his house in Washington Square and offered himself to the custody of the law.

'I don't like to have to do this, Mr. Governor,' Under-Sheriff McMorris had protested.

'You must do your duty, Mr. Under-Sheriff.'

The crowd had thereupon cheered loudly, and the wife of the ex-governor dissolved in tears had waved the Stars and Stripes from an upper window.

'Jug for the ex-governor and a jag for the under-sheriff,' said Sylvia. 'If only the same spirit could be applied to minor arrests. That may come; it's wonderful really how in this mighty republic they manage to preserve any vestige of personality, but they do.'

The play ran through the autumn, and went on the road in January. Sylvia did not add much to her appreciation of America in the course of it, because, as was inevitable with the short visits they paid to various towns, she had to depend for intercourse upon the members of the company. She reached New York again shortly before her twenty-eighth birthday: when nearly all her fellow-players returned to England, she decided to stay behind. The first impression she had received of entering upon a new phase of life when she landed in New York had not yet deserted her, and having received an offer from the owner of what sounded from his description a kind of hydropathic establishment to entertain the visitors during the late summer and fall, she accepted. In August therefore she left New York and went to Sulphurville, Indiana.

Sylvia had had glimpses of rural America in Vermont and New Hampshire during the tour; in such a cursory view it had not seemed to differ much from rural England; now she was going to see rustic America, if a distinction between the two adjectives might be made. At Indianapolis she changed from the great express into a smaller train that deposited her at a railway-station consisting of a tumble-down shed. Nobody came out to welcome the train, but the coloured porter insisted that this was the junction from which she would ultimately reach Sulphurville and denied firmly Sylvia's suggestion that the engine-driver had stopped here for breath. She was the only passenger who alighted, and she saw with something near despair the train continue on its way. The sun was blazing down; all around was a grasshopper-haunted wilderness of Indian corn. It was the hottest, greenest, flattest, most god-forsaken spot she had ever seen. The heat was so tremendous that she ventured inside the hut for shade; the only sign of life was a bug proceeding slowly across a greasy table. Sylvia went out and wandered round to the other side; here fast asleep was a man dressed in a pair of blue trousers, a neckerchief, and an enormous straw hat. As the trousers reached to his armpits, he was really fully dressed, and Sylvia was able to recognize him from an illustrated edition she possessed of Huckleberry Finn as a human being; at the same time she thought it wiser to let him sleep, and returned to the front of the shed. To her surprise, for it seemed scarcely possible that anybody could inhabit the second floor, she perceived a woman with curl-papers in a spotted green and yellow bed-wrapper looking out of what until now she had supposed to be a gap in the roof caused by decay. Sylvia asked the woman if this was the junction for Sulphurville. She nodded, but vanished from the window before there was time to ask her when the train would arrive.

Sylvia waited for an hour in the heat, and had almost given up hope of ever reaching Sulphurville when suddenly a train arrived, smaller than the one into which she had changed at Indianapolis, but still considerably larger than any European train. The hot afternoon wore away while this new train puffed slowly deeper and deeper into rustic America until it reached Bagdad. Hitherto Sylvia had travelled in what was called a parlour-car; but at Bagdad she had to enter a fourth train that did not possess a parlour-car and that really resembled a local train in England with oil lamps and semi-detached compartments. At every station between Bagdad and Sulphurville crowds of country folk got in, all of whom were wearing flags and flowers in their button-holes and were in a state of perspiring festivity: at the last station before Sulphurville the train was invaded by the members of a local band, whose instruments fought for a place as hard as their masters. Sylvia was nearly elbowed out of her seat by an aggressive ophicleide, but an old gentleman opposite with a saxhorn behind him and an euphonium on his knees told her by way of encouragement that the soldiers didn't pass through Indiana every day.

'The last time I saw soldiers like that was during the war,' he said, 'and I don't allow any of us here will ever see so many soldiers again.' He looked round the company defiantly, but nobody seemed inclined to contradict him, and he grunted with disappointment.

It seemed hard that the old gentleman's day should end so tamely, but fortunately a young man in the far corner proclaimed it not merely as his opinion, but supported it from inside information, that the regiment was being marched through Indiana like this in order to get it nearer to the Mexican border.

'Shucks!' said the old gentleman, and blew his nose so violently that everyone looked involuntarily at one of the brass instruments. 'Shucks,' he repeated; then he smiled at Sylvia, who, sympathizing with the happy close of his day, smiled back just as the train entered the station of Sulphurville.

The Plutonian Hotel, Sulphurville, had presumably been built to appease the same kind of human credulity that created the Pump Rooms at Bath or Wiesbaden or Aix-les-Bains. Sylvia had observed that one of the great elemental beliefs of the human race, a belief lost in primeval fog, was that if water with an odd taste bubbled out of the earth, it must necessarily possess curative qualities; if it bubbled forth without a nasty enough taste to justify the foundation of a spa, it was analyzed by prominent chemists, bottled, and sold as a panacea to the greater encouragement of lonely dyspeptics with nothing else to read at dinner. In the Middle Ages, and possibly in the classic times of Æsculapius, these natural springs had fortified the spiritual side of man; in later days they served to dilute his spirits. The natural springs at Sulphurville fully justi-fied the erection of the Plutonian Hotel and the lowest depths of mortal credulity, for they had a revolting smell, an exceptionally unpleasant taste, and a high temperature. Everything that balneal ingenuity could suggest had been done, and in case the internal cure was not nasty enough as it was, the first glass of water was prescribed for six o'clock in the morning.

Though it was necessary to test human faith by the most arduous and vexatious ordinances for human conduct, lest it might grow contemp-tuous of the cure, it was equally necessary to prevent boredom, if not of the devotees themselves, at any rate of their families. Accordingly there was an annexe to the ascetic hotel where everybody was driven to bed at eleven by the uncomfortable behaviour of the servants, and where break-fast was served not later than seven; this annexe possessed a concert hall, a small theatre, a gaming saloon with not merely roulette, but many apparently childish games of chance that nevertheless richly rewarded the management. Sylvia wondered if there was any moral intention on the part of the proprietors in the way they encouraged gambling, if they wished to accentuate the chances and changes of human life and thereby secure for their clients a religious attitude toward their bodily safety. Certainly at the Plutonian Hotel it was impossible to obtain anything except meals without gambling. In order to buy a cigar or a box of chocolates it was necessary to play dice with the young woman who sold them with more or less profit to the hotel according to one's luck. Every morning some new object was on view in the lobby to be raffled that evening: thus on the fourth night of her stay Sylvia became the owner of a large saratoga trunk, the emptiness of which was a continuous temptation.

The Plutonian was not merely a resort for gouty Easterners; it catered equally for the uric acid of the West. Sylvia liked the families from the West, particularly the girls with their flowing hair and big felt hats who rode on Kentucky ponies to see smugglers' caves in the hills, conforming invariably to the traditional aspect of the Western belle in the cinema; the boys were not so picturesque, in fact they scarcely differed from European boys of the same age. The East supplied the exotic note among the children; candy-fed, shrill and precocious with a queer gnome-like charm, they resembled expensive toys. These visitors to Sulphurville were much more affable with one another than their fellows in Europe would have been in similar circumstances. Sylvia had already noticed that in America stomachic subjects could inspire the dullest conversation; here, at the Plutonian the stomach had taken the place of the soul, and it was scarcely an exaggeration to say that in the lounges people rose up to testify in public about their insides.

The morning after Sylvia's arrival the guests were much excited by the visit of the soldiers, who were to camp for a week in the hotel grounds and perform various manœuvres. Sylvia observed that everybody talked as if a troupe of acrobats was going to visit the hotel; nobody seemed to have any idea that the American army served any purpose but the entertainment of the public with gymnastic displays. That afternoon the regiment marched past the hotel to its camping ground; the band played the *Star Spangled Banner;* all the visitors grouped upon the steps in front clapped their hands; the Colonel took off his hat, waved it at the audience, and bowed like a successful author. At first Sylvia considered his behaviour undignified and absurd; afterwards she rather approved of its friendliness, its absence of pomp and arrogance, its essentially democratic inspiration, in a word, its familiarity.

The proprietor of the Plutonian, a leading political 'boss,' was so much moved by the strains of the music, the martial bearing of the men, and the opportunity of self-advertisement that he invited the officers of the regiment to mess free in the hotel during their visit. Everybody praised Mr. O'Halloran's generosity and patriotism, the more warmly because it gave everybody an occasion to commiserate with the officers upon their absurdly small pay; such commiseration gratified the individual's sense of superiority and made it easy for him to brag about his own success in life. Sylvia resented the business man's point of view about his national army; it was almost as patronizing as an Englishman's attitude to an artist or a German's to a woman or a Frenchman's to anybody but a Frenchman. Snobbishness was only tolerable about the past; perhaps that was the reason why the Italians were the only really democratic nation she had met so far; the Italians were aristocrats trying to become tradesmen: the rest of mankind were tradesmen striving to appear aristocrats.

Sylvia had sung her songs and was watching the roulette, when a young lieutenant who had been playing with great seriousness turned to her and asked if she was not British.

'We came to know some British officers out in China,' he told her. 'We couldn't seem to understand them at first, but afterwards we found out they were good boys really. Only the trouble was we were never properly introduced at first, and that worried them some. Say, there's a fellow-countryman of yours sick in Sulphurville. I kind of found out by accident this morning, because I went into a drug-store where the store-keeper was handing out some medicine to a coloured girl who was arguing with him whether she should pay for it. Seems this young Britisher's expecting his remittance. That's a god-awful place to be stranded, Sulphurville.'

They chatted for a while together: Sylvia liked the simple good-fellowship of the young American, his inquisitiveness about her reasons for coming to sing at the Plutonian Hotel, and his frank anticipation of any curiosity on her side by telling her all about himself and his career since he left West Point. He was amused by her account of the excitement over the passage of the troops through the villages, and seized the occasion to moralize on the vastness of a country through one State of which a regiment could march and surprise half the inhabitants with their first view of an American soldier.

'Seems kind of queer,' he said.

'But very Arcadian,' Sylvia added.

When Sylvia went to bed, her mind reverted to the young Englishman; at the time she had scarcely taken in the significance of what the officer had told her. Now suddenly the sense of his loneliness and suffering overwhelmed her fancy. She thought of the desolation of that railway-junction where she had waited for the train to Sulphurville, of the heat and the grasshoppers and the flat endless greenery. Even that brief experience of being alone in the heart of America had frightened her. She had not taken heed of the vastness of it while she was travelling with the company, and here at the hotel, definitely placed as an entertainer, she had a certain security. But to be alone and penniless in Sulphurville; to be ill, moreover, and dependent on the charity of foreigners so much the more foreign, because though they spoke the same language, they spoke it with strange differences like the people in a dream: the words were the same, but they expressed foreign ideas.

Sylvia began to speculate upon the causes that had led to this young Englishman's being stranded in Sulphurville. There seemed no explanation, unless he were perhaps an actor who had been abandoned because he was too ill to travel with the company. At this idea she almost got out of bed to walk through the warm frog-haunted night to his rescue. She became sentimental about him in the dark. It seemed to her that nothing in the world was so pitiable as a sick artist; always the servant of the public's curiosity, he was now the helpless prey of it. He would be treated with the contempt that is accorded to sick animals whose utility is at an end. She pictured him in the care of a woman like the one who had leaned out of that railway-shed in a spotted green and yellow wrapper. Yet after all he might not be a mountebank; there was really no reason to suppose he was anything but poor and lonely, though that was enough indeed.

'I must be getting very old,' Sylvia said to herself. 'Only approaching senility could excuse this prodigal effusion of what is really almost maternal lust. I've grown out of any inclination to ask myself why I think things or why I do things. I've nothing now but an immense desire to do – do – do. I was beginning to think this desperate determination to be impressed, like a child whose father is hiding conspicuously behind the door, was due to America. It's nothing to do with America: it's myself. It's a kind of moral and mental drunkenness. I know what I'm doing. I'm entirely responsible for my actions. That's the way a drunken man argues. Nobody is so utterly convinced of his rightness and reasonableness and judgment as a drunken man. I might argue with myself till morning that it's ridiculous to excite myself over the prospect of helping an Englishman stranded in Sulphurville, but when worn out with self-conviction I fall asleep I shall wake on tiptoe as it were: I shall be quite violently awake at once. The fact is I'm absolutely tired of observing human nature. I just want to tumble right into the middle of its confusion and forget how to criticize anybody or anything. What's the good of meeting a drunken man with generalizations about human conduct or direction or progression? He won't listen to generalizations, because drunkenness is the apotheosis of the individual. That's why drunken people are always so earnestly persuasive, so anxious to convince the unintoxicated observer that it is better to walk on all-fours than upright. Eccentricity becomes a moral passion; every drunken man is a missionary of the peculiar. At the present moment I'm in the mental state that, did I possess an honest taste for liquor, would make me get up and uncork the brandy bottle. It's a kind of defiant self-expression. Oh, that poor young Englishman lying alone in Sulphurville. To-morrow, to-morrow! Who knows? perhaps I really shall find that I am necessary to somebody. Even as a child I conceived the notion of being indispensable. I want some-body to say to me, "You! You! what should I have done without you?" I suppose every woman feels that; I suppose that is the maternal instinct. But I don't believe many women can feel it so sharply as I do, because very few women have ever been compelled by circumstances to develop their personalities so early and so fully, and then find that nobody wants that personality. I could cry just at the mere notion of being wanted, and surely this young Englishman, whoever he is, will want me. Oh, Sylvia, Sylvia, you're deliberately working yourself up to an adventure! And who has a better right? Tell me that. That's exactly why I praised the drunkard; he knows how to dodge self-consciousness. Why shouldn't you set out to have an adventure? You shall, my dear. And if you're disap-pointed? You've been disappointed before. Damn those tree-frogs. Like all croakers they disturb oblivion. I wonder if he'd like my new trunk. And I wonder how old he is. I'm assuming that he's young, but he may be a matted old tramp.'

Sylvia woke next morning as she had prefigured herself on tiptoe; at breakfast she was sorry for all the noisy people round her, so important to her was life seeming. She set out immediately afterwards to walk along the hot dusty road to the town, elated by the notion of leaving behind her the restlessness and stark cleanliness of the big hotel. The main street of Sulphurville smelt of straw and dry grain; and if it had not been for the flies, she would have found the air sweet enough after the damp exha-lations of brimstone that permeated the atmosphere of the Plutonian and its surroundings. The flies, however, tainted everything: not even the drug-store was free from them. Sylvia inquired for the address of the Englishman, and the druggist looked at her sharply; she wondered if he was hoping for the settlement of his account.

'Madden's the name, ain't it?' the druggist asked.

'Madden?' she repeated mechanically. A wave of emotion flooded her mind, receded, and left it strewn with the jetsam of the past. The druggist and the drug-store faded out of her consciousness; she was in Colonial Terrace again, insisting upon Arthur's immediate departure.

'What a little beast I was,' she thought, and a desire came over her to atone for former heartlessness by her present behaviour. Then abruptly she realized that the Madden of Sulphurville was not necessarily, or even probably, the Arthur Madden of Hampstead. Yet behind this half-disappointment lay the conviction that it was he. 'Which accounts for my unusual excitement,' Sylvia murmured. She heard herself calmly asking the storekeeper for his address.

'The Auburn Hotel,' she repeated. 'Thank you.'

The store-keeper seemed inclined to question her farther; no doubt he wished to be able to count upon his bill's being paid, but Sylvia hurried from the shop before he could speak.

The Auburn Hotel, Sulphurville, was perhaps not worse than an hotel of the same class would have been in England, but the coloured servant added just enough to the prevailing squalor to make it seem worse. When Sylvia asked to see Mr. Madden, the coloured servant stared at her, wiped her mouth with her apron, and called:

'Mrs. Lebus!'

'O Julie, is that you, what is it you want?' twanged a voice from within that sounded like a cat caught in a guitar.

'You're wanted right now, Mrs. Lebus,' the servant called back.

The duet was like a parody of a coon song, and Sylvia found herself humming to ragtime:

> *Oh, Mrs. Lebus, you're wanted,*
> *Oh, yes, you're wanted, sure you're wanted, Mrs. Lebus,*
> *You're wanted, you're wanted,*
> *You're wanted – right now.*

Mrs. Lebus was one of those women whose tongues are always hunting like eager terriers. With evident reluctance she postponed the chase of an artful morsel that had taken refuge in some difficult country at the back of her mouth and faced the problem of admitting Sylvia to the sick man's room.

'You a relative?' she asked.

Sylvia shook her head.

'Perhaps you've come about his remittance? He told me he was expecting a hundred dollars any time. You staying in Sulphurville?'

Sylvia understood that the apparent disinclination to admit her was only due to unsatisfied curiosity and that there was not necessarily any suspicion of her motives. At this moment something particularly delicious ran across the path of Mrs. Lebus's tongue, and Sylvia took advantage of the brief pause during which it was devoured to penetrate into the lobby, where a melancholy citizen in a frock coat and a straw hat was testing the point of a nib upon his thumb, whether with the intention of offering it to Mrs. Lebus to pick her teeth or of writing a letter was uncertain.

'O Scipio,' said Mrs. Lebus. She pronounced it 'Skipio.'

'Wal?'

'She wants to see Mr. Madden.'

'Sure.'

The landlady turned to Sylvia.

'Mr. Lebus don't have any objections. Julie, take Miss – what did you say your name was?'

Sylvia saw no reason against falling into what Mrs. Lebus evidently considered was a skilfully laid trap, and told her.

'Scarlett,' Mr. Lebus repeated. 'We don't possess that name in Sulphurville. No, ma'am, that name's noo to Sulphurville.'

'Sakes alive, Scipio, are you going to keep Miss Scarlett hanging around all day whiles you gossip about Sulphurville?' his wife asked; aware of her husband's enthusiasm for his native place, she may have foreseen a dissertation upon its wonders unless she were ruthless.

'Julie'll take you up to his apartment. And don't you forget to knock before you open the door, Julie.'

On the way upstairs in the wake of the servant, Sylvia wondered how she could explain her intrusion to a stranger, even though he were an Englishman. She had so firmly decided to herself it was Arthur that she could not make any plans for meeting anybody else. Julie was quite ready to open the door of the bedroom and let Sylvia enter unannounced; she was surprised by being requested to go in first and ask the gentleman if he could receive Miss Scarlett. However, she yielded to foreign eccentricity, and a moment later ushered Sylvia in.

It was Arthur Madden; and Sylvia, from a mixture of penitence for the way she treated him at Colonial Terrace, of self-congratulation for being so sure beforehand that it was he, and of swift compassion for his illness and loneliness ran across the room and greeted him with a kiss.

'How on earth did you get into this horrible hole?' Arthur asked.

'My dear, I knew it was you, when I heard your name.' Breathlessly she poured out the story of how she had found him.

'But you'd made up your mind to play the good Samaritan to whoever it was – you never guessed for a moment at first that it was me.'

She forgave him the faint petulance because he was ill, and also because it brought back to her with a new vividness long bygone jealousies, restoring a little more of herself, as she once was, nearly thirteen years ago. How little he had changed outwardly, and much of what change there was might be put down to his illness.

'Arthur, do you remember Maria?' she asked.

He smiled.

'He only died about two years ago. He lived with my mother after I went on the stage.'

Sylvia wondered to him why they had never met all these years: she had known so many people on the stage, but then of course she had been a good deal out of England. What had made Arthur go on the stage first? He had never talked of it in the old days.

'I used always to be keen on music.'

Sylvia whistled the melody that introduced them to each other, and he smiled again.

'My mother still plays that sometimes, and I've often thought of you when she does. She lives at Dulwich now.'

They talked for a while of Hampstead and laughed over the escape.

'You were a most extraordinary kid,' he told her. 'Because after all, I was seventeen at the time – older than you. Good lord, I'm thirty now, and you must be twenty-eight.'

To Sylvia it was much more incredible that he should be thirty; he seemed so much younger than she, lying here in this frowsy room; or was it that she felt so much older than he?

'But how on earth *did* you get stranded in this place?' she asked.

'I was touring with a concert party. The last few years I've practically given up the stage proper. I don't know why really – for I was doing quite decently, but concert-work was more amusing somehow. One wasn't so much at the beck and call of managers.'

Sylvia knew by the careful way in which he was giving his reasons for abandoning the stage that he had not yet produced the real reason. It might have been baffled ambition, or it might have been a woman.

'Well, we came to Sulphurville,' said Arthur. He hesitated for a moment: obviously there had been a woman. 'We came to Sulphurville,' he went on, 'and played at the hotel you're staying at now – a rotten hole,' he added with retrospective bitterness. 'I don't know how it was, but I suppose I got keen on the gambling – anyway I had a row with the other people in the show, and when they left I refused to go with them. I stayed behind and got keen on the gambling.'

'It was after the row that you took to roulette?' Sylvia asked.

'Well, as a matter of fact I had a row with a girl. She treated me rather badly, and I stayed on. I lost a good deal of money. Well, it wasn't a very large sum as a matter of fact, but it was all I had, and then I fell ill. I caught cold and I was worried over things – I cabled to my mother for some money, but there's been no reply. I'm afraid she's had difficulty in raising it. She quarrelled with my father's people when I went on the stage. Damned narrow-minded set of yokels. Furious because I wouldn't take up farming. How I hate narrow-minded people,' and with an invalid's fretful intolerance he went on grumbling at the ineradicable characteristics of an English family four thousand miles away.

'Of course something may have happened to my mother,' he added. 'You may be sure that, if anything had, those beasts would never take the trouble to write and tell me. It would be a pleasure to them if they could annoy me in any way.'

A swift criticism of Arthur's attitude toward the possibility of his mother's death rose to Sylvia's mind, but she repressed it, pleading with herself to excuse him because he was ill and over-strained. She was positively determined to see henceforth nothing but good in people, and in her anxiety to confirm herself in this resolve she was ready not merely to exaggerate everything in Arthur's favour, but even to twist any failure on his side into actual merit. Thus, when she hastened to put her own resources at his disposal and found him quite ready to accept without protest her help, she choked back the comparison with Jack Airdale's attitude in similar circumstances and was quite angry with herself, saying how much more naturally Arthur had received her good will and how splendid it was to find such simplicity and sincerity.

'I'll nurse you till you're quite well, and then why shouldn't we take an engagement together somewhere?'

Arthur became enthusiastic over this suggestion.

'You've not heard me sing yet. My throat's still too weak, but you'll be surprised, Sylvia.'

'I haven't got anything but a very deep voice,' she told him. 'But I can usually make an impression.'

'Can you? Of course, where I've always been held back is by lack of money. I've never been able to afford to buy good songs.'

Arthur began to sketch out for himself a most radiant future, and as he talked, Sylvia thought again how incredible it was that he should be older than herself. Yet was not this youthful enthusiasm exactly what she required? It was just this capacity of Arthur's for thinking he had a future that was going to make life tremendously worth while for her, tremendously interesting – oh, it was impossible not to believe in the decrees of fate, when at the very moment of her greatest longing to be needed by somebody she had met Arthur again. She could be everything to him, tend him through his illness, provide him with money to rid himself of the charity of Mrs. Lebus and the druggist, help him in his career, and watch over his fidelity to his ambition. She remembered how years ago at Hampstead his mother had watched over him; she could recall every detail of the room and see Mrs. Madden interrupt one of her long sonatas to be sure Arthur was not sitting in a draught. And it had been she who had heedlessly lured him away from that tender mother: there was poetic justice in this opportunity of reparation now accorded to her. To be sure, it had been nothing but a childish escapade – reparation was too strong a word; but there was something so neat about this encounter years afterwards in a place like Sulphurville. How pale he was, which, nevertheless made him more romantic to look at; how thin and white his hands were. She took one of them in her own boy's hands, as so many people had called them, and clasped it with the affection that one gives to small helpless things, to children and kittens, an affection that is half gratitude because one feels good will rising like a sweet fountain from the depths of one's being, the freshness of which playing upon the spirit is so dear, that no words are enough to bless the wand that made the stream gush forth.

'I shall come and see you all day,' said Sylvia. 'But I think I ought not to break my contract at the Plutonian.'

'Oh, you'll come and live here?' Arthur begged. 'You've no idea how horrible it is. There was a cockroach in the soup last night, and of course there are bugs. For goodness' sake, Sylvia, don't give me hope and then dash it away from me. I tell you I've had a hell of a time in this cursed hole. Listen to the bed: it sounds as if it would collapse at any moment; and the bugs have got on my nerves to such a pitch that I spend the whole time looking at spots on the ceiling and fancying they've moved. It's so hot too; everything's rotted with heat. You mustn't desert me. You must come and stay here with me.'

'Why shouldn't you move up to the Plutonian?' Sylvia suggested. 'I'll tell you what I'll do. I'll get one of the doctors to come and look at you, and if he thinks it's possible, you shall move up there at once. Poor boy, it really is too ghastly here.'

Arthur was nearly weeping with self-pity.

'But, my dear girl, it's much worse than you think. You know those horrible birds' bath-tubs in which they bring your food at third-rate American hotels, loathsome saucers with squash and bits of grit in watery milk that they call cereals and bony bits of chicken – well, imagine being fed like that when you're ill, imagine your bed covered with those infernal saucers. One of them always gets left behind when Julie clears away, and it always falls with a crash on the floor, and I always wonder if the mess will tempt the cockroaches into my room. And then Lebus *will* come up and make noises in his throat and brag about Sulphurville, and I always know by his wandering eye that he is looking for what he calls the cuspidor, which I've put out of sight. And Mrs. Lebus *will* come up and suck her teeth at me until I feel inclined to strangle her.'

'The sooner you're moved away the better,' Sylvia said decidedly.

'Oh yes, if you think it can be managed. But if not, Sylvia, for god's sake don't leave me alone.'

'Are you really glad to see me?' she asked.

'Oh, my dear, it was like heaven opening before one's eyes.'

'Tell me about the girl you were fond of,' she said abruptly.

'What do you want to talk about her for? There's nothing to tell you really. She had red hair.'

Sylvia was glad Arthur spoke of her with so little interest; it certainly was definitely comforting to feel the utter dispossession of that red-haired girl.

'Look here,' said Sylvia. 'I'm going to let these people suppose that I'm your long-lost relative. I shall pay their bill, and bring the doctor down to see you. Arthur, I'm so glad I've found you. So you remember the cab-horse? Oh, and do you remember the cats in the area and the jug of water that splashed you? You were *so* unhappy, almost as unhappy as you were when I found you here. Have you always been treated unkindly?'

'I have had a pretty hard time,' Arthur said.

'Oh, but you mustn't be sorry for yourself,' she laughed.

'No, seriously, Sylvia, I've always had a lot of people against me.'

'Yes, but that's such fun. You simply must be amused by life, when you're with me. I'm not hard-hearted a bit really, but you really mustn't be offended with me when I tell you that really there's something a tiny bit funny in your being stranded in the Auburn Hotel, Sulphurville.'

'I'm glad you think so,' said Arthur in rather a hurt tone of voice.

'Don't be cross, you foolish creature.'

'I'm not a bit cross. Only I *would* like you to understand that my illness isn't a joke. You don't suppose I should let you pay my bills and do all this for me, unless it were really something serious.'

Sylvia put her hand on his mouth.

'I forgive you,' she murmured, 'because you really are ill. Oh, Arthur, *do* you remember Hube? What fun everything is.'

Sylvia left him and went downstairs to arrange matters with Mrs. Lebus.

'It was a relation after all,' she told her. 'The Maddens have been related to us for hundreds of years.'

'My! my! now isn't that real queer? O Scipio!'

Mr. Lebus came into view cleaning his nails with the same pen, and was duly impressed with the coincidence.

'Darned if I don't tell Pastor Gollick after next Sunday Meeting. He's got a kind of hankering after the ways of Providence. Gee! Why, it's a sermonizing cinch.'

There was general satisfaction in the Auburn Hotel over the payment of Arthur's bill.

'Not that I wouldn't have trusted him for another month or more,' Mrs. Lebus affirmed. 'But it's a satisfaction to be able to turn round and say to the neighbours, "what did I tell you?" Folks in Sulphurville were quite sure I'd never be paid back a cent. This'll learn them!'

Mr. Lebus, in whose throat the doubts of the neighbours had gathered to offend his faith, cleared them out for ever in one sonorous rauque.

The druggist's account was settled, and though when Sylvia first heard him he had been doubtful if his medicine was doing the patient any good, he was now most anxious that he should continue with the prescription. That afternoon, one of the doctors in residence at the Plutonian visited Arthur and at once advised his removal thither.

Arthur made rapid progress when he was once out of the hospitable squalor of the Auburn Hotel; and the story of Sylvia's discovery of her unfortunate cousin became a romantic episode for all the guests of the Plutonian, a never-failing aid to conversation between wives waiting for their husbands to emerge from their daily torture at the hands of the masseurs, who lived like imps in the sulphurous glooms of the bath below; maybe it even provided the victims themselves with a sufficiently absorbing topic to mitigate the penalties of their cure.

Arthur himself expanded wonderfully as the subject of so much discussion; it gave Sylvia the greatest pleasure to see the way in which his complexion was recovering its old ruddiness and his steps their former vigour; but she did not approve of the way in which the story kept pace with Arthur's expansion. She had confided to him how very personally the news of the sick Englishman had affected her and how she had made up her mind from the beginning that it was a stranded actor, and afterwards, when she heard in the drug-store the name Madden, that it actually was Arthur himself. He, however, was unable to stay content with such an incomplete telepathy; indulging human nature's preference for what is not true, both in his own capacity as a liar and in his listeners' avid and wanton credulity, he transferred a woman's intimate hopes into a quack's tale.

304

'Then you didn't see your cousin's spirit go up in the elevator when you were standing in the lobby? Now isn't that perfectly discouraging?' complained a lady with an astral reputation in Illinois.

'I'm afraid the story's been added to a good deal,' Sylvia said. 'I'm sorry to disappoint the faithful.'

'She's shy about giving us her experiences,' said another lady from Iowa. 'I know I was just thrilled when I heard it. It seemed to me the most wonderful story I'd ever imagined. I guess you felt pretty queer when you saw him lying on a bed in your room.'

'He was in his own room,' Sylvia corrected, 'and I didn't feel at all queer. It was he who felt queer.'

'Isn't she secretive?' exclaimed the lady from Illinois.

'Why, I was going to ask you to write it up in our Society's magazine *The Flash*. We don't print any stories that aren't established as true. Well, your experience has given me real courage, Miss Scarlett. Thank you.'

The astral enthusiast clasped Sylvia's hand and gazed at her as earnestly as if she had noticed a smut on her nose.

'Yes, I'm sure we ought to be grateful,' said the lady from Iowa. 'My! Our footsteps are treading in the unseen every day of our lives. You certainly are privileged,' she added, wrapping Sylvia in a damp mist of benign fatuity.

'I wish you wouldn't elaborate everything so,' Sylvia begged of Arthur when she had escaped from the deification of the two psychical ladies. 'It makes me feel so dreadfully old to see myself assuming a legendary shape before my own eyes. It's as painful as being stuffed alive – stuffed alive with nonsense,' she added with a laugh.

Arthur's expansion, however, was not merely grafted on Sylvia's presentiment of his discovery in Sulphurville; he blossomed upon his own stock, a little exotically perhaps like the clumps of fiery cannas in the grounds of the hotel, but with a quite conspicuous effectiveness. Like the cannas he required protection from frost, for there was a very real sensitiveness beneath all that flamboyance, and it was the knowledge of this that kept Sylvia from criticizing him at all severely. Besides, even if he did bask a little too complacently in expressions of interest and sympathy it was a very natural reaction from his wretched solitude at the Auburn Hotel, for which he could scarcely be held culpable, least of all by herself. Moreover, was not this so visible recovery the best tribute he could have paid to her care? If he appeared to strut, for indeed there was a hint of strutting in his demeanour, he only did so from a sense of well-being. Finally, if any further defence was necessary, he was an Englishman among a crowd of Americans; the conditions demanded a good deal of competitive self-assertion.

Meanwhile summer was gone; the trees glowed with every shade of crimson. Sylvia could not help feeling that there was something characteristic in the demonstrative richness of the American fall; though she was far from wishing to underrate its beauty, the display was oppressive. She sighed for the melancholy of the European autumn, a conventional emotion no doubt, but so closely bound up with old associations that she could not wish to lose it. This cremation of summer, these leafy pyrotechnics, this holocaust of colour seemed a too barbaric celebration of the year's death. It was significant that 'autumn' with its long-drawn-out suggestion of decline should here have failed to displace 'fall'; for there was something essentially catastrophic in this ruthless bonfire of foliage. It was not surprising that the aboriginal inhabitants should have been Redskins, nor that the gorgeousness of nature should have demanded from the humanity it overwhelmed a readjustment of decorative values, which superficial observers were apt to mistake for gaudy ostentation. Sylvia could readily imagine that if she had been accustomed from childhood to these crimson woods, these beefy robins, and these saucer-eyed daisies, she might have found her own more familiar landscapes merely tame and pretty; but as it was she felt dazzled and ill at ease. 'It's the little more and how much it is,' she told herself, pondering the tantalizing similarity that was really as profoundly different as an Amazonian forest from Kensington Gardens.

Arthur's first flamboyance was much toned down by all that natural splendour; in fact it no longer existed, and Sylvia found a freshening charm in his company amid these crimson trees and unfamiliar birds, and in this staring white hotel with its sulphurous exhalations. His complete restoration to health, moreover, was a pleasure and a pride that nothing could mar, and she found herself planning his happiness and prosperity as if she had already transferred to him all she herself hoped from life.

At the end of September, the long-expected remittance arrived from Mrs. Madden; and Sylvia gathered from the letter that the poor lady had been much puzzled to send the money.

'We must cable it back to her at once,' Sylvia declared.

'Oh well, now it's come, is that wise?' Arthur objected. 'She may have had some difficulty in getting it, but that's over now.'

'No, no, it must be cabled back to her. I've got plenty of money to carry us on till we begin work together.'

'But I can't go on accepting charity like this,' Arthur protested. 'It's undignified really. I've never done such a thing before.'

'You accepted it from your mother.'

'Oh, but my mother's different.'

'Only because she's less able to afford it than I am,' Sylvia pointed out. 'Look, she's sent you fifty pounds. Think how jolly it would be for her suddenly to receive fifty pounds for herself.'

Arthur warmed to the idea; he could not resist the picture of his mother's pleasure, nor the kind of inverted generosity with which it seemed to endow himself. He talked away about the arrival of the money in England, till it almost seemed as if he were sending his mother the accumulation of hard-earned savings to buy herself a new piano: that was the final purpose to which in Arthur's expanding fancy the fifty pounds was to be put. Sylvia found his attitude rather boyish and charming, and they had an argument on the way to cable back the money whether it would be better for Mrs. Madden to buy a Bechstein or a Blüthner.

Sylvia's contract with the Plutonian expired with the first fortnight of October, and they decided to see what likelihood there was of work in New York before they thought of returning to Europe. They left Sulphurville with everybody's good wishes, because everybody owed to their romantic meeting an opportunity of telling a really good ghost story at first hand with the liberty of individual elaboration.

New York was very welcome after Sulphurville; they passed the wooded heights of the Hudson at dusk in a glow of sombre magnificence softened by the vapours of the river; it seemed to Sylvia that scarcely ever had she contemplated a landscape of such restrained splendour, and she thought of that young New Yorker who had preferred not to travel more than fifty miles west of his native city, though the motive of his loyalty had most improbably been the beauty of the Hudson. She wondered if Arthur appreciated New York, but he responded to her enthusiasm with the superficial complaints of the Englishman, complaints that when tested resolved themselves into conventional formulas of disapproval.

'I suppose trite opinions are a comfortable possession,' Sylvia said. 'Yet a good player does not like a piano that is too easy. You complain of the morning papers appearing shortly after midnight, but confess that in your heart you prefer reading *them* in bed to reading a London evening paper, limp from being carried about in the pocket and with whatever is important in it illegible.'

'But the flaring headlines,' Arthur protested. 'You surely don't like them?'

'Oh, but I do,' she vowed. 'They're as much more amusing than the dreary column beneath as tinned tongue is nicer than the dry undulation for which you pay twice as much. Headlines are the poetry of journalism, and after all what would the Parthenon be without its frieze?'

'Of course, you'd argue black was white,' Arthur said.

'Well, that's a better standpoint than accepting everything as grey.'

'Most things are grey.'

'Oh, no, they're not. Some things are. Old men's beards and dirty linen and Tschaikowsky's music and oysters and Wesleyans.'

'There you go,' he jeered.

'Where do I go?'

'Right off the point,' said Arthur triumphantly. 'No woman can argue.'

'Oh, but I'm not a woman,' Sylvia contradicted. 'I'm a mythical female monster – don't you know – one of those queer beasts with claws like hayrakes and breasts like pegtops and a tail like a fish.'

'Do you mean a Sphinx?' Arthur asked in his literal way; he was always rather hostile toward her extravagant fancies, because he thought it dangerous to encourage a woman in much the same way as he would have objected to encouraging a beggar.

'No, I really meant a Grinx, which is a bit like a Sphinx, but the father was a griffin – the mother in both cases was a minx of course.'

'What was the father of the Sphinx?' he said rather ungraciously.

Sylvia clapped her hands.

'I knew you wouldn't be able to resist the question. A Sphere – a woman's sphere of course, which is nearly as objectionable a beast as a lady's man.'

'You do talk rot sometimes,' said Arthur.

'Don't you ever have fancies?' she demanded mockingly.

'Yes, of course, but practical fancies.'

'Practical fancies,' Sylvia echoed. 'Oh, my dear, it sounds like a fairy in Jaeger combinations. You don't know what fun it is talking rot to you, Arthur. It's like hoaxing a chicken with marbles. You walk away from my conversation with just the same disgusted dignity.'

'You haven't changed a bit,' Arthur proclaimed. 'You're just the same as you were at fifteen.'

Sylvia, who had been teasing him with a breath of malice, was penitent at once: after all, he had once run away with her, and it would be difficult for any woman of twenty-eight not to rejoice a little at the implication of thirteen undestructive years.

'That last remark was like a cocoanut thrown by a monkey from the top of the cocoanut-palm,' she said. 'You meant it to be crushing, but it was crushed instead, and quite deliciously sweet inside.'

All the time that Sylvia had been talking so lightly, while the train was getting nearer and nearer to New York, there had lain at the back of her mind the insistent problem of her relationship to Arthur. The impossibility of their going on together as friends and nothing more had been firmly fixed upon her consciousness for a long time now, and the reason of this was to be sought for less in Arthur than in herself. So far they had preserved all the outward semblances of friendship, but she knew that one look from her eyes deep into his would transform him into her lover. She gave Arthur credit for telling himself quite sincerely that it would be 'caddish' to make love to her while he remained under what he would consider a grave obligation; and because with his temperament it would be as much in the ordinary routine of the day to make love to a woman as to dress himself in the morning, she praised his decorum and was really half-grateful to him for managing to keep his balance on the very small pedestal that she had provided. She might fairly presume, too, that if she let Arthur fall in love with her he would wish to marry her. Why should she not marry him? It was impossible to answer without accusing herself of a cynicism that she was far from feeling, yet without which she could not explain even to herself her quite definite repulsion from the idea of marrying him. The future, really now the immediate future, must be flung to chance: it was hopeless to arrogate to her fore-thought the determination of it; besides, here was New York already.

'We'd better go to my old hotel,' Sylvia suggested. Was it the reflection of her own perplexity, or did she detect in Arthur's accents a note of relief, as if he too had been watching the palisades of the Hudson and speculating upon the far horizon they concealed?

They dined at Rector's and after dinner they walked down Broadway into Madison Square, where upon this mild October night the Metropolitan Tower, the best of all the Gargantuan baby's toys, seemed to challenge the indifferent moon. They wandered up Madison Avenue, which was dark after the winking sky-signs of Broadway, and with its not very tall houses held a thought of London in the darkness. But when Sylvia turned to look back, it was no longer London, for she could see the great illuminated hands and numerals of the clock in the Metropolitan flashing from white to red for the hour. This clock without a dial-plate was the quietest of the Gargantuan baby's toys, for it did not strike; one was conscious of the almost pathetic protest against all those other damnably noisy toys; one felt he might become so enamoured of its pretty silence that to provide himself with a new diversion he might take to doubling the hours to keep pace with the rapidity of the life with which he played.

'It's almost as if we were walking up Haverstock Hill again,' said Arthur.

'And we're grown up now,' Sylvia murmured. 'Oh, dreadfully grown up really.'

They walked on for a while in silence: it was impossible to keep back a temptation to cheat time by leaping over the gulf of years and to be what they were when last they walked along together like this. Sylvia kept looking over her shoulder at the bland clock hanging in the sky behind them: at this distance the fabric of the tower had melted into the night and was no longer visible, which gave to the clock a strange significance and made it a simulacrum of time itself.

'You haven't changed a bit,' she said.

'Do you remember when you told me I looked like a cow? It was after—' he breathed perceptibly faster, 'after I kissed you.'

She would not ascribe his remembering what she had called him to an imperfectly healed scar of vanity, but with kindlier thoughts turned it to a memento of his affection for her. After all, she had loved him then; it had been a girl's love, but did there ever come with age a better love than the first flushed gathering of youth's opening flowers?

'Sylvia, I've thought about you ever since. When you drove me away from Colonial Terrace, I felt like killing myself. Surely we haven't met again for nothing.'

'Is it nothing unless I love you?' she asked fiercely, striving to turn the words into weapons to pierce the recesses of his thoughts and blunt themselves against a true heart.

'Ah no, I won't say that,' he cried. 'Besides I haven't the right to talk about love. You've been – Sylvia, I can't tell you what you've been to me since I met you again.'

'If I could only believe – oh, but believe with all of me that was and is and ever will be – that I could have been so much.'

'You have, you have.'

'Don't take my love as a light thing,' she warned him. 'It's not that I'm wanting so very much for myself, but I want to be so much to you.'

'Sylvia, won't you marry me? I couldn't ever take your love lightly. Indeed. Really.'

'Ah, it's not asking me to marry you that means you're serious. I'm not asking you what your intentions are. I'm asking if you want me.'

'Sylvia, I want you dreadfully.'

'Now, now?' she pressed.

'Now and always.'

They had stopped without being aware of it; a trolley-car jangled by, casting transitory lights that wavered across Arthur's face, and Sylvia could see how his eyes were shining. She dreaded lest by adding a few conventional words he should spoil what he had said so well, but he waited for her, as in the old days he had always waited.

'You're not cultivating this love, as a convalescent patient does for his nurse?' Sylvia demanded.

She stopped herself abruptly, conscious that every question she put to him was ultimately being put to herself.

'Did I ever not love you?' he asked. 'It was you that grew tired of me. It was you that sent me away.'

'Don't pretend that all these years you've been waiting for me to come back,' she scoffed.

'Of course not. What I'm trying to explain is that we can start now where we left off, that is if you will.'

He held out his hand half timidly.

'And if I won't?'

The hand dropped again to his side, and there was so much wounded sensitiveness in the slight gesture that Sylvia caught him to her as if he were a child who had fallen and needed comforting.

'When I first put my head on your shoulder,' she murmured. 'Oh, how well I can remember the day – such a sparkling day with London spread out like life at our feet. Now we're in the middle of New York, but it seems just as far away from us two as London was that day – and life,' she added with a sigh.

VII

Circumstances seemed to applaud almost immediately the step that Sylvia had taken: there was no long delay caused by looking for work in New York, which might have destroyed romance by its interposition of fretful hopes and disappointments. A variety company was going to leave in November for a tour in Eastern Canada. At least two months would be spent in the French provinces, and Sylvia's bilingual accomplishment was exactly what the manager wanted.

'I'm getting on,' she laughed. 'I began by singing French songs with an English accent; I advanced from them to acting English words with a French accent; now I'm going to be employed in doing both. But what does it matter? The great thing is that we should be together.'

That was where Arthur made the difference to her life: he was securing her against the loneliness that at twenty-eight was beginning once more to haunt her imagination. What did art matter? It had never been anything but a refuge.

Arthur himself was engaged to sing, and though he had not such a good voice as Claude Raglan, he sang with much better taste and was really musical. Sylvia was annoyed to find herself making comparisons between Claude and Arthur: it happened at the moment that Arthur was fussing about his number on the programme, and she could not help being reminded of Claude's attitude towards his own artistic importance. She consoled herself by thinking that it should always be one of her aims to prevent the likeness growing any closer; then she laughed at herself for this resolve, which savoured of developing Arthur, that process she had always so much contemned.

They opened at Toronto, and after playing a week Arthur caught a chill and was out of the programme for a fortnight; this gave Sylvia a fresh opportunity of looking after him; and Toronto in wet raw weather was so dreary that to come back to the invalid after the performance, notwithstanding the ineffable discomfort of the hotel, was to come back home. During this time Sylvia gave Arthur a history of the years that had gone by since they parted, and it puzzled her that he should be so jealous of the past; she wondered why she could not feel the same jealousy about his past, and she found herself trying to regret that red-haired girl and many others on account of the obvious pleasure such regrets afforded Arthur. She used to wonder, too, why she always left out certain incidents and obscured certain aspects of her own past, whether for instance she did not tell him about Michael Fane on her own account, or because she was afraid that Arthur would perceive a superficial resemblance between himself and Claude and a very real one between himself and Lily, or because she would have resented from Arthur the least expression, not so much of contempt as even of mild surprise at Michael's behaviour. Another subject she could never discuss with Arthur was her mother's love for her father, notwithstanding that his own mother's elopement with a groom must have prevented the least criticism on his side; here again she wondered if her reserve was due to loyalty, or to a vague sense of temperamental repetition that was condemning her to stand in the same relation to Arthur as her mother to her father. She positively had to run away from the idea that Arthur had his prototype; she was shutting him up in a box and scarcely even looking at him, which was as good as losing him altogether really. Even when she did look at him, she handled him with such exaggerated carefulness for fear of his getting broken that all the pleasure of possession was lost. Perhaps she should have had an equal anxiety to preserve intact anybody else with whom she might have thrown in her lot; but when she thought over this attitude, it was dismaying enough, and seemed to imply an incapacity on her part to enjoy fully anything in life.

'I've grown out of being destructive: at least I think I have. I wonder if the normal process from jacobinism to the intense conservatism of age is due to wisdom, jealousy, or fear.'

'Arthur, what are your politics?' she asked aloud.

He looked up from the game of patience he was playing, a game in which he was apt to attribute the pettiest personal motives to the court-cards, whenever he failed to get out.

'Politics?' he echoed vaguely. 'I don't think I ever had any. I suppose I'm a conservative. Oh, yes, certainly I'm a conservative. That infernal Knave of Hearts is covered now!' he added in an aggrieved voice.

'Well, I didn't cover it,' said Sylvia.

'No, dear, of course you didn't. But it really is a most extraordinary thing that I always get done by the Knaves.'

'You share your misfortune with the rest of humanity, if that's any consolation.'

The conversation was interrupted by the entrance of Orlone. He was a huge Neapolitan with the countenance of a gigantic and swarthy Punch, who had been trying to get back to Naples for twenty years, but had been prevented at first by his passion for gambling and afterwards by an unwilling wife and a numerous family. Orlone made even Toronto cheerful, and before he had come two paces into a room Sylvia always began to laugh; he never said anything deliberately funny except on the stage, but laughter emanated from him infectiously, as yawning might. Though he had spent twenty years in America, he still spoke the most imperfect English; and when he and Sylvia had done laughing at one another they used to laugh all over again, she at his English, he at her Italian. When they had finished laughing at that, Orlone used to swear marvellously for Sylvia's benefit whenever she should again visit Sirene: and she would teach him equally tremendous oaths in case he should ever come to London. When they had finished laughing at this, Orlone would look over Arthur's shoulder and, after making the most ridiculous gestures of caution, would finally burst out into an absolute roar of laughter right in Arthur's ear.

'*Pazienza*,' Sylvia would say, pointing to the outspread cards.

'*Brava signora! Come parla bene!*'

And of course this was obviously so absurd a statement that it would set them off laughing again.

'You are a pair of lunatics,' Arthur would protest; he would have liked to be annoyed at his game's being interrupted, but he was powerless to repulse Orlone's good humour.

When they returned to New York in the spring and Sylvia looked back at the tour, she divined how much of her pleasure in it had been owed to Orlone's all-pervading mirth. He had really provided the robust and full-blooded contrast to Arthur that had been necessary. It was not exactly that without him their existence together would have been insipid – oh, no, there was nothing insipid about Arthur, but one appreciated his delicacy after that rude and massive personality. When they had travelled over leagues of snow-covered country, Orlone had always lightened the journey with gay Neapolitan songs, and sometimes with tender ones like *Torna da Surriento*. It was then that, gazing out over the white waste, she had been able to take Arthur's hand and sigh to be sitting with him on a Sirenian cliff, to smell again the rosemary, and crumble with her fingers the sun-burnt earth. But this capacity of Orlone's for conjuring up the long Parthenopean shore was nothing more than might have been achieved by any terra-cotta Silenus in a provincial museum. After Silenus, what nymph would not turn to Hylas somewhat gratefully? It had been the greatest fun in the world to drive in tinkling sledges through Montreal, with Orlone to tease the driver until he was as sore as the head of the bear that in his fur coat he resembled: it had been fun to laugh with Orlone in Quebec and Ottawa and everywhere else; but after so much laughter it had always been particularly delightful to be alone again with Arthur, and to feel that he too was particularly enjoying being alone with her.

'I really do think we get on well together,' she said to him.

'Of course we do.'

And was there in the way he agreed with her just the least suggestion that he should have been surprised if she had not enjoyed his company, an almost imperceptible hint of complacency, or was it condescension?

'I really must get out of this habit of poking my nose into other people's motives,' Sylvia told herself. 'I'm like a horrid little boy with a new penknife. Arthur could fairly say to me that I forced myself upon him. I did really. I went steaming into the Auburn Hotel like a salvage-tug. There's the infernal side of obligations – I can't really quite free myself from the notion that Arthur ought to be grateful to me. He's in a false position through no fault of his own, and he's behaving beautifully. It's my own cheap cynicism that's to blame. I wish I could discover some mental bitter-aloes that would cure me of biting my mind, as I cured myself of biting my nails.'

Sylvia was very glad that Arthur succeeded in getting an engagement that spring to act and that she did not; she was really anxious to let him feel that she should be dependent on him for a while. The result would have been entirely satisfactory but for one flaw – the increase in Arthur's sense of his own artistic importance. Sylvia would not have minded this so much, if he had possessed enough of it to make him oblivious of the world's opinion, but it was always more of a vanity than a pride, chiefly concerned with the personal impression he made. It gave him much more real pleasure to be recognized by two shopgirls on their afternoon out than to be praised by a leading critic. Sylvia would have liked him to be equally contemptuous of either form of flattery, but that he should revel in both, and actually esteem more valuable the recognition accorded him by a shopgirl's backward glance and a nudge from her companion seemed to be lamentable.

'I don't see why you should despise me for being pleased,' Arthur said. 'I'm only pleased because it's a proof that I'm getting known.'

'But they'd pay the same compliment to a man with a wen on his nose.'

'No doubt, but also to any famous man,' Arthur added.

Sylvia could have screamed with irritation at his lack of any sense of proportion. Why could he not be like Jack Airdale, who had never suffered from any illusion that what he was doing, so far as art was concerned, was not essentially insignificant? Yet after all was she not being unreasonable in paying so much attention to a childish piece of vanity that was inseparable from the true histrionic temperament?

'I'm sorry, Arthur. I think I'm being rather unfair to you. I only criticize you because I want you to be always the best of you. I see your point of view, but I was irritated by the giggles.'

'I wasn't paying the least attention to the girls.'

'Oh, I wasn't jealous,' she said quickly. 'Oh, no, darling Arthur, even with the great affection that I have for you, I shall never be able to be jealous of your making eyes at shopgirls.'

When Arthur's engagement seemed likely to come to an end in the summer, they discussed plans and decided to take a holiday in the country, somewhere in Maine or Vermont. Arthur as usual set the scene beforehand, but as he set it quite in accord with Sylvia's taste, she did not mind. Indeed, their holiday in Vermont on the borders of Lake Champlain was as near as she ever got to being perfectly happy with Arthur, happy that is to the point of feeling like a chill the prospect of separation. Sylvia was inclined to say that all Arthur's faults were due to the theatre and that when one had him like this in simple surroundings the best side of him was uppermost and visible, like a spun coin that shows a simple head when it falls.

Sylvia found that she had brought with her by chance the manuscript of the poems given to her by the outcast Englishman in Paris, and Arthur was very anxious that she should come back to her idea of rendering these: he had already composed a certain number of unimportant songs in his career, but now the Muses smiled upon him – or perhaps it might be truer to speak of her own smiles, Sylvia thought – with such favour that he set a dozen poems to the very accompaniment they wanted, the kind of music, moreover, that suited Sylvia's voice.

'We must get these done in New York,' he said; but that week a letter came from Olive Airdale, and Sylvia had a sudden longing for England: she did not think she would make an effort to do anything in America. The truth was that she had supplemented the Englishman's poems with an idea of her own to give impressions gathered from her own life; it was strange how abruptly the longing to express herself had arrived, but it had arrived with a force and fierceness that was undeniable. It had come, too, with that authentic fever of secrecy that she divined a woman must feel in the first moment of knowing that she has conceived; she could not have imparted her sense of creation to anyone else: such an intimacy of revelation was too shocking to be contemplated. Somehow she was sure that this strange shamefulness was right and that she was entitled to hug within herself the conception that would soon enough be turned to the travail of birth.

'By Jove, Sylvia, this holiday *has* done you good,' Arthur exclaimed.

She kissed him because, ignorant though he was of the true reason, she owed him thanks for her looks.

'Sylvia, if we go back to England, do let's be married first.'

'Why?'

'Why, because it's not fair on me.'

'On you?'

'Yes, on me. People will always blame me, of course.'

'What has it got to do with anybody else except me?'

'My mother—'

'My dear Arthur,' Sylvia interrupted sharply, 'if your mother ran away with a groom, she'll be the first person to sympathize with my point of view.'

'I suppose you're trying to be cruel,' said Arthur.

'And succeeding to judge by your dolorous mouth. No, my dear, let the suggestion of marriage come from me. I shan't be hurt if you refuse.'

'Well, are we to pretend we're married?' Arthur asked hopelessly.

'Certainly not, if by that you mean that I'm to put *Mrs. Arthur Madden* on a visiting card. Don't look so frightened. I'm not proposing to march into drawing-rooms with a big drum to proclaim my emancipation from the social decencies. Don't worry me, Arthur; it's all much too complicated to explain, but I'll tell you one thing: I'm not going to marry you merely to remove the world's censure of your conduct, and as long as you feel about marrying me as you might feel about letting me carry a heavy bag, I'll never marry you.'

'I don't feel a bit like that about it,' he protested. 'If I could leave you, I'd leave you now. But the very thought of losing you makes my heart stop beating. It's like suddenly coming to the edge of a precipice. I know perfectly well that you despise me at heart. You think I'm a wretched actor with no feelings off the stage. You think I don't know my own mind, if you even admit that I've got a mind at all. But I'm thirty-one; I'm not a boy. I've had a good many women in love with me. Now don't begin to laugh. I'm determined to say what I ought to have said long ago, and should have said, if I hadn't been afraid the whole time of losing you. If I lose you now, it can't be helped. I'd sooner lose you than go on being treated like a child. What I want to say is that, though I know you think it wasn't worth while being loved by the women who've loved me, I do think it was. I'm not in the least ashamed of them. Most of them at any rate were beautiful, though I admit that all of them put together wouldn't have made up for missing you. You're a thousand times cleverer than me. You've got much more personality. You've every right to consider you've thrown yourself away on me. But the fact remains that you've done it. We've been together now a year. That proves that there *is* something in me. I'm prouder of this year with you than of all the rest of my life. You've developed me in the most extraordinary way.'

'I have?' Sylvia burst in.

'Of course you have. But I'm not going to be treated like a mantis.'

'Like a what?'

'A mantis. You can read about it in that French book on insects. The female eats the male. But I'm damned well not going to be eaten. I'm not going back to England with you unless you marry me.'

'I'm not going to marry you,' Sylvia declared.

'Very well, then I shall try to get an engagement on tour and we'll separate.'

'So much the better,' she said. 'I've got a good deal to occupy myself at present.'

'Of course you can have the music I wrote for those poems,' said Arthur.

'Damn your music,' she replied.

Sylvia was so much obsessed with the conviction of having at last found a medium for expressing herself in art that, though she was vaguely aware of having a higher regard for Arthur at this moment than she had ever had, she could only behold him as a troublesome visitor that was preventing her from sitting down to work.

Arthur went off on tour; Sylvia took an apartment in New York far away up town and settled down to test her inspiration. In six months she lived her whole life over again and of every personality that had touched her own and left its mark she made a separate presentation. Her great anxiety was to give to each sketch the air of an improvisation, and in the course of it to make her people reveal their permanent characters rather than their transient emotions. It was really based on the art of the impersonator who comes on with a cocked hat, sticks out his neck, puts his hands behind his back and his legs apart, leans over to the audience, and whispers 'Napoleon.' Sylvia thought she could extend the pleasures of recognition beyond the mere mimicry of externals to a finer mimicry of essentials. She wanted an audience to clap not because she could bark sufficiently like a real dog to avoid being mistaken for a kangaroo, but because she could be sufficiently Mrs. Gainsborough not to be recognized as Mrs. Beardmore – yet without relying upon their respective sizes in corsets to mark the difference. She did not intend to use even make-up: the entertainment was always to be an improvisation. It was also to be undramatic: that is to say, it was not to obtain its effect by working to a climax, so that, however well hidden the mechanism might have been during the course of the presentation, the machinery would reveal itself at the end. Sylvia wanted to make each member of the audience feel that he had dreamed her improvisation, or rather she hoped that he would gain from it that elusive sensation of having lived it before, and that the effect upon each person listening to her should be ultimately incommunicable like a dream. She was sure now that she could achieve this effect with the poems, not as she had originally supposed through their objective truthfulness, but through their subjective truth. That outcast Englishman should be one of her improvisations, and of course, the original idea of letting the poems be accompanied by music would be ruinous: one might as well illustrate them with a magic-lantern. As to her own inventions, she must avoid giving them a set form, because whatever actors might urge to the contrary, a play could never really be performed twice by the same cast. She would have a scene painted like those futurist Italian pictures: they were trying to do with colour what she was trying to do with acting: they were striving to escape from the representation of mere externals, and often succeeding almost too well, she added with a smile. She would get hold of Ronald Walker in London, who doubtless by now would be too prosperous to serve her purpose himself, but who would probably know of some newly fledged painter anxious to flap his wings.

318

At the end of six months Sylvia had evolved enough improvisations to make a start; she went to bed tired out with the last night's work, and woke up in the morning with a sense of blankness at the realization of there being nothing to do that day. All the time she had been working, she had been content to be alone; she had even looked forward to amusing herself in New York when her work was finished. Now the happy moment was come, and she could feel nothing but this empty boredom. She wondered what Arthur was doing, and she reproached herself for the way in which she had discarded him; she had been so thrilled by the notion that she was necessary to somebody: it had seemed to her the consummation of so many heedless years. Yet no sooner had she successfully imposed herself upon Arthur than she was eager to think of nothing but herself without caring a bit about his point of view. Now that she could do nothing more with her work until the test of public performance was applied to it, she was bored: in fact she missed Arthur. The truth was that half the pleasure of being necessary to somebody else had been that he should be necessary to her. But marriage with Arthur? Marriage with a curly-headed actor? Marriage with anybody? No, that must wait, at any rate until she had given the fruit of these six months to the world. She could not be hampered by belonging to anybody before that.

'I do think I'm justified in taking myself a little seriously for a while,' said Sylvia, 'and in shutting my eyes to my own absurdity. Self-mockery is dangerous beyond a certain point. I really will give this idea of mine a fair chance. If I'm a failure, Arthur will love me all the more through vanity, and if I'm a success – I suppose really he'll be vain of that too.'

Sylvia telegraphed to Arthur, and heard that he expected to be back in New York at the end of the month: he was in Buffalo this week. Nothing could keep her a moment longer in New York alone, and she went up to join him. She had a sudden fear when she arrived that she might find him occupied with a girl; in fact really when she came to think of the manner in which she had left him, it was most improbable that she should not; she nearly turned round and went back to New York; but her real anxiety to see Arthur and talk to him about her work made her decide to take the risk of what might be the deepest humiliation of her life. It was strange how much she wanted to talk about what she had done: the desire to do so now was as overmastering an emotion as had been in the first moment of conception the urgency of silence.

Sylvia was spared the shock of finding Arthur wrapped up in some one else.

'Sylvia, how wonderful! what a relief to see you again,' he exclaimed.

'I've been longing for you to see me in the part I'm playing now. It's certainly the most successful thing I've done. I'm so glad you kept me from wasting myself any longer on that concert work. I really believe I've made a big hit at last.'

Sylvia was almost as much taken aback to find Arthur radiant with the prospect of success as she would have been to find him head over ears in love. She derived very little satisfaction from the way in which he attributed his success to her; she was not at all in the mood for being a god-mother, now that she had a baby of her own.

'I'm so glad, old son. That's splendid. Now I want to talk about the work I've been doing all these six months.'

Forthwith she plunged into the details of the scheme to which Arthur listened attentively enough, though he only became really enthusiastic when he could introduce analogies with his own successful performance.

'You will go in front to-night?' he begged. 'I'm awfully keen to hear what you think of my show. Half my pleasure in the hit has been spoilt by your not having seen it. Besides, I think you'll be interested in noticing that once or twice I try to get the same effect as you're trying for in these impersonations.'

'Damn your eyes, Arthur, they're not impersonations: they're Improvisations.'

'Did I say impersonations? I'm sorry,' said Arthur, looking rather frightened.

'Yes, you'd better placate me,' she threatened. 'Or I'll spend my whole time looking at Niagara and never go near your show.'

However, Sylvia did go to see the play that night and found that Arthur really was excellent in his part, which was that of the usual young man in musical comedy who wanders about in a well-cut flannel suit followed by six young women with parasols to smother him with affection, melody, and lace. But how even in the intoxication of success, he had managed to establish a single analogy with what she proposed to do was beyond comprehension.

Arthur came out of the stage-door, wreathed in questions.

'You were in such a hurry to get out,' said Sylvia, 'that you haven't taken off your make-up properly. You'll get arrested if you walk about like that. I hear the sumptuary laws in Buffalo are very strict.'

'No, don't rag. Did you like the Hydrangea song? Do you remember the one I mean?'

He hummed the tune.

'I warn you, Arthur, there's recently been a moral uplift in Buffalo. You will be sewn up in a barrel and flung into Niagara, if you don't take care. No, seriously I think your show was capital. Which brings me to the point. We sail for Europe at the end of April.'

'Oh, but do you think it's wise for me to leave America now that I've really got my foot in?'

'Do you still want to marry me?'

'More than ever,' he assured her.

'Very well then. Your only chance of marrying me is to leave New York without a murmur. I've thought it all out. As soon as I get back, I shall spend my last shilling on fitting out my show; when I've produced it and when I've found out that I've not been making a fool of myself for the last six months, perhaps I'll marry you. Until then – as friends we met, as anything more than friends we part. Got me, Steve?'

'But, Sylvia—'

'But me no buts, or you'll get my goat. Understand my meaning, Mr. Stevenson?'

'Yes, only—'

'The discussion's closed.'

'Are we engaged?'

'I don't know. We'll have to see our agents about that.'

'Oh, don't rag me. Marriage is not a joke. You are a most extraordinary girl.'

'Thanks for the discount: I shall be thirty in three months, don't forget. Talking of the advantages of rouge, you might get rid of some of yours before supper if you don't mind.'

'Are we engaged?' Arthur repeated firmly.

'No, the engagement ring and the marriage bells will be pealed simultaneously. You're as free as Boccaccio, old son.'

'You're in one of those moods when it's impossible to argue with you.'

'So much the better. We shall enjoy our supper all the more. I'm so excited at the idea of going back to England. After all, I shall have been away nearly three years. I shall find god-children who can talk. Think of that. Arthur, don't you want to be back?'

'Yes, if I can get a shop. I think it's madness for me to leave New York, but I daren't let you go alone.'

The anticipation of being in England again and of putting to the test her achievement could not charm away all Sylvia's regrets at leaving America, most of all New York. She owed to New York this new stability that she discovered in her life. She owed to some action of New York upon herself the delight of inspiration, the sweet purgatory of effort, the hope of a successful end to her dreams. It was the only city of which she had ever taken a formal farewell, such as she took from the top of the

Metropolitan Tower upon a lucid morning in April. The city lay beneath with no magic of smoke to lend a meretricious romance to its chequered severity; a city encircled with silver waters and pavilioned by huge skies, expressing modern humanity as the great monuments of ancient architecture express the mighty dead.

'We too can create our Parthenons,' thought Sylvia, as she sank to earth in the florid elevator.

They crossed the Atlantic in one of the smaller Cunard liners; the voyage was uneventful; nearly all the passengers in turn told Sylvia why they were not travelling in one of the large ships, but nobody suggested as a reason that the smaller ships were cheaper.

When they reached England, Arthur went to stay with his mother at Dulwich; Sylvia went to the Airdales; she wanted to set her scheme in motion, but she promised to come and stay at Dulwich later on.

'At last you've come back,' Olive exclaimed on the verge of tears. 'I've missed you dreadfully.'

'Great Scott, look at Sylvius and Rose,' Sylvia exclaimed. 'They're like two pigs made of pink sugar. Pity we never thought of it at the time, or they could have been christened Scarlet and Crimson.'

'Darlings, isn't godmamma horrid to you?' said Olive.

'Here! Here! What are you teaching them to call me?'

'Dat's godmamma,' said Sylvius in a thick voice.

'Dat's godmamma,' Rose echoed.

'Not on your life, cullies,' their godmother announced. 'Unless you want a thick ear each.'

'Give me one,' said Sylvius stolidly.

'Give me one,' Rose echoed.

'How can you tease the poor darlings so?' Olive exclaimed.

'Sylvius will have one,' he announced in the same thick monotone.

'Rose will have one,' echoed his sister.

Sylvia handed her godson a large painted ball.

'Here's your thick ear, Pork.'

Sylvius laughed fatly: the ball and the new name both pleased him.

'And here's yours,' she said, offering another to Rose, who waited to see what her brother did with his and then proceeded to do the same with the same fat laugh: suddenly, however, her lips puckered.

'What is it, darling?' her mother asked anxiously.

'Rose wants to be said Pork.'

'You didn't call her Pork,' Olive translated reproachfully to Sylvia.

'Give me back the ball,' said Sylvia. 'Now then; here's your thick ear, Porka.'

Rose laughed ecstatically: after two ornaments had been broken Jack came in, and the children retired with their nurse.

Sylvia found that family life had not spoilt Jack's interest in that career of hers; indeed he was so much excited by her news that he suggested omitting for once the ceremony of seeing the twins' being given their bath in order not to lose any of the short time available before he should have to go down to the theatre. Sylvia, however, would not hear of any change in the domestic order, and reminded Jack that she was proposing to quarter herself on them for some time.

'I know, it's terrific,' he exclaimed.

The excitement of the bath was always considerable, but this evening with Sylvia's assistance it became acute: Sylvius hit his nurse in the eye with the soap, and Rose wrought up to a fever of emulation managed to hurl the sponge into the grate.

Jack was enthusiastic about Sylvia's scheme: she was not quite sure that he understood exactly at what she was aiming, but he wished her so well that in any case his criticism would have had slight value; he gave instead his devoted attention, and that seemed a pledge of success. Success! Success! it sounded like a cataract in her ears, drowning every other sound. She wondered if the passion of her life was to be success. On no thoughts urged so irresistibly had she ever sailed to sleep, nor had she ever wakened in such a buoyancy, greeting the day as a swimmer greets the sea.

'Now what about the backing?' Jack asked.

'Backing? I'll back myself. You'll be my manager. I've enough to hire the Pierian Hall for a day and a night. I've enough to pay for one scene. Which reminds me, I must get hold of Ronald Walker. You'll sing, Jack, two songs? Oh, and there's Arthur Madden. He'll sing too.'

'Who's he?' Olive asked.

'Oh, didn't I tell you about him?' said Sylvia, almost too nonchalantly she feared. 'He's rather good. Quite good really. I'll tell you about him some time. By the way I've talked so much about myself and my plans that I've never asked about other people. How's the Countess?'

Olive looked grave.

'We don't ever see them, but everybody says that Clarehaven is going the pace tremendously.'

'Have they retreated to Devonshire?'

'Oh no, didn't you hear? I thought I told you in one of my letters. He had to sell the family place. Do you remember a man called Leopold Hausberg?'

'Do I not?' Sylvia exclaimed. 'He took a flat once for a chimpanzee instead of Lily.'

'Well, he's become Lionel Houston this year, and he's talked about with Dorothy a good deal. Of course, he's very rich, but I do hope there's nothing in what people say. Poor Dorothy!'

'She'll survive even the Divorce Court,' Sylvia said. 'I wish I knew what had become of Lily. She might have danced in my show. I suppose it's too late now though. Poor Lily! I say, we're getting very compassionate, you and I, Olive. Are you and Jack going to have any more kids?'

'Sylvia darling,' Olive exclaimed with a blush.

Sylvia had intended to stay a week or two with the Airdales and after having set in motion the preliminaries of her undertaking to go down to Dulwich and visit Mrs. Madden; but she thought she would get hold of Ronnie Walker first, and with this object went to the Café Royal, where she should be certain of finding either him or a friend who would know where he was.

Sylvia had scarcely time to look round her in the swirl of gilt and smoke and chatter, before Ronald Walker himself, wearing now a long pale beard, greeted her.

'My dear Ronald, what's the matter? Are you tired of women? You look more like a grate than a great man,' Sylvia exclaimed. 'Cut it off and give it to your landlady to stuff her fireplace this summer.'

'What shall we drink?' he asked imperturbably.

'I've been absinthe for so long that really—'

'It's a vermouth point,' added Ronald.

'Ronnie, you devil, I can't go on, it's too whisky. Well, of course after that we ought both to drink port and brandy. Don't you find it difficult to clean your beard?'

'I'm not a messy feeder,' said Ronnie.

'You don't paint with it then?'

'Only Cubist pictures.'

Sylvia launched out into an account of her work, and demanded his help for the painting of the scene.

'I want the back-cloth to be a city – not to represent a city, mark you, but to be a city.'

She told him about New York as beheld from the Metropolitan Tower, and exacted from the chosen painter the ability to make the audience think that.

'I'm too old-fashioned for you, my dear,' said Ronald.

'Oh you, my dear man, of course! If I asked you for a city, you'd give me a view from a Pierrot's window of a Harlequin who'd stolen the first five numbers of the Yellow Book from a Pantaloon who kept a secondhand bookshop in a street-scene by Steinlen and whose daughter

Columbine, having died of grief at being deserted by the New English Art Club, had been turned into a bookplate. No, I want some fierce young genius of to-day.'

Over their drinks, they discussed possible candidates; finally Ronald said he would invite a certain number of the most representative and least representational young modern painters to his studio, from whom Sylvia might make her choice. Accordingly, two or three days later Sylvia visited Ronald in Grosvenor Road. For the moment when she entered, she thought that he had been playing a practical joke upon her, for it seemed impossible that such extraordinary people could be real. The northerly light of the studio, severe and virginal, was less kind than the feverish exhalation of the Café Royal.

'They are real?' she whispered to her host.

'Oh yes, they're quite real, and in deadly earnest. Each of them represents a school and each of them thinks I've been converted to his point of view. I'll introduce Morphew.'

He beckoned to a tall young man in black, who looked like a rolled-up umbrella with a jade handle.

'Morphew, this is Miss Scarlett. She's nearly as advanced as you are. Sylvia, this is Morphew the Azurist.'

Walker maliciously withdrew when he had made the introduction.

'Ought I to know what an Azurist is?' Sylvia asked. She felt that it was an unhappy opening for the conversation, but she did not want to hurt his religious feelings if Azurism was a religion, and if it was a trade she might be excused for not knowing what is was, such a rare trade must it be.

Mr. Morphew smiled in a superior way.

'I think most people have heard about me by now.'

'Ah, but I've been abroad.'

'Several of my affirmations have been translated and published in France, Germany, Russia, Spain, Italy, Sweden, Hungary, and Holland,' said Mr. Morphew in a tone that seemed to imply that if Sylvia had not grasped who he was by now she never would, in which case it was scarcely worth his while to go on talking to her.

'Oh dear, what a pity,' she exclaimed. 'I was in Montenegro all last year, so I must have missed them. I don't *think* you're known in Montenegro yet. It's such a small country; I should have been sure to hear about anything like that.'

'Like what?' thought Sylvia, turning up in her mind's eyes to heaven.

Mr. Morphew was evidently not sure what sort of language was spoken in Montenegro, and thought it wiser to instruct Sylvia than to expose his own ignorance.

'What colour is that?' he suddenly demanded, pointing to the orange coverlet of a settee.

'Orange,' said Sylvia. 'Perhaps it's inclining to some shade of brown.'

'Orange! Brown!' Mr. Morphew scoffed. 'It's blue.'

'Oh, but it's not,' she contradicted. 'There's nothing blue about it.'

'Blue,' repeated Mr. Morphew. 'All is blue. The Azurists deny that there is anything but blue. Blue,' he continued in a rapt voice. 'Blue! I was a Blanchist at first; but when we quarrelled, most of the Blanchists followed me. I shall publish the nineteenth affirmation of the Azurists next week. If you give me your address, I'll send you a copy. We're going to give the Ovists hell in a new magazine that we're bringing out. We find that affirmations are not enough.'

'Will it be an ordinary magazine?' Sylvia asked. 'Will you have stories, for instance?'

'We don't admit that stories exist. Life-rays exist. There will be life-rays in our magazine.'

'I suppose they'll be pretty blue,' said Sylvia.

'All life-rays are blue.'

'I suppose you don't mind wet weather?' she suggested. 'Because it must be rather difficult to know when it's going to clear up.'

'There are degrees of blue,' Mr. Morphew explained.

'I see. Life isn't just one vast reckless blue. Well, thank you very much for being so patient with my old-fashioned optical ideas. I do hope you'll go to America and tell them that their leaves turn blue in autumn. Anyway, you'll feel quite at home crossing the ocean, though some people won't even admit that's blue.'

Sylvia left the Azurist and rejoined Ronald.

'Well,' he laughed. 'You look quite frightened.'

'My dear, I've just done a bolt from the blue. You are a beast to rag my enthusiasms. Isn't there anybody here whose serious view of himself I can endorse?'

'Well, there's Pattison the Ovist. He maintains that everything resolves itself into ovals.'

'I think I should almost prefer Azurism,' said Sylvia. 'What about the Blanchists?'

'Oh, you wouldn't like them: they maintain that there's no such thing as colour; their pictures depend on the angle at which they're hung.'

'But if there's no such thing as colour, how can they paint?'

'They don't: their canvasses are blank. Then there are the Combinationists. They don't repudiate colour, but they repudiate paint. The most famous Combinationist picture exhibited so far consisted of half a match-box, a piece of orange peel, and some sealing-wax, all stuck upon a slip of sugar-paper. The other Combinationists wanted to commit suicide because they despaired of surpassing it. Roger Cadbury wrote a superb introduction, pointing out that it must be either liked or disliked, but that it was impossible to do both or neither. It was that picture which inspired Hezekiah Penny to write what is considered one of his finest poems. You know it perhaps?

> *Why do I sing?*
> *There is no reason why I should continue:*
> *This image of the essential bin is better*
> *Than the irritated uvulas of modern poets.*

'That caused almost as great sensation as the picture, because some of his fellow-poets maintained that he had no right to speak for anybody but himself.'

'But this is madness,' Sylvia exclaimed, looking round her at the studio, where the representatives of modernity eyed one another with surprise and distaste like unusual fish in the tank of an aquarium. 'Behind all this rubbish surely something truly progressive exists. You've deliberately invited all the charlatans and impostors to meet me. I tell you, Ronnie, I saw lots of pictures in New York that were eccentric, but that were striving to rediscover life in painting. You're prejudiced, because you belong to the decade before all this, and you've taken a delight in showing me all the extravagant side of it. You should emulate Tithonus.'

'Who was he?'

'Now don't pretend you can't follow a simple allusion. The gentleman who fell in love with Aurora.'

'Didn't he get rather tired of living for ever?'

'Oh well, that was because he grew a beard like you. Don't nail my allusions to the counter: they're not lies.'

'I'll take pity on you,' said Ronnie. 'There is quite a clever youth, whom I intended for you from the beginning. He's coming in later, when the rest have gone.'

When she and Ronnie were alone again and before Lucian Hope, the young painter, arrived, Sylvia looking through one of his sketch-books came across a series of studies of a girl in the practice-dress of the ballet; he told her it was Jenny Pearl.

'Maurice Avery's Jenny,' she murmured. 'What happened to her?'

'Didn't you hear about it? She was killed by her husband. It was a horrible business. Maurice went down to see her where she lived in the country, and this brute shot her. It was last summer. The papers were full of it.'

'And what happened to Maurice?'

'Oh, he nearly went off his head. He's wandering about in Morocco probably.'

'Where I met him,' said Sylvia.

'But didn't he tell you?'

'Oh, it was before. More than three years ago. We talked about her.'

Sylvia shuddered: one of her improvisations had been Maurice Avery: she must burn it.

Lucian Hope arrived before Sylvia could ask any more questions about the horrible event; she was glad to escape from the curiosity that would have turned it into a tale of the police-court. The newcomer was not more than twenty-two, perhaps less – too young at any rate to have escaped from the unconventionality of artistic attire that stifled all personality. But he had squirrel's eyes, and was not really like an undertaker. He was shy, too; so shy that Sylvia wondered how he could tolerate being stared at in the street on account of his odd appearance. She would have liked to ask him what pleasure he derived from such mimicry of a sterile and professional distinction, but she feared to hurt his young vanity; moreover, she was disarmed by those squirrel's eyes, so sharp and bright even in the falling dusk. The three of them talked restlessly for a while; Sylvia seeing that Ronald was preparing to broach the subject for which they were met anticipated him with a call for attention, and began one of her improvisations: it was of Concetta lost in a greater city than Granada. By the silence that followed she knew that her companions had cared for it, and she changed to Mrs. Gainsborough: then she finished up with three of the poems.

'Could you paint me a scene for that?' she asked quickly to avoid any comment.

'Rather,' replied the young man very eagerly; though it was nearly dark now, she could see his eyes flashing real assurance.

They all three dined together that evening, and Lucian Hope, ever since Sylvia had let him know that she stood beside him to conquer the world, lost his early shyness and talked volubly of what she wanted and of what he wanted to do. Ronald Walker presided in the background of the ardent conversation, and as they came out of the restaurant he took Sylvia's arm for a moment.

'All right?'

'Quite all right, thanks.'

'So's your show going to be. Not so terribly modern as you gave me to suppose. But that's not a great fault.'

Sylvia and Lucian Hope spent a good deal of time together, so much was there to talk about in connection with the great enterprise: she brought him to the Airdales' that he might meet Jack, who was supposed to have charge of the financial arrangements. The sight of the long-haired young man made Sylvius cry, and as a matter of course Rose also, which embarrassed Lucian Hope a good deal, especially when he had to listen to an explanation of himself by Oliver for the children's consolation.

'He's a gollywog,' Sylvius howled.

'He's a gollywog,' Rose echoed.

'He's come to gobble us,' Sylvius bellowed.

'To gobble us, to gobble us,' Rose wailed.

'He's not a gollywog, darlings,' their mother declared. 'He makes pretty pictures, oh, such pretty pictures of—'

'He *is* a gollywog,' choked Sylvius in an ecstasy of rage and fear.

'A gollywog, a gollywog,' Rose insisted.

Their mother changed her tactics.

'But he's a kind gollywog. Oh, such a kind gollywog, the kindest nicest gollywog that was ever thought of.'

'He *is*-ent,' both children proclaimed. 'He's bad!'

'Don't you think I'd better go?' asked the painter. 'I think it must be my hair that's upsetting them.'

He started towards the door, but unfortunately he was on the wrong side of the children, who seeing him make a move in their direction, set up such an appalling yell that the poor young man drew back in despair. In the middle of this the maid entered, announcing Mr. Arthur Madden who followed close upon her heels. Sylvius and Rose were by this time obsessed with the idea of an invasion by an army of gollywogs, and Arthur's pleasant face took on for them the dreaded lineaments of the foe. Both children clung shrieking to their mother's skirts: Sylvia and Jack were leaning back, incapable through laughter: Arthur and Lucian Hope surveyed miserably the scene they had created. At last the nurse arrived to rescue the twins, and they were carried away without being persuaded to change their minds about the inhuman nature of the two visitors.

Arthur apologized for worrying Sylvia, but his mother was so anxious to know when she was coming down to Dulwich that, as he had been up in town seeing about an engagement, he had not been able to resist coming to visit her.

Sylvia felt penitent for having abandoned Arthur so completely since they had arrived in England, and she told him she would go back with him that very afternoon.

'Oh, but Miss Scarlett,' protested Lucian. 'Don't you remember? We arranged to explore Limehouse to-morrow.'

Arthur looked at the painter very much as if he were indeed the gollywog for which he had just been taken.

'I don't want to interfere with previous arrangements,' he said with such a pathetic haughtiness that Sylvia had not the heart to wound his dignity, and told Lucian Hope that the expedition to Limehouse must be postponed; the young painter looked disconsolate, and Arthur blossomed from his fading. However, Lucian had the satisfaction of saying in a mysterious voice to Sylvia before he went:

'Well, then while you're away, I'll get on with it.'

It was not until they were half-way to Dulwich in the train that Arthur asked Sylvia what he was going to get on with.

'My scene,' she said.

'What scene?'

'Arthur, don't be stupid. The set for my show.'

'You're not going to let a youth like that paint a set for you? You're mad. What experience has he had?'

'None. That's exactly why I chose him. *I'm* providing the experience.'

'Have you known him long?' Arthur demanded. 'You can't have known him very long. He must have been at school when you left England.'

'Don't be jealous,' said Sylvia.

'Jealous? Of him? Huh!'

Mrs. Madden had changed more than Sylvia expected. Arthur had seemed so little altered that she was surprised to see his mother with white hair, for she could scarcely be fifty-five yet. The drawing-room of the little house in Dulwich recalled vividly the drawing-room of the house in Hampstead: nor had Mrs. Madden bought herself a new piano with the fifty pounds that was cabled back to her from Sulphurville. It suddenly occurred to Sylvia that this was the first time she had seen her since she ran away with Arthur fifteen years ago, and she felt that she ought to apologize for that behaviour now; but after all Mrs. Madden had run away herself once upon a time with her father's groom and could scarcely have been greatly astonished at her son's elopement.

'You have forgiven me for carrying him off from Hampstead?' she asked with a smile.

Mrs. Madden laughed gently.

'Yes, I was frightened at the time. But in the end it did Arthur good, I think. It's been such a pleasure to me to hear how successful he's been lately.' She looked at Sylvia with an expression of marked sympathy.

Before supper Mrs. Madden came up to Sylvia's room, and taking her hand said in her soft voice:

'Arthur has told me all about you two.'

Sylvia flushed and pulled her hand away.

'He'd no business to tell you anything about me,' she said hotly.

'You mustn't be angry, Sylvia. He made it quite clear that you hadn't made up your mind yet. Poor boy,' she added with a sigh.

Sylvia, when she understood that Arthur had not said anything about their past, had a strong desire to tell Mrs. Madden that she had lived with him for a year: she resented the way she had said 'poor boy.' She checked the impulse, and assured her that if Arthur had spoken of their marriage, he had had no right to do so. It was really most improbable that she should marry him: oh, but most improbable.

'You always spoke so severely about love when you were a little girl. Do you remember? You must forgive a mother, but I must tell you that I believe Arthur's happiness depends upon your marrying him. He talks of nothing else and makes such plans for the future.'

'He makes too many plans,' Sylvia said severely.

'Ah, there soon comes a time when one ceases to make plans,' Mrs. Madden sighed. 'One is reduced to expedients. But now that you're a woman – and I can easily believe that you're the clever woman Arthur says you are, for you gave every sign of it when you were young – now that you're a woman, I do hope you'll be a merciful woman; it's such a temptation – you must forgive my plain speaking – it's such a temptation to keep a man like Arthur hanging on. You must have noticed how young he is still – to all intents and purposes quite a boy: and believe me he has the same romantic adoration for you and your wonderfulness as he had when he was seventeen. Don't, I beg of you, treat such devotion too lightly.'

Sylvia could not keep silent under this unjustified imputation of heartlessness and broke out:

'I'm sure you'll admit that Arthur has given quite a wrong idea of me when I tell you that we lived together for a year; and you must remember that I've been married already and know what it means. Arthur has no right to complain of me.'

'Sylvia, I'm sorry,' Mrs. Madden almost whispered. 'Oh dear, how could Arthur do such a thing?'

'Because I made him, of course. Now you must forgive *me* if I say something that hurts your feelings, but I must say it. When you ran away with your husband, you must have made him do it. You *must* have done.'

'Good gracious me,' Mrs. Madden exclaimed. 'I suppose I did. I never looked at it in that light before. You've made me feel quite ashamed of my behaviour. Quite embarrassed. And I suppose everybody has always blamed me entirely: but because my husband was one of my father's servants, I always used to be defending him. I never thought of defending myself.'

Sylvia was sorry for stirring up in Mrs. Madden's placid mind old storms; it was painful to see this faded gentlewoman in the little suburban bedroom, blushing nervously at the unladylike behaviour of long ago. Presently Mrs. Madden pulled herself up and said with a certain decision:

'Yes, but I did marry him.'

'Yes, but you hadn't been married already. You hadn't knocked round half the globe for twenty-eight years. It's no good my pretending to be shocked about myself. I don't care a bit what anybody thinks about me, and anyway it's done now.'

'Surely you'd be happier if you married Arthur after – after that,' Mrs. Madden suggested.

'But I'm not in the least unhappy. I can't say whether I shall marry Arthur until I've given my performance. I can't say what effect either success or failure will have on me. My whole mind is concentrated on the Pierian Hall next October.'

'I'm afraid I can't understand this modern way of looking at things.'

'But there's nothing modern about my point of view, Mrs. Madden. There's nothing modern about the egotism of an artist. Arthur is as free as I am. He has his own career to think about. He does think about it a great deal. He's radically much more interested in that than in marrying me. The main point is that he's free at present. From the moment I promise to marry him and he accepts that promise he won't be free. Nor shall I. It wouldn't be fair on either of us to make that promise now, because I must know what October is going to bring forth.'

'Well, I call it very modern. When I was young we looked at marriage as the most important event in a girl's life.'

'But you didn't, dear Mrs. Madden. You, or rather your contemporaries, regarded marriage as a path to freedom – social freedom, that is. Your case was exceptional. You fell passionately in love with a man beneath you, as the world counts it. You married him, and what was the result? You were cut off by your relations as utterly as if you had become the concubine of a Hottentot.'

'Sylvia dear, what an uncomfortable comparison!'

'Marriage to your contemporaries was a social observance. I'm not religious, but I regard marriage as so sacred that, because I've been divorced and because so far as I know my husband is still alive, I have something like religious qualms about marrying again. It takes a cynic to be an idealist: the sentimentalist gets left at the first fence. It's just because I'm fond of Arthur in a perfectly normal way when I'm not immersed in my ambition that I even contemplate the *notion* of marrying him. I've got a perfectly normal wish to have children and a funny little house of my own. So far as I know at present, I should like Arthur to be the father of my children. But it's got to be an equal business. Personally I think that the Turks are wiser about women than we are; I think the majority of women are only fit for the harem, and I'm not sure that the majority wouldn't be happier under such conditions. The incurable vanity of man, however, has removed us from our seclusion to admire his antics, and it's too late to start shutting us up in a box now. Woman never thought of equality with man until he put the notion into her head.'

'I think perhaps supper may be ready,' Mrs. Madden said. 'It all sounds very convincing as you speak, but I can't help feeling that you'd be happier if you wouldn't take everything to pieces to look at the works. Things hardly ever go so well again afterwards. Oh dear, I wish you hadn't lived together first.'

'It breaks the ice of the wedding-cake, doesn't it?' said Sylvia.

'And I wish you wouldn't make such bitter remarks. You don't really mean what you say. I'm sure supper must be ready.'

'Oh, but I do,' Sylvia insisted, as they passed out into the narrow little passage and down the narrow stairs into the little dining-room. Nevertheless in Sylvia's mind there was a kindliness toward this little house, almost a tenderness, and far away at the back of her imagination was the vision of herself established in just such another house.

'But even the Albert Memorial would look all right from the wrong end of a telescope,' she said to herself.

One thing was brought home very vividly during her stay in Dulwich, which was the difference between what she had deceived herself into thinking was that first maternal affection she had felt for Arthur and the true maternal love of his mother. Whenever she had helped Arthur in any way, she had always been aware of enjoying the sensation of her indispensableness; it had been an emotion altogether different from this natural selflessness of the mother; it was really one that had always reflected a kind of self-conscious credit upon herself. Here in Dulwich with this aspect of her affection for Arthur completely overshadowed, Sylvia was able to ask herself more directly if she loved him in the immemorial way of love; and though she could not arrive at a finally positive conclusion, she was strengthened in her resolve not to let him go. Arthur himself was more in love with her than he had ever been, and she thought

333

that perhaps this was due to that sudden and disquieting withdrawal of herself: in the midst of possession he had been dispossessed, and until he could pierce her secret reasons he would inevitably remain deeply in love, even to the point of being jealous of a boy like Lucian Hope. Sylvia understood Arthur's having refused an engagement to tour as juvenile lead in a successful musical piece and his unwillingness to leave her alone in town: he was rewarded, too, for his action, because shortly afterwards he obtained a good engagement in London to take the place of a singer who had retired from the cast of the Frivolity Theatre. At that rate he would soon find himself at the Vanity Theatre itself.

In June Sylvia went back to the Airdales', and soon afterwards took rooms near them in West Kensington. It was impossible to continue indefinitely to pretend that Arthur and herself were mere theatrical acquaintances, and one day Olive asked Sylvia if she intended to marry him.

'What do you advise?' Sylvia asked. 'There's a triumph, dearest Olive. Have I ever asked your advice before?'

'I like him. Jack likes him too, and says that he ought to get on fast now, but I don't know. Well, he's not the sort of man I expected you to marry.'

'You've had an ideal for me all the time,' Sylvia exclaimed. 'And you've never told me.'

'Oh, no, I've never had anybody definite in my mind, but I think I should be able to say at once if the man you had chosen was the right one. Don't ask me to describe him, because I couldn't do it. You used to tease me about marrying a curly-headed actor, but Arthur Madden seems to me much more of a curly-headed actor than Jack is.'

'In fact you thoroughly disapprove of poor Arthur?' Sylvia pressed.

'Oh dear, no. Oh, not at all. Please don't think that. I'm only anxious that you shouldn't throw yourself away.'

'Remnants always go cheap,' said Sylvia. 'However, don't worry. I'll be quite sure of myself before I marry anybody again.'

The summer passed away quickly in a complexity of arrangements for the opening performance at the Pierian Hall. Sylvia stayed three or four times at Dulwich and grew very fond of Mrs. Madden, who never referred again to the subject of marriage. She also went up to Warwickshire with Olive and the children, much to the pleasure of Mr. Fanshawe, who was now writing a supplementary volume called *More Warwickshire Worthies*. In London she scarcely met any old friends; indeed she went out of her way to avoid people like the Clarehavens, because they would not have been interested in what she was doing: by this time Sylvia had reached the point of considering everybody either for the interest and belief he evinced in her success or by the use he could be to her in securing it. The first rapturous egoism of Arthur's own success in London had worn off with time, and he was able to devote himself entirely to running about for Sylvia, which gradually made her regard him more and more as a fixture. As for Lucian Hope, he thought of nothing but the great occasion, and would have fought anybody who had ventured to cast a breath of doubt upon the triumph at hand. The set that he had painted was exactly what Sylvia required, and though both Arthur and Jack thought it would distract the audience's attention by puzzling them, they neither of them on Sylvia's account criticized it at all harshly.

At last in mid-October the very morning of the day arrived, so long anticipated with every kind of discussion that its superficial resemblance to other mornings seemed heartless and unnatural. It was absurd that a milkman's note should be the same as yesterday, that servants should shake mats on front-door steps as usual, and that the maid who knocked at Sylvia's door should not break down beneath the weightiness of her summons. Nor, when Sylvia looked out of the window, were Jack and Arthur and Ronald and Lucian pacing with agitated steps the pavement below – an absence of enthusiasm, at any rate on the part of Arthur and Lucian, that hurt her feelings, until she thought for a moment how foolishly unreasonable she was being.

As soon as Sylvia was dressed, she went round to the Airdales: everybody she met on the way inspired her with a longing to confide in him the portentousness of the day, and she found herself speculating whether several business men who were hurrying to catch the nine o'clock train had possibly the intention of visiting the Pierian Hall that afternoon. She was extremely annoyed to find when she reached the Airdales' house that neither Jack nor Olive was up.

'Do they know the time?' she demanded of the maid in a scandalized voice. 'Their clock must have stopped.'

'Oh no, miss, I don't think so. Breakfast is at ten as usual. There's Mr. Airdale's dressing-room bell going now, miss. That'll be for his shaving-water. Shall I say you're waiting to see him?'

What a ridiculous time to begin shaving, Sylvia thought.

'Yes, please,' she added aloud. 'Or no, don't bother him; I'll come back at ten o'clock.'

Sylvia saw more of the streets of West Kensington in that hour than she had ever seen of them before, and decided that the neighbourhood was impossible. Nothing so intolerably monotonous as these rows of stupid and meaningless houses had ever been designed: one after another of them blinked at her in the autumnal sunshine with a fatuous complacency that made her long to ring all the bells in the street. Presently she found herself by the playing fields of St. James's School, where the last boys were hurrying across the grass like belated ants. She looked at the golden clock in the school buildings: half-past nine! In five hours and a half she would be waiting for the curtain to go up: in seven hours and a half the audience would be wondering if it should have tea in Bond Street, or cross Piccadilly and walk down St. James's Street to Rumpelmayer's. This problem of the audience began to worry Sylvia; she examined the alternatives with a really anxious gravity. If it went to Rumpelmayer's, it would have to walk back to the Dover Street Tube, which would mean re-crossing Piccadilly, though it would be on the right side for the omnibuses. On the other hand, it would find Rumpelmayer's full, because other audiences would have arrived before it, invading the tea-shop from Pall Mall. Sylvia grew angry at the thought of these other audiences robbing her audience of its tea – her audience, some members of which would have read in the paper this morning:

PIERIAN HALL.
This afternoon at 3 p.m.
SYLVIA SCARLETT
IN
IMPROVISATIONS

and would actually have paid, some of them as much as seven shillings and sixpence to see Sylvia Scarlett. Seven hours and a half: seven shillings and sixpence: $7\frac{1}{2}$ plus $7\frac{1}{2}$ made fifteen. When she was fifteen, she had met Arthur. Sylvia's mind rambled among the omens of numbers, and left her audience still undecided between Bond Street and Rumpelmayer's, left it upon the steps of the Pierian Hall, the sport of passing traffic, hungry, thirsty, homesick. In seven and a half hours she should know the answer to that breathless question asked a year ago in Vermont. To think that the exact spot on which she had stood when she asked was existing at this moment in Vermont! In seven and a half hours, no, seven hours and twenty-five minutes: the hands were moving on. It was really terrible how little people regarded the flight of time: the very world might come to an end in seven hours and twenty-five minutes.

'*Have you seen Sylvia Scarlett yet?*'

'*No, we intended to go yesterday, but there were no seats left. They say she's wonderful.*'

'Oh, my dear, she's perfectly amazing. Of course it's something quite new. You really must go.'

'Who is she like?'

'Oh, she's not like anybody else. I'm told she's half French.'

'Oh, really, how interesting.'

'Good morning, have you used Pears' soap?'

'V-vi-vin-vinó-vinól-vinóli-vinolia!'

Sylvia pealed the Airdales' bell, and found Jack in the queer mixed costume which a person wears on the morning of an afternoon that will be celebrated by his best tail-coat.

'My dear girl, you really mustn't get so excited,' he protested when he saw Sylvia's manner.

'Jack, do you think I shall be a success?'

'Of course you will. Now, do for goodness' sake drink a cup of coffee or something.'

Sylvia found that she was hungry enough to eat even an egg, which created a domestic crisis, because Sylvius and Rose quarrelled over which of them was to have the top. Finally it was adjusted by awarding the top to Sylvius, but by allowing Rose to turn the empty egg upside down for the exquisite pleasure of watching Sylvia tap it with ostentatious greed, only to find that there was nothing inside after all, an operation that Sylvius watched with critical jealousy and Rose saluted with ecstatic joy. Sylvia's disappointment was so beautifully violent that Sylvius regretted the material choice he had made and wanted Sylvia to eat another egg, of which Rose might eat the top and he offer the empty shell: but it was too late, and Sylvius learnt that often the shadow is better than the substance.

It had been decided in the end that Jack should confine himself to the cares of general management, and Arthur was left without a rival. Sylvia had insisted that he should only sing old English folk songs, a decision which he had challenged at first on the ground that he required the advertisement of more modern songs and that Sylvia's choice was not going to help him.

'You're not singing to help yourself,' she told him. 'You're singing to help me.'

In addition to Arthur there was a girl whom Lucian Hope had discovered, a delicate creature with red hair, whose chief claim to employment was that she was starving, though incidentally she had a very sweet and pure soprano voice. Finally there was an Irish pianist whose technique and good humour were alike unassailable.

Before the curtain went up, Sylvia could think of nothing but the Improvisations that she ought to have invented instead of the ones that she had: it was a strain upon her common sense to prevent herself from cancelling the whole performance and returning its money to the audience. The more she contemplated what she was going to do, the more she viewed the undertaking as a fraud upon the public. There had never been any *chiqué* like the *chiqué* she was presently going to commit. What was that noise? Who had given the signal to O'Hea? What in hell's name did he think he was doing at the piano? The sound of the music was like water running into one's bath while one was lying in bed: nothing could stop it from overflowing presently. Nothing could stop the curtain from rising. At what a pace he was playing that Debussy! He was showing off, the fool! A ridiculous joke came into her mind that she kept on repeating while the music flowed: *Many a minim makes a maxim. Many a minim makes a maxim.* How cold it was in the dressing-room: and the music was getting quicker and quicker. There was a knock at the door: it was Arthur. How nice he looked with that red carnation in his buttonhole.

'How nice you look, Arthur, in that buttonhole,'

The flower became tremendously important; it seemed to Sylvia that if she could go on flattering the flower O'Hea would somehow be kept at the piano.

'Well, don't pull it to pieces,' said Arthur ruthfully. But it was too late: the petals were scattered on the floor like drops of blood.

'Oh, I'm so sorry. Come along back to my dressing-room. I'll give you another flower.'

'No, no, there isn't time now. Wait till you come off after your first set.'

Now it was seeming the most urgent thing in the world to find another flower for Arthur's buttonhole: at any cost the rise of that curtain must be delayed. But Arthur had brought her on the stage, and the notes were racing toward the death of the piece. It was absurd of O'Hea to have chosen Debussy: the atmosphere required a ballade of Chopin, or better still Schumann's *Noveletten*. He could have played all the *Noveletten*. Oh dear, what a pity she had not thought of making that suggestion: the piano would have been scarcely half-way through by now.

Suddenly there was silence: then there followed the languid applause of an afternoon audience for an unimportant part of the programme.

'He's stopped,' Sylvia exclaimed in horror. 'What *has* happened?'

She turned to Arthur in despair, but he had hurried off the stage. Lucian Hope's painted city seemed to press forward and stifle her; she moved down stage to escape it; the curtain went up, and she recoiled as from a chasm at her feet. Why on earth was O'Hea sitting in that idiotic attitude, as if he were going to listen to a sermon, looking down like that with his right arm supporting his left elbow and his left hand propping up his chin? How hot the footlights were; she hoped nothing had happened, and looked round in alarm; but the fireman was standing quite calmly in the wings. Just as Sylvia was deciding that her voice could not possibly escape from her throat which had closed upon it like a pair of pincers, the voice tore itself free and went travelling out toward that darkness in front, that nebulous darkness scattered with hands and faces and programmes. Like Concetta in a great city, Sylvia was lost in that darkness: she *was* Concetta. It seemed to her that the applause at the end was not so much approval of Concetta as a welcome to Mrs. Gainsborough. When isolated laughs and volleys of laughter came out of the darkness and were followed sometimes by the darkness itself laughing everywhere, so that O'Hea looked up very personally and winked at her, then Sylvia fell in love with her audience. The laughter increased, and suddenly she recognized at the end of each volley that Sylvius and Rose were supplementing its echoes with rapturous echoes of their own; she could not see them, but their gurgles in the darkness were like a song of nightingales to Sylvia. She ceased to be Mrs. Gainsborough, and began to say three or four of the poems; then the curtain fell, and came up again, and fell, and came up again, and fell, and came up again.

Jack was standing beside her and saying:

'Splendid, splendid, splendid, splendid.'

'Delighted, delighted, delighted, delighted.'

'Very good audience, splendid audience, delighted audience. Success! Success! Success!'

Really how wonderfully O'Hea was playing, Sylvia thought, and how good that Debussy was.

The rest of the performance was as much of a success as the beginning. Perhaps the audience liked best Mrs. Gowndry and the woman who smuggled lace from Belgium into France. Sylvius and Rose laughed so much at the audience's laughter at Mrs. Gowndry that Sylvius announced in the ensuing lull that he wanted to go somewhere, a desire which was naturally loudly endorsed by Rose; the audience was much amused, because it supposed that Sylvius's wish was a tribute to the profession of Mrs. Gowndry's husband, and whatever faint doubts existed about the propriety of alluding in the Pierian Hall to a lavatory-attendant were dispersed.

Sylvia forgot altogether about the audience's tea when the curtain fell finally: it was difficult to think about anything with so many smiling people pressing round her on the stage. Several old friends came and reminded her of their existence, but there was no one who had quite such a radiant smile as Arthur Lonsdale.

'Lonnie! How nice of you to come.'

'I say, topping I mean, what? I say, that's a most extraordinary back-cloth you've got. What on earth is it supposed to be? It reminds me of what you feel like when you're driving a car through a strange town after meeting a man you haven't seen for some time and who's just found out a good brand of fizz at the hotel where he's staying. I was afraid you'd get bitten in the back before you'd finished. I say, Mrs. Gowndry was devilish good. Some of the other lads and lasses were a bit beyond me.'

'And how's business?'

'Oh, very good. We've just put on the neatest little 90 h.p. torpedo-body two-seater on the market. I'll tootle you down to Brighton in it one Sunday morning. Upon my word, you'll scarcely have time to wrap yourself up before you'll have to unwrap yourself to shake hands with dear old Harry Burnley coming out to welcome you from the Britannia.'

'Not married yet, Lonnie?'

'No, not yet. Braced myself up to do it the other day, dived in, and was seized with cramp at the deep end: she offered to be a sister to me, and I sank like a stone. My mother's making rather a nuisance of herself about it. She keeps producing girls out of her muff like a conjurer whenever she comes to see me. And what girls! Heather mixture most of them, like Guggenheim's Twelfth of August. I shall come to it at last, I suppose. Mr. Arthur Lonsdale and his bride leaving St. Margaret's, Westminster, under an arch of spanners formed by grateful chauffeurs whom the brilliant and handsome young bridegroom has recommended to many titled readers of this paper. Well, so long, Sylvia, there's a delirious crowd of admirers waiting for you. Send me a line where you're living, and we'll have a little dinner somewhere—'

Sylvia's success was not quite so huge as in the first intoxication of her friends' enthusiasm she had begun to fancy; however, it was unmistakably a success, and she was able to give two recitals a week through the autumn with certainly the prospect of a good music-hall engagement for the following spring, if she cared to accept it. Most of the critics discovered that she was not as good as Yvette Guilbert. In view of Yvette Guilbert's genius, of which they were much more firmly convinced now than they would have been when Yvette Guilbert first appeared, this struck them as a fairly safe comparison: moreover, it gave their readers an impression that they understood French, which enhanced the literary value of their criticism. To strengthen this belief most of them were inclined to think that the French poems were the best part of Miss Sylvia

Scarlett's performance: one or two of the latter definitely recalled some of Yvette Guilbert's early work, no doubt by the number of words they had not understood, because somebody had crackled a programme or had shuffled his feet or had coughed. As for the English character studies, or *études*, as some of them carried away by reminiscences of Yvette Guilbert into oblivion of their own language preferred to call them, they had a certain distinction, and in many cases betrayed signs of an almost meticulous observation, though at the same time like everybody else doing anything at the present moment except in France, they did not have as much distinction or meticulousness as the work of forerunners in England or contemporaries abroad. Still that was not to say that the work of Miss Sylvia Scarlett was not highly promising and of the greatest possible interest: the *timbre* of her voice was specially worthy of notice and justified the italics in which it was printed. Finally two critics, who were probably sitting next to one another, found a misprint in the programme, no doubt in searching for a translation of the poems.

If Sylvia fancied a lack of appreciation in the critics, all her friends were positive that they were wonderful notices for a beginner.

'Why, I think that's a splendid notice in the *Telegraph*,' said Olive. 'I found it almost at once. Why, one often has to read through a paper before one can find the notice.'

'Do you mean to tell me that the most self-inebriated egotist on earth ever read right through *The Daily Telegraph*? I don't believe it. He'd have been drowned like Narcissus.'

Arthur pressed for a decision about their marriage, now that Sylvia knew what she had so long wanted to know; but she was wrapped up in ideas for improving her performance and forbade Arthur to mention the subject until she raised it herself: for the present she was on with a new love twice a week. Indeed, they were fascinating to Sylvia, these audiences each with a definite personality of its own. She remembered how she had scoffed in old days at the slavish flattery of them by her fellow actors and actresses: equally in the old days she had scoffed at love. She wished that she could feel towards Arthur as she felt now towards her audiences, which were as absorbing as children with their little clevernesses and precocities. The difference between what she was doing now and what she had done formerly when she sang French songs with an English accent, was the difference between the realism of an old knotted towel that is a baby and an expensive doll that may be a baby, but never ceases to be a doll. Formerly she had been a mechanical thing and had never given herself, because she had possessed neither art nor truth, but merely craft and accuracy; she had thought that the personality was degraded by depending on the favour of an audience. All that old self-consciousness and false shame were gone; she and her audience communed through art as spirits might commune after death. In the absorption of studying the audience as a separate entity, Sylvia forgot that it was made up of men and women: when she knew that any friends of hers were in front, they always remained entirely separate in her mind from the audience. Gradually, however, as the autumn advanced, several people from long ago re-entered her life, and she began to lose that feeling of seclusion from the world, and to realize the gradual setting up of barriers to her complete liberty of action. The first of these visitants was Miss Ashley, who in her peacock-blue gown looked much as she had looked when Sylvia last saw her.

'I could not resist coming round to tell you how greatly I enjoyed your performance,' she said. 'I've been so sorry that you never came to see me all these years.'

Sylvia felt embarrassed, because she dreaded presently an allusion to her marriage with Philip, but Miss Ashley was too wise.

'How's Hornton House?' asked Sylvia rather timidly; it was like enquiring after the near relation of an old friend, who might have died.

'Just the same. Miss Primer is still with me. Miss Hossack now has a school of her own; Miss Pinck became very ill with gouty rheumatism and had to retire. I won't ask you about yourself; you told me so much from the stage. Now that we've been able to meet again, won't you come and visit your old school sometime?'

Sylvia hesitated.

'Please,' Miss Ashley insisted. 'I'm not inviting you out of politeness. It would really give me pleasure. I have never ceased to think about you all these years. Well, I won't keep you, for I'm sure you must be tired. Do come. Tell me, Sylvia. I should so like to bring the girls one afternoon. What would be a good afternoon to come?'

'You mean, when will there be nothing in the programme that—'

'We poor schoolmistresses,' said Miss Ashley with a whimsical look of deprecation.

'Come on Saturday fortnight, and afterwards I'll go back with you all to Hornton House. I'd love that.'

So it was arranged.

On Wednesday of the following week it happened that there was a particularly appreciative audience, and Sylvia became so much enamoured of the laughter that she excelled herself; it was an afternoon of perfect accord, and she traced the source of it to a group somewhere in the middle of the stalls, too far back for her to recognize its composition.

After the performance a pack of visiting-cards was brought to the door of her dressing-room. She read: *Mrs. Ian Campbell: Mrs. Ralph Dennison: who on earth were they? Mr. Leonard Worsley*—

Sylvia flung open the door, and there they all were, Mr. and Mrs. Worsley, Gladys and Enid, two good-looking men in the background, two children in the foreground.

'Gladys! Enid!'

'Sylvia!'

'Oh, Sylvia, you were priceless. Oh, we enjoyed ourselves no end. You don't know my husband. Ian, come and bow nicely to the pretty lady,' cried Gladys.

'Sylvia, it was simply ripping. We laughed and laughed. Ralph, come and be introduced, and this is Stumpy, my boy,' Enid cried simultaneously.

'Fancy, he's a grandfather,' the daughters exclaimed, dragging Mr. Worsley forward, who looked younger than ever.

'Hercules is at Oxford, or of course he'd have come too. This is Proodles,' said Gladys, pointing to the little girl.

'Sylvia, why did you desert us like that?' Mrs. Worsley reproachfully asked. 'When are you coming down to stay with us at Arbour End? Of course the children are married . . .' she broke off with half a sigh.

'Oh, but we can all squash in,' Gladys shouted.

'Oh, rather,' Enid agreed. 'The kids can sleep in the coal-scuttles. We shan't notice any difference.'

'Dears, it's so wonderful to see you,' Sylvia gasped. 'But do tell me who you all are over again. I'm so muddled.'

'I'm Mrs. Ian Campbell,' Gladys explained. 'And this is Ian. And this is Proodles, and at home there's Groggles who's too small for anything except pantomimes. And that's Mrs. Ralph Dennison, and that's Ralph, and that's Stumpy, and at home Enid's got a girlie called Barbara. Mother hates being a grandmother four times over, so she's called Aunt Victoria, and of course father's still one of the children. We've both been married seven years.'

Nothing had so much brought home to Sylvia the flight of time as this meeting with Gladys and Enid, who when she last saw them were only sixteen: it was incredible. And they had not forgotten her; in what seemed now a century they had not forgotten her! Sylvia told them about Miss Ashley's visit and suggested that they should come and join the party of girls from Hornton House. It would be fun, would it not? Miss Primer was still at the school.

Gladys and Enid were delighted with the plan, and on the day fixed about twenty girls invaded Sylvia's dressing-room, shepherded by Miss

343

Primer, who was still melting with tears for Rodrigo's death in the scene. Miss Ashley had brought the carriage to drive Sylvia back; but she insisted upon going in a motor-bus with the others and was well rewarded by Miss Primer's ecstasies of apprehension. Sylvia wandered with Gladys and Enid down well-remembered corridors, in and out of bedrooms and classrooms; she listened to resolutions to send Prudence and Barbara to Hornton House in a few years: for Sylvia it was almost too poignant, the thought of these families growing up all round her, while she after so many years was still really as much alone as she had always been. The company of all these girls with their slim black legs, their pigtails and fluffy hair tied back with big bows, the absurdly exaggerated speech and the enlaced loves of girlhood – the accumulation of it all was scarcely to be borne.

When Sylvia visited Arbour End and talked once again to Mrs. Worsley sitting at the foot of her bed about the wonderful lives of that so closely self-contained family, the desolation of the future came visibly nearer; it seemed imperative at whatever cost to drive it back.

Shortly before Christmas a card was brought round to Sylvia: *Mrs. Prescott-Merivale, Hardingham Hall, Huntingdon.*

'Who is it?' she asked her maid.

'It's a lady, miss.'

'Well of course, I didn't suppose a cassowary had sent up his card. What's she like?'

The maid strove to think of some phrase that would describe the visitor, but she fell back hopelessly upon her original statement.

'She's a lady, miss.' Then with a sudden radiancy lighting her eyes, she added, 'and there's a little boy with her.'

'My entertainment seems to be turning into a children's treat,' Sylvia muttered to herself. '*Sic itur ad astra.*'

'I beg pardon, miss, did you say to show her in?'

Sylvia nodded.

Presently a tall young woman in the late twenties with large and brilliant grey eyes, rose-flushed and deep in furs, came in accompanied by an extraordinarily handsome boy of seven or eight.

'How awfully good of you to let me waste a few minutes of your time,' she said; and as she spoke, Sylvia had a fleeting illusion that it was herself speaking, a sensation infinitely rapid, but yet sufficiently clear to make her ask herself the meaning of it, and to find in the stranger's hair the exact replica of her own. The swift illusion and the equally swift comparison were fled before she had finished inviting her visitor to sit down.

'I must explain who I am. I've heard about you – oh, of course, publicly – but also from my brother.'

'Your brother?' repeated Sylvia.

'Yes, Michael Fane.'

'He's not with you?'

'No, I wish he had been. Alas, he's gone off to look for a friend who, by the way, I expect you know also – Maurice Avery? All sorts of horrid rumours about what had happened to him in Morocco were being brought back to us, so Michael went off last spring and has been with him ever since.'

'But I thought he was a monk,' Sylvia said.

Mrs. Merivale laughed with what seemed rather like relief.

'No, he's neither priest nor monk, thank goodness; though the prospect still hangs over us.'

'After all these years?' Sylvia asked in astonishment.

'Oh, my dear Miss Scarlett, don't forget the narrow way is also long. But I didn't come to talk to you about Michael. I simply most shamelessly availed myself of his having met you a long time ago to give myself an excuse for talking to you about your performance. Of course, it's absolutely great. How lucky you are.'

'Lucky?' Sylvia could not help glancing at the handsome boy beside her.

'He's rather a lamb, isn't he?' Mrs. Merivale agreed. 'But you started all sorts of old, forgotten, hidden away, burnt-out fancies of mine this afternoon, and – you see, I intended to be a professional pianist once, but I got married instead. Much better really, because unless – oh, I don't know. Yes, I *am* jealous of you. You've picked me up and put me down again where I was once. Now the conversation's backed into me, and I really do want to talk about you. Your performance is the kind about which one wonders why nobody else ever did it before: that's the greatest compliment one can pay an artist, I think. All great art is the great expression of a great commonplace: that's why it always looks so easy. I do hope you're having the practical success you deserve.'

'Yes, I think I shall be all right,' Sylvia said. 'Only I expect that after the New Year I shall have to cut my show considerably and take a music-hall engagement. I'm not making a fortune at the Pierian.'

'How horrid for you. How I should love to play with you. Oh dear! It's heartrending to say it, but it's much too late. Well, I mustn't keep you. You've given me such tremendous pleasure and just as much pain with it as makes the pleasure all the sharper . . . I'll write and tell Michael about you.'

345

'I expect he's forgotten my name by now,' Sylvia said.

'Oh, no, he never forgets anybody, even in the throes of theological speculation. Good-bye. I see that this is your last performance for the present. I shall come and hear you again when you re-open. How odious about music-halls. You ought to have called yourself Sylvia Scarlatti, told your press agent that you were the direct descendant of the composer, vowed that when you came to England six months ago you could speak nothing but Polish, and you could have filled the Pierian night and day for a year. We're queer people, we English. I think, you know, it's a kind of shyness, the way we treat native artists: you get the same thing in families. It's not really that the prophet has no honour, etc.: it really is, I believe, a fear of boasting, which would be such bad form, wouldn't it? Of course we've ruined ourselves as a nation by our good manners and our sense of humour. Why, we've even insisted that what native artists we do support shall be gentlemen first and artists second. In what other country could an actor be knighted for his trousers or an author for his wife's dowry? Good-bye, I do wish you great, great success.'

'Anyway, I can't be knighted,' Sylvia laughed.

'Don't be too sure. A nation that has managed to turn its artists into gentlemen will soon insist on turning its women into gentlemen too, or at any rate on securing their good manners in some way.'

'Women will never really have good manners,' Sylvia said.

'No, thank God, there you're right. Well, good-bye. It's been so jolly to talk to you, and again I've loved every moment of this afternoon. Charles,' she added to the handsome boy, 'after bragging about your country's good manners, let's see you make a decent bow.'

He inclined his head with a grave courtesy, opened the door for his mother and followed her out.

The visit of Michael's sister, notwithstanding that she had envied Sylvia's luck, left her with very little opinion of it herself. What was her success after all? A temporary elation dependent upon good health and the public taste, financially uncertain, emotionally wearing, radically unsatisfying and insecure, for however good her performance was, it was always mummery really, as near as mummery could get to creative work perhaps, but mortal like its maker.

'Sad to think this is the last performance here,' said her maid.

Sylvia agreed with her: it was a relief to find a peg on which to hang the unreasonable depression that was weighing her down. She passed out of her dressing-room; as the stage door swung to behind her, a figure stepped into the lamplight of the narrow court: it was Jimmy Monkley. The spruceness had left him; all the colour too had gone from his face,

346

which was now a sickly white – an evil face with its sandy moustache streaked with grey and its lack-lustre eyes. Sylvia was afraid that from the way she started back from him, he would think that she scorned him for having been in prison, and with an effort she tried to be cordial.

'You've done damned well for yourself,' he said, paying no attention to what she was saying. She found this meeting overwhelmingly repulsive and moved towards her taxi; it was seeming to her that Monkley had the power to snatch her away and plunge her back into that life of theirs; she would really rather have met Philip than him.

'Damned well for yourself,' he repeated.

'I'm sorry, I can't stay. I'm in a hurry. I'm in a hurry.'

She reached the taxi and slammed the door in his face.

This unexpected meeting convinced Sylvia of the necessity of attaching herself finally to a life that would make the resurrection of a Monkley nothing more influential than a nightmare. She knew that she was giving way to purely nervous fears in being thus affected by what, had she stopped to think, was the natural result of her name's becoming known. But the liability to nervous fears was in itself an argument that something was wrong. When had she ever been a prey to such hysteria before? When had she allowed herself to be haunted by a face, as now she was being haunted by Monkley's face? Suppose he had seated himself behind the taxi and that when she reached the Airdales' house he should once more be standing on the pavement in the lamplight?

In Brompton Road Sylvia told the driver to stop: she wanted to do some Christmas shopping. After an hour or more spent among toys she came out with a porter loaded with packages, and looked round her quickly; but of course he was not upon the pavement. How absurd she had been! In any case, what could Monkley do? She would forget all about him. To-morrow was Christmas Eve: there was going to be such a jolly party at the Airdales'. The taxi hummed toward West Kensington; Sylvia leaned back huddled up with her thoughts, until they reached Lillie Road. She had passed Mrs. Meares' house so many times without giving it a second look; now she found herself peering out into the thickening fog in case Monkley should be standing upon the doorstep. She was glad when she reached the Airdales' house, warm and bright, festooned with holly and mistletoe; there were pleasant little household noises everywhere, comfortable little noises, and a rosy glow from the silken shades of the lamps; the carpet was so quiet and the parlourmaid in a clean cap and apron so efficient, so quick to get in all the parcels and shut out the foggy night.

Olive was already in the drawing-room, and because this was to be a specially unceremonious evening in preparation for the party to-morrow, Olive was in a pink tea-gown that blended with the prettiness of her cosy house and made her more essentially a part of it all. How bleak was her own background in comparison with this, Sylvia thought. Jack was dining out most unwillingly and had left a great many pleas to be forgiven by Sylvia on the first night of her Christmas visit. After dinner they sat in the drawing-room, and Sylvia told Olive about her meeting with Monkley; she said nothing about Michael Fane's sister: that meeting did not seem to have any bearing upon the subject she wanted to discuss.

'Can you understand,' Sylvia asked, 'being almost frightened into marriage?'

'Yes, I think so,' Olive replied as judicially as the comfort of her surroundings would allow; it was impossible to preserve a critical attitude in this room; in such a suave and genial atmosphere one accepted anything.

'Well, do you still object to my marrying Arthur?' Sylvia demanded.

'But, my dear, I never objected to your marrying him. I may have suggested when I first saw him that he seemed rather too much the type of the ordinary actor for you, but that was only because you yourself had always scoffed at actors so haughtily. Since I've known him, I've grown to like him. Please don't think I ever objected to your marrying him. I never felt more sure about anybody's knowing her own mind than I do about you.'

'Well, I am going to marry him,' Sylvia said.

'Darling Sylvia, why do you say it so defiantly? Everybody will be delighted. Jack was only talking the other day about his perpetual dread that you'd never give yourself a chance of establishing your position finally, because you were so restless.'

Sylvia contemplated an admission to Olive of having lived with Arthur for a year in America, but in this room the fact had an ugly look and seemed to belong rather to that evil face of the past that had confronted her with such ill omen this evening, rather than to anything so homely as marriage.

'Arthur may not be anything more than an actor,' she went on. 'But in my profession what else do I want? He has loved me for a long time; I'm very fond of him. It's essential that I should have a background so that I shall never be shaken out of my self-possession by anything like this evening's encounter. I've lived a life of feverish energy, and it's only since the Improvisations that I can begin to believe it wasn't all wasted. I made a great mistake when I was seventeen, and when I was nineteen I tried to repair it with a still greater mistake. Then came Lily: she was a mistake.

Oh, when I look back at it all, it's nothing but mistake after mistake. I long for such funny ordinary little pleasures – Olive darling, I've tried, I've tried to think I can do without love, without children, without family, without friends – I can't.'

The tears were running swiftly, and all the time more swiftly down Sylvia's cheeks while she was speaking; Olive jumped up from her soft and quilted chair and knelt beside her friend.

'My darling Sylvia, you have friends, you have, indeed you have.'

'I know,' Sylvia went on. 'It's ungrateful of me. Why, if it hadn't been for you and Jack I should have gone mad. But just because you're so happy together and because you have Sylvius and Rose and because I flit about on the outskirts of it all like a timid, friendly, solitary ghost, I must have someone to love me. I've really treated Arthur very badly. I've kept him waiting now for a year; I wasn't brave enough to let him go, and I wasn't brave enough to marry him. I've never been undecided in my life. It must be that the gipsy in me has gone for ever, I think. This success of mine has been leading all the time to settling down properly. Most of the people who came back to me out of the past were the nice people, like my old mistress and the grown-up twins, and I want to be like them. Oh, Olive, I'm so tired of being different, of people thinking that I'm hard and brutal and cynical – I'm not, indeed I'm not. I couldn't have felt that truly appalling horror of Monkley this evening, if I were really bad.'

'Sylvia, dear, you're working yourself up needlessly. How can you say that you're bad? How can you say such things about yourself? You're not religious perhaps.'

'Listen, Olive: if I marry Arthur, I swear I'll make it a success. You know that I have a strong will. I'm not going to criticize him. I'm simply determined to make him and myself happy. It's very easy to love him really. He's like a boy – very weak, you know – but with all sorts of charming qualities, and his mother would be so glad if it were all settled – Olive, I meant to tell you a whole heap of things about myself, about what I've done, but I won't. I'm going to forget it all and be happy; I'm glad it's Christmas time. I've bought such ripping things for the kids. When I was buying them to-night, there came into my head almost my first adventure when I was a very little girl and thought I'd found a ten-franc piece which was really the money I'd been given for the marketing. I had just such an orgy of buying to-night. Did you know that a giraffe could make a noise? Well, it can, or at any rate the giraffe I bought for Sylvius can. You twist its neck, and it protests like a bronchial calf.'

The party on Christmas Eve was a great success: Lucian Hope burnt a hole in the table cloth with what was called a drawing-room firework:

Jack split his coat trying to hide inside his bureau; Arthur, sitting on a bottle with his legs crossed, lit a candle twice running: the little red-haired singer found the ring in the pudding: Sylvia found the sixpence: nobody found the button, so it must have been swallowed. It was a splendid party: Sylvius and Rose did not begin to cry steadily until after ten o'clock.

When the guests were getting ready to leave about two o'clock on Christmas morning and while Lucian Hope was telling everybody in turn that somebody must have swallowed the button inadvertently, to prove that he was quite able to pronounce 'inadvertently,' Sylvia took Arthur down the front-door steps and walked with him a little way along the foggy street.

'Arthur, I'll marry you when you like,' she said, laying a hand upon his arm.

'Sylvia, what a wonderful Christmas present!'

'To us both,' she whispered.

Then on an impulse she dragged him back to the house and proclaimed their engagement, which meant the opening of new bottles of champagne and the drinking of so many healths that it was three o'clock before the party broke up: nor was there any likelihood of anybody's being able to say 'inadvertently' by the time he had reached the corner of the street.

Arthur had begged Sylvia to come down to Dulwich on Christmas Day, and Mrs. Madden rejoiced over the decision they had reached at last. There were one or two things to be considered, the most important of which was the question of money. Sylvia had spent the last penny of what was left of Morera's money in launching herself, and she owed nearly two hundred pounds besides; Arthur had saved nothing. Both of them, however, had been offered good engagements for the spring – Arthur to tour as lead in one of the Vanity productions, which might mean an engagement at the Vanity itself in the autumn, Sylvia to play a twenty minutes' turn at all the music-halls of a big circuit. It seemed unsatisfactory to marry and immediately afterwards to separate, and they decided each to take the work that had been offered, to save all the money possible, and to aim at both playing in London next autumn, but in any case to be married in early June when the tours would end: they should then have a couple of months to themselves. Mrs. Madden wanted them to be married at once; but the other way seemed more prudent. Sylvia, having once made up her mind, was determined to be practical and not to run the risk of spoiling by financial worries the beginning of their real life together; her marriage in its orderli-ness and forethought and simplicity of intention was to compensate for everything that had gone before. Mrs. Madden thought they were both of them being too deliberate, but then she had run away once with her father's groom and must have had a fundamentally impulsive, even a reckless temperament.

The engagement was announced with an eye to the most advantageous publicity that is the privilege of being servants of the public. One was able to read everywhere of a theatrical romance or more coldly of a forthcoming theatrical marriage; nearly all the illustrated weeklies had two little oval photographs underneath which ran the legend:

INTERESTING ENGAGEMENT

We learn that Miss Sylvia Scarlett, who recently registered such an emphatic success in her original entertainment at the Pierian Hall, will shortly wed Mr. Arthur Madden, whom many of our readers will remember for his rendering of 'Somebody is sitting in the sunset' at the Frivolity Theatre.

In one particularly intimate paper was a short interview headed:

ACTRESS'S DELIGHTFUL CANDOUR

'No,' said Miss Scarlett to our representative who had called upon the clever and original young performer to ascertain when her marriage with Mr. Arthur Madden of 'Somebody is sitting in the sunset' fame would take place. 'No, Arthur and I have decided to wait till June. Frankly we can't afford to be married yet . . .'

and so on, with what was described as a portrait of Miss Sylvia Scarlett inset, but which without the avowal would probably have been taken for the thumb-print of a paper-boy.

'This is all terribly vulgar,' Sylvia bewailed; but Jack, Arthur, and Olive were all firm in the need for thorough advertisement, and she acquiesced woefully. In January she and Arthur parted for their respective tours. Jack before she went away begged Sylvia for the fiftieth time to take back the money she had settled on her god-children; he argued with her until she got angry.

'Jack, if you mention that again, I'll never come to your house any more. One of the most exquisite joys in all my life was when I was able to do that and when you and Olive were sweet enough to let me, for you really were sweet and simple in those days and not purse-proud *bourgeois*, as you are now. Please, Jack!' She had tears in her eyes. 'Don't be unkind.'

'But supposing you have children of your own?' he urged.

'Jack, don't go on. It really upsets me. I cannot bear the idea of that money's belonging to anybody but the twins.'

'Did you tell Arthur?'

'It's nothing to do with Arthur. It's only to do with me. It was my present. It was made before Arthur came on the scene.'

With great unwillingness Jack obeyed her command not to say anything more on the subject.

Sylvia earned a good enough salary to pay off all her debts by May, when her tour brought her to the suburban music-halls, and she was able to amuse herself by house-hunting for herself and Arthur. All her friends, and not the least old ones, like Gladys and Enid, took a profound interest in her approaching marriage; wedding presents even began to arrive. The most remarkable omen of the gods' pleasure was a communication she received in mid-May from Miss Dashwood's solicitors to say that Miss Dashwood had died and had left to Sylvia in her will the freehold of Mulberry Cottage with all it contained. Olive was enraptured with her good fortune and wanted to telegraph to Arthur, who was in Leeds that week; but Sylvia said that she would rather write:

Dearest Arthur,

You remember my telling you about Mulberry Cottage? Well, the most wonderful thing has happened. That old darling, Miss Dashwood, the sister of Mrs. Gainsborough's Captain, has left it to me with everything in it. It has of course for me all sorts of memories, and I want to tell you very seriously that I regard it as a sign, yes, really a sign of my wanderings and restlessness being for ever finished. It seems to me somehow to consecrate our marriage. Don't think I'm turning religious: I shall never do that. Oh no, never! But I can't help being moved by what to you may seem only a coincidence. Arthur, you must forgive me for the way in which I've often treated you. You mustn't think that because I've always bullied you in the past, I'm always going to in the future. If you want me now, I'm yours really, much more than I ever was in America, much, much more. You shall be happy with me. Oh, it's such a dear house with a big garden for London – a very big garden – and it held once two such true hearts. Do you see the foolish tears smudging the ink? They're my tears for so much. I'm going to-morrow morning to dust our house. Think of me when you get this letter as really at last
Your Sylvia

The next morning arrived a letter from Leeds, which had crossed hers:

My dear Sylvia,

I don't know how to tell you what I must tell. I was married this morning to Maimie Vernon. I don't know how I let myself fall in love with her. I never looked at her when she sang at the Pierian with you. But she got an engagement in this company and – well, you know the way things happen on tour. The only thing that makes me feel not an absolutely hopeless cad is that I've a feeling somehow that you were going to marry me more out of kindness and pity than out of love. Forgive me.
Arthur

'That funny little red-haired girl,' Sylvia gasped. Then like a surging wave the affront to her pride overwhelmed her. With an effort she looked at her other letters. One was from Michael Fane's sister:

HARDINGHAM HALL,
HUNTINGDON
May 20, 1914.

Dear Miss Scarlett,

My brother is back in England and so anxious to meet you again. I know you're playing near town at present. Couldn't you possibly come down next Sunday morning and stay till Monday? It would give us the greatest pleasure.
Yours sincerely,
Stella Prescott-Merivale

'Never,' Sylvia cried, tearing the letter into small pieces. 'Ah no – that, never, never!'

She left her rooms, and went to Mulberry Cottage. The caretaker fluttered round her to show her sense of Sylvia's importance as her new mistress. Was there nothing that she could do? Was there nothing that she could get?

Sylvia sat on the seat under the mulberry tree in the still morning sunlight of May; it was impossible to think, impossible to plan, impossible, impossible; the ideas in her brain went slowly round and round; nothing would stop them; round and round they went, getting every moment more mixed up with one another. But gradually from the confusion one idea emerged, sharp, strong, insistent: she must leave England. The moment this idea had stated itself, Sylvia could think of nothing but the swiftness and secrecy of her departure. She felt that if one person should ever fling a glance of sympathy or condolence or pity or even of mild affection, she should kill herself to set free her outraged soul. She made no plans for the future; she had no reproaches for Arthur; she had nothing but the urgency of flight as from the Furies themselves. Quickly she went back to her rooms and packed; all her big luggage she took to Mulberry Cottage and placed with the caretaker; she sent a sum of money to the solicitors and asked them to pay the woman until she came back.

At the last moment in searching through her trunks, she found the yellow shawl that was wrapped round her few treasures of ancestry. She decided to leave it behind, but on second thoughts she packed it in the only trunk she took with her: she was going back perhaps to the life of which these treasures would be the only solid pledge of continuity.

'This time, yes, I'm off with the raggle-taggle gipsies in deadly earnest!'

'Charing Cross,' she told the taxi-driver.

SYLVIA AND MICHAEL

BOOK III

I

By the time that Sylvia reached Paris she no longer blamed anybody but herself for what had happened. Everything had come about through her own greed in trying simultaneously to snatch from life artistic success and domestic bliss: she had never made a serious attempt to choose between them, and now she had lost both; for she could not expect to run away like this and succeed elsewhere to the same degree or even in the same way as in London. No doubt all her friends would deplore the step she had taken and think it madness to ruin her career; but after so much advertisement of her marriage, after the way she had revealed her most intimate thoughts to Olive, after the confidence she had shown in Arthur's devotion, there was nothing else but to run away. Yet now that the engagement had been definitely broken she felt no bitterness towards Arthur: the surprising factor was that he should have waited so long. Moreover, behind all her outraged pride, behind her regret for losing so much, deep in her mind burned a flickering intuition that she had really lost very little, and that out of this new adventure would spring a new self worthier to demand success, and more finely tempered to withstand life's onset. Even when she was sitting beneath the mulberry-tree in the first turmoil of the shock, she had felt a faint gladness that she was not going to live in Mulberry Cottage with Arthur. Already on this May morning of Paris with the chestnuts in their flowery prime she could fling behind her all the sneers and all the pity for her jilting; and though she had scarcely any money she was almost glad of her poverty, glad to be plunged once again into the vortex of existence with all the strength and all the buoyancy that time had given her. She thought of the months after she left Philip. This was a different Sylvia now, and not even yet come to what Sylvia might be. It was splendid to hear already the noise of waters round her, from which she should emerge stronger and more buoyant than she had ever imagined herself before.

Immediately upon her arrival – for with the little money she had there was not a day to be lost – Sylvia went in this mood to visit her old agent; like all parasites he seemed to know in advance that there was little blood to suck. She told him briefly what she had been doing, let

357

him suppose that there was a man in the case, and asked what work he could find for her.

The agent shook his head: without money it was difficult, nay, impossible to attempt in Paris anything like she had been doing in London. No doubt she had made a great success, but a success in London was no guarantee of a success in Paris, indeed rather the contrary. It was a pity she had not listened to him when she had the money to spend on a proper *réclame*.

'*Bref, il n'y a rien à faire, chère madame.*'

There was surely the chance of an engagement for cabaret work? The agent looked at Sylvia; and she could have struck him for the way he was so evidently pondering her age and measuring it against her looks. In the end he decided that she was still attractive enough, and he examined his books. She still sang of course and no doubt still enjoyed dancing? Well, they wanted French girls in Petersburg at the Trocadero cabaret. It would work out at four hundred and fifty francs a month, to which of course the commission on champagne would add considerably. She would have to remain on duty till three a.m., and the management reserved the right to dispense with her services if she was not a success.

'*Comme artiste ou comme grue?*' Sylvia demanded.

The agent laughed and shrugged his shoulders: he was afraid that there was nothing else remotely suitable. Sylvia signed the contract, and so little money was left in her purse that from Paris to Petersburg she travelled third class, an unpleasant experience.

The change from the Pierian Hall to the place where she was now singing could scarcely have been greater. For an audience individual, quiet, attentive, was substituted a noisy gathering of people that was not an audience at all. It had been difficult enough in old days to sing to parties drinking round a number of tables; but here to the noise of drinking was added the noise of eating, the clatter of plates, and the shouting of waiters. In a way Sylvia was glad, because she did not want anybody to listen to the songs she was singing: she preferred to come on the small stage as impersonally as an instrument in the music of the restaurant orchestra, and retire to give way to another singer without the least attention being paid either to her exit or to her successor's entrance.

Sylvia wished that the rest of the evening could have passed away as impersonally; she found it terribly hard to endure again after so long the sensation of being for sale, of being pulled into a seat beside drunken officers, of being ogled by elderly German Jews, of being treated as an equal by waiters, of feeling upon her the eyes of the manager as he reckoned her net value in champagne. There were moments when she despaired of her ability to hold out and when she was on the verge of cabling to England for money to come home. But pride kept her back and sustained her; luckily she had to do nothing at present except talk in order to induce her patrons to buy champagne by the dozen. She knew that it could not last, that sooner or later she should acquire the general reputation of being no good for anything except to sit and chatter at a table and make a man spend money on wine for nothing, and that then she should have to go because nobody would invite her to his table. She was grateful that it was Russia and not America or France or England, where a quicker return for money spent would have been expected.

When Sylvia first arrived at Petersburg, she had stayed in solitary misery at a small German hotel that lacked even the merit of being clean. After she had been performing a week, one of her fellow-artistes recommended her to a pension kept by an Englishwoman, the widow of a *chancelier* at the French Embassy: it was a long way from the cabaret, beyond the race-course, but there was the tram, and one would always find somebody to pay for the drozhky home.

Sylvia visited the pension, which was a tumble-down house in a very large garden of the rankest vegetation, a queer embrangled place; but the first impression of the guests appealed to her, and she moved into it the same afternoon. Mère Gontran, the owner, was one of those expatriated women that lose their own nationality and acquire instead a new nationality compounded of their own, their husband's, and the country they inhabit. She was about fifty-five years old, nearly six feet in height, excessively lean, with a neck like a turkey's, a weather-beaten veinous complexion, very square shoulders, and thin colourless hair done up in a kind of starfish at the back. Her eyes were very bright of an intense blue, and she had a habit of wearing odd stockings, which like her hair were always coming down, chiefly because she used her garters to keep her sleeves above her elbows. One of the twin passions of her life was animals; but she also had three sons, loutish young men who ate or smoked cigarettes all day and could hardly speak a word of English or French. Their mother on the contrary, though she had come to Petersburg as a governess thirty-five years ago and had lived there ever since, could speak hardly any Russian and only very bad French. Mère Gontran's animals were really more accomplished linguists than she, if it was true, as she asserted, that a collie she possessed could say 'good-bye,' 'adieu,' and 'proschai.' Sylvia suggested that the Russian salute had really been a sneeze, but Mère Gontran defied her to explain away the English or the French, and was angry at any doubts being cast on what she had heard with her own ears. In addition to Samuel the talking collie there was a senile bulldog called James who on a pillow of his own slept beside Mère Gontran in her bed, which was in a hut two hundred yards away from the house, at the other end of the garden. High up round the walls were hung boxes for nine cats: into these they ascended by ladders, and none of them ever attempted to sleep anywhere but in his own box, an example to the rest of the pension. There were numerous other animals about the place, the most conspicuous of which were a pony and a goat that spent most of their time in the kitchen with the only servant, a stunted Tartar who went muttering about the house and slept in a cupboard under the stairs. Mère Gontran's other great passion was spiritualism; but Sylvia did not have much opportunity to test her truthfulness in this direction, because at first she was more interested in the guests at the pension, accepting Mère Gontran as one accepts a queer fact for future investigation at the right moment.

The outstanding boarder in Sylvia's eyes was a French aviator called Carrier, who had come to give lessons and exhibitions of his skill in Petersburg. He was a great bluff creature with a loud voice and what at first seemed a boastful manner, until one realized that his brag was a kind of game which he was playing with fate. Underneath it all there lay a deep melancholy and a sense of always being very near to death; but since he would have considered the least hint of this a disgraceful display of cowardice, he was careful to cover what he might do with what he had done, which was, even allowing for brag, a great deal. It was only when Sylvia took the trouble to make friends with him that he revealed to her his fierce ambition to finish with flying as soon as possible and with the money he had made to buy a little farm in the country.

'*Tu sais, la terre vaut mieux que le ciel,*' he told her.

He was superstitious, and boasted loudly of his materialism: venturing upon what was still largely an unknown element he relied upon mascots, while preserving a profound contempt for God.

'I've not ever seen him yet,' he used to say, 'though I've flown higher than anybody.'

His chest of drawers was covered with small talismans, some the pledges of fortune given him by ladies, others picked up in significant surroundings or conditions of mind. He wore half-a-dozen rings, not one of which was worth fifty francs, but all of which were endowed with protective qualities. By the scapulars and medals he carried round his neck he should have been the most pietistic of men, but however sacred their inscriptions they counted with him as merely more portable guarantees than the hideous little monkeys and mandarins that littered his room.

'When I've finished,' he told Sylvia, 'I shall throw all this away. When I'm digging in the good earth, my mascot will be my spade, nothing else, *je t'assure*.'

Sylvia asked him why he had ever taken up flying.

'When I was small I adored my *bécane*: afterwards I adored my *automobile*. *On arrive comme ça.* Ah, if the fools hadn't invented biplanes, how happy I should be.'

Then perhaps a few moments later he would find himself in the presence of an audience, and one heard him at his boasting:

'*Bigre!* I am sorry for the man who cannot fly. One has not lived if one has not flown. The clouds! One would say a feather-bed beneath. To-morrow I shall loop the loop at five thousand *mètres*. One might say that all Petersburg will be regarding me.'

There were two young acrobatic jugglers staying at the pension, who performed some extremely dangerous acts, but who performed them with such ease that they seemed like nothing, especially as the acrobats themselves were ladylike to a ludicrous degree.

'Oh, Bobbie, say, wouldn't it be fine to fly? Would you be terribly frightened? I should. Oh, I should be frightened.'

'Don't you ever feel s-sick?' Bobbie asked the aviator.

For these two young men Carrier reserved his most hair-raising tales, which always ended in Willie's saying to Bobbie:

'Oh, Bobbie, I s-s-simply can't listen to any more. So now! Oh, it does make me feel so funny. Doesn't it you, Bobbie?'

Then arm-in-arm, giggling like two girls, they used to trip out of hearing, and Carrier would spit in bewilderment. Once he invited Bobbie to accompany him on a flight, at which Willie screamed, flung his arms round Bobbie's neck, and created a scene. Yet that same evening they both balanced themselves with lamps on a high ladder, until the audience actually stopped eating for a moment and held its breath.

Sylvia found the long hours of the cabaret very fatiguing: even in old days she had never thought the life anything but the most cruel exaction made by the rich man for his pleasure. She was determined to survive the strain that was being put upon her, but she had moments of depression during which she saw herself going under with the female slaves round her. Her fatigue was increased by having to take the long tram-ride down to the cabaret, when the smell of her fellow-passengers was a torture: she could not afford, however, to pay the fare of a drozhky twice in one day, and she did not always find somebody to pay for her drive home. The contract with the management stipulated that she should be released from her nightly task at three o'clock; but she was very often kept until five o'clock when the champagne was flowing and when it would have been criminal in the eyes of the management to break up a profitable party. She found that the four hundred and fifty francs a month was not enough to keep her in Petersburg; it had sounded a reasonably large salary in Paris, but it barely paid the board at Mère Gontran's: she was therefore dependent for everything above this on the commission of about five francs she received on each bottle of champagne opened under her patronage. Fortunately it seemed to give pleasure to the wild frequenters of this cabaret when a bottle was knocked over on the floor; yet with every device it was not always possible to escape drinking too much.

One day at the beginning of July Sylvia discussed the future with Carrier, and he advised her to surrender and return to England; he even offered to lend her the money for the fare. It was a hot day, and she had a bad headache; she called it a headache, but it was less local than that. her whole body ached beneath a weight of despair. Sylvia had taken Carrier into her confidence about her broken marriage and explained why it was impossible to return to England yet awhile; he contested all her arguments, and in the mood that she was in she gave way to him. They spoke in French, and arguments always seemed more incontestable in a language that refused to allow anything in the nature of a vague explanation: besides, her own body was responding against her will to the logic of surrender.

'Pride is all very well,' said Carrier. 'I am proud of being the greatest aviator of the moment, but if I fall and smash myself to pulp, what becomes of my pride? It's impossible for you to lead the life you are leading now without debasing yourself, and then where will your pride be? Listen to me. You have been at the cabaret very little over a month, and already it is telling upon you. It is very good that you are able even for so long to keep men at a distance, but are you keeping them at a distance? For me it is the same thing logically if you drink with men or—' he shrugged his shoulders. 'You sell your freedom in either case. N'est-ce pas que j'ai raison, ma petite Sylvie? For me it would be a greater pride to return to England and walk with my head in the air and laugh at the world. Besides, you have a je ne sais quoi that will prevent the world from laughing, but if you continue you will have nothing. When I fall and smash myself to pulp, I shan't care about the world's laughter. Nor will you.'

Indeed he was right, Sylvia thought: that first impulse of defiance seemed already like a piece of petulance, the gesture of a spoilt child.

'And you will let me as a good copain lend you the money for your fare back?'

'No,' Sylvia said. 'I think I can just manage to earn it by going once more to-night to the cabaret. I've arranged to meet some count with an unpronounceable name, who will probably open at least twenty-four bottles. I get my week's salary to-night also. I shall have with what I have saved enough to travel back as I came, third-class. It has been a thoroughly third-class adventure, *mon vieux*. A thousand thanks for your kindness, but I must pay my pride the little solace of earning enough to get me home again.'

Carrier shrugged his shoulders.

'It must be as you feel. That I understand. But it gives me much pleasure that you are going to be wise. I wish you *de la veine* to-night.'

He pressed upon her a mascot to charm fortune into attendance: it was a little red devil with his tongue sticking out.

Sylvia went down to the cabaret that evening with the firm intention of its being the last occasion; her headache had grown worse all the afternoon and the gloom upon her spirit was deepening. What a fool she had been to run away with so much assurance of having the courage to endure this life, what a fool she had been! For the first time the thought of suicide presented itself to her as a practical solution of everything. In her present state she could perceive not one valid argument against it. Who had attacked existence with less caution than she, and who had deserved more from it in consequence? Had she once flinched? Had she once taken the easier path? Yes, there had been Arthur: that was the first time she had given way to indecision, and how swiftly the punishment had followed. Was it really worth while to seek now to repair that mistake? Was anything worth while? Except to go suddenly out of it all, passing as abruptly from life to death as she had passed from one society to another, one tour to another, one country to another. She would abide by to-night's decision: if fortune put it into the head of the count with the unpronounceable name to buy enough bottles of champagne to make up what was still wanting to her fare, she would return to England, devote herself to her work, turn again to books, watch over her godchildren, and live at Mulberry Cottage. If on the other hand the fare should not be made up on this night, why then she should kill herself. To-night should be a night of hell. How her body was burning: how vile the people smelt in this tram: how wearisome was this garish sunset. She took from her velvet bag the red devil that Carrier had given her: in this feverish atmosphere it had a certain fitness, a portentousness even: one could almost believe it really was a tribute to fate.

The cabaret was crowded that evening; never before had there been such a hurly-burly of greed and thirst. Sylvia by good luck was feeling thirsty; for the dust from the tram had parched her mouth, and her tongue was like cork: so much the better, because if she was going to win that champagne she must be able herself to drink. The tintamarre of plates, knives, and forks; the chickerchack as of multitudinous apes; the blare and glare would have prevented the loudest soprano in the world from sounding more than the squeak of a slate-pencil; and Sylvia sang with gestures alone, forming with her lips mute words. 'I'm paid for my body not for my voice; so let my body play the antic,' she muttered angrily.

When her turn was over, Sylvia came down and joined the two young Russians, who were waiting for her with another girl at a table on which already the bottles of champagne were standing like giant pawns.

'*Ils ont la cuite*,' the girl whispered to Sylvia. '*Alors, il faut briffer, chérie; autrement ils seront trop soûlés.*'

This seemed good advice, because if their hosts were too drunk too soon they might get tired of the entertainment; and Sylvia proposed an adjournment to eat, though she had little enough appetite. As a matter of fact the men wanted to drink vodka when supper was proposed, and not merely to drink it themselves, but to make Sylvia and the other girl keep them company glass by glass. In Sylvia's condition to drink vodka would have been to drink liquid fire, and she managed to plead thirst with such effect that the Count benevolently ordered twenty-four bottles of champagne to be brought immediately for her to quench it. The other girl was full of admiration for Sylvia's strategy: if the worse came to the worst they would have earned seventy-five francs each, and could boast of a successful evening. Sylvia, however, wanted a hundred and fifty francs for herself, and invoking the little red devil she showed a way of breaking a bottle in half by filling it with hot water, saturating a string in methylated spirits, tying the string round the bottle, setting light to it, and afterwards tapping the bottle gently with a knife until it broke. The Count was delighted with this trick, but thought, as Sylvia hoped he would think, that the trick would be much better if practised on an unopened bottle of champagne. In this way twenty-six bottles were broken in childish rage by the Count, because the trick only worked with the help of hot water. He was by now in a state of drunken obstinacy, and being determined to show the superiority of the human mind over matter he ordered twenty-four more bottles of champagne, as a Roman Emperor might have ordered two dozen slaves to test an empirical method of execution. By a fluke he managed to succeed with the twenty-fourth bottle, and having by now gathered round him an audience, he challenged the onlookers to repeat the trick. Other women were anxious for their hosts to excel, particularly with such profit to themselves; soon at every table in the cabaret champagne-bottles were being cracked like eggs. The Count was afraid that there might not be enough wine left to carry them through the evening and ordered another two dozen bottles to be held in reserve for his table.

Sylvia, though she was feeling horribly ill by now, was nevertheless at peace, for she had earned her fare back to England. Unluckily she could not quit the table and go home, because unless she waited until three she would not be paid her commission on the champagne. She felt herself receding from the noise of breaking glass all round her, and thought she was going to faint, but with an effort she gathered the noise round her again and tried to believe that the room still existed. She seemed to be catching hold of the great chandelier that hung from the middle of the ceiling, and fancied that it was only her will and courage to maintain her hold that was keeping the cabaret and everybody in it from destruction.

'*Tu es malade, chérie?*' the other girl was asking.

'*Rien, rien,*' she was whispering. '*La chaleur.*'

'*Oui, il fait très chaud.*'

The laughter and shouts of triumph rose higher: the noise of breaking glass was like the waves upon a beach of shingle.

'*Pourquoi il te regarde?*' she found herself asking.

'*Personne ne me regarde, chérie,*' the other girl replied.

But somebody was looking at her, somebody seated in one of the boxes for private supper-parties that were fixed all round the hall, somebody tall with short fair hair sticking up like a brush, somebody in uniform. He was beckoning to her now and inviting her to join him in the box. He had slanting eyes, cruel eyes that glittered and glittered.

'*Il te regarde. Il te regarde,*' said Sylvia hopelessly. '*Il te veut. Oh, mon dieu, il te veut. Quoi faire? Il n'y a rien à faire. Il n'y a rien à faire. Il t'aura. Tu seras perdue. Perdue!*' she moaned.

'*Dis, Sylvie, dis, qu'est-ce que tu as? Tu me fais peur. Tes yeux sont comme les yeux d'une folle. Est-ce que tu as pris l'éther ce soir?*'

It seemed to Sylvia that her companion was being dragged to damnation before her eyes, and she implored her to flee while there was still time.

Somebody stood up on a table and shouted at the top of his voice:

'*Il n'y a plus de champagne!*'

The Count was much excited by this and demanded immediately how they were going to spend the money they had brought with them. If there was no more champagne, they should have to drink vodka, but first they must play skittles with the empty bottles that were not already broken to pieces. He picked a circular cheese from the table and bowled it across the room.

'*Encore du fromage! Encore du fromage!*' everybody was shouting, and soon everywhere crimson cheeses were rolling along the floor.

'The cheeses belong to me,' the Count cried. 'Nobody else is to order cheeses. *Garçon! Garçon!* bring me all the cheeses you have. The cheeses are mine. Mine! Mine!'

His voice rose to a scream.

'*Mon dieu, il vont se battre à cause du fromage,*' cried the other girl, holding her hand to her eyes and cowering in her chair.

By this time the management thought it would soon lose what it had made that evening and ordered the cabaret to be closed. The girls, who were anxious to escape, ran to be paid for their champagne. Sylvia swayed and nearly fell in the rush; her companion kept her head and exacted from the management every kopeck. Then she dragged Sylvia with her to a drozhky, put her in, and said good-night.

'*Tu ne viens pas avec moi?*' Sylvia cried.

'*Non, non, il faut que j'aille avec lui.*'

'*Avec l'homme qui te regardait de la loge?*'

'*Non, non, avec mon ami.*'

She gave the address of the pension to the driver and vanished in the confusion. Sylvia fancied that this girl was lost for ever, and wept to herself all the way home, but without shedding a single tear: her body was like fire. There was nobody about in the pension when she arrived back; she dragged herself up to her room and lay down on the bed fully dressed. It seemed that all reality was collapsing fast, and she clutched the notes stuffed into her corsage as the only solid fact left to her, the only link between herself and home. Once or twice she vaguely wondered if she were really ill, but her mental state was so much worse than the physical pain that she struggled feebly to quieten her nerves and kept on trying to assure herself that her own unnatural excitement was nothing except the result of the unnatural excitement at the cabaret. She found herself wondering if she were going mad, and trying to piece together the links of the chain that would lead her to the explanation of this madness.

'What could have made me go mad suddenly like this?' she kept moaning.

It seemed that if she could only discover the cause of her madness she should be able to cure it. All her attention was soon taken up in watching little round red devils that kept rising out of the floor beside the bed, little round red devils that swelled and ripened like tomatoes, burst, and vanished. Her faculties concentrated upon discovering a reasonable explanation for such a queer occurrence; many explanations presented themselves, hovered upon the outskirts of her brain, and escaped before they could be stated. There was no doubt in Sylvia's mind that a reasonable explanation existed, and it was tantalizing never to be able to catch it, because it was quite certain that such an explanation would have been very interesting; at any rate it was a relief to know that there was an explanation and that these devils were not figments of the imagination. As soon as she had settled that they had an objective existence, it became rather amusing to watch them: there was a new variety now that floated about the floor like bubbles before they burst.

Suddenly Sylvia sat up on the bed and listened: the stairs were creaking under the footsteps of some heavy person who was ascending. It must be Carrier. She should go out and call to him: she should like him to see those devils. She went out into the passage dove-grey with the dawn, and called. Ah, it was not Carrier: it was that man who had stared from the box at her friend! She closed the door hurriedly and bolted it; every sensation of being ill had departed from her; she could feel nothing but an unspeakable fear. She put her hand to her forehead: it was dripping wet, and she shivered. The devils were nowhere to be seen; dawn was creeping about the room in a grey mist. The door opened, and the bolt fell with a clatter upon the floor: she shrank back upon the bed, burying her face in the pillow. The intruder clanked up and down the room with his sword, but never spoke a word; at last Sylvia, finding that it was impossible to shut him out by closing her eyes and ears to his presence, sat up and asked him in French what he wanted and why he had broken into her room like this. All her unnatural mental excitement had died away before this drunken giant who was staring at her from glazed eyes and leaning unsteadily with both hands upon his sword; she felt nothing but an intense physical weariness and a savage desire to sleep.

'Why didn't you wait for me at the cabaret?' the giant demanded in a thick voice.

Sylvia estimated the distance between herself and the door, and wondered if her aching legs would carry her there quickly enough to escape those huge freckled hands that were silky with golden hairs. Her heart was beating so loudly that she was afraid he would hear it and be angry.

'You didn't ask me to wait,' she said. 'It was my friend whom you wanted. She's still there. You've made a mistake. Why don't you go back and look for her?'

He banged his sword upon the floor angrily.

'A trick! A trick to get rid of me,' he muttered. Then he unbuckled his sword, flung it against a chair, and began to unbutton his tunic.

'But you can't stay here,' Sylvia cried. 'Don't you understand that you've made a mistake? You don't want *me*. Go away from here.'

'Money?' the giant muttered. 'Take it.'

He put his hand in his pocket, pulled out a bundle of notes and threw them on the bed, after which he took off his tunic.

'You're drunk or mad,' Sylvia cried, now more exasperated than frightened. 'Go out of my room before I wake up the house.'

The giant paid not the least attention, and seating himself on a chair bent over to pull off his boots. Sylvia again tried to muster enough strength to rise, but her limbs were growing weaker every moment.

'And if you're not the girl I wanted,' said the giant looking up from his boots, 'you're a *girl*, aren't you? I've paid you, haven't I? A splendid state the world's coming to when a cocotte takes it into her head to argue with a Russian officer who pays her the honour of his intentions. The world's turning upside-down. The people must have a lesson. Come, get off that bed and help me undo these boots.'

'Do you know that I'm English?' Sylvia said. 'You'll find that even Russian officers cannot insult English women.'

'A cocotte has no nationality,' the giant contradicted solemnly. 'She is common property. Come, if you had wished to talk, you should have joined my table earlier in the evening. One does not wish to talk when one is sleepy.'

The English acrobats slept next door to Sylvia, and she hammered on the partition.

'Are you killing bugs?' the giant asked. 'You need not bother. They never disturb me.'

Sylvia went on hammering: her arms were getting weaker, and unless help came soon she would faint. There was a tap on the door.

'Come in,' she cried. 'Come in at once – at once!'

Willie entered in purple silk pyjamas, rubbing his eyes.

'Whatever is it, Sylvia?'

'Take this drunken brute out of my room.'

'Bobbie! Bobbie!' he called. 'Come here, Bobbie! Bobbie! Will you come. You are mean. Oh, there's such a nasty man in Sylvia's room. Oh, he's something dreadful to look at.'

The drunken officer stared at Willie in amazement, trying to make up his mind if he were an alcoholic vision: his judgment was still further shaken by the appearance of Bobbie in pyjamas of emerald green silk.

'Oh, Willie, he's got a sword,' said Bobbie. 'Oh, doesn't he look fierce. Oh, he does look fierce. Most alarming, I'm sure.'

The intruder staggered to his feet.

'*Foutez-moi le camp*,' he bellowed, making a grab for his sword.

'For heaven's sake get rid of the brute,' Sylvia moaned. 'I'm too weak to move.'

The two young men pirouetted into the middle of the room, as they were wont to pirouette upon the stage, with arms stretched out in a curve from the shoulder and fingers raised minicingly above an imaginary teacup held between the first finger and thumb. When they reached the giant, they stopped short to sustain the preliminary pose of a female acrobat: then turning round they ran back a few steps, turned round again and with a scream flung themselves upon their adversary; he went down with a crash, and they danced upon his prostrate form like two butterflies over a cabbage.

The noise had wakened the other inhabitants of the pension, who came crowding into Sylvia's room; with the rest was Carrier and they managed to extract from her a vague account of what had happened. The aviator in a rage demanded an explanation of his conduct from the officer, who called him a *maquereau*. Carrier was strong; with help from the acrobats he had pushed the officer half-way through the window when Mère Gontran, who notwithstanding her bedroom being two hundred yards away from the pension had an uncanny faculty for divining when anything had gone wrong, appeared on the scene. Thirty-five years in Russia had made her very fearful of offending the military, and she implored Carrier and the acrobats to think what they were doing: in her red dressing-gown she looked like an insane cardinal.

'They'll confiscate my property. They'll send me to Siberia. Treat his excellency more gently, I beg. Sylvia, tell them to stop. Sylvia, he's going – he's going – he's gone!'

He was gone indeed, head first into a clump of lilacs underneath the window, whither his tunic and sword followed him.

The adventure with the drunken officer had exhausted the last forces of Sylvia; she lay back on the bed in a semi-trance soothed by the unending bibble-babble all round. She was faintly aware of somebody's taking her hand and feeling her pulse, of somebody's saying that her eyes were like a dead woman's, of somebody's throwing a coverlet over her. Then the bibble-babble became much louder; there was a sound of crackling and a smell of smoke, and she heard shouts of 'fire!' 'fire!' 'he has set fire to the outhouse!' There was a noise of splashing water, a rushing sound of water, a roar of a thousand torrents in her head; the people in the room became animated surfaces, cardboard figures without substance and without reality; the devils began once more to sprout from the floor;

she felt that she was dying, and in the throes of dissolution she struggled to explain that she must travel back to England, that she must not be buried in Russia. It seemed to her in a new access of semi-consciousness that Carrier and the two acrobats were kneeling by her bed and trying to comfort her, that they were patting her hands kindly and gently. She tried to warn them that they would blister themselves if they touched her, but her tongue seemed to have separated itself from her body. She tried to tell them that her tongue was already dead, and the effort to explain racked her whole body. Then suddenly, dark and gigantic figures came marching into the room: they must be demons, and it was true about hell. She tried to scream her belief in immortality and to beg a merciful God to show mercy and save her from the Fiend. The sombre forms drew near her bed. From an unimaginably distant past she saw framed in fire the picture of The Impenitent Sinner's Deathbed that used to hang in the kitchen at Lille, and again from the past came suddenly back the text of a sermon preached by Dorward at Green Lanes. *Though your sins be as scarlet, they shall be as white as snow*. It seemed to her that if only she could explain to God that her name was really Snow and that Scarlett was only the name assumed for her by her father, all might even now be well. The sombre forms had seized her, and she beat against them with unavailing hands; they snatched her from the bed and wrapped her round and round with something that stifled her cries; with her last breath she tried to shriek a warning to Carrier of the existence of hell, to beg him to put away his little red devils lest he when he should ultimately fall from the sky should fall as deep as hell.

Sylvia came out of her delirium to find herself in the ward of a hospital kept by French nuns; she asked what had been the matter with her, and smiling compassionately they said it was a bad fever. She lay for a fortnight in a state of utter lassitude, watching the nuns going about their work as she would have watched birds in the cool deeps of a forest. The lassitude was not unpleasant; it was a fatigue so intense that her spirit seemed able to leave her tired body and float about among the shadows of this long room. She knew that there were other patients in the ward, but she had no inclination to know who they were or what they looked like; she had no desire to communicate with the outside world, nor any anxiety about the future. She could not imagine that she should ever wish to do anything except lie here watching the nuns at their work like birds in the cool deeps of a forest. When the doctor visited her and spoke cheerfully, she wondered vaguely how he managed to keep his very long black beard so frizzy, but she was not sufficiently interested to ask him. To his questions about her bodily welfare, she let her tired body answer automatically, and often, when the doctor was bending over to listen to her heart or lungs, her spirit would have mounted up to float upon the shadows of sunlight rippling over the ceiling, that he and her body might commune without disturbing herself. At last there came a morning when the body grew impatient of being left behind and when it trembled with a faint desire to follow the spirit. Sylvia raised herself up on her elbow, and asked a nun to bring her a looking-glass.

'But all my hair has been cut,' she exclaimed. She looked at her eyes: there was not much life in them, yet they were larger than she had ever seen them, and she liked them better than before, because they were now very kind eyes: this new Sylvia appealed to her.

She put the glass down and asked if she had been very ill.

'Very ill indeed,' said the nun.

Sylvia longed to tell the nun that she must not believe all she had said when she was delirious: and then she wondered what she had said.

'Was I very violent in my delirium?' she asked.

The nun smiled.

'I thought I was in hell,' said Sylvia seriously. 'When are my friends coming to see me?'

The nun looked grave.

'Your friends have all gone away,' she said at last. 'They used to come every day to enquire after you, but they went away when war was declared.'

'War?' Sylvia repeated. 'Did you say war?'

The nun nodded.

'War?' she went on. 'This isn't part of my delirium? You're not teasing me? War between whom?'

'Russia, France, and England are at war with Germany and Austria.'

'Then Carrier has left Petersburg?'

'Hush,' said the nun. 'It's no longer Petersburg. It's Petrograd now.'

'But I don't understand. Do you mean to tell me that everybody has changed his name? I've changed my name back to my real name. My name is Sylvia Snow now. I changed it when I was delirious, but I shall always be Sylvia Snow. I've been thinking about it all these days while I've been lying so quiet. Did Carrier leave any message for me? He was the aviator, you know.'

'He has gone back to fight for France,' the nun said, crossing herself. 'He was very sorry about your being so ill. You must pray for him.'

'Yes, I will pray for him,' Sylvia said. 'And there is nobody left? Those two funny little English acrobats with fair curly hair. Have they gone?'

'They've gone too,' said the nun. 'They came every day to enquire for you, and they brought you flowers, which were put beside your bed, but you were unconscious.'

'I think I smelt a sweetness in the air sometimes,' Sylvia said.

'They were always put outside the window at night,' the nun explained.

The faintest flicker of an inclination to be amused at the nun's point of view about flowers came over Sylvia; but it scarcely endured for an instant, because it was so obviously the right point of view in this hospital where even flowers not to seem out of place must acquire orderly habits. The nun asked her if she wanted anything and passed on down the ward when she shook her head.

Sylvia lay back to consider her situation and to pick up the threads of normal existence, which seemed so inextricably tangled at present that she felt like a princess in a fairy tale who has been set an impossible task by an envious witch.

In the first place, putting on one side all the extravagance of delirium, Sylvia was conscious of a change in her personality so profound and so violent, that now with the return of reason and with the impulse to renewed activity she was convinced of her rightness in deciding to go back to her real name of Sylvia Snow. The anxiety that she had experienced during her delirium to make the change positively remained from that condition as something of value that bore no relation to the grosser terrors of hell she had experienced. The sense of regeneration that she was feeling at this moment could not entirely be explained by her mind's reaction to the peace of the hospital, to the absence of pain, and to her bodily well-being. She was able to set in its proportion each of these factors, and when she had done so there still remained this emotion that was indefinable unless she accepted for it the definition of regeneration.

'The fact is I've eaten roseleaves and I'm no longer a golden ass,' she murmured. 'But what I want to arrive at is when exactly I was turned into an ass and when I ate the roseleaves.'

For a time her mind unused since her fever to concentrated thinking wandered off into the tale of Apuleius. She wished vaguely that she had the volume so inscribed by Michael Fane with her in Petersburg, but she had left it behind at Mulberry Cottage. It was some time before she brought herself back to the realization that the details of the Roman story had not the least bearing upon her meditation and that the symbolism of the enchanted transformation and the recovery of human shape by eating roseleaves had been an essentially modern and romantic gloss upon the old author. This gloss, however, had served extraordinarily well to symbolize her state of mind before she had been ill, and she was not going to abandon it now.

'I must have had an experience once that fitted in with the idea, or it would not recur to me like this with such an imputation of significance.'

Sylvia thought hard for a while; the nun on day duty was pecking away at a medicine-bottle, and the busy little noise competed with her thoughts so that she was determined before the nun could achieve her purpose with the medicine-bottle to discover when she became a golden ass. Suddenly the answer flashed across her mind; at the same moment the nun triumphed over her bottle, and the ward was absolutely still again.

'I became a golden ass when I married Philip and I ate the roseleaves when Arthur refused to marry me.'

This solution of the problem, though she knew that it was not radic-ally more satisfying than the defeat of a toy puzzle, was nevertheless wonderfully comforting, so comforting that she fell asleep and woke up late in the afternoon, refreshingly alert and eager to resume her unravel-ling of the tangled skein.

'I became a golden ass when I married Philip,' she repeated to herself.

For a while she tried to reconstruct the motives that fourteen years ago had induced her toward that step. If she had really begun her life all over again, it should be easy to do this. But the more she pondered herself at the age of seventeen, the more impossibly remote that Sylvia seemed. Certain results, however, could even at this distance of time be ascribed to that unfortunate marriage: amongst others the three months after she left Philip. When Sylvia came to survey all her life since, she saw how those three months had lurked at the back of everything, how really they had spoilt everything.

'Have I fallen a prey to remorse?' she asked herself. 'Must I for ever be haunted by the memory of what was after all a necessary incident to my assumption of assishness? Did I not pay for them that day at Mulberry Cottage when I could not be myself to Michael, but could only bray at him the unrealities of my outward shape?'

Lying here in the cool hospital Sylvia began to conjure against her will the incidents of those three fatal months, and so weak was she still from the typhus that she could not shake off their obsession. Her mind clutched at other memories; but no sooner did she think that she was safely wrapped up in their protecting fragrance than like Furies those three months drove her mind forth from its sanctuary, and scourged it with cruel images.

'This is the sort of madness that makes a woman kill her seducer,' said Sylvia, 'this insurgent rage at feeling that the men who crossed my path during those three months still live without remorse for what they did.'

Gradually, however, her rage died down before the pleadings of reasonableness; she recalled that somewhere she had read how the human body changes entirely every seven years: this reflection consoled her, and though she admitted that it was a trivial and superficial consolation, since remorse was conceived with the spirit rather than with the body, nevertheless the thought that not one corpuscle of her present blood existed fourteen years ago restored her sense of proportion and enabled her to shake off the obsession of those three months, at any rate so far as to allow her to proceed with her contemplation of the new Sylvia lying here in this hospital.

'Then of course there was Lily,' she said to herself. 'How can I possibly excuse my treatment of Lily, or not so much my treatment of her as my attitude towards her? I suppose all this introspection is morbid, but having been brought up sharp like this and having been planked down on this bed of interminable sickness, who wouldn't be morbid? It's better to have it out with myself now, lest when I emerge from here – for incredible as it seems just at present I certainly shall emerge one fine morning – I start being introspective instead of getting down to the hard facts of earning a living and finding my way back to England. Lily!' she went on. 'I believe really when I look back at it that I took a cruel delight in watching Lily's fading. It seemed jolly and cynical to predestine her to maculation, to regard her as a flower, an almost inanimate thing that could only be displayed by somebody else and was incapable of developing herself. Yet in the end she did develop herself. I was very ill then; but when I was in the clinic at Rio I had none of the sensations that I have now. What sensations did I have then? Mostly I believe, they were worries about Lily, because she did not come to see me. Strange that something so essentially insignificant as Lily could have created such a catastrophe for Michael, and that I, when she went her own way, let her drop as easily as a piece of paper from a carriage. The fact was that having smirched myself and survived the smirching I was unable to fret myself very much over Lily's smirching. And yet I did fret myself in a queer irrational way. But what use to continue? I behaved badly to Lily, but I can't excuse my attitude towards her by saying that I behaved badly to myself also.'

The longer Sylvia went on with the reconstruction of the past, the more deeply did she feel that she was to blame for everything in it.

'And yet I had the impudence to resent Arthur's treatment of me,' she cried.

The nun hastened to her bedside and asked her what she wanted.

'I'm so sorry, sister, I was talking to myself. I think I must really be very much better to-day.'

374

The nun shook her forefinger at Sylvia and retired again to her table at the end of the ward.

'Why, I deserved a much worse humiliation,' Sylvia went on. 'And I got it too. The fact was that when I ate those roseleaves and became a woman again I was so elated really that I thought everything I had done in the shape of an ass had been obliterated by the disenchantment. Ah, how much, how tremendously I deserve the humiliation which that Russian officer inflicted. And then mercifully came this fever on top of it, and I have got to rise from this bed and confront life from an entirely different point of view. I'm going to start from where I was that afternoon in Brompton Cemetery, when I was speculating about the human soul. Obviously, now I look back at it, I was just then beginning to apprehend that I might after all possess a soul with obligations to something more permanent than the body it inhabited. What a fool Philip was! If he'd only nurtured my soul instead of my body. If he'd only not bit by bit dried it up to something so small that it became powerless to compete with the arrogant body that held it. I wonder if he's still alive. But of course he's still alive. He's only forty-six now. Really I'd like to write and explain what happened. However, he'd only laugh – he was always so very contemptuous of souls. Anyway, nothing will ever induce me to believe that my soul hasn't grown in the most extraordinary way during this fever. What a triumph she has had over her poor body. Where's that looking-glass?'

She called to the nun and begged her to bring her the looking-glass again. The nun brought it and tried to console Sylvia for the loss of her hair.

'But I'm rejoicing in it,' Sylvia declared. 'I'm rejoicing in the sight I present to the world. Look here, can't you sit down beside me and tell me something about your religion? I'm absolutely bursting for a revelation. You fast, don't you, and spend long nights and days in prayer? Well, I am in the sort of condition in which you find yourself at the end of a long bout of fasting and prayer. I'm as light as a feather. I could achieve levitation with very little difficulty.'

The nun regarded Sylvia in perplexity.

'Have you thanked Almighty God for your recovery?' she asked.

'No, of course I haven't. I can't thank somebody I know nothing about,' said Sylvia impatiently. 'Besides, it's no good thanking God for my recovery unless I am sure I ought to be grateful. Mere living for the sake of living seems to me as sensual as any other appetite. Sister, can't you give me the key to life?'

The nun sheltered herself beneath an array of pious phrases; she was

375

like a person who has been surprised naked and hurriedly flings on all the clothes in reach.

'All that you're saying means nothing to me,' said Sylvia sadly. 'And the reason of it is that you've never lived. You've only looked at evil from the outside; you've only heard of unbelief.'

'I'll make a Novena for you,' said the nun hopelessly. She said it in the same way as she would have offered to knit a woollen vest. 'To-day is the Assumption.' It was as if she justified the woollen vest by a change in the weather.

Sylvia thanked her for the Novena just as she would have thanked her for the woollen vest.

'Or perhaps you'd like a priest?' the nun suggested.

Sylvia shook her head.

'I don't feel I require professional treatment yet,' she said. 'Don't look so sad, little sister, I expect your Novena will help me to what I'm trying to find – if I'm trying to find anything,' she added pensively. 'I think really I'm waiting to be found.'

The nun retired disconsolate; the next day Sylvia's spiritual problems vanished before the problem of getting up for the first time, of wavering across the ward and collapsing into a wicker chair among three other convalescent patients who were talking and sewing in the sunlight.

The uniformity of their grey shawls and grey dressing-gowns made Sylvia pay more attention to the faces of her fellow sufferers than she might otherwise have done; she sat in silence for a while, exhausted by her progress across the ward, and listened to their conversation which was carried on in French, though as far as she could make out none of them was of French nationality. Presently a young woman with a complexion like a slightly shrivelled apple turned to Sylvia and asked in her own language if she were not English.

Sylvia nodded.

'I'm English too. It's pleasant to meet a fellow-countrywoman here. What are you going to do about the war?'

'I don't suppose much action on my part will make any difference,' said Sylvia with a laugh. 'I don't suppose I could stop it, however hard I tried.'

The Englishwoman laughed because she evidently wanted to be polite; but it was mirthless laughter like an actor's at rehearsal, a mere sound that was required to fill in a gap in the dialogue.

'Of course not,' she agreed. 'I was wondering if you would go back to England as soon as you got out of hospital.'

'I shall if I can rake together the money for my fare,' Sylvia said.

'Oh, won't your family pay your fare back? Didn't you get that in the agreement?'

'I don't possess a family,' Sylvia said.

'Oh, aren't you a governess? How funny.'

'It would be very much funnier if I was,' said Sylvia.

'My name is Eva Savage. What's yours?'

Sylvia hesitated a moment and then plunged.

'Sylvia Snow.'

Immediately afterwards with an access of timidity she supplemented this by explaining that on the stage she called herself Sylvia Scarlett.

'On the stage,' repeated the little governess. 'Are you on the stage? You are lucky.'

Sylvia looked at her in surprise, and realized how much younger she was than a first glance at her led one to suppose.

'I came out to Russia when I was nineteen,' Miss Savage went on. 'And of course that's better than staying in England to teach, though I hate teaching.'

Sylvia asked how old she was now, and when she heard that she was only twenty-four she decided that illness must be the cause of that shrivelled rosy skin that made her look like an old maid of fifty.

They talked for a while of their illness and compared notes, but it seemed that Miss Savage must have had a mild attack, for she had been brought into the hospital some time after Sylvia and had already been up a week.

'I'm going to ask the sister-in-charge to let me sleep in the bed next to yours,' said Miss Savage. 'After all, we're the only two English girls here.'

Sylvia did not feel at all sure that she liked this plan, but she did not want to hurt her companion's feelings and agreed without enthusiasm. Presently she asked if the other two women spoke English, and Miss Savage told her that one was a German-Swiss, the wife of a pastry cook called Benzer, and that the other was a Swedish masseuse; she did not think that either of them spoke English, but added in a low voice that they were both very common.

'Interesting?'

'No, common, awfully common,' Miss Savage insisted.

Sylvia made a gesture of impatience: her countrywomen always summed up humanity with such complacent facility. At this moment a little girl of about thirteen habited like the rest in a grey shawl came tripping down the ward, clapping her hands with glee.

'How lovely war is,' she cried in French. 'I am longing to be out of hospital. I've been in the other ward, and through the window I saw thousands and thousands of soldiers marching past. *Maman* cried yesterday when I asked her why *papa* hated soldiers. He hates them. Whenever he sees them marching past he shakes his fist and spits. But I love them.'

This child had endeared herself to the invalids of the hospital; she was a token of returning health, the boon of which she seemed to pledge to everyone in the company. Even the grim Swedish masseuse smiled and spoke gently to her in barbaric French. Moreover, here in this quiet hospital the war had not yet penetrated, it was like a far distant thunderstorm, which had driven a number of people who were out of doors to take shelter at home; as Miss Savage said to Sylvia:—

'I expect everybody got excited and afraid; yet it all seems very quiet really, and I shall stay here with my family. There's no point in *making* oneself uncomfortable.'

Sylvia agreed with Miss Savage and decided not to worry about her fare back to England, but rather to stay on for a while in Russia and get up her strength after leaving the hospital; then when she had spent her money she should work again, and when this war was over she should return to Mulberry Cottage with one or two Improvisations added to her repertory. Now that she was out of bed life seemed already simple again, and perhaps she had exaggerated the change in herself; she wished she had not spoken to the nun so intimately; one of the disadvantages of being ill was this begetting of an intimacy between the nurse and the patient, which grows out of bodily dependence into mental servitude: it was easy to understand why men so often married their nurses.

'I am not sure,' said Sylvia to herself, 'that the right attitude is not the contempt of the healthy animal for one of its kind who is sick. There's a sort of sterile sensuality about nursing and being nursed.'

Sylvia's feelings about the war were confirmed by the views of the doctor who attended her. He had felt a little nervous until England had taken her place beside Russia and France, but once she had done so, the war would be over at the latest by the middle of October.

'It's easy to see how frightened the Germans are by the way they are behaving in Belgium.'

'Why, what are they doing?' Sylvia asked.

'They've overrun it like a pack of wolves.'

'I have a sister in Brussels,' she said suddenly.

The doctor shook his head compassionately.

'But of course nothing will happen to her,' she added.

The doctor hastened to support this theory: Sylvia was still very weak, and he did not want a relapse brought on by anxiety. He changed the conversation by calling to Claudinette, the little girl who thought war was so lovely.

'Seen any more soldiers to-day?' he asked jovially.

'Thousands,' Claudinette declared. 'Oh, *monsieur*, when shall I be able to leave the hospital? It's terrible to be missing everything. Besides, I want to make *papa* understand how lovely it is to march along with everybody thinking how fine and brave it is to be a soldier. Fancy, *maman* told me he has been invited to go back to France and that he has actually refused the invitation.'

The doctor raised his eyebrows and flashed a glance at Sylvia from his bright brown eyes to express his pity for the child's innocence.

At this point Madame Benzer intervened.

'The only thing that worries me about this war is the food: it's bound to upset custom. People don't order so many tarts when they're thinking of something else. And the price of everything will go up. Luckily I've told my husband to lay in stores of flour and sugar. It's a comfort to be a neutral.'

The Swedish masseuse echoed Madame Benzer's self-congratulation:

'Of course one doesn't want to seem an egoist,' she said, 'but I can't help knowing that I shall benefit. As a neutral I shan't be able to go and nurse at the front, but I shall be useful in Petersburg.'

'Petrograd,' the doctor corrected her with marked irritation.

'I shall never get used to the change,' said the masseuse. 'When do you think I shall be strong enough to begin my work again?'

The doctor shrugged his shoulders.

'November perhaps.'

'Why, the war will be over by then,' said the masseuse indignantly.

'They're calling for volunteers in England,' Miss Savage observed to Sylvia. 'I'm sure my two brothers have gone. They've always been mad about soldiering. They're like you, Claudinette.'

'If only I could be a *vivandière*,' cried the child. She was unable to contain her romantic exultation at the idea, and snatching the doctor's stethoscope, she marched up and down the ward pursing her lips to a shrill Marseillaise.

'Children are children,' said Madame Benzer fatly.

'It's true,' sighed the doctor.

'*She's* quite well again,' said the masseuse enviously.

'I love children,' Sylvia exclaimed.

'Do you?' said Miss Savage. 'Wait till you've had to teach them. You'll hate them then!'

Claudinette's march was interrupted by the nun on duty, who was horrified at the ward's being used so noisily: though there were no fresh patients, the rule of stillness could not be broken like this. Claudinette having been deprived of her bugle, went and drummed out her martial soul upon a window-pane; the doctor, who felt a little guilty, stroked his beard and passed on.

The governess carried out her intention of having her bed moved next to Sylvia; on the first night of the change she whispered across to her in the darkness, which seemed the more intense round their beds, because at the far end of the ward a lamp burned before the image of the Virgin and enclosed by two screens the nun on night-duty sat in a dim golden mist.

'Are you awake?'

Sylvia answered in a low voice in order not to disturb the other patients; she could not bring herself to answer in a whisper, because it would have made this conversation seem surreptitious.

'Hush! Don't talk so loud. Are you a Catholic?'

'I'm nothing,' said Sylvia.

'Do tell me about your life.'

'We can talk about that in the morning.'

'Oh no, one can't talk secrets in the morning. I want to ask you something. Do you think that everybody in Russia will go and fight? You see Prince Paul isn't a soldier. You remember I told you that Prince George and Prince Paul, the two elder sons of the family, were both very handsome? Well, Prince George is in the army, but Prince Paul isn't. They both made love to me,' she added with a stifled giggle.

Sylvia lay silent.

'Are you shocked?'

'Neither shocked nor surprised,' said Sylvia coldly. 'The nobility of Russia seems to think of nothing else but making love.'

'Paul gave me a book once. I've got it here with me in my box. It's called the *Memories of a German Singer*. Would you like to read it?'

'That book,' Sylvia exclaimed scornfully. 'Why, it's the filthiest book I ever read.'

'You are shocked then,' the governess whispered. 'I thought you'd be more broad-minded. I shan't tell you now about Prince Paul. He makes love divinely. He said it was so thrilling to make love to somebody like me who looked so proper. I'm dreadfully afraid that when I get back I shall find he's gone to fight. It's awful to think how dull it will be without either George or Paul. Haven't you had any interesting love-affairs?'

'Good god,' exclaimed Sylvia angrily. 'Do you think there's anything to be proud of in having love-affairs like yours? Do you think there's anything fine in letting yourself be treated like a servant by a lascivious boy? You make me feel sick. How dare you assume that I should be interested in your – oh, I have no word to call it that can be even spoken in a whisper.'

'You *are* proper,' the governess murmured resentfully. 'I thought girls on the stage were more broad-minded.'

'Is this muttering going to continue all night?' an angry voice demanded. Further along the ward could be heard the sound of a bed rattling with indignation.

The nun pushed back her screen, and the candlelight illumined Madame Benzer sitting up on her ample haunches.

'One must not talk,' said the nun reproachfully. 'One disturbs the patients. Besides, it is against the rules to talk after the lights are put out.'

'Well, please move me away from here,' Sylvia asked, 'because if Mademoiselle stays here I shall have to talk.'

'I'm sure I'd much rather not stay in this bed,' declared Miss Savage in an injured voice. 'And *I* was only whispering. There was no noise until Mademoiselle began to talk quite loudly.'

'Is this discussion worth while?' Sylvia asked wearily.

'Am I ever to be allowed to get to sleep?' Madame Benzer demanded.

'I should like to sleep too,' protested the masseuse. 'If I'm to get strong enough to resume work in November, I need all the sleep I can get. I'm not like a child that can sleep through anything.'

'*I'm* not asleep,' cried Claudinette shrilly. 'And I'm very content that I'm not asleep. I adore to hear people talking in the night.'

The nun begged for general silence, and the ward was stilled. Sylvia lay awake in a rage, listening to Madame Benzer and the masseuse while they turned over and over with sighs and groans and much creaking of their beds. At last, however, all except herself fell asleep; their united breathing seemed like the breathing of a large and placid beast. Behind the screens in that dim golden mist the pages of the nun's breviary whispered now instead of Miss Savage; the lamp before the image of the Virgin sometimes flickered and cast upon the insipid face subtle shadows that gave humanity to what by daylight looked like a large pale blue fondant.

'Or should I say "divinity"?' Sylvia asked herself.

She lay on her side staring at the image, which was the conventional representation of Our Lady of Lourdes with eyes upraised and hands clasped to heaven. Contemplated thus the tawdry figure really acquired a supplicatory grace, and in the night the imagination dwelling upon this form began to identify itself with the attitude and to follow those upraised eyes towards an unearthly quest. Sylvia turned over on her other side with a perfectly conscious will not to be influenced externally by what she felt was an unworthy appeal. But when she had turned over she could not stay averted from the image; a restless curiosity to know if it was still upon its bracket seized her, and she turned back to her contemplation.

'How ridiculous all those stories are of supernatural winkings and blinkings,' she thought. 'Why I could very easily imagine the most acrobatic behaviour by that pathetic little blue figure. And yet it has expressed the aspirations of millions of wounded hearts.'

The thought was overwhelming: the imagination of what this figure reduplicated innumerably all over the earth had stood for descended upon Sylvia from the heart of the darkness about her, and she shuddered with awe.

'If I scoff at that,' she thought, 'I scoff at human tears. And why shouldn't I scoff at human tears? Because I should be scoffing at my own tears. And why not at my own?'

'You dare not,' the darkness sighed.

Sylvia crept out of bed and bending over the governess waked her with soft reassurances, as one wakes a child.

'Forgive me,' she whispered, 'for the way I spoke. But oh, do believe me when I tell you that love like that is terrible. I understand the dullness of your profession, and if you like I will take you with me on my gipsy life when we leave the hospital. You can amuse yourself with seeing the world; but if you want love, you must demand it with your head high. Every little governess who behaves like you creates another harlot.'

'Did you wake me up to insult me?' demanded Miss Savage.

'No, my dear, you don't understand me. I'm not thinking of what you make yourself. *You* will pay for that. I'm thinking of some baby now at its mother's breast, for whose damnation you will be responsible by giving another proof to man of woman's weakness, by having kindled in him another lust.'

'I think you'd do better to bother about your own soul instead of mine,' said Miss Savage. 'Please let me go to sleep again. When I wanted to talk, you pretended to be shocked. I asked you if you were a Catholic, and you told me you were nothing. I particularly avoided hurting your susceptibilities. The least you can do is to be polite in return.'

Sylvia went back to bed, and thinking over what the governess had said decided that after all she was right: she ought to bother with her own soul first.

Three weeks later Sylvia was told that she was now fit to leave the hospital. The nuns charged her very little for their care; but when she walked out of the door she had only about eighty roubles in the world. With rather a heavy heart she drove to Mère Gontran's pension.

II

The pension was strangely silent when Sylvia returned to it; the panic of war had stripped it bare of guests. Although she had known that Carrier and the English acrobats were gone and had more or less made up her mind that most of the girls would also be gone this complete abandonment was tristful. Mère Gontran's influence had always pervaded the pension; even before her illness Sylvia had been affected by that odd personality and had often been haunted by the unusualness of the whole place; but the disconcerting atmosphere had always been quickly and easily neutralized by the jolly mountebanks and Bohemians with whose point of view and jokes and noise she had been familiar all her life. Sylvia and the other guests had so often laughed together at Mère Gontran's eccentricity, at the tumbledown house, at the tangled garden, at the muttering handmaid, and at the animals in the kitchen, that through this careless merriment the pension had come to be no more than one of the incidents of the career they followed, something to talk of when they swirled on and lodged in another corner of the earth's surface. There would be no city in Europe at which in some cabaret one would not find a *copain* with whom to laugh over the remembrance of Mère Gontran's talking collie. But how many of these gay mountebanks dispersed by the panic of war would not have been affected by the Pension Gontran, had they returned to it like this, alone?

The garden with its rank autumnal growth was more like a jungle than ever; the unpopulous house reasserted its very self, and there was not a crack in the stucco nor a broken tile nor a warped plank that did not now maintain a haunting significance. The Tartar servant with her unintelligible mutterings, her head and face muffled in a stained green scarf, her bent form, her feet in pattens clapping like hoofs, the animals that sniffed at her heels, and her sleeping cupboard beneath the stairs heaped with faded rags, seemed an incarnation of the house's reality. For a moment when Sylvia was making signs to her that she should fetch her mistress from where buried in docks and nettles she was performing one of her queer solitary operations of horticulture, she was inclined to turn round and search anywhere else in Petrograd for a lodging rather than expose herself to the night-time here. But the consciousness of her

383

uncertain position soon scattered such fancies, and she decided that the worst of them would not be so unpleasant as to find herself at the mercy of the material horrors of a fourth-rate hotel while she was waiting for vigour to resume work; at any rate Mère Gontran was kind-hearted and English. As Sylvia reached this conclusion, the mistress of the pension followed by two cats, a hen, two pigeons, a goat, and a dog came to greet her; putting the table-fork with which she had been gardening into the pocket of her overall, she warmly embraced Sylvia, which was like being flicked on the cheek by a bramble when driving.

'Why, Sylvia, I *am* glad to see you again. Everybody's gone. Everything's closed. No more vodka allowed to be sold in public, though of course it can always be got. The war's upon us, and I'm sowing turnips under Jupiter in case we starve. All your things are quite safe. Your room hasn't been touched since you left it. I'll tell Anna to make your bed.'

Anna was not the maid-servant's real name; but one of Mère Gontran's peculiarities was, that though she could provide an individual name for every bird or beast in the place without using the same one twice, all her servants had to be called Anna in memory of her first cook of thirty years ago – a repetition that could hardly have been due to sentiment, because the first Anna, when she ran away to be married, took with her as much of her mistress's plate as she could carry.

'Hasn't my bed been made all these weeks?' Sylvia asked with a smile.

'Why should it have been made?' Mère Gontran replied. 'There hasn't been a single newcomer since you were taken off in the ambulance.'

Sylvia asked if the drunken officer had done much damage.

'Oh no, it was quite easy to extinguish the fire. He burned half the tool-shed and frightened the guinea-pigs; that was all. I was quite relieved when war was declared, because otherwise the police would probably have taken away my licence; but there again, if they had taken it away, it wouldn't have mattered much for I haven't had any lodgers since; but there again I've been able to use Carrier's room for the owls, and they're much happier in a nice room than they were nailed up to the side of the house in a packing-case. If you hear them hooting in the night, don't be frightened: you must remember that owls being night birds can't be expected to keep quiet in the night, and when they hoot it shows they're feeling at home.'

'There's nothing in the acrobats' room?' Sylvia asked anxiously; the partition between her and them had been thin.

'Such a reek of scent,' Mère Gontran exclaimed. 'Phewff! Benjamin went in after they'd gone, and he regularly shuddered. Cats are very sensitive to perfumes, as no doubt you've observed.'

'Mère Gontran,' Sylvia began. 'I want to explain my position.'

'Don't do that,' she interrupted. 'Wait till the evening and you shall throw the cards. What's the good of anticipating trouble? If the cards are unfavourable to any immediate enterprise, settle down and help me with the garden until they're favourable again. When favourable, make the journey.'

Sylvia, however, insisted on anticipating the opinion of the cards, and explained to Mère Gontran that it would be impossible for her to attempt any work for at least another six weeks on account of her weakness, and also because of her short hair which, though it was growing rapidly with close chestnut curls, was still remarkably short.

Mère Gontran asked what day it had been cut, and Sylvia said she did not know, because it had been cut when she was unconscious.

'Depend upon it they cut it when the moon was waning.'

'I hope not,' said Sylvia.

'I hope not too. I sincerely hope not,' said Mère Gontran fervently.

'It would be serious?' Sylvia suggested.

'Anything might happen. Anything!'

Mère Gontran's vivid blue eyes fixed a far horizon lowering with misfortune, and Sylvia took the opportunity of her temporary abstraction to go on with the tale of present woes.

'Money?' Mère Gontran exclaimed. 'Put it in your pocket. You were overcharged all the weeks you were with me when you were well. Deducting overcharges, I can give you six weeks' board and lodging now.'

Sylvia protested, but she would take no denial.

'At any rate,' said Sylvia finally, 'I'll avail myself of your goodness until I can communicate with people in England and get some money sent out to me.'

'Useless to communicate with anybody anywhere,' said Mère Gontran. 'No posts. No telegraphs. Everything stopped by the war. And that's where modern inventions have brought us. If you want to communicate with your friends in England, you'll have to communicate through the spirits.'

'Isn't that rather an uncertain method too?' Sylvia asked.

'Everything's uncertain,' Mère Gontran proclaimed triumphantly. 'Life's uncertain. Death's uncertain. But never mind, we'll talk to Gontran about it to-night. I was talking to him last night, and I told him to be ready for another communication to-night. Now it's time to eat.'

In old days at the Pension Gontran the meals had always been irregular, though a dozen clamorous and hungry boarders had by the force of their united wills evoked the semblance of a set repast. With the departure of her guests Mère Gontran had copied her animals in eating whenever inclination and opportunity coincided. One method of satisfying herself was to sit down at the kitchen-table and rattle an empty plate at the servant, who would either grunt and shake her head (in which case Mère Gontran would produce biscuits from the pocket of her apron) or would empty some of the contents of a saucepan into the empty plate. On this occasion when they visited the kitchen there was something to eat, a fact which was appreciated not only by the dogs and cats, but also by Mère Gontran's three sons, who lounged in and sat down in a corner, talking to each other in Russian.

'They don't know what to do,' said their mother. 'It hasn't been decided yet whether they're French or Russian. They went to the Embassy to see about going to France, but they were told that they were Russian; and when they went to the military authorities here, they were told that they were French. The work they were doing has stopped, and they've nothing to do except smoke cigarettes and borrow money from me for their trams. I spoke to their father about it again last night, but his answer was very irrelevant, very irrelevant indeed.'

'What did he say?'

'Well, he was talking about one of his fellow-spirits called Dick at the time and he kept on saying "*Dick's picked a daisy*," till I got so annoyed that I threw the planchette board across the room. He was just the same about his sons when he was alive. If ever I asked him a question about their education or anything, he'd slip out of it by talking about his work at the Embassy. He was one of the most irrelevant men I ever knew. Well, I shall have to ask him again to-night, that's all, because I can't have them hanging about here doing nothing for ever. It isn't as if I could under-stand them or they me. Bless my soul, it's not surprising that I come to rely more and more on so-called dumb animals. Yesterday they smoked one hundred and forty-six cigarettes between them. I shall have to go and see the Ambassador myself about their nationality. He knows it's not my fault that Gontran muddled it up. In my opinion they're Russian. Anyway they can't say "bo" to a goose in any other language, and it's not much good their fighting the Germans in what French *they* know.'

The three young men ate solidly throughout this monologue, oblivious of its bearing upon their future, indifferent to anything but the food before them.

After the neatness and regularity of the hospital the contrast of living at the Pension Gontran made an exceptionally strong impression of disorder on Sylvia. It vaguely recalled her life at Lillie Road with Mrs. Meares, as if she had dreamt that life over again in a nightmare: there was not even wanting to complete the comparison her short hair. Yet with all the grubbiness and discomfort of it she was glad to be with Mère Gontran, whose mind long attuned to communion with animals had gained thereby a simplicity and sincerity that communion with mankind could never have given her. Like the body after long fasting, the mind after a long illness was peculiarly receptive, and Sylvia rejoiced at the opportunity to pause for a while before re-entering ordinary existence in order to contemplate the life of another lonely soul.

The evening meal at the Pension Gontran was positively formal in comparison with the haphazard midday meal; Mère Gontran's three sons rarely put in an appearance, and the maid used to come in with set dishes and lay them on the table in such a close imitation of civilized behaviour that Sylvia used to watch her movements with a fascinated admiration, as she might have watched the performance of an animal trained to wait at table. The table itself was never entirely covered with a white cloth, but that even half of it should be covered seemed miraculous after the kitchen-table. The black and red chequered cloth that covered the dining-room table for the rest of the day was pushed back to form an undulating range of foothills, beyond which the relics of Mère Gontran's incomplete undertakings piled themselves in a mountainous disarray: stockings that ought to be mended, seedlings that ought to be planted out, garden-tools that ought to be put away, packs of cards, almanacs, balls of wool, knitting-needles, flower-pots, photograph-frames, everything that had been momentarily picked up by Mère Gontran in the course of her rest-less day had taken refuge here. The dining-room itself was long, low, and dark with a smell of birdcages and withering geraniums; sometimes when Mère Gontran had managed to concentrate her mind long enough upon the trimming of a lamp, there would be a lamp with a shade like a draggled petticoat; more frequently the evening meal (dinner was too stringent a definition) was lighted by two candles, the wicks of which every five minutes assumed the form of large fiery flies' heads and danced up and down with delight like children who have dressed themselves up, until Mère Gontran attacked them with a weapon that was used indif-ferently as a nutcracker and a snuffer, but which had been designed by its maker to extract nails. Under these repeated assaults the candles themselves deliquesced and formed stalagmites and stalactites of grease, which she used to break off, roll up into balls, and drop on the floor, where they perplexed the greed of the various cats, whose tails upright with an expectation of food could dimly be seen waving in the shadows like seaweed.

On the first night of Sylvia's arrival she had been too tired to sit up with Mère Gontran and attend the conversation with her deceased husband, nor did the widow over-persuade her because it was important to settle the future of her three sons by threatening Gontran with a visit to the Embassy, a threat that might disturb even his astral liberty. Sylvia gathered from Mère Gontran's account of the interview next morning that it had led to words, if the phrase might be used of communication by raps, and it seemed that the spirit had retired to sulk in some celestial nook as yet unvexed by earthly communications; his behaviour as narrated by his wife reminded Sylvia of an irritated telephone subscriber.

'But he'll be sorry for it by now,' said Mère Gontran. 'I'm expecting him to come and say so every moment.'

Gontran, however, must have spent the day walking off his wife's ill-temper in a paradisal excursion with a kindred spirit, for nothing was heard of him, and she was left to her solitary gardening, as maybe often in life she had been left.

'I hope nothing's happened to Gontran,' she said gravely, when Sylvia and she sat down to the evening meal.

'Isn't the liability to accident rather reduced by getting rid of matter?' Sylvia suggested.

'Oh, I'm not worrying about a broken leg or anything like that,' Mère Gontran explained. 'But supposing he's reached another plane?'

'Ah, I hadn't thought of that.'

'The communications get more difficult every year since he died,' the widow complained. 'The first few months after his death, hardly five minutes used to pass without a word from him, and all night long he used to rap on the head of my bed, until James used to get quite fidgety.' James was the bulldog who slept with Mère Gontran.

'And now he raps no longer?'

'Oh, yes, he still raps,' Mère Gontran replied, 'but much more faintly. But there again, he's already moved to three different planes since his death. Hush! what's that?'

She stared into the darkest corner of the dining-room.

'Is that you, Gontran?'

'I think it was one of the birds,' Sylvia said.

Mère Gontran waved her hand for silence.

'Gontran! Is that you? Where have you been all day? This is a friend of mine who's staying here. You'll like her very much when you know her. Gontran! I want to talk to you after dinner. Now mind, don't forget. I'm glad you've got back. I want you to make some enquiries in England to-morrow.'

Sylvia was distinctly aware of a deep-seated amusement all the time at

Mère Gontran's matter of fact way of dealing with her husband's spirit, and she could never make up her mind how with her sense of amusement could exist simultaneously a credulity that led her to hear at the conclusion of Mère Gontran's last speech three loud raps upon the air of the room.

'He's got over last night,' said Mère Gontran in a satisfied voice. 'But there again, he always had a kind nature at bottom. Three nice cheerful raps like that always mean he's going to give up his evening to me.'

Sylvia's first instinct was to find in what way Mère Gontran had tricked her into hearing those three raps; something in the seer's true gaze forbade the notion of trickery, and a shiver roused by the inexplicable, the shiver that makes a dog run away from an open umbrella blown across a lawn, slipped through her being.

Although Mère Gontran was puffing at her soup as if nothing had happened, the house had changed, or rather it had not changed so much as revealed itself in a brief instant. All that there was of queerness in this tumbledown pension became endowed with deliberate meaning, and it was no longer possible to ascribe the atmosphere to the effect of weakened nerves upon a weakened body. Sylvia began to wonder if the form her delirium had taken had not been directly due to this atmosphere; more than ever she was inclined to attach a profound significance to her delirium and perceive in it the diabolic revelation with which it had originally been fraught.

When after dinner Mère Gontran took a pack of cards and began to tell her fortune, Sylvia had a new impulse to dread; but she shook it off almost irritably and listened to the tale.

'A long journey by land. A long journey by sea. A dark man. A fair woman. A fair man. A dark woman. A letter.'

The familiar rigmarole of a hundred such tellings droned its course accompanied by the flip-flap, flip-flap of the cards. The information was general enough for any human being on earth to have extracted from it something applicable to himself; yet against her will, and as it were bewitched by the teller's solemnity, Sylvia began to endow the cards with the personalities that might affect her life. The King of Hearts lost his rubicund complacency and took on the lineaments of Arthur: the King of Clubs parted with his fierceness and assumed the graceful severity of Michael Fane: with a kind of impassioned egotism Sylvia watched the journeyings of the Queen of Hearts, noting the contacts and biting her lips when she found her prototype associated with unfavourable cards.

'Come, I don't think the outlook's so bad,' said Mère Gontran at the end of the final disposition. 'If your bed's a bit doubtful, your street and your house are both very good, and your road lies south. But there again, this blessed war upsets everything, and even the cards must be read with half an eye on the war.'

When the cards had been put away, Mère Gontran produced the *planchette* and set it upon a small table covered in red baize round the binding of which hung numerous little woollen pompons.

'Now we shall find out something about your friends in England,' she announced cheerfully.

Sylvia had not the heart to disappoint Mère Gontran, and she placed her hands upon the heart-shaped board, which trembled so much under Mère Gontran's eager touch that the pencil affixed made small squiggles upon the paper beneath. The *planchette* went on fidgeting more and more under their four hands like a restless animal trying to escape, and from time to time it would skate right across the paper leaving a long pencilled trail in its path, which Mère Gontran would examine with great intentness.

'It looks a little bit like a Y,' she would say.

'A very little bit,' Sylvia would think.

'Or it may be an A. Never mind. It always begins rather doubtfully. I *won't* lose my temper with it to-night.'

The *planchette* might have been a tenderly loved child learning to write for the first time by the way Mère Gontran encouraged it and tried to award a shape and purpose to its most amorphous tracks. When it had covered the sheet of paper with an impossibly complicated river-system, Mère Gontran fetched a clean sheet and told Sylvia severely that she must try not to urge the *planchette*. Any attempt at urging had a very bad effect on its willingness.

'I didn't think I was urging it,' Sylvia said humbly.

'Try and sit more still, dear. If you like, I'll put my feet on your toes and then you won't be so tempted to jig. We may have to sit all night, if we aren't careful.'

Sylvia strained every nerve to sit as still as possible in order to avoid having her toes imprisoned all night by Mère Gontran's feet, which were particularly large even for so tall a woman. She concentrated upon preventing her hands from leading the *planchette* to trace the course of any more rivers toward the sea of baize, and after sitting for twenty minutes like this she felt that all the rest of her body had gone into her hands. She had never thought that her hands were small, but she had certainly never realized that they were as large and as ugly as they were; as for Mère Gontran's, they had for some time lost any likeness to hands and lay upon the *planchette* like two uncooked chops. At last when Sylvia had reached the state of feeling like a large pincushion that was being rapidly pricked by thousands of pins, Mère Gontran murmured:

'It's going to start.'

Immediately afterwards the *planchette* careered across the paper and wrote a sentence.

'*Dick's picked a daisy,*' Mère Gontran read out. 'Drat the thing! Never mind, we'll have one more try.'

Again a sentence was written, and again it repeated that Dick had picked a daisy.

Suddenly Samuel the collie made an odd noise.

'He's going to speak through Samuel,' Mère Gontran declared. 'What is it, dear? Tell me what it is?'

The dog, who had probably been stung by a gnat, got up and putting his head upon his mistress's knee gazed forth ineffable sorrows.

'You heard him trying to talk?' she asked.

'He certainly made a noise,' Sylvia admitted.

There was a loud rap on the air – an unmistakable rap, for the five cats which had remained in the room all twitched their ears toward the sound.

'Gone for the night,' said Mère Gontran. 'And he's very angry about something. I suppose this daisy that Dick picked means something important to him, though *we* can't understand. Perhaps he'll come back later on when I've gone to bed and tell me more about it.'

'Mère Gontran,' said Sylvia earnestly. 'Do you really believe in spirits? Do you really think we can talk with the dead?'

'Of course I do. Listen! they're all round us. If you want to feel the dead, walk up the garden with me now. You'll feel the spirits whizzing round you like moths.'

'Oh, I wonder, I wonder if it's true,' Sylvia cried. 'I can't believe it, and yet . . .'

'Listen to me,' said Mère Gontran solemnly. 'Thirty-five years ago I left England to come to Petersburg. I was twenty years old and very beautiful. You can imagine how I was run after by men. You've seen something of the way men run after women here. Well, one summer I went with my family to Finland, and I foolishly arranged to meet Prince Paul in the forest after supper. He was a fine handsome young man as bold and as wicked as the devil himself. But there again, I haven't got to give details. Anyway he said to me, "What are you afraid of? Your parents?" I can hear his laugh now after all these years, and I remember the bough of a tree was just waving very slightly, and the moonlight kept glinting in and out of his eyes. I thought of my parents in England when he said this, and I remember challenging them in a sort of defiant way to interfere. You see

I'd never got on well at home. I was a very wayward girl and they were exceptionally old-fashioned. And when Prince Paul held me in his arms I reproached them. It's difficult to explain, but I was trying to conjure them up before me to see if the thought of home would have any effect. And then Prince Paul laughed and said "Or another lover?" Now with the exception of flirting with Prince Paul and Prince George, the two eldest sons, I'd never thought much about lovers. Even in those days I was more interested in animals really, and of course I was very fond of children. But when Prince Paul said "Or your lover?" I saw Gontran leaning against a tree in the forest. He was looking at me, and I pushed Prince Paul away and ran back towards the house.

'Now when this happened I'd never seen my husband. He was working at the Embassy even in those days, and never went to Finland in his life. The next day the family was called back to Petersburg on account of the death of the grandmother, and I met Gontran at some friends'! We were married about six months afterwards.

'So there again, if I could see Gontran when he was alive before I'd ever met him, you don't suppose I'm not going to believe that I've seen him any number of times since he was dead? Until quite recently when he reached this new plane, we talked together as comfortably as when he was still alive and sitting in that chair.'

Sylvia looked at the chair uneasily.

'It's only since he's met this Dick that the communications are so unsatisfactory. Why, of course I know what's happened,' cried Mère Gontran in a rapture of discovery. 'Why didn't I think of it sooner? It's the war!'

'The war?' Sylvia echoed.

'Aren't there thousands of spirits being set free every day? Just as all the communications on earth have broken down, in the same way they must have broken down with the spirits. Fancy my not having understood that before! Well, aren't I dense?'

Five raps of surpassing loudness signalled upon the air.

'Gontran's delighted,' she exclaimed. 'He was always delighted when I found out something for myself.'

Soon after this Mère Gontran, having gathered up from the crowded table a variety of implements that could not possibly serve any purpose that night, wandered out into the garden, followed by Samuel and the five cats; Sylvia thought of her haunted passage through the dark autumnal growth of leaves toward that strange room she occupied, and went upstairs to bed rather tremulously. Yet on the whole she was glad that Mère Gontran left her like this every night at the pension with the Tartar servant in her cupboard under the stairs, and with the three ungainly sons, who used to sleep in a barrack at the end of the long passage on the ground floor. Sylvia had peeped into this room when the young men were out and had been surprised by its want of resemblance to a sleeping-chamber. There were to be sure three beds, but they had the appearance of beds that had been long stowed away in a remote part of a warehouse for disused furniture: the whole room was like that, with nothing human appertaining to it save the smell of stale tobacco-smoke. Yet really now that the migratory guests had gone on their way it would have been even more surprising to find in the pension signs of humanity, so much had its permanent inhabitants, both animals and human beings, approximated to one another. The animals were a little more like human beings; the human beings were a little more like animals: the margin between men and animals was narrow enough in the most distinguishing circumstances, and at the pension these circumstances were lacking.

Before Sylvia undressed, she opened the window of her bedroom and looked down into the moonlit garden. Mère Gontran's light was already lit, but she was still wandering about outside with her cats. Eccentric though she was, Sylvia thought, she was nevertheless typical. Looking back at the people who had crossed her path, she could remember several adumbrations of Mère Gontran – superstitious women with a love of animals. Of such a kind had been Mrs. Meares; and attached to every cabaret and theatre there had always been an elderly woman who had served as commission agent to the careless artistes, whether it was a question of selling themselves to a new lover or buying somebody else's old dress. These elderly women had invariably had the knack of telling fortunes with the cards, had been able to interpret dreams and omens, and had always been the slaves of dogs and birds. The superficial ascription of their passion for animals would have been to a stifled or sterile maternity; but as with Mère Gontran and her three sons Sylvia could recall that many of these elderly women had been the prey of their children. If one went back beyond one's actual experience of this type, it was significant that the witches of olden times were always credited with the possession of familiar spirits in the shape of animals; she could recollect no history of a witch that did not include her black cat. Was that too a stifled maternal instinct, or would it not be truer to find in the magic arts they practised nothing but a descent from human methods of intelligence to those of animals, a descent (if indeed it could be called a descent) from reason to instinct?

Here was Mère Gontran fulfilling in every particular the old conventional idea of a witch, and might not all this communion with spirits be nothing but the communion of an animal with scents and sounds imperceptible to civilized man? It could be a kind of atavism really, a return to disused senses, so long obsolete that their revival had a supernatural effect. Sylvia thought of the unusual success that Mère Gontran always had with her gardening; no matter where she sowed in the great dark jungle she gathered better vegetables than a gardener, who would have wasted his energy in wrestling with the weeds that seemed to forbid any growth but their own. Mère Gontran always paid greater attention to the aspects of the moon and the planets than to the laws of horticulture, and her gardening gave the impression of being nothing but a meaningless ritual: yet it was fruitful. Might there not be some laws of attraction of which in the course of dependence upon his own inventions man had lost sight, some laws of which animals were cognizant and by which many of the marvels of instinct might be explained? Beyond witches and their familiar spirits were fauns and centaurs, more primitive manifestations of this communion between men and animals, with whom even the outward shape was still a hybrid. Had scientists in pursuing the antics of molecules and atoms beneath the microscope become blind to the application of their theories? Might not astronomy have displaced astrology unjustly? Sylvia wished she had read more widely and more deeply that she might know if her speculations were after all nothing but the commonplaces of empirical thought. So much could be explained by this theory of attraction, not least of all the mystery of love and the inscrutable caprices of fortune.

Behold Mère Gontran out there in the garden bobbing to the moon. Were all these gestures meaningless like an idiot's mutterings? And was even an idiot's muttering really meaningless? Behold Mère Gontran in the moonlit garden with cats: it would be hard to say that her behaviour was more futile than theirs: they were certainly enjoying themselves.

Sylvia was conscious of trying to arrive at an explanation of Mère Gontran that, while it allowed her behaviour a certain amount of reasonableness, would prevent herself from accepting Mère Gontran's own explanation of it. There was something distasteful, something cheap and vulgar, in the conception of Gontran's spiritual existence as an infinite prolongation of his life upon earth; there was something radically fatuous in the imagination of him at the end of a ghostly telephone-wire still at the beck and call of human curiosity. If indeed in some mysterious way the essential Gontran was communicating with his wife, the translation of his will to communicate must be a subjective creation of hers; it was somehow ludicrous, and even unpleasant, to accept Dick's gathering of a daisy as a demonstration of the activity of mankind in another world, it was too much a finite conception altogether. Without hesitation Sylvia rejected spiritualism as a useful adventure for human intelligence. It was impossible to accept its more elaborate manifestations with bells and tambourines and materializing mediums, when one knew the universal instinct of mankind to lie; and in its simpler manifestations, as with Mère Gontran, where conscious or deliberate deceit was out of the question, it was merely a waste of time, being bound by the limitations of an individual soul that would always be abnormal and probably in most cases idiotic.

Sylvia pulled down the blind and, leaving Mère Gontran to her nocturnal contemplation, went to bed.

Notwithstanding her abrupt rejection of spiritualism, Sylvia found when she was in bed that the incidents of the evening and the accessories of the house were affecting her to sleeplessness. That succession of raps declined to come within the natural explanation that she had attempted. Were they due to some action of overcharged atmosphere, a kind of miniature thunderclap from the meeting of two so-called electrical currents generated by herself and Mère Gontran? Were they merely coincidental creakings of furniture in response to the warmth of the stove? Or had Mère Gontran mesmerized her into hearing raps that were never made? The cats had also heard them; but Mère Gontran's intimacy with her animals might well have established such a mental domination, even over them.

Naturally with so much of her attention fixed upon the raps downstairs Sylvia began to fancy renewed rappings all round her in the darkness, and not merely rappings, but all sorts of nocturnal shufflings and scrapings and whisperings and scratchings, until she had to relight her candle. The noises became less, but optical delusions were substituted for tricks of hearing, and there was not a piece of furniture in the room that did not project from its outward form the sense of its independent reality. The wardrobe for instance seemed to challenge her with the thought that it was no longer the receptacle of her skirts and petticoats: it seemed to be asserting its essential 'wardrobeishness' for being the receptacle for anything it liked. Sylvia set aside as too obviously and particularly silly the fancy that someone might be hidden in the wardrobe, but she could not get rid of the fancy that the piece of furniture had an existence outside her own consciousness. It was a mere Hans Andersen kind of fancy, but it took her back to remote childish apprehensions of inanimate objects, and after her meditation upon instinct she began to wonder whether after all the child was not quite right to be afraid of everything, which grown-ups called being afraid of nothing; and whether that escape from childish terrors which was called knowledge was nothing but a drug that blunted the perceptions and impeded the capacity for esteeming whatever approximated to truth. Yet why should a child be afraid of a wardrobe? Why should a child be afraid of everything? Because in everything there was evil. Sylvia recalled – and in this room it was impossible to rid herself of that diabolic obsession – that the Devil was known as the Father of Lies. Was not all evil anti-truth, and did not man with his preference for anti-truth create the material evil that was used as an argument against the Divine ordering of matter? Paradoxical as it might seem, the worse ordered the world appeared, the more did such an appearance of pessimism involve the existence of God. Whither led all this theosophistry? Toward the only perfect revelation of God in man: toward Jesus Christ.

How foolish it was to prefer to such divine speech the stammering of spiritualists. For the first time in her life Sylvia prayed deliberately that what she saw as in a glass darkly might be revealed to her more clearly; and while she prayed, there recurred from the hospital that whispered confession of the little English governess. It was impossible not to compare it with the story of Mère Gontran: the coincidence of the names and the similarity of the situation were too remarkable. Then why had Mère Gontran been granted what if her story were accepted was a supernatural intervention to save her soul? By her own admission she had practically surrendered to Prince Paul when she had the vision of her future husband. It seemed very unjust that Miss Savage should have been utterly corrupted and that Mère Gontran should have escaped corruption. Sylvia went back in her thoughts to the time when she left Philip and abandoned herself to evil. Yet she had never really abandoned herself to evil, for she had never had any will to sin; the impulse had been to save her soul, not to lose it. It had been an humiliation of her body like pain, and a degradation of her personality like death. Pride which had cast her out had been her undoing. Looking back now she could see that everything evil in her life had come from her pride: pride by the way was another attribute of the Devil.

Sylvia had a longing to go back to England and talk to the Vicar of Green Lanes. From the past kept recurring isolated fragments of his sermons, texts mostly, which had lain all this while dormant within her consciousness, until the first one had sprung up to flower amid her delirium. In all her reading she had never paid proper attention to the doctrines of Christianity, and she longed to know if some of these dim facts after which she was now groping were not there set forth with transparent brightness and undeniable clarity. Good or evil must present themselves to every soul in a different way, and it was surely improbable that the accumulated experience of the human mind gathered together in Christian writings would not contain a parallel by which she might be led toward the truth, or at least be granted the vision of another lonely soul seeking for itself salvation.

The sense of her loneliness, physical, spiritual, and intellectual overwhelmed Sylvia's aspirations. How could truth or faith or hope or love concern her until she could escape from this isolation? She had always been lonely, even before she came to Russia; yet it had always been possible up to a point to cheat herself with the illusion of company, because the loneliness had been spiritual and intellectual, a loneliness that would be immanent in any woman whose life was ordered on her lines and who had failed to find what was vulgarly called the 'right man.' Now there was added to this the positive physical loneliness of her present position. It would have been bad enough to recover from an illness and wake in a familiar world; but to wake like this in a world transformed by war was indeed like waking in Hell. The remembrance of England, of people like Jack and Olive, was scarcely more distinct now than the remembrance of Lille; everything in her past had receded to the same immeasurable distance. News of England in any familiar form now reached Russia by such devious ways that in a period of violent daily events the papers had, when they did arrive, the air of some ancient, bloody, and fantastic chronicle. No letters came, because nobody could know where she was; her friends must think that she was dead, and must have accepted her death as the death of a sparrow amid the slaughter that was now proceeding. To-morrow she should send a cablegram, which might some day arrive, to say that she was alive and well. And then she had a revulsion from such a piece of egotism in the midst of a world's catastrophe. Who could wish to be reminded of Sylvia Scarlett at such a moment? Besides, if this determination of hers to begin her life over again was to be made effective, Sylvia Scarlett must preserve this isolation and accept it as the grace of God. How what had once been phrases were now endowed with life! Any communication between her and the people she had known would be like communication between Gontran and his wife; it would be the stammering of spiritualism comparable with that absurd Dick gathering his daisies in the Elysian fields. Unless all these 'soul-spasms,' as once she would have called them, were the weakness of a woman who had been sick unto death, meaningless babblings without significance, her way would be indicated. Whatever the logicians might say, it was useless to expect faith, hope, or love unless one went to meet them: the will to receive them must outweigh the suspicion of receiving. Faith like any other gift-horse must not be looked in the mouth; pride had robbed her long enough, and for a change she would try humility.

When she made this decision, it seemed to Sylvia that what had formerly been evil and terrifying in the inanimate objects of her candle-lit room now lost their menacing aspect and wished her well. Suddenly she accused herself of the most outrageous pride in having all this time thought of nothing but herself, whose misery amid the universal havoc was indeed only the twittering of a sparrow. An apocalypse of the world's despair blazed upon her. This was not the time to lament her position, but rather to be glad very humbly that at the moment when she had been given this revelation of her pride, this return of herself, she was given also the moment to put the restored self to the test of action.

When Sylvia woke in the morning, her ideas that during the night had stated themselves with such convincing logic seemed less convincing; the first elation had been succeeded by the discouragement of the artist at seeing how ill his execution supports his intention. Riddles had solved themselves one after another with such ease in the darkness, that when she had fallen asleep she had been musing with astonishment at the failure of human nature to appreciate the simplicity of life's intention; now all those darkling raptures burned like a sickly fire in the sunlight. Yet it was consoling to remember that the sun did not really put out the fire, and therefore that the fire kindled within herself last night might burn not less brightly and warmly for all its appearance of being extinguished by the sun of action.

These fiery metaphors were ill-suited to the new day, which was wet enough to make Sylvia wonder if there had ever been so completely wet a day. The view from her window included a large piece of sky which lacked even thunder-clouds or wind to break its leaden monotony. The vegetation of the garden had assumed a universal hue of dull green, the depressing effect of which was intensified by the absence of any large trees to mark autumnal decay with their more precocious dissolution. Weather did not seem to affect Mère Gontran, whose clothes even upon the finest days had the appearance of a bundle of drenched rags; and if the dogs and cats preferred to remain indoors, she was able to paddle about the garden with her ducks and devote to their triumphant quacking a sympathetic attention.

'I'm going to see the Ambassador this morning,' she called up to Sylvia. 'Something must be decided about the boys' nationality and it's bound to be decided more quickly if they see me dripping all over the marble entrance of the Embassy.'

Not even the sight of that elderly Naiad haunting the desks of overworked *chanceliers* could secure a determination to which country her sons' military service was owed; it seemed as if they would remain unclassified to the end of the war, borrowing money for tram-tickets and smoking cigarettes while husbands were torn from the arms of wives, while lovers and parents mourned eternal partings.

Autumn drew on, and here in Russia hard upon its heels was winter; already early in October there was talk at the pension of the snow's coming soon, and Sylvia did not feel inclined to stay here in the solitude that snow would create. Moreover, she was anxious not to let Mère Gontran wish for her going on account of the expense, and she would not have stayed as long as she had, if her hostess had not been so obviously distressed at the idea of her leaving before she could be accounted perfectly well again. In order to repay her hospitality, Sylvia assisted gravely – and one might say reverently – at all her follies of magic. Nor under the influence of Mère Gontran's earnestness was it always possible to be sure about the foolish side. There were often moments when Sylvia was frightened in these fast-closing daylights and long wintry eves by the unending provocation of the dead that was as near as Mère Gontran got to evocation; although she claimed to be always seeing apparitions, of which Sylvia fortunately for her nerves was never granted a vision.

The climax was reached on the night of the first snowfall soon after the middle of October, when Mère Gontran came to Sylvia's bedroom, her crimson dressing-gown dusted with dry flakes of snow, and begged her to come out in the garden to hear Gontran communicating with her from a lilac-bush. It was in vain that Sylvia protested against being dragged out of bed on such a cold night; Mère Gontran candle in hand towered up above her with such a dominating excitement that Sylvia let herself be over-persuaded and followed her out into the garden. From what had formerly been Carrier's room the owls hooted at the moon; Samuel the talking collie was baying dolefully; the snowfall, too light to give the nocturnal landscape a pure and crystalline beauty, was enough to destroy the familiar aspect of the scene and to infect it with a withered papery look, turning house and garden to the colour of dry bones.

'He's in the lilac-bush by the outhouse,' Mère Gontran whispered. 'When I went past, one of the boughs caught hold of my hand, and he spoke in a queer crackling voice, as of course somebody would speak if he were speaking through a bush.'

Sylvia could not bear it any longer; she suddenly turned back and ran up to her bedroom, vowing that to-morrow she would make a serious effort to leave Petrograd.

'However short my hair,' she laughed, 'there's no reason why it should be made to stand on end like that.'

She supposed that Petrograd had not sufficiently recovered from the shock of war to make an engagement there pleasant or profitable; besides, after her experience at the cabaret she was disinclined to face another humiliation of the same kind. The Jewish agent whom she consulted suggested Kieff, Odessa, and Constantinople as a good tour; from Constantinople, she would be able to return home more easily and comfortably if she wished to return. He held up his hands at the idea of travelling to England by Archangel at this season. She could sing for a week at Kieff just to break the journey, take two months at Odessa, and be almost sure of at least four months at Constantinople: it was a great nuisance this war, but he was expecting every day to hear that the English fleet had blown Pola to pieces, and perhaps after Christmas there would be an opportunity of an engagement at Vienna. With so many troops in the city such an engagement would be highly remunerative; and he winked at Sylvia. She was surprised to find that it was so easy to secure an engagement in war-time and still more surprised to learn that she would be better paid than before the war. Indeed if she had been willing to remain in Petrograd, she could have earned as much as a thousand francs a month for singing, so many of the French girls had fled to France and so rare now were foreign artistes. As it was, she would be paid eight hundred francs a month at Kieff and Odessa. For the amount of her salary in Constantinople the agent would not answer, because on second thoughts he might observe that there was just a chance of war between Russia and Turkey, a very small chance; but in the circumstances it would be impossible to arrange a contract.

Sylvia returned to the pension to announce her success.

'Well, if you get ill,' said Mère Gontran, 'mind you come back here at once. You're *not* a good medium; in fact I believe you're a deterrent; but I like to see you about the place, and of course I *do* like to talk English, but there again, when shall I ever see England?'

When Sylvia had heard Mère Gontran speak of her native country formerly, it had always been as the place where an unhappy childhood had been spent, and she had seemed to glory in her expatriation. Mère Gontran answered her unspoken astonishment:

'I think it's the war,' she explained. 'It's seeing so much about England in the newspapers; I've got a feeling I'd like to go back, and I will go back after the war,' she proclaimed. 'Some kind of nationality my three sons shall have, if it's only their mother's. Which reminds me. Poor Carrier has been killed.'

400

'Killed,' Sylvia repeated. 'Already?'

In the clutch of apprehension she knew that other and dearer friends than he might already be dead.

'I thought we could celebrate your last night by trying to get into communication with him,' said Mère Gontran.

It was as if she had replied to Sylvia's unvoiced fear.

'No, no,' she cried. 'If they are dead, I don't want to know.'

So Carrier with all his mascots had fallen at last, and he would never cultivate that little farm in the Lyonnais; she remembered how he had boasted of the view across the valley of the Saône to the long line of the Alps: far wider now was his view, and his room at the pension was the abode of owls. She read the paragraph in the French paper: he had been killed early in September very gloriously. If Paradise might be the eternal present of a well-beloved dream, he would have found his farm; if human wishes were not vanity, he was at peace.

The brief snow had melted, and through a drenching afternoon of rain Sylvia packed up; it was pleasant to think that at any rate she should travel southward, for the pension was unbearable on these winter days and long nights filled with a sound of shadows. Again Sylvia was minded to brave the journey north and return to England, but again an overmastering impulse forbade her. Her destiny was written otherwise, and if she fought against the impulse not to go back, she felt that she should be cast up and rejected by the sea of life.

Mère Gontran having caught a slight chill went to bed immediately after dinner, and invited Sylvia to come and talk to her on her last evening. It was an odd place, this bedroom that she had chosen; and very odd she looked lying in the old four-poster, her head tied up in a bandana scarf and beside her with his wrinkled head on the pillow, James the bulldog. The four-poster seemed out of place against the matchboarding with which the room was lined, and the rest of the furniture gave one the impression of having been ransacked by burglars in a great hurry. On the wall opposite the bed was a portrait of Gontran, which by sheer bad painting possessed a sinister power like that of some black Byzantine Virgin; on either side of him were hung the cats' boxes from which they surveyed their mistress with the same fixed stare as her painted husband.

'Of course I should go mad if I slept in this room all by myself, and two hundred yards away from any habitation,' Sylvia exclaimed.

'Oh, I'm very fond of my room,' said Mère Gontran. 'But there again, I like to be alone with one foot in the grave.'

'I want to thank you for all your kindness,' Sylvia began.

'If you start thanking me, you'll make me fidget; and if I fidget, it worries James.'

'Still even at the risk of upsetting James, I must tell you that I don't know what I should have done without you these six weeks. Perhaps one day when the war is over you'll come to England and then you'll have to stay with me in my cottage.'

'Ah, I shall never be able to leave the cats, not to mention the pony. I just happened to have a fancy for England to-day, but it's too late; I'm established here; I'm known. People in England might stare, and I should dislike that very much.'

Sylvia wanted rather to talk again about spiritualism in order to find out if Mère Gontran's speculations coincided at any point with her own; but a discussion of spiritual experience with her was like a discussion of the liver; she was almost grossly insistent upon the organic machinery, almost brutal in her zest for the practical, one might almost say the technical details. The mysteries of human conduct on earth left her utterly uninterested except when she could obtain a commentary upon them from the spirits for a practical purpose; the spirits took the place for her of the solicitor and the doctor rather than of the priest. Systems of philosophy and religion had no meaning for Mère Gontran; her spiritual advice never concerned itself with them; and the ultimate intention of immortality was as well concealed from her as the justification of life on earth. It was this very absence of the high-falutin' which impressed Sylvia with the genuineness of the manifestations that she procured, but which at the time discouraged her with the sense that death merely substituted one irrational form of being for another.

'What's it all for?' Sylvia had once asked.

'For?' Mère Gontran had repeated in perplexity: she had never considered the utility of this question hitherto.

'Yes, why for instance did you marry Gontran? Did you love him? Are your children destined to fulfil any part in the world? And *their* children after them?'

'Why do you want to worry your head with such questions?' Mère Gontran had asked compassionately.

'But you deny me the consolation of oblivion. You accept this endless existence after death with its apparently meaningless prolongation of human vapidity and pettiness, and you're surprised that I resent it.'

But it was impossible to carry on the discussion with somebody who was as contented with what is as an animal and whose only prayer was *Give us this day our daily bread*. It was a disappointing contribution to the problem of life from one who had spent so long on the borderland of the grave. Yet it was Mère Gontran's devotion to this aspiration that had made her lodge Sylvia all these weeks.

'How can you who are so kind, want to see your sons go to the war not for any motives of honour or patriotism, but apparently just to keep them away from cigarettes and idleness? What does their nationality really matter?'

'They must do something for themselves,' Mère Gontran replied. 'Just at the moment the war offers a good opening.'

'But suppose they are killed?'

'I hope they will be. I shall be on much better terms with them than I am now. Gontran talks to me in English nowadays; so would they, and we might get to know one another. Cats don't worry about their kittens, after they're grown up; in fact they're anxious to get rid of them. And kingfishers chase their young ones away, or so I was informed by an English ventriloquist who was interested in natural history.'

'Well, I always congratulated myself on being free from sentimentality,' Sylvia said. 'But beside you I'm like a keepsake-album.'

'If you'd get out of the habit of thinking that death is of any more importance than going to sleep, you wouldn't bother about anything,' Mère Gontran declared.

'Oh, it isn't death that worries me,' Sylvia answered. 'It's life.'

Very early in the twilight of a wet dawn Sylvia started for Kieff. All day she watched the raindrops trickling down the windows of the railway carriage and wondered if her impulse to travel south was inspired by any profounder reason.

III

On the day after she reached Kieff, Sylvia went for a walk by herself. Since she was going to stay only a week in this city and since she still felt somewhat remote from the world after her long seclusion, she had not bothered to make friends with any of her fellow artistes. Presently she grew tired of walking alone and, looking about her, she saw on the other side of the road a cinema theatre, where she decided to spend the rest of a dreary afternoon. She was surprised to find that the lowest charge for entrance was two roubles; but when she went inside and saw the film, she understood the reason. The theatre was full of men, and she could hear them whispering to one another their astonishment at seeing a woman enter the place; she was thankful that the dim red light concealed her

403

blushes, and she escaped as quickly as possible, quenching the impulse to abuse the door-keeper for not warning her what kind of an entertainment was taking place inside.

This abrupt and violent reminder of human beastliness shocked Sylvia very deeply at a moment when she was trying to induce in herself an attitude of humility; it was impossible not to feel angrily superior to those swine grovelling in their mess. Ordinarily she might have obliterated the incident with disdain, or at any rate have seen its proportion to the whole of human life. But now with war closing upon the world, and with all the will she had to idealize the abnegation of the individual that was begotten from the monstrous crime of the mass, it was terrible to be brought up sharply like this by the unending and apparently unassailable rampart of human vileness. It seemed to her that the shame she had felt on finding herself inside that place must even now be marked upon her countenance, and there was not a passer-by whose criticism and curiosity she could keep from fancying intently directed towards herself. Anxious to elude the sensation of this commentary upon her action, she turned aside from the pavement to stare into the first shop-window that presented itself, until her blushes had burnt themselves out. The shop she chose happened to be a jeweller's, and Sylvia who never cared much for precious stones was now less than ever moved by any interest in the barbaric display that winked and glittered under the artificial stimulus of shaded electric lamps. She tried to see if she could somehow catch the reflection of her cheeks and ascertain if indeed they were flaming as high as she supposed. Presently a voice addressed her from behind, and looking round she saw a slim young soldier well over six feet tall with slanting almond eyes and wide nostrils. He pointed to a row of golden handbags set with various arrangements of precious stones and asked her in very bad French if she admired them. Sylvia's first impulse, when her attention was drawn to these bags for the first time, was to say that she thought them hideous; but a sympathetic intuition that the soldier admired them very much and would be hurt by her disapproval tempted her to agree with him in praising their beauty. He asked her which of them all she liked the best; and in order not to spoil this childish game of standing outside a shop-window and making imaginary purchases, she considered the row for awhile and at last fixed upon one that was set with emeralds, the gold of which had a greenish tint. The soldier said that he preferred the one in the middle that was set with rubies, sapphires, diamonds and emeralds, which was obviously the most expensive and certainly the most barbaric of the whole collection. Was Sylvia sure that she had chosen the one she liked the best? She assured him that her choice was unalterable, and the soldier taking her arm bade her enter the shop with him.

'I can't afford to buy a bag,' Sylvia protested.

'I can,' he replied. 'I want to buy you the bag you want.'

'But it's impossible,' Sylvia argued. 'Even if I could give you anything in return, it would still be impossible. That bag would cost two thousand roubles at least.'

'I have three thousand roubles,' said the soldier. 'Of what use are they to me? To-night I go to the front. You like the bag. I like to give it to you. Come. Do not let us argue in the street like this. We will buy the bag, and afterwards we will have tea together, and then I shall go my way and you will go your way. It is better that I spend two thousand roubles on buying you a bag that you want than to gamble them away. You are French. It is necessary that I do something for you.'

'I'm English,' Sylvia corrected. 'Half English – half French.'

'So much the better,' the soldier said. 'I have never met an Englishwoman. None of the soldiers in my company have met an Englishwoman. When I tell them that in Kieff I met an Englishwoman and gave her a golden bag, they will envy me my good fortune. Are we not suffering all of us together? And is that not a reason why I should give you something that you very much want?'

'Why do you think I am suffering?' she asked.

'There is sorrow in your eyes,' the soldier answered gravely.

The simplicity of the man overcame her scruples; she felt that her acceptance of his gift would give him a profound pleasure of which for a motive of petty pride she had no right to rob him. As for herself the meeting with this young soldier had washed away like purest water every stain with which Russia had marked her – from the brutality of the drunken officer to the vileness of that cinema theatre. Sylvia hesitated no longer; she accompanied him into the shop and came out again with the golden bag upon her wrist. Then they went into a confectioner's shop and ate cakes together; outside in the darkness sleet was falling, but in her mood of elation Sylvia thought that everything was beautiful.

'It is time for me to go back to the barracks,' the soldier announced at last.

While they were having tea, Sylvia had told him of many events in her life, and he had listened most seriously, though she doubted if he were able to understand half of what she told him. He in his turn had not told her much; but he was still very young, only twenty-one, and he explained that in his village not much could have happened to him. Soon after war was declared his father had died, and having no brothers or sisters or mother, he had sold all he had and quitted his village with 3500 roubles in his pocket. Five hundred roubles he had spent riotously and without satisfaction; and he still rejoiced in the money he had spent on the bag and was even anxious to give Sylvia the thousand roubles that were left, but she begged him to keep them.

'And so you must really go?' she said.

She walked with him through the darkness and sleet towards the barracks; soon there was a sound of bugles, and he exclaimed that he must hurry.

'Good-bye,' Sylvia said. 'I shall never forget this meeting.' She stood on tiptoe, and putting her arm round his neck pulled him towards her and kissed him.

'Good-bye. May you be fortunate and happy,' she repeated.

'It rests with God,' said the soldier; and he vanished into the noise of bugles and the confusion of a regimental muster.

The memory of this casual encounter rested in Sylvia's heart with all the warmth it had originally kindled; nay rather it rested there with a warmth that increased as time went on, and the golden bag came to be regarded with that most essential and sacred affection which may be bestowed upon a relic of childhood, an affection that is not sentimental or comparable in any way to the emotions aroused by the souvenirs of an old love. The bag possessed indeed the recreative quality of art; it was emotion remembered in tranquillity, and as such fiercely cherished by its owner. It was a true mascot, a monstrance of human love; for Sylvia it had a sacramental, almost a Divine significance.

From Kieff much heartened by the omen of fortune's favour Sylvia travelled gladly towards Odessa through leagues of monotonous country shrouded in mist and rain, which seen thus by an unfamiliar visitant was of such surpassing gloom that the notion of war acquired in contrast an adventurous cheerfulness. Often at railway stations that appeared to exist along the track without any human reason for existence Sylvia used to alight with the rest of the passengers and drink glasses of tea sweetened by spoonfuls of raspberry jam; in a luxury of despair she would imagine herself left behind by the train and be sometimes half tempted to make the experiment in order to see how life would adapt itself to such eccentricity. The only diversion upon this endless journey was when the train stopped before crossing a bridge to let soldiers with fixed bayonets mount it and stand in the corridors that they might prevent any traveller from leaving his seat or even from looking out of the window. These precautions against outrages with dynamite affected her at first with a sense of great events happening beyond these mournful steppes; but when she saw that the bayonets were so long that in any scuffle they would have been unmanageable, she had a revulsion from romantic fancies and told herself a little scornfully what children men were and how much playing at war went on behind the bloody scenes of action.

Sylvia reached Odessa on October 28, and the long front looking towards a leaden sea held a thought of England in its salt rain. The cabaret at which she was going to work was like all other cabarets, but being situated in some gardens that opened on the sea it had now a sad and wintry appearance of disuse. A few draggled shrubs, a few chairs not worth the trouble of putting into shelter, a deserted bandstand and open-air theatre served to forbid rather than invite gaiety. However, since the cabaret itself could be reached from a street behind the sea-front and visitors were not compelled to pass through the ghosts of a dead summer, this melancholy atmosphere was obviated. The *pension d'artistes* at which Sylvia stayed was kept by a certain Madame Eliane, a woman of personality and charm with a clear-cut rosy face and snow-white hair who limped slightly and supported herself upon two ebony canes. Madame Eliane objected to being called Mère, which would have been the usual prefix of ironical affection awarded to the owner of such a pension; although she must have been nearly sixty, she had an intense hatred of age and a remarkable faculty for remaining young without losing her dignity. For all the girls under her roof she felt a genuine affection that demanded nothing in return except the acceptance of herself as a contemporary, the first token of which was to call her Eliane; from the men she always exacted Madame. Her nationality was believed to have originally been Austrian, but she had become naturalized as a Russian many years before the war, when she was the mistress of an official who had endowed her with the *pension* before he departed to a remote Baltic province and the respectability of marriage. Sylvia found that Eliane was regarded by all the girls as an illustration of the most perfect success to which anyone of their profession might aspire.

'She's lucky,' said a small cockney called Ruby Arnold, who sang in English popular songs of four years ago that when Sylvia first heard them shocked her with their violent resuscitation of the past. 'Yes, I reckon she's lucky,' Ruby went on. 'There isn't no one that doesn't respect her as you might say. Isn't she cunning too to let her hair go white instead of keeping it gold like what it was once? Anybody can't help talking to anybody with white hair. I reckon with white hair and a house of my own I'd chuck up this life to-morrow, *I* would. *N'est-ce pas que j'ai raison?*' she added in French with a more brutal disregard of pronunciation than Sylvia had ever heard.

'*Oui, petite, tu as raison*,' agreed Odette, a vast French blonde with brilliant prominent eyes, those bulging myopic eyes that are generally the mirrors of vanity and hysteria. 'I have a friend here,' she continued in French, '*une femme du monde avec des idées très larges*, who assured me that if she did not know what Eliane was, she might easily have mistaken her for a *femme du monde* like herself.'

'She and her lady friends,' Ruby muttered contemptuously to Sylvia. 'If you ask me, these French girls don't know a lady when they see one. She had the nerve to bring her in here to tea one day, an old crow with a bonnet that looked as if a dog had worried it. She's bound to ask you to meet her. She can't talk of anything else since she met her in a tram.'

'Well, how's the war getting on? What do they say about it now?' asked a dancer called Flora, flashing a malicious glance at her partner, a young Belgian of about twenty-five with a pale and unpleasantly debauched face, who glared angrily in response. 'Armand cannot suffer us to talk about the war,' she explained to Sylvia.

'She hates him,' Ruby whispered. 'And whenever she can, she gets in a dig because he hasn't tried to fight for his country. Funny thing for two people to live together for three years and hate each other like they do.'

Sylvia said that she had no more information about the war than they had in Odessa, and there followed groans from all the artistes gathered together over coffee for the havoc which the war had brought in their profession.

'I was always *anti-militariste*,' Armand proclaimed, 'even before the war. Why, once in France I was arrested for singing a song that made fun of the army. It's a fine thing to talk about valour and glory and *la patrie* when you're *du premier grade*, but when you're not—' he shook his fist at a world of generals. '*Enfin*, Belgium no longer exists. And who first thought of stopping the Germans? The king! Does he have to dance for a living? *Ah, non alors!* She is always talking about the war,' he went on looking at Flora. 'But if I applied for a passport to go back, she'd be the first to make a row.'

'*Menteur!*' Flora snapped. '*Je m'en fiche.*'

'*Alors, ce soir je n'irai pas au cabaret.*'

'*Tant mieux! Qu'est-ce que ça peut me ficher? Bon dieu!*'

'*Alors, nous verrons, ma gosse.*'

'*Insoumis!*' she spat forth. '*Comme t'es lâche.*'

'They always carry on like that,' Ruby whispered. 'But they'll be dancing together to-night just the same as usual.'

When Sylvia came down from the dressing-room for her turn she found that Ruby had prophesied truly. Armand and Flora were dancing together on the stage, but though their lips were smiling the eyes of both were sullen and hateful. The performance at the Cabaret de l'Aube could not be said to differ in any particular from that of any other cabaret. Sylvia when she was brought face to face with such evidences of international bad taste wondered how the world had ever gone to war. All over Europe people slept in the same kind of wagon-lits (though here in Russia with a broad gauge they slept more comfortably), ate the same kind of food in the same kind of hotel, clapped the same mediocre artistes, and drank the same sweet champagne: yet they could talk about the individuality of nations. How remote war seemed here in Odessa: it was perhaps wrong of her to escape from it like this, and she pondered the detached point of view of Armand. Had she the right to despise his point of view? Did she not herself merit equal contempt?

'I'm too comfortable,' she decided, 'while there is so much misery in the distance.'

However comfortable Sylvia felt when at a quarter-past three she let herself into the Pension Eliane, she felt extremely uncomfortable about an hour later, when the sound of an explosion and the crash of falling glass made those inmates of the pension who were still gossiping downstairs in the dining-room drop their cigarettes and stare at one another in astonishment.

'Whatever's that?' Ruby cried.

'It must be the gas,' said Armand, who could not turn paler than he was, but whose lips trembled.

Another crash followed; outside in the street rose a moan of frightened voices and the clatter of frightened feet.

Two more explosions still nearer drove everybody that was in the pension out of doors, and when it became certain that warships were bombarding Odessa there was a rush to join the inhabitants who were fleeing to what they supposed was greater safety in the heart of the town. In vain Sylvia protested that if the town was really being bombarded, they were just as safe in a pension near the sea-front as anywhere else; the mere idea of propinquity to the sea set everybody running faster than ever away from it. She could hear now the shells whinnying like nervous horses, and with every crash she kept saying to herself in a foolish way:

'Well, at any rate there's no more danger from that one.'

At first in the rush of panic she had not observed any particular incident; but now as shell after shell exploded without any visible sign of damage she began to look with interest at non-combatant humanity in the presence of danger. She did not know whether to be glad or sorry that on the whole the men behaved worse than the women; she put this observation on one side to be argued out later with Armand, who had certainly run faster than anyone else in the pension. The number of the shells was already getting less; yet there were no signs of the populace's recovery. Fear was begetting fear with such rapidity that to stand still and listen to the moans and groans of the uninjured was awe-inspiring. In one doorway a distraught man with nothing on but a shirt and slippers was dancing about with a lighted candle, evidently in a quandary of terror whether to join the onflowing mob or to stay where he was. An explosion quite close made up his mind, and he dived down the steps into the street where the candle was immediately extinguished; nevertheless he continued to hold it as if it were still alight while he ran with the crowd. In another doorway stood a woman confronted with a triple problem. Wearing nothing but a wrapper and carrying in her arms a pet dog, she was trying at the same time to keep her wrapper fastened, to avoid letting the dog drop, and to shut the door behind her. The problem was a nice one: she could either keep her wrapper fastened, maintain the dog, and leave the door open, in which case she would lose her silver; or she could keep her wrapper close, shut the door, and drop the dog, in which case she would lose the dog; or she could keep the dog, shut the door, and let go of her wrapper, in which case she would lose her modesty. Sylvia's anxiety to see how she would solve the problem made her forget all about the shells; and it was only when the perplexed lady in a last desperate attempt slammed the door, so that her wrapper came flying open and the dog went bolting down the street that Sylvia realized the bombardment was over. She turned back toward the pension with a last look over her shoulder at the lady, who was vanishing into the darkness, gathering the wrapper round her nakedness as she ran and calling wildly to her pet.

Next day the military and civil population set out to find who could possibly have told the Turkish destroyers that such a place as Odessa existed. Armand, the Belgian dancer, was particularly loud on the subject of spies; Sylvia suspected it was he who had suggested to the police that Madame Eliane as a reputed Austrian should be severely examined with a view to finding out if the signals of which all were talking could be traced to her windows. If he did inform the police, his meanness recoiled upon his own head, for the examination of Madame Eliane was succeeded by an examination of all her guests, in the course of which Armand's passport was found to be slightly irregular, and he was nearly expelled to Roumania in consequence. The authorities made up their minds that no Turkish destroyer should ever again discover the whereabouts of their town, and the most stringent ordinances against showing lights were promulgated; but a more important result of the declaration of war by

Turkey than the lighting of Odessa was its interference with the future plans of the mountebanks at the Cabaret de l'Aube. There was not one of them who had not intended to proceed from here to Constantinople, a much more profitable winter engagement than this Black Sea port.

'*C'est assommant*,' Armand declared. '*Zut! On ne peut pas rester ici tout l'hiver. On crèvera.*'

'But at any rate one should be thankful that one was not hit by an *obus*,' said Odette. 'I nearly died of fright.'

'It wasn't the fault of the Turks that we weren't hit,' Armand grumbled. 'They did their best.'

'Luckily the shells didn't travel so fast as you,' Sylvia put in.

Flora laughed at this; but when everybody began to tease Armand about his cowardice she got angry, and invited any girl present to produce a man that would have behaved differently.

At last the flotsam that had been stirred up by the alarm of the bombardment drifted together again and stayed idly in what was after all still a backwater to the general European unrest. The manager of the cabaret was glad enough to keep his company together for as long as they would stay. It was getting more difficult all the time to import new attractions; and since as much money was being made out of human misery in Odessa as everywhere else, the champagne flowed not much less freely because since the Imperial edict some bribery of the police was required in order to procure it. Sylvia was puzzled to find what was fate's intention in thus keeping her from moving farther south: it seemed a tame end to all her expectation to be stranded here, lost to everything except the petty life of her fellow players. However, she sang her songs every night; somehow her personality attracted the frequenters of the cabaret, and when after a month she informed the manager that she must leave and go north again, he begged her to stay at any rate for another two months – after that he would arrange for her to travel north and sing at Kieff, Warsaw, and Petrograd, whence she could make her way back to England.

'Or you might go to Siberia,' he suggested.

'Siberia?' she echoed.

That anyone should propose a tour in Siberia seemed a joke at first; when Sylvia found the suggestion was serious, she plunged back with a shiver into the warmer backwater of Odessa. Deciding that with a comfortable pension, a friendly management, and an appreciative audience, it would be foolish to risk her health by moving about too much, she settled down to read Russian novels and study the characters of her associates.

'You are a funny girl,' Ruby said. 'Don't you care about fellows?'

'Why should I?' Sylvia countered.

'Oh, I don't know. It seems more natural somehow. I left home over a fellow and went with a musical comedy to Paris. That's how I started touring the continong. Funny you and I should meet like this in Odessa.'

'Why?'

'Well, I don't know. We're both English. Talk about the World's End, Chelsea! I wonder what they'd call this? Do you know, Sylvia, I sometimes say to myself – supposing if I was to go back to England and find it didn't really exist any more? I'm a funny girl. I think a lot when I'm by myself, which isn't often, thank god, or I should get the willies worse than what I do. I don't know: when I look round and see that I'm in Odessa, I can't somehow believe that there's such a place as London. Do you know, sometimes I'd go mad to hear a bus-driver call out to a cabbie, "You bloody—, where the— hell do you think you're shoving yerself!" Well, after seven years without seeing England, anyone does get funny fancies.'

'There aren't any cab-drivers now,' Sylvia said.

'I suppose that's a fact. Taxis were only just beginning to bob up when I went away. Oh well, I reckon the language is still just as choice. But I would love to hear it. Of course I might hear you swear in the dressing-room over your corsets or anything, but it's the tone of voice I hanker after. Oh well, it'll all come out in the wash, and I don't suppose they notice the war much in England. Still I hope the squareheads won't blow London to pieces. I once did a tour in Germany, and a fellow with a moustache like a flying trapeze wanted to sleep with me for ten marks. They've got nerve enough for anything. What's this word "boche"? I suppose it's French for rubbish.' She began to sing softly:

> 'Take me back to London Town,
> London town, London town!
> That's where I want to be,
> Where the folks are kind to me.
> Trafalgar Square, oh, ain't it grand?
> Oxford Street, the dear old Strand!
> Anywhere, anywhere, I don't care . . .

'Oh god, it gives anyone the hump to think about it. Fancy England at war. Wonders will never cease. I reckon my brother Alf's well in it. He was never happy without he was fighting somebody.'

It was curious, thought Sylvia that evening, as she watched Ruby

Arnold singing her four-year-old songs, how even to that cynical rat-faced little Cockney in her red velvet baby's frock the thought of England at war should bring such a violent longing for home. She tried to become intimate with Ruby; but after that single unfolding of secret aspirations and regrets, she drew away from Sylvia, who asked the reason of her sudden reserve.

'It's not that I don't like you,' Ruby explained. 'I reckon no girl could want a better pal than you if she was your sort. Only I'm not. I like fellows. You don't. Besides, you're different. I won't say you're a lady, because when all's said and done we're both of us working girls. But I don't know. Perhaps it's because you're older than me, only somehow you make me feel fidgety. That's flat, as the cook said to the pancake; but you asked me why I was a bit stand-offish and I've got to speak the truth to girls. I should go barmy otherwise with all the lies I tell to men. I reckon you'd get on better with Odette and her fam dee mond.'

Sylvia was vexed by her inability to bridge the gulf between herself and Ruby; it never occurred to her that the fault lay with anyone but herself, and she felt humiliated by this failure that was so crushing to her will to love; it seemed absurd that in a few minutes she should have been able to get so much nearer the heart of that Russian soldier who accosted her in Kieff than to one of her own countrywomen.

'Perhaps I've learnt how to receive good will,' she told herself, 'but not yet how to offer it.'

It was merely to amuse herself that Sylvia approached Odette for an introduction to her famous *femme du monde*. The suggestion, while it gratified Odette's sense of importance, caused her nevertheless several qualms about Sylvia's fitness for presentation to Madame Corvelis.

'*Elle a des idées très larges, tu sais, mais—*' Odette paused. She could not bring herself to believe that Madame Corvelis' broad-mindedness was broad enough to include Sylvia. '*Pourtant*, I will ask her quite frankly. I will say to her, "*Madame*, there is an artiste who wishes to meet a *femme du monde*." *Ses idées sont tellement larges que peut-être elle sera enchantée de faire ta connaissance*. She has been so charming to me that if I make a *gaffe* she must forgive me. *Enfin*, she came to take tea with me *chez Eliane*, and though of course I was careful not to introduce anybody else to her, she assured me afterwards that she had enjoyed herself. *Alors, nous verrons.*'

Madame Corvelis was a little French Levantine who had married a Greek of Constantinople. Odette had made her acquaintance one afternoon by helping to unhitch her petticoats, which had managed to get caught up while she was alighting from a tram. Her gratitude to Odette for rescuing her from such a blushful situation was profuse and had culminated in an invitation to take tea with her 'in the wretched little house she and her husband temporarily occupied in Odessa,' owing to their flight from Constantinople at the rumour of war.

'What was M. Corvelis?' Sylvia asked, when she and Odette were making their way to visit madame.

'Oh, he was a man of business. I believe he was secretary to some large company. You must not judge them by the house they live in here; they left everything behind in Constantinople. But don't be frightened of M. Corvelis. I assure you that for a man in his position he is very simple.'

'I'll try not to be very frightened,' Sylvia promised.

'And madame is charming. She has the perfect manners of a woman of forty accustomed to the best society. When I think that eight years ago – don't tell anybody else this – but eight years ago, *chérie*,' Odette exclaimed dramatically, '*je faisais le miché autour des boulevards extérieurs! Ma chérie*, when I think of my *mauvais début*, I can hardly believe that I am on my way to take tea with a *femme du monde. Enfin, on arrive!*'

Odette flung proud glances all round her; Sylvia marvelled at her satisfied achievement of a life's ambition, nor did she marvel less when she was presented to Madame Corvelis, surely the most insignificant piece of respectability that had ever adorned a cocotte's dream. It was pathetic to see the way in which the great flaunting creature worshipped this plump *bourgeoise* with her metallic Levantine accent: anxious lest Odette's deference should seem too effusive Sylvia found herself affecting an equally exaggerated demeanour to keep her friend in countenance, though when she looked at their hostess she nearly laughed aloud, so much did she resemble a little squat idol receiving the complimentary adoration of some splendid savage.

'I am really ashamed to receive you in this miserable little house,' Madame Corvelis protested. '*Mais que voulez-vous?* Everything is in Constantinople. Carpets, mirrors, china, silver. We came away like beggars. *Mais que voulez-vous?* My husband is so nervous. He feared the worst. But of course he's nervous. *Que voulez-vous?* The manager of one of the largest companies in the East! Well, I say manager, but of course when a company is as large as his, one ought to say secretary. "Let us go to Odessa, Alceste," he begged. My name is Alceste, but I've no Greek blood myself. Oh no, my father and mother were both Parisian. *Enfin*, my father came under the glamour of the East and called me Alceste. *Que voulez-vous?*'

All the time that Madame Corvelis was talking, Odette was asking

Sylvia in an unbroken whisper if she did not think that madame was *charmante, aimable, gentille*, and every other gracious thing she could be.

'Have you ever been to Constantinople? Have you ever seen the Bosphorus?' Madame Corvelis went on, turning to Sylvia. 'What, you've never seen the most enchanting city in the world? Oh, but you must! Not now, of course. The war! It robs us all of something. Don't, please don't think that Odessa resembles Constantinople.'

Sylvia promised she would not.

'*Mais non*, Odessa is nothing. Look at this house! Ah, when I think of what we've left behind in Constantinople. But M. Corvelis insisted, and he was right. At any rate we've brought a few clothes with us, though of course when we came to this dreadful place we never thought that we shouldn't be back home in a month. It was merely a precaution. But he was right to be nervous, you see: the Turks have declared war. When I think of the poor Ambassador. You never saw the Ambassador?'

Sylvia shook her head.

'I remember he trod on my toe – by accident, of course, oh yes, it was entirely an accident. But he was so apologetic. What manners! But then I always say, if you want to see good manners you must frequent good society. What a pity you never saw the Ambassador!'

'*N'est-ce pas que c'est merveilleux?*' Odette demanded.

'*Merveilleux*,' Sylvia agreed fervently.

'*Encore, madame!*' Odette begged. '*Vos histoires sont tellement intéressantes.*'

'Ah well, one can't live all one's life in Constantinpole without picking up a few stories.'

'Adhesive as burrs,' Sylvia thought.

'But really the best story of all,' Madame Corvelis went on, 'is to find myself here in this miserable little house. That's a pretty bag you have,' she added to Sylvia. 'A very pretty bag. Ah, *mon dieu*, when I think of the jewellery I've left behind!'

At this moment M. Corvelis came in with the cunningly detached expression of a husband who has been hustled out of the room by his wife at the sound of a bell in order to convey an impression, when he has had time to change his clothes, that he habitually dresses *en grande tenue*. It was thus that Odette described her own preparatory toilet, and she was ravished by M. Corvelis' reciprocity, whispering to Sylvia her sense of the compliment to his humble visitors.

'*Homme chic! homme du monde! homme élégant! Mais ça se voit. Dis, t'es contente?*'

Sylvia smiled and nodded.

415

The mould of form who had drawn such an ecstasy of self-congratulatory admiration from Odette treated the two actresses as politely as his wife had done, and asked Sylvia the same questions. When his reduplication of the first catechism was practically complete, Odette gave the signal for departure, and in a cyclone of farewells and compliments they left.

'*Elle est vraiment une femme du monde?*' Odette demanded.

'*De pied en cap,*' Sylvia replied.

'*Ton sac en or lui plaisait beaucoup,*' said Odette a little enviously. 'Ah, when I think of myself eight years ago,' she went on, 'it seems *incroyable*. I should like to invite them both to tea again *chez Eliane*. If only the other girls were like you! And last time I put too much sugar in her tea! *Non, je n'ose pas!* One sees the opportunity to raise oneself, but one does not dare grasp it. *C'est la vie,*' she sighed.

Moved by the vision of herself thwarted from advancing any higher Odette poured out to Sylvia the story of her life, a sad squalid story lit up here and there by the flashes of melodramatic events and culminating in the revelation of this paradise that was denied her.

'What would you have done if you had been invited to her house in Constantinople where the carpets and the mirrors are?'

'She would never have invited me there,' Odette sighed. 'Here she is not known. However broad her ideas, she could not defy public opinion at home. *À la guerre comme à la guerre! Enfin, je suis fille du peuple, mais on me regarde: c'est déjà quelque chose.*'

The *pension* that to Odette appeared so mean after the glories of Madame Corvelis' little house had never been so welcome to Sylvia, and it was strange to think that anyone could be more impressed by that pretentious little *bourgeoise* with her figure like apples in a string bag than by Madame Eliane who resembled a mysterious lady in the background of a picture by Watteau.

It was in mediation upon such queer contrasts that Sylvia passed away her time in Odessa, thus and in pondering the more terrifying profundities of the human soul in the novels of Dostoievsky and Tolstoy. She was not sorry, however, when the time came to leave; she could never exclude from her imagination the hope of some amazing event immemorially predestinate that should decide the course of the years still to come. It would have been difficult for her to explain or justify her conviction, but it would have been impossible to reject it, and it was with an oddly superstitious misgiving that she found herself travelling north again, so strong had been her original impulse to go south. If anything had been wanting to confirm this belief, her arrival in Warsaw at the beginning of February would have been enough.

Sylvia left Kieff on the return visit without any new revelation of human vileness or human virtue, and reached Warsaw to find a mad populace streaming forth at the sound of the German guns. She had positively the sensation of meeting a great dark wave that drove her back, and her interview with the distracted Jew who managed the cabaret for which she had been engaged was like one of those scenes played in a front set of a provincial drama to the sounds of feverish preparation behind the cloth.

'Don't talk to me about songs,' the manager cried. 'Get out! Can't you hear the guns? Everything's closed. Oh, my God, my God, where have I put it? I had it in my hands a moment ago. Get out, I say.'

'Where to?' Sylvia demanded.

'Anywhere. Listen, don't you think they sound a little nearer even in these few minutes? Oh, the Germans! They're too strong. What are you waiting for? Can't you understand me when I say that everything's closed?'

He wiped the perspiration from his big nose with a duster that left long black streaks in its wake.

'But where shall I go?' Sylvia persisted.

'Why don't you go to Bucharest? Why in the devil's name does anyone want to be anywhere but in a neutral country in these times? Go to the Roumanian consul and get your passport *visé* for Bucharest and for the love of God leave me in peace. Can't you see I'm busy this evening?'

Sylvia accepted the manager's suggestion and set out to find the consul: by this time it was too late to obtain a visa that night, and she was forced to sleep in Warsaw – a grim experience that remained as a memory of distant guns booming through a penetrating reek of onions. In the morning the guns were quieter, and there was a rumour that for the third time the German thrust for Warsaw had been definitely foiled. Sylvia, however, could not get over the impression of the evening before, and what the manager had suggested to rid himself of an importunate woman she accepted as a clear indication of the direction she ought to follow.

In the waiting-room of the Roumanian Consulate there was an excessively fat girl who told Sylvia that she was an accompanist anxious like herself to get to Bucharest. Sylvia took the occasion to ask her if she thought there was a certainty of being engaged in Bucharest, and the fat girl was fairly encouraging. She told Sylvia that she was a Bohemian from Prague who had been warned by the Russian police that she would do well to seek another country.

'And will you get an engagement?' Sylvia asked.

417

'Oh well, if I don't, I may as well starve in Bucharest as in Warsaw,' she replied.

There seemed something ludicrous in the notion of anyone so fat as this starving; the accompanist seemed to divine Sylvia's thoughts, for she laughed bitterly.

'I daresay you think I'm pretending, but ever since I was warned, I've been scraping together the money to reach Bucharest somehow; I haven't eaten a proper meal for a month. But the less I eat, the fatter I seem to get.'

Sylvia was vexed that the poor girl should have guessed what she was thinking, and she went out of her way to ask her advice on the smallest details of the proposed journey; she knew that there was nothing that restored a person's self-respect like a request for advice. The fat girl whose name inappropriately for a Bohemian appeared to be Lottie, cheered up, as Sylvia had anticipated, and brimmed over with recommendations about work in Bucharest.

'You'd better go to the management of the Petit Maxim. You're a singer, aren't you? Of course Bucharest is very gay and terribly expensive. You're English, aren't you? You are lucky. But fancy leaving England now! Still, if you don't get any work you'll be able to go to your consul and he'll send you home. I'll be able to get home too from Bucharest, but I don't know if I want to. All my friends used to be French and English girls. I never cared much for Austrians and Germans. But now I get called *sale boche* if I open my mouth. How do you explain this war? It seems very unnecessary, doesn't it?'

'I don't want to be inquisitive,' said Sylvia. 'But I wish you'd tell me why you're called Lottie.'

'Ah, lots of people ask that.' It was evident by the way she spoke that the ability of her name to arouse the curiosity of strangers was one of the chief pleasures life had brought to this fat girl. 'Well, I had an *amant de cœur* once, who was English. At least his mother was English: his father was from Hamburg, in fact I think he was more Jewish than anything. He didn't treat me very well and he threw me over for an English dancer called Lottie who died of consumption. It seems a funny thing to tell you, but the only way I could be revenged was to take her name when she died. You'd have been surprised to see how much my taking her name seemed to annoy him. He threatened me with a pistol once, but I stuck to the name, and then I got fond of it, because I found it created *beaucoup de réclame*. You see, I travelled all over Europe, and people remember me as the fat girl Lottie; so I've never gone back to my own name. It's just as well, because nobody can pronounce Bohemian names.'

The long formalities at the consulate were finished at last, and as they came out Sylvia suggested to the fat girl that they should travel together. She looked at Sylvia in astonishment.

'But I'm an Austrian.'

'Yes, I know. I daresay it's very reprehensible, but unfortunately I can't feel at war with you.'

'Thank you for your kindness,' said Lottie, 'which I'm not going to repay by travelling with you. After we get out of Russia, yes. But till we're over the frontier, I shan't know you for your own sake. You'd only have trouble with the Russian police.'

'Even police could surely not be so stupid as that?' Sylvia argued.

'*À la guerre comme à la guerre,*' the fat girl laughed. '*Au revoir, petite chose.*'

Sylvia left Warsaw that night. Having only just enough money to pay her fare second-class she found the journey down through Russia almost unendurable, especially the first part when the train was swarmed with fugitives from Warsaw, notwithstanding the news of the German failure to pierce the line of the Bzura, which was now confirmed. Yet with all the discomfort she was sustained by an exultant relief at turning south again; and her faculties were positively strained to attention for the disclosure of her fate. She was squeezed so tightly into her seat, and the atmosphere of the compartment was so heavy with the smell of disturbed humanity that it was lucky she had this inner assurance over which she could brood hour after hour. She was without sleep for two nights, and when toward dusk of a dreary February afternoon the frontier station of Ungheny was reached and she alighted from the third train in which she had travelled during this journey, she felt dazed for a moment with the disappointment of somebody who arrives at a journey's end without being met.

However, there was now the frontier examination by the Russian authorities of passengers leaving the country to occupy Sylvia's mind, and she passed with an agitated herd towards a tin-roofed shed in the middle of which a very large stove was burning. She had noticed Lottie several times in the course of the journey, and now finding herself next her in the crowd she greeted her cheerfully; but the fat girl frowned and whispered:

'I'm not going to speak to you for your own sake. Can't you understand?'

Sylvia wondered if she were a spy, who from some motive of charity wished to avoid compromising her; but there was no time to think about such problems, because an official was taking her passport and waving her across to the stacked up heaps of luggage. There was something redolent of old sensational novels in this frontier examination, something theatrically sinister about the attitude of the officials when they commanded everybody to turn everything out of the trunks and bags. The shed took on the appearance of a vast rag-heap and the accumulated agitation of the travellers was pitiable in its subservience to these machines of the State; it seemed incredible that human beings should consent to be treated thus. Presently it became evident that the object of this relentless search was paper; every scrap of paper, whether it was loose or used for wrapping and packing, was taken away and dropped into the stove. The sense of human ignominy became overwhelming when Sylvia saw men going down on their knees and weeping for permission to keep important documents; yet no appeal moved the officials, and the stove burned fiercely with the mixed records of money, love, and business; with contracts and receipts and title deeds; even with toilet-paper and old greasy journals. Sylvia fought hard for the right to keep her music, and proclaimed her English nationality so insistently that for a minute or two the officials hesitated and went out to consult the authorities who had taken charge of her passport; but when it was found that she was entered there as a music-hall artiste, the music was flung into the stove at once. Confronted with the proofs of her right to carry music, this filthy spawn of man's will to be enslaved took from her the only tools of her craft; orang-outangs would have been more logical. And all over the world the human mind was being debauched like this by war, or would it be truer to say that war was turning ordinary stupidity into criminal stupidity? Oh, what did it matter? Sylvia clasped her golden bag to reassure herself that nobility still endured in spite of war. Now they were throwing books into the stove! Sylvia sat down and laughed so loudly that two soldiers came across and took her arms to lead her outside: they evidently thought she was going to have hysterics, which would doubtless have been unlawful in the shed. She waved aside their attentions and went across to pick up her luggage.

When Sylvia had finished and was passing out to find the office where she had to receive back her passport inscribed with illegible permits to leave Russia, she saw Lottie being led through a curtained door on the far side of the shed. The sight made her feel sick: it brought back with horrible vividness her emotion when years ago she had seen on the French frontier the woman with the lace being led away for smuggling contraband. What were they going to do? She paused, expecting to hear a scream issue from that curtained doorway. She could not bring herself to go away, and with an excuse of having left something behind in the shed she went back. The curtain was pulled aside a moment for someone within to call the assistance of someone without, and Sylvia had a brief vision of the fat girl half undressed, with her arms held high above her head while two police officers prodded her like a sheep in a fair.

'Oh, God!' Sylvia murmured. 'God! God! Grant these people their revenge some day!'

The passengers were at last free to mount another train and Sylvia saw with relief that Lottie was taking her place with the rest. She avoided speaking to her, because she was suffering herself from the humiliation inflicted upon the fat girl and felt awed at the idea of any intrusion upon her shame. The train steamed out of the station, crossed a long bridge and pulled up in Roumanian Ungheny, where everybody had to alight again for the Roumanian officials to look for the old-fashioned contra-band of the days before the war. They did this as perfunctorily as in those happy days; and the quiet of the neutral railway-station was like the sudden lull that sheltering land gives to the stormiest seas. If she only had not lost all her music, if only she had not seen the fat girl behind that curtain, Sylvia could have clapped her hands for pleasure at this unim-pressive little station, which merely because it belonged to a country at peace had a kind of innocence and jollity that gave it a real beauty.

'Well, aren't you glad I wouldn't have anything to do with you?' said Lottie, coming up to her with a smile. 'You'd have had to go through the same probably. The Russian police are brutes.'

'All policemen are brutes,' Sylvia declared.

'I suppose they have their orders, but I think they might have a woman searcher.'

'Oh don't talk about it,' Sylvia cried. 'Such things crucify the soul.'

'You're very *exageree* for an English girl,' said Lottie. 'Aou yes! Aou yes! I never met an English girl who talked like you.'

The train arrived at Jassy about nine o'clock; here they had to change again, and since the train for Bucharest did not leave till about eleven and she was feeling hungry, Sylvia invited Lottie to have dinner with her. While they were walking along the platform toward the restaurant there was a sound of hurried footsteps behind them, and a moment later a breathless voice called out in English:

'Excuse me, please! Excuse me, please! They told me there was being an English artiste on the train.'

That voice reproduced so many times by Sylvia at the Pierian Hall was the voice of Concetta and turning round she saw her.

'Concetta!'

The girl drew in her breath sharply.

'How was you knowing me? My name is Queenie Walters. How was

421

you calling me Concetta? Ah, the English girl! Oh, my dear, I am so content to see you.'

Sylvia took her in her arms and kissed her.

'Oh, Sylvia! You see I remember your name. I can't get away from Jassy. I was being expelled from Moscow, and I had no money to come more than here, and the man I am with here I hate. I want to go to Bucharest, but he isn't wanting to let me go and gives to me only furs, no money.'

'You're not still with Zozo?'

'*Ach*, no! He – how do you say – he shooted me in the leg three years from now and afterwards we were no more friends. The man I am with her was of Jassy. I had no money. What else must I do?'

Sylvia had not much money either; but she had just enough to pay Concetta's fare to Bucharest, whither at midnight they set out.

'And let no one ever tell me again that presentiments don't exist,' murmured Sylvia, falling asleep for the first time in forty-eight hours.

IV

Concetta's history – or rather Queenie's, for it was by this name that she begged Sylvia to call her now – had been a mixture of splendour, misery, and violence during the six years that almost to a day had elapsed since they met for the first time at Granada. She told it in the creeping light of a wet dawn while the train was passing through a flat colourless country and while in a corner of the compartment Lottie's snores rose above the noise, told it in the breathless disjointed style that was so poignantly familiar to the one who listened. There was something ghostly for Sylvia in this experience; it was as if she sat opposite a Galatea of her own creation, a double-ganger from her own brain, a dream prolonged into the cold reality of the morning. All the time that she was listening she had a sensation of being told about events that she ought to know already, as if in a trance she herself had lived this history through before; and so vivid was the sensation that when there were unexplained gaps in Queenie's narrative she found herself puzzling her own brain to fill them in from experience of her own, the recollection of which had been clouded by some accident.

When Queenie told how she was carried away by Zozo from Mrs. Gainsborough at the railway-station of Granada, she gave the impression of having yielded to a magical and irresistible influence, and it was evident that for a long while the personality of the juggler had swayed her destiny by an hypnotic power that was only broken when he wounded her with the pistol-shot. Even now after three years of freedom his influence, when she began to talk of him, seemed to regather its volume and to be about to pour itself once more over her mind. Sylvia perceived this danger, and forbade her to talk any more about Zozo. This injunction was evidently a relief to the child – she must be twenty-one by now, though she seemed still a child – but it was tantalizing to Sylvia who could not penetrate beyond her own impression of the juggler as an incredible figure, incredible because only drawn with a kind of immature or tired fancy. He passed into the category of the Svengalis, and became one of a long line of romantic impossibilities with whom their creators had failed to do much more than can be done by a practical joker with a turnip, a sheet, and some phosphorus. Zozo had always been the weakest part of Sylvia's improvisation of Concetta, a melodramatic climax that for her had spoilt the more simple horror of the childhood; she determined that later on she would try to extract from Queenie bit by bit enough to complete her performance.

Although Queenie had managed to break away from the man himself, she had paid in full for his direction of her life, and Sylvia rebelled against the whim of destiny which at the critical moment in this child's career had snatched her from herself and handed her over to the possession of a Zozo. What could have been the intention of fate in pointing a way to safety and then immediately afterward barring it against her progress? The old argument of free will could not apply in her case, because it was the lack of that, and of that alone, which had caused her ruin. What but a savage and undiscerning fate could be held accountable for this tale that had for fit background the profitable and ugly fields through which on this tristful Roumanian day the train was sweeping? Queenie seemed to have had no lovers apart from the purchasers of youth, and to be able to look back with pride and pleasure at nothing except furs and dresses and jewellery with which she had been purchased. In the rage that Sylvia felt for this wanton corruption of a soul, she suddenly remembered how long ago she had watched with a hopeless equanimity and a cynical tolerance the progress of Lily along the same road as Queenie; and this memory of herself as she once was and felt revived the torments of self-reproach that had haunted her delirium in Petrograd. Then, as Queenie's tale went on, there gradually emerged from all the purposeless confusion of it one clear ambition in the girl's mind, which was a passion to be English – a passion feverish, intense, absorbing.

When in France Sylvia had first encountered continental music-hall artistes, she had found amongst them universal prejudice against English girls; later on, when she met in cabarets the expatriated and cosmopolitan mountebanks that were the slaves rather than the servants of the public, she had often been envied for her English nationality: Lottie sleeping over there in the corner was an instance in point. But she had never found this fleeting envy crystallized to such a passionate ambition as it was become for Queenie. The circumstances of her birth in Germany from an Italian father of a Flemish mother, her flight from a cruel stepmother, her life with the juggler whose nationality seemed as indeterminate as her own, her speech compounded of English, French, German, and Italian each spoken with a foreign accent, her absence of any kind of papers, her lack of any sort of home, had all combined to give her a positive belief that she was without nationality, which she coveted as some Undine might covet a soul.

'But why do you want to be English so particularly?' Sylvia asked.

'Don't you know? Why, yes, of course you know. It was you was first making me to want. You were so sweet, the sweetest person I was ever meeting, and when I lost you I was always wanting to be English.'

So after all, her own swift passage through Queenie's life had not been without consequence.

'People were always saying that I looked like an English girl,' Queenie went on. 'And I was always talking English. I will never speak other languages again. I will not know other languages. Until this war came it was easy; but when they asked me for my passport I had only a *billet de séjour* given to me by the Russian police, and after six months I was expelled. When I was coming to Roumania, there was a merchant on the train who was kind to me, but he made me promise that if he helped me I was never to leave him until he was wanting. He was very kind. He gave me these furs. They are nice, yes? But I was always going to the station at Jassy to see if some English girl would be my sister. There was once in Constantinople an English girl who would be my sister – but Zozo was jealous. If I was becoming her sister, I would be having a passport now, and England is so sweet!'

'But you've never been in England,' Sylvia observed.

'Oh yes, I was going there with another English girl, and we lived there three months. I was dancing into a club – a nice club, all the men were wearing smokings – but she was ill and I wanted to be giving her money, so I was going to Russia, and then came the war. And now you must be my sister, because that other sister will be perhaps dead, so ill she was. *Ach* yes, so ill, so very ill! When I will have my English passport we will go to England together and never come away again. Then for the first time I shall be happy.'

Sylvia promised that she would do all she could to achieve Queenie's purpose.

'Tell me, why did your call yourself Queenie Walters?' she asked.

'Because the girl who was my sister in England had once a real little baby sister who was called Queenie. Oh, dead long ago, long ago! Her mother who I was calling *my* mother told me about this baby Queenie. So I was Queenie Walters and my sister was Elsie Walters.'

'And your real brother, Francesco?' Sylvia asked. 'Did you ever see him again?'

That dreamlike and inexplicable meeting between the brother and the sister in the streets of Milan had always remained in Sylvia's memory.

'No, never yet again. But I am so sure he is being in England and that when we go there we will find him. And if he is English too, what fun we will have.'

Sylvia looked at these two companions who had both assumed English names. Not even the cold and merciless grey light of the Roumanian morning could destroy Queenie's unearthly charm, and the longer she looked at her, the more like an Undine she thought her. Her eyes were ageless, limpid as a child's; and that her experience of evil should have left no sign of its habitation Sylvia was tempted to ascribe to the absence of a soul for evil to mar. The only indication that she was six years older than when they met in Granada was her added gracefulness of movement, the impulsive gracefulness of a gazelle rather than that serene gracefulness of a cat which had been Lily's beauty. Her hair of a natural pale gold had not been dimmed by the fumes of cabarets, and even now all tangled after a night in the train it had a look of hovering in this railway-carriage like a wintry sunbeam. In the other corner sat Lottie snoring with wide-open mouth, whose body relaxed in sleep seemed fatter than ever. She too had suffered, perhaps more deeply than Queenie, certainly more markedly; and now in dreams what fierce Bohemian passions were aroused in the vast airs of sleep, what dark revenges of the spirit for the insults that grotesque body must always endure?

At this point in Sylvia's contemplation Lottie woke up and prepared for the arrival of the train at Bucharest by making her toilet.

'Where's the best place to stay?' Sylvia enquired.

'Well, the best place to stay is in some hotel,' Lottie replied. 'But the hotels are so horribly expensive. Of course, there are plenty of *pensions d'artistes*, and—' she broke off and looked at Sylvia curiously, who asked her why she did so.

'I was thinking that it's a pity you can't share a room together,' she said after a momentary hesitation.

'So we can,' Sylvia answered sharply.

'Well, in that case I should go to a small hotel,' Lottie advised. 'Because all the *pensions* here are run by old thieves. There's Mère Valérie – she's French and almost the worst of the lot – and there's one kept by a Greek who's not so bad, but they say most of her bedrooms have bugs.'

'We'll go to an hotel,' Sylvia decided. 'Where are you going yourself?'

'Oh, I shall find myself a room somewhere. I don't stand a chance of being engaged at any first-rate cabaret, and I shan't have much money to spend on rooms. *Entre nous, je ne dis plus rien aux hommes. Je suis trop grasse. A quoi sert une jolie chambre?*'

Sylvia had a feeling that she ought to ask Lottie to share a room with Queenie and herself, and after a struggle against the notion of this fat girl's ungainly presence she keyed herself to the pitch of inviting her.

'No, no' said Lottie. 'It wouldn't do for two English girls to live with an Austrian.'

Sylvia could not help being relieved at her refusal; perhaps she showed it, for Lottie smiled cynically.

'I think you'll feel a little less charitable to everybody,' she said, 'before much longer. You've kept out of this war so far, but you won't be able to keep out of it for ever. I've often noticed about English girls that they begin by thinking such a lot of themselves that they have quite a store of pity for the poor people who aren't like them; and then all of a sudden they turn round and become very unpleasant; because they discover that other people think themselves as good as they are. Mind you, I'm not saying you'll do that, but I don't want to find myself *de trop* after being with you a week. Let's part as friends.'

Sylvia in the flurry of arrival did not pay much attention to Lottie's prophecies, and she was glad to be alone again with Queenie. They discovered a small hotel kept by Italians, which seemed clean and, if they obtained a reasonable salary at the Petit Maxim, not too expensive. When they had dressed themselves up to impress the manager of the cabaret and were starting out to seek an engagement, the wife of the proprietor called Sylvia aside.

'You mustn't bring gentlemen back to the hotel except in the afternoon.'

'We don't want to bring anybody back at any time,' said Sylvia indignantly.

The woman shrugged her shoulders and muttered a sceptical apology.

The interview with the manager of the cabaret was rather humiliating for Sylvia, though she laughed at it when it was all over. He was quite ready to engage Queenie both to dance *en scène* and afterwards, but he declared he had nothing to offer Sylvia; she proposed to sing him one of her songs, but he scarcely listened to her and when she had finished repeated that he had nothing to offer her. Whereupon Queenie announced that unless her sister was engaged the Petit Maxim would have to forgo her own performance. The manager argued for a time, but he was evidently much impressed by Queenie's attraction as a typical English girl and finally rather than lose her he agreed to engage Sylvia as well.

'It's a pity you look so unlike an English girl,' he said to Sylvia in an aggrieved voice. 'The public will be disappointed. They expect an English girl to look English. You'll have to sing at the beginning of the evening, and I can't pay you more than three hundred *lei* – three hundred francs that is.'

'I was getting eight hundred in Russia,' Sylvia objected.

'I daresay you were, but girls are scarcer there. We've got thousands of them in Bucharest.'

Sylvia was furious at being offered so little, but Queenie promptly asked nine hundred and when the manager objected suggested that he might engage them both for twelve hundred: it was strange to find Queenie so sharp at business. In the end Sylvia was offered three hundred and fifty *lei* and Queenie seven hundred and fifty, which they accepted.

'You can have a band rehearsal to-morrow,' he said, 'and open on Monday week.'

Sylvia explained about the loss of her music; and the manager began to curse, demanding how she expected an orchestra to accompany her without band parts.

'I'll accompany myself,' she answered.

'Oh well,' he agreed, 'being the first item on the programme, it doesn't really matter what you do.'

It was impossible for the moment not to feel the sting of this when Sylvia remembered herself a year ago, fresh from her success at the Pierian and inclined to wonder if she were not dimming her effulgence as a moderately large star by appearing at English music-halls. Now here she was being engaged for the sake of another girl and allowed on sufferance to entertain the meagre listless audience at the beginning of a cabaret performance – for the sake of another girl who owed to her the fare to Bucharest and whom all the way in the train she had been pitying while she made plans to rescue her from a degrading existence. There was a brief moment of bitterness and jealousy; but it passed almost at once and she began to laugh at herself.

'There's no doubt you'll have to establish your English nationality,' she told Queenie, as they left the manager's office. 'I really believe he thought it was I who was pretending.'

'It's what I was saying you,' Queenie answered. 'They was all thinking that I was English.'

'Well, now we must decide about our relationship. Of course, you don't look the least like my sister, but I think the best way will be for you to pass as my sister. My name isn't really Sylvia Scarlett, but Sylvia Snow; so what I suggest is that you shall go on calling yourself Queenie Walters on the stage, though when we try to get our passport you must be Queenie Snow. Trust me to get round the English authorities here, if it's necessary. We can always go back to England through Bulgaria and Greece, but we must save up enough money, and it'll take us a good many weeks to do that in Bucharest.'

Sylvia did not tell Queenie that she could always write to England and borrow the money to go back, because the child would not have understood her disinclination to be helped home. Indeed, she never confided anything about herself to Queenie, one of whose charms was a complete lack of curiosity about other people, a quality which she shared with Lily, and which looking back on their life together Sylvia decided must have been Lily's great charm for her. This absence of curiosity about other people gave Queenie a kind of unworldliness – apart from the bargain she knew how to drive with a manager – and made her accept with the philosophy of an animal anything that did not positively hurt her. She wanted Sylvia to think for her, and the way in which she yielded up her will with an affectionate surrender brought home vividly the danger of exposing her to any external influence. After they had lived together for a while, Sylvia began to realize that no great hypnotic power had been required by the juggler to make Queenie his slave; she seemed to have a natural propensity toward slavery, and Sylvia often had to check herself from assuming too much of Queenie's character upon herself, partly because she thought it was deleterious to her own character, partly because she was trying hard to create in Queenie a conception of egoism. The girl's absence of nationality seemed to have deprived her of this to such an extent that often when she talked about herself she gave the impression of talking about a third person; it was extraordinary, but Queenie's conception of her own individuality was hardly as strong as Sylvia's conception of herself as Queenie in the days when she used to give the Improvisations. Indeed Sylvia could easily have claimed that she was more of Queenie than Queenie herself, and this assumption of another person's being made her fear anything that might befall her more acutely than she would have feared for herself.

428

'Which must she be given first?' Sylvia asked herself. 'A soul or a nationality? The ultimate reason of nationality is civilization, and the object of civilization is the progress and safety of the State. The more progressive and secure is the State, the more utterly is the individual soul destroyed, because the State compels the individual to commit crimes for which as an individual he would be execrated. Hence the crime of war, to which the individual is lured by a virtue created by appealing to mankind's sense of property, a virtue called patriotism that somehow or other I'm perfectly sure must be anti-divine, though it's a virtue for which I have a great respect. *What shall it profit a man if he shall gain the whole world and lose his own soul?* That's surely the answer to civilization, which after all has no object except the physical comfort of humanity. I suppose one might call the civilization that is of the spirit and not of the flesh 'salvation'. I wonder what the Germans mean by Kultur – really I suppose the aggregate soul of the German people. I think Kultur in their sense must be a hybrid virtue like patriotism. I think it's their own ascription of a divine origin to a civilization which has been as rapid and as poisonous and as ugly as a toad-stool. We other civilized nations revile the Germans as barbarians, particularly we English, because in England, thank heaven, we've always had an uncomfortable feeling that man is a greater thing than men, and we perceive in war a sacrifice of the individual that no State has the right to demand. I wonder why the Russians went to war. I can't understand a country that has produced Tolstoy and Dostoievsky going to war. If I had not met that soldier in Kieff I might have been sceptical about Russian idealism after my adventures in Petrograd, after that filthy cinema, and the scene in the station at Ungheny; but having met him I know that Tolstoy and Dostoievsky *are* Russia.

'All of which has taken me a long way from Queenie who is neither ready for civilization nor for salvation. It's a most extraordinary thing, but I've suddenly got an idea that she has never been baptized. If she has not, I shall persuade her to be baptized. Baptism – the key to salvation! A passport – the key to civilization! The antithesis is not so ludicrous nor so extravagant as it sounds at first. Without a passport Queenie has no nationality and does not possess elementary civic rights. She is liable to be expelled from any country at any moment, and there is no certainty that any other country will receive her. In that case she will spend the rest of her life on earth in a kind of Limbo comparable to the Limbo which I believe is reserved for the souls of those unbaptized through no fault of their own. I shall be able to procure her a passport and introduce her to the glories of nationality by perjuring myself, but I can't give her a soul

429

by perjuring myself, and I've got so strongly this intuition that she was never baptized that I shall dig out a priest and talk to him about it. And yet why am I bothering whether she was baptized or not? What have I to do with churches and their ceremonies? No doubt I was baptized, confirmed, and made my communion; yet for more than twenty years I have never entered a church except as an onlooker. Is this anxiety about Queenie's soul only another way of expressing an anxiety about my own soul? Yes, I believe it is. I believe that by a process of sheer intellectual exhaustion I am being driven into Christianity. Oh, I wish I could talk it all out! It's a damned dishonest way of satisfying my own conscience, to go to a priest and ask questions about Queenie. Why can't I go and ask him straight out about myself? But she is just as important as I am. I think that was brought home to me rather well, when the manager engaged me because he wanted her. There was I in a condition of odious pride because I had been given the chance of helping her by paying the beggarly fare to Bucharest, and boomph! as dear Gainsborough used to say, there was she given the chance of paying me back a hundred-fold within twenty-four hours.'

Queenie was out, and Sylvia was lying down with a headache which was not improved by the procession of these vagrant speculations round and round her brain. She got up presently to look for some aspirin, and, opening the drawer of the table between the two beds, she found a bundle of pictures – little coloured lithographs of old masters. She was turning them over idly, when Queenie came back.

'*Ach*, you was looking at my pictures. They are so nice, yes? See, this is the one I love the best.'

It was the Primavera, and Sylvia was astonished for a moment that Queenie's childlike and undeveloped taste should care for something so remote from the crudities that usually appealed to such a mind. Then she remembered that Botticelli as a painter must have appealed to contemporaries who by modern standards were equally childlike and undeveloped; and also that Queenie, whose nationality by the standards of civilization did not exist, had an Italian father, the inheritor perhaps of Botticelli's blood. Queenie sat on the bed and looked at her pictures with the rapt expression of a child poring over her simple treasures. From time to time she would hold up one for Sylvia's admiration.

'See how sweet,' she would say, kissing the grave little Madonna or diminished landscape that was drawing her out of Bucharest into another world.

'I've got a book somewhere about pictures,' Sylvia said. 'You must read it.'

Queenie hid her face in her arms; when she looked up again she was crimson as a carnation.

'I can't read,' she whispered.

'Not read?' Sylvia echoed.

'I can't read or write,' she went on. '*Ach*? Now you hate me, yes? Because I was being so stupid.'

'But when you went to the school in Dantzig, didn't they teach you anything?'

'They taught me ballet dancing and acrobatic dancing and step dancing. Now I must go to have my hair washed, yes?'

Queenie got off the bed and hurried away, leaving Sylvia in a state of bewilderment before the magnitude of the responsibility that she represented.

'It's like giving birth to a grown-up baby,' she said to herself; on a sudden irresistible impulse, she knelt down upon the floor and began to pray, with that most intense prayer of which a human being is capable, that prayer which transcends all words, all space, all time, all thought, that prayer which substitutes itself for the poor creature who makes it. The moment of prayer passed, and Sylvia, rising from her knees, dressed herself and went in search of a priest.

When she reached the door of the little Catholic mission church to which the proprietor of the hotel had directed her, she paused upon the inner threshold before a baize door and asked herself if she were not acting in a dream. She had not been long enough in Bucharest for the city to be reassuringly familiar; by letting her fancy play around the unreality of her present state of mind she was easily able to transform Bucharest to a city dimly apprehended in a tranced voyage of the spirit and to imagine all the passers-by as the fantastic denizens of another world. She stood upon the threshold and yielded a moment to what seemed like a fainting of reason, while all natural existence swayed round her mind and while the baize door stuck thick with pious notices, funereal objurgations, and the petty gossip as it were of a new habitation at which she was looking with strange eyes, seemed to attend her next step with a conscious expectancy. She pushed it open and entered the church; a bearded priest, escaping the importunities of an aged parishioner with a voluble grievance, was coming towards her; perceiving that Sylvia was looking round in bewilderment, he took the occasion to get rid of the old woman by asking in French if he could do anything to help.

'I want to see a priest,' she replied.

Although she knew that he was a priest, in an attempt to cheat the force that was impelling her she snatched at his lack of resemblance to

431

the conventional priestly figure of her memory and deluded herself with vain hesitations.

'Do you want to make your confession?' he asked.

Sylvia nodded, and looked over her shoulder in affright; it seemed that the voice of a wraith had whispered 'yes.' The priest pointed to the confessional, and Sylvia with a final effort to postpone her surrender asked with a glance at the old woman if he were not too busy now. He shook his head quickly and spoke sharply in Italian to the parishioner who retired grumbling; Sylvia smiled to see with what an ostentation of injured dignity she took the holy water and crossed herself before passing out through the baize door. The old woman's challenging humanity restored to Sylvia her sense of reality; emotion died away like a falling gale at eve, and she walked to the confessional imbued with an intention as practical as if she had been walking upstairs to tidy her hair. The priest composed himself into a non-committal attitude and waited for Sylvia, who now that she was kneeling felt as if she were going to play an unrehearsed part.

'I ought to say before I begin that, though I was brought up a Catholic, I've not been inside a church for any religious duties since I was nine years old. I'm now thirty-one. I know that there is some set form of words, but I've forgotten it.'

Sylvia half expected that he would tell her to go away and come back when she had learnt how to behave in the confessional; now that she was here, she felt that this would be a pity, and she was relieved when he began the *Confiteor* in an impersonal voice, waiting for her to repeat every sentence after him. His patience seemed to her almost miraculous in the way it smoothed her difficulties.

'I shall have to give you a short history of my life,' Sylvia began. 'I can't just say baldly that I've done this or not done that, because nearly all the sins I've committed weren't committed in their usual classification.'

As she said this, she had a moment of acute self-consciousness and wondered if the priest were smiling, but he merely said in that far-away impersonal voice:

'I am listening, my daughter.'

'I was brought up a Catholic. I was baptized and confirmed and I made my first communion. It was the only communion I ever made, because somehow or other at home there was always work to be done in the house instead of going to mass. My mother was French and she married an Englishman much younger than herself. Of this marriage I was the only child. My mother had six other daughters, two by a lover who died and four by her first husband who was a Frenchman. My mother was

432

illegitimate; her father was also an Englishman. I only knew this after she died. The man who married my grandmother always acknowledged her as his own daughter. My mother was very strict and, though she was not at all religious, she was really good: I don't want to give the idea that she was responsible for anything I did. The only thing is, perhaps, that being passionately in love with my father she was very demonstrative in front of me, which made the idea of passion shocking to me when I was still young. Therefore for whatever sins of the flesh I have committed I cannot plead a natural propensity. I don't know whether this would be considered to make them worse or not. My father was a weak man; when my mother died, he robbed his employers and had to leave France, taking me with him. I was twelve at the time. I suppose if I wanted to justify myself, I could say that no child could have spent a more demoralizing childhood from that moment. But though when I look back at it now and realize some of the horrible actions that my father and a friend of his who lived with us committed, I can't think that at the time they influenced me towards evil. I suppose that any kind of moral callousness *is* a bad example, and certainly I had no conception that swindling people out of money was anything but a perfectly right and normal procedure for anybody who was without money. My mother was angry with me once because by accident I spent some money of hers, but she was angry with me because it was a serious loss to the household accounts: there was no suggestion of my having spent money that did not belong to me. Other things that my father and his friend did I never understood at the time, and so I can't pretend that they set me a bad example. My father took a woman to live with him, and I was angry because it upset what had hitherto seemed a comfortable existence, but the revelation of the passionate side of it disgusted me still more with the flesh. I was a mixture of precocity and innocence. Looking back at myself as a child I am amazed at the amount I knew and the little I understood – the amount I understood and the little I knew. I read all sorts of books and accepted everything I read as the truth: I read dozens of novels, for instance, before I understood the meaning of fiction. I should say that no child was ever exposed so naturally to the full tide of human existence, and why or how I managed to escape degradation and damnation I've never been able to explain until now. As a matter of fact it's not true really to say that I did escape degradation, but I will come to that presently.

'Well, my father killed himself on account of this woman, and I was left with his friend when I was fifteen. Once I happened to be left altogether alone when this man was away turning a dishonest penny somewhere, and I suppose I fell mildly in love with a youth two years older than myself. This made my father's friend jealous, and one night he tried to make love to me. I was as much disgusted by this as if I had really been the innocent child I might have been. I ran away with the youth, and nothing happened. I ran away from him and lived with a young Jew, but nothing happened. I met the woman who had lived with my father, and – which shows how utterly unmoral I was – I made great friends with her and even went to live with her. She used to have all sorts of men, and I just accepted her behaviour as a personal taste of her own which I could neither understand nor share. Then I met a gentleman, a man fifteen years older than myself who was attracted by my unusualness and sent me to school with the idea of marrying me. Well, I married him, and I think that was the first sin I committed. I was seventeen at the time. I think if my husband had understood how stunted my emotional development was in proportion to my mental acquisitiveness he would have behaved differently. But he was fascinated by my capacity for cynicism and encouraged me to think as I liked with himself for audience; at the same time he tried to make me for outsiders' eyes a conventional young miss whom he had rather apologetically married. He demanded from me the emotional wisdom to sustain this part, and of course I could see nothing in his solicitude but a sort of snobbish egotism. He was delighted by my complete indifference to any kind of religion, supernatural or natural, and when I made friends with an English priest – not a Catholic – but half a Catholic – it's impossible to explain to a foreigner – I don't think anybody would understand the Church of England out of England, and very few people can there – he was afraid of my turning religious. I don't know – perhaps I might have done; but somebody sent an anonymous letter to my husband, suggesting that this priest and I were having a love affair, and my husband forbade me to see him again. So I ran away. I suppose my running away was the direct result of my bringing up, because whenever I had been brought face to face with a difficult situation I ran away. However, this time I was determined from some perverted pride to make myself more utterly myself than I had ever done. It's hard to explain how my mind worked. You must remember I was only nineteen, and already at thirty-one I am as far from understanding all my motives then as if I were trying to understand somebody who was not myself at all. Anyhow, I simply went on the streets. For three months I mortified my flesh by being a harlot. Can you understand that? Can you possibly understand the deliberate infliction of such a discipline, not to humiliate one's pride but to exalt it? Can you understand that I emerged from that three months of incredible horror with a complete personality? I was defiled: I was degraded: I was embittered: I hated mankind: I vowed to revenge myself on the world: I scoffed at love: and yet now, when I feel that I have at last brushed from myself the last speck of mud that was still clinging to me, I feel that somehow all that mud has preserved me against a more destructive corruption. This does not mean that I do not repent of what I did, but can you understand how without a pride that could lead me to such depths I could not have come through humility to a sight of God?'

Sylvia did not wait for the priest to answer this question, partly because she did not want to be disillusioned by finding so soon that he had not comprehended anything of her emotions or actions, partly because there seemed more important revelations of herself still to be made.

'I stayed a common harlot until I was offered by chance an opportunity to rescue myself by going on the stage. Then I sent my husband as much money as I had saved and the evidences of my infidelity, so that he might divorce me, which he did. Now comes an important event in my life. I met a girl – a very beautiful girl doomed from the creation of the universe to be a plaything of man.'

The priest held up his hand to protest.

'Ah, I know you'll say that no one can possibly be so foredoomed, and indeed I know the same myself now, or rather I'm trying hard to believe it, because predestination without free will seems to me a doctrine of devils. At the time, however, I could see nothing that would save this girl, and with a perverted idealism I determined that she should step gracefully downhill. I think the hardest thing to do is to go downhill gracefully. We can climb uphill, and a certain awkwardness is immaterial, because the visible effort lends a dignity to our progress, and the air of success blows freshly at the summit. We can walk along the level road of mediocrity with an acquired gracefulness that is taught us by our masters of the golden mean – particularly in England, where it's particularly easy to walk gracefully along the flat. Very well, instead of using my influence to prevent this girl descending at all, I was entirely occupied with the æsthetic aspects of her descent. I'm not going to pretend that I could have stopped her – a better person than I tried and failed – but that doesn't excuse my attitude. And there's worse to my account. When this other person wanted to marry her, I did all I could to stop the marriage at first, and it was not until the engagement between them was broken off that I discovered that my true reasons for hating it sprang entirely from my own jealousy. I felt that if this man had loved me, I could have regained myself, the self that was myself before those three months of prostitution. I should say here that I had nothing to do directly with the destruction of the other marriage, but I hold myself to blame ultimately, because, if from the beginning I had bent my whole will to its being carried through, it *would* have been carried through. Looking back at the business now, I am convinced that what happened happened for the best, and that such a marriage would have been fatal to the happiness of the man and useless to the girl, but that does not excuse my own share in the smash.

'Well, the man left this girl in my charge, and finally she threw me over and married a foreigner, since when I have never heard that she even still lives. I had the good fortune to be given enough money by somebody to enable me to be independent, and for two or three years I looked at life from the outside. I had nothing to do with men, and as a result I began to be afraid that youth would pass without my ever knowing what it was to love. Friends of mine married and were happy. Only I seemed fated to be always alone.

'I wonder sometimes if when we judge the behaviour of others we pay enough attention to this loneliness that haunts the lives of so many men and women. You will say that no one can be lonely with God; unfortunately thousands of lonely souls are destitute of the sense of God from birth to death, and these lonely souls are far more exposed to temptation than the rest. Faith they have not: hope has died in their hearts: love slowly withers. All the vices of self-destruction surround their path. Pride flourishes in such soil, and jealousy and envy. I believe their only compensation is the fact that lies and self-deception find small nourishment in such spiritual wastes. I'm sure that, if the pride of such people could be pierced, there would gush forth a cry of despair that ascribed everything in this life to a feeling of loneliness. In my own case in addition to the inevitable loneliness fostered by such a childhood as mine – the natural loneliness caused by living with two men who were perpetually on the verge of imprisonment – there was the loneliness of my own temperament. I know that every human being claims for himself the right to be misunderstood and unappreciated; it's not that kind of loneliness of which I speak. Mine was the loneliness of someone who is so masculine and so feminine simultaneously that reason is sapped by emotion and emotion is sterilized by reason. The only chance for such a temperament is self-expression either in love, art, or religion. I tried vaguely to express myself in art, but without success at first; and I was too proud and not vain enough to persevere. I then fell back on love. I let myself get into a condition of wanting to be in love, and at this moment of emotional collapse I met by accident the youth – now a man of thirty – with whom I had effected one of my childish elopements. With this man I lived for a year. I can't pretend that I did not take pleasure in the passionate relationship, though I always felt it was a temporary surrender to the most feminine side of me that I despised. I think I can best explain my emotions by saying that all the time I was with him I was like a person under the influence of a sedative drug.

'Now there are people who pass from drug to drug with increase of pleasure, but there are others to whom the notion of being drugged becomes suddenly obnoxious and in whom the reaction creates an abnormal activity. Quite suddenly I abandoned my pleasure and became ambitious to express myself in art. I succeeded. I was for one who begins so late in life exceptionally successful, and then behold, my very success took on the aspect of yielding to another sedative drug. It never seemed anything but a temporary expedient to defeat the claims of existence. Just as love had seemed a surrender to the exclusively feminine side of me, so art seemed a surrender to the exclusively masculine side. There was always an unsatisfied unexpressed part of me that girded at the satisfied part. As a result of this, I made up my mind that a happy marriage with children and a household to look after was a better thing than artistic success. Here was obviously another experiment for the benefit of the feminine side. I knew perfectly well that if I had carried out my intention I should not have remained content when the sedative action of the new drug began to cease, and I am grateful now that circumstances interfered. I was jilted by the man who was going to marry me, and the fact that I had already lived with him and refused to marry him dozens of times made the injury to my pride intolerable. In a fit of rage I flung behind me everything – success, love, marriage, friends – and left England to take up again at the age of thirty-one a life I had forsaken for several years. And now I found that even the mere externals of such a life were horrible. I could not bear the idea of being for sale; while I had no intention of ever giving myself to a man again, I had to drink for my living and dance with drunkards for my cab fare, which though it may not be a technical prostitution differs only in degree from the complete sale of the body.

'Scarcely a month had passed when I became seriously ill, and in the dreadful delirium of my fever I imagined that I was damned. I do not think that anybody has the right to accept seriously the mental revelations that are made to a mind beside itself; I think indeed it would be a blasphemy to accuse God of taking such a method to rouse a soul to a sense of its being, its duties, and its dangers; and I dread to claim for myself any supernatural intervention at such a time, partly because my reason shies at such a thought and partly because I think it is presumptuous to suppose that God should interest Himself so peculiarly in an individual. It seems to me almost vulgarly anthropomorphic.'

'Are not five sparrows sold for two farthings, and not one of them is forgotten before God?' the priest murmured.

'Yes, yes,' Sylvia agreed. 'I have expressed myself badly, and of course when I think of it I have been driven ever since the delirium really to accept just that. You can understand, can't you, the dread of presumption in my revolt against pride?

'But by insisting upon what seemed to happen in my delirium I am giving you a wrong impression. It was when I came to myself again in the hospital that I felt changed. I longed then for knowledge of God, but I was afraid that my feeling was simply the natural result of weakness after a severe illness. I almost rejected God in my fear of supposing myself hysterical and egotistical. However, I did try hard to put myself into a state of resignation, and when I came out of the hospital I felt curiously awake to the sense of God and simultaneously an utter indifference to anything in my old life that might interrupt my quest by restoring me to what I was before this illness. While I was ill war had broken out, and I found myself utterly alone. Ordinarily I am sure that such a discovery would have terrified me; now I rejoiced in such loneliness. I deliberately turned my back on England and waited for something from my new life to fill this loneliness. I felt like someone who has swept and garnished a room that he may receive guests. My chief emotion was a tremendous love of the whole world and an illimitable desire to make up for all my cynicism in the past by the depth of this love. I went back to the pension where I had lived before I was ill, and it seemed to me a coincidence that the woman who kept it should be a spiritualist and that for two months my mind should be continuously occupied by what I might call the magic side of things. The result was that, though I was often puzzled by inexplicable happenings, I conceived a distaste for all this meddling with the unknowable, this kind of keyhole peeping at infinity: it seemed to me vulgar and unpleasant. Nevertheless I was driven back all the time in my meditations on the only satisfactory revelation of God, the only rational manifestation, which was Jesus Christ. Every other explanation crumbled away in my brain except that one fact. Then, although I believe it was only some fortune-telling with cards that first put the notion into my head, I was obsessed with the idea that I must go south. On my way I met a soldier at Kieff who bought me a golden bag for no other reason than because it seemed to him that to give pleasure to somebody else was a better way of spending his money than in gambling or self-indulgence. In the state of mind I was in I accepted this as a sign that I was right to go south. So you see that I had really arrived at the point of view of accepting the theory of a Divine intervention in my favour.

'After three months at Odessa – where I read Tolstoy and Dostoievsky and found in them, ah, such profundities of the human soul lighted up – against my instinct I went north again; the Germans were advancing upon Warsaw, and circumstances brought me here. On the way, at Jassy, an extraordinary thing happened. I met a girl whom I had tried to adopt six years ago at Granada, but who was taken from me by a blackguard and who since then has what people call sunk very low. It seemed to me that in finding this child again, for she is still really a child, I was being given an opportunity of doing what I had failed to do for that first girl of whom I told you. Then suddenly I conceived the idea that she had never been baptized; when I began to think about her soul, I was driven by an unknown force to this church. When I came in I did not know what to do, and when you asked me if I wanted to make my confession the force seemed to say "yes." '

Sylvia was silent, and the priest finished the *Confiteor* which she repeated after him.

'My daughter,' he said, 'it is the grace of God. I do not feel that in this solemn moment – a moment that fills me as a priest with humility at being allowed to regard such a wonderful manifestation of God's infinite mercy – any poor words of mine can add anything. It is the grace of God: let that suffice. But wonderful as has been God's mercy to a soul that was deaf so long to His voice, do not forget that your greatest danger, your greatest temptation, may be to rely too much upon yourself. Do not forget at this solemn moment that you can only enjoy this Divine grace through the Sacraments. Do not forget that only in the Church can you preserve the new sense of security that you now feel. One who has been granted such mercy must expect harder struggles than less fortunate souls. Do not by falling back into indifference and neglect of your religious duties succumb to the sin of pride. By the height of your uplifting will be measured the depth of your fall, if in your pride you think to stand alone.'

When the priest had given her absolution, Sylvia asked him about Queenie; and when he seemed a little doubtful of Queenie's willingness to be a catechumen, she wondered if he were deliberately trying to discourage her in order to mortify that pride he had seemed to fear so much.

'But if she wants to be baptized?' Sylvia persisted.

'Of course I will baptize her.'

'You think that I'm too much occupied with her when I have still so much to learn myself?' she challenged.

They were walking down the church toward the door, and Sylvia felt

439

rather like the importunate parishioner whom she had interrupted by her entrance.

'No, no, I think you are quite right. But I fear that you will expect miracles of God's grace all round you,' said the priest. 'What has happened to you may not happen to her.'

'But it must,' Sylvia declared. 'It shall.'

The priest shook his head, and there was a smile at the back of his eyes.

'If you fail?'

'I shan't fail.'

'Is God already put on one side?'

'I shall pray,' said Sylvia.

'Yes, I think that is almost better than relying too much upon the human will.'

Two things struck Sylvia when she had left the church and was walking back to the hotel. The first was that the priest had really said very little in response to that long outpouring of her history, and the second was that here in this street it did not seem nearly as easy to solve the problem of Queenie's soul as it had seemed in the church. Yet when she came to think over the priest's words she could not imagine how he could have spoken differently.

'I suppose I expected to be congratulated as one is congratulated upon a successful performance,' she said to herself. 'That's the worst of a histrionic career like mine: one can't get rid of the footlights even in the confessional. As a matter of fact I ought to be grateful that he accepted the spirit of my confession without haggling over the form, as from his point of view he might have done most justifiably. Perhaps he was tired and didn't want to start an argument. And yet no, I don't think it was that. He came down like a hammer on the main objection to me – my pride. He was really wonderfully unecclesiastical. It's a funny thing, but I seem to be much less spiritually exalted than I ought to be after such a reconciliation. I seem to have lost for the moment that first fine careless rapture of conversion. Does that mean that the whole business was an emotional blunder and that I'm feeling disappointed? No, I don't feel disappointed: I feel practical. I suppose my friend the priest wouldn't accept the comparison, but it reminds me of how I felt when after I had first conceived the idea of my Improvisations I had to set about doing them. Everything has its drudgery: love produces household cares, art endless work, religion religious duties. The moment of attraction, the moment of inspiration, the moment of conversion, if they could only endure! Perhaps Heaven is the infinite prolongation of such moments.

'And then there's Queenie. It's not much use my leading her to the font as one leads a horse to water, because though I should regard it as Infant Baptism, the priest would not. Yet I don't see why he shouldn't instruct her like a child. Poor priest! He could hardly have expected such problems as myself and Queenie when he was so anxious to get rid of that old woman who was pestering him. I think I won't bother about Queenie for a bit, until I have practised a little subordination of myself first. She's got to acquire a soul of her own; it's no use my presenting her with a piece of mine.'

Queenie had been back from the hairdresser's for a long time when Sylvia reached the hotel and was wondering what had become of her friend.

'You've been out alone,' she said reproachfully. 'Your headache is better, I think. Yes?'

'My headache?' Sylvia repeated. 'Yes, it's much better. I've been indulging in spiritual aspirin.'

'I'm glad it's better, because it is our first night at the Petit Maxim to-night. I wonder if I will be having much applause.'

'So it is,' Sylvia said. 'I'd forgotten my approaching triumph with the waiters; it's not likely that there'll be any audience when I appear. At 9 p.m. sharp the programme of the Petit Maxim opened with Miss Sylvia Scarlett's three songs. The gifted young lady – I've reached the age when it's a greater compliment to be called young than beautiful – played and sang with much *verve*. Several waiters ceased from dusting the empty tables to listen and at the close her exit was hailed by a loud flourish of *serviettes*. The solitary visitor who clapped his hands explained afterwards that he was trying to secure some attention to himself, and that thirst not enthusiasm had dictated his action.'

'How you were always going on, Sylvia,' said Queenie. 'Nobody was ever going to understand you when you talk so quick as that.'

'Miss Sylvia Scarlett's first song was an old English ballad set to the music of Handel's Dead March.'

'If we were ever going to have any dinner, we must go and eat now,' Queenie interrupted.

'Yes, I don't want to miss the sunset with my last song.'

'But what does it matter if you are paid to sing, if you sing first or last?'

'The brightest star, my dear, cannot shine by daylight.'

'But you are stupid, Sylvia. It is no more daylight at nine o'clock.'

'Yes, I am very stupid,' Sylvia agreed and, catching hold of Queenie's arms, she looked deep into her eyes. 'Believe me, you little fairy thing, that I should be much more angry if you were put first on a programme than because I am.'

The cabaret Petit Maxim aimed at expressing in miniature the essence of all the best cabarets in Paris, just as Bucharest aimed at expressing in miniature the essence of Paris. The result, though pleasant and comfortable enough, was in either case as little like Paris as a scene from one of its own light operas is like Vienna. What Bucharest and the Petit Maxim did both manage to effect, however, was an excellent resemblance to one of those light operas. Sylvia in the course of her wanderings had once classified the capitals she had visited as metropolitan, cosmopolitan, and neapolitan. Bucharest belonged very definitely to the last group; it stood up like a substantially built Exhibition in the middle of a ring of industrial suburbs which by their real squalor heightened the illusion of its unreality. The cupolas of shining bronze and the tiled domes shimmering in the sun like peacocks' tails dazzled the onlooker with an illusion of barbaric splendour; but the city never escaped from the self-consciousness of an Exhibition, which was heightened by the pale blue and silver uniforms of the officers, the splendid equipages for hire, and the policemen dressed in chocolate like commissionaries, and accentuated by the inhabitants' pride in the expensiveness and 'naughtiness' of their side-shows, of which not the least expensive and 'naughty' were the hotels. One might conceive the promoter of the Exhibition taking one aside and asking if one did not think he had been successful in giving Paris to the Balkans, and one might conceive his disappointment on being told that magnificent though it all looked it was no more Paris than Offenbach was Molière.

At the time when Sylvia visited Bucharest the sense of being one of the chorus in a light opera was intensified by the dramatic plot that was provided by the European war. Factions always grew more picturesque with every mile away from England, the mother of Parliaments, where they ceased to be picturesque three hundred years ago when the chief punchinello's head tumbled into the basket at Whitehall. The comedy of kingship had been prolonged for another century and a half in France, and in France they were a century and a half nearer to the picturesque and already two or three hundred miles away from England. In Italy the picturesqueness grew still more striking with such anachronisms as the Camorra and the Mafia. But it was not until the Balkans that factions could be said to be vital in the good old way. Serbia had shown not so long ago what could still be done with a thoroughly theatrical regal murder; and now here was Roumania jigging to the manipulation of the French faction and the German faction with just enough possibility of all the plots and counter-plots ending seriously by plunging the country into war on one side or the other to give a background of real drama to the operatic form.

At the Petit Maxim the Montagues and Capulets came to blows nightly. Everything here was either Ententophile or Germanophile: there were pro-German waiters, pro-German tables, pro-German tunes, for the benefit of the Germans and pro-Germans who occupied one half of the cabaret and applauded the Austrian performers. Equally there was the Ententist complement. If the first violin was pro-French and played sharp for an Austrian singer, the cornet was pro-German ready to break time to disconcert a French dancer. On the whole, as was natural in what is called 'a centre of amusement,' the pro-French element predominated, and though it was possible to sing the *Marseillaise* at the cost of a few broken glasses, the solitary occasion when *Deutschland über Alles* was attempted ended in several broken heads, a smashed chandelier, and six weeks in bed for an Austrian contralto whose face was scratched with a comb by a French artiste under the influence of ether and patriotism.

Nor was this atmosphere of plot and faction confined to general demonstrations of friendliness or hostility. Bucharest was too small a city to allow deep ramifications to either party; the gossip of the Court on the day before became the gossip of the cabaret on the evening after; scarcely one successful conveyance of war material from Germany to Turkey but was openly discussed at the Petit Maxim. Intrigues and flirtations with the great powers increased the self-esteem of Roumania, who took on the air of a coquettish schoolgirl that finds herself surrounded by the admiration of half a dozen elderly rakes. Her dowry and good looks seemed both so secure that any little looseness of behaviour would always be overlooked by the man she chose to marry in the end.

Sylvia could not help teasing some of the young officers that frequented the Petit Maxim. They changed their exquisite operatic uniforms so many times in the day: they accepted with such sublime effrontery the salute of the goose step from a squad of magnificent peasants dressed up as soldiers; they painted and powdered their faces, wore pink velvet bands round their *képis* under nodding *panaches*; and not one but could display upon his breast the ribbon of the bloodless campaign against Bulgaria of two years before. When they came jangling into the cabaret, one felt that the destinies of Europe were attached to their sword-belts, as comfort hangs upon the tinkling of a housekeeper's *châtelaine*.

'If Italy declares war, we shall declare war; for we are more Roman than they are. If Italy remains neutral we shall remain neutral; because the Latin races must hold together,' the patrons of the Entente avowed.

'Italy will not declare war; and we shall have to fight the Russians. We won Plevna for them and lost Bessarabia as a reward. As soon as Austria understands that she must give us Transylvania we shall declare war,' said the patrons of the Central Powers.

'We shall remain neutral. Our neutrality is precious to both sides,' murmured a third set.

And after all, Sylvia thought, the last was probably the wisest view, for it would be a shame to spoil the pretty uniforms of the officers and a crime to maim the bodies of the nobler peasants they commanded.

In such an atmosphere Sylvia had to postpone any solution of the spiritual side of Queenie's problem and concentrate upon keeping her out of immediate mischief. The manager of the Petit Maxim had judged the tastes of his clients accurately, and Queenie had not been dancing at the cabaret for a fortnight when one read on the programme: QUEENIE, LA JEUNE DANSEUSE ANGLAISE ET L'ENFANT GÂTÉE DE BUCURESTI. Chocolates and flowers were showered upon her, and her faintest smile would uncork a bottle of champagne. But every morning at three o'clock when the cabaret closed, Sylvia snatched her away from all the suitors and took her home as quickly as possible to their hotel. She used to dread nightly the arrival of the moment when Queenie would refuse to go with her, but the moment did not come; and the child never once grumbled at Sylvia's sigh of relief to find themselves back in their own bedroom. In order as much as possible to distract her from the importunities of hopeful lovers Sylvia would always aim at surrounding herself and Queenie with the political schemers, so that the evening might pass away in speculation upon the future of the war and the imminence of Roumanian intervention. She impressed upon Queenie the necessity of seeming interested in the fate of the country of which she was supposed to be a native. They were the only English girls in the cabaret, in fact the only English actresses apparently anywhere in Bucharest; Sylvia finding that man is much more of a political animal in the Balkans than elsewhere took advantage of the general curiosity about England's personality to get as many bottles of champagne opened for information from her own lips as out of admiration and desire for Queenie's.

From general political discussions it was a short way to the more intimate discussions of faction's intrigue; and Sylvia became an expert on the ways and means of the swarm of German agents who corrupted Bucharest as bluebottles taint fresh meat. She sometimes wondered if she ought not to convey some of the knowledge thus acquired to the British Legation; but she supposed on second thoughts that she was unlikely to know anything that the authorities therein did not already know much better, and being averse from seeming to put herself forward for personal advantage, she did not move in the matter.

One of the chief frequenters of their company was a young lieutenant of the cavalry called Philidor with whom Sylvia made friends. He was an enthusiast for the cause of the Entente, and she learnt from him a great deal about the point of view of a Balkan state, so that when she had known him for a time she was able to judge both Roumania as a whole and the individual extravagances and vanities of Roumanians more generously.

'I don't think you quite understand,' he once said to her, 'the fearful responsibility that will rest upon the Balkan statesman who decides the policy of his country in this crisis. Whatever happens, England will remain England, France will remain France, Germany will remain Germany; but in Roumania, although our sympathies are with you, our geographical position makes us the natural allies of the Germans. Suppose we march with you and something goes wrong. Nothing can prevent us from being Germanized for the rest of our history. You mustn't pay too much attention to the talk you hear about the great power of Roumania and the influence we shall have upon the course of the war. Such talk springs from a half-expressed nervousness at the position in which we find ourselves. We are trying to bolster ourselves up with the sense of our own importance in the hope that we shall have the wisdom to direct our policy rightly. We are not a great power; we are a little power; and our only chance of becoming a great power would be that Austria should break up, that Russia should crumble away, and that the whole vile country of Bulgaria should be obliterated from the surface of the earth. It is certain that Bulgaria will march with Germany; nothing can stop that except the defeat of Germany this year. Possibly Italy may come in on your side this spring, but tied as we are to her by blood, we are separated from her by miles of alien populations, and Italy cannot help us. Greece is in the same plight as we are – not quite perhaps, because she can depend for succour upon the sea: we can't. Ah, if you could only open the Dardanelles! If you only had a statesman to see that there lies the key to certain victory in this war. But statesmen no longer exist among you great powers. You've become too big for statesmen and can only produce politicians. The only statesmen in Europe nowadays are to be found in the Balkans, because since every man here is a politician it requires a statesman to rise above the ruck. Paradox though it may seem, statesmen create states; they are not created by them. We have all our history before us in the Balkans, if we can only survive being swallowed up in this cataclysm; but I doubt if we can. To you this country of mine is like a comic opera, but to me, one of the players, it is as tragic as *Pagliacci*.

'You are right in a way to mock at our aristocracy, though much of that aristocracy is not truly Roumanian, but bastard Greek; yet we have such a wonderful peasantry, and an idealist like myself dreads the effect of this war. All our plans of emancipation, all our schemes for destroying the power of the great landowners,' and in a whisper he added, 'all our hopes of a republic are doomed to failure. I tell you, my dear, it's tragic opera, not comic opera.'

'But if you are a republican, why do you wear the uniform of a crack cavalry regiment?' Sylvia asked.

'Oh, I've thought that out,' Philidor replied. 'I belong to a good family. If I proclaimed my opinions openly, I should merely be put on one side. Aristocratic rule is more powerful in Roumania than anywhere in Europe except Prussia. The aristocrats have literally all the capital of the country in their hands; our peasants are serfs. As an avowed republican I could do nothing to spread the opinions that I believe to be the salvation of my country and the preservation of her true independence; we are a young state – not a state at all in fact, but a limited liability company with a director imported from the chief European firm of king-exporters – and we have still to realize our soul as by fire.'

'The soul of a country,' Sylvia murmured. 'It's only the aggregate of the human souls that make it, but each soul could be the microcosm of the universe.'

'True, true,' Philidor agreed. 'And the soul of Roumania is the soul of a girl who's just out, or of a boy in his first year at college. Hence all the prettiness and all the complacent naughtiness and all the imitation of older and more worldly people and all the tyranny and contempt for the rights of the poor, the want of consideration for servants really. Though I must be young like the rest and dress myself up and lead the life of my friends, I am always hoping to influence them gradually, very gradually. Perhaps if I were truly a great soul I should fling over all this pretence; but I know my own limitations, and all I pray is that when the man arises who is worthy to lead Roumania toward liberty and justice I shall have the wit to recognize him and the courage to follow his lead.'

'But you said just now,' Sylvia reminded him, 'that all the European statesmen were to be found in the Balkans.'

'I still say that, but our statesmen – we have only two – dare not in the presence of this war think of anything except the safety of the country. Republicanism would be of little use to a Roumania absorbed either into the Dual Monarchy or into the Tsardom of Russia or ravaged by the hellish Bulgarians. I tell you that we see precipices before our steps whichever way we turn for the path; but because we are young we dress ourselves up and gamble and sing and dance and swagger and boast; we are young, my dear girl, very very young, perhaps not old enough for our death to be anything but pathetic.'

'You're in a very pessimistic mood to-night,' Sylvia said.

'Who could be anything but gloomy when he looks round a room like this? A crowd of French, Roumanian, and Austrian cocottes dancing to *Tipperary* in this infernal tinkling din – forgive my frankness, but you know I don't include *you* in the *galère* – while over there I see a cousin of my own, a member of one of our greatest families, haggling with a dirty German agent over the price of sending another six aeroplanes to Turkey disguised as agricultural implements; and over there I see a man, who I had always hoped was an honest editor, selling his pen to the fat little German baron that will substitute poison for ink and banknotes for honest opinions; and over there are three brother officers with three girls on their knees singing the words of *Tipperary* with as much intelligence as apes, while they brag to their companions of how in six weeks they will be marching to save France.'

'They don't miss much by not understanding the words,' Sylvia said with a smile.

'I don't understand how a woman like you can tolerate or endure this life,' Philidor exclaimed fanatically. 'Why don't you take that pretty little sister of yours out of it and back to England? I don't understand how you can stay here with your country at war.'

'That's too long a story to tell you now,' Sylvia said. 'But between ourselves she's not really my sister.'

'I never supposed she was,' Philidor answered. 'She's not English either is she?'

Sylvia looked at him sharply.

'Have you heard anyone else say that?' she asked.

'Nobody else here knows English as well as I do.'

The dance stopped, and Queenie leaving her partner came up to their table with a smile.

'You're happy anyway,' said Philidor.

'Oh, yes. I'm so happy. She is so sweet to me,' Queenie cried, embracing Sylvia impulsively.

A French girl sitting at the next table laughed and murmured an epithet in *argot*. Sylvia's cheeks flamed; she was about to spring up and make a quarrel, but Philidor restrained her.

'Do you wonder that I protest against your exposing yourself to that sort of thing?' he said. 'What are you going to do? It wouldn't be quite

447

you, would it, to hit her over the head with a champagne bottle? Let the vile tongue say what it pleases.'

'Yes, but it's so outrageous, it's so – ah, I've no words for the beastliness of people,' Sylvia exclaimed.

'May I dance this dance?' Queenie interrupted timidly.

'Good heavens, why do you ask me, girl? What has it to do with me? Dance with the devil if you like.'

Queenie looked bewildered by Sylvia's emphasis and went off again in silence.

'And now you see the only person that's really hurt is your little friend,' Philidor observed. 'You're much too sure of yourself to care about a sneer like that, and she didn't hear what the woman called you or perhaps understand it if she heard.'

Sylvia was silent; she was thinking of once long ago when Lily had asked her if she could dance with Michael; now she blushed after nine years lest he might have thought for a moment what that woman had said.

'You're quite right,' she agreed with Philidor. 'This is a damnable life. Would you like to hear Queenie's story?'

'There's no need for you to defend yourself to me,' he laughed.

'Ah, don't laugh about it. You mustn't laugh about certain things. You'll make me think less of you.'

'I was only being *gauche*,' he apologized. 'Yes, tell me her story.'

So Sylvia told him the sad history, and when she had finished asked his advice about Queenie.

'You were talking just now about your country as if she were a child,' she said eagerly. 'You were imagining her individuality and independence destroyed. I feel the same about this girl. I want to make her really English. Do you think that I shall be able to get her a passport? We're saving up our money now to go to England.'

Philidor said he did not know much about English regulations, but that he could not imagine that any consul would refuse to help when he heard the story.

'And the sooner you leave Roumania the better. Look here. I'll lend you the money to get home.'

Sylvia shook her head.

'No, because that would interfere with my part of the story. I've got to get back without help. I have a strong belief that if I accept help I shall miss my destiny. It's no good trying to argue me out of a superstition, for I've tried to argue myself out of it a dozen times and failed. No, if you want to help me, come and talk to me every night and open a bottle or two of champagne to keep the manager in a good temper; and stand by me, if there's ever a row. I won't answer for myself if I'm alone and I hear things said like what was said to-night.'

Philidor promised he would do that for her as long as he was quartered in Bucharest, and presently Queenie came back.

'Don't be so frightened. I'm sorry I was cross to you just now.'

'You were being so savage,' said Queenie with wide-open wondering eyes. 'What was happening?'

'Something stung me.'

'Where?'

'Over the heart,' Sylvia answered.

When they were back in their room Queenie returned to the subject of Sylvia's ill-temper.

'I could not be thinking it was you,' she murmured. 'I could not be thinking it.'

'It was something that passed as quickly as it came,' Sylvia said. 'Forget about it, child.'

'Were you angry because I was being too much with that boy? If you like I shall say to him to-morrow that I cannot dance with him longer.'

'Please, Queenie, forget about it. Somebody said something that made me angry, and I vented my anger on you. It was of no importance.'

Queenie looked only half convinced and when she was in bed she turned for consolation to the little chromolithographs that were always at hand. She had the custom of wearing a lace night-cap and, sitting up thus in bed while her rapt gaze sought in those fairy landscapes the reflection of her own visions, she was remote and impersonal as a painted figure in some adoring angelic company. Sylvia felt that the moment was come to raise the question of the spiritual mood with which Queenie's outward appearance seemed in harmony, and that it was her duty to suggest a way of positively capturing and for ever enshrining the half revealed wonders of which these pictures spoke to her. Sylvia fancied that Queenie's development had now only reached as far as her own at about fifteen and, looking back to herself at that age, she thought how much it might have meant to her if somebody could have given expression to her capacity for wonder then. Moreover, it was improbable that Queenie would grow much older mentally, and it was impossible for Queenie to reach her own present point of view by her own long process of rejecting every other point of view in turn. Queenie would never reject anything of her own accord, and it seemed urgent to fortify her with the simple and in some eyes childish externals of religion, which precisely on account of such souls have managed to endure.

'The great argument in favour of the Church seems to me,' Sylvia thought, 'that it measures humanity by the weakest and not by the strongest link, which of course means that it never overestimates its power and survives assaults that shatter more ambitious and progressive organisations of human belief. Well, Queenie is a weak enough link, and I shan't feel happy until I have secured her incorporation first into the Church and secondly – I suppose into the State. Yet why should I want to give her nationality? What is the aim of a state? Material comfort really – nothing else. I'm tempted to give her to the Church, but deny her to the State. Alas, it's a material world, and it's not going to be spiritualized by me. The devil was sick, etc. No doubt at present everything promises well for a spiritual revival after this orgy of insane destructiveness. But history with its mania for repetition isn't encouraging about the results of war. As a matter of fact I've got no right to talk about the war at present. I choked and spluttered for a while in some of its vile backwash, and Bucharest hasn't managed to get the taste out of my mouth. Queenie,' she said aloud, 'you know that during these last weeks I've been going to church regularly?'

Queenie extricated herself from whatever path she was following in her pictures and looked at Sylvia with blue eyes that were intensely willing to believe anything her friend told her.

'I knew you were always going out,' she said. 'But I thought it was to see a boy.'

'Great heavens, child, do you seriously think that I should so much object to men's getting hold of you if I were doing the same thing myself in secret? Haven't you yet grasped that I can't do things in secret?'

'Don't be cross with me again. I think you are cross, yes?'

Sylvia shook her head.

'What I want to know is: did you ever go to church in your life, and if you did do you ever think about wanting to go again?'

'I was going to church with my mother when I was four; my stepmother was never going to church, and so I was never going myself until two years ago at Christmas. There was a girl who asked me to go with her, and it was so sweet. We looked at all the dolls, and there was a cow, but some woman said quite loudly: "Well, if this is the sort of women we was meeting on Christmas night, I'm glad Christmas only comes once in the year." My friend with me with very *maquillée*. Too much paint she was having really, and she said to this woman such rude things, and a man came and was asking us to move along further. And then outside my friend sat down on the steps and cried and cried. *Ach*, it was dreadful. She was making a scene. So I was not going more to church, because I was always remembering this and being unhappy.'

On the next day Sylvia took Queenie to the mission-church and intro-duced her to the priest; afterwards they often went to mass together. It was like taking a child; Queenie asked the reason of every ceremony, and Sylvia, who had never bothered her head with ceremonies, began to wish she had never exposed herself to so many unanswerable questions. It seemed to her that she had given Queenie nothing except another shadowy land in which her vague mind would wander without direction; but the priest was more hopeful and undertook to give her instruction so that she might be confirmed presently. When the question was gone into, there was no doubt that she had been baptized, for by some freak of memory she was able to show that she understood the reason of her being called Concetta from being born on the eighth of December. However, the revelation of her true name to the priest gave Queenie a horror of his company, and nothing would induce her to go near him again, or even to enter the church.

'This was going to bring me bad luck,' she told Sylvia. 'That name! that name! How was you so unkind to tell him that name?'

Sylvia was distressed by the thought of the fear she had roused and explained the circumstances to the priest, who rather to her irritation seemed inclined to resort placidly to prayer.

'But I can only pray when I am in the mood to pray,' she protested; and though she was aware of the weakness of such a habit of mind, she was anxious to shake the priest out of what she considered his undue resigna-tion to her failure with Queenie.

The fact was that the atmosphere of the Petit Maxim was getting on Sylvia's nerves. Apart from the physical revolt that it was impossible not to feel against the fumes of tobacco and wine, the scent of Eau de Chypre and Quelques Fleurs, the raucous chatter of conversation and the jangle of fidgety tunes, there was the perpetual inner resentment against the gossip about herself and Queenie. Sylvia did not lose any of her own joy at being able to rest in the high airs of Christian thought away from all this by reading the books of doctrine and ecclesiastical history that the priest lent her; but she was disappointed at her inability to provide any alternative for Queenie except absolute dependence upon herself. She was quite prepared to accept the final responsibility of guardianship, and she made it clear to the child that her ambition to have a permanent sister might be considered achieved. What she was not prepared to do was to invoke exterior aid to get them both back to England. She reproached herself sometimes with an unreasonable egotism; yet when it came to the point of accepting Philidor's offer to lend her enough money to return home, she always drew back. Life with Queenie at Mulberry Cottage shone steadily upon the horizon of her hopes, but she had no belief in the value of that life unless she could reach it unaided and offer its freedom as the fruit for her own perseverance and indomitableness. She was annoyed by Queenie's forebodings over the revelation of her name, and her annoyance was not any the less because she had to admit that her own behaviour in holding out against accepting the means of escape from Roumania was based on nothing more secure than a superstitious fancy.

The Petit Maxim closed at Easter; at the beginning of May the whole company was re-engaged for an open air theatre called the Petit Trianon. Sylvia and Queenie were still many francs short of their fares to England and were forced to re-engage themselves for the summer. The new place was an improvement on the cabaret, because at any rate during the first half of May it was too cold for the public to enjoy sitting about in a garden and drinking sweet champagne. After a month, however, all Sylvia's friends went away, some to Sinaia whither the court had moved; others, and amongst them Philidor, were sent to the Austrian frontier; the expedition to the Dardanelles and the intervention of Italy had brought Roumania much nearer to the prospect of entering the war. Meanwhile in Bucharest the German agents worked more assiduously than ever to promote neutrality and secure the passage of arms and munitions to Turkey.

At the end of May the manager of the Petit Trianon, observing that Sylvia had for some time failed to take advantage of the warmer weather by gathering to her table a proper number of champagne drinkers and having received complaints from some of his clients that she made it impossible to cultivate Queenie's company to the extent they would have liked, announced to her that she was no longer wanted. Her songs at the beginning of the evening were no attraction to the thin audience scattered about under the trees, and he could get a cheaper first number. This happened to be Lottie, who was engaged to thump on the piano for half an hour at two hundred francs a month.

'I never knew that I was cutting you out,' Lottie explained. 'But I've been playing for nearly four months at a dancing-hall in a low part of the town and I only asked two hundred in desperation. He'll probably engage you again if you'll take less.'

Sylvia forced herself to ask the manager, if he would not change his mind. She hinted as a final threat that she would make Queenie leave if he did not, and he agreed at last to engage her again at three hundred francs instead of three hundred and fifty, which meant that she could not save a sou towards her going home. At the same time the manager dismissed Lottie, and everybody said that Sylvia had played a mean trick. She would not have minded so much if she had not felt really sad about the fat girl, who was driven back to play in a low dancing-saloon at less than she had earned before; but she felt that there was no time to be lost in getting Queenie away from this life, and if it were a question of sacrificing Queenie or Lottie, it was certainly the fat girl who must go under.

Since the manager's complaint of the way she kept admirers away from her friend, Sylvia had for both their sakes to relax some of her discouraging stiffness of demeanour. One young man was hopeful enough of ultimate success to send Queenie a bunch of carnations wrapped up in a thousand-franc note. Normally Sylvia would have compelled her to refuse such a large earnest of future liberality; but these months upon the verge of penury had hardened her, and she bade Queenie keep the money, or rather she kept it for her to prevent its being frittered away in petty extravagance. Queenie could not hold her tongue about the offering; and the young man, when he found that the thousand francs had brought him no nearer to his goal than a bottle of champagne would have done, was loud in his advertisement of the way Sylvia had let Queenie take the money and give nothing in return. Everybody at the Petit Trianon was positive that Sylvia was living upon her friend, and much unpleasant gossip was brought back to them by people who of course did not believe it themselves, but thought it right that they should know what all the world was saying.

This malicious talk had no effect upon Queenie's devotion, but it added greatly to Sylvia's disgust for the tawdry existence they were both leading, and she began to play with the idea of using the thousand francs to escape from it and get back to England. She was still some way from bringing herself to the point of such a surrender as would be involved by temporarily using this money, but each time that she argued out the point with herself the necessity of doing so presented itself more insistently. In the middle of July something occurred which swept on one side every consideration but immediate flight.

All day long a warm and melancholy fog had suffused the suburbs of Bucharest, from which occasional scarves of mist detached themselves to float through the high centre of the town dislustring the air as they went, like steam upon a shining metal. Sylvia had been intending for some time to visit Lottie and explain to her the circumstances in which she had been supplanted by herself; such a day as this accorded well with such an errand. As with all cities of its class a few minutes after one left the main streets of Bucharest to go downhill one was aware of the artificiality of its metropolitan claims. Within five hundred yards of the sumptuous Calea Victoriei the side-turnings were full of children playing in the gutter, of untidy women gossiping to one another from untidy windows, and of small rubbish-heaps along the pavement: and a little farther on were signs of the unquiet newness of the city in the number of half-constructed streets and half-built houses.

Lottie lived in one of these unfinished streets in a tumbledown house that had survived the fields by which not long ago it had been surrounded. A creeper-covered doorway opened into a paved triangular courtyard shaded by an unwieldy tree, along one side of which at an elevation of about two feet ran Lottie's room. As Sylvia crossed the courtyard she could see indistinct forms moving about within; and she stopped for a moment listening to the drip of the fog above the murmur of human voices. She did not wish to talk to Lottie in front of strangers and turned to go back; but the fat girl had already observed her approach and was standing on the rotten threshold to receive her.

'You're busy,' Sylvia suggested.

'No, no. Come in. One of my friends is an English girl.'

'But I wanted to talk to you alone. I wanted to explain that I couldn't refuse to sing again at the Trianon; I've been worrying about you all this time.'

'Oh, that's all right,' Lottie said cheerfully. 'I never expected anything else.'

'But the other girls—'

'Oh, the other girls,' she repeated with a contemptuous laugh. 'Don't worry about the other girls. People can always afford to be generous in this world if it doesn't hurt themselves and does hurt somebody else. One or two of them came here to condole with me, and I'm sure they got more pleasure out of seeing my wretched lodging than I got out of their sympathy. Come in and forget all about them.'

Sylvia squeezed her pudgy hand gratefully; it was a relief to find that the object of so much commiseration had grasped the shallowness of it.

'Who are your friends?' she whispered.

'The man's a juggler who wants an engagement at the Trianon. He's a Swiss called Krebs. The girl's an English dancer and singer called Maud. You'll see them both up there to-night for certain. You may as well come in. What a dreary day, isn't it?'

Sylvia agreed and was aware of ascribing to the weather the faint malaise that she experienced on following Lottie into her room, which smelt of stale wallpaper and musty wood and which on account of the overhanging tree and the dirty French windows was dark and miserable enough.

'Excuse me getting up to shake hands,' said Krebs in excellent English. 'But this furniture is too luxurious.'

He was lying back smoking a cigarette in an armchair, all the legs of which were missing and the rest of it covered with exudations of flocculence that resembled dingy cauliflowers. Sylvia saw that he was a large man with a large undefined face of dark complexion. He offered a huge hand, brutal and clumsy in appearance, an inappropriate hand for a juggler, she thought vaguely. His companion, crudely coloured and shapeless as a quilt, sprawled on another chair. Everything about this woman was defiant; her harsh accent, the feathers in her hat, her loose mouth, her magenta cheeks, her white boa, and her white boots affronted the world like an angry housemaid.

'This is a fine hole, this Roumania,' she shrilled. 'Gawd! I went to the English consul at Galantza expecting to be treated with a little consideration, and the — pushed me out of his office. Yes, we read a great deal about England nowadays, but I've been better treated by everybody than what I have by the English. Stuck-up la-di-da set of —, that's what they are, and anybody as likes can hear me say so.'

She raised her voice for the benefit of the listeners without that might be waiting anxiously upon her words.

'Don't kick up such a row,' Krebs commanded; but Maud paid no attention to him and went on.

'England! Yes, I left England ten years ago, and if it wasn't for my poor old mother I'd never go back. Treat you as dirt that's what the English do. That consul threw me out of his office the same as a commissionaire might throw any old two-and-four out of the Empire. Yes, they talk a lot about patriotism and all pulling one way, but when you ask a consul to lend you the price of your fare to Bucharest you don't hear no more about patriotism. As I said to him, "I suppose you don't think I'm English?" and he sat there grinning for answer. Yes, I reckon when they christened that talking chimpanzee at the Hippodrome "Consul," it was done by somebody who'd had a bit of consul in his time. What's a consul for? that's what I'm asking. As I said to him, "What are you for? Are you paid," I said, "to sit there smoking cigarettes for the good of your country?" "This ain't a workhouse," he answered very snotty. "You're right," I said. "No fear about anyone ever making that mistake. Why, I reckon it's a bloody sleeping-car, I do." And with that I slung my hook out of it. Yes, I could have been very rude to him; only it was beneath me, the uneducated la-di-da savage! Well, all he's done is to put me against my own country. That's *his* war work.'

The tirade exhausted itself, and Sylvia unwilling to be Maud's sponsor at the Petit Trianon that evening made some excuse to leave. While she was walking across the courtyard with Lottie, she heard:

'And who's she? I'll have to tell *her* off, that's very plain. Did you see the way she looked down her nose at me? Nice thing if anyone can't say what they think of a consul without being stared at like a mummy by *her*.'

Sylvia asked Lottie if she had known this couple long.

'I've known him a year or two, but she's new. I met them coming up from the railway-station this morning. The girl was stranded without any money at Galantza, and Krebs brought her on here. He's a fine juggler and conjurer. Zozo he calls himself on the stage.'

Sylvia's heart throbbed as she climbed the streets that led toward the high centre of the city away from the hot mists below; it was imperative to get Queenie out of Roumania at once, and while she walked along she began to wonder if she could not procure an English passport, the delight of possessing which would counter-balance for Queenie the shock of hearing that the dreaded Zozo was in Bucharest.

'It's such a ridiculous name for a bogey,' Sylvia thought. 'And the man himself was not a bit as I pictured him. I'd always imagined someone lithe and subtle. I wonder what his object was in helping that painted hussy he was with. Queer rather.'

She reached the British Consulate, but was told rather severely to direct herself to the special office that occupied itself with passports.

'Do you want a visa for England?' the clerk enquired.

'Yes, and I also want to enquire about a new passport for my sister who's lost hers.'

'Lost her passport?' the clerk echoed; he shuddered at the information.

'It seems to upset you,' Sylvia said.

'Well, it's a pretty serious matter in war time,' he explained. 'However, we have nothing to do with passports at the consulate.'

The clerk washed his hands of Sylvia's past and future; and she left the consulate to discover the other office. By the time she arrived it was nearly five o'clock, and the clerk looked hurt at receiving a visitor so late.

'Do you want a visa for England?' he asked.

She nodded, and he pointed to a printed notice that hung above his desk.

'The morning is the time to make such applications,' he told her fretfully.

'Then why are you open in the afternoon?' Sylvia asked.

'If the application is favourably entertained, the recommendation is granted in the afternoon. You must then take your passport to the consulate for the consular visa, which can only be done in the morning between twelve and one.'

It was like the eternal competition between the tube-lifts and the tube-trains, she thought.

'But they told me at the consulate that they have nothing to do with passports.'

'The consulate *has* nothing to do with passports until the applicant for a visa has been approved here.'

'Then I must come again to-morrow morning?' Sylvia asked.

'To-morrow morning,' the clerk repeated, bending over with intrepid fervour to the responsible task upon which he was engaged. Sylvia wondered what it was: the whole traffic of Europe might hang upon these few minutes.

'I'm sorry to interrupt you again,' she said. 'But in addition to requiring a visa, my sister wants a new passport.'

She decided not to say anything about a lost passport, the revelation of which had so much shocked the man at the consulate.

'Miss Johnstone,' the clerk called in a weary voice to somebody in an inner office. 'Kindly bring Form AQ – application for renewal of expired passport.'

A vague looking young woman, who seemed to have been collecting native jewellery since her arrival in Bucharest, tinkled into the office.

'There aren't any AQ forms left, Mr. Mathers,' she said, plaiting as she spoke a necklace of coins into another of what looked like broken pieces of mosaic.

'It really is too bad that the forms are not given out more regularly,' Mr. Mathers cried in exasperation. 'How am I to finish transferring these Greeks beginning with C to K? You know how anxious Mr. Iredale is to get the index in order, and the F's haven't been checked with the *Ph's* yet.'

'Well, it's Miss Henson's day off,' said Miss Johnstone, 'so it's not my fault, is it? I'm sure I hate the forms! They're always a bother. Won't an AP one do for this lady? We've a lot of them left, and there's only a difference in one question.'

'Excuse me,' Sylvia asked. 'Did you mention a Mr. Iredale?'

'Mr. Iredale is the O.C.P.T.N.C. for Bucharest,' said Mr. Mathers.

'Not Mr. Philip Iredale by chance?' she went on.

That transposition of Greek initials had sounded uncommonly like Philip.

'That's right,' the clerk replied.

'Oh well, I know him. I should like to see him personally.'

'See Mr. Iredale? But he's the O.C.P.T.N.C.'

'Does that confer invisibility?' she asked. 'I tell you I'm a friend of his. If you send up my card, I'm sure he'll see me.'

'But he never sees anybody,' Mr. Mathers objected. 'I'm afraid you didn't understand that he's the Officer Controlling Passenger Traffic from Neutral Countries in Bucharest. If he was to see everybody that came to this office, he wouldn't be able to control *himself*, let alone passenger traffic. No really, joking apart, madam, Mr. Iredale is very busy and by no means well.'

'He's worn out,' put in Miss Johnstone, who having by now plaited four necklaces into a single coil was swinging the result round and round like a skipping-rope. 'His nerves are worn out. But if you like I'll take up your card.'

'You might ask him at the same time if he wants all the Greek names entered unter *Y* transferred to *G*, will you?' said Mr. Mathers. 'Oh, and Miss Johnstone,' he called after her, 'there seems to be some confusion between *Tch* and *Ts*. Ask him if he's got any preference. Awful names the people in this part of Europe get hold of,' he added to Sylvia. 'Even Mr. Iredale can't transpose the Russians, and of course the War Office likes accuracy. There was rather a strafe the other day because a man travelling from here to Spain got arrested three times on the way owing to his name being rather like a suspect spelt differently by us, the French, and the Italians. As a matter of fact, the original suspect's dead, but his name was spelt a fourth way in the notification that was sent around, and so it's not realized yet.'

'It must be rather like that whispering game,' Sylvia said. 'You know, where somebody at one end of the room starts a sentence and it comes out quite differently at the other.'

Sylvia could not make out why she did not feel more nervous when she was following Miss Johnstone upstairs to meet Philip for the first time since she had run away from him thirteen years ago. The fact was that her anxiety to escape from Roumania with Queenie outweighed everything else, and she was so glad to find somebody she knew in a position of authority who would be able to help her in the matter of Queenie's passport that any awkwardness was quenched in relief. The discovery of Philip was such an encouraging answer by destiny to the reappearance of Zozo.

He came forward to greet her from behind a large rolltop desk, and she saw that he looked tired and ill, yet except for his baldness not really much older.

'Would you have recognized me, Philip?' she asked.

He was far more nervous than she was, and he stumbled a good deal over Mr Mathers' questions.

'I'll tell him you're too busy now to answer,' said Miss Johnstone at last in a cheerful voice.

This was a happy solution of the problem of *Ts* and *Tch*, and Philip gratefully accepted it.

'And I daresay I might find time to help him with the transpositions, if you're very anxious to get them done.'

'Oh, will you? Yes, thank you, that would be excellent.'

Miss Johnstone turned to leave the room; one of her necklaces broke under the strain of continuous plaiting, and a number of tiny green shells peppered the floor.

'There, that's the third time it's done that to-day,' she exclaimed. 'I'm so sorry.'

Sylvia, Philip and she gathered up as many as were not trodden upon in the search, and at last Miss Johnstone managed to get out of the room.

'No wonder you're worn out,' said Sylvia with a smile. It seemed quite natural to comment rather intimately like this upon Philip's health. 'But you haven't answered my question. Would you have recognized me?'

'Oh yes, I should have recognized you. I saw you only last year at the Pierian Hall.'

'Did you go to see me there?' she exclaimed, touched by his having wanted to see her act without letting her know anything about his visit.

'Yes, I enjoyed the performance; it was excellent. I wonder why you're in Bucharest. Wouldn't you be better in England in war time?'

'I think it's much more surprising to find you here,' she said.

'Oh, I was sent out here to look after passports.'

'But, Philip, why were you chosen as an expert on human nature?'

She could not resist the little stab; and he smiled sadly.

'I knew the country,' he explained. 'I'd done some excavating here, so the War Office made me an honorary captain and sent me out.'

'Are you a captain? What fun! Do you remember when I wanted you to enlist for the South African war and you were so annoyed? But I suppose you're shocked by my reviving old memories like this. Are you shocked, Philip?'

'No, no, I'm not shocked. I'm still rather overcome by the suddenness of your visit. What are you doing here?'

'I'm singing at the Trianon. All the winter I was at the Petit Maxim.'

'Those places,' he said with a look of distaste.

'It would take too long to explain to you why,' she went on. 'But you can't disapprove of my being there more than I do myself; and it's for that very reason that I want a visa for England.'

'Of course you shall have one immediately. You're much better at home in these detestable times.'

'But I also want something else. I want a passport for a friend – an English girl.'

'Hasn't she got a passport? Does she want hers renewed?'

'I'd better tell you the whole story. I expect that since you've become the U.V.W.X.Y.Z. of Bucharest, you've listened to plenty of sad stories, but you must pay special attention to this one for my sake. I don't know why I say "for my sake" – it's rather an improper remark for a divorced wife. Philip, do you remember in my show at the Pierian an Improvisation about a girl who had been horribly ill-treated as a child and was supposed to be lost in a great city?'

'Yes, I think I do, in fact I'm sure I do. I remember that at the time I was reminded of our first meeting in Brompton Cemetery.' He blinked once or twice very quickly, and coughed in his old embarrassed way.

'Well, that's the girl for whom I want a passport.'

Sylvia told him Queenie's story in detail from the time she met her first in Granada to the present moment under the shadow of Zozo's return.

'But, my dear Sylvia, I can't possibly procure an English passport for her. She's not English.'

'I want her to be my sister,' Sylvia pursued. 'I'm prepared to adopt her and to be responsible for her. Any difference in the name she had been generally known by can easily be put down to the needs of the stage. I myself want to take once more my own name Sylvia Snow, and I thought you could issue two passports, one to Sylvia Snow professionally known as Sylvia Scarlett, and the other to Queenie Snow known professionally as Queenie Walters. Surely you won't let mere pedantry interfere with a deed of charity?'

'It's not a question of pedantry. This is war time. I should render myself liable to – to – a court-martial for doing a thing like that. Besides, the principle of the thing is all wrong.'

'But you don't seem to understand.'

'Indeed I understand perfectly,' Philip interrupted. 'This girl was born in Germany.'

'Of an Italian father.'

'What papers has she?' he asked.

'None at all. That's the whole point. She couldn't get even a German passport if she wanted to. But she doesn't want one. She longs to be English. It's the solitary clear ambition that she has. She was living in England before war broke out, and she only came away to help this girl who was kind to her. Surely the most rigid rule can be unbent to fit a special case?'

'I could not possibly assume the responsibility,' Philip declared.

'Then you mean to say you'll condemn this child to damnation for that's what you're doing with your infernal rules and regulations? You're afraid of what will happen to you.'

'Excuse me, even if I were certain that nothing could possibly be known about the circumstances in which this passport was issued, I should still refuse the application. Everybody suffers in this war; I suffer myself in a minor degree by having to abandon my own work and masquerade in this country as what you well call an U.V.W.X.Y.Z.'

'But even if we grant that in some cases suffering is inevitable,' Sylvia urged eagerly, 'here's a case where it is not. Here's a case where by applying a touch of humanity you can save a soul. But I won't put it that way, because I know you have no use for souls. Here's a case where you can save a body for civilization, for that fetish on whose account you find yourself in Bucharest and half Europe is slaughtering the other half. You are not appealing to any divine law when you refuse to grant this passport; you are appealing to a human law. Very well then. You are in your own way at this moment fighting for England; yet when somebody longs to be English you refuse her. If there is any reality behind your patriotism, if it is not merely the basest truckling to a name, a low and cowardly imitation of your next door neighbour whose opinion of yourself you fear as much as he fears your opinion of him, if your patriotism is not just this, you'll be glad to give this child the freedom of your country. Philip, you and I made a mess of things. I was to blame for half the mess; but when you married me, though you married me primarily to please yourself, there was another motive behind – the desire to give a lonely little girl a chance to deal with the life that was surging round her more and more dangerously every day. Now you have another opportunity of doing the same thing, and this time without any personal gratification. It isn't as if I were asking you to do something that could possibly hurt England. I tell you I will be responsible for her. If the worst came to the worst and anything were found out, I could always take the blame and you could never be even censured for accepting my word in such a case.'

Sylvia could see by Philip's face that her arguments were doing nothing to convince him, yet she went on desperately:

'And if you refuse this, you don't merely condemn her, you condemn me too. Nothing will induce me to abandon her to that man. By your bowing down to the letter of the regulation, you expose me for the second time to the life that you drove me to before.'

Philip made a gesture of protest.

'Very well, then I won't accuse you of being responsible on the first occasion, certainly not wantonly. But this time, if I'm driven to the same life, it *will* be your fault and your fault alone. I'm not going to bother about my body, if I think that by destroying it I can save a soul. I shall stick at nothing to preserve Queenie – at nothing, do you hear? You have the chance to send us both safely back to England. Philip, you won't refuse!'

'I'm sorry. It's terribly painful for me to say "no." But it's impossible. Only quite recently the Foreign Office sent round a warning that we were to be specially careful in this part of the world. No papers of naturalization are issued in time of war. Why, I'm sent here to Bucharest for the express purpose of preventing people like your friend obtaining fraudulent passports.'

'The Foreign Office!' Sylvia scoffed. 'How can you expect people not to be Christians? It was just to redeem mankind from the sin that creates Foreign Offices and War Offices and bureaucrats and shoddy kings and lawyers and politicians that Christ died. Oh, you can sneer; but your unbelief is condemned out of your own mouth. You puny little U.V.W.X.Y.Z. with your nose buried in your own waste-paper basket, with a red tapeworm gnawing at your vitals, with some damned fool of a narrow-headed general for an idol, you have the impertinence to sneer at Christianity. Do you think that after this war people are going to be content with the kind of criminal state that you represent? Life is not a series of rules, but a set of exceptions. Philip, forgive me if I have been rude, and let this girl have a passport, please, please!'

'You must not think,' Philip answered, 'that because I plead the necessities of war in defence of what strikes you as mere bureaucratic obscurantism that therefore I am defending war itself; I loathe war from the bottom of my heart. But just as painful operations are often necessary in accidents which might easily have been avoided, yet which having happened must be cured in the swiftest way: so in war time for the good of the majority the wrongs of the nation must take precedence over the wrongs of the individual. I sympathize profoundly with the indignation that you feel on account of this girl, but the authorities in England after due consideration of the danger likely to accrue to the State from the abuse of British nationality by aliens have decided to enforce with the greatest strictness the rules about the granting of passports.'

'Oh, don't explain the reasons to me as if I were a baby,' Sylvia burst in. 'The proposition of the Foreign Office is self-evident in its general application. My point is with you personally. You are not a professional bureaucrat who depends for his living on his capacity for de-humanizing himself. In this case you have a special reason to exercise your rights and

462

your duties as an amateur. You are as positive as you can ever hope to be positive about anything, even your absurd positivist creed, that while no harm can result to your country, a great mercy will be conferred upon an individual as the result of enlightened action.'

'It is precisely this introduction of the personal element,' Philip said, 'that confirms me in refusing your request. You are taking advantage of – our – of knowing me to gain your point. As a stranger you would not stand the least chance of doing this, and you have no business to make the matter a personal one. You don't seem to realize what such a proceeding would involve. It is not merely a question of issuing a passport as passports used to be issued before the war on the applicant's bare word. A whole set of searching questions has to be answered in writing, and you ask me to put my name to a tissue of lies. Go back to England yourself. You have done your best for this girl, and you must bow before circumstances. She has reached Roumania, and if she does not try to leave it, she will be perfectly all right.'

'But have you appreciated what I told you about this man who has just arrived? He's a German-Swiss, and if he's not a spy, he has all the makings of one. Suppose he gets hold of Queenie again? Can't you see that on the lowest ground of material advantage you are justified – more than justified, you owe it to your country to avoid the risk of creating another enemy?'

'My dear Sylvia,' said Philip more impatiently than he had spoken yet. 'It is none of my business to interfere with potential agents of the enemy. I have quite enough to do to keep pace with the complete article. If your little friend is in danger of being turned into a spy, it seems to me that you have stated the final argument against granting your request.'

'If she were with me, she could never become a spy; but if I were to leave her helpless here, anything might happen. I am struggling for this child's soul, Philip, more bitterly than I ever struggled for my own. Your mind is occupied with the murder of human bodies: my mind is obsessed with the destruction of human souls.'

'Well, if I accept your own definition of your attitude,' Philip answered, 'perhaps you will admit that logically a passport occupies itself with the body, and that Christians do not consider nationality necessary to salvation. I can't make out your exalted frame of mind. You used to be rather sensible on this subject. But if, as I gather, you have taken refuge in that common weakness of humanity – religion, let me recommend you to find therein the remedy for your friend's future.'

'Yes, I suppose logically you've scored,' Sylvia said slowly.

'But please don't think I want to score,' Philip went on in a distressed voice. 'Please understand that for me to refuse is torture. I've often wondered about a judge's emotions when he puts on the black cap; but since I've faded out of real life into this paper world, I've worn myself out with worrying over private griefs and miseries. It's only because I feel that, if everyone on our side does not martyr himself for a year or so, the future of the world will be handed over to this sort of thing; and that is an unbearable thought.'

'You're very optimistic about the effect upon your own side,' Sylvia said. 'Have you such faith in humanity as to suppose that this war will cure it more radically than all the wars that have gone before? I doubt it. When I listened to our arguments this afternoon, I began to wonder if either side is fighting for anything but a sterile nominalism. I can't argue any more. It's not your fault, Philip. You lack the creative instinct. I'll fight out this Queenie business by myself without invoking state aid. I am rather ashamed of myself really. I feel as if I'd been compelled to ask a policeman the way. Perhaps I've got everything out of proportion. Women usually manage to do that somehow. There must be something very satisfying about personal conflict – bayonet to bayonet I mean: but even in the trenches I suppose men get taken out and shot for cowardice. Even there you wouldn't escape from the grim abstract heartlessness that hangs like a fog over a generalized humanity – generalized is doubly appropriate in this connection. What a wretched thing man is in the mass and how rare and wonderful in the individual. The mass creates that arch-bureaucrat God, and the individual seeks the heart of Christ. Good-bye, Philip, I'm sorry you look so ill. I'm afraid I've tired you. No, no,' she added seeing that he was bracing himself up to talk about themselves. 'This wasn't really the personal intrusion you accuse me of making. We were never very near to one another, and we are more remote than ever now.'

'But what about your own visa?' he asked.

'It's no use to me at present. When I want it, I'll apply in the morning to Mr. Mathers and come for it in the afternoon most correctly. I promise to attempt no more breaches in the formality of your office. By the way, one favour I would ask: please don't come to the Trianon. You wouldn't understand the *argot* in my songs, and if you did you wouldn't understand my being able to sing them. Get better.'

'Yes, I'm taking Sanatogen,' Philip said hopefully. At this moment Miss Johnstone entered with a cup on a small tray, which just escaping being lassoed by one of her chains was set down on his desk.

'I'm afraid I haven't got it quite so smooth as Miss Henson does,' said Miss Johnstone.

'Oh never mind, please. It was so kind of you to remember.'

'Well, I didn't think you ought to miss it on Miss Henson's day off.'

Sylvia waved her hand and left him with Miss Johnstone; he seemed to be hesitating between the injury to her feelings if he did not take the lumpy mixture and the harm to his digestion if he did.

'Even offices are subject to the clash of temperament on temperament,' said Sylvia to herself. 'A curious thing really that Philip should be prepared to choke himself over a cup of badly mixed Sanatogen rather than wound that young woman's feelings, and yet that he should be able to refuse me what I asked him to do this afternoon.'

She nodded to Mr. Mathers, as she passed through the outer office, who jumped up and opened the door for her. He had evidently been impressed by the length of her interview with the O.C.P.T.N.C. in Bucharest.

'I believe I've had the pleasure of hearing you sing,' he murmured. 'Are you staying long at the Trianon?'

'I hope not,' she answered.

'Quite, quite,' he murmured, nodding his head with an air of deep comprehension, while he bowed her forth with marked courtesy.

The fog had cleared away when Sylvia started to walk back to her hotel, and though it was still very hot there was a sparkle in the air that made it seem fresher than it really was. The argument with Philip had braced her point of view to accord with the lightening of the weather; it had thrown her so entirely back upon her own resources that the notion of ever having supposed for an instance that he could help her in the fight for Queenie now appeared ludicrous. Although her arguments had been unavailing, and although at the end Philip had actually defeated her by the very logic on which she had prided herself, she nevertheless felt wonderfully elated at the prospect of a struggle with Zozo and no longer in the least sensible of that foreboding dejection which was lying so heavily upon her heart when she left Lottie's house three hours ago.

Poor Philip! he had spoken of his own sufferings in a minor degree from the war. Yet to be rooted up at his age – he was nearly fifty after all – and to be set down in Roumania to dig for human motives, he who had no instinct to dig for anything but dry bones and ancient pottery, it was surely for him suffering in a major degree. He had been so pathetically proud of being a captain, and at the same time so obviously conscious of the radical absurdity of himself in such a position; it was like a prematurely old child playing with soldiers to gratify his parents. And here in a neutral country he was even debarred from dressing up in uniform. When she first saw him she had been surprised to find that he did not

465

appear much older than thirteen years ago; now looking back at him in his office he seemed to her a very old man. Poor Philip, he did not belong to the type that is rejuvenated in war time by a sense of his official importance. Sylvia had seen illustrations in English newspapers of beaming old gentlemen 'doing', as it was called, 'their bit,' proud of the nuisance they must be making of themselves, incorrigible optimists about the tonic effects of war because they had succeeded in making their belts meet round their fat paunches, pantaloons that should have buried themselves out of sight instead of pirouetting while young men were being killed in a war for which they and their accursed Victorianism were responsible by licking the boots of Prussia for fifty years.

Sylvia found Queenie in a state of agitation at her long absence; she did not tell her anything about Zozo at once in the hope that he would not come to the Trianon on the first night of his arrival. She did think it advisable, however, to tell Queenie of her failure to secure the passport.

'Then we can't be going to England?' Queenie asked.

'Well, not directly from here,' Sylvia answered. 'But we'll move on as soon as we can into Bulgaria. We can get down to the Piraeus from Dedeagatch. I don't think these neutral countries are very strict about passports. We'll manage somehow to get away from here.'

'But if we cannot be going to England why must we be going from Bucharest? Better to stay, I think. Yes?'

'We might want to go,' Sylvia said. 'We might get tired of the Trianon. It wouldn't be difficult.'

'I shall never be going to England now,' said Queenie in a toneless voice. 'Never shall I be going! I shall learn a new song and a new dance, yes?'

Sylvia felt tired after her long afternoon and thought she would rest for an hour before getting ready for the evening's work. The mist gathered again at sunset, and the gardens of the theatre, though they were unusually full, lacked any kind of gaiety. When they were walking down the narrow laurel-bordered path that screened the actors from the people sitting at their tables under the trees, Sylvia was sure that Zozo would be standing by the stage door at the end of it; but he was nowhere to be seen. After the performance, however, when they came out, as the custom was, to take their seats in the audience, the juggler made a dramatic appearance from behind a tree; Queenie seemed to lose all her fairy charm and become a terrified little animal.

'I don't think there's room at our table for you,' Sylvia said.

'There are plenty of chairs,' Maud insisted stridently; she had followed the juggler into the lamplight round the table.

'I'm quite sure there's no room for you,' said Sylvia sharply; and taking advantage of Queenie's complete limpness she dragged her away by the wrist and explained quickly to the manager who was walking up and down by the entrance gate that Queenie was ill and must go home at once.

'Ill!' he exclaimed sceptically. 'Well, I shall have to fine you both your evening's salary. Why, it's only half-past eleven!'

Sylvia did not wait to argue with him, but hurried Queenie to a carriage, in which they drove back immediately to their hotel.

'I said to you that it was going to bring me bad luck when you said to that priest my real name. *Ach!* what shall I be doing? What shall I be doing now?' Queenie wailed.

'You must pay no attention to him,' Sylvia told her; but she found that Queenie did not recover herself as she usually did at the tone of command. 'What can he do to you while you're with me?' she continued.

'You don't know him,' Queenie moaned. 'He's very strong. Look at the mark on my leg where he was shooting me. *Ach*, if we could be going to England, but we cannot. We are here and he is here. You are not strong like he was, Sylvia.' ·

'If you're going to give way like this before he has touched you and frighten yourself to death in advance, of course he'll do what he likes, because I can do nothing without support from you. But if you'll try to be a little bit brave and remember that I can protect you, everything will be all right and we'll get away from Roumania at the first opportunity.'

'*Ach*, you have papers. You are English. Nobody will protect me. Anyone was being able to do what they was liking to do with me.'

Sylvia tried to argue courage into her until early morning; but Queenie adopted an attitude of despair, and it was impossible to convince her that Zozo could not at whatever moment he chose take her away and, if he wished, murder her without anyone's interfering or being able to interfere. In the end Sylvia fell asleep exhausted, resolving that if Queenie was not in a more courageous frame of mind next day she should not move from the hotel. When Sylvia woke up she found that Queenie was already dressed to go out, and for an instant she feared that the juggler's power over her was strong enough to will her to go back to him by the mere sense of his being near at hand. She asked her almost angrily why she had dressed herself so quietly and where she was going.

'To the hairdresser's,' Queenie answered in a normal voice.

Sylvia was puzzled what to do. She did not like to put the idea into Queenie's head of the juggler's being able to mesmerize her into following him apparently of her own accord, and if she really intended to go to the hairdresser's, it might imply that the terror of the night before had burnt itself out. Certainly she did not seem very nervous this morning. It was taking a risk, but probably the only way out of the situation was by taking risks, and in the end she decided not to oppose her going out by herself.

Two hours passed; when Queenie had not returned to the hotel Sylvia went out and made enquiries at the hairdresser's. Yes, she had been there earlier that morning and had bought several bottles of scent. Sylvia made a gesture of disapproval; scent was an extravagance of Queenie's, and she was strictly rationed in this regard on account of the urgency of saving all the money they could for their journey. She returned to the hotel; Queenie was still absent, and she opened her bag to look for the address of a girl whom Queenie occasionally visited; she found the card, but the thousand-franc note that she was guarding for her had vanished. Queenie must have joined that infernal Swiss after all, and the old instinct of propitiating him with money had been too strong for her.

'Fool that I was to let her go this morning,' Sylvia cried. As she spoke, Queenie came in, her cheeks flushed with excitement, her arms full of packages.

'Where have you been and what have you been doing?' she demanded.

'Oh, you must pardon me for taking the money from your bag,' Queenie cried. 'I was taking it to buy presents for all the girls.'

'Presents for the girls?' Sylvia echoed in amazement.

'Yes, yes, it was the only way to make them on my side against him. To-night in the dressing-room I shall give these beautiful presents. I was spending all of my thousand francs. It was no use any longer, because we cannot be going to England. Better that I was buying these presents to make all the girls be on my side.'

Sylvia was between laughter and tears, but she could not bring herself to be angry with the child; at least her action showed that she was taking her own part against the juggler. Queenie spent the rest of the day quite happily, arranging how the presents were to be allotted. Those that were small enough she put into chocolate boxes that she had bought for this purpose; the larger ones were tied up with additional pink and blue silk ribbons to compensate for the lack of a box. To each present – there were fifteen of them – a picture postcard was tied, on which Sylvia had to write the name of the girl for whom it was intended *with heaps of love and kisses from Queenie:* it was like a child preparing for her Christmas party.

They went down to the Trianon earlier than usual in order that Queenie might get ready in time to sit at the entrance of the dressing-room and hand each girl her present as she came in. Sylvia tried to look as cheerful as possible under the ordeal, for she did not want to confirm the tale that she was living on Queenie's earnings by seeming to grudge her display of generosity. The girls were naturally eager to know the reason of the unexpected entertainment. When Queenie took each of them aside in turn and whispered a long confidence in her ear, Sylvia supposed that she was explaining about the advent of Zozo; but it turned out Queenie was explaining that, having no longer any need for the money since she could not get a passport for England, she was doing now what she had wanted to do before, but had been unable to do on account of saving up for the journey. Sylvia remonstrated with her for this indiscretion, and she said:

'I think it was you that was being silly not me, yes? If I say to the girls "here is a silver brush, help me against Zozo," they was thinking that I was buying them to help me. But when he tries to take me, I shall call out to them and they will be loving me for these presents and will be fighting against him I think, yes?'

Sylvia had her doubts, but she had not the heart to discourage such trust in the grateful appreciation of her companions.

Neither Zozo nor Maud came to the Trianon that evening; nevertheless, outside on the playbill was an announcement that next Sunday would appear zozo: LE MEILLEUR PRESTIDIGITATEUR DU MONDE.

'It was always so that he was writing himself,' said Queenie, when Sylvia read her the announcement; she spoke in a voice of awe as if the playbill had been inscribed by a warning fate. In due course the juggler made a successful first appearance, dressed in green with a snake of shimmering tinsel wound round him. They watched the performance from the wings; when he came off he asked Queenie with a laugh if she would stand for his dagger act, as in the old days she had stood.

'You've got Maud for that,' Sylvia interposed quickly.

'Maud!' he scoffed.

Earlier in the evening she had thundered about the stage in what she described as the world famous step-dance of the world famous American cow-girl Maud Moffat to the authentic and original native melody, which happened this year to be *On the Mississippi* and might just as easily have been *A Life on the Ocean Wave*.

Sylvia was puzzled by the relationship between Zozo and Maud, for there was evidently nothing even in the nature of affection between them, and as far as she could make out they had never met until the day he paid her fare from Galantza to Bucharest. Her first idea had been that he was a German agent and intended to use Maud in that capacity, her patriotism, judging by her loud denunciations of England and everything

English, not being very deep. But Sylvia had already outlived the habit of explaining as a spy everyone in war time that is not immediately and blatantly obvious. She could imagine nobody less fitted to be a spy than Maud, who was attractive neither to her compatriots nor to foreigners and who even had she possessed attraction would have had no brains to take advantage of it. Yet she came back to the theory that Zozo was a German agent when she saw with whom he consorted in Bucharest, and she decided that when he had brought Maud here he had done so in the hope of having found a useful recruit, but that on discovering her dull coarseness he had come to the conclusion that her hostility to England was counter-balanced by England's hostility to her. Sylvia decided that if her surmises were at all near to being correct she must be particularly on her guard against any attempt on the part of the Swiss to corrupt Queenie. She had supposed at first that she should only have to contend with his lust or with his desire of personal domination; now it seemed that the argument she had used with Philip to procure Queenie a passport had really been a sound argument. Superficially Queenie might not strike anybody as a valuable agent; knowing her charm for men, her complete malleableness, and her almost painful simplicity, Sylvia could imagine that she might be a practical weapon in the hands of an unscrupulous adventurer like the Swiss, who was finding like so many other rascals of his type that in war natural dishonesty is a lucrative asset. She wondered to what extent her ideas about his intentions were based upon his behaviour at Granada and whether after all she was not attributing to him all sorts of schemes of which he was entirely innocent. Really he had always been for her a symbol of evil that she was inclined to turn into a crude personification. It was strange the way that one was apt in changing one's mode of life to abandon simultaneously the experience one had gathered formerly. Most probably she was giving this juggler with an absurd name an importance quite beyond his power, simply because she herself was giving her present surroundings a permanence far more durable and extensive than they actually possessed. After all, could one but perceive it, the way from the Petit Trianon to Mulberry Cottage did exist as a material fact: there was no impassable gulf of space or time between them.

After Zozo had been juggling for about a fortnight in Bucharest without having given the least sign of wanting to interfere with Queenie, Sylvia began to think that she had worked herself up for nothing, though the problem of his relationship to Maud with whom he remained on terms of contemptuous intimacy still puzzled her. She thought of making a report on the queer association to Philip, but she was afraid he might think it was an excuse to meet him again; and since Philip himself had made no effort to follow up their interview, she gave up speculating upon Zozo and Maud and took to speculating instead upon Philip's want of curiosity, as she called it. Unreasonable as she admitted to herself that the emotion was, she could not help being piqued by his indifference, and she resented now the compassion she had felt for him when she left the office that afternoon. She could not understand any man, however badly a woman had treated him – and she had not treated Philip badly – being able to contemplate so calmly that woman's existence as a cabaret singer without wanting to know what had brought her to it so short a time after her success. No, certainly she should not trouble Philip with her suspicions of Zozo and Maud; it was inviting a rebuff.

Just when Sylvia was beginning to feel reassured about Queenie and not to worry about anything except the waste of that thousand francs and the continuous difficulties in the way of saving any money, the girls at the Trianon began to whisper among themselves. Queenie's presents had given her a brief popularity that began to fade when it was evident that no more presents were coming; her attempt to secure the friendship of her companions, inasmuch as it seemed a token of weakness, reacted against her and made her in the end less popular than before. The story about the refusal of a passport by the British authorities was soon magnified into a demand for her expulsion from Roumania as a German agent masquerading as an English girl. Hence the whispers. The French girls were naturally the most venomous; but the Austrian girls were nearly as bad, because having lived for months under the perpetual taunt of being spies they were anxious to re-establish their own virtue at Queenie's expense. Zozo commiserated with her on the unfairness of the whispers, and one evening to Sylvia's dismay Queenie told her that he had offered to secure her a passport and take her with him when he left Bucharest.

'He was really being very nice to me,' Queenie said. 'Oh, Sylvia, what shall I do? I cannot stay here with these girls who are so unkind to me.'

The following evening Sylvia asked Zozo straight out about the kind of passport he proposed to find for Queenie and where he proposed to take her.

The juggler sneered.

'That's my business I think. What can you do for her? If the kid's anything, she's German. What the hell's the good of you trying to make her English? Why don't you let her alone instead of stopping her from earning good money?'

Sylvia kept her temper with a great effort and contented herself with denying that Queenie was German and with asking who had first made the assertion. The juggler spat on the floor and walked away without replying.

After the performance that night, a hot thunderous night in August, Zozo with Maud and two well-known pro-German natives took the next table to Sylvia and Queenie. Maud was drinking heavily and presently she began to talk in a loud voice:

'Well, I may have spoken against England once or twice, but thank gawd, I'm not a bloody little yellow-haired German pretending to be English. I never went and tried to pass off a dirty little German as my sister the same as what some people who's proud of being English does. Yes, I earn my living honestly. I've never heard anyone call me a spy and any— as did wouldn't do it twice. My name's Maud Moffat, born and bred a cockney, and proud I am when I see some people who think their-selves superior and all the time is dirty German spies betraying their country. Does anyone presume to say I'm not English?' she shouted, rising unsteadily to her feet. 'And if he does, where is he so as I can show him he's a bloody liar by breaking his head open?'

Her companions made a pretence of restraining her, but it was plain that they were enjoying the scene, and Maud continued to hold forth.

'German! And calls herself English. Goes around giving presents to honest working girls so as she can carry on her dirty work of spying. Goes around trying to get a girl's boy away from her by low dirty mean tricks as she's learnt from the bloody Germans who she belongs to. Yes, it's you I'm talking to,' she shrieked at Queenie. White as paper she sprang up from her seat and began to answer Maud, notwithstanding Sylvia's efforts to silence her.

'You was being a bad wicked girl,' she panted. 'You dare to say I was being German! I hate the Germans! I *am* English. I *am* English. You dare to say I was being German!'

Upon this an Austrian girl at another table began to revile Queenie from her point of view for abusing the Germans; before ten seconds had passed the gardens were in an uproar.

A fat French Jewess stood on a table and shouted:

'*Oh, les sales boches! Oh, les sales boches!*'

Whereupon an Austrian girl pushed her from behind, and she crashed down into a party of Francophile young Roumanians who instantly began to throw everything within reach at a party of Germanophile young Roumanians. Glasses were shivered; fairy lamps were pulled out of the trees and hurtled through the air like Roman candles; some-body snatched a violin from the orchestra and broke it on the head of his assailant; somebody else climbed on the stage and made a speech in Roumanian calling upon the country to intervene on behalf of the Entente, until two pro-Germans seized him and flung him down on top of the melancholy dotard who played the double-bass; the manager and the waiters rushed into the street to find the police; everybody argued with everybody else.

'Tu dis que je suis boche, moi? Merde pour toi!'

'La ferme! La ferme! Espionne! Type infecte!'

'Moi, je suis Roumaine. Si tu dis que je suis Hongroise, je dis que t'es une salope. Tu m'entends?'

'Oh, la vache! Elle m'a piquée!'

'Elle a bien fait! Elle a bien fait!'

Some French girls began to sing–

> Les voyez-vous?
> Les hussards! Les dragons! la gar-rrde!
> Glorieux fous . . .

and a very shrill little soprano who was probably a German, but declared she was a Dane, sang:

> It's a larway to Tipperary,
> It's a larway to go,
> It's a larway to Tipperary,
> It's a la-a-way to go!
> Gooba, Piccadilli,
> Farwa lar-sa sca-aa!
> It's a lar-lar-way to Tipperary
> Ba-ma-ha's ra-tha.

After which somebody hit her on the nose with a vanilla ice: then the police came in and quieted the uproar by arresting several people on the outskirts of the riot.

The next evening, when Sylvia and Queenie presented themselves for the performance, the manager told them that they were dismissed: he could not afford to let the Petit Trianon gain a disorderly reputation. Sylvia was glad that the decision of taking a definite step had been settled over her head. As they were passing out, they met Lottie looking very happy.

'I've been engaged for three hundred francs to play the piano in the orchestra. The accompanist broke his wrist last night in the row,' she told them. 'So they sent for me in a hurry.'

473

'We've been sacked,' Sylvia said.

'Oh, I am sorry,' the fat girl exclaimed, trying to curb her own pleasure. 'What will you do?'

Sylvia shrugged her shoulders.

'Why don't you go to Galantza and Bralatz and Avereshti? You ought to be able to get engagements there in the summer-time – especially at Avereshti.'

Sylvia nodded thoughtfully.

'Yes, that's rather an idea. But Lottie, don't tell Zozo where we've gone. Good-bye, good luck. I'm glad you've got an engagement.'

'Yes, I shall leave that room now. It smells rather, as the summer gets on.'

The next morning Sylvia and Queenie left Bucharest for Galantza.

V

Neither in Galantza nor in Bralatz did Sylvia and Queenie perceive any indication of a fortune. They performed for a week at the Varietés High Life in Bralatz; but the audience and the salary were equally low, the weather was hot and misty, and the two hotels they tried were full of bugs. In Galantza they performed for two days at the Varietés Tiptop; but here both the audience and the salary were lower still, the weather was hotter and more misty, and there were as many bugs in the one hotel as in the two hotels at Bralatz put together. Sylvia thought she should like to visit the British vice-consul who had angered Maud so much by his indifference to her future. He was a pleasant young man, not recognizable from her description of him except by the fact that he certainly did smoke incessantly. He invited them both to dine and grumbled loudly at the fate which had planted him down in this god-forsaken corner of Roumania in war time. He was disappointed to hear that they could not stay in Galantza, but agreed with them about the audience and the salary.

'I can't think who advised you to come here,' he exclaimed. 'Though I'm glad you did come; it has cheered me up a bit.'

'It wasn't Maud,' Sylvia said with a smile.

'Maud?' he repeated. 'Who is she?'

'An English girl who took a great fancy to you. She wanted you to pay her fare to Bucharest.'

'Oh, my hat, a most fearful creature,' he laughed. 'A great pink blowsy woman with a voice like two trains shunting. I had a terrible time with

474

her. Upon my word I had actually to push her out of the consulate. Oh, an altogether outrageous phenomenon! What became of her finally? In Bucharest, is she? Well, she's not a good advertisement of our country in these times. What part of England do you come from?' he added, turning to Queenie.

'London,' Sylvia said quickly. She always answered this kind of question before Queenie could blush and stammer something unintelligible. 'But she's been on the continent since she was a little girl, and can't speak any language except with the accent of the one she spoke last.' Then she changed the subject by asking him where he advised them to go next.

'I should advise you to go back to England. These are no times for two girls to be roaming about Europe.'

'You'd hardly describe me as a girl,' Sylvia laughed. 'Even I can no longer describe myself as one. Passports have been fatal to some cherished secrets. No, we can't get back to England chiefly because we haven't saved enough money for the fare, and secondly because the passport-office in Bucharest didn't consider me a good enough voucher for Queenie's right to a British passport.'

'Wouldn't they recommend the consul to issue one?'

Sylvia shook her head.

'Too bad,' said the vice-consul in a cheerful voice. 'But that's one of the minor horrors of war, this accumulation of a new set of officials begotten by the military upon the martial enthusiasm of non-combatants. It's rather ridiculous, isn't it, to assume that all consuls are incapable of their own job? . . . but I suppose I've no business to be displaying professional jealousy at such a moment,' he broke off.

'Would you have given her a passport?' Sylvia asked.

The vice-consul looked at Queenie with a smile.

'I could hardly have refused, eh?'

But Sylvia knew that once inside his consulate he would probably be even more pedantic than Philip, and this affectation of gallantry over coffee rather annoyed her.

'But what *are* you going to do?' he went on.

'Oh, I don't know,' said Sylvia curtly. 'Leave things to arrange themselves, I suppose.'

'Yes, that's a very good attitude to take up when your desk is untidy, but seriously I shouldn't advise you to leave things to arrange themselves by touring round Roumania. These provincial towns are wretched holes.'

'What's Avereshti like?'

'I don't know. I've never been there. It's not likely to be any better than Galantza or Bralatz, except for being a good deal nearer to Bucharest.

475

Oh dear, everything's very gloomy. That Suvla business will keep out the Roumanians for some time. In fact I don't think myself they'll ever come in now, unless they come in with the Germans. Why don't you take a week's holiday here?'

But the vice-consul, who had seemed agreeable at first, was getting on Sylvia's nerves with his admiration for Queenie, and she told him that they should leave next day.

'Too bad,' he exclaimed. 'But that's the way of the world. When a consul would like to be thoroughly bothered by somebody, nothing will induce that person to waste five minutes of his precious time. Your friend Maud on the contrary haunted me like a bluebottle.'

Avereshti turned out to be a much smaller place than Sylvia had expected. She had heard it spoken of in Bucharest as a favourite summer resort, and had pictured it somehow with a casino, gardens, good hotels, and pretty scenery: the very name had appealed to her with a suggestion of quietude. She had deliberately not gone there at once with Queenie when they left Bucharest, because being not more than sixty kilometres from the capital she had had an idea that Zozo might think it a likely place for them to visit and take it into his head to seek them out. Even in the train coming back from Galantza she had doubts of the wisdom of turning on their tracks so soon; but their taste of Galantza and Bralatz had been so displeasing that Avereshti with its prefigured charm of situation promised a haven with which the risk of being worried by their enemy could not interfere. They would take a week's holiday before engaging themselves to appear at the casino or whatever the home of amusement was called in Avereshti; then after a short engagement they might perhaps venture back to Bucharest and start saving up money again.

'For what good?' Queenie asked sadly.

'Oh, something will turn up,' Sylvia replied. 'Perhaps the war will come to a sudden end, and you'll be able to go to England without a passport.'

'You are always dreaming, Sylvia. Happy things cannot come to me so easily as you was thinking.'

Since the night of the row at the Trianon Queenie had settled down to a steady despair about the whole of her future, and it was partly Sylvia's powerlessness to restore her to the childish gaiety that was so attractive in one whom she was conscious of protecting which had made her conceive such a distaste for the two towns they had just left. She was beginning indeed to doubt if her intervention between Queenie and the life she had been leading was really worth while. She upbraided herself with a poor spirit, with a facile discouragement, with selfishness and want of faith; yet all the way in the train she was on the verge of proposing that they should go back at once to Bucharest and there definitely part company. The dreary country through which they were travelling and the moist heat of the September afternoon created such a desire for England that the thought of remaining five minutes longer in Roumania was becoming intolerable. Sylvia began to make plans to telegraph home for money, and while she pondered these she began to think about Jack and Olive and the twins. Jack of course would be a soldier by now; but Olive would be in Warwickshire. Perhaps at this moment she was walking through a leafy path in Arden and wondering what her lost friend was doing. Sylvia tried to conjure familiar English scents – the smell of bluebells and young leaves, the smell of earth in a London window-box after being watered, and most wistfully of all the smell of the seaside on a breathless day of late summer when the sun was raining diamonds into the pale blue water – that so poignantly English seaside smell of salt sand and pears in paper bags, of muslin frocks and dusty shrubs and warm asphalt. It might be such a day in England now, such a day at Eastbourne or Hastings. The notion of enduring any longer these flat Roumanian fields, this restless and uncertain existence upon the fringe of reality, this pilgrimage in charge of a butterfly that must soon or late be caught, clouded her imagination.

'In seeking to direct Queenie's course I am doing something that is contrary to my dearest theory of behaviour. When I met her again at Jassy I was in an abnormal and hysterical condition. The sense of having failed myself led me to seize desperately upon her salvation to justify this long withdrawal from the activity of my own world. This world of gipsies is no longer my world. Why, I believe that the real reason I feel annoyed with Philip is because, having roused in me a sense of my unsuitableness to my present conditions and actions, he does not trouble to understand the effect that talking to him had upon me. Here I am at thirty-two thinking like an *exaltée* schoolgirl. Thirty-two! Just when I ought to be making the most tremendous efforts to anchor myself to some stable society that will carry me through the years to come, the years that without intellectual and spiritual pleasures will be nothing but a purgatory for my youth, I find myself more hopelessly adrift than ever before. It will end in my becoming a contemplative nun in one last desperate struggle to avoid futility. It is a tragedy for the man or woman who comprehends futility without being able to escape from it. That's where the Middle Ages were wiser than we. Futility was impossible then. That's where we suffer from that ponderous bog of Victorianism.

When one pauses to meditate upon the crimes of the Victorian era! And it's impossible not to dread a revival of Victorianism after this war. It's obvious that unless we defeat the Teuton quickly – and there's no sign of it – we shall be Teutonized in order to do it. And then indeed, O grave where *is* thy victory? Will the Celtic blood in England be enough to save her in ten years' time from a base alliance with these infernal Germans in order that the two stupidest nations in the world may combine to overlay it? Will this war at last bring home to Europe the sin of handing herself over to lawyers? Better the Middle Ages priest-ridden than To-day lawyer-ridden. At least if we are going to pay these rascals who exploit their country, let us have it well exploited. Don't let us call in one political plumber after another whose only object is to muddle the State for his successor to muddle it still more that he may be called in again to muddle it again – and muddle – and muddle eternally! When one reads in the papers the speeches of politicians, of what can one be reminded but of children playing cat's cradle over the tortured body of their mother? Yet what business have I to be abusing lawyer and politician when I lack the strength of mind to persevere in a task which I set myself with my eyes open? Unless I suffer in achieving it, it will not be worth the achievement. Surely the human soul that has suffered deeply can never again acknowledge futility? O England, perhaps it is a poor little pain to be away from you now, a mean little egotistical ache at the best, but away from you I see your faults so much more clearly and love you for them all the more.'

The train entered the station, and Sylvia perceived that there was nothing beautiful about Avereshti in the way she had fancied. Yet she was ashamed now of the temptation to desert Queenie; therefore, though the train was going on to Bucharest, she hurried her out on the platform, and when they reached the Hotel Moldavia she took a room for two weeks, paying for it in advance lest she should be tempted by her disappointment with Avereshti to hurry back to Bucharest again, the inevitable result of which in her present mood would be to abandon her friend.

Avereshti instead of being situated amid the romantic scenery that one expected from a celebrated summer resort was surrounded by oilfields which disfigured still more the flat environment. It was too large for genuine rusticity, too small for its assumption of European civilization, and too commercial for gaiety. Possibly during the season shareholders and owners of the oilfields came here to gloat for a week upon the sources of their prosperity; if they did, they had all of them left by the middle of September; The Varietés Alcazar was closed and the playbills were already beginning to peel off the walls. Whatever life there was in Avereshti displayed itself in the Piatza Carol I, the pavement of which was planted with trees clipped out of any capacity to cast a pleasant shade. The Hotel Moldavia flanked by cafés occupied one side of it, a row of respectable shops another, a large municipal hall of the crudest Germanic architecture fronted the hotel, and along the remaining side ran a row of market booths, the insult of which to the progress of Avereshti was greatly resented by the inhabitants and always apologized for and explained in the first few minutes of conversation.

The appearance of Sylvia and Queenie in this square on the morning after their arrival created an interest that soon developed into a pertinacious and disconcerting curiosity. If they entered a shop to make some small purchases, a crowd gathered outside and followed them to the next shop, and finally became such a nuisance that they retired to the balcony outside their room – a long wooden balcony of a faded tint of green – and watched the populace gathering to stare at them from below. When the sun became too hot for this entertainment, they took refuge in the big bedroom which had the unusual merit of being free from bugs. Queenie dreamed away the morning with her lithographs; Sylvia read *War and Peace*. Late in the afternoon they went out again on the balcony and were amused to see that the frequenters of the cafés on either side of the hotel had moved their chairs hornwise far enough out into the square to obtain a view of their movements. Sylvia suggested to the waiter that they should give a musical performance from the balcony, but he replied quite seriously that it was not strong enough: otherwise, he left them to understand, there would have been no objection.

'Yet really after all it's not so bad here,' Sylvia declared. 'We'll stay a few days, and then I'll go into Bucharest and prospect. Perhaps Zozo will be gone by now.'

Avereshti possessed at any rate the charm of making one feel lazy; to feel lazy and to be able to gratify one's laziness was after nearly a year of ceaseless work pleasant enough. On the third afternoon the waiter came up with six visiting-cards from local gentlemen who desired their acquaintance. Sylvia told him that they were not anxious to make any friends; he smiled and indicated two names as those that would best repay their choice.

'We wish to be left quite alone,' Sylvia repeated irritably.

'Then why do you walk about on the balcony?' the waiter asked.

'We walk on the balcony because it's the only place where we can walk without being annoyed by a crowd. You don't expect us to remain in our room day and night, do you?'

The waiter smiled and again called attention to the desirable qualifications of the two visiting-cards he had first thrust into prominence. He added that both the gentlemen, M. Stefan Florilor and M. Toma Enescu, were particularly anxious to make the acquaintance of the fair young lady; that M. Florilor was young, handsome, and the son of the richest man in Avereshti; and that though M. Enescu was not young he was very rich. Perhaps the ladies would invite them to take coffee? It would be easy to get rid of the other four visiting-cards.

Sylvia told the waiter to get rid of all six and never again to have the impudence to refer to the subject; but he continued to extol his clients, until at last Sylvia in a rage knocked the card-tray out of his hand with the volume of *War and Peace* that he was interrupting, upon which he retired muttering abuse.

About ten minutes afterwards the waiter came back and told Sylvia that all the gentlemen were gone away except M. Florilor who insisted upon being received.

'Insists?' cried Sylvia. 'But is he the crown-prince of Avereshti?'

The waiter shrugged his shoulders.

'His father has a mortgage on the hotel,' he explained. 'And the proprietor would be very much upset to think that any discourtesy had been shown to the son.'

'Have we paid for this room?' Sylvia demanded.

The waiter agreed with her that they had paid for it.

'Very well, when we ask for free board and lodging it will be time enough to talk about the proprietor's annoyance at our refusal to receive his creditors.'

She indicated the direction of the door with a contemptuous inclination of the head, and the waiter retired.

'I don't know how you can be so strong to talk like that,' Queenie marvelled. 'If I was being alone here I should be too frightened to speak so to the waiter. Suppose they was all to murder us to-night?'

When Queenie spoke like this, Sylvia's old sense of guardianship flowed again as fast as ever, and any impulse to abandon her was drowned in a flood of rage against the arrogance of money with its sale and purchase of human lives. There was something less distasteful about the domination of Zozo than about the attempted domination of this young Roumanian puppy yelping in his backyard of a town. If the juggler were to arrive in Avereshti to-night and in a frenzy of baulked passion were to murder both herself and Queenie, there would be a kind of completeness about the action that made the presentiment of it a sane and feasible terror; but that Queenie should have been reduced to a condition of semi-idiocy merely by the fact that the accidents of her childhood had put her for sale on the market of life did seem to Sylvia inexpressibly revolting.

'And we credit ourselves with the abolition of slavery! I am not sure that the frank slavery of the past was not more moral than the unadmitted slavery of the present. At any rate it carried with it its own penalty in the demoralization and decay of the owners; but I perceive no prospective penalty for this sort of thing. A young barbarian whose father has grown rich and fat upon petroleum sees a girl that takes his fancy and sends up his card; the proprietor of the hotel threatens us through that pimping waiter with the enmity of his father's debtor. This happens to be a crude case because we are living temporarily in a crude country; but less crudely the same thing goes on in England. It is true that we shrink there from the licensed brothel, and that we are still able to shrink from that is something to be grateful for; yet though we refrain from inflicting an open shame upon womanhood, we pay very little attention to the rights of the individual woman and child, or for the matter of that to the rights of the individual man. We no longer allow the bodies of children to be slowly murdered in factories, but we offer not the least objection to their employment in nice healthy amusing occupations such as selling newspapers for great monopolies or dancing in the theatres. There *can* be no defence of employing child-labour, and the man who defends it is the equal of the most brutalized and hardened *souteneur*. I still think that the greater part of humanity is so naturally inclined to be enslaved that the bestowal of freedom will in a short time land the world in the same state as before; but what I don't understand is the necessity for a reformer or the philanthropist to be anything except profoundly cynical. It always seems to be assumed that a desire to help other people implies a belief that other people will benefit from the help. I should like to meet an unadvertising philanthropist who was willing to admit that his philanthropy was a vice like secret drinking. One occasionally perceives signs of a sick conscience in some large anonymous contribution to charity; I always suspect the donor of expiating a monstrous crime. I can imagine being haunted by the fear of a peerage in return for the expenditure upon a Lord Mayor's fund of the superfluous savings of a wicked life.'

'Of what are you thinking?' Queenie asked.

'I'm thinking, my dear, that visits from the *jeunesse dorée* of Avereshti tend to infect me with an odious feeling of self-righteousness. The result of reading Tolstoy and arguing with a waiter about the sale of your body to M. Florilor has reduced me to a state of morbid indignation with the human race. But the problem that's bothering me is my ultimate ineffectiveness. I'm like a chained-up dog, and I am realizing that noise to be a real weapon of defence requires listeners. I'm a little afraid, Queenie, that unless I can do more than bark, I shall lose you.'

'When shall you lose me?'

'When the web of my theory in which I'm sitting like a spider gets swept away by something more powerful than you, my butterfly, whom even without interference I can scarcely retain. You'll escape me then and be caught finally in a net, and I shall scuttle off and hide myself in a dark corner until I die of inanition and chagrin.'

'I was not understanding one word of what you were saying,' said Queenie. 'First you were being a dog. After you were being a spider. Who was ever to understand you?'

'Who indeed?' Sylvia murmured with half a sigh, as she went out on the balcony and looked down upon the frequenters of the cafés, whose heads when she appeared were simultaneously lifted to regard her with a curiosity that her elevated position made impersonal as the slow glances of cattle at pasture.

That evening after dinner the first sign of the proprietor's displeasure at the snub administered to the heir of his chief creditor was visible in a bill for their board of three days. The sum was not large, but by using up their small cash it involved breaking into the five-hundred-franc note that represented the last of the money they had saved since February. Sylvia had always kept this note in a pocket of her valise; now when she went up to their room to fetch it it was gone. The discovery of the loss was such a blow at this moment that she could not speak of it to Queenie when she came downstairs again; she paid what was owing with the last halfpenny they had, and sat back revolving internally in her mind how, when, and where that five-hundred-franc note could possibly have been lost. Suddenly she had an idea that she might have moved it to another pocket and, leaving a half-smoked cigarette balanced against the saucer of her coffee-cup, she ran upstairs again to verify the conjecture. Alas, it was the emptiest of conjectures, and in a fever of exasperation she searched wildly in all sorts of unlikely places for the missing money. When the bedroom was scattered with her clothes to no purpose, she went back to the dining-room, where she found that the waiter had taken the half-smoked cigarette in clearing away the coffee-cups.

'Didn't you keep that cigarette?' she demanded.

Queenie looked at her in surprise.

'Why to keep a cigarette?' she asked.

'Because I haven't another.'

'Well, ring for the waiter. He shall bring one for you.'

'No, no, it doesn't matter,' Sylvia muttered; but the waste of that last precious cigarette brought home to her more than anything else that there was absolutely not even a halfpenny left in her purse after paying for the food they had had, and abruptly with the transmutation of that insignificant object to something of immense value arrived a corresponding change in Sylvia's attitude to the whole of life.

In the first case the larger share of the money she had lost so carelessly – with an effort she drove from her brain the revolving problem of how, when, and where – belonged to Queenie. Hence her responsibility toward Queenie was doubled, because if in certain moods of disillusionment she had been able to set aside her former responsibility as nothing but a whim, there was now a positive and material obligation that no change of sentiment could obliterate. Any harm that threatened Queenie now must be averted by herself, no matter at what cost to herself; somehow money must be obtained. It was plain that they could expect no consideration from the proprietor of the hotel; the way in which he had demanded payment for their day's board proved as much. Having accepted the money in advance for this room, he could not eject them into the street; but unless it suited him he was under no obligation to feed them. What a precipitate fool she had been to pay for a fortnight's lodging in advance! Seventy francs flung away! She might ask him for them back, or at any rate for the fifty francs' worth of lodging of which they would not have availed themselves if they left to-morrow. With fifty francs they would reach Bucharest, where something might turn up. But supposing nothing did turn up? Suppose that damned juggler found Queenie and herself without a halfpenny? Even that was better than starving here or surrendering to M. Stefan Florilor.

Sylvia went out to ask the proprietor if he would give her back the money she had paid in advance for a room she and her friend found themselves unable any longer to occupy. The proprietor shrugged his shoulders, informed her in his vile French that he had never demanded the sum in advance, assured her that he had refused the room twice to important clients who had wanted it for next week, and altogether showed by his attitude that he had been too much embittered by the reception of M. Florilor to stand upon anything except his strict rights. It was clear that these rights would include refusal of any food that was not paid for at the time. Such behaviour might be unjust and unreasonable, she thought, but after all it was not to be expected than an empty pocket was going to tempt the finer side of human nature. Sylvia went back to Queenie, who was looking in bewilderment at the clothes strewn about the bedroom. She explained what had happened, and Queenie ejaculated:

'There, fancy! We have no money now. Never mind, I can be friends with that gentleman who was asking to know me. He will give me the money, because if he wants me very much he will have to give much money. Yes, I think?'

Sylvia could have screamed aloud her rejection of such a course.

'What, after keeping you away from men for six months to let you go back to them on account of my carelessness? Child, you must be mad to think of it.'

'Yes, but I have been thinking, Sylvia. I have been thinking very much. When I was going to be English and you were saying to me that I should have a passport and be going to England and be English myself, it was good for me to care nothing at all for men; but now what does it matter? I am nothing. I am just being somebody lost, and if I am going with men or not going with men I am still nothing. Why to be worried for money? I shall show you how easy it is for me to have money. It is true what I am speaking. You could be having no idea how much money I can have. And if I am nothing, always nothing, why must I be worrying any more about money? You are so sweet to me, Sylvia, so kind. No one was ever being so kind to me before. So I must be kind to you now. Yes, I think? Are you crying about that money? I think you are stupid to cry for such a little thing as money.'

'There are things, my rose, that must not, that shall not happen,' Sylvia cried, clasping the child in her arms. 'And that you should ever again sell yourself to a man is one of them.'

'But I am nothing.'

'Ah,' thought Sylvia, 'here is the moment when I should be able to say that everyone to God is everything; but if I say it she will not understand. What hope is there for this child?' Then aloud she added, 'Are you nothing to me?'

'No, to you I am something, and if my brother was here I would be something to him.'

'Very well then, you must not think of selling yourself. I lost the money. I shall find a way of getting more money. I have a friend in Bucharest. I will telegraph to him to-morrow and he will send us money.' And to herself she thought: 'This is indeed the ultimate irony, that I should ask a favour of Philip. Yet perhaps I am glad, for if I did him the least injury years ago, no priest could have imagined a more appropriate penance. Yes, perhaps I deserve this.'

The next morning, when Sylvia ordered coffee, the waiter presented the bill for it at the same time, and when she tore it up he seemed inclined to take away the coffee; he retreated finally with a threat that in future nothing should be served to them that was not paid for in advance.

'They are being nasty with us,' Queenie solemnly enunciated.

'Never mind. We shall have some money to-night, or at any rate to-morrow morning. We must put up with fasting to-day. It's Friday appropriately enough. Good heavens,' Sylvia exclaimed, 'I haven't even got the money to send a telegram. We must raise a few francs. Perhaps I could borrow some money with a trinket. Good gracious, I never realized until this moment that I haven't a single piece of jewellery! It takes the sudden affliction of extreme poverty to discover one's abnormality and to prove how essential it is to be different from everybody else. Come, Queenie, you must lend me your two brooches.'

Sylvia took the daisy of brilliants set around a topaz, and the swallow of sapphires – all that Queenie had kept after her disastrous expulsion from Russia – and visited the chief local jeweller, who shrugged his shoulders and refused to buy them.

'But at least you can lend me twenty francs upon them until to-morrow,' Sylvia urged.

He shrugged his shoulders again and bent over to pick at the inside of a watch with that maddening indifference of the unwilling purchaser. Sylvia could not bring herself to believe in his refusal and suggested a loan of fifteen francs. Nothing answered her except the ticking of a dozen clocks and the scraping of a small file. There was a smell of drought in the shop that seemed to symbolize the personality of its owner.

'Ten francs?' Sylvia begged.

The jeweller looked up slowly from his work and regarded her with a fishy eye, the fishiness of which was many times magnified by the glass that occupied it. He raised his chin in a cold negative and bent over his work more intently. Every clock in the shop told a different time and ticked away more loudly than ever. Sylvia gathered up the trinkets and went away. She tried two other jewellers without success, and she even proposed the loan to a chemist who had a pleasant exterior; finally she had to go back to the hotel without obtaining the money. The day dragged itself along; not even *War and Peace* could outlast it, and Sylvia wondered why she had never grasped before how much of life radiated from lunch, the absence of which dislocated time itself. Toward six o'clock she came to a sudden resolution, and going out into the square she began to sing outside the café. Four lean dogs came and barked; a waiter told her that the singing was not required. Somebody threw a stone at one of the dogs and cut open its leg; whereupon the other three set upon it, until it broke away and fled howling across the square, leaving a trail of blood in its wake. The drinkers outside the café looked at Sylvia over the tops of their newspapers, until she went back to the hotel. Such a retirement would ordinarily have made her hot with shame; but she was already hardened by the first pangs of hunger and had only a savage contempt for the people who had thought to humiliate her; she had not been hungry long enough to feel the pathos of a broken spirit; after all, she had only missed her lunch.

Dinner consisted of two stale chocolate creams that were found in a pocket of one of Queenie's jackets; even the bits of silver paper adhering to them seemed to possess a nutritive value.

'But we cannot be going on like this,' Queenie protested.

'There must be some way of raising money enough to get to Bucharest,' Sylvia insisted. 'There must be. There must be. If we really starve, the police will send us there to avoid a death in this cursed hole of a town.'

'We must ask that gentleman to tea with us to-morrow,' Queenie declared, as she put out the light.

Want of food prevented Sylvia from sleeping, and in her overwrought spirit those good-night words of Queenie seemed to presage the collapse of everything.

'It shall not be. It shall not be,' she vowed to herself. 'I will not be defeated by squalid circumstances in this dreary little Roumanian town. If thirteen years ago I could sell my body to save my soul, now I can sell my body to save the soul of another. Surely that sacrifice will defeat futility. I had a presentiment of this situation when I was arguing with Philip that afternoon. I warned him that nothing should stand in my way over this girl. And nothing shall! To-morrow I will invite this youth who is the son of the richest man in Avereshti. He will not refuse me twenty francs for my body. If I cannot do this I am worth no more than those trinkets that the jeweller refused to buy for ten francs. I will do this, and accept its accomplishment as the sign that I have fought long enough. Then I will go to Philip and tell him what his refusal has brought about. I will *make* him give me the passport. But suppose that he is no longer capable of being horrified? Suppose that my behaviour of thirteen years ago has rendered him proof against such an emotion? Oh well, we shall see. Am I light-headed? No, no, no. On the contrary, hunger makes one clear-sighted. It must be. It shall be. The duty of the human soul lies in such a complete, such a reckless, such a relentless, such a victorious self-will as can only be assuaged by self-sacrifice. This is the great paradox of life. This is the Divine egotism.'

Toward dawn Sylvia slept, and woke at sunrise from dreams that were strangely serene in contrast with the tormenting fevers of the night to find that Queenie was still fast asleep. The beauty of her lying there in this lucid and golden morn was like the beauty of a flower that blooms at daybreak in a remote garden. It was a beauty that caught at Sylvia's

486

heart, a beauty that could only be expressed with tears; which were silent as the dew and which like the dew sparkled in the daybreak of the soul.

'It is through such tears that people have seen the fairies,' she murmured.

Sylvia half raised herself in bed, and leaning upon her elbow she watched the sleeping girl so intently that it seemed as if some of herself was passing away to Queenie. This still and virginal hour was indeed time transmuted to the timelessness of dreams, in which absolute love like a note of music rose quivering upon its own shed sweetness to such an ecstasy of sustained emotion that the barest memory of it would secure the wakeful one for ever against disillusionment.

'Call it hunger or the Divine vision, the result is the same,' she murmured. 'I was lifted out of myself, and I take it that is the way martyrs died for their faith. From an outsider's point of view I may be only worthy of a footnote in a manual of psychology; but I 'on honeydew have fed and drunk the milk of paradise.' Another queer thought: the fasting saint and the drunken sinner both achieve ecstasy by subduing the body, the one with mortification, the other with indulgence. Those whom the gods love die young – they drink too deep and too often of honeydew and become intoxicated even unto death. Wine must serve the man who would live long. Perhaps I am one of those less rare spirits that depends too much on purely material beauty; yet even in defence of so little I can act. Some nightingales love roses: the rest of them love other nightingales. Which do I love? Ah, whether Queenie be rose or nightingale what does it matter? Nobody that would not stoop to save a woodlouse in his path can claim to love. And I will stoop as low as hell to save this rosebud that has already been gathered and wired and worn in a buttonhole and dropped by the roadside, but surely not yet trodden underfoot.'

Queenie woke with a bad headache, and Sylvia went downstairs to see if she could persuade the waiter to let her have some coffee. He was going to refuse, but when she asked him if he would tell M. Florilor that a visit would be welcomed that afternoon, his manner changed, and presently he came back from an interview with the proprietor to say that he would serve coffee at once. At the same time he brought the bill of fare for lunch, and seemed anxious that they should choose some special delicacy to fortify themselves against the ill effects of the day before. There was no talk of paying for the meal, and the best wine was indicated with that assumption of subservient greed which is common to all good waiters.

After lunch Sylvia told Queenie that she was going out to send off the delayed telegram to Bucharest and left her lying down with her pictures.

487

Then she consulted the waiter about a room. The waiter agreed that it would be inconvenient to receive M. Florilor in their own, and informed her that the best room in the hotel was ready, adding that he had ordered plenty of cakes and put flowers in the vases.

'I'll go there now,' Sylvia announced. 'When he comes, bring him straight up.'

The brightness of the early morning had been dimmed by a wet mist, and the room allotted for the reception of M. Florilor which was on the other side of the hotel looked out over houses covered with sodden creepers and down into gardens of dishevelled sunflowers; it was a view that suited the mood Sylvia was in, and for a long time she stood gazing out of the window, trying to detect beyond the immediate surroundings of the hotel some definition of a landscape in the distance. In the light of the morning her resolution had not presented itself as morbidly as now; then it had appeared essentially poetic – a demonstration really of the creative power of the human will; now like the dejected flowers in the gardens below it hung limp and colourless. She turned away from the window and sat down in a tight new armchair, the back of which seemed to be enclosed in corsets. Everything in this room was new, and like all hotel rooms it depressed one with that indeterminate bleakness which is the property of never having been touched by the warmth of personality. It was bleak as an abandoned shell on the beach and stirred by nothing save the end of the tide's ebb and flow. The waiter's attempt to give it the significance of human life by cramming bunches of dahlias into a pair of fluted vases only added to the desolate effect. For want of something to do Sylvia began to arrange the flowers with a little consideration for their native ugliness, as one tries to smarten an untidy woman with a bad figure; but when she poured some water into a china bowl and saw floating upon its surface the ends of burnt-out matches and cigarettes, she gave up the task. These burnt-out relics of transitory occupants seemed typical of the room's effect upon the pensive observer. A confused procession of personalities made up its history, and as these had cast away their burnt-out cigarettes and matches, so had they cast behind them the room where they had lodged, preserving no memory of its existence and leaving behind not a single emotion to vitalize the bleak impersonal shell they had thankfully forsaken.

Yet Sylvia, waiting here for the beginning of the heartless drama that would be wrought of her heart's blood pulsing to reinforce her will, rejoiced in this sterility of the setting; it helped her to achieve a similar effect in her own attitude. Just as this room had succeeded in preserving itself from any impression of having ever been lived in by human beings, so she when the drama was played through should retain of it no trace. That in it which was real – the lust of man – should be left behind, an ignominious burnt-out thing less than a cigarette-stump at the bottom of a china bowl.

The waiter came in with a basket of cakes, the cold and sugary forms of which were no more capable than the dahlias of imparting life to the merciful deadness. And how dead it all was! Those red plush curtains eternally tied back in symmetrical hideousness – they had never lived since the time when some starved and withered soul had sewn those pompons along their edges one after another, pompons as numerous and monotonous as the days of their maker. Indeed, there was not a single piece of furniture, not an ornament nor a drapery that was not stamped with the hatred of its maker. There was no trace of the craftsman's joy in his handiwork either in thread or tile or knob. There was nothing except the insolence of profit and the dreary labour of slaves. Yet a world stifled by such ugliness talked with distasteful surprise of men who profited by war. With the exploitation of the herd and the sacrifice of the individual that was called civilization what else could be expected? Nowadays even man's lust had to be guaranteed pure and unadulterated like his beer. Better that the whole human race should rot on dunghills with the diseases they merited than that they should profit from an added shame imposed upon the meanest and most miserable tinker's drab. People were shocked at making a hundred per cent upon a shell to blow a German to pieces; but they regarded with equanimity the same profit at the expense of a child's future. Wherever one looked, there was nothing but material comfort set as the highest aim of life at the cost of beauty, religion, love, childhood, womanhood, virtue, everything. Then two herds met in opposition, and there was war; the result had made everybody uncomfortable, and everybody had declared there must never again be war. But so long as the individual submitted to the herd, war would go on; and the most efficient herd with the greatest will for war would succeed because it would be able to offer greater comfort at the time and higher profits afterwards. Yet the individual had nearly always much that was admirable; the most sordid profiteer possessed a marvellous energy and perception that might be turned to good, if he could but grasp that virtue is the true egotism and that vice is only a distorted altruism.

'I've always hated ants and loathed bees,' Sylvia cried. 'And in certain aspects the human race makes one shudder with that sense of co-operative effort running over one which I believe is called formication.'

The waiter came to announce M. Florilor's arrival.

'Now we get the individual at his worst just when I've been backing him against the herd. This is formication spelt with an "n." '

Stefan Florilor resembled a figure in a picture by Guido Reni. A superficial glance would have established him as a singularly handsome, well-built, robust, and attractive young man; a closer regard showed that his good looks owed too much to soft and feminine contours, that the robustness of his frame was only the outward form of strength with all the curves but nothing of the hardness of muscle, and that his eyes flashed not as the mirrors of an inward fire but with liquid gleams of sensuous impressions caught from outside. He really was extremely like one of Guido Reni's triumphant and ladylike archangels.

They talked in French, a language that Florilor spoke without distinction but with a pothouse fluency – no doubt much as one of Guido Reni's archangels might have picked it up from one of Guido Reni's devils.

'What a fatally seductive language it is,' Sylvia exclaimed at last, when she had complimented him as he evidently expected to be complimented upon his ease. 'Whenever I hear a tea-table conversation in French I suspect everyone of being a poet or a philosopher: whenever I read a French poet I want to ask him if he likes his tea strong or weak.'

'Your friend is English also?' Florilor enquired.

He took advantage of the ethnical turn in the conversation to express his own interest in a problem of nationality.

'Yes, she is English.'

'And no doubt she will be coming down soon?'

'She's not coming down. She has a headache.'

'But perhaps she will be well enough to dine this evening with me?'

'No, I don't think she will be well enough,' said Sylvia.

The young man's face clouded with the disappointment; his features seemed to thicken, so much did their fineness owe to the vitality of sensual anticipation.

'Perhaps to-morrow, then?'

'No, I don't think she will ever be well enough,' Sylvia continued. Then abruptly she put her will to the jump and cleared it breathlessly. 'You'll have to make the best of me as a substitute.'

Afterwards when the reality that stood at the back of this scene had died away Sylvia used to laugh at the remembrance of the alarm in Florilor's expression when she made this announcement. She must have made it in a way so utterly different from any solicitation that he had ever known. At the moment she was absurdly positive that she had offered herself to him with as much freedom and as much allurement as his experience was able to conjecture in a woman. When therefore he

490

showed by his temper that he had no wish to accept the offer, it never struck her that, even had he felt the least desire, her manner of encouragement would have frozen it. A secondary emotion was one of swift pride in the detachment of her position, which was brought home to her by the complete absence of any chagrin – such as almost every woman would have felt – at the obvious dismay caused by her proposal to substitute herself for her friend.

'I'm afraid I must go. I'm busy,' he muttered.

'But you haven't had any cake,' Sylvia protested.

'*Vous vous fichez de moi*,' he growled. '*Vous m'avez posé un sale lapin*.'

He looked like a greedy boy, a plump spoilt child that has been deprived of a promised treat.

'What did she come here for,' he demanded, 'if she's not prepared to behave like any other girl? You can tell her from me that finer girls – girls in Paris – have been glad enough to be friends with me.'

'Caprice and mystery are the prerogatives of woman,' Sylvia said.

'I'm glad she can afford to be capricious when she has not enough money to pay for her food.'

'I'm not going to argue with you about your behaviour, though I could say a good deal about it. At present I can't be as rude as I should like. You see, you've just paid me the compliment of declining to accept the offer of myself. The fact that either I am sufficiently inhuman or that you are too bestial for the notion of any intercourse between us leaves me with a real hope in my heart that there is a difference between you and me. You've no idea of the lowering effect, nay more, of the absolute despair it would cast over my view of life, had I to regard you as belonging to the same natural order as myself. It would involve belief in the universal depravity of man.'

'*Ah, vous m'emmerdez*,' he shouted, as he ran from the room. Sylvia cried after him to remember the fate of the Gadarene swine and to avoid going downstairs too fast. Then to herself she added:

'Ecstasies and dreams of self-abnegation! What are they beside the pleasure of conflict face to face? The pleasure would have been keener though, if I could have hurt him physically.'

In the first elation of escaping from the fulfilment of her intention Sylvia overlooked all the consequences involved in Florilor's withdrawal. Soon in the stillness shed by this bleak room, in the sight of the frozen cakes upon the table, in the creeping obscurity of the afternoon, she was more sharply aware than before of the future, aware of it not as a vague and faintly disturbing horizon too far away still to affect anything except her moods of depression, but as the immediate future in the shape of a chasm at her feet, a future so impassable that she could scarcely think of it in other terms than those of space. It had positively lost the nebulous outlines of time and acquired in their stead the sharp materialism of hostile space. The future! Calculations of how to bridge or leap this gap went whirling through Sylvia's brain, calculations that even included projects of fantastic violence, but never one that envisaged the surrender of a single scruple about Queenie. The resolve she had made that morning, however its practical effect seemed to have been nullified by Florilor's rejection of her sacrifice, had woven each separate strand of her thought and emotion so tightly round the steel wire of her will that nothing could have snapped the result. There was not a bone in her body, not a nerve nor a corpuscle that did not thrill to the command of her will, and wait upon its fresh intention with a loyalty that must endow it with an invincible tenacity of purpose.

The sense of an omnipotent force existing in herself was so strong that when Sylvia saw a golden ten-franc piece lying in the very middle of the fiddle-backed armchair on which Florilor had been sitting, she had for a moment the illusion of having created the coin out of air by the alchemy of her own will.

'Many miracles have deserved the name less than this,' she murmured, picking up the piece of gold. For the second time in her life she was able to enjoy the sensation of illimitable wealth; by a curious coincidence the sum had been the same on both occasions. She preened her nail along the figured edge, taking a delight in the faint luxurious vibration.

'Misers may get very near to paradise by fingering their gold,' she thought. 'But the fingering of gold preparatory to spending it is paradise indeed.'

She went back to Queenie, clasping the coin so tightly that even when she had put it in her purse it seemed to be resting in her palm.

'Will you be leaving me here?' Queenie exclaimed in dismay, when she heard of Sylvia's plan for going to Bucharest to-morrow morning and interviewing Philip.

'There's not enough money to take us both there, but I shall come back to-morrow evening; and then we'll flaunt our wealth in the faces of these brutes here.'

'But I shall be so hungry to-morrow,' Queenie complained.

'Fool that I am,' Sylvia cried. 'The cakes!'

She rushed away and reached the other room a moment before the waiter arrived with his tray.

'These cakes belong to me,' she proclaimed, snatching up the china basket and hugging it to her breast.

The waiter protested that they had not been paid for; but she swept him and his remonstrances aside, and passed out triumphantly into the corridor, where the proprietor of the hotel, a short greasy man, began to abuse her for the way she had treated Florilor.

'*Va-t-en*,' she said scornfully.

'*Quoi? Quoi ditez? Moi bâton? Non! Vous bâton! Comprenez?*'

He was in such a rage at the idea of Sylvia's threatening him with a stick, which was the way he understood her French, that be began to dribble; all his words were drowned in a foam of saliva, and the only way he could express his opinion of her behaviour was by rapid expectoration. Again Sylvia tried to pass him in the narrow corridor, instinctively holding up the cakes beyond his reach. The proprietor evidently thought she was going to bring down the basket upon his head, and in an access of fear and fury he managed to knock it out of her hands.

'Those cakes are mine,' Sylvia really screamed. She felt like a cat defending her kittens when she plunged down upon the floor to pick them up. The proprietor jumped right over her, stamping upon the cakes and the pieces of broken china and grinding them underfoot into the carpet until it looked like a pavement of broken mosaics. Sylvia completely lost her temper at the sight of the destruction of her dinner; and when the proprietor trod upon her hand in the course of his violence she picked up the broken handle of the basket and jabbed his instep, which made him yell so loudly that all the hidden population of the kitchens came out like disturbed animals, holding in their hands the implements of the tasks upon which they had been engaged.

'*Vouz payez! Vous payez tout! Oui, oui, vous payez,*' the proprietor shouted.

The intensity of his anger made his veins swell and his nose bleed, and not being able to find a handkerchief he began to bellow for the attentions of his staff. This seemed an appropriate moment for the waiter to get himself back into his master's good graces, and with a towel in one hand and a chamber-pot in the other he came running out of the room where he had been hiding. At the sight of more china the proprietor uttered a stupendous Roumanian oath and kicked the pot out of the waiter's hand with such force that a piece of it flew up and cut his cheek. Sylvia left a momentarily increasing concourse of servants chattering round their master and the man, each of whom was stanching blood with his own end of the towel they held between them: they were all shovelling aside bits of china while they talked, so that they seemed like noisy hens scratching in a garden.

Queenie was standing with big frightened eyes when Sylvia got back to their room.

'Whatever was happening?'

'An argument over our dinner,' Sylvia laughed.

Then suddenly she began to cry, because at such a moment the loss of the cakes was truly a disaster and the thought of Queenie alone without food waiting here for her return from Bucharest was too much after the strain of the afternoon. She caught the child to her heart and told the story of what had happened with Florilor.

'Now do you understand?' she asked fiercely. 'Now do you understand how much I want you never – but never never again – even so much as to think of the possibility of selling yourself to a man? You must always remember when the temptation comes what I was ready to do to prevent such a horror. You must always believe that I am your friend and that if the war goes on for twenty years I will never leave you. You *shall* come back to England with me. With the money that I'm going to borrow in Bucharest we'll get as far as Greece anyway. But whatever happens I will never leave you, child, because I bear on my heart the stigmata of what I was ready to do for you.'

'I was not understanding much of what you are talking,' Queenie sighed.

'There is only one thing to understand – that I love you. You see this golden bag? The man who gave it to me left inside it a part of his soul; and if he has been killed, if he is lying at this moment a dreadful and disfigured corpse, what does it matter? He lives for ever with me here. He walks beside me always, because he obeyed the instinct of pure love. For you I was ready to do an action to account for which when I search deep down into myself I can find no motive but love. You must remember that and let the memory of that walk beside you always. Let me go on talking to you. You need not understand anything except that I love you and I must not lose you. I shall be thinking of you to-morrow when I'm in Bucharest, and I shall eat nothing all day, because I could not eat while you are waiting here hungry. It won't be for long. I shall be back to-morrow night with money. You don't mind my leaving you? And promise me, promise me that you won't unlock your door for a moment. Don't let that horrible youth have his way when I'm gone for the sake of a lunch. You won't, will you? Promise me, promise me.'

'Of course I would never do anything with him,' Queenie said.

Sylvia held up the ten-franc piece.

'Isn't it a wonderful little coin?' she laughed. 'It will take us so far from here. Once when I was a very small girl I found just such another.'

'You were being a small girl long ago,' Queenie exclaimed. 'Fancy! I was always forgetting that anybody else except me was ever being small.'

'What a lonely world she lives in,' Sylvia thought. 'She is conscious of nothing but herself, which is what makes her desire to be English such a tragedy, because she is feeling all the time that she has no real existence. She is like a ghost haunting the earth with incommunicable desires.'

Sylvia passed away the supperless evening for Queenie by telling her stories about her own childhood, trying to instil into her some apprehension of the continuity of existence, trying to populate the great voids stretching between her thoughts that so terrified her with the idea of being lost. Queenie really had no conception of her own actuality, so that at times she became positively a doll dependent upon the imagination of another for her very life. In the present stage of her development she might be the plaything of men without suffering; but Sylvia was afraid that if she again exposed her to the liability by deserting her at this point, Queenie might one day suddenly wake up to a sense of identity and find herself at the moment in a brothel. People always urged in defence of caging birds that if they were caged from the nest they did not suffer. Yet it was hard to imagine anything more lamentable than the celestial dreams of a lark that never had flown. Sylvia knew that at last she had been able to frame clearly the fear she had for Queenie; it lent new strength to her purpose. The horror of the brothel had become an obsession ever since earlier in the year she had passed by a vast and gloomy building which seemed a prison, but which she had been told was the recognized pleasure-house of soldiers. In this building behind high walls were two hundred women, most of whom in a Catholic country would have been cherished as penitents by nuns. Instead of that they were doomed to expiate their first fault by serving the State and slaking the lust of soldiers at the rate of a franc or a franc and a half. These women were fed by the State; they were examined daily by State doctors; everybody agreed that such forethought by the State was laudable. People who protested against such a debasement of womanhood were regarded as sentimentalists: so were people who believed in hell.

'This Promethean morality that enchains the world and sets its bureaucratic eagle to gnaw the vitals of humanity,' Sylvia cried. 'Prometheus himself was surely only another personification of Satan, and this is his infernal revenge for what he suffered in the Caucasus. The future of the race! Or is my point of view distorted and am I wrong in mocking at the future of the majority? No, no, it cannot be right to secure the many by debasing the few. Am I being Promethean myself in trying to keep hold of you, Queenie? You came back into my life at such a moment that I feel as if you were a part of myself. Yet I can't help divining that there's a weakness in my logic somewhere.'

The next morning Sylvia went to Bucharest. She did not remember until she was in the train that it was Sunday; but the passport-office was open and Mr. Mathers was at work as usual. She asked if Mr. Iredale was too busy to see her.

'Mr. Iredale?' the clerk repeated. 'I'm sorry to say that Mr. Iredale's dead.'

Sylvia stared at him; for a moment the words had no more meaning than a conventional excuse to unwelcome visitors.

'But how can he be dead?' she exclaimed.

'I'm sorry to say that he died very suddenly. In fact he was taken ill almost immediately after you were here last. It was a stroke. He never recovered consciousness. Mr. Abernethy is in charge temporarily. If you're anxious about your visa, I'm sure Mr. Abernethy will do everything in his power – subject of course to the regulations. Oh certainly yes, everything in his power.'

Mr. Mathers tried by the tone of his voice to convey that, though his late chief was dead, he could not forget the length of the interview he had granted to Sylvia and that the present rulers of the office would pay a tribute to the dead by treating her with equal condescension.

'No, I wanted to see Mr. Iredale privately.'

The clerk sighed his sympathy with her position in face of the unattainable.

'Perhaps I shall be wanting a visa presently,' she added.

The clerk brightened. Sylvia fancied that in the remote and happy days before the war he must have had experience of the counter. He had offered her the prospect of obtaining a visa instead of seeing Philip again much as a shop assistant might offer one shade of ribbon in the place of another no longer in stock.

Sylvia left the passport-office and without paying any heed in what direction she walked she came to the Cimisgiu Gardens and sat down upon a seat beside the ornamental lake. It was a hot morning, and there was enough mist in the atmosphere to blur the outlines of material objects and to set upon the buildings of the city a charm of distance that was as near as Bucharest ever approximated to the mellowing of time. The shock of the news that she had just heard, coming on top of the fatigue caused by her journey without even a cup of coffee to sustain her body, blurred the outlines of her mental attitude and made her glad of the fainting landscape that accorded with her mood and did not jar upon her with the turmoil of a world insistently, almost wantonly alive.

So Philip was dead. Sylvia tried to imagine how the news of his death would have affected her, if he had not lately re-entered her life. Poor

Philip! Death out here seemed to crown the pathos of his position, had she wished that she had not parted from him so abruptly, that she had not tried so hard to make him aware of his incongruity in Bucharest, and now most of all that she had let him talk, as he had wanted to talk, about their life together. If she had only known that he was near to death she should have told him of her gratitude for much that he had done for her; had he lived to hear the request that she had been going to make him this morning, she was sure that he would have taken pleasure in his ability to be of use once more. She had been wrong to blame him for his attitude toward Queenie. After all, his experiment with herself had not encouraged him to make other experiments in the direction of obeying impulses that took him off the lines he had laid down for his progress through life. She was really the last person who should have asked him to forgo another convention in favour of a girl like Queenie. How had he been paid for marrying a child whom he had met casually in a London cemetery? Very ill, he might consider. Poor Philip! Early next month it would be the fifteenth anniversary of their marriage. He had never known how to manage her; yet how preposterous it should have been to expect anything else. The more Sylvia meditated upon their marriage, the more she felt inclined to blame herself for its collapse; and in her present state of weakness the thought that it was now for ever too late to tell Philip how sorry she was fretted her with the poignancy of missed opportunity. Beneath that weight of pedagogic ashes there had always been the glow of humanity; if only she could have fanned it to a flame before she left Bucharest by giving him the chance of feeling that he was helping her! Yet she had regarded the favour she was about to ask as such an humiliation that almost she had been inclined to put it on the same level of self-sacrifice as the offer of herself to that Roumanian youth. Now that she had failed with both her self-imposed resolves, how easy it was to see the difference in their degree! Her appeal to Philip would have been the just payment she owed him for that letter she wrote when she ran away; it would have washed out that callow piece of cruelty. But Philip was dead, and the relation between them must remain eternally unadjusted.

In meditating upon her married life and in conjuring scenes that had long been tossed aside into the lumber room of imagination, Sylvia's spirit wandered again in the green English country and forgot its exile. The warmth and mystery of the autumnal air drowsed all urgency with dreams of the past; for a minute or two she actually slept. She was disturbed by the voices of passing children, and she woke up with a shiver to the imperative and tormenting facts of the present – to the complete lack of money, to the thought of Queenie waiting hungry in Avereshti, and to Roumania clouding with the fog of war.

'What on earth am I going to do?' she murmured. 'I must sell my bag.'

The decision seemed to be made from without; it was like the voice of a wraith that had long been waiting incapable of speech, and involuntarily she turned round as if she could catch the spirit in the act of interfering with her affairs.

'Were I a natural liar, I should vow it was a ghost and frame the episode of Philip's death with a supernatural decoration. How many people who have penetrated to the ultimate confines of themselves have preferred to perceive the supernatural and in doing so destroyed the whole value of their discovery! Yet lying is the first qualification of every explorer.'

But setting aside considerations of the subconscious self, Sylvia was for a while horrified at the damnable clarity with which her course of action presented itself. There was no possible argument against selling the bag, and yet to sell it would demand a greater sacrifice than borrowing money from Philip or selling herself to Florilor. The fact that during all this time of strain the idea had never suggested itself before showed to what depths of her being it had been necessary to pierce before she could contemplate the action. Her feeling for the bag far transcended anything in the nature of sentiment; without blasphemy she could affirm that she would as soon have attributed her sense of God in the sacrifice of the Mass to sentiment. But without incurring an imputation of idolatry by such a comparison she could at least award the bag as much value as devout women awarded a wedding-ring; for this golden bag positively was the outward sign that she had affirmed her belief in human love. In whatever tirades she might indulge against the natural depravity of man when confronted by the evidence of it so repeatedly as lately she had been, this bag was a continual reminder of his potential nobility. Certainly a critic of her extravagant reverence might urge that the value of the bag was created by the man who gave it and that any transference of such an emotion to a natural object was nothing but a surrender to sentiment which involved her in the common fault of seeking to express the eternal in terms of the temporal. But certain acts of worship lay outside the destructive logic of an unmoved critic; the circumstances in which the gift had been made were exceptional and her attitude towards it must remain equally exceptional. And now it must go; its talismanic and sacramental power must rest unappreciated in the hands of another. Yet in selling the bag was she not giving final and practical expression to the impulse of the donor? He had told her when she had protested against his generosity that before he was lost in the war his money would be better spent in giving someone something that was desired than in gambling it all away. Equally now would he not say to her that the money was better spent in helping a Queenie than in serving as a symbol rather than as an instrument of love? Or was the intrusion of Queenie into this intimacy of personal communion a kind of sacrilege? The soldier had never intended the bag to acquire any redemptive signification; he had merely chosen Sylvia by chance as the vehicle of one of those acts of sacred egotism which illuminate the Divine purpose. It was not to be supposed that the woman with the cruse of ointment was actuated by anything except self-expression, which was precisely what gave her impulse value as an act of worship. The commonplace and utilitarian point of view on that occasion was perfectly expressed by Judas.

'And my own point of view about Queenie is not in the least altruistic. I want to give her something of which I have more than my fair share. I am burdened with an overflowing sense of existence. I have attached Queenie to myself and assumed a responsibility for her in exactly the same way as if I had brought a child into the world. There is no false redemptionism about the mother's relation to her child: there is merely a passion to bequeath to the child the sum of her own experience. My feeling about Queenie partakes of the passionate guardianship with which a loose woman so often shields her child. Certainly I must sell the bag. Who knows what chain of good may not weave itself from that soldier's action? To me he gave an imperishable store of love at the very moment when without the assurance of love my faith must have withered. I in turn give all that I can give to balance Queenie's life in the way I think it should be balanced. The next purchaser of the bag may, I should like to think without superstition, inherit with it a sacramental of love that will carry on the influence. And the one who first gave it to me? That almond-eyed soldier swept like a grain of chaff before the winnowing-fan of war? At this very moment perhaps the bullet has struck him. He has fallen. His company presses forward or is pressed back. He will lie rotting for days between earth and sky, and when at last they come to bury him they will laugh at the poor scarecrow that was a man. They will speculate neither whence he came nor who may weep for him; but his reward will be in his handiwork, for he will have shown love to a woman and he will have died for his country; such men like stars may light a very little of the world's darkness, but they proclaim the mysteries of God.'

With all her conviction that she was right in selling the bag, it was with a heavy heart that Sylvia left the Cimisgiu Gardens to seek a jeweller's shop; when she found that all the shops were shut except those open for the incidental amusements of the Sunday holiday, she nearly abandoned in relief the idea of selling the bag in order to go back to Avereshti and trust to fate for a way out of her difficulties. On reflection, however, she admitted the levity of such behaviour, if she wished to regard her struggle as worth anything at all, and she sharply brought herself back to the gravity of the position by reminding herself that it was she who had lost the five hundred francs, a piece of carelessness that was the occasion if not the cause of what had happened afterwards. If anything was to be left to hazard, it must be Queenie to-night alone in that hotel; besides, if further argument were necessary, there was not enough change from the ten francs to get back. Sylvia had promised Queenie that she would not eat until she saw her again, but she had not counted upon the effect of this long day to be followed by another long day to-morrow. How much money had she? Three francs twenty-five. Oh, she must eat; and she must also send a telegram to Queenie. Otherwise the child might do anything. But she *must* eat; and suddenly she found herself sitting at a table outside a café with a waiter standing by on tiptoe for her commands. The coffee tasted incredibly delicious, but the moment she had finished it she was overcome by a sensation of nausea and pierced by remorse for her weakness in giving way. She left the café and went to the post-office, where she spent all that was left of her money in a long telegram of exhortation and encouragement to Queenie.

The problem of how to pass the rest of the day weighed upon her. She did not want to meet any of the girls at the Trianon; she did not want to meet anybody she knew until she could meet them with money in her pocket. To-night she would stay at their old hotel in Bucharest; she would say that she had missed the train back to Avereshti, if they wondered at the absence of luggage. Oh, but what did it matter if they did wonder? It was her sensitiveness to such trifles as these that brought home to Sylvia how much the strain of the last week had told upon her. Walking aimlessly along, she found herself near the little mission church and turned aside to enter it. At such an early hour of the afternoon the church was empty, and the incense of the morning mass was still pungent. There was the same sort of atmosphere that exists in a theatre between a matinée and an evening performance; the emotion of the departed worshippers was mingled with the expectation of more worshippers to come. Sylvia sat contemplating the images and wondering about the appeal they could make. She tried to put herself in the position of the humble and faithful soul that could derive consolation and help from praying before that tawdry image of the Sacred Heart. She wished that she could be given the mentality of a poor Italian girl whose sense of awe was so easily satisfied and could behold those flames of cheap gold paint around the Heart burning like the eyes of Seraphim.

'Yet after all,' she thought, 'are we superior people, who suppose that such representations hurt the majesty of God, any nearer to Him with our equally pretentious theories of His manifestation? What in the ultimate sum of this world's history, when the world itself hangs in the sky like a poor burnt-out moon, will mark the difference between the greatest philosopher with his words and the most degraded savage with his idols? And am I with my perception of God's love in a golden bag less hopelessly material than the poor Italian girl who bows before that painted heart?'

The influence of the church began to penetrate Sylvia's mind with a tranquillizing assurance of continuity, or rather with the assurance of silent and universal forces undisturbed by war. The sense of the individual's extinction in the strife of herd with herd had been bound to affect her very deeply, coming as it did at a time when she had once again challenged life as an individual by refusing any co-operation with the past.

'The worst of feeling regenerated,' she thought, 'is that such an emotion or condition of mind implies the destruction of all former experience. Of course, former experience must still produce its effect unconsciously; but one is too sensible of trying to bring the past into positively the same purified state as the present. When I was thinking about Philip this morning and re-living bygone moments, I was all the time applying to them standards which I have only possessed for about a year. Certainly I perceive that what I call my regeneration must be the fruit of past experience – otherwise the description would be meaningless – but it is the fruit of individual experience ripening at the very moment when individual experience counts for less than it has ever counted since the beginning of the world. Had I always been a social and political animal the idea of the war would not have preyed on my mind as it does; I should have been educated up to the point of expecting it. I remember when I was first told in the Petrograd hospital that a war had broken out what a trifling impression the news made compared with my own discovery of the change in myself. Gradually during this past year I have found at every turn my new progress barred by the war. My individual efforts perpetually shrink into insignificance before the war, and I am beginning to perceive, unless I can in some way fall into step with the rest of mankind, that what I considered progress is really the retreat of my personality along a disused bypath where I am expending all my energy in cutting away briers that were better left alone, at any rate at such a moment in history. Certainly one of the effects of an ordered religion is to restore the individual to the broad paths along which mankind is marching. An ordered religion is equally opposed either to short cuts or to cul-de-sacs, or to what by their impenetrability to the individual are equivalent to cul-de-sacs. My first instinct about Queenie was certainly right when I was anxious to entrust her to religion rather than to rely upon my personal influence. I think I must have lacked conviction in the way I approached the subject, I must have been timid and self-conscious; and the sceptical side of me that has just been wondering about the appeal of that image of the Sacred Heart may have defeated my purpose without my noticing its intrusion. I was all the time like a grown-up person who plays with children in order to get pleasure from their enjoyment rather than from his own.

'Yes, sitting here in this tawdry little church, I am beginning to make a few discoveries. I must positively lose the slightest consciousness of being superior to Queenie in any way whatsoever. Equally I must get over the slightest consciousness of being superior to any of the worshippers in this church. I must get over the habit of being injured by the monstrousness of this war until I have been personally injured by it in the course of sharing its woes with the rest of mankind. I have got to find an individualism that while it abates nothing of its unwillingness to be injured by the State is simultaneously always careful in its turn never to injure or impede the State, which from the individual's point of view must be regarded not as a state but as another individual. Presumably the chief function of an ordered religion is by acting through the individual to apply the sum of mankind's faith, hope, and love under the guidance of the Holy Ghost to the fulfilment of the Divine purpose. In such a way the self-perfection of the individual will create the self-perfection of the State, and oh, what a long time it will take! God is a great conservative; yet when He was incarnate He was a great radical. I wonder if I had ever had a real logical training or indeed any formal education at all whether I should be tossed about as I am from one paradox to another. The Church was significantly enough built upon Peter, not upon John nor upon Thomas; it was founded upon the most human of the apostles. If one might admit in God what in men would be called an afterthought, it might be permissible to look upon Paul as an afterthought to leaven some of the ponderousness of Peter's humanity. Anyway the point is that the paradoxes began in the very beginning, and it's quite obvious that I'm not going to help myself or anybody else by exposing myself to them rather than to the mighty moral, intellectual, and spiritual fabric into which they have all been absorbed or by which they have all been rejected.'

During Sylvia's meditation the church had gradually filled with worshippers to receive the Benediction of the Blessed Sacrament.

Generally, that strangely wistful concession to the pathetic side of human nature had not made a deep appeal to Sylvia's instinct for worship; but this afternoon the bravery of self had fallen from her. For the first time she felt in all its force – not merely apprehending it as a vague discomfort – the utter desolation of the soul without God. In such a state of mind faith shrank to infatuate speculation, hope swelled to arrogance, and even love shivered in a chill and viewless futility, until the mystical sympathy of other souls, the humblest of whom was a secret only known to God, led her to identify herself with them and to cry with them:

> *O salutaris Hostia,*
> *Quæ cœli pandis ostium:*
> *Bella premunt hostilia,*
> *Da robur, fer, auxilium.*

They were very poor people, these Albanians and Italians who knelt round her in this church; and Sylvia bowed before the thought that all over the world in all the warring nations somewhere about this hour poor people were crying out to God the same words in the same grave Latin. The helplessness of humanity raged through her like a strong wind, and her self-reliance became as the dust that was scattered before it. When the priest held the monstrance aloft, and gave the Benediction, it seemed that the wind died away; upon her soul the company of God was shed like a gentle rain, which left behind it faith blossoming like a flower, and hope singing like a bird, and above them both love shining like a sun.

Sylvia went out of the church that afternoon with a sense of having been personally comforted; she was intensely aware of having made more spiritual progress in the last hour than in all the year that had gone by since the first revelation of God.

'Without Him I am nothing, I am nothing, I am nothing,' she murmured.

That evening – an evening that she had dreaded indescribably – she sat by the window of her bedroom, happier than she could remember that she had ever been; when the chambermaid on her way to bed came to ask her if she wanted anything, Sylvia nearly kissed her in order that perhaps so she might express a little of her love towards all those who in this world serve.

'For such a girl with the eyes of a nymph to be serving you and for you to have presumed to consider yourself above all service that did not gratify your egotism,' she exclaimed aloud to her reflection in the glass.

The next morning Sylvia sold her golden bag for fifteen hundred francs. On the way to the station she felt very faint, and finding when she arrived that she would have to wait an hour for the train to Avereshti she drank some coffee. She told herself that it was only the weakness caused by fasting which made her regard so seriously this second breach of her promise to Queenie; nevertheless nothing could put out of her head the superstitious dread that the surrender caused her. The drinking of coffee while her friend was still hungry took on a significance quite out of proportion to what it actually possessed; she felt like the heroine of a fairy story who disobeys the warnings of her fairy godmother. While she was waiting in the *salle d'attente* and reproaching herself for what she had done, she heard a familiar voice behind her and looking round saw Philidor in uniform. He was travelling to Bralatz on military duty, and she was glad of his company as far as Avereshti, for all sorts of fears about what might have happened to Queenie during her absence were assailing her fancy. Philidor was surprised to find her still in Roumania and spoke seriously to her about the necessity of leaving at once if she did not want to travel home by Russia.

'You must get away. No one knows what may happen in the Balkans presently. You must get within sight of the sea. You English are lost away from the sea. I assure you that Bulgaria will come in soon. There is no doubt of it. I cannot understand the madness of your English politicians in making speeches to deceive everybody that the mobilization is in self-defence. It is in self-defence, but not on the side of the Entente. You have been poisoned in England by the criminal stupidity of the Englishmen who come out here and see reflected in the eyes of the Bulgarian peasant their own liberal ideals. It is a tradition inherited from your Gladstone. To us out here such density of vision is incomprehensible. The Bulgarian is the Prussian of the Balkans: he is a product of uncompromising materialism. One of your chief Bulgarian propagandists was shot in the jaw the other day; it was a good place to wound him, but it's a pity he wasn't hit there before he did so much harm with his activities. We in Roumania were blamed by idealistic politicians for the way we stabbed Bulgaria in the back in 1913: you might as well blame a man for shooting at a slightly injured wild beast. You have always been too sporting in England, as you say; and not even war with Germany seems to have cured you of it. The Austrians are preparing to invade Serbia, and this time there will be no mistake. Get out of Roumania and get through Bulgaria before the carnage begins.'

The conviction with which he spoke gave Sylvia a thrill; for the first time the active side of the war seemed to be approaching her.

'And what is Roumania going to do?' she asked.

The young officer made a gesture of bewilderment.

'Who knows? Who knows? It will be a struggle between sentiment and expediency. I wish that the cry of the rights of small nations was not being so loudly shouted by the big nations. Battle cries are apt to die down when the battle is over. An idea that presents itself chiefly as a weapon of offence has little vitality; ideas, which are abstractions of liberty, do not like to be the slaves of other ideas. There is one idea in the world at this moment which overshadows all the rest – the idea of victory: the idea of the rights of small nations does not stand much chance against that. God fights on the side of the big battalions. Perhaps I'm too pessimistic. We shall see what happens in Serbia. But to put aside ideas for the moment, don't waste time in following my advice. You must leave Roumania now, if you want to leave at all. And I do not recommend you to stay. A woman like you following your profession should be in her own country in times of war. You are too much exposed to the malice of any private person, and in war justice like everything else is only regarded as a contribution to military efficiency.'

'You mean I might be denounced as a spy?'

'Anybody without protection may be denounced as a spy. Probably nothing would follow from it except expulsion, but expulsion would be unpleasant.'

'I wonder what is the fundamental reason for spymania,' said Sylvia. 'Is it due to cheap romanticism or a universal sense of guilt? Or is it the opportunity for the first time to give effect to vulgar gossip? I think it's the last probably. It must be very pleasant to glorify the meanest vice with the inspiration of a patriotic impulse.'

'I said that justice was subordinated to military efficiency.'

'Yes, and even slander has a temporary commission and is dressed up in a romantic uniform and armed with anonymous letters. Bullets are not the only things with long noses.'

'I suppose you can get away? You have money?' Philidor asked.

'Oh, I'm rich,' she declared.

'And your little friend, how is she?'

'She's waiting for me at Avereshti.'

Sylvia gave an account of her adventures, and Philidor shook his head.

'But it has all ended satisfactorily,' he said.

'I hope so.'

'It only shows how right I was to warn you of the spy danger – the double danger of being made the victim of a genuine agent and the risk of a frivolous accusation. You may be sure that now when you go back to the hotel with money, you will be accused everywhere of being a spy. If you have any trouble telegraph to me at Bralatz. Here's my address.'

'And here's Avereshti,' Sylvia said. 'Good-bye and good luck. *Et vive la Roumanie!*'

She waved her hand to him and walked quickly from the station to the hotel. It was good to see the waiter on the threshold and to be conscious of being able to rule him with the prospect of a tip. How second-rate the hotel looked, with money in one's pocket! How obsequiously it seemed to beg one's patronage! There was not a single window that did not have the air of cringing to the new arrival.

'Lunch for two at once,' Sylvia cried, flinging him a twenty-franc note.

'For two?' the waiter repeated.

'For myself and Mademoiselle Walters – my friend upstairs,' she added, when the waiter stared first at her and then at the money. 'What's the matter? Is she ill? *Cretin*, if she's ill you and your master shall pay.'

'The lady who was staying here with madame left this morning with a gentleman.'

'*Crapule, tu mens!*'

'Madame may look for herself. The room is empty.'

Sylvia caught the waiter by the throat and shook him.

'You lie! You lie! Confess that you are lying. She was starved by you. She has died, and you are pretending that she has gone away.'

She threw the waiter from her, and ran upstairs. Her own luggage was still in the room; of Queenie's nothing remained except a few pieces of pink tissue-paper trembling faintly in the draught. Sylvia rang the bell, but before anyone could answer her summons she had fainted.

When she came to herself her first action – an action that seemed when afterwards she thought about it to mark well the depths of her disillusionment – was to feel for her money lest she might have been robbed during her unconsciousness. The wad of notes had not shrunk; the waiter was looking at her with all the sympathy that could be bought for twenty francs; a blowsy chambermaid dragged for the operation from a coal-cellar to judge by her appearance was sprinkling water over her.

'What was the man like?' she murmured.

The waiter bustled forward.

'A tall gentleman. He left no name. He said he brought a message. He paid a few little items on the bill that were not paid by madame. They took the train for Bucharest. Mademoiselle was looking ill.'

Sylvia mustered all that will of hers, which lately had been tried hardly enough, to obliterate Queenie and everything that concerned Queenie from her consciousness. She fought down each superstitious reproach for not having kept her word by drinking the coffee in Bucharest: she drove forth from her mind every speculation about Queenie's future: she dried up every regret for any carelessness in the past.

'Clear away all this paper, please,' she told the chambermaid; then she asked the waiter for the menu.

He dusted the grimy card and handed it to her.

'*J'ai tellement faim*,' said Sylvia. '*Que je saurais manger même toi sans beurre.*'

The waiter inclined his head respectfully as if he would intimate his willingness to be eaten; but he tempered his assent with a smile to show that he was sensible that the sacrifice would not be exacted.

'And the wine?' he asked.

She chose half-a-bottle of the best native wine; and the waiter hurried away like a lame rook.

After lunch Sylvia carefully packed her things and put all her professional dresses away at the bottom of her large trunk. In the course of packing, the golden shawl that contained the records of her ancestry was left out of the trunk by accident, and she put it in the valise, which so far on her journeys she had always managed to keep with her. Philidor's solemn warning about the political situation in the Balkans had made an impression, and thinking it was possible that she might have to abandon her trunk at any moment she was glad of the oversight that had led her to making this change; though if she had been asked to give a reason for paying any heed to the shawl now she would have found it difficult. When she had finished her packing she sat down and wrote a letter to Olive.

HOTEL MOLDAVIA,
AVERESHTI,
Sept. 27, 1915

My darling Olive,

This is not a communication from the other world as you might very well think. It's Sylvia herself writing to you from Roumania with a good deal of penitence, but still very much the same Sylvia. I'm not going to ask you for your news, because by the time you get this you may quite easily have got me with it. At any rate you can expect me almost on top. I shall telegraph when I reach France, if telegrams haven't been made a capital offence by that time. I've wondered dreadfully about you and Jack. I've a feeling the dear old boy is in Flanders or likely soon to go there. Dearest thing, I need not tell you that though I've not written I've thought terribly about you both during all this ghastly time. And the dear babies! I'm longing to see them. If I started to tell you my adventures I shouldn't know where to stop, so I won't begin. But I'm

507

very well. Give my love to anybody you see who remembers your long lost Sylvia.

How colourless the letter was, she thought, on reading it through. It gave as little indication of herself as an electric bell gives of the character of a guest when he is waiting on the doorstep. But it would serve its purpose like the bell to secure attention.

Sylvia intended to leave Avereshti that evening, but feeling tired she lay down upon her bed and fell fast asleep. She was woken up three hours later by the waiter, who announced with an air of excitement that Mr. Porter had arrived at the hotel and was intending to spend the night.

'What of it?' she said coldly. 'I'm leaving by the nine o'clock train for Bucharest.'

'Oh, but Mr. Porter will invite you to dinner.'

'Who is Mr. Porter?'

'He's one of the richest men in Roumania. He is the head of many big petroleum companies. I told him that there was an English lady staying with us, and he was delighted. You can't leave to-night. Mr. Porter will never forgive us.'

'Look here. Is this Florilor the Second?'

The waiter held up his hands in protest.

'Ah, no, madame! This is an Englishman. He could buy up M. Florilor ten times over. Shall I say that madame will be delighted to drink a cocka-taila with him?'

'Get out,' said Sylvia, pointing to the door.

But afterwards she felt disinclined to make a journey that night, and notwithstanding Philidor's urgency she decided to waste one night more in Avereshti. Moreover, the notion of meeting an Englishman was not so dull after all. Ten minutes later, she strolled downstairs to have a look at him.

Mr. Porter was a stout man of about sixty, who was sometimes rather like Mr. Pickwick in appearance, but generally bore a greater resemblance to Tweedledum. He was dressed in a well-cut suit of pepper and salt check and wore a glossy collar with a full black cravat, in which a fine diamond twinkled modestly; a clear somewhat florid face with that priestly glimmer of a very close shave, well-brushed boots, white spats, and a positive impression of having clean cuffs completed a figure that exhaled all the more prosperity and cheerfulness because the background of the hotel was so unsuitable.

'Going to introduce myself. Ha-ha! Apsley Porter's my name. Well known hereabouts. Ha-ha! Didn't expect to meet a compatriot in these times at Avereshti. Ugly little hole. Business before pleasure, though, by George, I don't see why pleasure should be left out in the cold altogether. What are you going to have? Ordered a Martini here the other day. "What's that?" I said to the scoundrel who served it. "Martini? Pah! Almost as dangerous as a Martini-Henry," I said. Ha-ha-ha-ha! But of course the blackguard didn't understand me. Going to have dinner with me, I hope? I've ordered a few special dishes. Always bring my own champagne with me in case of accidents. I forced them to get ice here though. Ha-ha! By George I did. I said that if there wasn't ice whenever I came I should close down one of the principal wells I control. Did I tell you my name? Ah, glad I did. I've got a deuced bad habit of talking away without introducing myself. Here comes the villain with your cocktail. You must gin and bear it. What? Ha-ha-ha-ha-ha-ha-ha!'

Sylvia liked Mr. Porter and accepted his invitation to dinner. He was distressed to hear that a friend had been staying with her in the hotel so recently as this morning and that he had had the bad luck to miss entertaining her.

'What, another little Englishwoman in Avereshti? By George, what a pity I didn't turn up yesterday! I shan't forgive myself. Come along, waiter. Hurry up with that champagne. Fancy! Another jolly little Englishwoman and I missed her. Too bad!'

There was irony in meeting upon the vigil of her return to England this Englishman redolent of the Monico. Sylvia had spent so much of her time intimately with people at the other pole of pleasure that she had forgotten how to talk to this type and could only respond with monosyllables to his boisterous assaults upon the present. He was so much like a fine afternoon in London that she sunned herself as it were in his effluence and let her senses occupy themselves with the noise of the traffic, as if she had suddenly been transplanted to the Strand and was finding the experience immediately on top of Avereshti pleasant, but rather bewildering. And now he was talking about the war.

'Nothing to worry about. Nothing to worry about at all. Pity about the Dardanelles. Great pity, but we had no luck. They are making a great fuss here over this coming Austrian attack upon Serbia. Don't believe in it. Shan't believe in it until it happens. But it won't happen, and if it does happen – waiter, where's that champagne? – if it does happen, it won't alter the course of the war. Not a bit of it. I'm an optimist. And in times like these I consider that optimism is of as much use to my country at my age as a rifle would have been if I were a younger man. Pessimism in times like these is a poison.'

'But isn't optimism apt to be an intoxicant?' Sylvia suggested.

She felt inclined to impress upon Mr. Porter the difference between facing misfortune with money and without it, and she told him a few of her adventures in the past year, winding up with an account of the behaviour of the proprietor of this very hotel.

'You don't mean to say old Andrescu refused to serve you with anything to eat?'

The notion seemed to shake Mr. Porter to the depths of his being.

'Why, I never heard anything like it. Waiter, go and tell M. Andrescu to come and speak to me at once. I shall give him a piece of my mind.'

The jovial curves of his face had all hardened: his bright little eyes were like steel: even the dimple in his chin had disappeared in the contraction of his mouth. When Andrescu came in, he began to abuse him in rapid Roumanian, while his complexion turned from pink to crimson, and from crimson in waves of colour to an uniform purple. In the end he stopped talking for a moment, and the proprietor begged Sylvia's intercession.

'That's the way to deal with rascally hotel-keepers,' said Mr. Porter, fanning himself with a red and yellow bandana handkerchief and drinking two glasses of champagne.

'What annoyed me most of all,' he added, 'was that his behaviour should have made me miss the chance of asking another jolly little English girl to dinner. Too bad!'

Sylvia had not told him more than the bare outlines of the story; she had not confided in him about Florilor or the sale of her bag or the fact that she had lost Queenie for ever. Her tale could have seemed not much more than a tale of temporary inconvenience, and she was therefore only amused when Mr. Porter deduced from it as the most important result his own failure to entertain Queenie.

After dinner she and her host sat talking for awhile, or rather she sat listening to his narratives of holidays spent in England, which evidently appealed to him as a much more vital part of his career than his success in the Roumanian oilfields. When about eleven o'clock she got up to take her leave and go to bed, he expressed his profound dismay at the notion of thus breaking up a jolly evening.

'Tell you what we'll do,' he announced. 'We'll make a night of it. We will, by George we will. A night of it. We'll have half-a-dozen bottles put on ice and take them up to my room. I can talk all night on champagne. Now don't say no. It's a patriotic duty, by George it's a patriotic duty when two English people meet in a god-forsaken place like this, it's a patriotic duty to make a night of it. Eat and drink to-day, for to-morrow we die.'

Sylvia was feeling weary enough, but the fatuous talk had cheered her by its sheer inanity, and the thought of going to bed in that haunted room – her will was strong, but the memory of what she had endured for Queenie was not entirely quenched – and of perhaps not being able to sleep was too dismal. She might just as well help this amiable old buffoon's illusion that champagne was the elixir of eternal life and that pleasure was nothing but laughing loudly enough.

'All right,' said Sylvia. 'But I'd rather we made the night of it in my room. I'll get into a wrapper and make myself comfortable, and when dawn breaks I can tumble into bed.'

Mr. Porter hesitated a moment.

'Right you are, my dear girl. Of course. Waiter! Where's the ruffian hidden himself?'

'I'll leave you to make the arrangements. I shall be ready in about a quarter of an hour,' Sylvia said.

She left him and went upstairs.

'I believe the silly old fool thought I was making overtures to him when I suggested we should make merry in my room,' she laughed to herself. 'Oh dear, it shows how much one can tell and how little of oneself need be revealed in the telling of it. Stupid old ass! But rather pleasant in a way. He's like finding an old Christmas number of the *Graphic* – coloured heartiness, conventional mirth, reality mercifully absent, and O *mihi præteritos* printed in Gothic capitals on the cover. I suppose these pre-war figures still abound in England. And I'm not sure he isn't right in believing that his outlook on life is worth preserving as long as possible. Timbered houses, crusted port, and Dickens are nearer to fairyland than anything else that's left nowadays. To what old age will this blackened, mutilated, and agonized generation grow? Efficiency and progress have not spared the monuments of bygone art except to imprison them in libraries, museums, and iron-railings. Will it spare the Englishman? Or will the generations of a century hence read of him only, and murmur "This was a Man." Will they praise him as the last and noblest individual, turning with repulsion and remorse from the sight of themselves and their fellows, the product of the triumphant herd eternally sowing where it does not reap? Night thoughts of the young on perceiving a relic of insular grandeur in an exceptionally fine state of preservation – preserved in oil! And here he comes to interrupt my sad soliloquy.'

The night passed away just as the evening had passed away. Mr. Porter sustained his joviality in a fashion that would have astounded Sylvia, if all capacity for being astounded had not been exhausted in watching him drink champagne. It was incredible not so much that his head could withstand the fumes as that his body, fat though it was, should be expansive enough to contain the cubic quantity of liquor. It was four o'clock before he had finished the last drop, and was shaking Sylvia's hand in cordial farewell.

'Haven't enjoyed an evening so much for months. By George, I haven't. Ha-ha-ha! Well, you'll forgive an old man – always accuse myself of being old when the wine is low, but I shall be as young as a chicken again after three hours' sleep – you'll excuse an old man. Little present probably damned useful in these hard times. Ha-ha-ha! Under your pillow. Good girl. Never made me feel an old man by expecting me to make love. I've often set out to make a night of it, and only succeeded in making a damned fool of myself. Sixty-four next month. Youth's the time! Ha-ha-ha. Good-bye. God bless you. Shan't see you in the morning. By George! I *shall* have a busy day.'

He shook her warmly by the hand, avoided the ice-stand with a grave bow, and left her with a smell of cigar-smoke. Under the pillow she found four five-hundred franc notes.

'Really,' Sylvia exclaimed. 'I might be excused for thinking myself a leading character in a farce by fate. I fail to make a halfpenny by offering myself when the necessity is urgent and make two thousand francs by not embarrassing an old gentleman's impotence. Meanwhile, it's too late – it's just too late. But I shall be able to buy back my golden bag. I suppose fate thinks that's as good a curtain as I'm entitled to in a farce.'

Sylvia left Avereshti next morning with a profound conviction that whatever the future held nothing should induce her to put foot in that town again. There was some satisfaction in achieving even so much sense of finality, negative though the achievement might be.

'I don't advise you to go to Dedeagatch,' said Mr. Mathers when Sylvia presented herself at the passport-office for the recommendation for a visa. 'I may tell you in confidence that the situation in Bulgaria is very grave – very grave indeed. Anything may happen this week. The feeling here is very tense too. If you are determined to take the risk of being held up in Bulgaria, I counsel you to travel by Rustchuk, Gorna Orechovitza, and Sofia to Nish. From Nish you'll get down to Salonika, and from there to the Piræus. At the same time I strongly advise you to keep away from Bulgaria. With the mobilization, passenger traffic is liable to be very uncertain.'

'But if I go back through Russia I may find it just as hard to get back to England. No, no. I'll risk Bulgaria. To-day's Tuesday the 28th. When can I have my visa?'

'Well, strictly speaking it's already too late to-day to entertain applications, but as you were a friend of Mr. Iredale, I'll ask Mr. Abernethy to put it through for you. If you come in to-morrow morning at ten, I will give you a letter for the Consulate. There will be the usual fee to pay there. Oh dear me, you haven't brought the four photographs that are necessary. I must have them, I'm afraid. Two for us, one for the Consulate, and one for the French authorities. The Italians don't insist upon a photograph at present. I'm afraid I shan't be able to put it through for you to-day. The French are very strict and insist on a minimum of four days. But in view of the Bulgarian crisis I'll get them to relax the rule. Luckily one of the French officers is a friend of mine – a very nice fellow.'

Three days elapsed before Sylvia was finally equipped with her passport *visé* for Bulgaria, Serbia, Greece, Italy, France, and England. The representatives of the first two nations, who seemed most immediately concerned with her journey, made the least bother; the representative of Italy, the nation that seemed least concerned with it, made the most.

While she was waiting for the result of the accumulated contemplation upon her age, her sex, her lineaments, and her past history, Sylvia bought back her gold bag for eighteen hundred francs, which left her with just over fifteen hundred francs for the journey – none too much, but she should no longer have any scruples in telegraphing to England for help if she found herself stranded.

On Friday afternoon she called for the last time at the passport-office to get a letter of introduction that Mr. Mathers had insisted on writing for her to a friend of his in the American Tobacco Company at Cavalla.

'You're not likely to go there,' he said, 'but if you do, it may be useful.'

The clerk handed her the letter, and there was something magnificently protective in the accompanying gesture; he might have been handing her a personal letter to the Prime Minister and giving her an assurance that the Foreign Secretary would personally meet her at Waterloo and see that she did not get into the wrong tube.

When Sylvia was leaving the office, Maud Moffat came in, at the sight of whom Mr. Mathers' spectacled benevolence turned to an aspect of hate for the whole of humanity.

'It's too late, madam, to-day. Nothing can be done until further enquiries have been made,' he said sharply.

'Too late be damned,' Maud shouted. 'I'm not going to be— about any longer. My passport's been stolen and I want another. I'm an honest English girl who's been earning her living on the continent and I want to go home and see my poor old mother. Perhaps you'll say next that I'm not English?'

'Nobody says that you're not English,' Mr. Mathers replied through set teeth. 'And please control your language.'

At this moment Maud recognized Sylvia.

'Oh, you've come back, have you? I suppose *you* didn't have any difficulty with *your* passport. Oh, no, people as frequents the company of German spies can get passports for nothing, but me who's travelled for seven years on the continent without ever having anyone give me so much as a funny look, me I repeat gets cross-examined and messed about as if I was a murderer instead of an artiste. Yes, war's a fine thing for some people,' she went on. 'Young fellows that ought to be fighting for their country instead of bullying poor girls from the other side of a table thoroughly enjoys *their*selves. Nice thing when an honest English girl – and not a German spy – can't mislay her passport without being—'

'I must repeat, madam,' Mr. Mathers interrupted, 'that the circumstances have to be gone into.'

'Circumstances? I'm in very good circumstances, thank you. But I shan't be if you keep me mucking about in Bucharest so as I forfeit my engagement at the White Tower, Saloniker. You'll look very funny, Mr. Nosey Parker, when my friend the Major who I know in Egypt and still writes to me lodges a complaint about your conduct. Why don't you ask this young lady about me? She knows I'm English.'

'I keep telling you that nobody questions your nationality.'

'Well, you've asked me enough questions. You know the size of my corsets and the colour of my chemise and how many moles I've got, and whether my grandmother was married and if it's true my uncle Bill ran away to Africa because he couldn't stand my aunt Jane's voice. Nationality! I reckon you couldn't think of any more questions, unless you became a medical student and started on my inside. Why don't you tell him you know all about me?' she added, turning to Sylvia.

'Because I don't,' Sylvia replied coldly.

'Well, there's a brazen-faced bitch!' Miss Moffat gasped.

Sylvia said good-bye hurriedly to Mr. Mathers and left him to Maud. When she was in the train on the way to Rustchuk, it suddenly struck her that Zozo might be able to explain the missing passport.

VI

The more Sylvia pondered the coincidence of Queenie's flight with the loss of Maud's passport, the more positive she became that Zozo had committed the theft. And with what object? It seemed unlikely that the passport could be altered plausibly enough to be accepted as Queenie's own property in these days when so much attention was being given to passports and their reputed owners. Probably he had only used it as a bait with which to lure her in the first instance; he would have known that she could not read and might have counted upon the lion and the unicorn to impress her with his ability to do something for her that Sylvia had failed to do. Queenie must have been in a state of discouragement through her not having come back to Avereshti on the Sunday evening, as she had promised. The telegram she sent had really been a mistake, because Queenie would never have asked anyone in the hotel to read it for her, and Zozo would assuredly have pretended whatever suited his purpose if by chance it had been shown to him.

At first Sylvia had been regretting that she had not divined sooner the explanation of Maud's missing passport, so that she could have warned Mr. Mathers; but now she was glad, because whatever Queenie did the blame must be shared by herself and the British regulations. She reproached herself for the attitude she had taken toward Queenie's disappearance; she had done nothing in these days at Bucharest to help the poor child, not even as much as to find out where she had gone. If Zozo were indeed a German agent, what might not be the result of that callousness? Yet after all he might not be anything of the kind; he might merely have been roused by her own opposition to regain possession of Queenie. Really it was difficult to say which explanation was more galling to her own conscience. However, it was useless to do anything now; there was as little probability of Queenie's being still in Bucharest as of her being anywhere else. If Zozo were in German pay he would find it easy enough to secure Queenie's entrance into a neutral country; and if he were once more enamoured of his power over her, he would certainly have taken precautions against any new intervention by herself.

Late in the afternoon of Saturday the third of October Sylvia arrived at Giurgiu, the last station in Roumania before crossing the Danube to enter Bulgaria. It had been a slow journey owing to the congestion of traffic caused by the concentration of Roumanian troops upon the frontier. When she was leaving the station to take the ferry she caught sight of Philidor upon the platform.

'You here? I thought you were at Bralatz,' she cried.

She was thinking that Philidor's presence was of good omen to her journey; and as they walked together down to the quay she was glad that her last memory of Roumania should be of this tall figure in his light blue cloak appearing indeed of heroic mould in the transmuting fog of the Danube that enmeshed them.

'You've left it very late,' he said. 'We expect every hour the Bulgarian declaration of war upon the Entente. Ah, this disastrous summer! The failure at the Dardanelles! The failure of the Russians! And now I doubt if we shall do anything but cluster here upon the frontier like birds gathering to go south.'

'I am going south,' Sylvia murmured.

'I wish that I were,' he sighed. 'Now is the moment to strike. When I think of the Bulgarians on the other side of the river, and of my troop – such splendid fellows – waiting and waiting! Sylvia, I am filled with intuitions of my country's fate. Wherever I look the clouds are black. If when you are back in England you read one day that Roumania is fighting with you, do not remember the tawdry side of her, but think of us waiting here in the fog, waiting and waiting. If – and God forbid that you should read this – if you read that Roumania is fighting against you, think that one insignificant lieutenant of cavalry will hope to fall very early upon a Russian bayonet.'

He held her for a moment in the folds of his bedewed cloak, while they listened to the slow lapping of the river; then she mounted the gangway, and the ferry glided into the fog.

There was a very long wait at Rustchuk; but Sylvia did not find the Bulgarian officials discourteous; in fact for the representatives of a country upon the verge of going to war with her own they were pleasant and obliging. It was after midnight before the train left Rustchuk, and some time before dawn that it reached Gorna Orechovitza where it seemed likely to wait for ever. A chill wind was blowing down from the Balkans, which had swept the junction clear of everybody except a squat Bulgarian soldier who marched up and down in his dark-green overcoat, stamping his feet; so little prospect was there of the train starting again that all the station officials were dozing round a stove in the buffet and the passengers had gone back to their *couchettes*. To Sylvia the desolation was exhilarating with a sense of adventure. Roumania had already receded far away – at any rate the tawdy side of it – and the only picture that remained was of Philidor upon the bank of the misty river. It seemed to her now that the whole of the past eighteen months had been a morbid night, such a new and biting sense of reality was blown down from the mountains upon this windy October dawn, such magical horizons were being written across this crimson sky.

The train did not reach Sofia until the afternoon; the station was murmurous with excitement on account of the rumour of an ultimatum presented that morning by the Russian Minister; Sylvia as an Englishwoman became the object of a contemplative stare of curiosity, in which was nothing insolent or hostile, but which gave her the sensation of being just a material aid to dim unskilful meditations, like a rosary in the hands of a converted savage. There was not such a long wait at Sofia as she had expected, and toward dusk after changing trains they reached Slivnitsa; but at Zaribrod, the last station before crossing the Serbian frontier, the train pulled up and showed no sign of proceeding. The platform was thronged with Bulgarian troops, the sound of whom all talking excitedly was like a prolonged sneeze.

At Slivnitsa a tall fair man had got into Sylvia's compartment. In excellent French he told her that his name was Rakoff and that he was a rose-grower. Sylvia expressed her astonishment that a Bulgarian rose-grower should travel to Serbia at such a time, but he laughed at the notion of war between Bulgaria and the Entente, avowed that the agrarian party to which he belonged was unanimously against such a disastrous step, and spoke cheerfully of doing good business in Salonika. At Zaribrod he went off to make enquiries about the chance of getting on that night, but he could obtain no information, and invited Sylvia to dine with him at the station buffet. He also helped her to change her *lei* and *lewa* into Serbian money and generally made himself useful in matters of detail such as putting her clock back an hour to mid-European time. Upon these slight courtesies Sylvia and he built up, as travellers are wont, one of those brief and violent friendships that colour the memory of a voyage like brilliant fugacious blooms. Rakoff expressed loudly his disgust at seeing the soldiers swarming upon the frontier; they had had quite enough war in Bulgaria two years ago, and it was madness to think of losing the advantages of neutrality, especially on behalf of the Germans. He talked of his acres of roses, of the scent of them in the early morning, of the colour of them at noon, and gave Sylvia a small bottle of attar that drenched with its stored up sweetness even the smell of the massed soldiery. Sylvia in her turn talked to him of her life on the stage, described her success in London, and even confided in him her reason for abandoning it all.

'One has these impulses,' he agreed. 'But it is better not to give way to them. That is the advantage of my life as a rose-grower. There is always something to do. It is a tranquil and beautiful existence. One becomes almost a rose oneself. I hate to leave my fields, but my brother was killed in the last war, and I have to travel occasionally since his death. Ah, war! It is the sport of kings; yet our King Ferdinand is a great gardener. He is only happy with his plants. It is terrible that a small group of *arrivistes* should deflect the whole course of our national life, for I'm sure that a gardener must loathe war.'

Sylvia thought of Philidor's denunciations of Englishmen who had found that the Bulgarians were idealists, and sympathized with their partiality when she listened to this gentle rose-grower.

At last about two o'clock in the morning the train was allowed to proceed to Serbia. As it left the station the Bulgarian soldiers shouted 'Hourrah! Hourrah! Hourrah!' in accents between menace and triumph. She turned to her companion with lifted eyebrows.

'They don't sound very pastoral,' she said.

'Some Serbians in the train must have annoyed them,' Rakoff explained.

'Well, I hope for the sake of the Serbians that we're not merely shunting,' Sylvia laughed.

The train went more slowly than ever after they left Pirot, the first station in Serbia, where there had been an endless searching of half the passengers, of which apparently everybody had suddenly got tired, because the passengers in their portion of the train were not examined at all.

'I doubt if this train will go beyond Nish,' said Rakoff. 'The Austrians are advancing more rapidly than was expected. There is a great feeling in Serbia against us. I shall travel back by sea from Salonika.'

They reached Nish about seven o'clock in the morning. When Rakoff was standing outside the window of the compartment to help Sylvia with her luggage he was touched on the shoulder by a Serbian officer, who said something to him at which he started perceptibly. A moment later, however, he called out to Sylvia that he should be back in a moment and would see her to the hotel. He waved his hand and passed on with the officer.

Sylvia turned round to go out by the corridor, but was met in the entrance by another Serbian officer who asked her to keep her seat.

'*Mais je suis Anglaise*,' she protested.

'No doubt there's some mistake,' he answered politely in excellent English. 'But I must request you to stay in the compartment.'

He seated himself and asked her permission to smoke. The passengers had all alighted, and the train seemed very still. Presently another officer came and demanded her papers, which he took away with him. Half an hour went by, and Sylvia began to feel hungry. She asked the officer in the compartment if it would be possible to get some coffee.

'Of course,' he answered with a smile, calling to someone in the corridor. A soldier with fixed bayonet came along and took his commands; presently two cups of black coffee and a packet of cigarettes arrived.

The officer was young and had a pleasant face, but he declined to be drawn into conversation beyond offering Sylvia her coffee and the cigarettes. An hour passed in this way.

'How long am I likely to be kept here?' she asked irritably.

The young officer looked uncomfortable, and invited her to have another cup of coffee, but he did not answer her question. At last, when Sylvia was beginning to feel thoroughly miserable, there was a sound of voices in the corridor, and an English captain in much-stained khaki appeared in the entrance to the compartment.

'Good morning,' he said. 'Sorry you've been kept waiting like this. My fault, I'm afraid. Fact is I won a bath at piquet last night, and not even the detention of a compatriot would make me forgo one exquisite moment of it.'

He was a tall thin man in the early thirties with a languid manner of speech and movement that, though it seemed at first out of keeping with the substance of his conversation, nevertheless oddly enhanced it somehow. Sylvia had an impression that his point of view about everything was worn and stained like his uniform, but that like his uniform it preserved a fundamentally good quality of cloth and cut. His arrival smoothed away much of her annoyance, because she discerned in him a capacity for approaching a case upon its own merits and a complete indifference to any professionalism real or assumed for the duration of the war. In a word she found his personality sympathetic, and long experience had given her the assurance that wherever this was so she could count upon rousing a reciprocal confidence.

'Good morning, Antitch,' he was saying to the young Serbian officer who had been keeping guard over her. And to Sylvia he added: 'Antitch was at Oxford and speaks English like an Englishman.'

'I've had very little chance of knowing if he could even speak his own language,' she said sharply.

Her pleasure in finding an English officer at Nish was now being marred, as so many pleasures are marred for women, by consciousness of the sight she must present at this moderately early hour of the morning after thirty-six hours in the train.

The Englishman laughed.

'Antitch takes an occasion like this very seriously,' he said.

'It's the only way to treat half-past eight in the morning,' Sylvia answered. 'Even after a bath.'

'I know. I must apologize for my effervescence at such an hour. We try to assume this kind of attitude toward life when we assume temporary commissions. I'm a parvenu to such an hour and don't really know how to behave myself. Now at dawn you would have found my manner as easy as a doctor's by a bedside. Well, what have you been doing?'

'Really, I think that's for you to tell me,' Sylvia replied.

'Where did you meet your fellow-traveller – the Bulgarian?'

'The rose-grower?'

'Oh, you think he *is* a rose-grower?'

'I didn't speculate upon the problem. He got into the train at Slivnitsa and did all he could to make himself useful and agreeable,' Sylvia said.

'That's one for you, Antitch,' the Englishman laughed. 'Another Bulgarophile. We're hopeless, aren't we? Upon my soul, people like Prussians and Bulgarians are justified in thinking that we're traitors to our convictions when they witness the affinity between most of them and most of us. I say, you must forgive me for being so full of voluble buck this morning,' he went on to Sylvia. 'It really is the effect of the bath. I feel like a general who's been made a knight commander of that most honourable order for losing an impregnable position and keeping his temper. Well, I'm sorry to bother you, but I think you'd better be confronted by your accomplice. We have reason to doubt his bona fides, and Colonel Michailovitch, our criminal expert, would like to have your testimony. You'll entrust this lady to me?' he asked Antitch, who saluted ceremoniously. 'All right, old thing, you'll bark your knuckles if you try to be too polite in a railway-carriage. Come along then, and we'll tackle the Colonel.'

'I think I will come as well,' said Antitch.

'Of course, of course. I don't know if it's etiquette to introduce a suspected spy to her temporary gaoler, but this is Lieutenant Antitch, and my name's Hazlewood. You've come from Roumania, haven't you? Here, let me carry your valise. Even if you are condemned by the court, you won't be condemned to travel any more in this train. What an atrocious sentence! *Voyages forcés* for twenty years!'

'Roumania was very well,' said Sylvia, as they passed along the corridor to the platform.

'Still flirting with intervention, I suppose?' Hazlewood went on. 'Odd effect this war has of making one think of countries as acquaintances. All Europe has been reduced to a suburb. I was sent up here from Gallipoli, and I find Nish – which with deep respect to Antitch, I had always regarded as an unknown town consisting of mud and pigs, or as one of the stations where it was possible to eat between Vienna and Constantinople – as crowded and cosmopolitan as Monte Carlo. The whole world and his future wife is here.'

Sylvia was trying to remember how the name Hazlewood was faintly familiar to her, but the recollection was elusive, and she asked about her big trunk.

'If you're going on to Salonika,' he advised. 'You'd better get on as soon as possible after the stain of suspicion has been erased from your passport. Nish is full up now, but presently—' he broke off, and looked across at Antitch with an expression of tenderness.

The young Serbian shrugged his shoulders; and they passed into the office of Colonel Michailovitch, who was examining Sylvia's passport with the rapt concentration of gaze that could only be achieved by someone who was incapable of understanding a single word of what he was apparently reading. The Colonel bowed to Sylvia when she entered and invited her to sit down. Hazlewood asked him if he might look at the passport.

'It's quite in order, I think, *mon colonel*,' he said in French. The Colonel agreed with him.

'You have no objection to its being returned?'

'*Pas du tout, pas du tout! Plaisir, plaisir,*' exclaimed the Colonel.

'And I think you would like to hear from—' Hazlewood glanced at the passport – 'from Miss Scarlett? Sylvia Scarlett?' he repeated, looking at her. 'Why, I believe we have a friend in common. Aren't you a friend of Michael Fane?'

Sylvia realized how familiar his name should be to her; and she felt that her eyes brightened in assent.

'He's in Serbia, you know,' said Hazlewood.

'Now?' she asked.

'Yes. I'll tell you about him. *Je demande pardon, mon colonel, mais je connais cette dame.*'

'*Enchanté, enchanté,*' said the Colonel getting up and shaking hands cordially. '*Le Capitaine Antonivitch. Le Lieutenant Lazarevitch,*' he added, indicating the other officers, who saluted and shook hands with her.

'They're awful dears, aren't they?' murmured Hazlewood. Then he went on in French: 'But, *mon colonel*, I beg you will ask Miss Scarlett any questions you want to ask about this man Rakoff.'

'*Vous me permettez, madame?*' the Colonel enquired. '*Desolé, mais vous comprenez, la guerre c'est comme ça, n'est-ce pas? Ah oui, la guerre.*'

Everybody in the office sighed in echo: '*Ah oui, la guerre!*'

'Where did this man get into the train?'

'At Slivnitsa, I believe.'

'Did he talk about anything in particular?'

'About roses mostly. He said he did not believe there could be war with Serbia. He spoke very bitterly against Germany.'

Sylvia answered many more questions in favour of her fellow traveller. The Colonel talked for a few moments in Serbian to his assistants; presently a grubby looking peasant was brought in, at whom the Colonel shouted a number of questions, the answers to which seemed to reduce him to a state of nervous despair. One of the officers retired and came back with the Bulgarian rose-grower; after a great deal of talking the peasant was sent away, and Rakoff's passport was handed back to him.

'*Je suis libre?*' asked the Bulgarian, looking round him.

The Colonel bowed stiffly.

'This lady has spoken of your horticultural passion,' said Hazlewood, looking at Rakoff straight in the eyes.

'*Je suis infiniment reconnaissant,*' the Bulgarian murmured with a bow. Then he saluted the company and went out.

'I daren't precipitate the situation,' the Colonel told Hazlewood. 'He must leave Nish at once, but if he tries to alight before the Greek frontier, he can always be arrested.'

Renewed apologies from the Colonel and much cordial saluting from his staff ushered Sylvia out of the office, whence she was followed by Hazlewood and Antitch, the latter of whom begged her to show her forgiveness by dining with him that night.

'My dear fellow,' Hazlewood protested. 'Miss Scarlett has promised to dine with me.'

In the end she agreed to dine with both, and begged them not to bother about her any more, lest work should suffer.

'No, I'll see you into town,' Hazlewood said. 'Because I don't know if there's a room in any hotel. You ought really to go on to Salonika at once, but I suppose you want to see Nish on the eve of its calvary.'

She looked at him in surprise: there was such a depth of bitterness in his tone.

'I should hate to be a mere sight-seer.'

'No, forgive me for talking like that. I'm sure you're not, and to show my penitence for the imputation let me help you about your room.'

Sylvia and Hazlewood bowed to Antitch and walked out of the station.

'They've started to commandeer every vehicle and every animal,' Hazlewood explained. 'So we shall have to walk. It's not far. This youth will carry your bag. Your heavy luggage had better remain in the *consigne*. I suppose you more or less guessed what was Michailovitch's difficulty about your friend the Bulgarian rose-grower?'

'No, I don't think I did really.'

Sylvia did not care anything about the Bulgarian or the Colonel; she was only anxious to hear something about Michael Fane; but because she was so anxious she could not bring herself to start the topic and must wait for Hazlewood.

'Well, this fellow Rakoff was identified by that peasant chap who was brought in – or at any rate so almost certainly recognized as to amount to identification – as one of the most bloodthirsty comitadji leaders.'

'What do they do?'

She felt that she must appear to take some interest in what Hazlewood was telling her, after the way he had helped and was helping her and perhaps would help her.

'Their chief mission in life,' he explained, 'is the Bulgarization of Macedonia, which they effect in the simplest way possible by murdering everybody who is not Bulgarian. They're also rather fond of Bulgarizing towns and churches by means of dynamite. Altogether the most unpleasant ruffians left in Europe, and in yielding them the superlative I'm not forgetting Orangemen and Junkers. The Colonel did not believe that he was a rose-grower, but he was afraid to arrest him, because at this moment it is essential not to give the least excuse for precipitating the situation. We expect to hear at any moment that Bulgaria has declared war on Serbia; but all sorts of negotiations are still in progress. One of the characteristics of our policy during this war is to give a frenzied attention to the moulding of a situation after it has hopelessly hardened. This Austrian advance is bad enough, but there's probably worse to follow, and we don't want the worst yet. The people here are counting on French and English help, and they are frightened to death of doing anything that will upset us. As a matter of fact your evidence was a godsend to the Colonel, because it gave him an excuse to let Rakoff go without losing his dignity. And of course there's always a chance that the fellow is what he claims to be – a peaceful rose-grower, though I doubt it: I can't imagine anyone of that trade travelling through Serbia at such a moment. I believe myself that the Germans furnish condemned criminals with sufficiently suspicious accessories to occupy the Allied Intelligence, while they get away with the real goods. Do you ever read spy-novels? Our spy-novels and spy-plays must have been of priceless assistance to the Germans in letting them know how to coach their condemned criminals for the part. There's only one thing on earth that bears less resemblance to its original than the English novelist's spy and that is his detective.'

'Where is Michael Fane?' Sylvia asked; she could bear it no longer.

'He's out here with Lady What's-Her-Name's Red Cross unit. I don't really know where he is at the moment – probably being jolted by a mule on a track leading south from Belgrade. His sister's out here too. Her husband – an awfully jolly fellow – was killed at Ypres. When did you see Michael last?'

'Oh, not for – not for nearly nine years,' she answered.

There was a silence; Sylvia wished now that she had let Hazlewood lead up to the subject of Michael; he must be thinking of the time when his friend was engaged to Lily; he must be wondering about herself, for that he had remembered her name after so many years showed that Michael's account of her had impressed itself upon him.

'If he's on his way south, he'll be in Nish soon,' Hazlewood said, breaking the silence abruptly. 'You'd better wait and see him. Nine years last month: September 1906.'

'No, it was June,' Sylvia said. 'Early June.'

'Sorry,' he said. 'I was thinking of Michael in relation to myself.'

He sighed, and at that moment coming down the squalid street appeared a band of children shepherded by a fussy schoolmaster and carrying bouquets of flowers, who at the sight of Hazlewood cheered shrilly.

'You seem to be very popular here already,' Sylvia observed.

'Do you know what those flowers are for?' he asked gravely.

She shook her head.

'They're for the British and French troops that these poor dears are expecting to arrive by every train to help them against the Austrians. I tell you it makes me feel the greatest humbug on earth. They are going to decorate the station to-morrow. It's like putting flowers on their country's tomb. Ah, don't let's talk about it – don't let's think about it,' he broke out passionately. 'Serbia has been one of my refuges during the last nine years, and I stand here now like a mute at a funeral.'

He walked on, tugging savagely at his moustache, until he could turn round to Sylvia with a laugh again.

'My moustache represents the badge of my servitude. I tug at it as in the old Greek days slaves must have tugged at their leaden collars. The day I shave it off I shall be free again. Here's the hotel where I hang out – almost literally, for my room is so small and so dirty that I generally put my pillow on the window-sill. The hotel is full of bugs and diplomats, but the coffee is good. However, it's no good raising your hopes, because I know that there isn't a spare room. Never mind,' he added. 'I've got another room at another hotel which is equally full of bugs, but unfrequented by diplomats. It is being reserved for my lady-secretary, but she hasn't turned up yet, and so I make you a present of it till she does.'

'Why are you being so kind?' Sylvia asked.

'I don't know,' Hazlewood replied. 'You amused me, I think, sitting there in that railway-carriage with Antitch. It's such a relief to arrest somebody who doesn't instantly begin to shriek "Consul! Consul!" Most women regard consuls as Gieve waistcoats, that is to say something which is easily inflated by a woman's breath, has a flask of brandy in one pocket, and affords endless support. No, seriously, it happens that Michael Fane talked a great deal about you on a memorable occasion in my life, and since he's a friend of mine I'd like to do all I can for you. For the moment – here's the other hotel, nothing is far apart in Nish, not even life and death – for the moment I must leave you, or rather for the whole day, I'm afraid, because I've got the dickens of a lot to do. However, it's just as well the lady-secretary hasn't turned up, because it's really impossible to feel very securely established in Nish. I expect as a matter of fact, she's been kidnapped by some white slavery of the Staff en route. Miss Potberry is her name. It's a depressing name for a secretary, but true romance knows no laws of nomenclature, so I still have hope. Poor lady;

> Miss Potberry muttered, "Oh, squish!
> I don't want to go on to Nish.
> I like Malta better!"
> The General said, "Let her
> Remain here, if that is her wish,

and send a telegram to London to say that she has been taken ill and is unable to proceed further, but that her services can be usefully employed here." I say, I must run! I'll come and fetch you for dinner about half-past seven.'

He handed her over to the care of the hotel-porter and vanished.

The room that Hazlewood had lent to Sylvia possessed a basin, a bed, five hooks, a chair, the remains of a table, an oleograph of a battle between Serbians and Bulgarians that resembled a fire at a circus, and a balcony. At such a time in Nish a balcony made up for any absence of comfort, so much was there to look at in the square full of stunted trees and mud, surrounded by stunted houses, and crammed with carts, bullocks, donkeys, horses, diplomats, soldiers, princes, refugees, peasants, poultry, newspaper correspondents, and children, the whole mass flushed by a spray of English nurses as a pigsty by a Dorothy Perkins rambler.

Sylvia searched the crowd for a glimpse of Michael Fane, though she knew that he was almost certainly not yet arrived. Yet if the Serbians were evacuating Belgrade and if Michael had been in Belgrade, he was bound to arrive ultimately in Nish. She wondered how long she could keep this room and prayed that Miss Potberry would not appear. The notion of travelling all the way here from Petrograd, only to miss him at the end was not to be contemplated; his sister was in Serbia too, that charming sister who had flashed through her dressing-room at the Pierian like a lovely view seen from a train. After the last eighteen months she was surely justified in leaving nothing undone that might bring about another meeting. Hazlewood had spoken of being overworked. Could she not offer her services in place of Miss Potberry? Anything, anything to have an excuse to linger in Nish, an excuse that would absolve her from the charge of a frivolous egotism in occupying space that would soon be more than ever badly needed. She had thought that destiny had driven her south from Petrograd to Kieff, from Kieff to Odessa, from Odessa to Bucharest, from Bucharest to Nish for Queenie and for Philip, but surely it was for more than was represented by either of them.

'Incredible ass that I am,' she thought. 'What is Michael to me and what am I to Michael? Not so easily is time's slow ruin repaired. If we meet, we shall meet for perhaps a dinner together: that will be all. What romances must this war have woven and what romances must it not have shattered as swiftly! Romances! Yet how dare I use such a word about myself? Nine years, nine remorseless deadening years lie on top of what was never more than a stillborn fancy, and I am expecting to see it burst forth to bloom in Nish. It's the effect of isolation. Time goes by more slowly when one only looks at oneself, and one forgets the countless influences in other people's lives. But I should like to see him again. Oh yes, quite ordinarily and unemotionally I should like to shake hands with him and perhaps talk for a little while. There is nothing extravagantly sentimental in thinking so much.'

Sylvia had often enough been conscious of her isolation from the world and often enough she had tried to assuage this sense of loneliness by indulging it to the utmost – to such an extent indeed that she had reached the point of hating not merely anything that interfered with her own isolation, but even anything that interfered with the isolation of other people. She had turned the armour of self-defence into a means of aggression, although by doing so she had destroyed the strength of her position. Her loneliness that during these last months seemed to have acquired the more positive qualities of independence was now only too miserably evident as loneliness; and unless she could apply the vital suffering she had undergone recently so that the years of her prime might bear manifest fruit, she knew that the sense of futility in another nine years would be irreparable indeed. At present the treasure of eighteen months of continuous and deliberate effort to avoid futility was still rich with potentiality; but the human heart was a deceptive treasure-house never very strong against the corruption of time, which when unlocked might at any moment display nothing except coffers filled with dust.

'But why do I invite disillusionment by counting upon this meeting with Michael Fane? Why should he cure this loneliness and how will he cure it? Why in two words do I want to meet him again? Partly, I think, it's due to the haunting incompleteness of our first intercourse, to which is added the knowledge that now I am qualified to complete that intercourse, at any rate so far as my attitude towards him is concerned. And the way I want to show my comprehension of him is to explain about myself. I am really desperately anxious that he should hear what happened to me after we parted. For one thing he is bound to be sympathetic with this craving for an assurance of the value of faith. I want to find how far he has travelled in the same direction as myself by a different road. I divine somehow that his experience will be the complement to my own, that it will illumine the wretched cross-country path which I've taken through life. If I find that he, relying almost entirely upon the adventures of thought, has arrived at a point of which I am also in sight, notwithstanding that I have taken the worst and roughest road, a road moreover that was almost all the time trespassing upon forbidden territory, then I shall be able to throw off this oppression of loneliness. But why should I rely more upon his judgment than anybody else's?'

Sylvia shrugged her shoulders.

'What is attraction?' she asked herself. 'It exists, and there's an end of it. I had the same sense of intimacy with his sister in a conversation of five minutes. Then am I in love with him? But isn't being in love a condition that is brought about by circumstances out of attraction? Being in love is merely the best way of illustrating affinity. Ah, that word! When a woman of thirty-two begins to talk about affinities, she has performed half her emotional voyage; the sunken rocks and eddies of the dangerous age may no longer be disregarded. Thirty-two, and yet I feel younger than I did at twenty-three. At twenty-three experience most bitter was weighing me down; at thirty-two I know that experience must not be regarded as anything more important than food or drink or travelling in a train or any of the incidental aids to material existence. Then what is important? I should be rash to hazard a statement while I am looking at this heterogeneous mob below. One cannot help supposing that the war will bring about a readjustment of values.'

The feeling of unrest and insecurity in the square at Nish on that Monday morning was almost frightful in its emotional actuality; it gave Sylvia an envy to fling herself into the middle of it, as when one sits upon a rock lashed by angry seas and longs to glut an insane curiosity about the extent of one's helplessness. This squalid Serbian town gave her the illusion of having for the moment concentrated upon itself the great forces that were agitating the world.

'I don't believe anybody realizes yet how much was let slip with the dogs of war,' she said to herself. 'People are always talking about the vastness of this war, but they are always thinking in terms of avoirdupois; they have never doubted that the decimal system will express their most grandiose calculations. The biggest casualty-list that was ever known, the longest battle, the heaviest gun, all these flatter poor humanity with a sense of its importance: but when all the records have been broken and when all the congratulations upon outdoing the past have been worn thin, to what will humanity turn from the new chaos it has created? And this is one of the fruits of the great nineteenth century, this miserable square packed with the evidence of civilization. Perhaps I'm too parochial: at the other end of the universe planets may be warring upon planets. If that be so, we lose even the consolation of a universal record and must fall back upon a mere world-record; in eternity our greatest war will have sunk to a brawl in a slum. How can mankind believe in man? How can mankind reject God?' she demanded passionately.

Sylvia did not dine with Hazlewood or Antitch that evening, because they were both too busy. Hazlewood begged her to stay on in the room and promised that he would try to make use of her; though he was too busy at present to find time to explain how she could be useful. Sylvia did not like to worry him with enquiries about Michael, and she spent the next few days watching from her balcony the concourse of distracted human beings in the square. On Saturday when news had arrived that the Austrians had entered Belgrade and when every hour was bringing convoys of refugees from the north, a rumour suddenly sprung up that thousands of British and French troops were on their way from Salonika, that the Greeks had invaded Bulgaria and that Turkey had made peace. Such an accumulation of good news meant that the miseries of Serbia would soon be over. The railway station was hung with more flags and scattered with more flowers than ever; and an enterprising coffee-house keeper anticipated the arrival of British troops by hanging out a sign inscribed GUD BIIR IS FOR SEL PLIS TO COM OLD ENGLAND BIRHOUS.

Sylvia was reading this notice, when Hazlewood came up and asked her to dine with him that evening.

'I'm so sorry I've had to leave you entirely to yourself, but I've not had a moment, and I hate dining when I can't talk. To-night there seems a lull in the stream of telegraphic questions to which I've been subjected all this week.'

'But please don't apologize. I feel guilty in staying here at all, especially when I'm doing nothing but stare.'

'Well, I was going to talk to you about that. You ought to leave to-morrow or the next day. The Bulgarians are sure to move, now that the Austrians have got Belgrade, and that means fresh swarms of fugitives from the east; it may also mean that communications with Greece will be cut.'

'But the British advance?'

Hazlewood looked at her.

'Ah yes, the British advance,' he murmured.

'And you promised that you'd find me some work,' Sylvia said.

'Frankly it's no good your beginning to learn now.'

She must have shown as much disappointment as she felt, for he added:

'Well, after dinner to-night you shall take down the figures of one or two long telegrams.'

'Anything,' offered Sylvia eagerly.

'It's all that Miss Potberry could have done at present. I'm not writing any reports; so her expert shorthand of which I was assured would have been wasted. Reports! One of the revelations of this war to me was the extraordinary value that professional soldiers attach to the typewritten word. I suppose it's a minor manifestation of the impulse that made Wolfe say he would rather have written Gray's *Elegy* than take Quebec. If typewriters had been invented in his time he might have said, "I would rather be in the War Office and be able to read my report of the capture of Quebec than take it." I'm sure that the chief reason of a knowledge of Latin being still demanded for admission to Sandhurst is the hope universally cherished in the Army that every cadet's haversack contains a new long Latin intransitive verb which can be used transitively to supplant one of the short Saxon verbs that still disfigure military correspondence. I can imagine such a cadet saying, "Sir, I would sooner have been the first man that wrote of evacuating wounded than take Berlin." The trouble with men of action is that something written means for them something done. The labour of writing is so tremendous and the consequent mental fatigue so overwhelming that they cannot bring themselves to believe otherwise. The general public, even after fifteen months of war, has the same kind of respect for the printed word. How long does it take you to read a letter? I imagine that two readings would give you the gist of it? Well, it takes a British general at least five readings, and even then he only understands a word here and there, unless it's written in his own barbaric departmental English. If I had a general over me here – which thank heaven I've not – and I were to make a simple suggestion, he would invite me to put it on paper. This he would do because he would presume that life would be too short for me to succeed and that therefore he should be for ever spared having to make up his mind in response to any prompting on my side. If on the other hand I did by chance embody my suggestion in typescript, he would be amazed at the result, and by some alchemy of thought, if he could write on the top "Concur," he would feel that he had created the suggestion himself. The effort even to write "Concur" represents for the average British general the amount of labour involved by a woman in producing a child, and . . . but look here – to-night at half-past seven. So long!'

Hazlewood hurried away; at dinner that night he went on with his discourse.

'You know that among savages certain words are taboo and that in the middle ages certain words possessed magic properties? The same thing applies to the Army and to the Navy. For instance the Navy has a word of power that will open anything. That word is "submit." If you wrote "submitted" at the top of a communication I believe you could tell an admiral that he was a damn fool, but if you wrote "suggested" you'd be shot at dawn. In the same way a naval officer endorses your "submission" by writing "approved," whereas a soldier writes "concur." I've often wondered what would happen to a general who wrote "agree." Certainly any junior officer who wrote "begin" for "commence" or "allow" for "permit" would be cashiered. I was rather lucky because, after being suspected for the simplicity of my reports, I managed to use the word "connote" once. My dear woman, my reputation was made. Generals came up and congratulated me personally, and I'm credibly informed that all the new military cyphers will include the word, which was just what was wanted to supplant "mean," a monosyllable that had been a blot on military correspondence for years.'

'Are you talking seriously?' Sylvia asked. 'You can't really connote what you say.'

Hazlewood indicated the room where they were dining.

'Which are the English diplomats?' he demanded.

'That's perfectly easy to tell,' she replied.

'And why?' he went on. 'Simply because they've made no concession to being in Nish at a moment of crisis. I invite you to regard my friend Harry Vereker. See how he defies any Horatian regret for lapsed years. Positively he is still at Oxford. Can't you hear above all this clatter of cosmopolitanism in a pigsty the suave insistency of his voice impressing upon you by its quality of immutable self-assurance that whatever happens to the rest of the world nothing vitally deformative ever happens to England?'

'But what has the voice of a Secretary to do with the military abuse of Latin derivations?'

'Not much, I admit, except in its serene ruthlessness. An English officer compels a Latin verb to fit in with his notion of what a Latin verb ought to do just in the same way as he expects a Spaniard to regard with pleasure his occupation of Gibraltar: any protest by a grammarian or an idealistic politician would strike him as impertinent. Harry Vereker's voice is a still more ineradicable manifestation of the spirit. Listen! He is asking the waiter in Serbian for salt, but he does so in a way that reminds one of mankind's concession to animals in using forms of communication that the latter can understand. It is not to be supposed that the dog invented patting: Harry's Serbian is his way of patting the waiter: it is *his* language, not the waiter's. Personally I can't help confessing that I admire this attitude to the world, and I only wish that it could be eternally preserved. The great historical tragedy of this war – I'm putting on one side for the moment the countless personal tragedies that are included in it, and trying to regard the war as Mr. Buckle regarded civilization – the great historical tragedy will be the Englishman's loss of his personality. When we look back at the historical tragedy of the fall of the Roman Empire, we think less of the *civis Romanus sum* than of the monuments of architecture, law, political craft, and the rest that remain imperishably part of human progress. In the same way a thousand years hence I assume that the British Empire will be considered to have played a part only second to the Roman Empire in the manifest results of its domination. But what has been lost and what will be lost is the individual Roman's attitude and the individual Englishman's. Not all the remains of the Roman Empire have been enough really to preserve for us the indefinable flavour of being a Roman, and with much more material at his disposal I defy the perfect cosmopolitan of mixed Aryan, Mongol, and Semitic blood to realize a thousand years from now Harry Vereker's tone of voice in asking that waiter for the salt. No, no, the cosmopolitan of the future will turn aside from the records of the past and in Esperanto murmur sadly to himself that something is missing from his appreciation. Perhaps I can illustrate my meaning better if I compare the Athenians with the French. I feel that the Art of both enduring through time to come will be enough. I have no regret for the personal attitude of the Athenian, and in the same way I don't feel that the cosmopolitan of a thousand years hence will lose anything by not meeting the

Frenchman of to-day. It is Athens and France rather than the Athenian or the Frenchman of which the world is enamoured. How often have I heard a foreigner say "The politics of England do not please me: I find it a brigand policy, but the individual Englishman is always a gentleman." An individual Englishman like Byron is worth more to England than twenty Chamberlains or Greys, who yet have more right to represent their country: he comes as such a romantic surprise. A Frenchman like Lafayette is taken for granted. The word of an Englishman is proverbial; the perfidy of Albion equally so.'

'And the Germans?' Sylvia asked.

'Oh, they have never been thought worthy of a generalization. We have apprehended them vaguely as one apprehends pigs – as a nation of gross feeders and badly dressed women drinking a mixture of treacle and onions they call beer, with a reputation for guttural peregrination and philosophy.'

'Their music,' Sylvia protested.

'Yes, that is difficult to explain. Yes, I think we must give them that; but when we remember Bach and Schumann, we must not forget Wagner and the German band.'

'I think your characterization is rather crude,' Sylvia said.

'It is crude. But there is no bygone civilization with which Germanic *Kultur* can be compared. So as with any novelty one depends upon a sneer to hide one's own ignorance.'

'The Italians interest me more,' Sylvia said.

'The Italians seem to me rather to resemble the English, and naturally, because they are the most direct heirs of Rome. I'm bound to say that I don't believe in an imperial future for them now. It's surely impossible to revive Rome. They still preserve an immense capacity for political craft, but it is an egotism that lacks the sublime unconsciousness of English egotism. The Italians have never recovered from *Il Principe* of Machiavelli. It's an eclectic statecraft; like their painting from Raphael onwards it's too *soigné*. Moreover, Italy suffers from the perpetual sacrifice of the Southern Italian to the Northern. The real Italians belong to the South, and for me the *risorgimento* has always been a phœnix rising from the ashes of the South: the bird is most efficient, but I distrust its aquiline appearance. One of the most remarkable surprises of this war has been the superior fighting quality – the more quickly beating heart – of the Neapolitans and Sicilians. I found the same surprising quality in the Greeks during the last Balkan war. To me who regard the Mediterranean as still *the* civilized sea of the world the triumph of Naples has been a delight.'

'And the Russians?' Sylvia went on.

'Ah, the future of Russia is as much an unknown quantity as the future of womanhood. Personally I am convinced that the next great civilization will be Slavonic, and my chief grudge against mortality is that I must die long before it even begins to draw near, for it is still as far away as Johannine Christianity will be from the Petrine Christianity to which we have been too long devoted. But when it does come, I am sure that it will easily surpass all previous civilizations, because I believe it will resolve the eternal dualism in humanity that hitherto we have expressed roughly by Empire and Papacy or by Church and State. I envisage Russia as containing the civilization of the soul, though God knows through what agony of blood and tears it may have to pass before it can express what it contains. In Russia there still exists a genuine worship of the Czar as a superior being, and a nation that respects the divinity about a king is still as deep in the mire of fetichism as the most debased Melanesians. We worship kings in England, I admit, but only snobbishly; we significantly call the pound a sovereign. Not even our most exalted snobs dream of paying divine honours to kingship; we are too much heirs of Imperial Rome for that. I always attribute Magna Carta to an inherited consciousness of Cæsarian excesses.'

'And now you've only Austria left,' said Sylvia.

'Austria,' Hazlewood exclaimed. 'A battered cocotte who sustains herself by devoting to pietism the settlements of her numerous lovers – a cocotte with a love of finery, a profound cynicism, and an acquired deportment. Austria! rouged and raddled, plumped and corseted, a suitable mistress for that licentious but still tragic old buffoon who rules her.'

'What a wonderful sermon on so slight a text as a friend's asking a Serbian waiter for salt,' Sylvia said.

'Ah, you led me away from the main thread by asking me direct questions. I meant to confine myself to England.'

'*On peut toujours revenir à ses moutons*,' Sylvia said.

'New Zealand mutton, eh?' Hazlewood laughed. 'Wasn't it a New Zealander who was to meditate upon the British Empire a thousand years hence amid the ruins of St. Paul's?'

'Well, go on,' she urged.

'You're one of those listening sirens so much more fatal than the singing variety,' he laughed.

'Oh, but I'm very rarely a good listener,' she protested. Hazlewood bowed.

'And don't forget that sirens have always an *arrière pensée*,' she went on. 'However well you talk, you'll find that I shall demand something in return for my attention. Don't looked alarmed; it won't involve you personally.'

Sylvia was getting a good deal of pleasure out of his monologue; it was just what her nerves needed, this sense of being entertained while all the time she preserved, so far as any reality of personal intercourse was concerned, a complete detachment. She was quite definitely aware of wanting Hazlewood to exhaust himself that she might either bring her part of the conversation round to Michael or at any rate extract from him an excuse for lingering in Nish until Michael should come here. Now her host was off again:

'Have you ever thought,' he was asking her, 'about the appropriateness of our national animal – the British lion? We are rather apt to regard the lion as a bluff, hearty sort of beast with a loud roar and a consciousness of being the finest beast anywhere about. But after all, the lion *is* one of the great cats. He's something much finer than the British bulldog, which with most unnecessary self-depreciation we have elected as our secondary pattern or prototype among the animals. There are few animals so profoundly, so densely, so hopelessly stupid as the bulldog. Its chief virtue is alleged to be its never knowing when it is beaten, but this is only an incidental ignorance merged in its ignorance of everything. Why a dog that approximates in character to a mule and in appearance to an hippopotamus should be accepted as the representative of English character I don't know. The attribution takes its place with some of the great fundamental mysteries of human conduct; it is comparable with those other riddles of why a chauffeur always waits till you get into the car again before he turns round, or why kidneys are so rare in beefsteak-and-kidney pudding, or why every man in the course of his life has either wanted to buy or has bought a rustic summer-house. The lion, however, really is typical of the Englishman: somewhat blonde and very agile, physically courageous, morally timid, fierce, full of domestic virtues, tolerant of jackals, generous, cunning, graceful, arrogant, and acquisitive: he seems to me a perfect symbol of the British race.'

'Is your friend at the diplomats' table so very leonine?' Sylvia asked.

'Oh no, Harry is the individual Englishman; the lion represents the race.'

'But the race is an accumulation of individuals.'

'I say, don't listen too intelligently,' Hazlewood begged. 'It's not fair either to my babbling or to your own dinner.'

'Well, I want to bring you back to the point you made when you talked about the historical tragedy of this war.'

Hazlewood looked serious.

534

'I meant what I said. I've just come down from the grave of what was England, and already the deeds at Gallipoli have taken on the aspect of an heroic frieze. We might have repeated Gallipoli here in Serbia, but we shan't; we've learnt our lesson; I do not think that on such a scale such decorative heroism can ever happen again. Gallipoli saw the death of the amateur; and a conservative like myself feels the historical tragedy of such a death. I suppose there are few people who would be prepared to argue that such a spirit ought to be purchased at such a price, and yet I don't know – I believe I would. I wasn't in Flanders at the beginning; but I imagine the same spirit existed there. Don't you remember the child-like amateurish pleasure that all the soldiers took in being ferried across the Channel without anybody's knowing they had gone? The successful secrecy compensated them for all that hell of Mons. You'll never again hear of that childlike enjoyment. Very soon we shall have conscription, and from that moment the amateur in a position of responsibility who sacrifices any man's life to his own sense of exterior form will become a criminal. Surely it is an appalling tragedy that we shan't be able to carry on such a war as this without conscription? England, our England, disappears with conscription: nothing will ever be the same again. They accused us of decadence, but had you seen that landing last April – had you seen that immortal division of Englishmen, Scotsmen, Irishmen, and Welshmen literally dyeing the sea with their blood, you could never have thought of decadence again. And yet, mark my words, so much of England was lost upon that day that already the unthinking herd led by the newspapers, which are always waiting to hail the new king, talks of the landing as famous chiefly for the Australian share in it. My God, it enrages me to read about the Australians when I think of that deathless dead division. Whatever else may happen in this war, whatever our fate at the hands of intriguing politicians and backbiting generals, England was herself upon that day: it stands with Trafalgar and Agincourt in a trinity of imperishable glory.'

'But why do you say that so much of England was lost? You don't think we shall disgrace ourselves henceforth in this war?'

'We have already done so morally in failing to come to the help of the Serbians. Gallipoli turned us into professionals, and though I'm not saying that there is a single good professional argument in favour of helping Serbia, I still believe against all professionals that we shall pay for our failure in bitter years of prolonged war. The Dardanelles could have been forced. What stopped it? Professional jealousy at home.'

'It's a hard thing of which to accuse the people at home.'

'It was a hard thing to land that day at Sedd-el-bahr, but it was done.

535

No, we've fallen a prey to the glamour of Teutonism, and of being expedient and Hunnish. By the time the war is over I don't doubt we shall be a very pretty imitation of the real article that we're setting out to destroy. But, thank heaven, we shall always be able to point to Mons and to Antwerp and to Gallipoli: though we are fast forgetting to be gentlemen, we've already forgotten more than the Germans ever dreamed of in that direction. Mind you, I'm not attempting to say that we haven't got to hit below the belt: we have, because we are fighting with foul fighters; but that is what I conceive to be the historical tragedy of this war – the debasement of our ideals in order that we may compete with the Germans, and with the old men in morocco-chairs at home, and with the guttural press. I remember how the waning moon of dawn came up out of Asia while we were still waiting for news of the Suvla landing. There was a tattoo of musketry over the sea, a lisp of wind in the sandy grass; and in a moment of apprehensive chill I divined that with a failure at Suvla this waning moon was the last moon that would rise upon the old way of thinking, the rare old way of acting, the old, old merry England built in a thousand years.'

'But a greater England may arise from that failure.'

'Yes, but it won't be our England. The grave of our England was dug by the Victorians; this generation has planted the flowers upon it; the monument will be raised by the new generation. Oh yes, I know, it's an egotistical regret, a superficial and sentimental regret if you will, but you must allow some of us to cherish it; otherwise we could not go on. And in the end I believe history will endorse the school of thought I follow. In the end I'm convinced that it will blame the men who failed to see that England was great by the measure of her greatness, and that the real way to win this war was by what were sneeringly called side-shows. All our history has been the alternate failure and triumph of our side-shows; we made ourselves what we are by side-shows.'

Hazlewood swept aside from the table the pile of crumbs he had been building while he was talking, and smiled at Sylvia.

'It's your turn now,' he said.

'You've deprived me of any capacity for generalization. I think perhaps you may have got things out of focus. I know it's a platitude, but isn't one always inevitably out of focus nowadays? When I was still at a distance from the war the whole perspective was blurred to my vision by the intrusion of individual humiliations and sufferings. Now I'm nearer to it I feel that my vision is equally faulty from an indifference to them,' Sylvia said earnestly.

Then she told Hazlewood the story of Queenie and the passport, and asked for his opinion.

'Well, of course, there's an instance to hand of sterile professionalism. Naturally, had I been the official in Bucharest, I should have given the girl her passport. At such a moment I should have been too much moved by her desire of England to have done otherwise. Moreover, if her desire of England was not mere lust, I should have been right to do so.'

Sylvia finished her story by telling him of Queenie's escape with the juggler after the probable theft of Maud's passport.

'By Jove,' he exclaimed. 'I'll bet they've gone to Salonika. We'll send a telegram to our people there and warn them to keep a look out.'

'What a paradox human sympathy is,' Sylvia murmured. 'Ever since I got to Nish it's been on my conscience that I didn't tell you about this girl before, and yet in Bucharest the notion of doing anything like that was positively disgusting to my sense of decency. And look at you! A moment ago you were abusing the official in Bucharest for his red tape, and now your eyes are flashing with the prospect of hunting her down.'

'Not even Heraclitus divined quite the rapidity with which everything dissolves in flux,' said Hazlewood. 'That's another thing that will be brought home to people before the war's over – the intensity and rapidity of change, of course considerably strengthened and accelerated by the impulse that war has given to pure destruction. You can see it even in broad ideas. We began by fighting for a scrap of paper; we shall go on fighting for different ideas until we realize we are fighting for our existence. Then suddenly we shall think we are fighting about nothing, and the war will be over.'

Hazlewood sat silent; most of the diners had finished and left the room, which accentuated his silence with an answering stillness.

'Well, what is to be your reward for listening?' he asked at length.

'To stay on in Nish for the present,' she answered firmly.

'No, no,' he objected, with a sudden fretfulness that was the more conspicuous after his late exuberance. 'No, no, we don't want more women than are necessary. You'd better get down to Salonika on Monday. Look here, I must send a telegram about that friend of yours. Come round to my office and give me the details.'

Sylvia accompanied him in a state of considerable depression; she could not bear the idea of revealing so much of herself as to ask him directly to give her an excuse to remain in Nish because she wanted to see Michael; it was seeming impossible to introduce the personal element in this war-cursed town, and particularly now when she was quenching so utterly the personal element by thus allying herself with Hazlewood against Queenie. She waited while he deciphered a short telegram which had arrived during his absence and while he occupied himself with writing another.

'How will this do for their description?' he read. 'A *certain Krebs known professionally as Zozo, acrobatic juggler and conjurer, alleged Swiss nationality, tall, large face, clean shaven, very large hands, speaking English well, accompanied by Queenie Walters of German origin possibly carrying stolen passport of Maud Moffat, English variety artiste. Description, slim, very fair, blue eyes, pale, delicate, speaks German, Italian, French and English, left Bucharest at end of September. Probably travelled via Dedeagatch and Salonika. Nothing definite known against them, but man frequented company of notorious enemy agents in Bucharest and is known to be bad character. Suggest he is likely to use woman to get in touch with British officers.*'

'But what will they do to her?' Sylvia asked, dismayed by this metamorphosis of Queenie into a police-court case.

'Oh, they won't do anything,' Hazlewood replied irritably. 'She'll be added to the great army of suspects whose histories in all their discrepancies are building up the Golden Legend of this war. She'll exist in card-indexes for the rest of her life; and her reputation will circulate only a little more freely than herself. In fact really I'm doing her a favour by putting her down for the observation of our military psychologists and criminologists; her life will become much easier henceforth. The war has not cured human nature of a passion for bric-à-brac, and as a catalogued article *de vertu* – or should I say *de vice?* – she will be well looked after.'

'Then if that's all, why do you send the telegram?' Sylvia asked.

'I really don't know – probably because I've joined in the may-pole dance for ribbons with the rest of the departmental warriors. Card-indexes are the casualty-lists of officers commanding *embusqués*: the longer the list of names, the longer the row of ribbons.'

'You've become very bitter,' Sylvia said. 'It's like a sudden change of wind. I feel quite chilled.'

'Well, you shall warm yourself by taking down a few hundred groups. Come along.'

Sylvia listened for an hour to the endless groups of five figures that Hazlewood dictated to her, during which time his voice that began calmly and murmurously reached a level of rasping and lacerating boredom before he had done.

'Thank heaven, that's over, and we can go to bed,' he said.

He seemed to be anxious to be rid of her, and she went away in some disconsolation at his abrupt change of manner. Nothing that she could think of occurred to cause it, and ultimately she could only ascribe it to nerves.

'And after all why not nerves?' she said to herself. 'Who will ever again be able to blame people for having nerves?'

The next morning a note came from Hazlewood apologizing for his rudeness and thanking her for her help.

'*I was in a vile humour,*' he wrote, '*because when I got back to my room I found a refusal to let me leave Nish and join the Serbian Headquarters on the Serbian frontier. This morning they've changed their minds and I'm off at once. Keep the room, if you insist upon staying in Nish. If Miss Potberry by any unlucky chance turns up, say I've been killed and that she had better report in Salonika as soon as possible. If I see Michael Fane, which is very unlikely, I'll tell him you want to see him.*'

With all his talk Hazlewood had plumbed her desire; with all his talk about nations he had not lost his capacity for divining the individual. Sylvia wished now that he was not upon his way to the Bulgarian frontier; she should like to watch herself precipitated by his acid. Did acids precipitate? It did not matter; there was no second person's comprehension to be considered at the moment. Sylvia stayed on in the room, watching from the balcony the now unceasing press of refugees.

Three days after she had dined with Hazlewood, there was a murmur in the square, a heightened agitation that made a positive impact upon the atmosphere; Bulgaria had declared war. She had the sense of a curtain's rising upon the last and crucial act, the sense of an audience strung to such a pitch of expectancy, dread and woe, that it was become a part of the drama. During the next three days the influx of pale fugitives was like a scene upon the banks of Styx. The odour of persecuted humanity hung upon the air in a positively visible miasma; white exhausted women suckled their babies in the mud; withered crones dragged from bed sat nursing their ulcers; broken-hearted old men bowed their heads between their knees, seeming actually to have been trampled underfoot in the confused terror that had brought them here; the wailing of tired and hungry children never ceased for a single instant. The only thing that seemed to keep this dejected multitude from rotting in death where they lay was the assurance that everyone gave his neighbour of the British and French advance to save them. Two French officers sent up on some business from Salonika walked through the square in their celestial uniforms like angels of God, for the people fell down before them and gave thanks; faded flowers were flung in their path, and women caught at their hands to kiss them as they went by. Once there was a sound of cavalry's approach, and the despairing mob shouted for joy and pressed forward to greet the vanguard of rescue; but it was a Serbian patrol covered with blood and dust which had been ordered back to guard the railway line. The troopers rode through sullenly and the people did not even whisper about them, so deep was their disillusion, so bitter their resentment. And through all this fetid and pitiful mob the English nurses wound their way like a Dorothy Perkins rambler.

A week after Hazlewood had left Nish, Sylvia saw from her balcony a fair young Englishwoman followed by a ragged boy carrying a typewriter in a tin case. It struck her as the largest typewriter that she had ever seen, and she was thinking vaguely what a ridiculous weapon it was to carry about at such a moment when it suddenly flashed upon her that this might be the long expected Miss Potberry. She hurried downstairs and heard her asking in the hall if anyone knew where Captain Hazlewood could be found. Sylvia came forward and explained his absence.

'He did not really expect you, but he told me to tell you that if you did come you ought to go back immediately to Salonika.'

'I don't think I can go back to Salonika,' said Miss Potberry. 'Somebody was firing at the train as I came in, and they told me at the station that there would be no more trains to Salonika, because the line had been cut.'

The boy had put her typewriter upon a table in the hall; she stood by, embracing it with a kind of serene determination that reminded Sylvia of the images of patron saints that hold in their arms the cathedrals they protect.

'I'm surprised that they let you come up from Salonika,' Sylvia said. 'Didn't they know the line was likely to be cut?'

'I had to report to Captain Hazlewood,' Miss Potberry replied firmly. 'And as I had already been rather delayed upon my journey I was anxious to get on as soon as possible.'

The consciousness of being needed by England radiated from her eyes; it was evident that nothing would make her budge from Nish until she had reported herself to her unknown chief.

'You'd better share my room,' Sylvia said. She nearly blushed at her own impudence when Miss Potberry gratefully accepted the offer. However, she could no longer reproach herself for staying on in Nish without justification, for now it was impossible to go away in ordinary fashion.

'It seems funny that Captain Hazlewood shouldn't have left any written instructions for me,' said Miss Potberry, when she had waited three days in Nish without any news except the rumoured fall of Veles. 'I'm not sure if I oughtn't to try and join him wherever he is.'

'But he's at the front,' Sylvia objected.

'I had instructions to report to him,' said Miss Potberry seriously. 'I think I'm wasting time and drawing my salary for nothing here. *That* isn't patriotism. If he'd left something for me to type – but to wait here like this doing nothing seems almost wicked at such a time.'

Two more days went by; Uskub had fallen; everybody gave up the idea of Anglo-French troops arriving to relieve Nish, and everybody began to talk about evacuation. About six o'clock of a stormy dusk, four days after the fall of Uskub, a Serbian soldier came to the hotel to ask Sylvia to come at once to a hospital. She wondered if something had happened to Michael, if somehow he had heard she was in Nish, and that he had sent for her. But when she reached the schoolroom that was serving as an improvised ward she found Hazlewood lying back upon a heap of straw that was called a bed.

'Done a damned stupid thing,' he murmured. 'Got hit, and they insisted on my being sent back to Nish. Think I'm rather bad. Why haven't you left?'

'The line is cut.'

'I know. You ought to have been gone by now. You can take my horse. Everyone will evacuate Nish. No chance. The Austrians have joined up with the Bulgarians. Bound to fall. I want you to take the keys of my safe and burn all my papers. Don't forget the cypher. Go and do it now and let me know it's done. Quick, it's worrying me. Nothing important, but it's worrying me.'

Sylvia decided to say nothing to him about Miss Potberry's arrival in order not to worry him any more. Miss Potberry should have his horse: Nish might be empty as a tomb, but she herself should stay on for news of Michael Fane.

'What are you waiting for?' he asked fretfully. 'Damn it, I shan't last for ever. That's Antitch you're staring at in the next bed.'

Sylvia looked at the figure muffled in bandages. Apparently all the lower part of his face had been shot away, and she could see nothing but a pair of dark and troubled eyes wandering restlessly in the candlelight.

'We took our finals together,' said Hazlewood.

Sylvia went away quickly; if she had paused to compare this meeting with the first meeting in the railway-carriage not yet three weeks ago, she should have broken down.

When Miss Potberry heard of her chief's arrival in Nish she insisted upon going to see him.

'But, my dear woman, he may be dying. What's the good of bothering him now? I'll find out whatever he can tell me. You must get ready to leave Nish. Pack up your things.'

'He may be glad to dictate something,' Miss Potberry argued. 'Please let me come. I am anxious to report to Captain Hazlewood. I'm sure if you had told him that I was here he would have wished to see me.'

Sylvia did not feel that she could contest anything; with Miss Potberry's help she burnt the few papers that remained in the safe together with the cypher, which glowed and smouldered in the basin for what seemed an interminable time. When not a single record of Hazlewood's presence in Serbia remained, Sylvia and Miss Potberry went back to the hospital.

'You've burnt everything?' he asked.

Sylvia nodded.

'Is that a nurse? I can't see in this infernal candlelight and I'm chockful of morphia, which makes my eyelids twitch.'

'It's I, Captain Hazlewood – Miss Potberry. I had instructions from the War Office to report to you. I was unfortunately delayed upon my journey, and when I arrived from Salonika you had left. Is there anything you would like done?'

'Oh, my god,' he half groaned, half laughed. 'I see that even my deathbed is going to be haunted by departmental imbecility. Who on earth sent you to Nish from Salonika?'

'Colonel Bullingham-Jones to whom I reported in Salonika knew nothing about me and advised me to come on here as soon as possible.'

'Officious ass!' Hazlewood muttered. 'Why didn't you go back, when you found I wasn't here?' he added to his secretary.

'There was no way of getting back, Captain Hazlewood. I believe that the enemy has cut the line.'

'I'm sorry you've had all this trouble for nothing,' he said. 'However, you and Miss Scarlett must settle between you how to get away. You'd better hang on to one of the Red Cross units.'

'I'm afraid I may have to leave my typewriter behind,' said Miss Potberry. 'Have I your permission?'

'You have,' he said, smiling with his eyes through the glaze of the drug.

'You couldn't give me a written authorization?' asked Miss Potberry. 'Being government property—'

'No, I can only give you verbal instructions. Both my arms have been shot away, or as nearly shot away as doesn't make it possible to write.'

'Oh, I beg your pardon. Then to whom should I report next?'

'I don't know. It might be St. Peter, with winter coming on and Albania to be crossed. No, no, don't you bother about reporting. Just follow the crowd and you'll be all right. Good-bye, Miss Potberry. Sorry you've had such a long journey for nothing. Sorry about everything.'

He beckoned Sylvia close to him with his eyes.

'For heaven's sake get rid of her or I shall have another hemorrhage.'

Sylvia asked Miss Potberry to go back to the hotel and get packed. When the secretary had gone, she knelt by Hazlewood.

'Michael Fane arrived yet?' he asked.

She shook her head.

'I had something to give him.'

The wounded man's face became more definitely lined with pain in the new worry of Fane's non-appearance.

'I want you to give him a letter. It's under my pillow. If by chance he doesn't come, perhaps you'd be good enough to post it when you get an opportunity. Miss Pauline Grey, Wychford Rectory, Oxfordshire.'

Sylvia found the letter which was still unaddressed.

'If Michael comes, I'd like him to take it to her himself when he gets to England. Thanks awfully. Give him my love. He was a great friend of mine. Yes, a great friend. Thanks awfully for helping me. I don't like to worry the poor devils here. They've got such a lot to worry them. Antitch died while you were burning my papers.'

Sylvia looked at the muffled figure whose eyes no longer stared with troubled imperception.

'Of course I may last for two or three days,' he went on. 'And in that case I may see Michael. Mind you bring him if he comes in time. Great friend of mine, and I'd like him to explain something to somebody. By the way, don't take all my talk the other night too seriously. I often talk like that. I don't mean half I say. England's all right really. Perhaps you'll look me up in the morning, if I'm still here? Goodbye. Thanks very much. I'm sorry I can't shake hands.'

'Would you like a priest?' Sylvia asked.

'A priest?' he repeated in a puzzled voice. 'Oh no, thanks very much, priests have always bored me. I'm going to lie here and think. The annoying thing is, you know, that I've not the slightest desire to die. Some people say that you have at the end, but I feel as if I was missing a train. Perhaps I'll see you in the morning. So long.'

But she did not see him in the morning, because he died in the night, and his bed was wanted immediately for another wounded man.

'What a dreadful thing war is,' sighed Miss Potberry. 'I've lost two first cousins and four second cousins, and my brother is soon going to France.'

The evacuation of Nish was desperately hastened by the news of the swift advance of the enemy on three sides. Sylvia with the help of Colonel Michailovitch managed to establish her rights over Hazlewood's horse, and Miss Potberry fired with the urgency of reporting to somebody else and of explaining why she had abandoned her typewriter was persuaded to attach herself to a particularly efflorescent branch of Dorothy Perkins that had wound itself round Harry Vereker to be trained

543

into safety on the other side of the mountains. The last that Sylvia saw of her was when she drove out of Nish in a bullock-cart, still pink and prim, because the jolting had not yet really begun. The last Sylvia heard of Harry Vereker was his unruffled voice leaving instructions that if some white corduroy riding-breeches which he had been expecting by special courier from Athens should by chance arrive before the Bulgarians they were to follow him. One had the impression of his messenger and his breeches as equally important entities marching arm in arm toward the Black Drin in obedience to his instructions. The next day came news of the fall of Kragujevatz following upon that of Pirot, and the fever of flight was aggravated to panic.

In the evening when Sylvia was watching the tormented square, listening to the abuse and blasphemy that was roused by the scarcity of transport and trying to accept in spite of the disappointment the irremediable fact of Michael's failure to arrive, she suddenly caught sight of his sister pushing her way through the mob below. Her appearance alone like this could only mean that Michael had been killed; Sylvia cursed the flattering lamp of fortune, which had lighted her to Nish only to extinguish itself in this moment of confusion and horror. How pale that sister looked, how deeply ringed her eyes, how torn and splashed her dress: she must have heard the news of her brother and fled in despair before the memory. All Sylvia's late indifference to suffering in the actual presence of war was kindled to a fury of resentment against the unreasonable forces that the world had let loose upon itself; even the envelope that Hazlewood had given to her now burnt her heart with what it enclosed of eternally unquenched regret, of eternal unfulfilment. She hurried downstairs and out into the mad, screaming, weeping mob and bathed herself in the stench of wet and filthy rags and in the miasma of sick, starved, and verminous bodies. A child was sucking the raw head of a hen; it happened that Sylvia knocked against it in her hurry, whereupon the child grabbed the morsel of blood and mud, snarling at her like a famished hound. Wherever she looked there were children searching on all fours among the filth lodged in the cracks of the rough paving-stones; it was an existence where nothing counted except the ability to trample over one's neighbour to reach food or safety; and she herself was searching for Michael's sister in the fetid swarm, just as these children were shrieking and scratching for the cabbage-stalks they found among the dung. At last the two women met, and Sylvia caught hold of Mrs. Merivale's arm.

'What do you want? What do you want?' she cried. 'Can I help you?'

The other turned and looked at Sylvia without recognizing her.

544

'You're Mrs. Merivale – Michael's sister,' Sylvia went on. 'Don't you remember me? Sylvia Scarlett. What has happened to him?'

'Can't we get out of this crowd?' Mrs. Merivale replied. 'I'm trying to find an English officer – Captain Hazlewood.'

Before Sylvia could tell her what had happened a cart drawn by a donkey covered with sores interposed between them; it was impossible for either woman to ask or answer anything in this abomination of humanity that oozed and writhed like a bunch of earthworms on a spade. Somehow they emerged from it all, and Sylvia brought her upstairs to her room.

'Is Michael dead?' she asked.

'No, but he's practically dying. I've got him into a deserted house. He fell ill with typhus in Kragujevatz. The enemy was advancing terribly fast, and I got him here, heaven knows how, in a bullock-cart – I've probably killed him in doing so; he certainly can't be moved again. I must find this friend of ours – Guy Hazlewood. He'll be able to tell me how long we can stay in Nish.'

Sylvia broke the news of Hazlewood's death and was momentarily astonished to see how casually she took it. Then she remembered that she had already lost her husband, that her brother was dying, and that probably she had heard such tidings of many friends. This was a woman who was beholding the society in which she had lived falling to pieces round her every day; she was not like herself cloistered in vagrancy, one for whom life and death had waved at each other from every platform and every quay in partings that were not less final. There occurred to Sylvia the last utterance of Hazlewood about missing a train; he perhaps had found existence to be a destructive business; but even so she could not think that he had loved it more charily.

'Everybody is dying,' said Mrs. Merivale. 'Those who survive this war will really have been granted a second life and will have to begin all over again like children – or lunatics,' she added to herself.

'Could I come with you to see him?' Sylvia asked. 'I had typhus myself last year in Petrograd and I could nurse him.'

'I don't think it's any longer a matter for nursing,' the other answered hopelessly. 'It's just leaving him alone and not worrying him any more. Oh, I wonder how long we can count on Nish not being attacked.'

'Not very long, I'm afraid,' said Sylvia. 'Hardly any time at all in fact.'

They left the hotel with that sense of mechanical action which sometimes relieves a strain of accumulated emotion. Sylvia had the notion of finding a Serbian doctor whom she knew slightly, and was successful in bringing him along to the house where Michael was lying. It was dark when they arrived in the deserted side-street now strewn with the rubbish of many families' flight.

Michael was lying on a camp bed in the middle of the room. On the floor a Serbian peasant wearing a Red Cross brassard was squatting by his head and from time to time moistening his forehead with a damp sponge. In a corner two other Serbians armed with fantastic weapons sat cross-legged upon the floor, a winking candle and strewn playing-cards between them. Sylvia felt a sudden awe of looking at him directly, and she waited in the doorway while the doctor went forward with his sister to make his examination. After a short time the doctor turned away with a shrug; he and Mrs. Merivale rejoined Sylvia in the doorway and together they went in another room, where the doctor in sibilant French confirmed the impossibility of moving him if his life was to be saved. He added that the Bulgarians would be in Nish within a few days and that the town would be empty long before that. Then after giving a few conventional directions for the care of the patient he saluted the two women and went away.

Sylvia and Mrs. Merivale looked at each other across a bare table on which was set a lantern covered with cobwebs; it was the only piece of furniture left, and Sylvia had a sense of dramatic unreality about their conversation; standing up in this dim room, she was conscious of a make-believe intensity that tore the emotions more completely into rags than any normal procedure or expression of passionate feeling. Yet it was only because she divined an approach to the climax of her life that she felt thus; it was so important that she should have her way in what she intended to do that it was impossible for her to avoid regarding Michael's sister not merely as a partner in the scene, but also as the audience on whose approval success ultimately depended. The bareness of the room was like a stage, and the standing up like this was like a scene; it seemed right to exaggerate the gestures to keep pace with the emotional will to achieve her desire.

'Mrs. Merivale,' she began, 'I beg you to let me stay behind in Nish and look after Michael so far as anything can be done – and of course it will be better for him that a woman should oversee the devotion of his orderly. Nothing will induce me to leave Nish. Nothing. You must understand that now. There is nothing to prevent me from staying here; you must take Captain Hazlewood's horse and go to-morrow.'

'Leave my brother? Why, the idea is absurd. I tell you I almost dragged that cart through the mud from Kragujevatz. Besides, I'm a more or less qualified nurse. You're not.'

'I'm qualified to nurse him through this fever because I know exactly

546

what is wanted. If any new complication arose, you could do no more than I could do until the Bulgarian doctors arrived. If you stay here, you will be taken to Bulgaria.'

'And why not?' demanded the other. 'I'd much rather be taken prisoner with Michael than go riding off on my own and leave him here. No, no, the idea's impossible.'

'You have your mother – his mother to think of. You have your son,' Sylvia argued.

'Neither mother nor son could be any excuse for leaving Michael at such a moment.'

'Certainly not, if you could not find a substitute. But I shall stay here in any case, and you've no right to desert other obligations,' Sylvia affirmed.

'You're talking to me in a ridiculous way. There is only one obligation, which is to him.'

'Do you think you can do more for him than I can do?' Sylvia challenged. 'You can do less. You have already had the fearful strain of getting him here from the north. You are worn out. You are not fit to nurse him as he must be nursed. You are not fit to deal with the Bulgarians when they come. You are already breaking down. Why – there is no force in your arguments! They are as tame and conventional as if you were inventing an excuse to break a social engagement.'

'But by what right do you make this – this violent demand?' asked the other.

There suddenly came over Sylvia the futility of discussing the question in this fashion: this flickering room echoing faintly to the shouts of the affrighted fugitives in the distance lacked any atmosphere to hide the truth, for which in its bareness and misery it seemed to cry aloud. The question that his sister had put demanded an answer that would evade nothing in the explanation of her request; and if that answer should leave her soul stripped and desolate for the contemptuous regard of a woman who could not comprehend, why then thus was her destiny written and she should stand humiliated while the life that she had not been great enough to seize passed out of her reach.

'If my demand is violent, my need is violent,' she cried. 'Once in my dressing-room – the only time we met – you told me that you half regretted your rejection of art; you envied me my happiness in success. Your envy seemed to me then the bitterest irony, for I could not find in art that which I demanded. I have never found it until now in the chance to save your brother's life. That is exaggerating, you'll say. Yet I do believe – and if you could know my history you would believe it too – I do believe that my will can save him now not merely from death, but from the captivity that will follow. I know what it feels like to recover from this fever; and I know that he will not wish to see you and himself prisoners. He will fret himself ill again about your position. I am nothing to him. He will never know that we changed places deliberately. He will accept me as a companion in misfortune, and I will give all that love can give, love that feeds upon and inflames itself without demanding fuel except from the heart of the one who loves. You cannot refuse me now, my dear – so dear to me because you are his sister. You cannot refuse me when I ask you to let me stay because I love him.'

'Do you love Michael?' asked the other wonderingly.

'I love him, I love him, and one does not speak lightly of love at a moment like this. Do you remember when you asked me to come and stay with you in the country to meet him? It was eighteen months ago. Your letter arrived when I had just been jilted by a man I was going to marry in a desperate effort to persuade myself that domesticity was the cure for my discontent. My discontent was love for your brother. It has never been anything else since the moment we met, though I cried out "Never" when I read your invitation. I abandoned everything. I have lived ever since as a mountebank, driven always by a single instinct that sustained me. That instinct was merely a superstition to travel south. Whenever I travelled on, I had always the sense of an object. I have found that object at last, and I know absolutely that fate stood at your elbow and dragged with you at those weary bullocks in the mud to bring Michael here in time. I know that fate chained me to my balcony at Nish, where for nearly a month I have been watching for your arrival. You are wise; you have suffered; you have loved: I beseech you that just for the sake of your pride you will not rob me of this moment to which my whole life has been the mad overture.'

'What you say about my being a worry to him when he recovers consciousness is true,' said the sister. 'It's the only good argument you've brought forward. Ah, but I won't be so ungenerous. Stay then. To-night I will wait here and to-morrow you shall take my place.'

The flickering bareness of the room flashed upon Sylvia with unimaginable glory; the dark night of her soul was become day.

'I think you can hear the joy in my heart,' she whispered. 'I can't say any more.'

Sylvia fell upon her knees; bowing her head upon the table she wept tears that seemed to gush like melodious fountains in a new world.

'You have made me believe that he will not die,' the sister murmured. 'I did not think that I should be able to believe that; but I do now, Sylvia.'

An assurance that positively seemed to contain life came over both of them. Sylvia rose from her knees, and abruptly they began to talk practically of what should be done that night and of what it would be wise to provide to-morrow. Presently Sylvia left the house, and slept in her hotel one of those rare sleeps whence waking is a descent upon airy plumes from heights where action and aspiration are fused in a ravishing unutterable affirmative, of which somehow a remembered consciousness is accorded to the favoured soul.

The next morning, Michael's sister mounted her horse. The guns of the desperate army of Stephanovitch confronting the Bulgarian advance were now audible; their booming gave power of flight to the weakest that remained in Nish; and the coil of fugitives writhed over the muddy plain toward the mountains.

'I think he seemed a little better this morning,' she said wistfully.

'Don't be jealous of leaving me,' Sylvia begged. 'You shall never regret that impulse. Will you take this golden bag with you? I don't want it to adorn a Bulgarian; it was a token to me of love, and it has been a true token. At the end of your journey sell it and give the money to poor Serbians. Will you? And this letter for Captain Hazlewood. Please post it in England. Good-bye, my dear, my dear.'

Michael's sister took the bag and the letter. In the light of this grey morning her grey eyes were profound lakes of grief.

'I am envying you for the second time,' she said. Then she waved her crop and rode quickly away. Sylvia watched her out of sight, thinking what it must have cost that proud sister to make this sacrifice. Her heart ached with a weight of unexpressed gratitude, and yet she could not keep it from beating with a fierce and triumphant gladness when she went up to where Michael was lying and found him alone. The orderly and servants had fled from the fear that clung to Nish like the clouds of this heavy day, and Sylvia taking his hand bathed his forehead with a tenderness that she half dreaded to use, so much did it seem a flame that would fan the fever in whose embrace he tossed unconscious of all but a world of shadows.

For a week she stayed beside him, sleeping sometimes with her head against his arm, listening to the sombre colloquies of delirium, striving to keep the soul that often in the long trances seemed to flutter disconsolately away from the exhausted body. There was no longer any sound of people in Nish: there was nothing but the guns coming nearer and nearer every hour. Then suddenly the firing ceased: there was a clatter and splash of cavalry upon the muddy paving-stones. The noise passed. Michael sat up and said:

'Listen!'

She thought he was away upon some adventure of delirium and told him not to worry, but to lie still. He was so emaciated that she asked herself if he could really be living: it was like brushing a cobweb from one's path to make him lie down again. A woman's scream, the thin scream of an old woman, shuddered upon the silence outside; but the noise did not disturb him, and he lay perfectly still with his eyes fixed upon the ceiling. A few minutes later he again sat up in bed.

'Am I mad, or is it Sylvia Scarlett?' he asked.

'Yes, it's Sylvia. You're very ill. You must keep still.'

'What an extraordinary thing,' he murmured seriously to himself. 'I suppose I shall hear all about it to-morrow.'

He lay back again without seeming to worry about the problem of her presence; nor did he ask where his sister was. Sylvia remembered her own divine content in the hospital when the fever left her, and she wanted him to lie as long as possible thus. Presently, however, he sat up again and said:

'Listen, Sylvia, I thought I wasn't wrong. Do you hear a kind of whisper in the air?'

She listened to please him, and then upon the silence she heard the sound. From a whisper it grew to a sigh, from a sigh it rose to a rustling of many leaves: it was the Bulgarian army marching into Nish, a procession of silent-footed devils, mysterious, remorseless, innumerable.

VII

To Sylvia's surprise and relief, the conquerors paid no attention to the house that night. Michael, after he had listened for awhile to the damp-ered progress of that soft-shod army, fell back upon his pillow without comment and slept very tranquilly. Sylvia who had now not the least doubt of his recovery busied herself with choosing what she conceived to be absolute necessities for the immediate future and packing them into her valise. In the course of her preparations she put on one side for destruction or abandonment the contents of the golden shawl. Daguerrotypes and photographs; a rambling declaration of the circum-stances in which her alleged grandfather had married that ghostly Adèle her grandmother; and a variety of letters that illustrated her mother's early life: all these might as well be burnt. She lay down upon her bed of overcoats and skirts piled upon the floor and found the shawl a pleasant addition to the rubber hot-water bottle she had been using as a pillow. Michael was still sleeping; it seemed wise to blow out the candle and, although it was scarcely seven o'clock, to try to sleep herself. It was the first time for a week that she had been able to feel the delicious and inviting freedom of untrammelled sleep. What did the occupation of a Bulgarian army signify in comparison with the assurance she felt of her patient's convalescence? The brazier glowed before her path towards a divine oblivion.

When Sylvia woke up and heard Michael's voice calling to her, it was six o'clock in the morning. She blew up the dull brazier to renewed warmth, set water to boil, and in a real exultation lighted four candles to celebrate with as much gaiety as possible the new atmosphere of joy and hope in the stark room.

'It's all very mysterious,' Michael was saying. 'It's all so delightfully mysterious that I can hardly bear to ask any questions lest I destroy the mystery. I've been lying awake, exquisitely and self-admiringly awake for an hour, trying to work out where I am, why I'm where I am, why you're where you are, and where Stella is.'

Sylvia told him of the immediate occasion of his sister's departure, and when she had done so had a moment of dismay lest his affection or his pride should be hurt by her willingness to leave him in the care of one who was practically a stranger.

'How very kind of you,' he said. 'My mother would have been distracted by having to look after her grandson in the whirlpool of war-work upon which she is engaged. So you had typhus too? It's a rotten business, isn't it? Did you feel very weak after it?'

'Of course.'

'And we're prisoners?'

'I suppose so.'

The water did not seem to be getting on, and Sylvia picked up her family papers to throw into the brazier.

'Oh, I say, don't destroy without due consideration,' Michael protested. 'The war has developed in me a passionate conservatism for little things.'

'I am destroying nothing of any importance,' Sylvia said.

'Love-letters?' he murmured with a smile.

She flushed angrily and discovered in herself a ridiculous readiness to prove his speculation beside the mark.

'If I ever had any love-letters I certainly never kept them,' she avowed. 'These are only musty records of a past, the influence of which has already exhausted itself.'

'But photographs?' he persisted. 'Let me look. Old photographs always thrill me.'

She showed him one or two of her mother.

'Odd,' he commented. 'She rather reminds me of my sister. Something about the way the eyes are set.'

'You're worrying about her?' Sylvia put in quickly.

'No, no. Of course I shall be glad to hear she's safely by the sea on the other side, but I'm not worrying about her to the extent of fancying a non-existent likeness. There really is one; and if it comes to that, you're not unlike her yourself.'

'My father and my grandfather were both English,' Sylvia said. 'My mother was French and my grandmother was Polish. My grandfather's name was Cunningham.'

'What?' Michael asked sharply. 'That's odd.'

'Quite a distinguished person according to the old Frenchman whom the world regarded as my grandfather.'

She handed him Bassompierre's rambling statement about the circumstances of her mother's birth, which he read and put down with an exclamation.

'Well, this is really extraordinary! Do you know that we're second cousins? This Charles Cunningham became the twelfth Lord Saxby. My father was the thirteenth and last earl. What a trick for fate to play upon us both! No wonder there's a likeness between you and Stella. How strange it makes that time at Mulberry Cottage seem. But you know, I always felt that underneath our open and violent hostility there was a radical sympathy quite inexplicable. This explains it.'

Sylvia was not at all sure that she felt grateful toward the explanation; mere kinship had never stood for much in her life.

'You must try to sleep again now,' she said sternly.

'But you don't seem at all amazed at this coincidence,' Michael protested. 'You accept it as if it was a perfectly ordinary occurrence.'

'I want you to sleep. Take this milk. We are sure to have a nerve-racking day with these Bulgarians.'

'Sylvia, what's the matter?' he persisted. 'Why should my discovery of our relationship annoy you?'

'It doesn't annoy me, but I want you to sleep. Do remember that you've only just returned to yourself and that you'll soon want all your strength.'

'You've not lost your baffling quality in all these years,' he said, and lay silent when he had drunk the warm milk she gave him and while she tidied the floor of the coats that served for a bed. The letters and the photographs she threw into the brazier and drove them deep into the coke with a stick, looking round defiantly at Michael when they were ashes. He shook his head with a smile, but he did not say anything.

Sylvia was really glad when the sound of loud knocking upon the door downstairs prevented any further discussion of the accident of their relationship; nevertheless she found a pleasure in announcing to the Bulgarian officer her right to be found here with the sick Englishman, her cousin: it seemed to launch her once more upon the flow of ordinary existence, this kinship with one who without doubt belonged to the world actively at war. The interview with the Bulgarian officer took place in the stark and dusty room where she had argued with Stella for the right to stay behind with her brother. Now in the light of early morning it still preserved its scenic quality, and Sylvia was absurdly aware of her resemblance to the pleading heroine of a melodrama, when she begged this grimy, shaggy creature whose slate-grey overcoat was marbled by time and weather to let her patient stay here for the present, and further-more to accord her facilities to procure for him whatever was necessary and obtainable. In the end the officer went away without giving a more decisive answer than was implied by the soldier he left behind. Sylvia did not think he could have understood much of her French, so little had she understood of his, and the presence of this soldier with fixed bayonet and squashed Mongolian countenance oppressed her. She wondered what opinion of them the officer had reached and ached at the thought of how perhaps in a few minutes she and Michael should be separated, intolerably separated for ever. She made a sign to the guard for leave to go upstairs again; but he forbade her with a gesture, and she stood leaning against the table, while he stared before him with an expression of such unutterable nothingness as by sheer nebulosity acquired a sinister and menacing force. He was as incomprehensible as a savage beast encoun-tered in a forest, and the fancy that he had ever existed with his own little ambitions in a human society refused to state itself. Sylvia could make of him nothing but a symbol of the blind mad forces that were in opposition throughout the old familiar world, the blindness and madness of which were fitly expressed by such an instrument.

Half an hour of strained indifference passed, and then the officer came back with another who spoke English. Perhaps the consciousness of speaking English well and fluently made the newcomer anxious to be pleasant; one felt that he would have regarded it as a slight upon his own proficiency to be rude or intransigent. Apart from his English there was nothing remarkable in his appearance or his personality. He went upstairs and saw for himself Michael's condition, came down again with

Sylvia, and promised her that, if she would observe the rules imposed upon the captured city, nothing within the extent of his influence should be done to imperil the sick man's convalescence. Then after signing a number of forms that would enable her to move about in certain areas to obtain provisions and to call upon medical help, he asked her if she knew Sunbury-on-Thames. She replied in the negative, which seemed to disappoint him. Whereupon she asked him if he knew Maidenhead, and he brightened up again.

'I have had good days in the Thames,' he said, and departed in a bright cloud of riverside memories.

The next fortnight passed in a seclusion that was very dear to Sylvia. The hours rolled along on the easy wheels of reminiscent conversations, and Michael was gradually made aware of all her history. Yet at the end of it, she told herself that he was aware of nothing except the voyages of the body; of her soul's pilgrimage he was as ignorant as if they had never met. She reproached herself for this and wanted to begin over again the real history; but her own feelings towards him stood in the way of frankness and she feared to betray herself by the emotion that any deliberate sincerity must have revealed. Yet, as she assured herself rather bitterly, he was so obviously blind to anything but the coincidence of their relationship that she might with impunity have stripped her soul bare. It was unreasonable for her to resent his showing himself more moved by the news of Hazlewood's death than by anything in her own history, because anything in her own history that might have moved him she had omitted, and his impression of her now must be what his impression of her had been nine years ago – that of a hard and cynical woman with a baffling capacity for practical kindliness. She had often before been dismayed by a sense of life slipping out of her reach, but she had never before been dismayed by the urgent escape of hours and minutes. She had never before said *ruit hora* with her will to snatch the opportunity palsied, as if she stood panting in the stifling impotence of a dream. Already he was able to walk about the room, and like all those who are recovering from a serious illness was performing little feats of agility with the objective self-absorption of a child.

'Do people – or rather,' she corrected herself quickly, 'does existence seem something utterly different from what it was before you saw it fade out from your consciousness at Kragujevatz?'

'Well, the only person I've really seen is yourself,' he answered. 'And I can't help staring at you in some bewilderment, due less to fever than to the concatenations of fortune. What seems to me so amusing and odd is that, if you had known we were cousins, you couldn't have behaved in a more cousinly way than you did over Lily.'

'When I found myself in that hospital at Petrograd,' Sylvia declared, 'I felt like the Sleeping Beauty being waked by the magic kiss—' she broke off, blushing hotly and cursing inwardly her damned self-consciousness; and then blushed again because she had stopped to wonder if he had noticed her blush.

'I don't think anything that happened during this war to me personally,' Michael said, 'could ever make any impression now. The war itself always presents itself to me as a mighty fever, caught, if you will, by taking foolish risks or ignoring simple precautions, but ultimately and profoundly inevitable in the way that one feels all illness to be inevitable. Anything particular that happens to the individual must lose its significance in the change that he must suffer from the general calamity. I think perhaps that as a Catholic I am tempted to be less hopeful of men and more hopeful of God, but yet I firmly believe that I am more hopeful of men than the average – shall we call him humanitarian, who perceives in this war nothing but a crime against human brotherhood committed by a few ambitious knaves helped by a crowd of ambitious fools. I'm perfectly sure for instance that there is no one alive and no one dead that does not partake of the responsibility. However little it may be apprehended in the case of individuals, nothing will ever persuade me that one of the chief motive forces that maintain this state of destruction to which the world is being devoted is not a sense of guilt and a determination to expiate it. Mark you, I'm not trying to urge that God has judicially sentenced the world to war, dealing out horror to Belgium for the horror of the Congo, horror to Serbia for the horror of the royal assassination, horror to France, England, Germany, Austria, Italy, and Russia for their national lapses from grace – I should be very sorry to implicate Almighty God in any conception based upon our primitive notions of justice. The only time I feel that God ever interfered with humanity was when He was incarnate amongst us, and the story of that seems to forbid us our attribution to Him of anything in the nature of fretful castigation. The most presumptuous attitude in this war seems to me the German idea of God in a *pickelhaube*, of Christ bound to an Iron Cross, and of the Dove as a bloody-minded Eagle; but the Allies' notion of the Pope as a kind of diplomat with a licence to excommunicate seems to me only less presumptuous.'

'Then you think the war is in every human heart?' Sylvia asked.

'When I look at my own I'm positive it is.'

'But do you think it was inevitable because it was salutary?'

'I think blood-letting is old-fashioned surgery: aren't you confusing the disease with the remedy? Surely no disease is salutary, and I think it's morally dangerous to confuse effect with cause. At the same time I'm not going to lay down positively that this war may not be extremely salutary. I think it will be, but I acquit God of any hand in its deliberate ordering. Free will must apply to nations. I don't believe that war which, while it brings out often the best of people, brings out much more often the worst is to be regarded as anything but a vile exhibition of human sin. The selflessness of those who have died is terribly stained by the selfishness of those who have let them die. Yet the younger generation, or such of it as survives, will have the compensation when it is all over of such amazing opportunities for living as were never known, and the older generation that made the war will die less lamented that any men that have ever died since the world began. And I believe that their purgatory will be the greyest and the longest of all the purgatories. But as soon as I have said that I regret my words, because I think it will be fatal for the younger generation to become precocious Pharisees, and so I reiterate that the war is in every human heart, and you're not to tempt me any more into making harsh judgments about anyone.'

'Not even the great Victorians?' said Sylvia.

'Well, that will be a difficult and very penitential piece of self-denial, I admit. And it is hard not to hope that Carlyle is in hell. However, I can just avoid doing so, because I shall certainly go to hell myself if I do, where his Teutonic borborygmi would be an added woe, gigantic genius though he was. But don't let's joke about hell. It's – infernally credible since August, 1914. What were we talking about before we began to talk about the war? Oh, I remember, the new world that one gets up to face after a bad illness.'

'Perhaps my experience was peculiar,' Sylvia said.

But what did it matter how he regarded the world, she thought, unless he regarded her? Already the topic was exhausted; he was tired by his vehemence; once more the ruthless and precipitate hour had gone by.

During this period of seclusion Sylvia often had to encounter in its various capacities the army of occupation, by which generally she was treated with consideration, and even with positive kindness. Nish had been so completely evacuated that after the medley which had thronged the streets and squares it now seemed strangely empty. The uniformity of the Bulgarian characteristics added to the impression of violent change; there was never a moment in which one could delude oneself with the continuation of normal existence. At the end of the fortnight, the English-speaking officer came to make a visit of inspection in order to give his advice at headquarters about the future of the prisoners. Michael was still very weak and looked a skeleton, so much so indeed that the officer went off and fetched a squat little doctor to help his deliberation; the latter recommended another week, and the prisoners were once more left to themselves. Sylvia was half sorry for such considerate action; the company of Michael which had seemed to promise so much and had in fact yielded so little was beginning to fret her with the ultimate futility of such an association. She resented the emotion she had given to it in the prospect of a more definitely empty future that was now opening before her, and she gave way to the reaction against her exaggerated devotion by criticizing herself severely. The supervention of such an attitude made irksome what had been so dear a seclusion, and going beyond self-criticism she began to tell herself that Michael was cold, inhuman and remote, that she felt ill at ease with him and unable to talk, and that the sooner their separation came about, the better. Perhaps she should be released, in which case she should make her way back to England and become a nurse.

At the end of the third week Sylvia desperately tried to arrest the precipitate hour.

'I think I suffer from a too rapid digestion,' she announced.

He looked at her with a question in his eyes.

'You were talking to me the other day,' she went on, 'about your contemplative experiences, and you were saying how entirely your purely intellectual and spiritual progress conformed to the well-trodden mystical way. You added, of course, that you did not wish to suggest any comparison with the path of greater men, but allowing for conventional self-depreciation you left me to suppose that you were content with your achievement. At the moment war broke out you felt that you were ripe for action, and instead of becoming a priest after those nine years of contemplative preparation, you joined an hospital unit for Serbia. You feel quite secure about the war; you accept your fever, your possible internment for years in Bulgaria, and indeed anything that affects you personally without the least regret. In fact you're what an American might call in tune with the infinite. I'm not! And it's all a matter of digestion.'

'My illness has clouded my brain,' Michael murmured. 'I'm a long way from understanding what you're driving at.'

'Well, keep quiet and listen to my problems. We're on the verge of separation, but you're still my patient and you owe me your attention.'

'I owe you more than that,' he put in.

'How feeble,' she scoffed. 'You might have spared me such a pretty-pretty sentence.'

'I surrender unconditionally,' he protested. 'Your fierceness is superfluous.'

'I suppose you've often labelled humanity in bulk? I mean for instance

– you must have often said and certainly thought that all men are either knaves or fools?'

'I must have thought so at some time or another,' Michael agreed.

'Well, I've got a new division. I think that all men have either normal digestions, slow digestions, rapid digestions, or no digestions at all. Extend the physical fact into a metaphor and apply it to the human mind.'

'Dear Sylvia, I feel as if I were being poulticed. How admirably you maintain the nursing manner. I've made the application. What do I do now?'

'Listen without interrupting, or I shall lose the thread of my argument. I suppose you'll admit that the optimists outnumber the pessimists? Obviously they must, or the world would come to an end. Very well then, we'll say that the pessimists are the people with no digestions at all: on top of them will be the people with slow digestions, the great unthinking herd that is optimistic because the optimists shout most loudly. The people with good normal digestions are of course the shouting optimists. Finally come the people whose digestions are too rapid. I belong to that class.'

'Are they optimists?'

'They're optimists until they've finished digesting, but between meals they're outrageously pessimistic. The only way to illustrate my theory is to talk about myself. Imagine you're a lady-palmist and prepare for a debauch of egotism from one of your clients. All through my life, Michael, I have been a martyr to quick digestion. Your friend Guy Hazlewood suffered from that complaint, judging by the way he talked about the war. I can imagine that his life has been made of brief exquisite illusions followed by long vacuums. Am I right?'

Michael nodded.

'Cassandra, to take a more remote instance, suffered from rapid digestion – in fact all prophets have the malady. Isn't it physiologically true to say that the unborn child performs in its mother's womb the drama of man's evolution? I'm sure it's equally true that the life of the individual after birth and until death is a microcosm of man's later history, or rather I ought to say that it might be, for only exceptional individuals reproduce the history of humanity up to contemporary development. A genius – a great creative genius seems to me a man whose active absorption can keep pace with the rapidity of his digestion. How often do we hear of people who were in advance of their time! This figure of speech is literally true, but only great creative geniuses have the consolation of projecting themselves beyond their ambient in time. There remain a number of sterile geniuses, whom nature with her usual prodigality has put on the market in reserve, but for whom later on she finds she has no use on account of the economy that always succeeds extravagance. These sterile geniuses are left to fend for themselves and somehow to extract from a hostile and suspicious environment food to maintain them during the long dreary emptiness that succeeds their too optimistic absorption. Do you agree with me?'

'At one end of the pole you would put Shakespeare, at the other the Jubilee Juggins?' Michael suggested.

'That's it,' she agreed. 'Although a less conspicuous wastrel would serve for the other end.'

'And I suppose if you're searching for the eternal rhythm of the universe, you'd have to apply to nations the same classification as to individuals?' he went on.

'Of course.'

'So that England would have a good normal digestion and Ireland a too rapid digestion? Or better, let us say that all Teutons eat heartily and digest slowly, and that all Celts are too rapid. But come back to yourself.'

Sylvia paused for a moment, and then continued with swift gestures of self-agreement:

'I certainly ascribe every mistake in my own life to a rapid digestion. Why I've even digested this war that, if we think on a large scale, was evidently designed to stir up the sluggish liver of the world. I'm sick to death of the damned war already, and it hasn't begun yet really. And to come down to my own little particular woes, I've laboured toward religion, digested it with horrible rapidity, and see nothing in it now but a half truth for myself. In art the same, in human associations the same, in everything the same. Ah, don't let's talk any more about anything.'

In the silence that followed she thought to herself about the inspiration of her late theories; and looking at Michael, pale and hollow-eyed in the grim November dusk, she railed at herself because with all her will to make use of the quality she had attributed to herself she could not shake off this love that was growing every day.

'Why, in God's name,' she almost groaned aloud, 'can't it go the way of everything else? But it won't. It won't. It never will. And I shall never be happy again.'

A rainy nightfall symbolized for her the darkness of the future, and when in the middle of their evening meal, while they were hacking at a tin of sardines, a message came from headquarters that to-morrow they must be ready to leave Nish, she was glad. However, the sympathy of the English-speaking officer had exercised itself so much on behalf of the two prisoners that the separation which Sylvia had regarded as immediate was likely to be postponed for some time. The officer explained that it was inconvenient for them to remain any longer in Nish, but that arrangements had been made by which they were to be moved to Sofia and therefore that Michael's convalescence would be safe against any premature strain. They would realize that Bulgaria was not unmindful of the many links, now unfortunately broken, which had formerly bound her to England, and they would admit in the face of their courteous treatment how far advanced his country was upon the road of civilization.

'Splendid,' Michael exclaimed. 'So we shan't be separated yet for awhile and we shall be able to prosecute our philosophical discoveries. The riddle of life finally solved in 1915 by two prisoners of the Bulgarian Army! It would almost make the war worth while. Sylvia, I'm so excited at our journey.'

'You're tired of being cooped up here,' she said sharply. And then to mask whatever emotion might have escaped, she added: 'I'm certainly sick to death of it myself.'

'I know,' he agreed, 'it must have been a great bore for you. The invalid is always blissfully unconscious of time, and forgets that the pleasant little services which encourage him to go on being ill are not natural events like sunrise and sunset. You do well to keep me up to the mark; I'm not really forgetful.'

'You seem to have forgotten that we may have months, even years of imprisonment in Bulgaria,' Sylvia said.

He looked so frail in his khaki overcoat that she was seized with penitence for the harsh thoughts of him she had indulged, and with a fondling gesture tried to atone:

'You really feel that you can make this journey? If you don't, I'll go and rout out our officer and beg him for another week.'

Michael shook his head.

'I'm rather a fraud. Really, you know, I feel perfectly well. Quite excited about this journey, as I told you.'

She was chilled by his so impersonally cordial manner and looked at him regretfully.

'Every day he gets farther away,' she thought. 'In nine years he has been doing nothing but place layer after layer over his sensitiveness. He's a kind of mental coral-island. I know that there must still exist a capacity for suffering, but he'll never again let me see it. He wants to convince me of his eternal serenity.'

She was looking at him with an unusual intentness, and he turned away in embarrassment, which made her jeer at him to cover her own shyness.

'It was just the reverse of embarrassment really,' he said. 'But I don't want to spoil things.'

'By doing what?' she demanded.

'Well, if I told you—' he stopped abruptly.

'I have a horror of incomplete or ambiguous conditionals. Now you've begun, you must finish.'

'Nothing will induce me to. I'll say what I thought of saying before we separate. I promise that.'

'Perhaps we never shall separate.'

'Then I shall have no need to finish my sentence.'

Sylvia lay awake for a long time that last night in Nish, wondering, with supreme futility as she continually reminded herself, what Michael could have nearly said. Somewhere about two o'clock she decided that he had been going to suggest adopting her into his family.

'Damned fool,' she muttered, pulling and shaking her improvised bed as if it were a naughty child. 'Nevertheless he had the wit to understand how much it would annoy me. It shows the lagoon is not quite encircled yet.'

The soldiers who arrived to escort them to the railway station were like grotesques of hotel-porters; they were so ready to help with the baggage that it seemed absurd for their movements to be hampered by rifles with fixed bayonets. The English-speaking officer accompanied them to the station and expressed his regrets that he could not travel to Sofia; he had no doubt that later on he should see them again and in any case when the war was over he hoped to revisit England. Sylvia suddenly remembered her big trunk, which she had left in the *consigne* when she first reached Nish nearly two months ago. The English-speaking officer shrugged his shoulders at her proposal to take it with her to Sofia.

'The station was looted by the Serbs before we arrived,' he explained. 'They are a barbarous nation, many years behind us in civilization. We never plunder. And of course you understand that Nish is really Bulgarian? That makes us particularly gentle here. You heard, perhaps, that when the Entente Legations left we gave them a champagne lunch for the farewell at Dedeagatch? We are far in front of the Germans, who are a very strong but primitive nation. They are not much liked in Bulgaria: we prefer the English. But, alas, poor England!' he sighed.

'Why poor?' Sylvia demanded indignantly.

He smiled compassionately for answer, and soon afterwards in a first-class compartment to themselves Michael and she left Nish.

'Really,' Michael observed, 'when the conditions are favourable, travelling as a prisoner-of-war is the most luxurious travelling of all. I've never experienced the servility of a private courier, but it's wonderful to feel that other people are under an obligation to look after you. However, at present we have the advantages of being new toys. Our friend from Sunbury-on-Thames may be as compassionate as he likes about England, but there's no doubt it confers on the possessor a quite peculiar thrill to own English people – even two such non-combatant creatures as ourselves. It's typical of the Germans' newness to European society that they should have thought the right way to treat English prisoners was to spit at them. I remember once seeing a grandee of Spain who'd been hired as secretary by a Barcelona Jew, and by Jove! he wasn't allowed to forget it. The Bulgarians on the other hand have a superficial air of breeding, which they've either copied from the Turks or inherited from the Chinese. Didn't you love the touch about the champagne lunch at Dedeagatch? There's a luxurious hospitality about that, which you won't find outside the *Arabian Nights* or Chicago. Really the English nation should give thanks every Sunday, murmuring with all eyes on the East window and Germany: "There but for the grace of God blowing in the west wind goes John Bull." Yet I wonder if the hearts would be humble enough to keep the Pharisee out of the thanksgiving.'

The train went slowly with frequent stoppages, often in wild country far from any railway-station, where in such surroundings its existence seemed utterly improbable. Occasionally small bands of comitadjis would ride up and menace theatrically the dejected Serbian prisoners who were being moved into Bulgaria. There was a cold wind, and snow was lying thinly on the hills.

In the rapid dusk Michael fell asleep; soon after, the train seemed to have stopped for the night. Sylvia did not wake him up, but sat for two hours by the light of one candle stuck upon her valise and pored upon the moonless night that pressed against the window-panes of the compartment with a scarcely endurable desolation. There was no sound of those murmurous voices that make mysterious even suburban tunnels when trains wait in them on foggy nights. The windows were screwed up; the door into the corridor was locked; in the darkness and silence Sylvia felt for the first time in all its force the meaning of imprisonment. Suddenly a flaring torch carried swiftly along the permanent way threw shadowy grotesques upon the ceiling of the compartment, and Michael waking up with a start asked their whereabouts.

'Somewhere near Zaribrod as far as I can make out, but it's impossible to tell for certain. I can't think what they're doing. We've been here for two hours without moving, and I can't hear a sound except the wind. It was somebody's carrying a torch past the window that woke you up.'

They speculated idly for a while on the cause of the delay, and then gradually under the depression of the silence their voices died away into occasional sighs of impatience.

'What about eating?' Sylvia suggested at last. 'I'm not hungry, but it will give us something to do.'

So they struggled with tinned foods, glad of the life that the fussy movement gave to the compartment.

'One feels that moments such as these should be devoted to the most intimate confidences,' Michael said, when they had finished their dinner and were once more enmeshed by the silence.

'There's a sort of portentousness about them, you mean?'

'Yes, but as a matter of fact one can't even talk about commonplace things, because one is all the time fidgeting with the silence.'

'I know,' Sylvia agreed. 'One gets a hint of madness in the way one's personality seems to shrink to nothing. I suppose there really is somebody left alive in the world? I'm beginning to feel as if it was just you and I against the universe.'

'Death must come like that sometimes,' he murmured.

'Like what?'

'Like that thick darkness outside and oneself against the universe.'

'I'd give anything for a guitar,' Sylvia exclaimed.

'What would you play first?' he enquired gravely.

She sang gently:

> '*La donna è mobile qual piuma al vento,*
> *Muta d'accento e di pensiero,*
> *Sempre un amabile leggiadro viso,*
> *In pianto o in riso, è menzognero—*

and that's all I can remember of it,' she said, breaking off.

'I wonder why you chose to sing that.'

'It reminds me of my father,' she answered. 'When he was drunk, fair cousin, he always used to sing that. What a charming son-in-law he would have made for our grandfather! Oh, are we ever going to move again?' she cried, jumping up and pressing her face against the viewless pane. 'Hark! I hear horses.'

Michael rose and joined her. Presently flames leapt up into the darkness, and armed men were visible in silhouette against the bonfire they had kindled, so large a bonfire indeed that, in the shadows beyond, the stony outcrop of a rough steep country seemed in contrast to be the threshold of titanic chasms. A noise of shouting reached the train, and presently Bulgarian regulars, the escort of the prisoners, joined the merry-makers round the fire. Slow music rumbled upon the air, and a circle of men shoulder to shoulder with interwoven arms performed a stately swaying dance.

'Or are they just holding one another up because they're drunk?' Sylvia asked.

'No, it's really a dance, though they may be drunk too. I wish we could get this window open. It looks as if all the soldiers had joined the party.'

The dance came to an end with shouts of applause, and one or two rifles were fired at the stars. Then the company squatted round the fire, and the wine circulated again.

'But where are the officers in charge?' Michael asked.

'Playing cards probably. Or perhaps they're dining with the rest. Anyway, if we're going to stay here all night, it's just as well to have the entertainment of this al fresco supper-party. Anything is better than that intolerable silence.'

Sylvia blew out the stump of candle, and they sat in darkness watching the fire-flecked revel. The shouting grew louder with the frequent passing of the wineskins; after an hour groups of comitadjis and regulars left the bonfire and wandered along the permanent way, singing drunken choruses. What happened presently at the far end of the train they could not see, but there was a sound of smashed glass followed by a man's scream. Those who were still sitting round the fire snatched up their weapons and stumbled in loud excitement toward the centre of the disturbance. There were about a dozen shots, the rasp of torn wood-work, and a continuous crash of broken glass with curses, cries, and all the sounds of quarrelsome confusion.

'The drunken brutes are breaking up the train,' Michael exclaimed. 'We'd better sit back from the window for a while.'

Sylvia cried out to him that it was worse and that they were dragging along by the heels the bodies of men and kicking them as they went.

'Good God!' he declared, standing up now in horror. 'They're murdering the wretched Serbian prisoners. Here, we must get out and protest.'

'Sit down, fool,' Sylvia commanded. 'What good will your protesting do?'

But as she spoke she gave a shuddering shriek and held her hands up to her eyes: they had thrown a writhing, mutilated shape into the fire.

'The brutes, the filthy brutes,' Michael shouted, and jumping upon

564

the seat of the compartment he kicked at the window-panes until there was not a fragment of glass left. 'Shout, Sylvia, shout. Oh, hell, I can't remember a word of their bloody language. We must stop them. Stop, I tell you. Stop!'

One of the prisoners had broken away from his tormentors and was running along the permanent way, but the blood from a gash in the forehead blinded him and he fell on his face just outside the compartment. Two comitadjis banged out his brains on the railway line; with clasp-knives they hacked the head from the corpse and merrily tossed it in at the window, where it fell on the floor between Sylvia and Michael.

'My God,' Michael muttered. 'It's better to be killed ourselves than to stay here and endure this.'

He began to scramble out of the window, and she seeing that he was nearly mad with horror at his powerlessness followed him in the hope of deflecting any rash action. Strangely enough, nobody interfered with their antics, and they had run nearly the whole length of the train, in order to find the officers in charge, before a tall man descending from one of the carriages barred their progress.

'Why, it's you,' Sylvia laughed hysterically. 'It's my rose-grower! Michael, do you hear? My rose-grower.'

It really was Rakoff, decked out with barbaric trappings of silver and bristling with weapons, but his manners had not changed with his profession and as soon as he recognized her, he bowed politely and asked if he could be of any help.

'Can't you stop this massacre?' she begged. 'Keep quiet, Michael, it's no good talking about the Red Cross.'

'It was the fault of the Serbians,' Rakoff explained. 'They insulted my men. But what are you doing here?'

The violence of the drunken soldiers and comitadjis had soon worn itself out, and most of them were back again round the fire, drinking and singing as if nothing had happened. Sylvia perceived that Rakoff was sincerely anxious to make himself agreeable and treading on Michael's foot (he was in a fume of threats) she explained their position.

Rakoff looked up at the carriage from which he had just descended.

'The officers in command are drunk and insensible,' he murmured. 'I'm under an obligation to you. Do you want to stay in Bulgaria? Have you given your parole?' he asked Michael.

'Give my parole to murderers and torturers?' shouted Michael. 'Certainly not, and I never will.'

'My cousin has only just recovered from typhus,' Sylvia reminded Rakoff. 'The slaughter has upset him.'

In her anxiety to take advantage of the meeting she had cast aside her own horror and forgotten her own inclination to be hysterical.

'He must understand that in the Balkans we do not regard violence as you do in Europe. He should remember that the Serbians would do the same and worse to Bulgarians.'

Rakoff spoke in a tone of injured sensibility, which would have been comic to Sylvia without the smell of burnt flesh upon the wind, and without the foul bloodstains upon her own skirt.

'Quite so. *À la guerre comme à la guerre*,' she agreed. 'What will you do for us?'

'I'm really anxious to return your kindness at Nish,' Rakoff said gravely. 'If you come with me and my men, we shall be riding southward, and you could perhaps find an opportunity to get over the Greek frontier. The officer commanding this train deserves to be punished for getting drunk. I'm not drunk, though I captured a French outpost a week ago and have some reason to celebrate my success. It was I who cut the line at Vrania. *Alors, c'est entendu? Vous venez avec moi?*'

'*Vous êtes trop gentil, monsieur.*'

'*Rien du tout. Plaisir! Plaisir!* Go back to your carriage now, and I'll send two of my men presently to show you the way out. What's that? The door is locked on the outside? Come with me then.'

They walked back along the train, and entered their compartment from the other side on which the door had been broken in.

'You can't bring much luggage. Wrap up well. *Il fait très froid.* Is your cousin strong enough to ride?'

At this point Rakoff stumbled over the severed head on the floor, and struck a match.

'What babies my men are,' he exclaimed with a smile.

He picked up the head and threw it out on the track. Then he told Sylvia and Michael to prepare for their escape and left them.

'What do you think of my æsthetic Bulgarian?' she asked.

'It's extraordinary how certain personalities have the power to twist one's standards,' Michael answered emphatically. 'A few minutes ago I was sick with horror – the whole world seemed to be tumbling to pieces before human bestiality – and now before the blood is dry on the railway-sleepers I've accepted it as a fact and – Sylvia – do you know what I was thinking the last minute or two – I'm in a way appalled by my own callousness in being able to smile – but I really was thinking with amusement what a pity it was we couldn't hand over a few noisy stay-at-home Englishmen to the sensitive Rakoff.'

'Michael,' Sylvia demanded anxiously, 'do you think you *are* strong enough to ride? I'm not sure how far we are from the Greek frontier, but it's sure to mean at least a week in the saddle. It seems madness for you to attempt it.'

'My dear, I'm not going to stay in this accursed train.'

'I've a letter of introduction for a clerk in Cavalla,' Sylvia reminded him with a smile.

'Let's hope he invites us to lunch when we present it,' Michael laughed.

The tension of waiting for the escape required this kind of feeble joking; any break in the conversation gave them time to think of the corpses scattered about in the darkness, which with the slow death of the fire was reconquering its territory. They followed Rakoff's advice and heaped extra clothes upon themselves, filling the pockets with victuals. Sylvia borrowed a cap from Michael and tied the golden shawl round her head; Michael did the same with an old college scarf. Then he tore the red cross brassard from his sleeve:

'I haven't the impudence to wear that during our pilgrimage with this gang of murderers. I've tucked away what paper money I have in my boots, and I've got twenty sovereigns sewn in my cholera belt.'

Two smiling comitadjis appeared from the corridor and beckoned the prisoners to follow them to where on the other side of the train ponies were waiting; within five minutes the wind blowing icy cold upon their cheeks, the smell of damp earth and saddles and vinous breath, the ragged starshine high overhead, the willing motion of the horses, all combined to obliterate everything except drowsy intimations of adventure. Rakoff was not visible in the cavalcade, but Sylvia supposed that he was somewhere in front. After riding for three hours, a halt was called at a deserted farmhouse, and in the big living-room he was there to receive his guests with pointed courtesy.

'You are at home here,' he observed with a laugh. 'This farm belonged to an Englishman before the war with Greece and Serbia. He was a great friend of Bulgaria; the Serbians knew it and left very little when their army passed through. We shall sleep here to-night. Are you hungry?'

The comitadjis had already wrapped themselves in their sheepskins and were lying in the dark corners of the room, exhausted by the long ride on top of the wine. A couple of men, however, prepared a rough meal to which Rakoff invited Sylvia and Michael. They had scarcely sat down, when to their surprise a young woman dressed in a very short tweed skirt and Norfolk jacket and wearing a Tyrolese hat over two long plaits of flaxen hair came and joined them. She nodded curtly to Rakoff and began to eat without a word.

'Ziska disapproves of the English,' Rakoff explained. 'In fact the only

567

thing she really cares for is dynamite. But she is one of the great comit-adji leaders and acts as my second in command. She understands French, but declines to speak it on patriotic grounds, being half a Prussian.'

The young woman looked coldly at the two strangers; then she went on eating. Her silent presence was not favourable to conversation; and a sudden jealousy of this self-satisfied and contemptuous creature over-came Sylvia. She remembered how she had told Michael's sister the secret of her love for him, and the thought of meeting her again in England became intolerable. She had a mad fancy to kill the other woman and to take her place in this wild band beside Rakoff, to seize her by those tight flaxen plaits and hold her face downwards on the table, while she stabbed her and stabbed her again. Only by such a duel could she assert her own personality, rescuing it from the ignominy of the present and the greater ignominy of the future. She had actually grasped a long knife that lay in front of her, and she might have given expression to the mad notion if at that moment Michael had not collapsed.

In a moment her fantastic passions died away; even Ziska's sidelong glance of scorn at the prostrate figure was incapable of rousing the least resentment.

'He should sleep,' said Rakoff. 'To-morrow he will have a long and tiring day.'

Soon in the shadowy room of the deserted farmhouse they were all asleep except Sylvia, who watched for a long time the dusty lanternlight flickering upon Ziska's motionless form; as her thoughts wavered in the twilight between wakefulness and dreams, she once more had a longing to grip that smooth pink neck and crack it like the neck of a wax doll. Then it was morning; the room was full of smoke and the smell of coffee.

Sylvia's forecast of a week's journeying with the comitadjis was too optimistic; as a matter of fact they were in the saddle for a month, and it was only a day or two before Christmas new style when they pitched their camp on the slopes of a valley sheltered from the fierce winds of Rhodope about twenty kilometres from the Bulgarian outposts beyond Xanthi.

'We are not far from the sea here,' Rakoff said significantly.

Whatever wind reached this slope had dropped at nightfall, and in the darkness Sylvia felt like a kiss upon her cheek the salt breath of the mighty mother to which her heart responded in awe as to the breath of liberty.

It had been a strange experience, this month with Rakoff and his band, and seemed already, though the sound of the riding had scarcely died away from her senses, the least credible episode of a varied life. Yet looking back at the incidents of each day, Sylvia could not remember that her wild companions had ever been conscious of Michael and herself as intruders upon their monotonously violent behaviour. Even Ziska, that riddle of flaxen womanhood, had gradually reached a kind of remote cordiality toward their company. To be sure, she had not invited Sylvia to grasp, or even faintly to guess, the reasons that might have induced her to adopt such a mode of life; she had never afforded the least hint of her relationship to Rakoff; she had never attempted to justify her cold, almost it might have been called her prim mercilessness. Yet she had sometimes advised Sylvia to withdraw from a prospective exhibition of atrocity, and this not from any motive of shame, but always obviously because she had been considering the emotions of her guest. It was in this spirit, when once a desperate Serbian peasant had flung a stone at the departing troop, that she had advised Sylvia to ride on and avoid the fall of mangled limbs that was likely to occur after shutting twenty villagers in a barn and blowing them up with a charge of dynamite. She had spoken of the unpleasant sequel as simply as a meteorologist might have spoken of the weather's breaking up. Michael and Sylvia used to wonder to each other what prevented them from turning their ponies' heads and galloping off anywhere to escape this daily exposure to the sight of unchecked barbarity; but they could never bring themselves to pass the limits of expediency and lose themselves in the uncertainties of an ideal morality; ultimately they always came back to the fundamental paradox of war and agreed that in a state of war the life of the individual increased in value in the same proportion as it deteriorated. Rakoff had taken pleasure in commenting upon their attitude, and once or twice he had been at pains to convince them of the advantages they now enjoyed of an intellectual honesty from which in England, so far as he had been able to appreciate criticism of that country, they would have been eternally debarred. But perhaps no amount of intellectual honesty would have enabled them to remain quiescent before the rapine and slaughter of which they were compelled to be cognizant if not actually to see, had not the journey itself healed their wounded conscience with a charm against which they were powerless. The air of the mountains swept away the taint of death that would otherwise have reeked in the very accoutrements of the equipage. The light of their bivouac fires stained such an infinitesimal fragment of the vaulted night above that the day's violence used to shrink into an insignificance which effected in its way their purification. However rude and savage their companions, it was impossible to eliminate the gift they offered of human companionship in these desolate tracts of mountainous country. In the stormy darkness they would listen with a kind of affection to the breathing of the ponies and to the broken murmurs of conversation between rider and rider all round them. There was always something of sympathy in the touch of a sheepskin coat, something of a wistful consolation in the flicker of a lighted cigarette, something of tenderness in the offer of a water-flask; and when the moon shone frostily overhead so that all the company was visible, there was never far away an emotion of wonder at their very selves being a part of this hurrying silver cavalcade, a wonder that easily was merged in gratitude for so much beauty after so much horror.

For Sylvia there was above everything the joy of seeing Michael growing stronger from day to day, and upon this joy her mind fed itself and forgot that she had ever imagined a greater joy beyond. Her contentment may have been of a piece with her indifference to the sacked villages and murdered Serbs; but she put away from her the certainty of the journey's end and surrendered to the entrancing motion through these winds of Thrace rattling and battling southward to the sea.

And now the journey was over. Sylvia knew by the tone of Rakoff's voice that she and Michael must soon shift for themselves. She wondered if he meant to hint his surprise at their not having made an attempt to do so already, and she tried to recall any previous occasion when they would have been justified in supposing that they were intended to escape from the escort. She could not remember that Rakoff had ever before given an impression of expecting to be rid of them, and a fancy came into her head that perhaps he did not mean them to escape at all, that he had merely taken them along with him to while away his time until he was bored with them. So insistent was the fancy that she looked up to see if any comitadjis were being despatched toward the Bulgarian lines, and when at that moment Rakoff did give some order to four of his men she decided that her instinct had not been at fault. Some of her apprehension must have betrayed itself in her face, for she saw Rakoff looking at her curiously, and to her first fancy succeeded another more instantly alarming that he would give orders for Michael and herself to be killed now. He might have chosen this way to gratify Ziska: no doubt it would be a very gratifying spectacle, and possibly something less passively diverting than a spectacle for that fierce doll. Sylvia was not really terrified by the prospect in her imagination; in a way she was rather attracted to it. Her dramatic sense took hold of the scene, and she found herself composing a last duologue between Michael and herself. Presumably Rakoff would be gentleman enough to have them killed decently by a firing party; he would not go farther toward gratifying Ziska than by allowing her to take a rifle with the rest. She decided that she should decline to let her eyes be bandaged; though she paused for a moment before the ironical pleasure of using her golden shawl to veil the approach of death. She should turn to Michael when they stood against a rock in the dawn, and when the rifles were levelled she should tell him that she had loved him since they had met at the masquerade in Redcliffe Hall and walked home through the fog of the Fulham Road to Mulberry Cottage. But had Mulberry Cottage ever existed?

At this moment Michael whispered to her a question so absurdly redolent of the problems of real life and yet so ridiculous somehow in present surroundings that all gloomy fancies floated away on laughter.

'Sylvia, it's quite obvious that he expects us to make a bolt for the Greek frontier as soon as possible. How much do you think I ought to tip each of these fellows?'

'I'm not very well versed in country-house manners,' Sylvia laughed, 'but I was always under the impression that one tipped the head game-keeper and did not bother oneself about the local poachers.'

'But it does seem wrong somehow to slip away in the darkness without a word of thanks,' Michael said with a smile. 'I really can't help liking these ruffians.'

At that moment Rakoff stepped forward into their conversation.

'I'm going to ride over to our lines presently,' he announced. 'You'd better come with me, and you'll not be much more than a few hundred metres from the Greek outposts. The Greek soldiers wear khaki. You won't be called upon to give any explanations.'

Michael began to thank him, but the Bulgarian waved aside his words.

'You are included in the fulfilment of an obligation, *monsieur*, and being still in debt to *mademoiselle* I should be embarrassed by any expression from her of gratitude. Come, it is time for supper.'

Throughout the meal, which was eaten in a ruined chapel, Rakoff talked of his rose-gardens, and Sylvia fancied that he was trying to reproduce in her mind her first impression of him in order to make this last meal seem but the real conclusion of their long railway journey together. She wondered if Ziska knew that this was the last meal and if she approved her leader's action in helping two enemies to escape. However, it was waste of time to speculate about Ziska's feelings: she had no feelings: she was nothing but a finely perfected instrument of destruction; and Sylvia nodded a casual good-night to her when supper was over, turning round to take a final glance at her bending over her rifle in the dim tumbledown chapel, as she might have looked back at some inanimate object which had momentarily caught her attention in a museum.

They rode downhill most of the way toward the Bulgarian lines, and about two hours after midnight saw the tents like mushrooms under the light of a hazy and decrescent moon.

'Here we bid one another farewell,' said Rakoff reining up.

In the humid stillness they sat pensive for a little while listening to the ponies nuzzling for grass, tasting in the night the nearness of the sea and straining for the shimmer of it upon the southern horizon.

'*Merci, monsieur, adieu,*' Michael said.

'*Merci, monsieur, vous avez été plus que gentil pour nous. Adieu,*' Sylvia continued.

'*Enchanté,*' the Bulgarian murmured: Michael and Sylvia dismounted. 'Keep well south of those tents and the moon over your right shoulders. You are about three kilometres from the shore. The sentries should be easy enough to avoid. We are not yet at war with Greece.'

He laughed, and spurred away in the direction of the Bulgarian tents; Michael and Sylvia walked silently toward freedom across a broken country where the dwarfed trees like the dwarfed Bulgarians themselves seemed fit only for savage hours and pathetically out of keeping with this tranquil night. They had walked for about half-an-hour, when from the cover of a belt of squat pines they saw ahead of them two figures easily recognizable as Greek soldiers.

'Shall we hail them?' Sylvia whispered.

'No, we'll keep them in view. I'm sure we haven't crossed the frontier yet. We'll slip across in their wake. They'd be worse than useless to us if we're not on the right side of the frontier.'

The Greeks disappeared over the brow of a small hill; when Sylvia and Michael reached the top they saw that they had entered what looked like a guard-house at the foot of the slope at the farther side.

'Perhaps we've crossed the frontier without knowing it,' Michael suggested.

Sylvia thought it was imprudent to make any attempt to find out for certain; but he was obstinately determined to explore and she had to wait in a torment of anxiety while he worked his way downhill and took the risk of peeping through a loophole at the back of the building. Presently he came back crawling up the hill on all fours until he was beside her again.

'Most extraordinary thing,' he declared. 'Our friend Rakoff is in there with two or three Bulgarian officers. The fellows we saw *were* Greeks – one is an officer, the other is a corporal. The officer is pointing out various spots on a large map. Of course one says "traitor" at first, but traitors don't go attended by corporals. I can't make it out. However, it's clear that we're still in Bulgaria.'

'Oh, do let's get on and leave it behind us,' Sylvia pleaded nervously.

But Michael argued the advisableness of waiting until the Greeks came out and of using them as guides to their own territory.

'But if they're traitors, they won't welcome us,' she objected.

'Oh, they can't be traitors. It must be some military business that they're transacting.'

In the end they decided to wait; after about an hour the Greeks emerged, passing once more the belt of pines where Sylvia and Michael were waiting in concealment. They allowed the visitors to get a long enough lead, and then followed them, hurrying up inclines while they were covered and lying down on the summits to watch their guides' direction. They had been moving like this for some time and were waiting above the steep bank of a ravine, the stony bed of which the Greeks were crossing, when suddenly the corporal leaped on the back of the officer, who fell in a heap. The corporal rose, looked down at the prostrate form for a moment, then knelt beside him and began to perform some laborious operation, which was invisible to the watchers. At last he stood upright and with outstretched fingers flung a malediction at the body, kicking it contemptuously; then with a gesture of despair to the sky he collapsed against a boulder and began to weep loudly.

Sylvia had seen enough violence in the last month to accept the murder of one Greek officer as a mere incident on such a night; but somehow she was conscious of a force of passion behind the corporal's action that lifted it far above her recent experience of bloodshed. She paused to see if Michael was going to think the same, unwilling to let her emotion run away with her now in such a way as to deprive them of making use of the deed for their own purpose. Michael lay on the brow of the cliff, gazing in perplexity at the man below whose form shook with sobs in the grey moonlight and whose victim seemed already nothing more important than one of the stones in the rocky bed of the ravine.

'I'm hanged if I know what to do,' Michael whispered at last.

'Personally,' Sylvia whispered back, 'it's almost worth while to spend the rest of our life in a Bulgarian prison-camp, if we can only find out the meaning of this murder.'

'Yes, I was rather coming to that conclusion,' he agreed.

'Don't think me absurd,' she went on hurriedly. 'But I've got a quite definite fancy that he's going to play an important part in our escape. Would you mind if I went down and spoke to him?'

'No, I'll go,' Michael said. 'You don't know Greek.'

'Do you?' she retorted.

'No. But he might be alarmed and attack you.'

'He'll be less likely to attack a gentle female voice,' Sylvia argued; and before Michael could say another word, she began to slide down the side of the gully, repeating very quickly 'Don't make a noise, we're English,' laughing at herself for the probable uselessness of the explanation, and yet all the time laughing with an inward conviction that there was nothing to fear from the encounter.

The corporal jumped up and held high his bayonet, which was gleaming black with moonlit blood.

'English?' he repeated doubtfully in a nasal voice.

'Yes, English prisoners escaped from the Bulgarians,' she panted as she reached him.

'That's all right,' said the corporal. 'You got nothing to be frightened of. I'm an American citizen from New York City.'

Sylvia called to Michael to come down, whereupon the corporal took hold of her wrist and reminded her that they were still in Bulgaria.

'Don't you start hollering so loud,' he said severely.

She apologized, and presently Michael reached them.

'Wal, mister,' said the Greek. 'I guess you saw me kill that dog. Come and look at him.'

He turned the dead man's face to the moon. On the forehead, on the chin, and on each cheek the flesh had been sliced away to form Π.

'$\Pi\rho o\delta \acute{o}\tau\eta\varsigma$,' explained the corporal. 'Traitor in American. I'm an American citizen, but I'm a Greek man too. I fought in the last war and was in Thessaloniki. I killed four Toiks and nine Voulgars in the last war. See here?' He pointed to the pale blue ribbons on his chest. 'I went to New York and was in a shoe-shine parlour. Then I learnt the barber-shop. I was doing well. Then I come home and fought the Toiks. Then I fought the Voulgars. Then I went back to New York. Then last September come the mobilizing to fight them again. Yes, mister, I put my razor in my pocket and come over to Piræus. I didn't care for submarines. Hundreds of Greek mens come with me to fight the Voulgars. The Greek mens hate the Voulgars. But things is different this time. They was telling tales how our officers was chummy with the Voulgar officers. I didn't believe it. Not me. But it was true. With my own eyes I see this dog showing the plans of Rupel and other forts. With my own ears I heard this sunnavabitch telling the Voulgars the Greek mens wouldn't fight. My heart swelled up like a water-melon. My eyes was bursting and I cursed him inside of me saying, "I wish your brains for to become beans in your head." But when we was alone I thought of what big means the Greeks was in old times, and I said to him "$\kappa\acute{v}\rho\iota\varepsilon\ \lambda\acute{o}\chi\alpha\gamma\varepsilon$," which is Mister Captain in American, "what means this what we have done

574

to-night?" And he says to me, "It means the Greek mens ain't going to fight for Venizelo who is a Senegalese and προδότης of his country." And he cursed the French and cursed the British and he said that the Voulgars must be let drive them into the sea. But I said nothing. I just spit. Then after a bit I said "κύριε λόχαγε, does the other officers think like you was?" And he says all Greek mens what is not traitors think like him, and if I tell him who is for Venizelo in our regiment I will be a sergeant good and quick. But I didn't say nothing: I am only spitting to myself. Then we come to this place, and my heart was bursting out of my body, and I killed him. Then I took my razor and marked his face for a προδότης.'

The corporal threw up his arms to heaven in denunciation of the dead man. They asked him what he would do, and he told them that he should hide on his own native island of Samothrace until he could be an interpreter to an English ship at Mudros or until Greece should turn upon the Bulgarians and free his soul from the stain of the captain's treachery.

'Can you help us to get to Samothrace?' they asked.

'Yes, I can help you. But what you have seen to-night swear not to tell, for I am crying like a woman for my country; and other peoples and mens must not laugh at Hellas, because to-night this σκυλάκι, this dog, has had the moon for eats.'

'And how shall we get to Samothrace?' they asked, when they had promised their silence.

'I will find a caique and you will hide by the sea where I show you. We cannot go back over the river to Greece. But how much can you pay for the caique? Fifty dollars? There are Greek fish-mens, sure, who was going to take us.'

Michael at once agreed to the price.

'Then it will be easy,' said the corporal, after he had calculated his own profit upon the transaction.

'And ten dollars for yourself,' Michael added.

'I don't want nothing out of it for myself,' the corporal declared indignantly; but after a minute's hesitation he told them that he did not think it would be possible to hire the caique for less than sixty dollars, and looked sad when Michael did not try to contest the higher figure.

They had started to walk seaward along the bed of the ravine, when the corporal ran back with an exclamation of contempt to where the dead officer was lying.

'If I ain't dippy,' he laughed. 'Gee! I 'most forgot to see what was in his pockets.'

He made up for the oversight by a thorough search and came back presently, smiling and slipping the holster of the officer's revolver on his

575

own belt. Then he patted his own pockets, which were bulging with what he had found, and they walked forward in silence. The end of the ravine brought them to an exposed upland, which they crossed warily, flitting from stunted tree to stunted tree, because the moonlight was seeming too bright here for safety. The upland gave place to sandy dunes, the hollows of which were marshy and made the going difficult; but the night was breathless and not a leaf stirred in the oleander thickets to alarm their progress.

'Not much wind for sailing,' Michael murmured.

'That's all right,' said the corporal, whose name was Yanni Psaradelis. 'If we find a caique, we can wait for the wind.'

Sylvia was puzzled by Rakoff's not having said a word about any river to cross at the frontier. She wondered if he had salved his loyalty thereby, counting upon their recapture, or if by chance they were to get away throwing the blame on providence. Yet had he time for such subtleties? It was hard to think he had, but by Yanni's account of the river it seemed improbable that they would ever have escaped without his help, and it was certainly strange that Rakoff if his benevolence had been genuine should not have warned them. And now actually the dunes were dipping to the sea; on a simultaneous impulse they ran down the last sandy slope and knelt upon the beach by the edge of the tide, scooping up the water as though it were of gold.

'Say, that's not the way to go escaping from the Voulgars,' Yanni told them reproachfully. 'We've got to go slow and keep out of sight.'

The beach was very narrow and sloped rapidly up to low cliffs of sand continually broken by wide drifts and water-courses; but they were high enough to mask the moonlight if one kept close under their lea, and one's footsteps were muffled by the sand. They must have walked in this fashion for a couple of miles when Yanni stopped them with a gesture and bending down picked up the cork of a fishing-net and an old shoe.

'Guess there's folk around here,' he whispered. 'I'm going to see. You sit down and rest yourselves.'

He walked on cautiously; the sandy cliffs apparently tumbled away to a flat country almost at once, for Yanni's figure lost the protection of their shadow and came into view like a grey ghost in the now completely clouded moonlight. Presumably they were standing near the edge of the marshy estuary of the river between Bulgaria and Greece.

'How will he explain himself to any of the enemy on guard?' Sylvia whispered.

'He must have had the countersign to get across earlier to-night,' Michael replied.

'It's nearly five o'clock,' she said. 'We haven't got so very much longer before dawn.'

They waited for ages, it seemed, before Yanni came back and told them that there was no likelihood of getting a caique on this side of the river, but that he should cross over in a boat and take the chance of finding one on the farther beach before his captain's absence was remarked. He should have to be careful because the Greek sentries would be men from his own regiment and his presence so far down the line might arouse suspicion.

'But if you find a caique, how are we going to get across the river to join you?' Michael asked.

'Say, give me twenty dollars,' Yanni answered after a minute's thought. 'The fish-mens won't do nothing for me unless I show them the money first. I'll say two British peoples want to go Thaso. We can give them more when we're on the sea to go Samothraki. They'd be afraid to go Samothraki at first. You must go back to where we come down to the sea. Got me? Hide in the bushes all day and before the φεγγάρι, what is it, before the moon is beginning to-morrow night, come right down to the beach and strike one match; then wait till you see me, but not till after the moon is beginning. If I don't come to-morrow, go back and hide and come right down the next night till the moon is beginning. And if I don't come the next night—' he stopped. 'Sure, Yanni will be dead.'

Michael gave him five sovereigns; he walked quickly away, and the fugitives turned on their traces in the sand.

'Do you feel any doubt about him?' Sylvia whispered after a spell of silence.

'About his honesty? Not in the least. If he can come, he will come.'

'That's what I think.'

They found by their old footprints the gap in the cliffs through which they had first descended and took the precaution of scrambling farther along so that there should remain only the marks of their descent. In the first oleander thicket they hid themselves by lying flat on the marshy ground; so tired were they that they both fell asleep until they were awakened by morning and a drench of rain.

'One feels more secluded and safe somehow in such weather,' said Sylvia with an attempt at optimism.

'Yes, and we've got a box of Turkish-delight,' said Michael.

'Turkish-delight?' she repeated in astonishment.

'Yes, one of Rakoff's men gave it to me about a week ago, and I kept it with a vague notion of its bringing us luck or something. Besides, another thing in the rain's favour is that it serves as a kind of bath.'

'A very complete bath, I should say,' laughed Sylvia.

They ate Turkish-delight at intervals during that long day when not for a single moment did the rain cease to fall. Sylvia told Michael about the Earl's Court Exhibition and Mabel Bannerman.

'I remember a girl called Mabel who used to sell Turkish-delight there, but she had a stall of her own.'

'So did my Mabel the year afterwards,' she said.

Soon they decided it must be the same Mabel. Sylvia thought what a good opening this was to tell Michael some of her more intimate experiences, but she dreaded that he would in spite of himself show his distaste for that early life of hers, and she could not bear the idea of creating such an atmosphere now – or in the future, she thought with a sigh. Nevertheless, she did begin an apostrophe against the past, but he cut her short.

'The past? What does the past matter? Without a past, my dear Sylvia, you would have no present.'

'And after all,' she thought, 'he knows already I have a past.'

Once their hands met by accident, and Michael withdrew his with a quickness that mortified her, so that she simulated a deep preoccupation in order to hide her chagrin, for she had outgrown her capacity to sting back with bitter words, and could only await the slow return of her composure before she could talk naturally again.

'But never mind, the adventure is drawing to a close,' she told herself, 'and he'll soon be rid of me.'

Then he began to talk again about their damned relationship and to speculate upon the extent of Stella's surprise when she should hear about it.

'I think, you know, when I was young,' Michael said presently, 'that I must have been rather like your husband. I'm sure I should have fallen in love with you and married you.'

'You couldn't have been in the least like him,' she contradicted angrily.

For a moment, so poignant in its revelation of a divine possibility as to stop her heart while it lasted, Sylvia fancied that he seemed disappointed at her abrupt disposal of the notion that he might have loved her. But even as the thought was born, it died upon his offer of another piece of Turkish-delight and of his saying:

'I *think* it's time for the eighth piece each.'

So that was the calculation he had been making, unless indeed their proximity and solitude through this long day in the face of danger had induced in him a sentimental desire to express an affection born of a conventional instinct to accord with favouring circumstance, bred of a kind of pity for a wasted situation. If that were so, she must be more than ever careful of her pride; and for the rest of the day she kept the conversation to politics, forcing it away from any topic that in the least concerned them personally.

A night of intense blackness and heavy rain succeeded that long day in the oleander thicket. Moonrise could not be expected by their reckoning much before three in the morning. The wet hours dragged so interminably that prudence was sacrificed to a longing for action; feeling that it was impossible to lie here any longer, sodden, hungry and apprehensive, they decided to go down to the beach and strike the first match at midnight and notwithstanding the risk to strike matches every half-hour. The first match evoked no response; but the plash of the little waves broke the monotony of the rain, and the sand, wet though it was, came as a relief after the slime in which they had been lying for eighteen hours. The second match gained no answering signal, neither did the third nor the fourth. They consoled themselves by whispering that Yanni had arranged his rescue for the hour before moonrise. The fifth and sixth matches flamed and went out in dreary ineffectiveness; so thick was the darkness over the sea it began to seem unimaginable for anything to happen out there. Suddenly Michael whispered that he could hear the clumping of oars and struck the seventh match. There was silence; then the oars definitely grew louder; a faint whistle came over the water: the darkness before them became tremulous with a hint of life, and their straining eyes tried to fancy the outline of a boat standing off from the shore. Presently low voices were audible; then the noise of a falling plank and a hurried oath for someone's clumsiness; a little boat grounded, and Yanni jumped out.

'Quick,' he breathed. 'I believe I heard footsteps coming right down to the shore.'

They pushed off the boat; and when they were about twenty strokes from the beach, what seemed after so much whispering and stillness a demoniac shout rent the darkness inland. Yanni and the fishermen beside him pulled now without regard for the noise of the oars; they could hear the sound of people's sliding down the cliff; there were more shouts, and a rifle flashed.

'Those Voulgars,' Yanni panted, 'won't do nothing except holler. They can't see us.'

Another rifle banged, and Sylvia was thrilled by the way their escape was conforming to the rules of the game; she revelled in the confused sounds of anger and pursuit on land.

'They don't know where we are,' laughed Yanni.

But the noise of the fugitives scrambling on board the caique and the hoisting of the little boat brought round them a shower of bullets, the splash of which was heard above the rain. One of these broke a jar of wine, and every man aboard bent to the long oars, driving the perfumed caique deeper into the darkness.

'I had a funny time getting this caique,' Yanni explained, when with some difficulty he had been dissuaded from firing his late captain's revolver at the country of Bulgaria, by this time at least two miles away. 'I didn't have no difficulty to get across, but I had to walk half-way to Cavalla before I found the old fish-man who owns this caique. I told him two British peoples wanted him and he says "Are them Mr. B's fellows for Cavalla?" I didn't know who Mr. B was anyway, so I says "Sure, they're Mr. B's fellows," but when we got off at dusk, he says his orders was for Porto Lagos and to let go the little boat when he could hear a bird calling. He didn't give a dern for no matches, Wal, Mr. B's fellows didn't answer from round about Lagos, and he said bad words and how it was three days too soon and who in hell did I think I was anyway telling him Mr. B's fellows was waiting. So I told him there was a mistake somewhere and asked him what about taking you Thaso for twenty dollars. We talked for a bit and he said "Yes." Now we got to make him go Samothraki.'

At this point the captain of the caique, a brown and shrivelled old man seeming all the more shrivelled in the full-seated breeches of the Greek islander, joined them below for an argument with Yanni that sounded more than usually acrimonious and voluble. When it was finished, the captain had agreed, subject to a windy moonrise, to land them at Samothraki on payment of another ten pounds in gold. They went on deck and sat astern, for the rain was over now. A slim rusty moon was creeping out of the sea and conjuring from the darkness forward the shadowy bulk of Thasos; presently with isolated puffs that frilled the surface of the water like the wings of alighting birds the wind began to blow; the long oars were shipped, and the crew set the curved mainsail that crouched in a defiant bow against whatever onslaught might prepare itself; from every mountain gorge in Thrace the northern blasts rushed down with life for the stagnant sea, and life for the dull decrescent moon, which in a spray of stars they drove glittering up the sky.

'How gloriously everything hums and gurgles,' Sylvia shouted in Michael's ear. 'When shall we get to Samothrace?'

He shrugged his shoulders and leant over to Yanni, who told them that it might be about midday if the wind held like this.

For all Sylvia's exultation, the vision of enchanted space that seemed to forbid sleep on such a night soon faded from her consciousness, and she did not rouse herself from dreams until dawn was scattering its roses and violets to the wind.

'I simply can't shave,' Michael declared, 'but Samothrace is in sight.'

The sun was rising in a fume of spindrift and fine gold, when Sylvia scrambled forward into the bows. Huddled upon a coil of wet rope, she first saw Samothrace faintly relucent like an uncut sapphire, where already it towered upon the horizon, though there might be thirty thundering miles between.

'I'm glad we ended our adventure with this glorious sea race,' shouted Michael, who had joined her in the bows. 'Are you feeling quite all right?'

She nodded indignantly.

'See how grey the sky is now,' he went on. 'It's going to blow even harder, and they're shortening sail.'

They looked aft to where the crew, whose imprecations were only visible so loud was the drumming of the wind, were getting down the mainsail; and presently they were running east-south-east under a small jib, with the wind roaring upon the port quarter and the waves champing at the taffrail. It did not strike either of them that there was any reason to be anxious until Yanni came forward with a frightened yellow face and said that the captain was praying to St. Nicholas in the cabin below.

'Samothraki bad place to go,' Yanni told them dismally. 'Many fishmens drowned there.'

A particularly violent squall shrieked assent to his forebodings, and the helmsman looking over his shoulder crossed himself as the squall left them and tore ahead, decapitating the waves in its course so that the surface of the water blown into an appearance of smoothness resembled the powdery damascene of ice in a skater's track.

'It's terrible, ain't it?' Yanni moaned.

'Cheer up,' Michael said. 'I'm looking forward to your shaving me before lunch in your native island.'

'We shan't never come Samothraki,' Yanni said. 'And I can't pray no more somehow since I went away to America. Else I'd go and pray along with the captain. Supposing I was to give a silver ship to the παναγία in Teno, would you lend me the money for the workmens to do it?'

'I'll pay half,' Michael volunteered. 'A silver ship to Our Lady of Tenos,' he explained to Sylvia.

'Gee!' Yanni shouted more cheerfully. 'I'm going to pray some right now. I guess when I get kneeling the trick'll come back to me. I did so much kneeling in New York to shine boots that I used to lie in bed on a Sunday. But this goddam storm's regular making my knees itch.'

He hurried aft in a panic of religious devotion, whither Michael and

Sylvia presently followed him in the hope of coffee. Everyone on board except the helmsman was praying, and there was no sign of fire; even the sacred flame before St. Nicholas had gone out. The cabin was in a confusion of supplicating mariners prostrate amid onions, oranges and cheese; the very cockroaches seemed to listen anxiously in the wild motion. The helmsman was not steering too well or else the sea was growing wilder, for once or twice a stream of water poured down the companion and drenched the occupants, until at last the captain rushed on deck to curse the offender, calling down upon his head the pains of hell should they sink and he be drowned.

Michael and Sylvia found the most sheltered spot in the caique and ate some cheese. The terror of the crew had reacted upon their spirits; the groaning of the wind in the shrouds, the seething of the waves, and the frightened litany below quenched their exultation and silenced their laughter.

Yanni, more yellow than ever, came up and asked Michael if he would mind paying the captain now.

'He says he don't believe he can get into port, but if he can't, he's going to try and get around on the south side of Samothraki, only he'd like to have his money in case anything should happen.'

Three hours tossed themselves free from time; and now in all its majesty and in all its menace the island rose dark before them, girdled with foam and crowned with snow above six thousand feet of chasms, gorges, cliffs, and forests.

'What a fearful leeshore,' Michael exclaimed with a shudder.

'Yes, but with a sublime form,' Sylvia cried. 'At any rate to be wrecked on such a coast is not a mean death.'

Yanni explained that the only port of the island lay on this side of the low-lying promontory that ran out to sea on their starboard bow. In order to make this the captain would have to beat up to windward first, which with the present fury of the gale and so lofty a coast was impossible. The captain evidently came to the same conclusion, though at first it looked as if he had changed his mind too late to avoid running the caique ashore before he could gain the southerly lee of the island. Sylvia held her breath when the mast lost itself against the darkness of land and breathed again when anon it stood out clear against the sky. Yet so frail seemed the caique in relation to the vast bulk before them that it was incredible this haunt of Titans should not exact another sacrifice.

'I think, as we get nearer, that the mast shows itself less often against the sky,' Sylvia shouted to Michael.

'About equal, I think,' he shouted back.

Certainly the caique still laboured on, and it might be that after all they would clear the promontory and gain shelter.

'Do you know what I'm thinking of?' Michael yelled.

She shook her head, blinking in the spray.

'The Round Pond!' he yelled again.

'I can't imagine that even the Round Pond's really calm at present,' she shouted back.

Suddenly astern there was a cry of despair that rose high above the howling of the wind; the tiller had broken, and immediately the prow of the caique swerving away from the sky drove straight for the shore. Two men leapt forward to cut the ropes of the jib, which flapped madly aloft; then it gave itself to the wind and danced before them till it was no more than a gull's wing against dark and mighty Samothrace.

The caique rocked alarmingly until the oars steadied her; the strength of the rowers endured long enough to clear the promontory, but unfortunately the expected shelter on the other side proved to be an illusion, and though a new tiller had been provided by this time, it was impossible for the exhausted men to do their part. The caique began to ship water, so heavily indeed that the captain gave orders to run her ashore where the sand of a narrow cove glimmered between huge towers of rock. The beaching would have been effected safely, had it not been for a sunken reef that ripped out the bottom of the caique, which crumpled up and shrieked her horror like a live sentient thing. Sylvia found herself, after she had rolled in a dizzy switchback from the summit of one wave to another, clinging head downward to a slippery ledge of rock, her fingers in a mush of sea-anemones, her feet wedged in a crevice; then another wave lifted her off and she was swept over and over in green somersaults of foam, until there came a blow as from a hammer, a loud roaring, and silence.

When Sylvia recovered consciousness, she was lying on a sandy slope with Michael's arms round her.

'Was I drowned?' she asked; then commonsense added itself to mere consciousness and she began to laugh. 'I don't mean actually, but nearly?'

'No, I think you hit your head rather a thump on the beach. You've only been lying here about twenty minutes.'

'And Yanni and the captain and the crew?'

'They all got safely ashore. Rather cut about of course, but nothing serious. Yanni and the captain are arguing whether Our Lady of Tenos or St. Nicholas is responsible for saving our lives. The others are making a fire.'

She tried to sit up; but her head was going round, and she fell back.

'Keep quiet,' Michael told her. 'We're in a narrow sandy cove from which a gorge runs up into the heart of the mountains. There's a convenient cave higher up full of dried grass – a goatherd's I suppose, and when the fire's alight the others are going to scramble across somehow to the village and send a guide for us to-morrow. There won't be time before dark to-night. Do you mind being left for a few minutes?'

She smiled her contentment, and closing her eyes listened to the echoes of human speech among the rocks above, and to the beating of the surf below.

Presently Yanni and Michael appeared in order to carry her up to the cave; but she found herself easily able to walk with the help of an arm, and Michael told Yanni to hurry off to the village.

Sylvia and he were soon left alone on the parapet of smoke-blackened earth in front of the cave, whence they watched the sailors toiling up the gorge in search of a track over the mountain. Then they took off nearly all their clothes and wandered about in overcoats, breaking off boughs of juniper to feed the fire for their drying.

'Nothing to eat but cheese,' Michael laughed. 'Our diet since we left Rakoff has always run to excess of one article. Still, cheese is more nutritious than Turkish-delight, and there's plenty of water in that theatrical cascade. The wind is dropping; though in any case we shouldn't feel it here.'

Shortly before sunset the gorge echoed with liquid tinklings, and an aged goatherd appeared with his flock of brown sheep and tawny goats, which with the help of a wild-eyed boy he penned in another big cave on the opposite side. Then he joined Sylvia and Michael at their fire and gave them an unintelligible, but obviously cordial salutation; after which he entered what was evidently his dwelling place and came out with bottles of wine and fresh cheese. He did not seem in any way surprised by their presence in his solitude, and when darkness fell he and the boy piped ancient tunes in the firelight until they all lay down on heaps of dry grass. Sylvia remained awake for a long while in a harmony of distant waves and falling water and of sudden restless tinklings from the penned flock. In the morning the old man gave them milk and made them a stately fare-well; he and his goats and his boy disappeared up the gorge for the day's pasturage in a jangling tintinnabulation that became fainter and fainter, until the last and most melodious bells tinkled at rare intervals far away in the dim heart of the mountain.

The cove and the gorge were still in deep shadow; but on the slopes above toward the east bright sunlight was hanging the trees with emeralds beneath a blue sky, and seaward the halcyon had lulled the waves for her azure nesting.

584

'Can't we get up into the sunlight?' Michael proposed.

For all the sparkling airs above them, it was chilly enough down here, and they were glad to scramble up through thickets of holm-oak, arbutus, and aromatic scrub to a grassy peak in the sun's eye. Here not even the buzzing of an insect broke the warm wintry peace of the South, and it was hard to think that the restless continent of Asia was lapped by that tender and placid sea below. The dark blue wavy line of Imbros and the dove-grey bulk of Lemnos were the only islands in sight, though like lines of cloud upon the horizon they could fancy the cliffs of Gallipoli and hear, so breathless was the calm, the faint grumbling of the guns.

'It was in Samothrace they set up the Winged Victory,' Michael said. Then suddenly he turned to Sylvia and took her hand. 'My dear, when I dragged you up the beach yesterday I thought you were dead, and I cursed myself for a coward because I had let you die without telling you. Sylvia, this adventure of ours, need it ever stop?'

'Everything comes to an end,' she sighed.

'Except one thing – and that sets all the rest going again.'

'What is your magic key?'

'Sylvia, I'm afraid to ask you to marry me, but will you?'

She stared at him; then she saw his eyes, and for a long while she was crying in his arms with happiness.

'My dear, my dear, you've lost your yellow shawl in the wreck.'

'The mermaids can have it,' she murmured. 'I shall wrap up the rest of my memories in you.'

Then she stopped in sudden affright.

'But, Michael, how can I marry you? I haven't told you anything really about myself.'

'Foolish one, you've told me everything that matters in these two months of the most perfect companionship possible for human beings.'

'Companionship?' she echoed, looking at him fiercely. 'And cousin-ship, eh?'

'No, no, my dear, you can't frighten me any longer,' he laughed. 'Surely telling things belongs to the companionship of a life together – love has no words except when one is still very young and eloquent.'

'But, Michael,' she went on, 'all these nine years of mystical speculation, are they going to end in the commonplace of marriage?'

'It won't be commonplace, and besides the war isn't over yet, and after the war there will be an empty world to fill with all we have learnt. Ah, how poor old Guy would have loved to fill it with his Spanish castles.'

'It seems wrong for us two up here to be so happy,' Sylvia sighed.

'This is just a halcyon day, but there will soon be stormy days again.'

'You mean you'll go back now to—' she stopped in a desperate apprehension. 'But of course, we can't live for ever in these days of war between a blue sky and a blue sea. Yet somehow, oh, my dearest and dearest, I don't believe I shall lose *you*.'

Like birds calling to one another, in the green thickets far away two bells tinkled their monotone; and a small grey craft flying the white ensign glided over the charmed sea toward Samothrace.